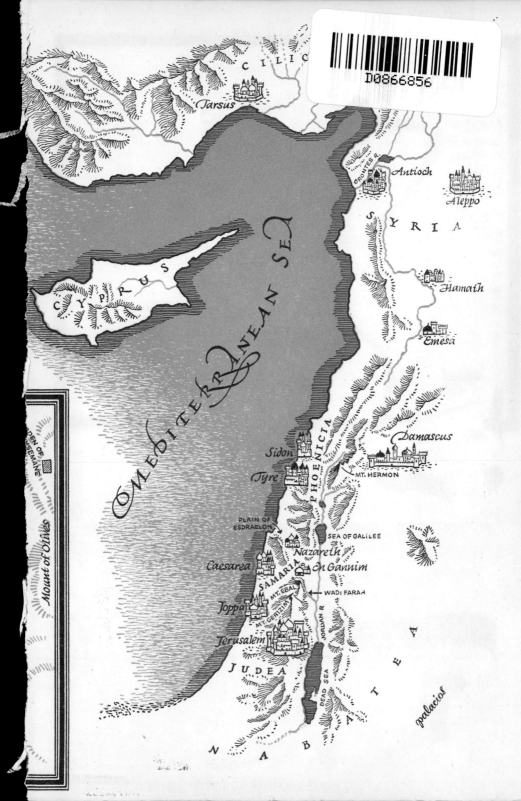

CILICIA

Tarsus

ORONTES R. Antioch

Aleppo

S Y R I A

CYPRUS

Hamath

Emesa

MEDITERRANEAN SEA

Damascus

Sidon

Tyre

MT. HERMON

PHOENICIA

PLAIN OF
ESDRAELON

SEA OF GALILEE

Nazareth

Caesarea

En Gannim

SAMARIA

WADI FARAH

Joppa

MT. EBAL

MT. GERIZIM

JORDAN R.

Jerusalem

JUDEA

DEAD SEA

N   A   B   A   T   E   A

Palacios

GARDEN OF
GETHSEMANE

Mount of Olives

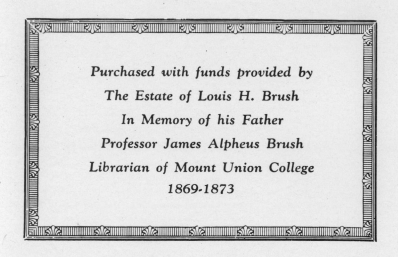

THE SILVER CHALICE

BOOKS BY
THOMAS B. COSTAIN

The Silver Chalice
The Magnificent Century: The Pageant of England
Son of a Hundred Kings
The Conquerors: The Pageant of England
High Towers
The Moneyman
The Black Rose
Ride with Me
For My Great Folly
Joshua: A Study in Leadership
(in collaboration with Rogers MacVeagh)

THE
SILVER CHALICE

a novel by

THOMAS B. COSTAIN

Garden City, New York

DOUBLEDAY & COMPANY, INC.

1952

Library of Congress Catalog Card Number 52-8754

COPYRIGHT, 1952, BY THOMAS B. COSTAIN
ALL RIGHTS RESERVED
PRINTED IN THE UNITED STATES OF AMERICA BY
KINGSPORT PRESS, INC., KINGSPORT, TENNESSEE

THE SILVER CHALICE

PROLOGUE

THE RICHEST MAN in Antioch, by common report, was Ignatius, the dealer in olive oil. He had groves that extended as far as the eye could see in every direction and he lived in a marble palace on the Colonnade. He had been born in the same Pisidian village as Theron, who supported his family by selling ink and pens made of the split ends of reed. Theron found it hard to support his family in a one-room lodging a quite considerable distance away from the Colonnade.

One day in the heat of summer, when no one ventured out to engage in trade, least of all to buy pens, the great man came on foot to the hole in the wall where Theron sat with his unwanted wares. The latter could not be convinced at first that he was being paid this great honor and was slow in returning the salutation, "Peace be with you."

The oil merchant, gasping for breath and slightly purple of cheek, stepped inside to escape the sun, which was beating down on the street with all the fury of the fires of atonement. Making room for himself beside his one-time friend, he went directly to the object of his visit.

"Theron, you have three sons. I have none."

Theron nodded. He realized that he was singularly blessed in the possession of three sons who had survived the hazards of childhood.

"Is my memory to be lost through lack of children?" asked Ignatius, his voice rising to an unhappy pitch. "Is my spirit to wander after death with no one to come back to, as a moth flies to the flame?"

The awe Theron had felt at the start was giving place to the ease of old acquaintance. After all, had not he and this corpulent merchant been raised in houses of equal size? Had they not stolen fruit together and fished in the same stream?

"It is perhaps your thought to adopt a son," said the seller of pens.

"My old friend," said Ignatius, "if you are willing, I shall buy one of your sons and adopt him as my own. He shall have as much love as though he came from my own loins. When the time comes for me to die, he shall inherit everything I possess."

Theron's heart gave an exultant tug, although he did not allow any of the excitement that had taken possession of him to show on the surface. What a wonderful chance for his first-born! To become a man of substance and wealth, to eat his meals off plate of gold and silver, to drink wine cooled by snow from the mountains of the north! Or would it be the second son on whom the favor of the great merchant had descended?

"Is it Theodore you want?" he asked. "My first-born is a boy of fine parts. He will make a strong man."

Ignatius shook his head. "Your Theodore will grow big and have a bulging stomach on him before he is thirty. No, it is not Theodore."

"It is Denis, then. My second son is a tall and handsome fellow. And also he is obedient and industrious."

The wealthy merchant shook his head a second time. Theron's heart sank and he said to himself, "It is my good little Ambrose he wants!" Ambrose was turning ten and lived in a thoughtful world of his own, never so happy as when modeling figures out of clay or carving bits of wood. The seller of pens had always known that in his heart he had a preference for Ambrose. The thought of losing him was like a dagger thrust.

There was nothing unusual about the proposal Ignatius was making. Men without sons sought to remedy the deficiency in this way. The law, as laid down in the Twelve Tables, made no distinction in the matter of inheritance between sons of the flesh and sons by adoption. It was unusual, however, for a man of wealth to think of an alliance with one as poor as a seller of pens. Ignatius could have found a willing candidate in any of the best families of Antioch. Theron, nevertheless, sought feverishly in his mind for some excuse to refuse the offer, saying to himself, "How sad life would be if I parted with my good little Ambrose!"

After a moment he shook his head. "My third son would not suit you. He is a dreamer, that Ambrose. He has no head on him for figuring. Oh, he is a fine boy and I am overly partial to him; but I can see his faults as well as his good points. He has only one desire in life, and that is to make his little statues out of clay and chalk and wood." Theron gave his head an emphatic shake as though to conclude the matter. "No, my Ambrose would not suit you."

The merchant was a thickset man, as broad across the shoulders as a carrier of water. His head was square, his features rugged. A man who fights his way to the top in trade, and stays there, sees more of warfare than a soldier; for life to him is one long battle, a continual round of buffeting and coming to grips, of tugging and sweating and scheming and hating, with none of the pleasant interludes a soldier enjoys around the campfire in the company of other soldiers, with a wineskin handy and the talk easy and vainglorious. Ignatius carried no scars on his body, but if it had been possible to hold up his soul for inspection like a garment, it would have been revealed as a thing of black bruises and scars, ridged and welted and as callused as a penitent's knee.

He leaned forward and placed a hand on the forearm of the seller of pens. If the latter had not been so concerned with the threat to his own happiness, he might have detected a note of supplication in the attitude of the great man.

"That, friend of my youth, is why I want him." Ignatius drew his brows into a troubled frown, because the need had now been reached of explaining himself and he doubted his ability to do so adequately. "The Greek nation was great when it had artists to make figures of marble and build beautiful temples of stone. It had men who wrote noble thoughts and who told the history of our race in—in glowing words. Is it not so?"

Theron nodded. "It is so." This was the thought that consoled him when troubles gathered around his head, when no one wanted to buy pens and the mother of his three sons railed at him as a good-for-nothing.

"But now," went on Ignatius, "we are traders, we are dealers in cattle and corn and ivory and olive oil. Koine has become the language of the world's trade. I suppose that when people think of Greece today, they think first of men like me." His eyes, usually so withdrawn and shrewd, had taken fire. "That is wrong, my Theron, and it must be changed. Greece must produce thinkers and tellers of stories and great artists again. And it is in my power, and that of men like me, to bring this about."

Theron was listening and watching with amazement. Could this be Ignatius talking, the man most feared in the markets and countinghouses and along the waterfront where the warehouses were so thick they cut off all view of the shipping at the wharves?

"When I die," went on the merchant, with a hint of pride in his manner, "there will be a great fortune to pass on. There will be no need for those who follow me to go on accumulating money and possessions. I want in my place then a man who will see things as I see them now and who will know how to use my wealth to restore some of the real glory of Greece."

Theron felt himself in the position of a defending captain who sees the high walls around him being battered down.

"But," he demurred, in an effort to find some ground for a last stand, "you know nothing about my third son. Why are you sure he is the one you want?"

"I never take a step until I know exactly what I want." Ignatius spoke confidently. "I saw your son once only, but I know much about him. I have seen to it that inquiries were made.

"I walked one day through the Ward of the Trades, and it was then I saw him," he went on. "There were a dozen boys together, hopping about and scuffling and fighting—and one who sat against a wall and whittled with a knife at a piece of wood. I stopped and watched him. He was different from the others. I could see that he had a fine and wide brow. The others tried to get him into their games, but he paid no attention. Then one of them went over and snatched away the piece of wood. The boy was on his feet in a trice and fighting to get it back. He fought well. I said to myself, 'He stands apart and asks only to be left alone, but he's willing to fight for what is important to him.' And then I said to myself, 'This is the boy I want as my son.' I felt very happy because I had been searching for a long time. I asked one of the other boys who he was and the boy said, 'His father is Theron, who can tilt a bottle with the best and who sells lampblack and calls it ink.' And so, Theron, my old friend, I have come to you today to talk of terms."

The seller of pens heaved a deep sigh. "You have opened your heart to me, Ignatius. Can I do less?" He spread out his hands in a gesture of reluctant surrender. "My fine little Ambrose is the light of my life. I love him so much that my house will be desolate without him. But what kind of a father is one who lets his own happiness stand in the way of his son's? It shall be as you desire." Then he turned with the fierce willingness to barter that the hot sun seems to foster. "There must be five witnesses."

"Yes." The oil merchant realized the distress in the mind of the other man and spoke in a kindly tone. "It will be made legal and tight. Three times you will offer to sell me your son in the presence of the five witnesses and each time one of them will strike the brass scales with the ingot of lead. It shall all be done as the laws prescribe so that your son—

no, it must now be said *my* son—will live with me and Persis, my wife, in full happiness and in the end be possessed of all my wealth."

Theron found it hard to speak because of the lump in his throat. "I place a high value on my son. I shall drive a hard bargain with you, Ignatius."

Accordingly five witnesses were summoned to hear Theron, clothed for the first time in his life in a spotless white toga (an extravagance at which his thrifty wife had protested bitterly), announce his willingness to sell his son Ambrose to Ignatius, son of Basil. Three times the scales were struck by one of the five, Hiram of Silenus. Hiram was an owner of small olive groves and made his profit by sailing in the wake of the lordly Ignatius; and he considered it the honor of a lifetime to officiate in this capacity. At the finish the new father said: "I shall name my son after my own father, Basil. It is the greatest honor I may pay him, for my father was a great man."

"Happy is the son," said Theron sadly, "who can look up with pride to his father. And happy is the father who can inspire such pride."

As he never did anything by halves, Ignatius not only handed over the full amount he was to pay, but he announced to the seller of pens that he had arranged for him and his family to move south to the city of Sidon, where much more remunerative employment had been found for him. Theron agreed at once that this was sensible. The boy, cut off from everything to do with his former life, would more easily fit himself into the new environment. "It will be better if you hear no word from me at all," he said to the new father. "The sooner the memory of me dims in the boy's mind, the easier it will be for all of us. Be good to him, old friend."

The one flaw in the ceremony had been the absence of the boy. It had been arranged that he was to be given over at once into the custody of his new parents. He had been thoroughly scrubbed and arrayed in the white tunic provided for him, and a handsome leather belt had been buckled about his waist. For a brief moment the boy had known a feeling of pride in the figure he cut; but when Theron was ready to leave, looking every bit as doleful as he felt, there was no trace to be found of the central figure in the transaction. The father went alone, therefore, to the frightening magnificence of the white palace beyond the four tiers of columns on the Great Colonnade while the boy's mother and his two older brothers (all furiously determined that nothing should prevent the paying over of the handsome sum that was to seal the bargain) went out to search. He was not found until late in the afternoon, crouched behind a pile of faggots in a river warehouse, his face black with soot and streaked with tears. He had not been idle while he remained in concealment. A lump of clay had been modeled into a caricature of the man into whose house he was to go, an unmistakable likeness, although the nose had been given a predatory hook and the ears had been enlarged to suggest extreme greed.

Theron arrived home on legs that were unsteady and with a wine stain on his white toga. His tongue was thick as he muttered: "I sell honest ink. Never have I given a customer plain lampblack. And I am never drunk."

"The wine drips from your ears now!" declared his wife.

Theron, at any rate, was sober enough to destroy the small bust before taking the boy to his new home.

2

Basil, to give him the name by which he was to be called for the rest of his life, had never been inside one of the stone palaces clustering in the neighborhood where the statue of Apollo perched atop the Omphalos and where stood also the gold-sheeted dome of the Temple of Jupiter. His eyes were wide with curiosity when he was led in under the elaborately carved *aliyyah* protruding out over the main entrance. The floor under his feet in the hall was of yellow stone, and the glowing colors of the tapestries on the walls drew an exclamation of wonder and delight from him. The house, which was three stories in height, was built around a luxuriously green garden, but the latticed windows had all been closed against the heat. There were no signs of life in the garden save the splash of water in a fountain and the occasional note of a bird. "This must be Paradise," thought the boy.

Theron bade his son farewell with an air of assumed dignity. "You are going to live in great splendor," he said. "But if you remember me, little son, let it not be with a sense of shame."

He left the boy then in the care of a fiercely handsome major-domo with bristling black whiskers. His name was Castor and there was a shade of condescension in his manner because he knew Basil had been born and raised in the Ward of the Trades. "Come, boy," he said. "I am to take you at once to the master. The master is a very rich man and one of great power. *You* will find things strange here."

Humility was a quality that was soon beaten out of boys who lived on the other side of the Colonnade. Basil scowled at the major-domo. "The only things strange here," he said, "is that a eunuch dares to speak thus to the son of the house."

Castor found this retort to his liking. He grinned at Basil and said, "We will get along together, you and I."

The cool halls of the house were filled with activity as the major-domo led the way up the wide stairs to the rooftop. Servants in fine robes were carrying up dishes of food and flagons of wine and bowls filled with pieces of ice, whispering as they passed each other; whispering about him, Basil realized at once, because there was a great deal of peering over shoulders in his direction and nodding of heads. "Children of filth!" said Castor, loosening the whip at his belt with furious relish. "Let one of them so much as smirk and they shall feel the sting of this on their behinds!"

Basil caught his breath in surprise when they reached the housetop. Curious mechanical aids were being used to supply comfort. Water pipes ran along the parapets and tiny streams were spouting forth from perforations in the metal. Fans then wafted the spray in all directions, so that a cool and pleasant mist filled the air with the effect of a perpetual breeze. At the far end, under a draped canopy of yellow silk, was a table of horseshoe shape, spread with silver and glass and an infinite variety of dishes made with a beautiful blue glaze. The table was dimly lighted, and at first the boy did not see the pretty lady reclining on a couch near the head.

His eyes instead were chained to the space inside the table where four girls in gauzy wide trousers were dancing on large glass balls. They were almost unbelievably expert, jumping from ball to ball like thistledown, spurning one with their feet while leaping to another, keeping all the glittering spheres in constant motion, their eyes laughing, their bare arms weaving to the music which came from instruments somewhere in the gloom. The glass balls tinkled with the clear, sharp sound of bells when they met, and they rolled with magic rhythm over the smooth plaster floor.

Then the boy became aware of the presence of the lady and he transferred his attention to her. She had, he saw, the fairest of hair and she was beautifully dressed in white and gold. He perceived also that she was taking no interest in the gay little dancers on the gyrating balls. This became apparent at the same time to a stout man who reclined on a couch beside her. He sat up with a resigned shake of his brown head.

"You are not watching, my loved one," he said. "It cost me heavily to engage them for your amusement. They come from the very far lands of the East."

"No," answered the lady in a languid voice, "I am not watching the dancers. I have been more interested in this boy. He is, I suppose, our son."

Ignatius had not been aware of Basil's arrival. He turned at once with a smile and motioned the boy to approach closer. Basil knew that this was his first great test. The lady in gold and white was studying him closely, and he realized that his chance for a happy life in this amazing household would depend on whether or not she liked him. He took a quick second glance in her direction and decided that it would be an easy matter to like her. She was slender, and this made a great impression on him, for he was accustomed to maternal outlines that bulged and sagged. She was gentle in manner and speech, and he was accustomed to shrillness and the heavy impact of callused hands.

The instinct bred in him by conditions in the Ward told him to face them boldly and speak with small respect. A still deeper instinct whispered to him that this would be wrong, that he must be quiet and respectful and have little to say for himself. Obeying this second prompting, he remained where he was, his head lowered, his feet shuffling nervously.

"Don't be afraid of us," said the lady. Her voice was kind. "Come closer so I may see you better."

Fighting down a desire to turn and run away, Basil moved forward on leaden feet. It became apparent at once, however, that he had passed muster, because the slender lady nodded her head and said to him, "I think you will make a nice son." Then she turned to the swarthy Ignatius. "You have chosen well."

The square countenance of the merchant lighted up immediately. He motioned Basil to take the couch on his other side.

"We are in great luck tonight, you and I, my son," he said. "I did not expect you to be approved so quickly. Your new mother is not easy to please. It took *me* two years to win her favor. You have done it in two minutes."

Basil had been accustomed to squatting on the floor and eating without ceremony and he was self-conscious when he found he was expected to stretch himself out on the couch and partake of the meal in a reclining position. The fare was so abundant and good, however, that the feeling of strangeness passed away. It was a matter of astonishment that the thick slices of cold mutton did not have to be counted or divided and that he could eat his fill of ripe dates and rich honey cakes. The wine, cooled in a deep jug in ice, was pure delight, and he swallowed it slowly. He watched his new mother and copied her manners, thereby saving himself from many mistakes.

After the meal a young Roman summoned the head of the household to a consultation with some visitors. Basil knew he was Roman because his manner was brisk and his tongue soft and drawling in its use of Koine. The merchant rose to his feet reluctantly and said, "Verily, Quintus Annius, I am the only slave in this establishment and you are my task-master."

"I don't believe your Quintus Annius ever eats or sleeps," said the lady Persis in an indifferent tone. "He is such a busy young man!"

The sky was now sprinkled with stars, and Basil found himself curious as to how the world would look at night from such a height. He looked at the lady Persis, who had partaken of supper substantially and was now showing signs of drowsiness, and asked in a respectful voice, "Is it permitted that I look over the parapet?"

She sat up at once and dabbed her eyes with perfumed water that a slave girl brought her in a jeweled glass. "Be careful, then," she said, straining to see him with shortsighted eyes. "We are so high from the ground that I never dare look over because of dizziness."

Basil, who had played games of hide-and-seek across the flat roofs of the poor section, leaping from house to house, saw no risk in surveying the world from the vantage point of his new home. The artistic soul of the boy responded at once to the magic spectacle of Antioch after the coming of darkness. All the families in this privileged section spent the evenings on their rooftops. He could see they were supping in much the same lavishness by lighted lamps that winked at him like fireflies. The profile of a lady with a beautiful Grecian nose and a nimbus of fluffy black hair swung directly into his line of vision from the next house as she moved her position, then vanished into the shadows, although he could still see her fingers toying with a bunch of grapes. On the roof beyond this a man was singing and accompanying himself on a cithara, a professional entertainer without a doubt, for his voice was sure and well trained. A slight breeze had sprung up, bringing to the boy the most delightful scents from the gardens below. He looked up at the sky and was sure that the stars were larger and brighter here than anywhere else.

Then he thought of the stifling heat in which his parents and his two brothers would be existing, and all sense of well-being left him. He was particularly concerned about his father. "I am sure he is sad," he thought, "because I am no longer there."

The slaves were removing the food and he became aware that one of them, a girl a year or two older than himself, was very attractive. She was watching him covertly, her eyes always turning in his direction as she moved about her tasks. Once, when Castor's back was turned, she gave him a smile. He allowed his mouth to twitch in response. Encouraged by this, she sauntered close enough to the parapet to address him in a whisper.

"Castor would whip me if he caught me speaking to you. But I don't care. He has whipped me many times and I scratch him and kick him in the shins. He is a beast."

A few minutes later, having accomplished so much without being detected, the girl sauntered close to him again, moving with a sinuous swing of her slender hips. She whispered with a catch of breath that came close to being a giggle, "I think you are a pretty boy."

This time she did not escape detection. The lady Persis raised herself from her couch and said in a sharp voice: "Attend to your duties, girl! Do you want me to report you to Castor for insolence?"

The girl disappeared in a great hurry at that, and the lady of the house called Basil to her and talked to him about the attitude he must adopt toward the slaves. He must never be familiar with them, particularly with the girls, of whom there were nearly a dozen. "Never lay a hand on any of them," she admonished. "It always leads to trouble. As for this one, she is an impudent slut. She was traded to us in redemption of a debt, and I am certain we made a mistake in taking her. Never speak to her or she will presume on it."

During the next few days, which were so exciting and full of surprises that he had no time to be homesick, Basil was always aware of this forward member of the household staff. Her name was Helena, and her sloe black eyes gave her an illusion of beauty. She never spoke to him, but he knew that she continued as aware of his presence as he was of hers and that only the fear of Castor's long black whip kept her from attempting more familiarities.

Then he missed her. For several weeks she was not in evidence; and finally he was told by Cassandra, a coal-black slave who did nothing but tend to the clothes of the lady Persis, that the girl had been sent to the "housing," which meant, he knew, that she was working in the warehouses. Sometimes slaves were sent to the housing and came back later in a subdued mood, in which case it was said they had been tamed. When Helena returned a full month later, Basil got up his courage to ask Castor about it. Had she—had she been tamed?

"Tamed?" Castor snarled with his whole face, his oily black whiskers curling upward under his nose. "Not that one. Nothing can tame her."

Basil's room was on the floor beneath the rooftop, a lofty and cool apartment with a sunken bath in one corner and with a couch that was beautiful to see but deceptively hard beneath its fancy coverings. The next night the heat was so great that sleep was impossible and, as he tossed about, he imagined that he had heard a voice call his name from the balcony of the floor below. The call was repeated, "Basil!" in a tone little above a whisper. He was sure it was the girl Helena and that she had climbed up from the slave quarters by means of the garden latticework.

Remembering the warning he had received from his mother, he did not respond at once. Then it occurred to him that she might be in need of help. He sat up on the side of his bed and wondered what to do. "Are you going to be a coward?" he asked himself. Finally he decided he must risk the consequences and, getting to his feet, tiptoed to the door opening on the inner corridor. As he did so, he fancied he detected a sound of rustling and creaking, as though she were making her way back by the same means she had employed in reaching the balcony. He whispered her name but received no response. The silence of the night remained unbroken after that, but the boy could not sleep. He was dissatisfied with himself. "I must be lacking in courage," he thought a dozen times.

The next day he heard that she had run away. When he asked Castor about it, the major-domo scowled and said: "I wish I knew where she has gone, the little slut! How I would like to get my hands on her. I would raise welts on that white back of which she is so proud!" He took out the whip that was always with him like a truncheon of office and cracked it viciously. "This much I know, she's not serving one master now. She will serve a different one every night of her life. *That* is what she has gone to, the lazy limb of wickedness!"

3

Basil soon fell into the new ways and found that living in luxury and being waited on hand and foot were quite pleasant. He became much attached to his new father. Quite often, when Ignatius was talking to other men about matters of trade in the high circular room opening on the garden that he reserved for such matters, his voice would be rough and domineering. None of this showed in his manner to his wife and new son, however. He would walk to the couch where Persis reclined (she never seemed to have enough energy to sit up) and stroke her hair while he asked, "Does my pretty little gray kitten feel any better today?" Unfortunately his pretty gray kitten never felt any better. Her usual answer, in fact, was that she felt worse. She would reach out a hand to touch the sleeve of his tunic, a gesture that would bare her arm to the shoulder and reveal its whiteness and slender purity of line, and say he must not worry, that she would not improve but was reconciled to her ill fortune. The broad and very brown face of the merchant would lose all of its content. He would sigh heavily and seat himself on the nearest couch, from which he would watch her with solicitude.

Basil became fond of his new mother also. He would fetch and carry for her and never failed to inquire about her well-being. Sometimes she would reward him with a smile of appreciation and even, on a few rare occasions, with a murmured admission that because of his kindness she felt a trifle better.

When the boy had lived in the white palace a matter of two years, he found himself so accustomed to his new life that the details of his earlier existence seldom came back to mind. Even the face of his real father was a blurred memory. He stopped asking questions about Theron.

He spent more of his time in the *aliyyah* above the entrance than anywhere else. Here he could look up and down the Great Colonnade and see the life of the city at high tide: the Roman official strutting pompously with toga over his left shoulder or clattering by in a chariot; the man from the desert on a handsome white Syrian camel with scarlet fringed harness from which a magic amulet dangled; the Jew who wore on his forehead a roll of parchment that was called a phylactery and was inscribed with holy texts; the Phoenician sailor, back from the Pillars of Hercules, with a brass ring in his nose and his hair curled in oily tufts.

Each day he would see rich neighbors (but none of them as wealthy as Ignatius) starting out for rides through the city. First a flag would be hoisted over the entrance and then there would be a loud beating of gongs and drums. The gate would swing back and two mighty horses would prance out, the reins held invariably in the proud black fists of a smiling driver. Behind, like an anticlimax, would come a tiny carriage with a fancy white canopy under which the members of the family would be closely packed.

Sometimes he witnessed a spectacle that caused the blood to course turbulently in his veins, a company of Roman soldiers on the march. He could always tell whether they were on parade or leaving for service in the frontier wars; in the latter event, they had "put on the saggum," a rough gray garment that was worn over the steel-plated habergeon and served also as a blanket at night. When this happened, he would watch the rhythmic marchers in their spiked Umbrian helmets and his eyes would take fire and his nostrils would flex themselves. He had no desire to be a soldier, but the color of war affected him like a fever.

One incident that occurred on the street below his post of observation always remained vividly in his memory. A vendor of sweetmeats had approached from the direction of the Omphalos, carrying his tray on his head. There was something about the man, an openness of eye and an almost benign cast of feature, that seemed out of keeping with the lowliness of his occupation. Basil, sensing this contrast, watched him closely, wondering about him and speculating as to his nationality. When the vendor reached a point immediately beneath, he was stopped by a customer. Looking down directly on them, the boy witnessed something that caused him to catch his breath. The hand of the vendor, raised ostensibly to make a selection from the tray, stopped instead to draw a piece of paper from a space immediately under the sweetmeats. The paper passed from one to the other and vanished into the sleeve of the purchaser so quickly that no pair of eyes save that of the watcher above could have become aware of what was happening. A small copper coin was tendered and accepted and the pair separated, to be lost at once in the thick traffic of the street.

Basil said to himself, "I am sure they are Christians."

He was recalling a visit he had paid with his real father when a boy of perhaps six years to a synagogue in the part of the city called Ceratium. It had once been handsomely adorned and a curious faith had been preached there openly, based on the teachings of someone called the Christ who had been a Jew. At the time when Theron, out of curiosity, took his youngest son, there had been a change of attitude on the part of the Roman authorities. The boy, who had seen multitudes of people bowing with covered heads before great bronze statues of the gods in the Gardens of Daphne, was astonished to see that the Christians held their heads up high as though watching something infinitely wonderful in the air above them. They sang together, simple airs about love and forgiveness, and their eyes were filled with so much content that Theron had whispered to his son: "These be strange people. But it is a strangeness about which we should know more."

A small man with a short blunt beard preached to them. Sometimes his voice was as shrill as the call of a bugle; sometimes it was deep like the thresh of waves over a stone reef; always it drew his listeners to him. His deep-set eyes had seen the miraculous things of which he spoke. He was not of Antioch, for his speech had more of the slurring note of the Romans. There were whispers about him in the audience which coupled the names of Paul and Tarsus.

The room was as still as a tomb in the rocks of sepulture while he spoke. Theron did not move as much as a hair of his bushy head. Once his hand tightened on the shoulder of the boy and he whispered, "My son, my son, can it be there is only one God and that He is a God of kindness and light?"

The discourse, however, was far over the head of a boy of six. Ambrose's attention became riveted instead on a second man, who stood off to one side of the gathering. He had a broad brow and a kindly eye and a smile of such gentleness that each strand in his great red beard seemed to curl in amiability. He was watching, familiarizing himself no doubt with the new faces in the gathering.

Theron was full of what they had witnessed when they reached the crowded room in the Ward of the Trades that served as home to his brood. "I have heard a great man deliver the most amazing message," he said, his eyes still veiled and withdrawn.

His wife had dampened his enthusiasm immediately. "Christians!" she said scornfully. "They are a bad lot. I saw one stoned to death in my native village. It was a woman, and I threw a stone myself. *That* is what happens to people who become Christians!"

"But the man Jesus performed miracles," protested Theron. "Those who follow Him cast out devils also and cause the lame to walk and the blind to see."

"Miracles!" scoffed his wife. "The face of that woman had turned black when I cast my stone. Why wasn't there a miracle to save her? There is one Simon the Magician who can perform miracles as well. They are all tricks."

They never returned to the synagogue, but one thing kept the meeting in Basil's memory. He recalled the face of the man with the red beard. It was still clear in his mind even when the contour of his own father's features had become dim and uncertain. What made it stay was a hint there of seeing things which other eyes missed, of hearing sounds, perhaps of music, in the stillest air.

There had been something of this same look on the face of the vendor of sweetmeats.

His hands were never idle while he sat in the latticed *aliyyah* and watched the rich spectacle below. He used bits of charcoal to make sketches on papyrus or on discarded fragments of cloth, catching with a few deft strokes the proud folds of a toga or the dignity of a red-and-white nomadic turban, the furtive leer of an unshaven beggar or the animal grace of a gladiator from the amphitheater that great Caesar himself had built. Later he would carry the sketches back to his room and mold figures in damp clay from the best of them.

Ignatius joined him once at his post of observation, seating himself with a hint of apology on the colored tiling of the floor. He studied the sketches with which the boy had surrounded himself, making a clucking sound with his tongue that conveyed approval.

"My son," he said, lifting up for closer inspection a figure done in wood of a slouching, bowlegged thief, "you have the gift the gods so seldom bestow. There is in this one the strong touch of Scopas. Sometimes I have seen in your work the ease and grace of Praxiteles, but this one is all Scopas; and for that reason I like it much. And yet you have never seen any of the work of these truly great men." He paused and indulged in a smile at the surprise on the face of the boy. "You did not guess how much I know about the glorious art of our race. You hear me railing and browbeating in that room of mine that is as round as the moon and you see me at meals filled with the troublesome problems of the day. Ah, my son, the glory that is so nearly lost to our race fills my mind oftener than the price of olive oil." He nodded his head slowly after several moments of reflection. "One day it will be necessary for you to learn something of the affairs of Ignatius the merchant so you will not be at a loss when the reins pass into your hands. But there is plenty of time for that. At the moment it is my earnest desire that you continue as you are doing."

There was a long pause then, and Basil knew that his father had something more to say and was finding it hard. Finally, in a defensively brusque manner, the merchant asked: "And what of you, my son? Are you happy here?"

The boy had no hesitation in answering, "Yes, I am very happy." Then he added, using the word for the first time since he had come to live in the high white palace, "Yes, Father."

Ignatius nodded his head several times, and it was clear that he was quite moved. "You are a good boy, my Basil," he said. "I think you are going to be worthy of the name I gave you. He was a truly great man, my father. When you get older I will tell you many things about him that will show what an honor it was for you when I gave you his name. Yes, my son, we shall have many talks."

Once when Basil was bathing in his sunken tub, the merchant came in and watched. It was always a matter of embarrassment to the boy that he was not permitted to take a bath by himself. Servants would always be about, some of them girls, to hold towels and pieces of soap (he had never lost his delight in having plenty of soap that gave so much lather and smelled so enticing), and he would have to drop off his tunic and the linen garment he wore next to his skin and then step naked into the water under the close observation of all these pairs of eyes. There were four attendants in the room on this occasion when Ignatius paid his visit.

The merchant watched in silence for several moments and then gave his head a shake. "It's clear you have no reason, my son, to be proud of your muscular development," he said. He seemed to find some discontent in this, and it was several moments later that he added: "But I didn't select you as a thrower of the discus. It was your spirit that I liked. Why should I be concerned now that you are as thin as a lath? You will be much like my father, who was never a strong man." He seemed to have discarded now all feeling of disparagement. "You are going to be tall, and that is what counts. I think you will be taller than all the sons of the men I call my friends."

4

Basil spent his seventeenth birthday finishing a gift for his father. He and his mother were making a joint offering of it. Persis had placed a fine ruby in his hand and suggested that he design a ring to hold it. He had decorated a narrow band with views of the Acropolis and had taken very special pains to make the stone show to advantage. To assist the red gold, which was to serve as the foil beneath, he had covered it with velvet of a deep wine shade and had placed the ruby on that, with the result that it glowed in an unnatural splendor. Delighted with the success of his experiment, Basil had said to his mother, "No king in the world has a ring on his finger to equal this one."

But the gift did not arouse in Ignatius the pleasure and gratification the two donors had anticipated. He looked at it so long in silence that Basil raised his own eyes from the ring to see what the matter could be. He discovered then that the face of the merchant was drawn and gray and that his neck, which had been as round and firm as a column of stone, had a flaccid look to it.

"Are you ill?" he asked with sudden anxiety.

"Blind! Blind!" said the merchant bitterly, as though speaking to himself. "I have been stupid, my son. I have wanted you to give all your time to making beautiful things like this, thinking that in due course I would teach you what you will need to know when you take my place. But will there be time? Here I am, with a pain like a hot iron in my side and the fear of death on me. And what do you know of the care of the groves, of the sailing of ships, of the accounts? I have been deliberately blind! And now perhaps it is too late."

Two days afterward he was dead. The white marble house fell into silence. No sound rose from the slave quarters; no one moved in the halls. A cautious hand had turned off the water which ran in the pipes, and so even the light ripple of the fountains ceased to be heard. The porters locked all the doors and stood guard in the shadows within. When Basil went to view his father's body, the scuffing of his felt heels echoed in the empty rooms as though a ghost were at large.

He approached the bier with a sense of dread. With his last breath Ignatius had issued a command against embalming. He did not want his brains drawn out through his nostrils, he had said; he had found them good brains and he wanted them left where they belonged inside his skull because he might have need of them in the strange land to which he was bound. In accordance with his wish, his body had been washed and scented with spices from the Far East and then bound in waxed cerements with such care that each finger and toe was wrapped separately.

Every care had been taken for the good of his soul. A tall candle had been lighted at the head of the bier and burned with a clear and steady flame. Salt had been sprinkled on the cerements in the hope of deceiving any evil spirits that might be lurking about, for salt was a concern solely of the living. A clenched fist was capable of fending off demons, and so the tightly wrapped fingers had been bent together.

Basil had become devoted to his father with the passing of the years. The sight of the white features above the close windings of the neck brought tears of pity into his eyes; pity for himself, in reality, because he had lost so kind a parent and so good a friend. The great merchant had looked vital and coarse in life, but death was lending dignity to his blunt features. It was as though he had captured for himself a moment of the beauty his race had done so much to create in the world.

Basil crept back through the ghostly stillness of the house to his own room, where he gave way to unrestrained grief. Persis found him there, having walked from her own extensive suite without any assistance. This was an unusual performance for her, the invalidism that she had so indolently practiced having finally become real. Basil, looking at her through eyes partly blinded with tears, noticed that she was very thin.

"My son," she said in a voice which contained a pleading note, "you are right to grieve for him. He was a good man, a kind husband and father. But, Basil, spare some of your compassion for me."

The youth raised his head and was surprised to find on her face an expression she had never worn before. He read there uncertainty and even fear. What surprised him was that the fear was of him.

"My gentle mother!" he protested. "You must know how much I love you."

"Yes," she said with quick eagerness. "I know that. But—but, my son, things will be different now. You will be the master. Will you love me enough still to be kind? As kind as *he* was?"

"I can never be anything but kind to you."

"It is easy to say such things." Her voice rose until it reached an almost shrill note. "But men change so much when they find all the wealth and power in their hands. I've seen it happen. My own father was like that, and then my brother. I was happy indeed when I found favor in the eyes of my husband and so escaped from the tutelage of my older brother. And now—and now—how can I be sure?"

Basil could not understand her anxiety. Why should she be so apprehensive of a change in his attitude? She had brought some wealth of her own when she wedded Ignatius. As his widow she would surely share in the estate. What hold could he have over her now?

He decided to discuss the point with Quintus Annius. The Roman was so capable in all things that his employer had once said of him, "This young man knows more than all the poets put together—I sometimes think he knows everything." Quintus had always been too busy to spare much time for the dreamy son of the family, but there had been an instinctive liking between them that both had recognized.

He found the secretary in the cubicle he used for his work. It opened unobtrusively off the magnificent circular room where Ignatius had received callers. The stone walls were lined with shelves, where papyrus rolls and written records bulged. The small marble-topped table was bare save for a document or two; and, for the first time perhaps since he had assumed his duties, Quintus was doing nothing. To his astonishment, Basil detected in him some of the hesitation and fear his mother had shown.

"You also?" he exclaimed. "Am I so much to be feared? I have just left my mother, who seems to think I will turn into a household tyrant. And now I suspect you of the same thought."

"Why are you surprised?" asked the secretary. "Don't you know what happens to widows who live under the law of the Twelve Tables? They are not recognized as human beings with rights of their own. Even when the widow has property she passes at once under the tutelage of the new head of the *gens,* the family. He may dispose of her property as he sees fit. He may refuse her the right to marry again if she has any such desire. On the other hand, he may make it hard for her to refuse a second husband of his own choosing. I hear that in some Eastern countries it is the custom to burn widows alive on the funeral pyres of their dead husbands. It sounds barbarous, but I sometimes wonder if it isn't kinder than our way."

Basil took a seat on the other side of the table and regarded his companion with a worried frown. It was a stifling hot day and his bodily discomfort equaled the mental distress he was feeling.

"I have heard a little about such matters, but I confess I gave them no serious thought," he said. He dipped his hands in a bowl of water standing beside the table and laved his face slowly. "I begin to see, Quintus, that I have much to learn."

"Much indeed, my master," answered Quintus. It was clear that he had some hesitation about pursuing the topic further. After a brief delay, however, he added: "You are in need of advice. There are pitfalls which perhaps you do not see."

The legally adopted son of the family had never questioned the future. It was easy enough to see the possibility of pitfalls for others, but how could they exist in his own carefully cleared path?

He leaned forward and placed his forearms on the cool marble of the table.

"To what do you refer?" he asked. "Do you expect—legal difficulties?"

When Quintus did not answer at once, Basil, whose mind, once aroused, was quick and aggressive, began to understand the difficulty in which his father's assistant now found himself. If some kind of legal complication lay ahead, it would be a matter of concern for the young Roman to ally himself with the winning faction. Could he be blamed for thinking of his own interests?

Quintus rubbed a finger thoughtfully down the length of his arched nose, keeping his eyes lowered. He was deep in consideration of the problem. When he looked up finally, it was clear he had made his decision. He smiled and nodded to his companion.

"You are the rightful heir," he declared, his voice once more precise and charged with conviction. "You were adopted legally with the five witnesses and the formula established in the Twelve Tables. I know your father considered you his son. It is my duty to stand by you and to give you such support as I may—if the need arises."

Basil rose to his feet and began in an agitated mood to pace about the room. As his father had predicted, he had grown tall, a full two inches above the average in height; but he was slenderly proportioned and fitted more, if strength were the test, for the sedentary life he had elected to live than the more active role which was devolving on him now. The doubts planted in his mind by Quintus Annius had brought a deep wrinkle of worry to his finely proportioned brow.

"You say you will support me—*if* the need arises," he declared, pausing at the table and gazing down unhappily at its occupant. "What do you mean by that, Quintus Annius?"

The secretary answered by propounding a question of his own. "What opinion do you hold of your father's brother?"

Ignatius had one surviving relation only, a brother named Linus. Ten years the junior in point of years, Linus had depended on the head of the family in everything, and it had been due to the guidance and the financial assistance of Ignatius that the younger brother had attained some degree of affluence in the shipping trade. The adoption of a son into the family had been a great blow to Linus, as Basil had been well aware.

"If your claim could be set aside," went on Quintus, speaking in a low tone, "this—this base brother of my noble employer would himself become the head of the *gens.*"

"But, Quintus," cried Basil, finding such doubts bitter to entertain, "there can be no doubt of my rights in the matter."

"None whatever. In my mind or in yours. In the minds of fair and honest men. But, my master, it happens that of the five witnesses three are now dead. The fourth—his name was Christopher and he was called Kester of Zanthus—has left Antioch and there seems some uncertainty as to his whereabouts. Some say he went to Jerusalem. He was over fifty when the ceremony took place. Can we be sure he is still alive? This leaves us with one of the five, and I consider it a great misfortune that the one should be Hiram of Silenus." He again ran a forefinger along the bridge of his nose. "Hiram of Silenus is a man of the most questionable character. I hear his financial standing at the moment is far from sound. If it entered the mind of Linus to dispute your right, this base Hiram might prove a very unsatisfactory witness. He might be persuaded to have lapses of memory, to have indeed a perversity of recollection to the undoing of your father's intent."

"Quintus!" cried Basil. "Why do you raise this terrible doubt?"

"The first lesson you must learn in the world of trade is to consider all possibilities. I may be alarming you without cause. But—I am afraid there is reason for fear. I would not be surprised if Linus had already begun his—his moves in the dark."

Basil resumed his seat, allowing his head to fall forward into the support of his cupped hands. He had been completely happy when his only concern was the making of clay figures and the carving of silver vessels. This contentious existence into which he had now been plunged was so obnoxious to him that he found it hard to continue the discussion.

"What can I do?" he asked finally.

"You must establish safeguards," declared Quintus briskly. He was now on familiar ground and quite sure of himself. "You must see Hiram of Silenus at once and sweeten his memory with a rich reward, richer than Linus can afford to offer. Then there are the magistrates. Their friendship will be necessary if Linus appeals to the law. They must be given presents at once. All this I can arrange for you if you have a reluctance to such matters."

"Must I bribe men to tell the truth?" cried Basil, his mind revolted at the need to begin a new life by such methods. "This is dishonest, base, unclean!"

The secretary seemed unwilling to acquaint this unworldly youth with the full peril of his position. He paused a long time before saying anything more.

"You were sold to Ignatius," he declared finally. "If Linus can convince the magistrates you were not sold for adoption, what, then, was the basis of the transaction? You were sold—as a slave." Quintus looked steadily into the eyes of the new head of the family, his mouth drawn into a tight, straight line. "There is no middle ground for you. Either you are master here or a slave, subject to the orders of Linus. Think of this well! It would be a mistake, a terrible mistake, not to take every step to protect yourself against the"—his composure left him suddenly and he allowed his voice to rise—"against the greed of this man, this unworthy brother who is like to a boar's snout, this hoof of a sick camel, this fester on a leper's skull!"

5

Angry, incredulous, filled with the bitterness of self-blame, Basil rose and left the court. Heads were turned carefully in the other direction as he strode out through the crowded room. No one looked up or nodded to him. The decision had left him an outcast, one to whom free men did not speak.

One thought filled his mind to the exclusion of everything else, even of speculation as to what lay before him now. He could not escape from the face of the magistrate who had presided. It represented the forces which had led to his undoing. It seemed to him the embodiment of everything evil, the face of a satyr run to seed. The eyes of this evil old man had been fixed on him from the moment the hearing began, filled with scorn and ill will. They seemed to be saying: "You have been the luckiest of all men, raised from the gutter of the Ward to untold wealth; you have everything in your favor; you are heir to the greatest fortune in Antioch, and people scrape before you and agree with what you say and declare you to be handsome and gifted; you can have your pick of friends and your choice of wives. But I, Marius Antonius, represent the law, and because you have been too blind and too haughty to seek my favor and pay me what it is worth, I have it in my power to break your pride, to cast you from the heights to the depths; and that is what I propose to do, O Basil, son so-called of Ignatius, who shall be forevermore now Basil, son of Theron, seller of pens and ink."

Whether Basil would have persuaded himself to the need of bribing the magistrates and the one important witness, as Quintus Annius had advised, was something he would never know himself. Linus, the brother of the dead merchant, had moved too fast. While the heir still debated the issue in his mind, rebelling at the dishonesty of it, the taurine brother had brought his action, claiming that he, Basil, was not an adopted son.

It had required no more than one glance at the face of Marius Antonius, who was called in the city the Bottomless Pocket, to convince the rightful heir that he had made a mistake. The magistrate was bitter and biting to him but affable to the plaintiff. He had shown himself from the first to be biased, directing the questions and prompting the witnesses when they seemed unsure of their answers. He had snapped off any tendency to give evidence friendly to the son of the house.

Hiram of Silenus was as unsatisfactory as a witness as the secretary had predicted. He remembered little, and everything he said was hostile to the son's claim. The brass scales had not been struck by the ingot of lead and so he was certain that the transaction he witnessed had not been an adoption. Acquaintances of the dead Ignatius testified that he had made no effort to put authority of any kind in the hands of the man who claimed to be his adopted son and that the position of the latter had seemed to be that of a beneficiary being supported while he developed his talents. Men in trade reported their impressions of the relationship, always unfavorable to Basil. Persis had not been allowed to attend and, when Quintus Annius did not appear, Basil's hopes expired. The young Roman, it seemed, had preferred at the last to consult his own interests.

Basil knew that his father had intended to summon a panel of witnesses and to acknowledge before them that he, Basil, was his adopted son. Because Ignatius had died too soon, it was now necessary to stand in court in front of a corrupt judge and listen to an unctuous statement of the decision.

He reached the street, where the sun blazed down on the white walls of the great buildings. "This is a world of cruelty and dishonesty," he said to himself, staring tautly at the crowds which passed along the Colonnade. "I, who should have been the richest man in Antioch, am now a slave. I own nothing and I have no rights in life."

Persis had dressed herself in the expectation of a rightful verdict. Over the intimate undergarment, which was white and sleeveless and of cool linen, she had draped her gayest *palla*. It was of Tyrian purple, the most prized of colors and the only one which aided her fading charms. Her hair had been curled and plaited and she wore a wreath of gold with precious stones in each leaf, the last gift of her uxorious husband.

But when she trailed her long draperies across the marble floor of her room to meet Basil on his return, her attire had fallen into sad disorder. Her hair hung on her forehead in straight, damp wisps. Her face looked wrinkled and thin.

"My poor boy, my poor boy!" she whispered, pressing her clenched knuckles to her lips. "What will become of you now? What—what will become of me?"

"I would have been a failure, Mother, as the head of the family." Basil paused and achieved a feeble smile. "I must not call you that again. The court has ruled I am not your son."

"You are my son!" She seemed to have taken fire at last. Her eyes lost their listlessness; she reached out to place a possessive hand on his shoulder. It was no more than a passing phase, and almost immediately she lapsed again into a mood of resignation. "He always resented you," she said in a low voice, as though afraid of being heard by other ears. "I could see it in his face. He intended to do this from the very first. Prying into the books and bribing the servants!" Her eyes were now filled with tears of self-pity. "He hated me because I complained to my husband of him once. Basil, Basil, is there nothing you can do to help us both?"

The dispossessed heir looked down at her with burning eyes. "Not immediately, Mother. Linus has won. He will be master here." His hands were so tightly clenched at his sides that he could feel the nails cut into his skin. "But I haven't given up hope, Mother. I am going to fight him. There is still one chance. I shall go on fighting him if—if they kill me for it!"

Persis was weeping loudly now. "Oh, why did my husband leave things like this? He was so careful about everything else. Ignatius, come back to your distracted wife and the son who has been robbed of his rights, and tell us what we should do!"

Basil was conscious of eyes on his back as he descended the stairs to the main floor and of anxious faces peering at him from around corners and out of darkened doorways. The silence of intense fear hung over the slave quarters. Castor met him in the lower hall, resentment in every line of his squat figure.

"He has come, stamping on his heels as though he owned everything," he said. "It was different once! He would come to me then and whisper out of the corner of his mouth, 'Help me in this, Castor,' or 'Get me those papers which came from the warehouses today when my brother is through with them.' He was like a cat with butter on his paws. When he came in just now, he stared at me and gave that grunt of his. 'You will be taking my orders, O once mighty Castor,' he said. 'Put away that whip because I am going to rule by the bastinado. How sensitive are the soles of *your* feet, my Castor?'" The major-domo stopped abruptly, as though realizing the danger to which he might be exposing himself with his frankness. He nodded to Basil in as friendly a manner as he dared assume. "You are wanted at once."

The new head of the *gens* was sitting in his brother's chair when the dispossessed heir entered the circular room. His head, which had once been covered with a thatch of tight-curling reddish hair, had been shaved as a sign of mourning, and it had something of the look of a ripe squash. Because of the heat of the day he had drawn the skirt of his tunic up around his hips, and his fat bare legs were spread out in front of him. There was a triumphant and malicious glitter in his pinkish-red eyes.

"You have been sold," he announced. "To Sosthene of Tarsus, the silversmith."

Basil had been expecting some such announcement and he was not much disturbed. Being sent back to the Ward of the Trades might be better than remaining here. He could detect sounds of activity in the room back of him, which the secretary occupied. "Quintus has lost no

time in changing sides," he thought. "I wish him joy of his new master."
He was fully aware, nevertheless, that the fault did not rest on the
shoulders of that capable young Roman but on his own.

"This knack of yours"—there was a slighting edge to the voice of Linus
—"gave you some small value. I drove as good a bargain as I could, but in
spite of that I got little enough for you. You will go to your master at
once. I don't want you here a moment longer than is necessary, so be on
your way, my once proud Ambrose, son of the laziest seller of pens in all
Antioch."

"The Romans would crucify me if I killed him now," said Basil to himself. "I must swallow everything he says—and wait."

"You understand, don't you, that you have no possessions now? Take
nothing with you but the clothes you wear. I would strip you to the skin
and send you on your way in sackcloth, but if I did there would be people
to find fault with me. The tools you used and the trinkets you made are
no longer yours. They belong here. They have been collected and put
away."

"They are mine!" Basil looked up at the new master of the household
for the first time. "I know something of the law and I can prove——"

Linus threw back his head and let out a loud guffaw. "So you want
more of the law, do you? More of Marius Antonius? You stupid ox, get
yourself gone before I invoke the law myself. A slave has no rights in a
Roman court. I think your stupidity exceeds your pride." He raised one
broad sleeve of his tunic and wiped the perspiration from his brow. "I
give you a word of warning. You are not to see any members of this
family. Most particularly, you are not to talk to the lady Persis. You must
not communicate with her in any way. Is that clear in your mind, slave?
If you come here on any excuse, I shall have you beaten and driven away
like a thief!"

BOOK ONE

CHAPTER I

I

FOR TWO YEARS the Great Colonnade, with its four rows of pillars like Roman soldiers on parade, had cut Basil off from everything that seemed worth while in life. He lived in the Street of the Silversmiths, which was narrow and turgid and filled at all hours with chaffering and expostulation. Here he sat at a rear window, in a sweltering hole under the roof, working through the hours of day and often into the night, with his hammers and chasing tools, his pots of wax and his soldering wicks. He was subject to the sullen humors of his master, who was called Sosthene of Tarsus, and the tinderlike temper of his mistress, who kept him under pressure to produce more and more.

From his window he could see the tops of the Colonnade columns and even a segment of parapet that he believed to be part of the house, once the property of Ignatius and now rightfully his.

Sosthene was small and black and at his trade he was quick and skillful. In the beginning he had been helpful. He would watch Basil at work and then suddenly he would shake his head and take the tools out of the boy's hands.

"No, no!" he would say with a rising intonation that made his voice seem to screech. "Not that way. By Zeus, by Apollo, by Pan! By Men! By all the gods! See, stupid one. Do it thus. And thus."

In spite of his great skill with the tools, the little man had no sense of beauty, and what he produced was dull and uninspired. It brought small prices in the shop below. The results were different when Basil had learned the tricks of the trade, for then everything he did glowed with beauty. Using the sketches he had made on the *aliyyah*, he produced busts and figurines that began to satisfy him in an increasing degree; but never completely, for he remained fiercely self-critical. They pleased the customers of the shop. Everything he made was sold, quickly and at good prices.

He never went out. This was due to a disinclination to meet old friends while wearing the cloth of servitude, but as time went on a more tangible reason had developed for remaining out of sight. He realized that his safety depended on not being seen. Linus knew that public opinion had been against him and that all Antioch was convinced he had robbed his brother's rightful heir. It required no special knowledge of the way that evil mind worked to be sure he would never be at rest as long as Basil remained a reproach to his possession.

Linus was not only increasing the wealth Ignatius had left but he was already a force in politics. He was hand in glove with the Roman authorities. It was being told around that he had great plans; that he was buying ships and organizing more and more camel trains; that he was setting up his personal agents everywhere. He would soon be in a position to enforce his desires.

Basil lived in fear of Linus from the day that a note reached him in the Street of the Silversmiths. A stranger slipped it into the hand of Agnes, the small Jewish girl, a slave like himself, who did such household work as was needed. The stranger had said in a hasty whisper, "Put this into the hand of Basil, son of Ignatius." Agnes had willingly risked the beating she would have received had her part in the transaction become known. She was a tiny wisp of a girl, flat-chested and thin, with unnatural spots of color in her cheeks. She waited until the time came to sweep out his room at the end of the working day. It was dark then and Basil was sitting at the open window. He was in a mood of the deepest dejection and paid no attention to her until she said in a whisper, holding out her broom of sturdy willow withes, "See, it is for you."

A piece of parchment was stuck in the osiers. He reached down quickly and took it. It proved to be an unsigned note, written in Koine, and in an unfamiliar hand.

> The head of the usurper lies uneasy on the pillow and he dreams of means to rid himself of the one he has wronged. Go not out on the streets. Have no speech with strangers. You will not be safe as long as you remain in Antioch.

Basil did not know who had sent him the warning. He was certain it had not come from his adopted mother. It was reported that her health was increasingly bad and, in any event, she lacked the energy for a step of such daring. He concluded finally that the note had come from Quintus Annius, who would be in the best position to know the designs of Linus. Perhaps the young Roman's conscience had prompted him to this one effort in his behalf. Whatever the motive had been, Basil believed the danger to be real. If he desired to live (sometimes he did not care), he must find some means of getting away.

Sosthene's wife brought him his meals. She was called Eulalia, which means fair of speech and was, therefore, the least suitable of all names for the double-tongued woman who bore it. She was the real head of the household, ruling her husband as rigidly as she did the two slaves. She never failed to be in the shop when a customer called, and it required an iron will to get away from her without making a purchase. All money went immediately into her hands, and it was one of the jokes in the Ward of the Trades that Sosthene never had as much as a half shekel or even a mite in his possession from one year's end to another.

There were two meals in this household of extreme frugality, the first at ten in the morning, the second at five in the evening. Eulalia would carry a battered tray up to Basil to save the time he would waste in walking up and down the stairs that were on the outside of the house. She would stand by and watch while he finished his meal, her eyes following each morsel of food from the dish to his mouth as though begrudging it. The fare was always of the plainest kind. Meat was provided twice a week only, and the usual dishes were vegetables, cheese, fruit, and coarse black bread. The wine was thin and sour, and of this he was allowed no more in a week than three and a half pints.

"The reward of diligence," she would invariably say as she picked up the tray. "Such bounteous meals will be forthcoming only if you stay close to your work."

On the day after the receipt of the warning he stopped her with a question before she reached the door with the empty tray.

"Do you sell all the things I make?"

Eulalia had stretched out an arm, so thin and withered that it resembled the stalk of a sunflower when the frosts are ready to cut it down, to open the door. She drew back at once.

"Is it concern of yours?" she demanded harshly.

Basil nodded. He had never been afraid of her and had won on that account a grudging measure of respect. "It is concern of mine. Would you like to make much more money out of the work I do?" He waited a moment before adding, "There is a way."

She placed the tray on the floor with a jolt that spilled what was left of the goat's milk, and walked back to confront him, hands on hips, her black eyes fixed as implacably on his as those of a hawk that sights below the slow beating of a victim's wings.

"What do you mean by that?" she demanded. "You are a slave. Everything you do belongs to us—to me, because I am the holder of the purse. Have you not been doing your best work? Is that what you are telling me?"

Basil shook his head. "No. I do the best I can. Always." He held out his hands, palms turned upward. They had changed from the soft white of the easy days when slaves had tended him, laving them with great care and rubbing them with costly unguents. They were now soiled with acids and callused from continuous work. He was finding it impossible to remove the grime with the niggardly fragment of soap allowed him. "There is so much these hands must learn. If I had the means of instruction, I am sure I could produce work such as has never before been seen in Antioch. Do you believe me? If not, ask the rich men to whom you are selling what I make now. They will open your eyes." He let his hands drop to his lap. "I can learn no more here. If I stay, I shall not be capable of doing much better than I do now."

"Your master shows you everything——" she began.

Basil brushed aside the suggestion of learning more from Sosthene of Tarsus. "He cannot show me the things I must know. I have already passed beyond him. He knows it, and so do you, as well as I do. Send me to one of the great silversmiths in Athens or Rome. Make an agreement with me that within a certain period I am to be a free man but that for as long as I live I am to pay you a share, a large share, of everything I earn. This I promise you: I will make you rich beyond any dream of wealth you may have in your head at this moment."

It was clear from the expression on the passionately acquisitive face of the woman that she grasped the possibilities in his proposal. She breathed heavily as she thought it over. But in the end she shook her head, bitterly reluctant to give up such a prospect, but too convinced of the drawbacks to consent.

"Such a risk!" she cried. "If we let you go, we might never see you again. No, no, no! How can I tell what schemes you are hatching in that mind of yours? You are a clever one. You are as sly as a fox. You are trying to get away, that is all. I can read things in your face. No, no, no! I must not listen to your schemes." It was clear she was working herself up into one of her rages over her inability to accept an idea that promised such rich rewards. "We are not getting good prices for what we sell. You may think so, but it is not true." She shook her head at him, fiercely, angrily. "I shall see to it, slave, that we do better out of you from now on. It is clear to me you have not been doing your best. There will be no shirking. You must get these notions out of your head or I will have my husband beat them out of you." She laughed shrilly. "You want to go to Rome, do you? Let me tell you, they know how to treat presumptuous slaves in Rome. They crucify them. They nail them to the cross upside down."

She whisked up the tray with an angry motion, spilling the milk on the floor, and stamped out.

Never in the two years that he had existed in the house of Sosthene had the bitter shrew who ruled it been unable to carry his meals to him. Yet it came about that the very day after this talk she was visited by a malady which chained her to her bed. The tray in the evening had to be taken up by Agnes. The latter came in proudly, carrying it above her head. She began to talk in cautious tones as soon as the food had been deposited on the workbench beside him.

"I think the mistress is possessed of a new devil, a *ruah ra'ah*," she said. "She tosses about and moans and I think her voice is different. Perhaps it is the *ruah ra'ah* which talks. Of course she has always had a devil in her. It may be the same one and that it is getting worse." She was silent for a moment and watched him as he munched on a piece of goat's-milk cheese. "Do you want to know what I think about this devil? I think she walked into the shadow of the moon under an acacia tree. That is where the *ruah ra'ah* always stays. As soon as she came there, the devil jumped right down her throat. If it stays inside her, she will be more cruel to us than ever."

Basil was more interested in her talk, he found, than in the food. He pushed the tray, which still contained most of his supper, to one side.

"Oh, Basil, aren't you hungry at all?" cried Agnes. She was on the point of tears because of his lack of appetite. "You *must* eat more. You will become ill, like me, if you don't. And you know what you leave tonight will be sent up to you tomorrow, and it will be stale then and tasteless. I took such pains with your supper tonight!"

He had been watching her with pity, noticing the hollows under her cheekbones and her unhealthy flush. She coughed continuously. To please her, he began to eat again.

"Basil," said the girl, hovering over him with a solicitude which was doubly unselfish in one so clearly in need of help herself, "you are very unhappy. I cry whenever I think of you. My poor Basil! I want to help you. And I can, if you will listen to me." She shook her head with emphasis and then asked a question. "Do you know anything about angels?"

"No," he answered. "It is a new word. What does it mean?"

"I didn't think you knew. You are not a Jew. You are a Greek, and the Greeks know nothing of the truth." She said this as a matter of course and with no intent to show superiority. "My father and mother were so poor they had to sell me as a slave. They were unhappy about it and my mother wept all the time before I left; but there would have been no food for the little brothers if they had not sold me. My mother told me many things I must always remember. She said I must never forget I am of the Jewish race and that the children of Israel are the chosen people of the great Jehovah. And she told me all about the angels." She paused to press a stalk of onion into his hand. It was crisp and young and undoubtedly she had experienced some difficulty in keeping it for him. "My mother told me that angels are wonderful beings who sit beside the great Jehovah and do His bidding. She said she had seen them herself. They have beautiful faces and they have wings to carry them back and forth between heaven and earth. When I was leaving, she began to weep harder than ever and she said, 'My poor little girl, always remember that Mefathiel is the angel to whom slaves pray. He is the Opener of Doors.'"

Everything Basil had heard about the Jewish people and their strange faith had interested him, but this talk about angels transcended everything he had been told before. If there was only one God, as the Jews said, it was easy to think that He would need an army of assistants to carry out His orders. Basil found himself ready to accept the existence of these beautiful, winged creatures.

"Agnes, there are doors which must be opened for me," he said earnestly. "Do you think your Mefathiel would help me?"

"Oh yes. Of course he would help you. He can open prisons. He can break down the sides of mountains. If you pray to him and he listens, he will open any door you want. Even"—she looked back at the entrance to the room before finishing—"even the door of this house."

Basil said to her: "Agnes, I shall pray to Mefathiel every night. Perhaps there are others who could help me also. Is there an angel of memory?"

She nodded quickly, delighted that she was able to be of help to him. "Yes, that is Zachriel. He is a very great angel, because if people did not remember they would not remain true to the one God. The most important thing of all is to remember God and the Laws, and so Zachriel sits close to Jehovah. My mother said he is always at God's right hand."

"Perhaps he would be too busy to listen if I prayed to him."

There seemed to be a doubt in her mind on this point. "He is a very busy angel," she conceded. "But you can try."

"You had better go now," he said, aware that time had been passing quickly. "The master's wife will be angry because we have been talking."

"She will twist my arm to make me tell her what was said. But I won't!" The child gave her head a defiant toss. "She has done it often, but I have never given in. She won't get anything out of me."

That night, following the instructions the slave girl had given him before leaving, Basil went to the open window and sank down on his knees. He turned his eyes in the direction of the stars.

"O Mefathiel," he said, "I have no right to speak to you because you are an angel of the Jews and I am not a Jew. I am Greek. Because I am Greek you may not hear my voice. But if you do hear me, most kind of angels, I want to tell you that a door must be opened for me if I am not to fall into the hands of my worst enemy. The door must be opened for me at once or it will be too late. If you look down and see me as I am, you will think me unworthy of your help. But remember this, O Mefathiel: I am a slave and I wear the clothes in which I came two years ago. I have worn nothing else since, and you will think me no better than a beggar at the city gate. Am I worth saving? you may ask, O generous Opener of Doors. I do not know. All I can tell you is that I have a certain gift for making things with my hands, and this I promise: If the doors of my prison swing open, I shall work very hard and I shall always strive to keep this gift from tarnish.

"And thou, O Zachriel," he went on, "of whose greatness I have just been told, do this much for a man who has never prayed to thee before. Never let me forget, Angel of Memory, those who have been kind to me and those who have taken great risks to be of help when I needed help. This I beg of you, as I do not want to be guilty of ingratitude, which is a great fault but a very easy one to commit."

The rest of his prayer was delivered with an intensity that told how deeply he felt.

"I beg that my memory will remain so clear that I shall forget none of the wrongs which have been done me. Keep the thought of my misfortunes so fresh in my mind that I may strive to undo the ill that has been done to me and to those who depended on me. Let my memory feed my resolution to be avenged on my enemies when the right day comes. This I beg of thee, Zachriel, Angel of Memory."

2

It was three nights later. Sosthene and his wife had climbed to their tiny rooftop, where a hint of breeze, tainted with the smells of the city, reached them over the huddle of parapets. It was so dark when the caller came, asking for the master of the house, that Agnes could see nothing of him, save that he was old and had a very long beard.

"You want the master?" she repeated. "Is it a matter to be talked over with him?"

"Yes. It is a matter to be talked over."

"Is there, perhaps, something to be decided?"

The visitor smiled, amused at her insistence. "There is something to be decided."

"Then," declared the girl, "I had better ask the mistress to come down too. When there is something to be decided, she does the deciding."

The old man laughed at this and patted her head. "You are bright, my child. I can see you will be one to do the deciding yourself when you grow up and become a woman."

Agnes shook her head and sighed. "Oh no. I am not well and I am not going to grow up."

The visitor moved closer to her so that he could see her face by the light of the small lamp she was carrying. He studied her carefully and with an air as sad as her own. "It is true, my child, that you are not well," he said. "You will not get better if you continue to live in a place as close and hot as this. You need much fresh air and rest and good food. And you need loving care, my good little child."

Agnes answered simply and without any intention of arousing his sympathies further, "I am a slave. A slave does not have these things. I must live here with my master and mistress."

The old man's manner became even more depressed. "In this life there are many things which are wrong, and of them, I believe, slavery is the worst. Someday, my child, there will be a great change in the world. A shining figure will come down out of the sky and after that there will be no more wickedness or slavery or bodily ills. I hope it will come to pass soon; even in time to save you from—from all the troubles I foresee."

Eulalia led the way down the outside stairs, followed by a grumbling Sosthene. "Well, and what is it you want?" she demanded. "Is there something you wish to buy?"

The visitor hesitated. "Yes," he said finally. "I think I may tell you there is something I want to buy. But we must not discuss it here. I feel there are ears in the darkness and that curiosity presses about us as closely as the heat of the night."

"Come inside," said Eulalia, all graciousness now that she saw the possibility of a sale.

She led the way into the shop on the ground floor and lighted a lamp suspended from the ceiling. By the limited illumination thus afforded it could be seen that the visitor was well advanced in years. He had a kind and understanding eye but with enough of an air of resolution to make it clear that he was not one to be imposed upon. For his part, he gave a quick glance about the small shop, noting the cheapness of most of the things for sale, the oriental masks, the daggers and bronze swords, the incense lamps, the jewel boxes from the desert country. Then he allowed his eyes to rest on the owner and his wife, studying them with great care.

"I must ask some questions," he said. "You have in your household one Basil, a worker in silver and gold. I understand he made himself, without aid or suggestion, a figure of Athena, which was sold to the Greek banker Jabez, who is a collector of works of art. This is true?"

Sosthene was on the point of answering, but his wife's sharp elbow nudged him into silence. "Yes," she said. "He is a slave and our property. He made the figure."

"And the silver vase with the head of Theseus in relief, which one of the magistrates in the city is fortunate enough to possess?"

"That also was of his fashioning."

"And the plaque with moonstones, which a Jewish merchant bought from you as a gift for his wife?"

Eulalia nodded. "He designed the plaque. Is there something you want him to make for you? We can promise that you will be more than satisfied."

The visitor continued his study of them, one hand smoothing the strands of his long silky beard. "It is not the work of his hands I desire to buy from you," he said finally. "It is his freedom. I come to offer you any reasonable amount you may name."

The woman of the house indulged in a cackling laugh. "The sum would be beyond your means, old man. My husband and I have our own idea of the value of this slave. It is high—very, very high."

There was a nod of agreement from the visitor. "The price might be fixed at a high figure if you had nothing in the future to consider. But what of tomorrow? Will it be high then, or the day after? You must be aware that—that this young man who is called Basil may have no value at all if you wait that long."

At this point Sosthene projected himself into the discussion. "The years have made you addled in the head," he declared roughly. A sense of resentment took possession of him. "What is your purpose, dotard, in coming to us with such talk? Do you count us as stupid as the partridge that can be run down and clubbed to death? You are too well seasoned for such joking!"

"I know the price you paid for the boy." The visitor was speaking now in tones so low that no ears beyond the confines of the stiflingly hot room could have heard him. "Linus made it low purposely because it was his thought to put more shame on the victim of his plotting. He is sorry now that he sold the young man at any price. Why? Because he wants nothing so much as to have his victim removed from his path. He will never feel secure as long as Basil is alive. He is powerful and the law nods at his say-so." There was a moment of silence. The visitor waited just long enough to let the full significance of what he had said sink deep into their selfish and acquisitive minds. "If the young man were killed tonight—or the day after—what compensation would Linus pay you? Would you dare go to law, thereby accusing him of murder? Or would you be wise enough to accept your loss and do nothing?"

The silence remained unbroken. The old man was conscious of the deep breathing of his two auditors and the conflict of fear and cupidity in their eyes.

"This may be stated as truth," he went on. "If the boy remains within reach of the agents of Linus, he will not be alive a week from today."

"What knowledge do you have that you speak so boldly?" asked Eulalia in a whisper.

"I am one who has no desire to see Linus succeed in his purpose. Need we probe any deeper?" The visitor glanced about him again and then took a seat at one end of the table where during the day most of the goods for sale were displayed. From somewhere in the folds of his spotless white tunic he produced a bottle of ink and a reed pen, then a sheet of parchment on which writing had been set down. "See," he said, holding up the parchment. "An order on Jabez, the banker. It will be honored when you present it to him, even tonight if the need to have the money presses on your minds. It is for double the amount you paid to Linus for the young man."

The faces of the silversmith and his wife seemed in the semidarkness of the room as drawn and grotesque as the dance masks which hung on the walls. Their eyes had drawn in to pin points, as sharp as the sword blades standing upright in a corner rack.

The visitor continued to speak quietly. "In an hour's time, when sleep has taken sway over your neighbors and there are neither ears nor eyes in the dark, the boy and I will slip away. You will not see either of us again."

Sosthene drew his wife to one side and whispered to her in desperate haste. "We would be mad to listen to him. What will Linus do if he finds we have let the boy go?"

His wife regarded him with fitting scorn. "Head of mutton! In the morning we go to the authorities and we say that a valuable slave has run away from us during the night. We demand aid of the law in finding him."

She had spoken in so low a tone that the visitor could not possibly have heard what was said. At this point, nevertheless, he interjected a comment that indicated he was aware of what had passed between them. "You will not dare go to the authorities with any such tale. You must sign a full release tonight, restoring to him his liberty without any restrictions. In the document I shall give you to sign, it will be stated that you relieve him of any obligations of *obsequium* and *officium* and that you will not oppose his restoration at once to the citizenship he enjoyed before."

Eulalia was too startled for several moments to make any move. Then she drew her husband aside and began to whisper in his ear. "This is what we must do. We must sign the paper and get our money. Then we shall go to Linus and say we were forced into it——"

"Do you not know," asked the old man, "that I can hear every word you say? Nay, I can do more. I can read the thoughts which enter your mind. My advice to you, false woman, is to cease for once your wicked conniving."

"You cannot frighten us!" she cried.

"You think I cannot do what I say?" The visitor's eyes held her, and she could neither avert her gaze from him nor move away. "This much I shall give you as a proof. You are thinking that when you have the money you will hide it in the bowl of brass at the bottom of the disused well in your cellar. The well so carefully covered that no one guesses its existence. You are thinking of the piece of land you will buy with the gold outside the city walls, the little farm of the Three Pear Trees."

Eulalia gasped in surprise and dismay. "Husband," she cried, "let us sign and get our money! We must not go against this old man. I am afraid of him!"

3

Basil had closed the curtain in his small window to protect himself from the insects which hummed in the darkness without. The breeze had died down completely and the curtain hung without a trace of movement. The atmosphere of the room was like a baker's oven when the fire is banked.

He sat perfectly still on the wooden bench where he spent his long working hours. If his body was inactive, his mind was feverishly busy. He was wondering when Linus would strike and what he might do to save himself.

"If he makes up his mind to have me killed," he thought, "he will send his men up over the rooftops. They will cross the Street of the Sailmakers and take to the roofs above the Bazaar. They will come to this window." He glanced about him in the darkness. "I might keep them from getting in if I had a weapon. It is a narrow space." After further thought he made up his mind to go downstairs when Sosthene was asleep and get the largest of the bronze swords. The swords had no trace of a cutting edge, but they were heavy.

He was so concerned with the danger in which he conceived himself to stand that he did not perceive at first the small light cast on the opposite wall by someone appearing in the door with a hand-shaded candle. He did not know that he had a visitor, in fact, until a voice said, "May I enter, my son?"

At first he thought this unexpected arrival had been sent by Linus and he sprang to his feet, fumbling in the dark for the largest of his knives that lay on the workbench.

"I have startled you," said the visitor. "I should have hailed you from the stairs as I climbed. I did not do so because it seemed wise not to rouse the neighbors."

Basil saw now that the newcomer was of venerable appearance. A multitude of fine lines had collected at the corners of his eyes, giving him a look of benevolence. There was something familiar about the face of the old man, and for a moment he believed this was because the miracle he had been hoping for had come to pass.

"I know who you are," he said eagerly. "You are the angel Mefathiel. You have come in answer to my prayers. You—you are the Opener of Doors."

A smile of great kindness lighted up the face of the visitor. "No, my son, I am not the angel Mefathiel. But I am happy to hear you have been making your prayers to him. It is well to pray when troubles perch on your back and your pillow is cheated of sleep. It is well to pray at all times, even when there are no troubles and no petitions to be made. But I am not an angel. I am a common man and my name will mean nothing to you. I am called Luke and I have some knowledge of herbs and the cure of sicknesses. Because of this some men speak of me as Luke the Physician."

Memory flooded back into Basil's mind. This was the tall and kindly man who had stood at the side of the congregation when his real father had taken him to the synagogue at Ceratium. He had failed to recognize him at once because his beard, which had been a fiery red, was now as white as snow.

"You are a Christian," said Basil. "I saw you once, many years ago. My father, my real father, whose name was Theron and who sold pens, took me to a beautiful temple to hear a man named Paul of Tarsus preach to the people. I could not have been more than seven years old at the time. But I have always remembered how you looked."

"Yes, I am a Christian." The visitor came into the room and placed the candle on the workbench. "You have been expecting a miracle. I am not a worker of miracles, my son. Sometimes, when I am about the work of my Master, I hear words spoken in my mind which I know to be instructions, but in what follows I am no more than an instrument. I am a plain man and my chief duty is to write about what other men, much greater men than I, are doing to spread the truth. I do not speak to the multitudes. I have no power of healing in my hands. The flame has never appeared above my head, nor have I been given the gift of tongues. Men in whose honesty I have every faith have told me of seeing angels, and so I have always believed them. But I must be honest with you and say that I, Luke the Physician, have never seen an angel with my own eyes."

He seated himself on the bench and motioned to Basil to do the same. Placing a reassuring hand on the boy's arm, he went on: "But it may be that we have played our parts in a miracle tonight. How do I know that my visit is not the result of the prayers you have addressed to the angel Mefathiel? I thought the plan had been conceived in my own mind, but the angel may have put the thought there in the first place. That, my son, is how most miracles come about. It is not necessary to have a bolt of fire from the sky or the sound of a heavenly Voice. Miracles are happening all the time, at all hours of the day and night; and they come about quietly, just like this, with two men talking together, perhaps, in a darkened room and the world asleep outside. This, at any rate, I may tell you: I have come tonight to take you away."

"Then you are the angel!" cried Basil, his spirits leaping for joy. "You are Mefathiel in disguise. You say it is not so, but I am sure of it. You are the Opener of Doors."

"I have no wings on my shoulders." Luke smiled so warmly that the boy felt his heart go out to him. All sense of fear and distress left his mind. For the first time since he had received the warning note he had a feeling of security. "There is no time to tell you everything," continued Luke, "but this much you should know. There is a man of great wealth, and of great years, whose granddaughter is the apple of his eye. Before he dies this fine old man desires that a likeness be made of him in silver for her to keep. Knowing that the arts flourish in Antioch, he sent word to Luke the Physician that he desired the best artificer in silver who could be obtained. I had heard of you and tonight I saw your master. I bought your freedom from him, so that you could go to do the bidding of this fondest of grandsires. Here is the document that restores to you your freedom."

Basil could scarcely believe that this had happened to him, that not only was he free again but that his escape from the power of Linus had been provided.

They had been conversing in Koine, the commercial Greek which was used very largely in Antioch. Luke now asked if he knew any other language and Basil answered that he spoke Aramaic. He had done some reading in the Greek classics and had a small smattering of Latin. "Very small," he added with a smile.

"It is the Aramaic you will use where you are to go," said Luke. "It is fortunate you can speak it."

"Before you came, my benefactor," declared Basil, "I was certain I would never see the outside again. But now I have no fear. I think I would risk walking into that circular room, where my father used to sit and which Linus now occupies in his place, and telling him to do his worst." His spirits had risen so high he found it impossible to remain still. He wanted to go out into the darkness of the rooftops and shout to the world that he was free and that the path to fame and fortune lay at his feet. "I will work hard to justify your choice of me," he went on. "And I shall be grateful to you all my life for putting this chance in my hands." He paused, aware that he must not weary this new friend with protestations, but conscious of a great curiosity as to the nature of the task ahead of him. "May I ask one question?"

"You want to know where you are being sent. It is to Jerusalem."

"Jerusalem!" Excitement boiled up again in Basil's veins. The name of Jerusalem was a potent one. Not Antioch the beautiful, not Rome the all-powerful, exerted the hold on the imaginations of men which this old city on the hills of Israel had gained. Apart from this, however, the boy had another reason for being glad he was to visit the city that clustered about the golden dome of the Temple of the One God. It was to Jerusalem that Kester of Zanthus had gone when he left Antioch, the missing witness who might enable him to have the verdict that deprived him of his fortune set aside.

Luke rose to his feet. "We should be on our way. There is much for us to do before the sun rises again."

Basil hesitated. "I will be sorry to go and leave my fellow slave here. Did you see a girl when you were below whose name is Agnes? She has been very good to me, so good that I wonder if it is in your power to do anything for her as well."

Luke's manner took on a new gravity. "I saw the child. She is quite ill, and I am compelled to tell you that she hasn't long to live. Less than a year, I am afraid. The wasting disease has its hold on her and nothing may now be done for her." He went on with every evidence of reluctance: "There are such cases all over the world. Much as we may want to help them, it is out of our power. The good friend in Jerusalem is a man of wealth, but we are making heavy demands on him now and I can see no reason for pressing the case of this poor child on his attention. It has cost a great deal more to buy your freedom than he had expected."

"Her freedom would take a very small sum," urged Basil. "Then she could have proper care for—for as long as she has to live. I know it is asking too much. But in all truth, I find it hard to persuade myself to go without her. Could there not be a miracle?"

"We may pray for a miracle, you and I." The physician ran his fingers thoughtfully over his long beard. "All I can say beyond that is that I will speak about it when I follow you to Jerusalem. The man in question has a kind heart, and he might be persuaded to do as you wish." He nodded his head slowly. "And now, are you ready, my son?"

Basil did not need further urging. "I have nothing to take," he said, springing to his feet. "A slave has no possessions. I wish there had been time to wash myself properly. I have had no chance here to keep myself clean."

"Where I take you," said Luke, "there will be a warm bath and a fresh linen tunic for you to don." He picked up the candle and raised it above his head for a closer survey of this youth on whom his choice had fallen. He seemed pleased at what he saw. "I think the gentle old man in Jerusalem will be in accord with what I have done, even though it has been a somewhat costly transaction."

Basil walked to the window and threw back the dirt-encrusted curtain. "It will be safer for us to leave by the roof," he said.

A change came over his visitor. Luke seemed to grow visibly taller. The human kindliness of his eyes disappeared and they became instead like deep and mysterious pools. He had denied that he communed with angels, but at this moment he seemed to have taken on himself the outward guide of a messenger from the world of the spirit.

"Listen to me, my son," he said. His voice also had changed and it now carried a deep and commanding tone. "It is not necessary for us to run away from danger. I shall walk down the stairs and through the door to the street, and you must follow me. It will not matter if that evil man Linus has placed assassins outside the house to do you harm. We shall walk through them unscathed as Daniel when he stood in the den of the lions." He laid a hand on the boy's arm and urged him toward the stairs. "Have no fear. We do not go alone. The Lord will go with us."

CHAPTER II

THE HEAT had been intense on the road to Aleppo and yet, curiously
enough, there had been something almost of benevolence about it, as
though its sole purpose was to be good to living creatures, even to men.
The old city had appeared at a distance like a saffron concoction on a
shallow platter of green held out in welcome by the bronze hands of the
gods of the hills. On close inspection the town proved to be a baffling
maze of narrow lanes with astonishing bazaars comparable only to Time,
which has no beginning and no end. Basil, child of the Ward of the
Trades, lost himself in these vastnesses and only through the help of a
beggar, whose sores were honest, found his way back, late and shamefaced, to the great khan inside the Antioch Gate.

He was there in time to witness the belated arrival of Adam ben Asher,
to whom they had been directed. The latter proved to be a study in in-
congruities; a figure of bulging girth and yet obviously as tough as leather;
his skin blackened by desert suns and his eyebrows the bushiest of black
penthouses, while his lively and roving eyes were of a most unusual shade
of gray. Contrasts were to be observed also in the matter of his dress.
With a flowing tunic bearing the red stripe of the desert nomad, he wore
high-laced shoes that suggested a Greek dandy and a belt that could have
come from nowhere but the distant and fabulous Cathay. He talked in the
high-pitched voice of the professional teller of tales, he gestured like a
camel trader, he fell in and out of rages as easily as a player of parts. His
talk never ceased, and it was amusing, blistering, and laudatory in turn. He
was openly and professedly a friend of every man on the caravan trails.

He crossed the courtyard of the khan, his voice shrill in greeting of
Luke the Physician. A clout on the chest knocked the latter off balance

and an immediate thump between the shoulder blades saved him from falling. "You look as cool as the snows of Ararat," Adam declaimed. "What errand brings you here? Do you go to prepare the way for the Brave Voices in a conquest of Bavil?"*

Luke had accepted the buffeting in good grace, but he protested what Adam had said. "It hurts me to hear you speak in this way," he said.

"Because I call Paul and Peter and the rest of your friends the Brave Voices? Come, what am I to call them? I stand by the old beliefs and the Law of Moses and I cannot bring myself to speak of these followers of the Nazarene as apostles. What then? Brave Voices is as good as any name. If it implies a small measure of disrespect, it indicates at the same time that the Christian leaders have courage. Can you expect me to do more?" He burst into a loud guffaw. Ending it abruptly, he shot a question at Luke. "What brings you to Aleppo?"

"I bring you this lad," said Luke. "He goes to Jerusalem, and it is the wish of Joseph of Arimathea that he make the journey in your train."

The light eyes of the mahogany-skinned nomad turned in Basil's direction. They took in every detail of his appearance, the youthful thinness, the wide brow, noting also the short-sleeved colobium of the free man, which the youth wore with such gladness.

"Who is he?" demanded Adam ben Asher, not lowering his voice. "He's too young, I think, to be one of the Brave Voices, but there's a suspicious glitter in his eye. There's something about him that makes me uneasy. What is it?"

"Adam ben Asher," said Luke in an urgent tone, "it will be better if you refrain from shouting about us to the rooftops. This young man comes from Antioch. He is an artist and he goes to carry out a commision for Joseph of Arimathea."

At this the caravan man gave over all other interests to a study of the youth. His manner lost all trace of joviality and became intense and critical.

"I think ill of artists," he remarked. "There have been too many of them in the world, painting on walls and carving idols out of stone. So, this one is an artist and he goes to work for Joseph of Arimathea! I have worked for Joseph of Arimathea all my life, and this is a matter of some concern to me."

The kindly eyes of Luke showed a faint trace of weariness. "My friend," he said, "this is a very small matter. It does not concern you in any way."

*The name commonly applied to Bagdad.

The curiously assorted trio sat down together in a corner of the court-yard with a copper dish between them, filled with rice and lamb and all manner of small surprises in the way of vegetables and nuts and spices from the Far East. Basil ate with the good appetite of youth. Adam ben Asher performed prodigiously, wiping his hands on a napkin each time he dipped into the dish but paying no immediate attention to the smearing of his lips and cheeks. Luke partook lightly and with a noticeable fastidiousness.

"You and I, O Luke," declared Adam, probing into the dish with a forefinger, "are much alike. You are not counted among the bravest of the Brave Voices, but I have observed how they depend on you in all things. You arrange the meetings, you talk to the magistrates, you see that there is food. When money is needed, you go to Joseph of Arimathea. You talk to the captains of ships, and jailers and innkeepers and tax collectors. I wonder if there would be as many believers today had it not been for the quiet work of one Luke who sits beside me at this moment and frowns with disapproval of what I say. You, old friend, have made yourself indispensable to them, and what is your reward? You have become the—the Cart Horse of Christianity!" The caravan captain threw back his black-thatched head and roared with appreciation of his own cleverness. "And now on the other hand. That wise old man in Jerusalem, Joseph of Arimathea, is counted the great merchant of the world. But for the last ten years I, Adam ben Asher, have done much of the work. I buy, I sell, I fight, I contrive. I take out caravans, I go as far east as India. I work from sunrise to sunset. I am the Titan of the Trails, the Pilgrim of the Pe Lu. It is Joseph of Arimathea who dispenses the wealth with such a generous hand, so that the Brave Voices may go out and preach, but it is Adam who provides the dinars."

Basil had finished his repast and was listening to this discourse with absorbed interest. Adam ceased talking at this point to give the youth another prolonged study.

"So, this boy is an artist!" he said finally. "I believe you, O Luke, because he could be nothing else with such useless hands. But what is this genius going to do for Joseph of Arimathea?"

"Your master is a very old man," said Luke, "and his granddaughter, the little Deborra——"

"The little Deborra," interrupted Adam with a loud and impatient snort, "is fifteen. The right age for marriage."

"Has her age any bearing?" asked Luke. "This is how it came about.

Deborra wants a likeness of Joseph in silver that she will always be able to keep. I was asked to find the best worker in silver in Antioch and I selected this young man."

Adam ben Asher had finished his meal. He dipped both hands in a bowl of water and clapped them over his face, rubbing vigorously to remove all traces of the repast, blowing the while like a sea monster. When he had finished, he rested his elbows on his knees and gave Basil a still more protracted stare.

"How long will this foolishness take?" he demanded, addressing the youth for the first time.

"A few weeks," answered Basil uneasily. It was not hard to read dislike in the shrewd eye of this strange individual. "Perhaps a little longer. It will depend on how much success I have. Sometimes the first attempts are not successful."

Adam turned to the older man. "Was it not possible to select one who would be successful from the first? Is this a pindling apprentice you send to Jerusalem? Where will he live?"

"He will live in the house of Joseph. It is the rule because it gives him a chance to study his subject."

"And for many other things. My venerable friend, do you consider this fellow good to look upon?"

"He is well favored."

The caravan captain glanced at Basil again and frowned. He changed his position, stole another look, and frowned with still greater violence. Finally he commented in a grumbling tone: "As I have said, I think poorly of artists. They are a weak-kneed lot. I could take this one in my two hands and crack all his ribs. It would be a pleasant way of exercising the muscles." He turned then and asked a question of Luke. "Where do you go when you have left this maker of images on my hands?"

"I return to join Paul," answered the physician. "He is getting together a party, as perhaps you have heard. A collection has been made in Macedonia for the use of the poor of Jerusalem, and Paul is taking it there."

A shrewd look came into the eyes of the caravan captain. "He uses it as an excuse," he declared. "Paul has other reasons for going."

Luke nodded. "You are right. Paul has other reasons."

This set Adam ben Asher off on a long harangue. "It is a rash thing for him to do. There will be trouble if he appears there again. Fighting and bloodshed and killing." He laid a hand on Luke's arm and gave a vigorous shake to compel attention to what he was saying. "You, Luke, have been a healer of bodies and now have made yourself into a healer of souls. You are kind and unselfish and I am fond of you. But in some matters you are no more than a child in a world of wicked men. I do not think you have any conception of the actual situation. You know that the high priests of the Temple hate Paul. Do you realize, O Healer of Men, that there are fires of discontent banked in every Jewish soul and that while the world lies quietly under Roman rule the day is being planned when the Jews will rise to throw off the shackles? The Zealots sharpen their knives and whisper of rebellion, and they hate Christians because a Jew who turns to your Jesus the Christ becomes a lover of peace. They hate Paul because he has been preaching peace all over the world—peace under the rule of Rome. If he goes to Jerusalem, there will be a Zealot dagger between his ribs before he can say 'Peace be with you.' "

"Paul is well aware of the danger," asserted Luke. "The daggers of the Zealots follow him wherever he goes."

"Keep him away!" exclaimed Adam. "There is trouble enough as it is. A riot over that master of indiscretion, Paul of Tarsus, might be the start of rebellion against Rome. I am a good Jew, I believe in the Law of Moses, but I am not a Zealot. I know how easily the Romans would crush an uprising in a great bath of Jewish blood."

"The hand of Jehovah beckons Paul back to Jerusalem."

"It is Paul himself who says so," declared Adam bitterly. "How can the rest of us be sure that the hand is not motioning him to stay away? Well, he will come; and it will be a black day for all of us when he does."

With an abruptness which startled his hearers, the caravan captain then jumped to another subject. "Simon the Magician was here last night. He appeared in the market place, and every man in Aleppo was out to see him perform his tricks."

Luke glanced up with a grave air. "I hear of this Simon everywhere. He gives us much trouble. Did you see him?"

"Of course I saw him." Adam nodded his head with gusto. "He is the greatest magician in the world and he makes miracles seem easy. Let me tell you this, O Luke: he wins followers wherever he goes and he takes them away from the Nazarene." He made an expansive gesture. "What can you expect? People believe Jesus to be the Messiah because He performed miracles. Then along comes Simon the Magician, who says to them: 'See, I can do miracles too. I can do greater miracles than He did.' So of course people begin to wonder and they say to themselves, 'It is true. Why, therefore, have we believed in the Nazarene?' "

Luke's manner had become graver with each word spoken. He had listened to Adam with a saddened air as one might take in the thoughtless chatter of a child.

"My son," he said, "you have not become one of us, and sometimes I fear you never will. You have lived under the influence of your saintly master all the years of your life. You know the apostles and you have heard them speak. It is possible that you saw Jesus when you were very young."

Adam shook his head. "It was after His death that my master engaged me as a camel driver. I heard then that He had been buried in Joseph's tomb and that He was supposed to have risen from the dead."

"It is true that He rose from the dead. Many of His followers saw Him."

"I am a Jew and I live by the Law of Moses," declared Adam. He grinned broadly and rapped his head with his knuckles. "My head is hard. Very hard."

"And, I fear, your heart."

"As hard," supplied the caravan man, "as the back of Ah-big, the crocodile."

Luke sighed deeply. "The comparison is only too accurate. None of us has been able to reach your soul." He fell into silence for a moment and then resumed speaking with passionate conviction. "You are not a Christian and so you do not understand that a belief in the miracles of Jesus is a very small matter indeed. I was denied the privilege of seeing Him, but it would make no difference to me if He had performed no miracles at all. It is what He taught, Adam ben Asher. He brought us the sublime truth that our God is the God of charity and forgiveness and that we may be redeemed and washed of our sins by the blood that was spilled on Calvary. When you ride on your camel, Adam, it is not the amulet around the animal's neck that supplies the strength to carry you from Aleppo to Jerusalem. This talk of miracles has no more importance to us than the amulet has to you."

"Then why do people come out in such crowds to see Simon the Magician? Why are they beginning to say he is the Messiah and not Jesus of Nazareth?"

"The number of deserters is small. No true Christian pays any attention to this trickster, this mountebank."

"It is not wise to pass him over lightly. There may be more than *keshef* in what he does. Oh, he is a wise one, that Simon. What do you suppose he did last night to make all the roving eyes of Aleppo pop right out of their sockets? He used a girl as a helper on the platform. Yes, O Luke, in full view of everyone and without even a veil over her face. A beautiful girl, with eyes like the stars and hair as black as midnight. She had a shape which turned the amorous bones of Aleppo to water. At first it seemed there might be a riot because women are not allowed to show their faces in public. But after a few moments it was apparent they were licking their lips and enjoying it."

"His heart is black with wickedness!" declared Luke. "I am surprised he was not struck down by a thunderbolt from the angry hand of Jehovah."

"Where do you suppose this man of black heart goes next to display his tricks? To Jerusalem."

"I cannot believe it!" cried Luke. "Simon is a Samaritan. He would not be allowed to appear publicly in the Holy City."

"I am not as sure of that as you. His aim is to make light of Jesus of Nazareth, and it may very well be that the high priests will welcome him. I would not be at all surprised if the great men of the Temple allowed him to do his tricks outside the very Gate of the Golden Bars."

Luke gave his head an anxious shake. "It is fortunate, then," he said, "that Paul is going to Jerusalem. Something must be done to prove this Simon a trickster and a cheat—this Bad Samaritan!"

That night, after Adam had fallen to snoring like the slow beat of a native fist on a taut drum, Luke said to Basil, who was stretched out beside him: "I shall stop in Antioch on my way to rejoin Paul and give notification to the courts of your release, and the terms. You are freer than is allowed under the Roman laws, but in Antioch, as in other provinces of the empire, they have begun to wink at such relaxations. Then I shall apply under a writ of *postliminium* to have your citizenship restored to you. I think it will be allowed because there is a general belief in the city that you were infamously treated. They have resented the corrupt methods that Linus used and they have nothing but contempt for him."

"I thought freedmen were held in scorn," said Basil.

"In Rome it is so. That city is filled with ex-slaves, and the old Romans resent their wealth and insolence. They still speak angrily of the marriage of Drusilla, a granddaughter of Antony and Cleopatra, to a freedman of Judea named Felix. They mutter a great deal because Nero admits so many freedmen to posts of authority under him. But outside of Rome it is different. Have you ever seen a *pileus* worn on the head of a freedman in Antioch?"

Basil shook his head. "I do not think so."

"They must still wear it in Rome." Luke paused reflectively. "In your case we have a definite advantage, for you were born free and your father was a citizen of Rome. I am sure, my son, that you may sleep easily and in full confidence that you will never have to don the *pileus!*"

2

Luke left the next day. For a week thereafter Adam ben Asher traded and bought and sold while Basil waited. After the talk to which he had listened between the two older men, Basil did not look forward to the long journey over the hot trails to Jerusalem in the company of Adam, who thought so ill of him.

"I hope you have a stout heart under those skinny ribs of yours," said Adam as they sat together over what they thought would be their last evening meal in Aleppo. "We will be two weeks at least on the road, and the heat will be enough to fry a lizard on a rock." He swallowed his last bite of food and wiped his lips with a quick flick of one hand. "We start at dawn."

But they did not start at dawn. Basil developed a fever during the night, the result, perhaps, of the state of anxiety in which he had existed, but more still of the undernourishment and overwork of two long years. For three days he tossed about in a stupor, his eyes closed, his brow hot and dry. Adam ben Asher, grumbling loudly about the delay and the absence of Luke in this emergency, dosed the sick youth with every medicine he could find. On the morning of the fourth day he detected a trace of moisture on the patient's forehead.

"Luke could not have done better," said the caravan captain to himself with a sense of pride in his success. "Was it the black hellebore or the pods of the carob I bought from that old Armenian? Whichever it was, he's going to live." Rubbing a hand over his unshaved jaw, he studied the patient with an eye which still lacked friendliness. "If he had stayed sick another day, I would have left him and gone on my way. It would have been necessary for Luke to find another artist, and he might have the good sense this time to pick a man of good round years, a fellow with a fat belly, perhaps, and a bald head. I would be easier in my mind if I were taking into the house of Joseph a chisel-wielder with a rheumy eye and a sourness of breath instead of this slim young sprig."

The day following, when the freshness of dawn was in the air, Basil was lifted to the back of a camel that had been fitted out with a *musattah,* a litter consisting of a small square tent and a comfortable back against which he could lean. He was still weak and ill but grimly determined not to cause the fuming caravan captain any further delay.

Adam watched an assistant tie the pale young artist to the rear cushions with tasseled cords of twisted goat's hair and grunted an order. The man gave the reins a jerk and said *"Khikh!"* in a sharp tone. The camel groaned, thrust its head forward, and rose slowly to its knees. Basil felt himself being tilted forward as the animal elevated its rear quarters without moving either foreleg. Lacking the strength to move his arms, he was certain that he was going to slip out of the front of the *musattah.* In the nick of time, however, one of the forelegs was raised until the foot touched the ground and the whole of the front quarter began to rise in turn. After what seemed a long time, and to the accompaniment of much groaning and grumbling, the front established equilibrium and the sick rider sighed with relief.

"Khikh!" cried the overseer, the leader of the train, who had come up to watch. He was a stout fellow with a bronze face and he looked around at Adam as the camel started off at a slow swinging gait. "Walk?" he asked.

"Walk," affirmed Adam. "For the next two days. If we try for more than twenty-five miles at first we will have an artist to bury. I would not object myself, but the old man in Jerusalem would not be pleased."

"There are times," said the overseer, "when we cannot consider our own pleasure and have to think about the old man in Jerusalem."

"He has some use for this young bag of bones," explained Adam.

The long train had swept out from the encampment, which lay under the walls of the city, and was moving slowly down the Jerusalem Road when Adam brought his camel up beside Basil's. He raised the flap of the tent and squinted in at the patient.

"You look as yellow as a mummy," he said. "Are you going to be sick again?"

"I think not," Basil answered without making the effort required to turn his head. "But I need more air."

"I will raise the canvas on this side where the sun does not strike. Keep your eyes straight ahead and you will get accustomed in time to the camel's gait."

He kept pace alongside and after a few moments of silence he began to talk, beginning with a question. "What do you know about Joseph of Arimathea?"

"I know nothing about him."

"Joseph," declared Adam with obvious pride, "is a very rich man. Some say he is the richest man in the world, and it may be true. Is it necessary to tell you that the Jews are the greatest people in the world? They are bright and sharp and they have the gift of understanding. Also, they are acquisitive and they make great fortunes, sometimes out of nothing. There was once a Jew named Job and he was so rich that he owned six thousand camels as well as great herds of cattle and flocks of sheep and enough horses to mount a Roman army. But that was a thousand years ago, and trade has grown so much since then that today Joseph of Arimathea is wealthier than half a dozen Jobs rolled into one. His connections are so wide that if he went bankrupt every business roof in Jerusalem would fall in. I am not boasting, young artist. I am trying to give you the truth about this great old man you are going to work for in Jerusalem.

"Joseph has one fault," he went on. "He is a Christian. He became one in the earliest days—when there was real danger in it. Joseph was sure his business would suffer if it was known and so he didn't go about beating his breast and singing hymns. It was not,". emphatically, "because he was afraid. After the crucifixion, he went to Pontius Pilate, that weak man, and asked for the body. He placed the body in his own tomb and rolled the stone over the entrance; and as to what happened after, I offer no opinion."

Basil was listening intently, but it would not have mattered if he had turned his head away: Adam had started to tell the story and nothing could stop him.

"Joseph has lived a long life. For over thirty years he has been the financial mainstay of the Christians. The Lord performs miracles, they say, but He does not cause the shekels to multiply in the purses of His people. There are others to help, but when it is said that 'Paul has been called into Macedonia' or 'Peter has decided to go to Rome,' it is Joseph of Arimathea they come to for help. He never refuses."

Adam paused, to catch his breath and to heave a deep sigh of regret. "He cannot live much longer, that fine old man. And when he dies his only son Aaron, the father of Deborra, will take his place. Things will be different then. Bismillah, what a difference there will be!

"How could it come about that a man like Joseph, who has glowed warmly all his life like a ball of fire in the sky, could sire a dried-up pod of seeds like Aaron? It was not necessary for Aaron to learn his arithmetic, he came into the world knowing how to add and multiply. If all the words spoken by the children of Israel over the ages had been written down and counted and put into columns, it would be found that our helpful, generous Aaron has said 'no' oftener than all the others put together. Have you ever camped on a high plain of a winter night and felt the cold turning you into a solid cake of ice? The heart of Aaron is colder than that, because you can always start a fire on the plains, but you cannot burn camel dung inside him to relieve the chill. When Joseph dies, the Christians will not get as much as one half shekel out of that man of small and shrivcled soul." It was clear that he did not fear the possible consequences of speaking with such freedom. "Why do I tell you this about the man who will sit over me someday? I will tell you, young artist. It is because I do not care. I have said all this before, and to Aaron's own face."

He continued to talk about the household of the great merchant in Jerusalem, but Basil had ceased to listen. The fever had resumed its hold and his mind had lost itself in strange and disjointed dreams.

3

The fever did not leave him finally until after ten days of continuous travel. They had progressed by that time beyond the lower tip of the Sea of Galilee and had camped by the ford of the Wadi Farah, which meanders slowly across the plain to join the fast-flowing waters of the Jordan. Basil had slept well and wakened with a clear head and a new feeling of energy in his veins. He gazed with wonder at the high hills to the west in which nestled, he had been told, the fruitful valleys of Samaria. It was pleasant in the cool of dawn, the air filled with the songs of birds in the palm trees and the mulberries, the sky shot across with brilliant streamers of color.

"What is the name of that highest peak?" he asked.

"Mount Ebal," answered Adam shortly. "Ask me no more questions about the land of the cursed Cutheans. Listen! They are stirring back there on the other side of the ford. In a moment there will be something worth your notice."

The night before a large party had come to the ford and had camped on the other side. "They are nearly through with their prayers," said Adam in a whisper of the deepest respect. "The Standing Man is ready to begin."

He had barely finished speaking when a voice was raised on the other side of the water, crying, "Arise ye! And let us go up to Zion and to Jehovah, our God!"

The rest of the company obeyed the summons by getting to their feet and beginning a chant, "I was glad when they said unto me, Let us go into the house of Jehovah."

This was a familiar spectacle to Adam. At this season of the year each of the twenty-four districts into which Palestine had been divided sent parties to Jerusalem, in charge of an official who was called the Standing Man, taking with them the First Fruits to be offered to God. It was the custom of the farmers to select the best of everything, the finest heads of grain, the largest and ripest grapes, the most succulent bunches of dates, and to place them in wicker baskets as white as snow or even in containers of gold or silver in which they would be carried to the Temple. But to Basil it was all strange and he watched with the greatest interest.

The company was now approaching the ford with the sound of flutes to set the pace of the march. They were beginning to chant the first of the Songs of Ascents.

Adam was filled with pride in this demonstration of the abiding faith of his people. He gave Basil a vigorous buffet on the shoulder and pointed to the files of earnest men marching down to the water.

"Look at them!" he said. "They all live by the Law of Moses. It was thus they came down behind Joshua for the Passover. These men slept in the open last night to avoid defilement, and some of them kept watch over the First Fruits. Now they will tread the long roads to the Holy City, singing as they go. Does it not stir your blood to see how faithfully they keep all the customs of their fathers? Listen to the words they are singing."

The pilgrims had reached the third of the Songs of Degrees and were reverently intoning the words:

> They that trust in the Lord shall be as Mount Zion
> Which cannot be removed but abideth forever.
> As the mountains are round about Jerusalem,
> So the Lord is round about his people,
> From henceforth, even forever.

Adam's eyes were gleaming happily. "When they come within sight of the hill on which the Temple stands," he said, "the priests and Levites will come out to bid them welcome, and as they climb the steps they will continue to sing songs of praise to Jehovah. And this they do each year."

The overseer had seen to it that the laborious packing for the day's journey had been done early. Basil climbed into his *musattah* briskly, calling to Adam, "I feel well enough to do fifty miles today."

Adam was still watching the procession of the First Fruits. "We, the children of Israel, take our religion seriously," he said. "And we are the only people in the world who do. I will tell you about that."

He proceeded to do so after the camel train had started and he had ranged himself beside the young artist. "One day," he began, "I was tempted to commit a sin. Not one of your puny sins, the kind that stupid little men commit every day, but a great, black, terrible sin. As I considered it, I felt that a hand was suspended over my head, ready to strike. I knew what it was: it was the hand of Moses. He has been dead for thousands of years, that wrathful man, and yet no Jew can commit a wrong today without fearing that Moses will punish him personally for it. It was Moses who taught us that the Sabbath must be kept. Master Basil, have you noticed that my left arm is stiff at the elbow? I get little use of it. When I was a boy I broke it on the Sabbath and my father would not permit anything to be done for it until the following day."

He was silent for a moment and then he began to deliver an address on the merits of his people. "To the Jew who lives abroad the Temple is the center of all spiritual life. He has his own synagogue, but it is to the Holy of Holies that he turns. He longs to share in its activities. It has become our custom to send out word from Jerusalem when the paschal moon rises. It's done by a string of beacon fires lighted on the tops of hills. As soon as the moon lifts its pale head above the horizon, the beacon fires flash and in a matter of minutes the Jews, even those as far away as Babylon, know that the paschal light is flooding the Holy City. They walk out on their housetops and stretch their arms toward Jerusalem. And a great peace and happiness take possession of them.

"But the cursed Cutheans"—a term of contempt the Jews used in speaking of Samaritans—"know of this and they envy us a custom in which they are not permitted to share. They try to interfere. They light other fires on hilltops—at the wrong times, of course. When this happens, the custodians of the sacred beacons become confused and do not know which lights to believe.

"Once," he continued with a note of satisfaction in his voice, "I was riding by night from Damascus. Off there in the direction of Mount Ebal I saw a light spring up on a hilltop and I knew they were playing their tricks again. I took my men to the hill, and there we found them, a score of grinning Cutheans, piling wood on the blaze and laughing and capering about." He threw back his head in a loud laugh of enjoyment. "We drubbed them from the hills and we trampled out the fire; and we sent down word into the smug valleys where they live in slothful ease that if they interfered again with the holy paschal fires we would set a torch to Shechem and Sebaste. That took away their appetite for tricks."

He seemed no longer aware that he had hearers. With eyes fixed straight ahead and his voice raised to an oratorical pitch, he declaimed the glories of his race. He recited stories from the Book of Jashar, gesticulating with his one good arm. He kept returning to the point of view with which he had started, that truth dwelt only in the Jew and that all other religions were no more than lip service to idols. This continued literally for hours. He seemed tireless. At the end of each story he would straighten himself and look up into the sky, where the sun was blazing, and he would shout out loudly, as though in defiance of the world, the words of the creed. To Basil, now half a dozen camel lengths behind, it seemed that everything in between was a jumble of words, and all he could distinguish was the phrase so often repeated:

Hear, O Israel, the Lord our God is One God!

CHAPTER III

I

IT WAS THE CUSTOM in Jerusalem to face the Temple when out of doors. To abide by this rule men had to control their walking and standing so that the great white building would always be partially in the eye, even looking back over the shoulder when going in the opposite direction.

This was a simple matter from the house of Joseph of Arimathea. It stood on the brink of the western hill above the Cheesemakers' Valley, and from there the horizon was dominated by the house of the one God on the slope of Mount Moriah, its marble walls brilliant against the turquoise of the sky, its gold-sheeted roof with tall spikes of the precious metal proclaiming the wealth and power and the reverence of the race which had raised it.

By way of contrast, the Cheesemakers' Valley was a belt of squalor separating the mount of the Temple from the activities of the upper and lower cities. As though striving to escape from its stifling heat and noisome discomfort, the houses of the cheesemakers climbed up the slopes, one on top of another, tiny structures of stone with flat roofs and a thick overgrowth of stout vines. It was a simple matter to mount from roof to roof, and many a fugitive from the law had escaped in that way, with the help of the repressed people who lived on the slope. The route most commonly taken was called the Goat's Walk; and at the end of it the climber found himself facing a door of imposing proportions in a wall of marble. This was the house of Joseph of Arimathea, the wealthiest man in Jerusalem, some said in the whole world. As Joseph had not placed a foot outside the great bronze-studded door in ten years, he had grown into a myth to the poor people whose homes clung precariously below him like pods on a beanstalk. Boys, who are always lacking in proper reverence, sometimes clambered up from the Valley in noisy groups and chanted in front of the door: "Ha, rich man, we are cubs of the poor cheesemakers; give us of your abundance." If they had not been doing this too often, the door would open and something satisfying would be distributed among them, dates, oaten cakes, sometimes even a copper coin for each.

It was to this splendid door that Adam ben Asher escorted Basil on the morning of their arrival in the Holy City. A current of air from the Cheesemakers' Valley came up blisteringly hot on their backs as they waited to be admitted. Adam did not seem to mind the discomfort. He turned so he could feast his eyes on the blazing white marble of the Temple at the far end of the bridge across the valley, being careful not to permit the Castle of Antonia to obtrude itself on his vision. This solid pile at the northwest corner had been built by the hated Herod and was now the headquarters of the Roman governor; and so no Jewish eye rested voluntarily on its high stone battlements.

They were escorted into a cool room off the entrance hall and in a few minutes they were greeted by Aaron. Remembering what Adam had told him about the son of the house, Basil was not surprised to find Aaron a middle-aged man of spare build with a face as arid as the desert lands beyond the Jordan and a quick darting eye that passed over each of them in turn with no indication of welcome or pleasure.

"You are back," said Aaron to Adam. "Has it been a successful journey?"

"Was I not in charge? Is it not certain, then, that the camels have brought wealth on their backs?"

"Perhaps," said Aaron dryly. "That will be seen." He glanced coldly at Basil. "Who is this?"

"This is the artist selected by Luke the Physician in Antioch. On instructions from your father."

Aaron had been holding both of his hands behind his back and at this point he made a loud snapping sound with his fingers. A servant had accompanied him into the room, carrying his head bent over so far that it was impossible to see much of his face. The click of his master's fingers conveyed some special intelligence to this attendant, for he turned immediately and left the room, the arch of his back and neck lending him a close resemblance to a condor.

"Ebenezer will tell my father you are here," declared Aaron. "If he

is in one of his more lucid moments, he will probably see you at once."
He studied Basil with an eye as cold as outer space and then said to
Adam, "He is very young. Were his qualifications weighed carefully
before he was selected?"

"I was so told by Luke." Adam's voice carried a bristling note. "Is it
not claimed that one Jesus disputed with learned doctors at the age of
twelve?"

"That has no bearing," declared the other sharply. He motioned toward
a room opening off the one where they were standing and then addressed
Basil. "You will find water there to remove the stains of travel. There will
be wine brought in. You," to Adam, "will have other matters to attend to
elsewhere, no doubt."

"When my master dies, this ungrateful son of a good father will have no
further use for my services," muttered Adam when Aaron had left.

Alone in the inner room, Basil looked about him with speculative eyes,
mentally comparing the house of Joseph of Arimathea with the palace on
the Antioch Colonnade. It was furnished with a beauty he found somewhat strange, although he realized that the hangings had a fineness of
color and texture that gave him a sense of voluptuous pleasure and that
the rugs were the best product of the weavers who wrought magic with
skilled fingers. It seemed to him that an air of mystery was fostered purposely, whereas the house of Ignatius had been kept wide open, a little
noisy by contrast, with the sunlight free to invade every nook and corner.
There were other differences. The ornamentation in Antioch had been
pure and with a certain feeling for the ascetic; here it approached the
point of overelaboration.

The nature of the message the fingers of Aaron had conveyed to the
ears of his servant became clear when the latter returned with a jug of
wine. It was *vinum acetum,* thin and metallic in flavor. Basil made a wry
face and replaced his cup after one taste.

A sound of voices from the interior court of the house drew him to the
window overlooking it. He was surprised at the size and beauty of the
garden upon which he found himself gazing. It was oblong in shape and
filled with a profusion of flowers and small trees. A magnificent fountain
stood in the center, throwing a spray of water into the air as high as the
latticed windows of the second floor. Birds of brilliant plumage nestled
sulkily in the green foliage and occasionally drew attention to themselves
with a flap of scarlet wings or an unmelodious cawing. Basil made a

mental acknowledgment to Joseph of Arimathea: in the matter of gardens Jerusalem ranked well above Antioch.

A very old man had entered the court, leaning on the arm of a girl, and progressing with slow and unsteady steps. Certain that this was the great Hebrew merchant, Basil studied him with eager eyes. The brow of Joseph of Arimathea was unusually broad, and his deep-sunk eyes had both nobility and intelligence. It was a beautiful and generous face. Basil's fingers itched for his finely balanced hammers and the coolness of his modeling clay.

He was so concerned with the countenance of the venerable merchant that he did not notice the girl with him. This was an oversight, for she was worth a long glance: a small figure in a white *palla* that covered her from neck to sandaled foot; her hair, as black as midnight, in braids hanging over her shoulders; her eyes so concerned with guiding her grandfather's steps that it was only when she glanced up for a casual moment that they were seen to be bright under finely arched brows.

The voices of the pair in the garden carried clearly to the room where the visitor waited, and Basil realized that they were engaged in an affectionate bickering.

"My dear child!" the old man was saying. "You are getting to be the same kind of tyrant as your grandmother. I must do this, I must not do that. Why must I be blamed so much because I had a good meal this morning?"

"You are no better than a disobedient boy," protested the girl in a high but pleasant voice. "Why, oh why, did you allow yourself a cucumber? Did not the kind physician who came to see you no more than three days ago tell you to be more careful? He mentioned cucumbers particularly. You will suffer for this! And you will have to take those medicines he left. Young hemlock and syrup of squills——"

"They turn my stomach," complained the old man. "Such things are unfit for wild dogs!"

"And now you insist on seeing this artist," went on the girl. "Do you think you have the strength today? There is plenty of time. The artist can wait."

"He has come all the way from Antioch, my child, on the bidding of my good friend Luke. And there are reasons, of which you do not know, for showing him every courtesy."

The girl's voice displayed more interest at once. "What is there about him that I haven't been told, Grandfather? You must let me know now."

Without waiting for any response, she linked an arm firmly in his. "I shall go with you, then. And I shall see that the talk is a short one. You are getting tired, I can tell, and ready for a nice long nap."

Joseph of Arimathea shook his snow-white head sadly in agreement. "Yes, a very long nap, my little Deborra."

Basil had transferred his attention finally to the girl, and he found himself admiring the purity of her white throat and the animation of her eyes. He had little time to study her because Adam ben Asher joined him at the window.

"You like her?" asked the caravan captain in a brusque tone.

Basil answered cautiously. "Yes—if one may judge at this distance."

"You think her attractive?"

"Yes, of course."

"I knew you did. I could see it in your eye." Adam was keeping his gaze fixed on Basil's face. "And now what will she think of you? I am more concerned about that." His breathing seemed labored, an indication that his emotions were deeply involved. "I give you a word of warning, young silversmith. You must stick to your hammers and tools. We want no airs here, no posturing and posing."

Basil turned and looked steadily at him. "I know no reason for accounting to you for my conduct."

Adam seemed on the point of explosion. "I shall find a reason," he said.

2

The girl's solicitude over her grandfather's health had prevailed. It was two hours before Basil was summoned to the bedroom of the head of the household. Joseph was sitting up in a huge bed, looking small and thin on its snowy expanse, but refreshed and receptive. On a table beside him there was a half-empty wine cup of silver and a platter with the remains of a light meal. His granddaughter sat close at hand. She gave Basil one glance and seemed surprised to find him so young. Then she studiously lowered her eyes.

"You are a boy," said the old man in a voice that seemed too deep and full to issue from a frame so frail. He did not appear to be disturbed, however, for he did not labor the point. "You left my friend Luke in good health, I trust?"

"He was fatigued with the journey from Antioch to Aleppo," answered

Basil. "But after one night's rest he started back alone to join one Paul of Tarsus. They are coming to Jerusalem together."

Joseph of Arimathea nodded his head gravely. "I wrote to Paul and advised against coming at this time, but I did not expect he would heed my warning. He scents danger and rushes always to meet it." His eyes, which shone benignly in a forest of wrinkles, turned back to his youthful visitor. "I see you have brought your clay with you. Set to work at once. I am well rested today. When your subject is as old as I am, you must take advantage of every moment."

Basil heard this suggestion with a feeling of panic. He invariably had difficulty in the first stages and he feared that nervousness would steal from his fingers all power to catch and imprison a likeness in the damp clay. If he failed, this shrewd old man in the enormous bed might decide he would not do for the task. What would happen to him then? He was a free man now, of course. He kept the document attesting his release from bondage in the belt under his tunic, and he could not be returned to slavery. But failure might rob him of his one great chance, and he would find himself condemned to a lifetime of ill-paid labor at a workman's bench.

He took a seat with open reluctance at the foot of the bed and set his fingers to work. At first his worst fears were justified. He could do nothing with the clay, and the face that emerged from the probing of his nervous hands bore small resemblance to Joseph of Arimathea. "I am going to fail!" he thought in a panic. "I shall be sent away in disgrace. Luke will be blamed and Adam ben Asher will be so pleased that he will laugh at me."

A second effort was more successful. The noble brow began to show, and under it the weary eyes came into a semblance of life. A deep sense of relief took possession of the boy and communicated itself to the tips of his sensitive fingers. He began to work then in real earnest and with a full share of the concentration of the artist.

He became so absorbed that he paid little attention to the talk carried on between Joseph and the girl. They were discussing Paul and a certain errand of much urgency that was bringing him to Jerusalem. There was mention also of others whose names meant nothing to the youth, James and Philip and Jude. It was clear that Joseph had reservations in his mind as to the attitude these men would take when the unwanted but intrepid Paul arrived. All this seemed of small importance to Basil; of minute concern, in fact, when compared with his feverish desire to transfer the stamp of the merchant's noble head to the damp material in his hands.

He became aware that a silence had fallen on the room and saw then that the girl had deserted her seat beside the couch, vanishing from the range of his vision. It was not until he heard her voice behind him that he realized she was still in the room.

"It is perfect!" she cried. "Oh, Grandfather, it is exactly like you."

Basil turned his head and saw that she had stationed herself at his shoulder so she could watch while he worked. Her eyes had widened with pleasure over what he was accomplishing. She was not beautiful, but when her face became lighted up thus she came close, he decided, to real beauty. Her lips were slightly parted with excitement and there was a hint of color in her cheeks. She smiled at him and repeated, "I think it is perfect."

"It is a beginning," said Basil. He studied his work with a critical eye and discovered that, although it had many good points, there was still a serious weakness. He turned on his stool to explain to her, "Getting a likeness, that human touch which can be recognized at first glance, depends nearly always on some one detail. It may be the width between the eyes. It may be as small a matter as the angle of the eyelid. Until you stumble on what it is, the face remains lifeless. Now I have one advantage here: I know what it is I need. The key to the likeness is the nose. Your grandfather has a most remarkable nose. It dominates his face. Oh, if I can only get it right! If I do, you will see this lump of clay come quickly to life before your eyes. But so far I have not succeeded." His fingers had gone back to work as he talked, changing the clay this way and that with the slightest possible pressure of the fingers. Suddenly he stopped. "I think—— Yes, I have it! Here it is, that splendid nose. I did no more than make a slight change in the elevation, the merest fraction of space, and now it is right. At last it is a likeness!"

"Yes, yes!" cried the girl.

But Basil shook his head. "It is not enough yet," he said, speaking as freely as though no one else were in the room. "True, I have the likeness now. But I am getting him as he is today. There must be as well a hint of the power of his earlier years. It will be empty without that. And again the secret is in his nose—that fine, fighting proud nose. I shall have to work still harder. But," confidently, "it will come. When one has attained this stage, it can be taken as certain that the final goal will be reached."

"I am sure of it," said the girl.

"Perhaps you young people will suspend your discussion long enough to let me see it," said Joseph. "It is *my* face you are discussing with such frankness. It is *my* nose that seems to cause so much concern."

He reached out a hand. His fingers, which had almost the transparency of ivory, trembled slightly. He accepted the clay from Basil and frowned a little in his shortsighted study of it. There was at the same time, however, an almost immediate display of approval.

"Yes, Deborra," he said, "the young man has a likeness of me here. I think it is going to be good, very good indeed."

Basil warmed to this welcome praise from his employer. All doubt left him. He was going to succeed. He was so certain of it that he accepted the clay back and set to work again with a feeling of full confidence.

Deborra returned to her chair beside the couch. Her praise had increased Basil's interest in her, and he was now fully conscious of the grace of her movements and the fine line of her profile. As noses had been so much under discussion, he gave hers a close scrutiny. It was short and straight and with the merest indentation at the end, which made it the very pleasantest kind of nose, pretty and slightly pert. He decided that he liked it.

"How can you be so calm about this, Grandfather?" she asked. "I think it is quite wonderful!"

The eyes of the two young people met across the room, hers still wide with the pleasure she was taking in the success of his efforts. She smiled at Basil so warmly that he began to wonder if it was entirely her interest in the work that prompted her. Was she willing to let him see that he himself was included in the approbation she felt?

CHAPTER IV

I

FOR A WEEK Basil saw nothing more of Joseph of Arimathea or his granddaughter. Adam ben Asher, he learned, had departed from the city. He worked a little on the clay bust from memory but found it unwise to attempt much, fearing he might lose the likeness. It was at best an elusive thing and could be destroyed by the indiscreet pressure of a fingertip.

He had been consigned to a small room on what obviously was the wrong side of the house, an airless space within sound of warehousing activities and on a dark hall that swarmed with workmen at all hours of the day. He washed with the domestic staff, waiting in a long line for his turn at a stream of water spouting sluggishly from a pipe, and sharing a piece of soap with the others. At intervals he visited an open and somewhat malodorous trench in the slave quarters. This treatment was so different from the warmth of his reception that he could not understand it. Had Joseph, on second thoughts, been less pleased with the start he had made? Was the parsimonious son of the house responsible for this unfriendly accommodation?

He took his meals alone in a small underground room lighted by an oil lamp in a bracket close to a ceiling that dripped moisture. The food was wholesome but decidedly plain and by the third day had become monotonous. Through an open door he looked on a long and dark chamber where the slaves of the household sat down to meat at the same hours. They gathered around a table large enough to accommodate forty or more at a time. He watched them as they ate (their food the same as his) and was surprised at the cheerfulness they displayed. They were a motley gathering, with skins of many colors, but dressed without exception in the plain gray tunic and the brass collar of servitude. There was much chaffing and laughing and, as both sexes shared the table, a tendency to ogle and flirt. An official sat at the head; the overseer, no doubt, for a whip was tucked into his belt, which he wore outside his tunic. He was a heavyish individual but not without good nature. He indulged in much humor of a heavy, bludgeoning variety and did a great deal of winking at the women.

The food on which the servants subsisted was in ample quantity; there was always something left over, at any rate. As soon as they had filed out of the room, the doors would be opened and beggars who had gathered at the rear door in readiness would be brought in to finish it. They were always an unclean and gluttonous lot, eating with a savage relish and disputing bitterly over the filling of the wine cups.

Basil spent his mornings in rambles about the city, finding himself involved in the busiest phase of life in the Holy City. It was crowded with visitors who had come for Pentecost. They filled the streets at all hours of the day and far into the night. Every house was filled to overflowing and tents had been set up outside the walls for the accommodation of the earnest men and women from all parts of the Diaspora* who asked no more than two things: to watch the paschal moon rise over Jerusalem and to bow their heads in reverence in the Temple. It was difficult for him under these circumstances to pursue his quest for information about Kester of Zanthus, but he did not allow himself to become discouraged.

His first jaunt carried him down into the Cheesemakers' Valley to a gate in the southern wall of the city; surely the busiest of all the gates, he thought, for its iron-plated doors were swung far back to permit the crowds to stream through. For the most part, those who used it were farmers bringing leban to the city, the thickened milk which did not sour quickly and which, therefore, was used instead of sweet milk. They were a hairy-chested, black-skinned lot, unfriendly in manner and loud of tongue.

The first vendor of leban to whom Basil put his inquiry regarded him with a slight hint of good nature. "Kester of Zanthus?" he said. "No, I have not heard of such a one. What is his occupation?"

"He is concerned with supplies for the Roman army."

The tolerance of the native turned at once to scoffing. "A contractor! *Aiy, aiy!* Have you lost your wits? Even a Greek should know that the

*The Diaspora is a term applied to the Jewish people who had left Jerusalem in the dispersal.

Dung Gate is not the place to seek word of an army contractor." The farmer pointed with his elbow toward the northwest. "Go and ask your questions there. Go to that insult in stone which Herod the Accursed raised to flout the children of Israel."

So Basil went to Castle Antonia standing on a great stone escarpment, its four towers frowning high above the city. As he climbed the graded approach he could hear the sharp call of military orders and the tramp of feet in unison from the walled-in courtyard. A sentry stopped him at the gate.

"You seek word of an army contractor?" said the latter. "It is lucky for you, my foolhardy youth, that I am a man of kindly heart. Anyone who comes here seeking information about army matters is like to be carried within and treated to a questioning that is not pleasant at all and that a sliver of flesh like you might not survive. Get you gone!"

He had no better luck in the vicinity of the Temple. Penetrating into the Court of the Gentiles, from which he could see as far inside as the narrow terrace of the Hel, he found himself face to face with a forbidding notice, which read:

LET NO STRANGER ENTER
WITHIN THE BALUSTRADE
AND THE ENCLOSING WALL
SURROUNDING THE SANCTUARY.
WHOEVER MAY BE CAUGHT,
OF HIMSELF SHALL BE THE
BLAME FOR HIS CERTAIN DEATH.

The colonnade about the Temple was thronged at all times, mostly with Jews who never seemed to walk alone but in argumentative pairs or groups. Their eyes would be fixed straight ahead, their tongues clicking in rapid controversy; and they would brush by him as though saying, "Make way, young Greek, for those whose thoughts are far above your comprehension." His question unanswered, he would be forced to the side of the street by the brusque passage of the men of Jerusalem. The region surrounding the Temple was devoted to the priesthood and the work of the schools of philosophy and it was a hive of activity at all hours of the day, but only on rare occasions was he able to corner anyone to ask his unvarying query. The result was always the same. "Kester of Zanthus?" the impatient passer-by would say. "A Greek? No knowledge have I of Greeks and no concern in them." Or perhaps the reply would be more straight to the point. "Betake yourself and your quest for foreigners out of sight of the House of the One God!"

He went up and down the Streets of the Glassblowers, the Waterskin Makers, the Meat Sellers, the Goldsmiths, the Spice Dealers. He haunted the neighborhood of the great palace of Herod; he went to the Gate of Ephraim, through which flowed most of the northern traffic; he patrolled the market on the floor of the valley, asking his question of anyone who could be persuaded to halt for a moment, "Know you aught of one Kester of Zanthus?" He had no success at all.

Despite this lack of results, he continued his quest with undiminished zeal. He was so persistent that even in his dreams he pursued the elusive purveyor of army supplies. Where is one Kester of Zanthus? Where, tell me, I beg of you, where is he now?

2

On the last day of the week Basil was on the point of leaving through the dining hall of the household slaves, having completed his midday meal, when he saw Joseph enter, accompanied by Deborra. He returned at once to the small room where he took his meals in humbly solitary state and composed himself to watch. The visitors stood beside the overseer and smiled at the respectful but somewhat anxious faces about the table. It was apparent that the master of the household was expected to speak a few words, and when he failed to do so it became clear to the watcher that the old man had suddenly ceased to enjoy what his son had called his more lucid moments. His face had taken on a tired and blank look. His lips moved, but no words were forthcoming.

Deborra led him to a stone bench at the side of the room and seated him there. Then she returned to the head of the table.

"Your master is not well today," she said. "I will tell you what was in his mind to say to you. He has been watching the work of the household and has studied the warehouse records, and he feels you are giving him the very best of service. For this he thanks you. He wants to be sure you are happy and contented. That you are well fed and clothed and that you are allowed ample time for rest and recreation." She was speaking easily. Basil watched her with close attention. "My grandfather wants you to feel free to come to him if you have complaints to make and to be sure that you will not be punished in any way if you do come. As—as he is far from well today, it might be better if any complaints were brought to me. I will know how to deal with them."

"She is very capable," thought Basil. "I am sure she would know what to do."

Deborra hesitated before going on, having difficulty seemingly in expressing what was in her mind. "A time is coming——" she began. Then she stopped and glanced about her uncertainly. "I don't know how my grandfather would have said this. But—but—*be of good cheer.*"

What did she mean? Basil was certain that a promise was being conveyed, but the nature of it lay outside his knowledge. The household staff had no doubts as to what it meant. By common consent they got to their feet and began to sing exultantly. Everyone joined in, even the overseer, who had plucked the whip from his belt and thrown it to the floor. Joseph of Arimathea, rousing from his withdrawn mood, began to sing with the others, holding closely his granddaughter's arm. It was a simple air, and the words were about goodness and love and charity. Basil listened with the feeling of wonder that came over him whenever he witnessed a demonstration of religious feeling. What was the secret of their deep conviction? Why were they so happy in their faith?

In the middle of the hymn the eyes of Deborra turned in his direction for the first time. The look of surprise on her face turned at once to puzzlement, then to comprehension of the way in which he was being treated. Her cheeks flushed and she dropped her eyes.

An hour later Aaron came to Basil's room, the silent servant in attendance as usual. He glanced about him before speaking.

"I see nothing wrong with this," he said. "But a complaint has been made and something must be done about it."

The usual snap of concealed fingers caused the servant to gather up all of Basil's belongings, wrapping the tools and materials in a square of cloth. Leaving the room with the bundle on his bent back, the slave looked so much like a condor that he might have been expected to spread his wings and take to flight immediately. Aaron motioned Basil to follow.

It was to a spacious room on the top floor that they proceeded. It had windows looking out over the city on two sides and rich hangings on the walls. There was a luxurious couch on a raised platform over which a rich carpet had been spread. On a table beside the couch were an oil lamp and a silver laver with water spouting from holes in its sides. A repast consisting of cold meat, a loaf of bread, and a platter piled high with fruit was spread on another table. A breeze blew across the room, bringing instant relief from the oppressive heat of the downstairs.

Aaron looked about him and his nostrils twitched with annoyance. "This," he said, "is to be yours. It seems unnecessarily fine and I sus- pect—— Well, it is yours, for the time being." A snap of the fingers caused the servant to deposit his bundle on the floor and betake himself to the hall. "My father is very feeble and so I lay this command on you, that you finish your task as soon as possible."

3

At noon on the following day Basil was summoned to the bedroom of Joseph. Deborra met him at the door. "Have you forgiven us?" she asked in a whisper. "I knew nothing about it."

The sleeper stirred on his couch and called in a complaining tone, "You are not reading, my child."

"Grandfather always has a nap at this time," she whispered in explana- tion. "I read to him. I thought it might be of help to you if you could study his face in repose."

She returned to her seat beside the bed and proceeded to read from a parchment of formidable size. The old man sighed in content, and almost immediately the steady rhythm of his breathing indicated that he had fallen back into slumber.

The young artist hastened to take full advantage of this opportunity to study his subject. His fingers wrought on the clay in eager haste, adding detail to what he had achieved at the first attempt. Although absorbed in his work, he found himself following what the girl was reading. It was the story of a young shepherd who was captured and sold into slavery in the household of a wealthy man in the country about Babylon. He became so much interested, in fact, that he paused from his labors to ask a question.

"What is it you read from?"

Deborra answered in the same even tone, "This is the Book of Jashar. It is very, very old and made up of tales of early Hebrew heroes."

"Are all the stories true?"

"I don't know. But it has been read for centuries and no one questions its truth." She raised her eyes from the parchment to smile across the couch at him. "I read Grandfather to sleep every day at this time. He falls off at once, but if I stop he wakens."

"Do you never get tired?"

"Oh no. But I—I practice a deception on him. He has me read always from the Torah or perhaps from some legal documents. It is very dry, and as soon as he is safely asleep I change to something I find more interesting myself. Such as this." Her smile returned, lighting up her face. "Sometimes he wakens and catches me at it and then he is very angry with me. You see, he pretends he does not sleep and that he listens to every word."

The sleeper stirred and changed his position, turning his profile to the watchful eyes of the artist. Basil studied him from this angle, wondering at the beauty of modeling in the brow and nose. "He has such a splendid head!" he whispered. "I am afraid I shall never be able to do justice to it."

The reading went on steadily for another ten minutes. The story gained in intensity because the young slave was sent out to fight against invaders of the valley where the estates of his master were located, and returned loaded with honors. Basil suspended work to ask more questions.

"I may not be here when you finish the reading," he said. "Is the slave given his freedom?"

Deborra nodded. "Yes. And he is given some land and sheep and cattle. And a house of his own in the hills."

"And does he marry the daughter of his master?"

A slight trace of pink showed under the ivory of the girl's cheek. "Yes, he marries Tabitha. But not at first. He asks for her hand, but her father refuses him. So he goes back into the hills and wonders what he is to do. Then one night he rides down to her father's house and gathers her up in his arms and takes her back with him. She rides behind him with her arms about his waist."

"She goes willingly, then?"

"Oh yes, yes! Tabitha is very much in love with him. Then he sends down word to her father, saying, 'Tabitha is my wife, and if you come to take her back we shall both fight you to the death.' Her father goes up alone to the house in the hills and he asks his daughter, 'Is this true?' She answers that she loves her husband. Her father says, 'Stay then with him, but never expect any inheritance from me, having disobeyed my commands.' But when the father dies, they have almost as much property as he, and so it does not matter that nothing is willed to Tabitha. It is a beautiful story, is it not?"

The sleeper stirred again, roused himself, and sat up. He shook an accusing forefinger at her.

"You are at your tricks again. It is from the Book of Jashar that you read. Must I repeat that I have no liking for such light tales?"

"Grandfather, how many times must we talk about this? You know that I take up something different as soon as you go to sleep. Does it matter *what* I read as long as the sound of my voice keeps you from stirring?"

"It matters a great deal," protested the old man. "I hear every word you say and I have told you so a dozen times. You are becoming very self-willed, I am afraid."

"You have told me that many times too, Grandfather."

He became aware of a third person in the room. "Who is this, my child?"

"It is the artist. I asked him to come in so he could study your features in repose."

"I hope you will not think I have been presumptuous," said Basil, beginning to gather his materials together. "It has been very helpful."

He was summoned at the same hour for several days in succession and the work progressed rapidly, his acquaintance with Deborra keeping pace with it. On the fourth day, as he pressed with questing fingers around the line of the mouth, he realized that he had achieved a change of expression. He hastily withdrew his hands.

"It is finished," he said after a moment.

Deborra dropped the parchment and ran over to stand at his shoulder. The white sleeve of her *palla* touched his arm. He was aware that she was breathing quickly.

"Yes, yes!" she exclaimed. "Lay not another finger on it, Basil, for fear it may change for the worse. It is perfect now."

"Not as much as a fingertip." He spoke happily. "It is finished and ready for casting."

They had been speaking in excited tones. Joseph roused and sat up. "What is it?" he asked in the sharp tone he always used when first wakened. Basil had discovered that it meant nothing. The old man worshiped his granddaughter and thought her perfect in every respect.

"It is finished," announced the proud artist. "May I show it to you?"

Joseph studied it with critical attention and then nodded his head. "I am well content," he said. "Tomorrow Luke will be here, and then I shall have something to say to you."

Basil was so delighted with the approval bestowed on his work that he paid no attention at first to the news about his benefactor. Then he said: "I am happy that Luke will be here. I have missed him very much."

"Paul and his followers reached Caesarea several days ago and stayed there in the house of Philip. They are now approaching Jerusalem and will arrive at some time during the evening. I have sent word entreating him to slip quietly into the city, but it may not be possible. I very much fear that those who oppose him are as well informed of his movements as I am. There may be trouble tonight." Joseph's eyes returned to the clay bust. "I agree now with my granddaughter. It is perfect."

CHAPTER V

T HAT AFTERNOON Deborra paid a visit in his room on the top floor. She was accompanied by three women of the household and carried in her hand a large metal ring filled with keys. Pausing in the doorway, she held up the ring.

"I have messages for you. They could have been brought by a servant, of course. But I thought I would like to be in a position to judge of your comfort now by the evidence of my own eyes. And so," smiling, "I decided on a tour of inspection as an excuse to come."

"It is kind of you to take so much interest. As you see, I live in the greatest comfort and luxury."

After a moment's silence her eyes, which she had kept lowered, were raised to his face.

"I know all about you," she said in a low tone. "I know how you were robbed of your inheritance and how badly you were treated. I think you were—very brave about everything." Then, realizing that she was allowing herself to display too much emotional involvement, she went on, "Grandfather would like you to sup with us this evening. At five o'clock."

Basil had been learning something of the ways of the household. He knew that Aaron dined at five each day and that he made it a point to collect about him a group of notabilities, Roman officials, other merchants of rank and wealth, members of the Sanhedrin, the great Jewish council. This he did, it was said, to offset the well-known fact that Joseph was a Christian. Aaron entertained on a lavish scale.

While the son of the house dined in state, his father and daughter supped together, quietly and happily, in an apartment adjoining the bedroom of Joseph.

"It will be an honor," said Basil.

The girl hesitated again. "If you care to come with me now," she said, "there is someone below who has information for you. He told me of it before I came up. He is one of Grandfather's men. His name is Benjamin, but everyone calls him Benjie the Asker. You will soon understand why."

Benjie the Asker was waiting for them in a dark cubicle in the warehouse wing. He was small and wiry, with owl-like hollows around his eyes. In his hand he held a cup of *sorbitio,* a barley water that was considered cooling in hot weather.

He took a sip of this tepid mixture, his sharp eye studying Basil over the rim.

"I know everything that goes on in Jerusalem," he announced. "And that means a great deal in these times. It would take little to start a revolution in Jerusalem against Roman rule. Did you know that?"

"No. I am sorry to say I know little about such matters."

"That is what I thought."

"Benjamin is a gatherer of information," explained Deborra.

"O Lady of the House, I am more than that," exclaimed Benjie. He proceeded to display a degree of loquacity almost equal to that of Adam ben Asher. "I am also a disseminator of opinion. I am a harrier of Pharisees in open meeting, I am a thorn in the flesh of Sadducees. I burrow under surfaces, I dip into many curious sources of information. I am in the confidence of many of the leaders of the city, but at the same time I belong to clubs on the lowest level. Oh yes, there are such clubs, I assure you. They meet in dark cellars on Fish Street and in hot tenements under the walls of the Gymnasium. There is one which meets in a warehouse where the air reeks of oil and camphor. I hear revolution plotted by the Zealots. I am consulted in matters of religious strife. And this I may say without boasting: no door in Jerusalem is closed to me."

Deborra smiled at the puzzled manner with which Basil was listening. "Now that you know about him," she said, "he will give you the information he has for you."

"You are like your grandfather," grumbled Benjie. "You always want to come quickly to the point." He shifted on his wooden stool and addressed himself directly to the artist. "It came to my attention—in fact, it is my business to know all such things—that you spend your mornings wandering about the city and asking questions of everyone you can persuade to stop. One question, rather, and always the same. I decided, after consulting our lady here, to take your quest on my own shoulders and see what I could find about the elusive Kester."

Basil asked eagerly, "And what have you found?"

"I have found everything that is known about him," declared the little man in a pompous tone. "He came to Jerusalem seven years ago, being interested in army contracts. For three years he was quite active and was constantly in contact with the Roman officials in Castle Antonia. He became wealthy and in due course decided he should seek a wider field. He went to Rome."

Basil's interest was so intense that he found it hard to remain still. "Are you sure of this?" he asked. "I was almost ready to give up. I had not succeeded in finding anyone who had ever heard his name."

"I am never in error, young man. There can be no doubt that your missing witness removed to Rome four years ago. He was still alive, still in Rome, and still active as recently as three months ago. At that time he wrote a letter to an old acquaintance here in Jerusalem. I," importantly, "have seen the letter."

"To whom was it sent?" Basil laid an importunate hand on the hairy wrist of the small man. "Will it be possible for me to see it?"

"I am sure I could get the consent of the man who received it. But would there be any satisfaction in seeing a few lines scrawled in a far from scholarly hand? All the note proves is that the man was alive at the time it was written." Benjie paused for effect. "It was received here by one Dionysius of Samothrace. He also was interested in army contracts, and, if I am correct in the conclusions I draw from some references in the letter, he is still concerned in a small way in such matters. This Dionysius is as flabby as the sponges he ships in from his native island. But make no mistake in the man; he is in character a close relative of the devilfish." The seeker of information nodded his head. "It would do no good to see the man. You would come away, I am sure, nauseated with him. My advice is: stay away. He might wheedle something of value out of you and send it on to Linus."

Basil, clearly, was finding reason for discouragement in the picture drawn of Dionysius. "They were partners? What manner of man, then, is Kester of Zanthus?"

"All I can tell you," answered Benjie, "is that he left a reputation here for honesty; and that is an extraordinary thing for an army contractor to do."

Basil drew a breath of relief. "My future," he said, "is going to depend on how much of that honesty he has retained."

He remained silent for a moment, and it was apparent that he was suffering from a sudden embarrassment. Benjie the Asker had of his own accord done him a very great service and was entitled to a reward. But how could a reward be paid out of empty pockets?

While this thought was running through his mind he became aware that something had been dropped into the palm of his hand. It was round and cold. He opened his fingers cautiously and glanced down. It was a coin and, moreover, of gold. Deborra was standing beside him, and it was apparent that she had transferred the piece of gold into his possession without letting either of them see what she was doing. She was looking purposely away, and he could not catch her eye to convey his gratitude.

"I shall be forever in your debt," he said to the Asker, holding the coin. "Will you accept this from me?"

"Gold!" cried Benjie. Taking the money, he gave it an ecstatic spin in the air. "The rarest and finest of all material things in the world. It makes and unmakes empires. It is dangerous, it leads men into evil designs, it corrupts their souls. But at the same time," he declared, "I confess that it has a most grateful feel on the palm. I accept with gratitude. And I hope that someday, if Kester's honesty is equal to the test, you will sit in ease and great power, even as King Midas, with whole columns of this most wonderful of metals stacked about you. Columns as tall as the Temple that Herod carried up into the sky when the people of Jerusalem insisted he must build it on the foundations of the Temple of Solomon."

"If that day comes," said Basil, smiling, "there will be a column of it for you as well."

"I shall be well content with one as high as a camel can raise its rear heel." He nodded his head gratefully. "May you always eat off gold plate and say your prayers before a golden shrine. May you wear a sword of gold at your belt."

Basil's embarrassment returned when he left the room in the company of Deborra. "You were observant and very kind," he said. "For two years now I have had no money in my possession. Since I was sold as a slave, my pockets have been empty."

"Did not Luke have money for you when you left Antioch? My grandfather thought that plenty had been sent."

"It cost him more than had been expected to purchase my freedom," explained Basil. "My owner and his wife were a grasping pair and they held him to a hard bargain. He had nothing left when the transaction was completed except two copper coins."

The girl's eyes opened wide with surprise. "How then did you get to Aleppo to meet Adam?"

"Luke was not concerned. He said to me that the Lord would provide. And most truly He did. The first night we stopped at a small village and were directed to the house of a widow. My benefactor said to her, 'Christ is risen,' and she made an answer that seemed quite as strange but meant something to him——"

Deborra interrupted in a low voice, "I think what the widow said was, 'He sits at the right hand of God.' "

"Those were the exact words. It seems that this established an understanding between them."

"A complete understanding, I am sure."

Basil did not ask any questions but went on with his account of the journey to Aleppo. "We stayed in the widow's house that night. The same thing happened the following night when we went to the home of a maker of wheels, a humble man with a family of seven children. He gave us of his best nevertheless."

They parted in the hall, Basil returning to his room. He was filled with gratitude for the generosity and tact she had shown, but other considerations soon drove all thought of her from his head. Kester of Zanthus was alive. He, Basil, must get to Rome as soon as possible. How could such a long journey be accomplished? It occurred to him that Joseph might be generous enough to send him on his way with letters to people in Rome. The only other course open would be to join the crew of a ship sailing for the capital of the world. This he would be most reluctant to do, knowing that the lot of a sailor was no better than a step above slavery. He would not willingly place his wrists in chains again.

2

It developed that Joseph was unable to partake of any food that evening, and a female relative took his place at the round table where supper was served. She was large and billowy, and it seemed to Basil that she was regarding him with a hostile eye.

"She is a cousin," whispered Deborra, suppressing a smile with difficulty. "Her name is Hazzelelponi, but everyone calls her Old Gaggle. She is a great eater and will not pay much attention to anything else."

It was a spacious room, with windows opening on the north and east, and with fans swinging back and forth noiselessly on the ceiling. A servant in spotless white stood ready to serve them.

"I have saved three quail from below." Abraham, the servant, bent his head over the girl's shoulder to whisper this information. "They are cooked in wine and *very* good, mistress. They were fattened on curds and young grasshoppers."

Deborra, whose cheeks showed a slight tinge of excitement as though this were an event of some importance, nodded her head in approbation of the quail. Then she asked, "What fish have you for us?"

Abraham drew down the corners of his mouth in a disconsolate line. "None has been prepared," he said. "Perhaps I could get you some of the mullet they are eating downstairs. Red mullet with a crayfish sauce. Most tasty, mistress."

Deborra shook her head. "I would rather not depend entirely on crumbs from my father's table. What has been prepared for us?"

It was soon apparent that a most excellent supper was in readiness. After the bones of the tender quail had been picked clean, a platter of kid's meat was served on rice, with pearl barley sprinkled over it, a mound of capers in the center, and young blite chopped fine around the edge of the dish. This was followed by hard-boiled eggs with a sauce of cummin, cheese of goat's milk with preserved quince, and a heaping dish of fresh peaches. Throughout the meal their cups were kept replenished with the delightful honey wine called *mulsum*.

The appetite of the third member of the trio at table has already been commented on, and it is hardly necessary to say that she did full justice to this delicious supper. Both Deborra and Basil had the hearty capacity of youth and did not lag behind her. It was a long time before the last dish had been served and the towels and hot water provided. Hazzelelponi, who had become more silent as the meal progressed, showed no tendency to join them when they took their seats at a north window, where the last glint of the setting sun could be seen on the roof of the Temple. The sound of the *shofarim,* the horns with which the priests announced the coming of night, reached them with surprising clearness.

"I have heard it every night of my life, and yet it still excites me," said Deborra, listening intently. "Do you know much of our customs?"

"Very little, I am sorry to say."

"It is ram's horns the priests use, but they are heated and straightened out to get more length and tone. I have never seen them. No one sees them. The priests keep them covered always, even when they come out to sound the passing of day. All the sacred objects in the Temple are kept covered. Did you know that the High Priest has bells on his robe so people will know when he approaches and will turn their heads away? It is all very mysterious."

"I realize," said Basil, "that there is one question no one asks."

The girl's face became grave at once. "I am not afraid to answer," she said. "You mean, am I a Christian? Yes, yes! I was born in the faith. I was raised to believe in Jesus Christ. My mother, who died when I was quite small, taught me to say Jesus before any other words, even before *avva* or *imma,* and then she took me in to let my grandfather hear. He seemed very old even then. His beard was white and he had all those wrinkles of kindness about his eyes. The tears poured down his cheeks when he heard me say Jesus.

"He and my mother were very close," she went on. "I can remember how concerned they were over the state of my father's soul." She sighed deeply. "I love my father, but I am sure now that he will never see the light. Religion to him is all a matter of form." She glanced about her to make sure that none of the servants were in the room and that the third member of the party was not straining her ears to follow the conversation between them. "Father's guests today are all from the Temple. The High Priest is there and many of the men closest to him. I think they are discussing what they will do now that Paul is on his way. Is it not strange that there should be such talk in the house of Joseph of Arimathea?"

She had been speaking with great earnestness, but now she paused. Leaning her chin on her cupped hands, she watched him with a sudden smile. "We are being very serious, aren't we? We always seem to be so serious. Do you know that I have never seen you smile?"

"Am I as glum as that?"

"No, not glum. I think I would call you grave. And it is not surprising after all you have been through."

He studied her face. It was a very young face, with the unclouded eyes and the fresh color of her few years. She looked more appealing at the moment, and prettier, than he had realized before.

"You do not smile often yourself," he said.

She nodded at once in agreement. "I guess I have always been a little solemn. You see, I was a very small girl when Grandfather decided to be less active in trade. Then my mother died, and he has depended on me ever since. I was never allowed to play with toy children,* even when I was very small. I have never had any young friends. I don't know a girl of my own age. Perhaps that is the reason."

"We seem to be a pair of sobersides, don't we?"

She had been so serious about her plight that, without any conscious effort, he found himself smiling at her. She returned it with immediate delight. "There!" she cried. "You have! You have actually smiled at me. For the first time. And it was a very nice smile. I liked it."

She was realizing that perhaps she had liked it too well. Facing him at the window, she thought: "He has a very fine face. I think it is a beautiful face. It is so sensitive and full of imagination."

"I think," said Basil, "that we should make a compact, you and I. To do a lot more smiling. How often do you think? Once every half hour?"

"Perhaps that would be right for a start. If we should get to know each other better, we might begin to smile much oftener. We might even laugh."

"Yes, we might even laugh."

She nodded her head and smiled to such good effect that her whole face lighted up. "I am sure it is going to be very nice," she said.

"What a pleasant little scene," said a voice from the door.

It was Adam ben Asher, looking dusty and even a little weary, which was most unusual, for his powers of endurance seemed to have no bounds. He walked stiffly into the room, keeping his intense gray eyes fixed on them.

"One might even think you a quiet little family group, the two of

*A term used for dolls.

you sitting there with your heads so close together, and Old Gaggle still under the influence of a big supper." He had crossed the room and was standing above them. "You have been discussing, no doubt, the little piece of work this young genius is doing for the master."

"No," answered Deborra. "It has not been mentioned."

"*Aiy!* Relaxing from his labors. I expected this. They are great relaxers, these Greeks; and always, it seems, in the company of beautiful women."

"The bust is finished and ready for casting," declared Basil angrily.

"Now *that* is excellent news." Adam turned to look at Deborra. "Can you detach your mind sufficiently from what this undernourished Apollo has been saying to you to hear what I have been doing? I have been escorting someone of importance to Jerusalem."

"I know," said Deborra. "It is Paul."

"Paul, and none else. The great teacher of the Gentiles. The ardent Jew who is striving so hard to wreck the Law of Moses. He was as fierce of eye and of temper as ever. But somewhat less talkative.

"I brought him from Caesarea. He had gone there to see Philip, and something had happened to take the edge of loquacity from his tongue." Adam threw back his head and laughed. "I was even allowed to do some talking myself, which is a strange thing when Paul is around. Naturally he did not listen to anything I said."

Although he had laughed as loudly as ever, it was clear that he did not feel any sense of amusement. His eyes kept jumping from one to the other, trying to find the key to the relationship that had developed between them. They were full of anger and disappointment. When they rested on Basil the depth of feeling in them became more intense and they seemed to say, "You have been up to tricks, my young pagan!"

"Did you bring him here?" asked Deborra.

Adam ben Asher snorted loudly. "I would as soon bring a pack of hungry lions into this house as Paul," he declared. "It seems he had plans of his own. He disappeared almost as soon as we came through the gate. A humble-looking fellow fell into step beside the camel the great Paul was riding and they began to talk in whispers. Before I knew what had happened, he had slipped down from the back of the camel and had vanished without a word. All the rest of them disappeared at the same time. It's well that they did. Within a few minutes they were swarming around us, the underlings from the Temple, and asking questions about him. There was a great deal of curiosity as to the whereabouts of Master Paul. If he had stayed with me, they would have had him trussed and ready for a hearing before the governor."

Adam seemed to become conscious for the first time then that the absence of Joseph called for comment. He asked anxiously, "Is my good Master Joseph seriously ill that he could not come to supper?"

"No," answered Deborra. "He is not ill at all. He is in bed, but he enjoyed a good supper by himself."

Adam gave his thigh a slap and burst into a loud roar of laughter. "That means we have company tonight from the Temple. I should know by this time that our good old man is always indisposed when the great ones come to sup with Aaron. They have not laid an eye on him in ten years. *Aiy,* he is still the wisest fox of them all." A still louder laugh attested his pleasure in the successful maneuvering of his employer. "Then I may see him this evening? I have many bits of information for his ear."

"He will want to see you, of course."

The servant Abraham had returned and was collecting the dishes from the table. He was in a disturbed state of mind; his hands fumbled at their task and he even allowed a cup half full of wine to fall. Deborra gave him an anxious glance and saw that his face was white.

"Are you ill?" she asked.

The servant straightened up and began to collect the remains of the supper with more care. "No, mistress, I am not ill." Then he replaced the jug of *mulsum* on the table and asked in an angry voice: "Is it right that a Samaritan should be admitted to this house? One of the cursed Cutheans? Is it right that the master's son should tell me to place a chair for him at the table? One would think he was a great man and not mud under our feet!"

Adam walked over to the table. "A Samaritan? Abraham, who is it?"

Abraham answered in a reluctant voice, as though unwilling to reveal the full infamy of the situation. "Simon the Magician. He was not here for supper. He came later, and they said he was to be taken in to them. They are all down there now, talking and whispering with their heads close together."

"And the High Priest himself is there?"

The servant nodded his head. "He is sitting there in his jeweled *ippudah,* the closest of all to this Cuthean." His voice sank to a husky note of fear. "All the fiends and the wicked spirits came into the house with him. I could feel them in the air."

"I think I know what those old men of iron down there are plotting with Simon the Magician," muttered Adam. "I hope Moses hears them. He will not approve!"

CHAPTER VI

I

SEATED at one of his windows, Basil waited the next morning for the summons from Joseph of Arimathea. From here he could look across the bridge that spanned the Cheesemakers' Valley and ran straight as an arrow flight to the Temple. The bridge was a magnificent structure, as great in its way as the Temple itself; a span of white stone nearly four hundred feet long and wide enough to allow the passage of five chariots driving abreast. He had crossed it many times in his morning rambles and was finding that he fell naturally into the custom of keeping his eyes on the grandeur of marble and gold massed above and allowing his feet to take care of themselves. One aspect had kept him in a somewhat unhappy frame of mind, however: the squalor of the valley two hundred feet below. There was no reason, he realized, for him to carry any such burden of worry: the people of Jerusalem, even the humble workers themselves who lived in that hot and malodorous depression, seemed to give no thought to the contrast between the magnificence of the heights and the poverty of the depths. Or did they reserve their discontent for the meetings in the cellars of Fish Street that Benjie the Asker frequented?

As he watched the bridge this morning, Basil became aware of three men in particular. They had, quite apparently, visited the Temple and were now crossing back to the city. They walked abreast, and the one in the center was shorter than his two companions, a slight figure with bowed legs showing beneath his knee-length tunic. He was monopolizing the conversation, for even at that distance Basil could see the emphatic nod of his head, the frequent lift of his hand for emphasis. His fellow walkers paced along beside him in absorbed silence, their attention given to every word he uttered.

Basil's attention, nevertheless, was given mostly to the member of the trio who walked on the right. There was a familiarity about this figure that did not lead to an identification until some peculiarity about the man's gait solved the problem. It was Luke, a jaded and somewhat disheveled Luke, weary from his travels and walking with the suggestion of a limp. Basil got to his feet and leaned out of the window in order to see better. He was realizing how much he had missed this kindliest of men since they had parted at Aleppo.

A man crossing the bridge in the opposite direction stopped as the three passed him. He remained motionless for a few moments, his eyes fixed intently on their backs. Then he turned and began to follow. A few moments later another pedestrian did the same. Before the watcher in the window was fully aware of what was happening there were half a dozen people tramping in the wake of the small man with the bowed legs; and before the head of the procession had reached the end of the bridge there were at least twoscore. It was now possible to distinguish voices, and Basil could hear repeated one word time and again, "Paul—Paul—Paul."

The small man, then, was the fiery evangelist whose preaching to the Gentiles had gone so far to split the Christians into two camps and whose presence in Jerusalem was expected to lead to much trouble. Basil strove to recall the day when he had heard Paul preach at Ceratium; but time, he found, had now blurred that episode in his mind.

His interest was deeply engaged and he watched the small man with the most intense curiosity. Paul, it was clear, was fully aware of the excitement he was creating and of the steady growth of the following that trailed after him like the tail of a comet. His voice could be heard, deep and resonant and emphatic. He was no longer carrying on a part in a conversation but was delivering an oration that those behind him could hear. His gestures had become studied and occasionally he shot a quick glance back over his shoulder as though to estimate the effect of what he was saying.

When the slow procession reached the end of the bridge and poured onto the paved open space before the door of Joseph it was joined by members of the household. Basil was surprised to see the diminutive figure of Benjie the Asker among the newcomers. From a window to his right he perceived the bald head of Aaron peering out with a caution that suggested he did not want to be seen himself.

Luke whispered in Paul's ear. The latter listened intently and then nodded in agreement. Raising a hand above his head, he spoke directly to those who had followed him.

"It is not meet that we linger here before the door of a brave and good man in whose debt we stand," he began. Basil, sitting high up in his window, could hear every word clearly, for Paul's voice had a remarkable carrying quality. "Disperse now to your homes or to the occupations by which you earn your daily bread. There will be opportunities within the next few days for us to gather together so that ye may hear what I have to tell of my stewardship. I do not know when or where it will be. The hand of hostility is being raised against us and we must exercise caution. Go then: watch and wait for the time when it will be possible for us to meet." The apostle paused and glanced about him at the attentive faces. "Then you will hear a wondrous story, the story of a world yearning for the truth, a field ripe for the sickle."

2

Basil had expected to be summoned at ten o'clock. It was nearly twelve when Luke came to his room. The weariness that had been perceptible at a distance was unmistakable at close range. The physician's large and eloquent eyes had a gaunt look in them and he moved stiffly. It was with a return of animation, however, that he came into the room and placed a hand on each of Basil's shoulders.

"My boy," he said, his face lighting up with a smile, "I have received the best reports of you. Joseph is well content with what you have done—and equally with you. The small Deborra is convinced you are the greatest artist in the world. Even Aaron, whose capacity for enthusiasm is small, has no criticism to offer. I need not tell you how happy this makes me."

"I have missed you very much," said Basil.

"Have you, my son?" The smile grew in warmth. "I have been many places and seen many strange things since we parted company. Often I said to myself that I wished you were there. Truly the Lord Jehovah rode with us and watched over us; and the scroll of history was being filled by the winds that brought our ship to Caesarea. Someday I shall sit me down and tell on parchment all the things that befell us; and I think, my son, that the world will hearken to the strange and wondrous story." His mood changed then and he shook his head with a hint of depression.

"We have scattered since we arrived, and stay in the humblest of houses. Even Paul is for the moment reconciled to remaining in seclusion. But he keeps saying that the Lord did not summon him to Jerusalem to skulk in the Cheesemakers' Valley, and I am afraid he will soon issue forth and cry out his message for all the city to hear." The tired head nodded slowly. "What will happen? What will the next few days bring forth?"

"I saw from my window that Paul came with you," said Basil. "Is he still here?"

Luke nodded. "He has been with Joseph of Arimathea for two hours. The advice of our splendid old friend is always sound and welcome. Even Paul feels the need of it in this crisis. I betook myself away for a few moments in order to see you, my son, but now I must return. You will be sent for soon, I think." He had been on the point of leaving, but at this he checked his steps. "I have spoken to Joseph about the little child in Antioch. He agrees she should be bought out of slavery and will see that it is done."

Basil felt a warm flood of gratitude for both old men, his own benefactor who had not forgotten to intercede for Agnes and the generous one who had promised his aid. "I give you my thanks!" he said fervently. The eyes with which he smiled at Luke were partly filled with tears. "I fall more into your debt all the time. Will I ever be able to repay you?"

"Yes," said Luke. "And very soon, I think."

Shortly after Luke left, Deborra appeared for the second time in the doorway. The usual domestics were behind her, the same ring of keys was in her hand, the same apologetic smile on her lips. There was one difference: a thin mongrel pup stood apologetically at her heels.

She explained about the dog first, speaking in a low voice for his ears only. "I want to be gay, to laugh more, to—to have a good time. So I thought it would help to have a pet. Benjie the Asker found this one for me. He was a poor stray in the Bellows of Beelzebub. Now that he has a home he is very grateful. Of course he is not the kind I wanted. What I wanted was a—a very busy little dog who played and barked a great deal. This poor fellow is a mournful kind of dog."

Basil studied the sad eyes and drooping tail of the mongrel. "I am afraid he has seen much sorrow," he said.

"I think so too. Perhaps I should name him after one of the old prophets, the ones who always found life so black and full of sin— Jeremiah or Zephaniah or Habakkuk. A name like that would suit him.

But I don't care." She leaned down and patted the animal's head. "I like him already. I am going to keep him."

She then proceeded with the errand that had brought her to his door. "Paul is with my grandfather. He has been there all morning."

"I was told he seeks advice of your grandfather."

Deborra could not refrain from smiling. "Perhaps that was his intention. But in truth Grandfather has had no chance yet to give advice. Paul has done all the talking." She hastened then to correct what she feared was a wrong intention. "It has been quite wonderful. I was allowed to stay in the room and listen. I was carried away by the things he was telling." The smile struggled to regain possession of her face. "But it goes on and on, and I think there has been enough of it now. I can see that Grandfather is becoming very tired. And you, Basil, must be impatient with so much delay."

"A little," he acknowledged.

"I am impatient too. I have no idea what Grandfather is going to say to you. I questioned him last night and again this morning. He was quite stubborn about it. He just smiled and said it was a secret. I was angry with him, but it had no effect at all."

"We will have to wait a little longer, Deborra. It won't be hard."

She had turned to leave, but at this she came back, to stand in the doorway with her head leaning against the frame.

"Did you know that you called me by my name? You made it sound very nice. Perhaps Greek voices are more melodious than ours."

"Perhaps the reason is that the name is a very nice one."

Deborra hesitated. "I should not tell you, but—I know a little. Enough to be sure that what Grandfather has to say will please you."

The summons came at one o'clock, but the talking had not reached an end when Basil arrived at the spacious room of the head of the house. He recognized the deep voice of Paul as soon as the door opened to admit him.

"I will not compromise, Joseph of Arimathea," the apostle was saying. "I have come to Jerusalem with a message. A message for your stiff-necked leaders, for such they are in very truth. It is this, that the Gentiles must be received, not on our terms but on their own terms. They must not be compelled to accept everything in the Law of Moses. To us the Law is familiar. It seems to us perfect. We were born to it and we believe in it. But to the Gentiles it is strange and frightening and it would drive them away from Christ. If we say they must be circumcised before they may belong, they will turn their backs on the great truths which Jesus taught. No, no, Joseph of Arimathea, I must be firm and allow no tampering with the decision reached five years ago, at which time I was given a free hand. The second thoughts, the reservations, which now fill the minds of the presbyters of the faith, must be put aside."

"This is the young man," said Joseph, motioning Basil to enter.

As Basil made his way into the room he saw that Joseph was reclining on his couch as usual and that both Luke and Deborra were present, although seated at a distance. Paul, who was stationed close to Joseph, turned at his entrance and gave him the benefit of a quick but intent glance.

The first close glimpse that Basil was thus afforded of this remarkable man was in the nature of a shock. He was surprised to find how old the great apostle had become. Paul's hair and beard were white, and there were both fatigue and suffering in the lines clustering about his eyes and accenting the hollowness of his cheeks. It surprised the youth also that the face that had been turned to him was not an agreeable one. The features seemed to have been cut out of the hardest granite, and the expression was stern. But at the same time he realized it was a compelling face. The eyes under straight white brows were the color of the moon in a daylight sky, strange eyes, disturbing and at the same time fascinating.

Basil realized after one glance at this frail old man in his short and unadorned woolen tunic that no one else in the room seemed to matter.

Joseph cleared his throat. "I have already said that I am pleased with what this young man has done for me. There is something I have not told you." He motioned toward the clay bust, which stood on a pedestal beside him. "It was not for this alone that I had him come here. There is something of much more moment to be done. It is so vital that I had to be sure of the artist who would undertake it. This," indicating the clay head, "was a test. He has passed it so well that I am sure he is capable of the much greater work that is now to be done.

"I have been making another test," went on the venerable head of the house. "It was not enough to be sure of this young man's skill with his hands. I had to be equally sure of him—of his character, his loyalty, his patience, even his courage. Unknown to him, I think, he has been under observation. I wish to say now that he has satisfied me on every point."

Basil saw that Luke was smiling and nodding his head at him. Deborra was leaning forward, her lips slightly parted in anxious anticipation.

"Young man," said Joseph, addressing Basil directly, "I must tell you, before going any further, that the task I have in mind would entail the most careful study and the hardest of work. You must give years to it if necessary. You must travel, for there are many men to be seen, of whom you must make as good likenesses as you have of me. You must expect to meet opposition and to face danger."

"I shall be happy to undertake it," declared Basil. "And to give every moment of my time to it. If I have any reluctance at all, it is because I wonder if it will be possible to satisfy you." He paused and then asked, "Where would it be necessary for me to go?"

"To Caesarea, I think. To Ephesus. Perhaps to Rome."

Basil found it hard to prevent himself from crying out exultantly, "I will go!" That he would have to visit Rome was sufficient to make him accept instantly. The answer to the question that had been weighing heaviest on his mind had been found. He would get to Rome and he would find Kester of Zanthus.

The main explanation was now to be made. Joseph glanced first at Paul and then at Luke. "Some years ago an object came into my possession," he said. "It was of such a nature that I trembled at the responsibility that had been placed on me. The fear that it might suffer damage or that it might—ah, what a terrifying thought!—be stolen or lost weighed so on my mind that I had a special room made in which to keep it. There it has been ever since, as free of observation as though in the Holy of Holies. Today, for the first time, I propose to open the room."

Paul had listened to the explanation with interest but also with some impatience. It was clear he resented the interruption to the discussion of his views. "My good Joseph, what can this most mysterious object be?" he asked.

"Let me tell you first," said Joseph, "how it came into my hands. A woman brought it to me, a humble woman who had hidden it away, not being sure of her duty in the matter. She had feared it might get into the wrong hands and so she had waited. It was with the most solemn admonitions that she confided it to me. I was to keep it until I in turn could be sure of what was to be done. She was very poor, but I need hardly tell you that she refused any remuneration."

Joseph made an effort to rise from his couch but found that he needed assistance in getting to his feet. With Deborra supporting him on one side and Basil on the other, he began to cross the room.

"I am old," he said, sighing. "Old and stiff. May I say to you, Paul of Tarsus, and to you, my good friend Luke, that to have had this sacred object in my possession has been such an honor that I am conscious of my unworthiness."

He walked slowly to the far wall of the room and stretched out his hand in search of a spring concealed behind an old chest of acacia wood. The pressure of his fingers caused a panel in the wall to roll back. Behind it was a small, unlighted space, a few feet square only.

"A lamp, if you please, my child," said the old man.

Deborra brought one and held it inside the dark cubicle. It could be seen then that the space was occupied by a box of sandalwood standing on a pedestal of marble. Joseph reached an arm within and raised the gold-studded lid of the box. From it he produced a drinking cup, a small and very plain cup.

It was ovoid in shape and made of silver. The design was of the simplest, for the lip had been turned over with the hastiest workmanship and no attempt whatever at ornamentation. It had seen much service, obviously, for it was battered and marked, particularly on the lip.

He held it out for their inspection in hands that trembled with reverence and excitement.

"This," he said in a whisper, "is the Cup from which Jesus drank and then passed to His devoted followers at the Last Supper."

3

Joseph offered the Cup to Luke, and the latter, with tears streaming down his face, took it into his hands. "I have wondered so often," he said, "into whose keeping it had fallen. Or if it had been lost."

He offered it in turn to Paul, but the latter, instead of accepting it, went down on his knees.

"The bitterest blow that life has dealt me," said the great apostle, "is that I did not see Jesus. I have studied His words. I have sought earnestly to learn everything that is known about Him. I heard His voice on the road to Damascus. But I did not see Him." He reached out his hand and with the tips of his fingers touched the rim of the Cup. "It was here," he whispered, "that the lips of Jesus were pressed."

Nothing more was said for several moments. They remained in rapt silence about this most sacred of relics. Luke, Joseph, and Deborra were weeping without restraint. Although he did not allow his emotions to show to an equal extent, Paul's intent gaze never left the sacred Cup, and Basil could see that his hands were trembling.

Standing back of them, Basil watched this demonstration of faith with surprise. "Truly," he thought, "they are strange people. They must have loved this Jesus very much to be so overcome." His eyes turned most often to Paul, for he was already feeling himself drawn to that intense and masterful man. As usual he had brought a supply of clay with him, and his fingers set themselves to work on an impression of the unusual features of the apostle of the Gentiles.

It was Paul who first shook himself free of the spell. He asked Joseph, "What is it you propose to do?"

"A suitable frame must be designed for it," said Joseph. "I think it should be of openwork so the Cup will show through; perhaps a scroll of leaves around the figures of Jesus and those who were closest to him."

Paul nodded in approval. "This Cup will be kept until the day when Jehovah comes in His glory," he said. "The frame must be of the finest workmanship and each figure must be so true to the original that those who live after us will know how Jesus looked, and each of his followers. It may become the chief symbol of the Christian faith." He was speaking in natural tones now and, characteristically, had taken the problem into his own hands. "Yes, first of all, we must be sure that a beautiful receptacle is made. Then we shall have to decide where it is to be kept." He was frowning thoughtfully. "In another generation it may be that all men will believe in Jesus. If this comes about, it would be natural to have the Cup of the Last Supper in the Temple itself."

"No, no!" cried Joseph in an instinctive dissent. "It must always be possible for Gentiles to see it, and they must never be allowed within the Temple."

Paul shook his head at him with a wry expression. "Even thou, O Joseph of Arimathea," he said. "Why do I permit myself to be surprised when men refuse to turn from old beliefs? Even my good and enlightened friend here has not yet shaken off all of the traditions which prevail in this—yes, I must say it—this city where faith still gropes in the dark." He brushed aside the point with another frown and his manner changed, becoming incisive and direct. "Have you considered which of the followers of Christ are to be included in the group?"

"Is it not necessary to include those to whom the Cup was passed at the Last Supper?"

"That is not necessary." Paul's face flamed then with passionate disapproval. "Judas?" he cried. "Would you include the betrayer of Jesus?"

"No, not Judas," said Joseph hastily. "I confess to you, Paul, that I have given this point little thought."

"Since Judas is not to be included," declared Paul, "we find ourselves compelled to consider a plan of selection. Must we include all the others? Must we pretend and evade and refuse to speak our minds about a matter as vital as this? When the record of these days has been written and the new books have been compiled and made into a new testament, what names will be most familiar to the future generations who read it? I will tell you, Joseph of Arimathea—Matthew, Mark, Luke——"

"I?" cried Luke. "No, no! I am one of the least. I am a follower, not a leader. I, truly, am a nonentity. The power has not been given me."

Paul brushed his remonstrances aside. "The noble story you have written of the days of Jesus on this earth will win more followers in years to come than the gift of tongues. What you are preparing now on the preaching of the gospel will be the basis for all history of the Christian church. My modest friend, the name of Luke will resound down the ages; and the face of Luke should be among those chosen for the silver Chalice."

It was clear that Joseph did not agree with this method of selection, but he was allowed no opportunity to express himself. Paul proceeded briskly with the discussion. "Peter, of course. That stout soul must be the first. And John, the beloved disciple. James, the son of Zebedee, and James, the kinsman of Christ. Andrew, I feel, should be included. He brought Peter to the faith and he died most bravely on the cross himself."

"Philip?" hazarded Joseph. Having relinquished control, he now seemed content to make suggestions.

Paul frowned in absorbed thought. "We must have either Philip or Jude. They are equally active in the home church." He reached a reluctant conclusion. "Jude, it must be. He sits here in Jerusalem beside the kinsman of Christ. That I name him must make it clear to you, Joseph, that I strive to be impartial. Philip has a place in my heart, but he is at Caesarea and he is a very old man."

As Paul had detected by this time that Basil's fingers were at work, he reached out and took the clay into his own hands. His approval was conveyed quickly by a nod of the head.

"You have caught something of me. But there are faults. The brow is too high. My enemies—and I have many—say that my lack of true intellectuality shows in the low elevation of my forehead. They may be right. I realize that I am unimpressive to the eye." He turned then in Joseph's direction. "Tomorrow, as I have already told you, I will be received by James and Jude in the presence of the presbyters of Jerusalem. It will be advisable for our young artist to be present so that he may begin work at once."

"I shall have it arranged for him to have a good seat."

"And now," went on Paul briskly, "he will find Matthew and Mark in Antioch. John is at Ephesus, and he above all must be seen. John is so different from the rest that no description would convey any idea of him. The hand of Jehovah has touched him, and he is filled with visions of the strange things which will come to pass. He must be visited at once. Peter, that sweet and violent man, is in Rome. I fear that the hands of the executioner hover above him, for Peter speaks out as though he deliberately courts martyrdom. It will be wise for this young man to go to Rome as soon as possible—if he is to find that lion-like head still carried on mortal shoulders."

"I am willing to go," declared Basil. His heart was thumping with excitement, and to himself he was saying, "How willing I am to go! I would start for Rome within the hour."

Paul's manner changed, completely and abruptly. For several moments he had nothing to say. His fingers toyed with the tephillah attached to his brow and the leather strap which bound it to the back of his head. In a musing voice he quoted a phrase from the texts on the parchment inside the leather case, "'And it shall be for a token upon thine hand . . .'

"It is not only in the case of Peter that there is need for haste," he said finally. "The end draws on for me. At each place where I stopped on my way here I bade my friends farewell, knowing I would see none of them again. Soon now the wings will brush my shoulder. Agabus knew it at once. He came to see me when I was with Philip at Caesarea and he called for my girdle. When I took it off and gave it to him, he bound his own hands and feet with it and said, 'So shall the Jews at Jerusalem bind the man that owneth this girdle, and shall deliver him into the hands of the Gentiles.' He meant I would be delivered to the Romans." Paul sighed wearily, as though the road which would end in this way had been a long and hard one. "It will be here in Jerusalem that the Jews will bind me and hand me to the Romans. There are few days of freedom left me; and so, if I am to appear on the Chalice, I must be done first of all." His eyes had lost their fire and seemed still and cold. "Let your fingers be diligent, then, for this may be your last chance."

4

At the eastern end of the house, on the level of the second floor, there was a stone balcony. For an hour before the evening meal a quiet group, Luke and Deborra and Basil, occupied this pleasant space where the reed screens kept out the insects but did not exclude the breezes. The air was thinning and there was a faint hint of coolness.

The street below was thronged with people, a noisy crowd which had assembled when the word spread throughout the turbulent city that Paul was in the house of Joseph of Arimathea. Despite the hostile demonstrations of the people below, the quiet trio could hear the voice of the apostle addressing the servants of the household in the service court. A few of the staff only were listening to him. Ebenezer, the servant of Aaron, obeying one of the cryptic messages from the snapping fingers of his master, had seen to it that the bulk of them were summoned away for work in the warehouse.

At about the same moment that the *shofarim* sounded clearly but thinly from the Temple there was a diversion below. The angry watchers began to disappear, with much waving of arms and vituperative shouting. In the space of a few minutes the street below became cleared.

Luke, who had put his head out under the reed screens to watch the exodus, turned back and smiled at his companions.

"A ruse of Adam ben Asher's," he explained. "He was to appear at the warehouse entrance with several horsemen and take away one of the staff with a cowl over his head. As you see, it has been successful. The word must have spread rapidly that an effort was being made to get Paul away. They have all gone to the other side."

"Will there be much trouble?" asked Deborra anxiously.

Luke did not think so. A few minutes only were needed for Paul to make his escape, and then Adam would let it be seen that he did not have the apostle in his train. In any case, Adam would know what to do if there was a violent demonstration.

The sound of Paul's passionate exhortation in the service court ceased and in a few moments two figures emerged suddenly from the main door of the house and flitted across the street.

"There he goes, and he has Benjie with him," said Deborra, who had hurried to the parapet with Basil. Their elbows touched as they leaned on the stone ledge to watch the two fugitive figures, but neither drew away. "Paul is safe now," continued the girl, "because Benjie knows every twist and corner in the city."

The pair below vanished from sight quickly, Benjie the Asker leading the way down into the Valley of the Cheesemakers. Deborra looked up into Basil's face in the dimming light and smiled her delight at the success of the ruse. "Adam has managed it well," she said.

Basil made no comment as they returned to their seats. It was in his mind that he would like to slip away from Jerusalem as easily and quickly as this. Nothing would please him more than to be off that night on the road to Rome. He wondered what the Imperial City would be like and where he would find the man whose aid was so vital to his future prospects.

"Basil!" He brought his vagrant thoughts back to more immediate concerns and realized that Joseph's granddaughter was watching him with a hint of entreaty in her eyes.

"Basil, I am happy they were all so satisfied with what you have done," she said. "And you know I am proud that you have been chosen to make the Chalice. No one in the world could do it as well as you." She was watching him with an air of unusual gravity, a pucker of worry on her white brow. "But—but there is something I must say. I have to tell you that I am disturbed."

"I am well aware of the difficulties," answered Basil.

"I am wondering what you will do when it comes to making the face of Christ. It will be the hardest test. Basil, have you any conception of how He looked?"

The young artist shook his head. "I will have to depend on what I am told. Can you help me?"

"My grandfather has told me about Him a hundred times," said Deborra eagerly. "Oh, if I could only help you to see Him as I do. He was not at all like other men. He was dark, very dark, but He did not wear His hair long as most people think. It did not touch his shoulders when He rode into Jerusalem for the last time. His brow was very wide and so His eyes were widely spaced. His nose was straight and not long. His mouth was sensitive and kind, but there was no trace of weakness in it. No, no, it was strong and firm! He had no beard, although most people think that he had."

Luke had been listening with the closest attention, his eyes turning from one to the other. Now he spoke. "That is how I have heard Him described."

"His eyes were wonderful!" cried Deborra. "I have always been able to see them in my mind. So gentle and compassionate, so very, very wise!"

"I am beginning to have a clear picture," said Basil, nodding his head to them. "I think I can see the brow, the nose, the mouth. But not the eyes. They elude me."

"Basil!" cried Deborra with so much earnestness that she reached out and touched both of his hands. "You will never see His eyes. Never, unless you can clear your mind of everything save the desire to see them. You must love Him as we do. When you have that love, He will come out of the darkness and you will see Him as though He stood before you."

There was a long moment of silence, and then Luke began to speak. "Although I have said nothing about it, my son, I have not been blind to the state of your mind. It is natural for you to hold resentment over the way you were cheated. I cannot say you have been wrong in letting yourself dwell on your misfortunes, even though it has been warping your mind and excluding healthier thoughts."

"Would you have me do nothing?" demanded Basil. He was keeping his eyes averted. "Until I have repaid Linus in coin of his own minting, I can have no peace of mind."

"There are things which count more in life," declared Luke, "than position and wealth and ease. Things that are even more pressing than revenge. I have never talked to you of these other things because I felt you had no desire to hear. Perhaps you will not resent it if I say this now. When the heart is given to Jesus, nothing else matters. The true Christian is only too happy to give up everything and follow Him, and in that surrender finds peace and compensation. If you could bring yourself to believe with us, your troubles would roll from your shoulders. You would be free and happy as never before. You might still strive to right the wrong that Linus did you, but it would cease to press so on your mind."

"I know nothing of Jesus," said Basil, "or what He preached."

"My son," said Luke, "I have said to you before that the part I am called upon to play is a small one. I have been content that it should be so. But tonight I wish I had the power to perform one of the miracles you have heard about. I wish I had the power to set things right for you with a wave of the hand. How happy I would be if I could bring you solace and drive away forever the black thoughts which are causing that crease on your brow. It makes me unhappy to see you so troubled in your mind.

And now, as Deborra has told you, there is the making of the Chalice to be considered."

Basil shifted his position uneasily, his eyes still fixed on the gray stone of the floor. A disturbing question had taken possession of his mind. Could it be that this small group was right and all the rest of the world wrong? "What am I to do?" he asked after a long pause. "What is the first step?"

"This child has told you the first step, my son," declared Luke. "Clear your mind of all other thoughts. Believe this in the mouth of an old man who has seen much of life: wealth is a burden which fosters pride at the expense of better things. Revenge may seem a sweet and heady drink. But, once quaffed, it is as harmful as a cup of hemlock."

"All I can promise," said Basil earnestly, "is that I will try. That I will try very hard—so that I may be able to see His eyes."

"Oh, Basil, Basil!" cried Deborra happily. "That is all we ask."

CHAPTER VII

I

Basil tossed on his hot couch that night. One train of thought ran continuously through his mind. Had these earnest people the secret of peace and happiness on earth? Would his success in making the silver Chalice depend on the state of mind with which he approached the task? Must he believe in Jesus of Nazareth before he could hope to achieve a mental picture of Him and mold it into perpetual form?

It took some time to reach a conclusion, but it came to him finally as he stared out at the sky where the stars seemed to hang low enough for a hand to reach. The Chalice was the most important thing in his life. It must be made for the ages, and the faces of Jesus and His disciples must look out from the silver frame for all the world to see and know. Nothing else must be allowed to concern him. His personal affairs must be forgotten. He must strive hard to reach the state of mind where he might see the eyes of Jesus. He had become sure that happiness would come to him at the same time.

He felt an immediate sense of peace. A breeze blew across the room and cooled his hot brow. He saw the benevolent face of Luke smiling at him in approval and a sense of something even deeper in the wide-spaced eyes of Deborra. He fell into sleep.

He roused himself early. A sultry morning: a heavy, moist blanket seemed to stretch across the sky, obscuring the outline of the Temple. There was such a deadness in the air that the slightest movement was an effort.

By seven o'clock Benjie the Asker was at his door, full of energy and bubbling with news.

"The Zealots were all over the city last night," he announced with zest.

"They were looking for Paul. If they had found him, he would have had as many daggers in him as a porcupine has quills. It was felt to be unsafe for him to venture on the streets in daylight, so he went to the hall, where the presbyters will meet, before dawn. Yes, there he is now, pacing up and down with a challenge in his eyes. 'Bring mine enemies to me,' he is saying to himself, 'and I will demolish them.'" The Asker beamed delightedly at Basil. "I am a lucky man today. I have been told to take you to the meeting and so I shall be there when the air is filled with the hailstones of invective. We must start as soon as you break your fast."

Basil began to bathe himself gratefully before the silver laver. "I have no desire for food on a day like this," he said, sloshing the water over his shoulders. "I have only one thought in my mind. To start work."

"That is wrong," declared Benjie emphatically. "The hotter the day, the bigger the meal. *That* is my rule. This morning I had a melon, a platter of grapes, the chop of a tender kid, and even a wedge of cheese. I feel as full of fight as David issuing forth to do battle with Goliath, whose spear was like a weaver's beam. Eat well, young artist, and your fingers will find a fresh magic in them."

In the hall they met Ebenezer, the servant of Aaron. He was walking with less stoop in his back and even a hint of animation on his usually expressionless face. Basil was surprised when this most silent of men stopped them and began to speak.

"What word does Benjie have for us?" he asked, his voice husky from lack of use. "Paul will not give in to them?"

"Have no fear, friend Ebenezer," answered Benjie. "Paul has come to Jerusalem for no other purpose than to fight. He will not give in."

The bent head nodded gravely. "It will be his last battle, O Asker. It is so written."

When they reached the street, where the sun, having broken through the clouds, greeted them with a blasting fury of heat, Basil asked his companion, "Can it be that the servant of Aaron is a Christian?"

Benjie nodded his head. "Ebenezer is one of the most devout of us all. He is a Gentile from the far North, and so he is a firm believer in everything that Paul preaches." He gave Basil a cautioning glance. "Aaron does not know that Ebenezer belongs to us."

Basil's mind was still filled with what Deborra and Luke had said to him. That this strange servingman, spending his days in obeying the instructions of his master's fingers, was a Christian also, interested him deeply.

"And the other slaves?" he asked.

"All of them. Even Uzziel, the overseer."

It proved to be a long walk. They did not go to the little room in the wall of David where the leaders of the church met, but turned their steps instead in the direction of the upper city. Basil found himself exhausted from the heat by the time Benjie stopped before the door of a warehouse in the Street of the Weavers. They were admitted to a dark cavern-like space which seemed cool after the furious onslaught of the sun. As their eyes were blinded by the sudden change, they remained by the door until a voice said, "This way, if you please, my masters." They followed the white tunic of the speaker, and Basil's eyes recovered their function sufficiently to see that the place was piled to the ceiling with bales of cloth. Passing through a door at the rear, they found themselves in an interior hall that was still darker. Their guide stopped abruptly and gave a rap with his knuckles on what seemed to be a blank wall. A panel slid back, and they became aware of light beyond and a murmur of voices.

"Who is it?" asked a custodian within.

"We come from Joseph of Arimathea," said Benjie.

The custodian said, "Enter," and swung back a narrow door. As they stepped into the room, which was lighted through the ceiling, Benjie whispered to his companion, "It is Paul speaking, and I can tell from his voice that he is wrapped in the toga of battle."

Basil was led to a seat behind a screen. He had opened out on his knees the cloth containing clay and had spread his tools in convenient array before his eyes became sufficiently adjusted to take in any of his surroundings. He sat back then and looked about him.

He saw that the hall, which was not large, was fitted up in a state of solemn and rather dingy splendor, as though at some earlier stage an effort had been made to match in a small degree the austere grandeur of the Temple. The walls were covered with hangings that had once been handsome, and there was an imposing dais at one end where, behind a pulpit of yellowing ivory, sat a small group of men in a matching solemnity.

A larger group, less stern of mien and containing a few women, sat on benches in front of the dais. Paul was standing in the midst of this second group and was filling the hall with the ardor of his words.

Benjie had stationed himself behind Basil. He gave the shoulder of the artist a twitch and whispered: "Look well at those two men on each side of the pulpit. James, on the right, is a kinsman of Jesus. The one on the other side is Jude."

Basil studied both men, noting particularly the face of Jude; the high forehead, the finely molded nose, the beard in which he took an obvious pride, for it was curled and oiled and quite handsome. Basil's fingers went busily to work.

After a time he said: "A face such as that of Jude presents small difficulty. Have you noticed how his nose curls? There is a hint of arrogance in his eye. Such physical traits are easy to get."

"You have him already," whispered Benjie. "It has taken no more than fifteen minutes. Truly this is astonishing."

Basil laid aside the head of Jude and took up another lump of clay. "That high pucker across the brow of James will make him an easy subject."

The features of the kinsman of Jesus came to life as the sensitive fingers flew at their task. Benjie watched closely, shaking his head at intervals to express his amazement. He even gave vent to a low whistle when the skilled hands created the nose of the apostle with no more than a moment of pressure on the clay. A second motion gave it a blunted end, and this seemed to be the finishing touch. A perfect likeness had been achieved.

They were both so absorbed that they had been paying small attention to Paul. In this respect they were alone, for everyone else in the long dark chamber had fallen under his spell. Paul had gathered the meeting into his thin, ivory-colored hands. Every eye was fixed on his face. Except for the rise and fall of his voice, there was no sound. James and Jude had become no more than spectators.

The great apostle was telling of his stewardship. With graphic words he described his journeys through the Gentile world, the pagan cities of the Greeks, the materialistic dominions of Rome, the hostile desert lands. It was a story of conquest he was telling, a conquest that would prove more complete than what Rome had accomplished with the might of her legions, one that would last forever. He was demonstrating to this most critical of audiences that he had been right, that the teachings of Jesus belonged to the whole human race and not exclusively to the one nation into which He had been born.

Paul had ceased speaking, and for several moments there was silence in the long dark chamber. His words had carried conviction and there could no longer be doubt that the presbyters would approve what he had done. Jude had listened impassively, without even the flicker of an eyelash, but James had responded, in some degree at least, to the eloquent pleading of the man from Tarsus. It was James who broke the silence.

"Brother Saul," he said, "it is clear to all of us that you have labored long and hard and that much has been accomplished. Those of us who have not seen eye to eye with you in the past still believe that it should be possible to extend the boundaries of the Lord's influence without deviating one inch from the just laws by which we live. We would prefer to go to the Gentiles with two great gifts in our hands, the teachings of Jesus and the Law of Moses.

"But you, who have been carrying the Word to the Gentiles, say it can only be done your way. It is clear you are sincerely convinced. Reluctantly I am disposed to say: Have it, then, your way, go on teaching in the future as you have done in the past."

The speaker stopped and glanced down at Jude but received no manner of response. His quick eye then skimmed the circle of presbyters, drawing a response in a general nodding of heads and a deep-toned chorus of "Yea!"

"Paul has won!" whispered Benjie, fairly bouncing on his seat in excitement. "He has talked them over. *Okhe!* What a victory it has been!"

The victory was not to be a complete one. James, it became clear, had more to say. He looked again with some evidence of uneasiness at the impassive form of Jude and then allowed his eyes to rest for a moment on the dark corner where troublesome counsel sat in the figure of the Mar.

"This must be said." The slender James had straightened up in his chair and his voice became high and a little shrill. "We have heard ill reports of your personal conduct, Brother Saul. It has been told us again and again that you have ceased to live by the Law of Moses. This is a charge which sits heavily on our minds."

"I declare it false!" cried Paul. "I declare to you, the elders of the church, that there is no truth in what my ill-wishers charge against me. I have not broken the Law."

"But you have condoned laxity in others," declared James. "This has been said of you on the testimony of many witnesses. Here in Jerusalem men are coming to fear you."

"James, James!" exclaimed the apostle to the Gentiles. "You sit here in a circle as small as the cupping of a child's hand. Can it be that you are more concerned with the trappings of truth than with truth itself?"

"We find joy in living as our fathers have lived before us," said James.

"But your fathers knew nothing of the teachings of Jesus." The voice of the apostle rose again to an oratorical pitch. "Can you not see that everything has been changed by the coming of the Master? The whole world must be taught, even as Jesus commanded. Can we obey that command if we still believe we must allow no deviation in the depth to which we dip our hands in water after eating meat? The salt of Sodom may cling to the date you eat on the desert—but if around you gather those who hunger for the Word, you must not delay in the telling of it until you have plunged your wrists in a tepid cleansing."

James rose up behind the ivory pulpit. It could be seen that he was thin and wasted from much fasting and that a palsy afflicted the hand he pointed accusingly at the apostle to the Gentiles. "Out of your own mouth you have sustained the charge!" he cried. "I say to you, Paul, that you must acknowledge the error of your ways and cleanse yourself publicly."

A deep chorus of "Yea!" rose from the circle of presbyters. One of them spoke up to say: "You have brought strangers with you who claim they should be allowed to enter the Temple beyond the Court of the Gentiles. There is profanation even in the wish!"

"I have been a Nazarite all my life," declared James. This was apparent in the curl of his long white hair and the softness of a beard that had never known the touch of the shears. "You, Paul, who sat at the feet of Gamaliel, know that the Code of the Nazarites calls for purification of body and heart. This, then, is what we demand of you, that you stand in the Dock of Atonement, where all men may see you, for the full number of days set by the Code. That in the end you submit your head to the shears and that your hair be publicly burned so that you may start afresh thereafter, clean of body and of mind."

Benjie could not keep his feelings under control. "No, no!" he cried aloud. It was so unexpected that his voice seemed to fill the hot chamber.

James was startled and glanced apprehensively toward the source of the interruption. "There must be order," he said with an air of affronted dignity.

Basil suspended work and waited for the effect of the interruption to pass.

"I have never so forgotten myself before," whispered Benjie, his face reflecting the shock he felt at his own presumption. "But this would be a fatal mistake. Paul to stand in the Dock of Atonement! The butt of every passer-by—spat upon, reviled, laughed at! What a mark his naked back would offer the daggers of the Zealots! There will be war on the streets of Jerusalem, and that is what Rub Samuel, the leader of the Zealots, wants."

There was a quick flurry of discussion among the princes of the church. At the end there was a general nodding of heads in assent.

Paul sat with bowed head. He neither glanced up nor sought counsel with his followers as speaker after speaker urged the ceremony of atonement. There was humiliation in the arch of his back, bitterness in the line of his jaw.

"So be it," he said when the last of the presbyters had spoken. "I have lived by the Law of Moses and I am not conscious of wrongdoing. But if this is necessary to keep peace in my Master's House, I shall do as you bid. I shall stand in nakedness and shame for sins of which I have not been guilty!"

2

On the fourth day of Paul's atonement, Basil arrived early at the Shushan, the Lily Gate of the Temple, having a little work still to do on the bust he was making of the apostle. He was desirous of finishing it before people came to stare at him and make audible and unfriendly comments as they breathed on the back of his neck. The twenty singers, whose duty it was to swing back the huge bronze doors of the gate (it could not be done with fewer hands), were still at work, and he could hear the agonized *"Aiy-waay!"* of the head porter as he urged them to greater efforts. He joined in the loud approval of the spectators when the task was completed and the doors, screeching and protesting in a metallic agony of unwillingness, fell back finally to each side, allowing a glimpse of the activities of the great outer court.

The naked torso and the sternly unemotional face of Paul could be seen at once above the railed-off space near the Court of the Women where Nazarites underwent the ceremony of purification. It had been four days of agony for the apostle. Filled with a sense of humiliation, he had kept his eyes closed and had tried to keep his ears shut as tightly to the exultant remarks of his ill-wishers. Hatred had ringed him about from the first moment, and it may have been that on this fourth day he failed to detect the more sinister note which filled the air. He was thinking of one thing only, that he must remain where he was for three days more, after which his hair would be cut and burned by the priests. On the eighth day he would repair to the Sanctuary of the Temple, taking with him two turtle doves and a lamb as a guilt offering.

For two days Basil had been striving to catch the spirit of Paul in the malleable clay. The previous evening, when darkness made it necessary to suspend work, he felt that he had achieved a real measure of success. The eyes had seemed to glow with life, the jutting bridge of the nose had become demanding, the mouth was cast in lines of wry eloquence. What remained was to catch the undertones, to give the commanding nose a hint of tolerance and the bitter mouth a shadow of tenderness.

That morning, as Basil left with his materials in a blue cloth bag over his shoulder, Deborra had met him to ask how the work progressed.

"Today I shall give it the final touches."

"May I come a little later and watch you finish it?"

He smiled at this. It was becoming an easier matter to smile, and he found himself indulging his feelings that way quite often. "Your presence will stimulate my hands to better efforts," he said. "You will find me close to the lattice which closes off the terrace of the Hel."

He looked about him now but saw no trace of her. Perhaps the extreme heat had influenced her to stay at home. He was so disappointed that he did not get along as well with his work as he had hoped.

He became sufficiently immersed in what he was doing, however, to be impervious to what happened around him. He failed to notice how rapidly the court had filled with men who stood about in silent groups, their eyes fixed on the occupant of the Dock of Atonement. They were not the visitors who had come to Jerusalem for Pentecost and who had departed already, on camelback, on horseback, on foot, revived in their faith but secretly glad to escape from the poverty, the dark moods, and the hint of violence under the surface of life in the Holy City. It was not until someone shouted an order in a high, keening voice that the young artist became aware of anything but his work. He looked up in time to see men from all parts of the court converging with exultant shouts on the Dock where Paul was standing with closed eyes.

At the same instant dagger blades gleamed in the morning sunlight. There was a sound of splintering wood. Paul, too proud to resist, with blood streaming down his face and over his bare shoulders, was dragged into the Court of the Gentiles, where Zealot dirks could finish the work they had begun.

Perhaps more observant eyes had sensed what was afoot and had seen to it that precautions were taken; perhaps it was no more than a coincidence. Whatever the reason, a company of Roman soldiers appeared on the scene at this moment. Attracted by the clamor, they marched into the court, scattering the stunned spectators with the arrogance an occupying force always feels for conquered people. They acted with such expedition that the weapons of the Zealots had no chance to complete the purpose to which they had been dedicated. The assassins were driven off with one organized rush. Paul, bewildered and bleeding, found his wrists and ankles manacled with Roman chains in a matter of seconds. He was led away at once as the heavy, cleaver-like swords drove a path through the mob.

At this point Basil saw Deborra. She was in the front of the mob that surged turbulently in the wake of the marching squad. It was easy to distinguish her, for she was wearing a red handkerchief over her head. Even at the distance it was possible to see that this was not the gentle and obedient Deborra who lived so quietly in her grandfather's house. Her usually tranquil eyes were blazing passionately.

He heard her cry, "Are we going to do nothing?"

Basil dropped the chisel into his kit of tools. This was going to be serious. Plunging vigorously into the crowd, he strove to overtake her before she could be guilty of further indiscretions.

The red handkerchief kept well ahead of him. He saw it weaving in and out, getting closer all the time to the forefront of the milling people. It was clear that Deborra was very much excited. He saw her raise an arm in the air.

"Will we let them take him away?" she demanded in a high and angry voice.

And then she did something that put a fevered determination into his efforts to reach her. She picked up a stone and threw it at the armed squad surrounding the figure of the chained apostle. Although it glanced harmlessly off the breastplate of one of the soldiers, the missile had accomplished its purpose. The voice of the people mounted from a mere hum of excitement to the full-mouthed roar of an angry mob. More stones began to fly. The Romans had to face about and fight off the peering men of Jerusalem with unsparing jabs of their heavy swords.

Basil was aware that others were forcing their way through the crowd. An authoritative voice said behind him: "Get that girl! She started this." He moved then in desperation, saying to himself, "The Romans will not spare her if she is caught!"

He reached her first. Tearing the red handkerchief from her head, he dropped it underfoot.

"Quick!" he said. "Come with me!"

Deborra recognized his voice. "Basil? I cannot leave now."

He seized one of her arms and dragged her aside. "You must come!" he insisted desperately.

"Do you think me a coward to run away?"

"You are behaving like a fool!" He gave her an angry shake. Then he drew her close and said in her ear: "Do you want to give the Romans an excuse to confiscate everything your grandfather possesses? Do you want him to live his last days in trouble and sorrow? As for you, if they get their hands on you now, the least you can expect is to be sold into slavery."

She gave in then and followed him when he made a way through the crowd at one side. The high pillars of Solomon's Porch loomed ahead of them. He noticed that the dog she had adopted a few days before was following at her heels.

They passed through the monoliths of white marble. They were now in a section of Mount Moriah that was new to him. He glanced about him in a state of desperate urgency.

"Where can we go?" he asked.

"Come," said Deborra. "I know a way."

They began to run, the dog prancing excitedly after them. They were closed in now by the homes of the pedagogues, which clustered thick about the Temple. As there was a limited amount of space on the Mount and an ever-increasing population, the houses had been drawn closer together and mounted high into the sky. It was said in other parts of the city that Moriah averaged one philosopher to each room and that the only commodity of which there was never any scarcity was erudition. This was quite true. The clay bins in the houses might lack cheese and honey and bread, and the limestone cisterns in the cellars might be dry, but the tongues of the household heads never failed to supply pearls of wisdom.

It was inevitable in a section such as this that the streets had not been cut straight through but had been allowed to follow the formation of the high ground, with the result that they were as crooked as the horns which the priests used in the Temple. This was fortunate, for it promised to make their escape easier.

"We must get down into the valley," said Deborra, breathing hard. "I know my way through it."

They were in a winding street that seemed as capable as a hoop snake of biting its own tail. Coming to a place where a low stone wall marked the edge of the cheesemakers' domain, Deborra slowed her steps. The clamor of pursuit could be heard behind them, but none of the pursuers was yet in sight. There was a narrow gate in the wall, and behind this a woman was standing.

"Christ is risen," whispered Deborra to the woman.

The latter seemed startled but answered quickly, "He sits on the right hand of God."

"There has been trouble and we must get down into the valley."

Without pausing to ask questions, the woman beckoned them to enter and closed the gate after them.

Deborra reached down and took the dog into her arms. "No barking now!" she commanded. "You must not give your mistress away."

They found themselves on the flat roof of a small stone house, the top-most of a succession that climbed in humility up the steep slope. A trap door admitted them to its single room below. The woman reached under a pile of clothing and drew out a knotted rope.

"Quick!" she said, dropping one end out of the window. "God go with you."

A man with a wasted face roused himself from a straw pallet on the roof of the house below. "Christ has risen," whispered Deborra. He gave the customary answer and motioned to a rope dangling over the parapet. They climbed down in desperate haste, for they could now hear voices at the gate in the stone wall above. Basil had taken the dog under one arm, which made his climbing slow and laborious.

The same course was followed at each house in their downward climb. Deborra would say, "We are being followed and must get into the valley." Help was given willingly and cheerfully in every case. No one hesitated; there was no tendency to count the cost, to consider what punishment might be their lot if they gave help. They ran instead to open trap doors for the fugitives and then to bar them against the oncoming officers, to get out the knotted ropes; always with earnest good will and a parting, "God go with you."

When they reached the last of the houses and came out on the level into a poor little garden where lizards basked on the wall and a fig tree endeavored in disconsolate solitude to provide shelter for the door, Basil asked, "Are all the cheesemakers Christians?"

"Nearly all."

"Is that the reason they are so poor?"

"Perhaps." She spoke with sudden gravity. "Such things do not matter. A Christian thinks of the life after death, and so poverty in this life is borne without complaining. They are all happy, even those who are so poor they have their homes on the slopes."

"Do they know they may be punished for this?"

They ran as they talked. "Christians live always on the threshold of punishment. None of them fear it. There is danger at all times. Right now, because the Zealots hate us so much, it is worse than ever. They attack us in the streets and sometimes they go about the city looking for victims. One night not long ago they went to many Christian homes and destroyed everything in them. Then they took the men and bound their arms and put crowns of thorns on their heads, and led them about the city, scourging them as they went. Two of the men died."

They could now hear their pursuers climbing down laboriously from above. Deborra plunged into a dark alley, running at top speed. The dog, as though sensing trouble, followed her silently. She was so fleet of foot that Basil found it hard to keep up with her.

"Now you are involved in this as deep as I am," she said over her shoulder. "I am sorry, Basil. I acted without thinking. And there will be trouble for many people." A moment later she turned her head again to ask, "Did you do this to protect Grandfather?"

"I did it for you," he protested.

The pursuit had reached the floor of the valley and was spreading out in all directions. They sought escape in a maze of dark streets, in which Deborra seemed completely at home, and the sounds grew fainter. Basil, feeling like a heavy-footed mortal in the company of a wood nymph, had scarcely enough breath to ask, "Didn't you realize that Paul was safest in the hands of the Romans?"

She made it clear that she did not understand. "They had taken him prisoner," she said. "They were leading him away."

"They were protecting him from the daggers of the Zealots."

They were traversing a street so narrow that housewives could exchange articles across it from the rooftops. Deborra spoke without looking back. "Then I was helping the Zealots when I threw that stone."

"Yes, I am afraid you were."

She stopped and faced him. "You called me a fool, and I see now that you were right. This has been a great folly."

Basil reached out and touched her hand. "A folly, Deborra, but a brave one. Now that you are safe, I find myself admiring you for what you did."

Their safety seemed less assured a moment later, for the dog raised his head and barked loudly in his anxiety to see them start again.

"Habby, Habby!" said Deborra. "You will lead them to us!" She reached down and took him up in her arms, holding a hand over his muzzle.

Finally they came to a low stone arch behind which there seemed no light at all. She reached back her free hand to take his, saying, "We must not get separated here." A man, naked to the waist and with eyes that seemed distended in the gloom, emerged from the depths, shaking a grimy fist at them and crying, *"Tooh! Tooh!"* Disregarding his demand that they betake themselves elsewhere, they plunged deeper into the shadows.

They floundered through families of pigs and goats, they felt their way carefully by wooden troughs filled with warm milk, they breathed an atmosphere acrid with rennet, they encountered more strange figures with shrill voices repeating *"Tooh!"* Finally they came out at another stone arch and ahead of them saw bright sunshine and the walls of the market place. They had reached the upper end of the valley.

All sounds of pursuit had died away. "We are quite safe now," said Deborra. She became aware that they were still holding hands and withdrew hers hastily. She dropped the dog at her feet.

They climbed the slope on the other side and progressed along the crest, passing the great Yard of the Doves, where Benaiah, son of Bimbal, sold the gentle birds by the hundreds each week for sacrifice in the Temple. Finally they came to the entrance of the house of Joseph and here, without a word being spoken, they paused. The noon sun was causing a shimmer so that even the outlines of the buildings seemed to move. The row of palm trees under which they stood were wilting, giving them only the poorest kind of shelter. The wood of their sandals was hot under the soles of their feet. Even the white splendor of the Temple looked sultry against the burnished glow of the sky.

Their glances met and held. At first it was with a consciousness of pleasure in a shared adventure that had come to a safe ending. Then their awareness of each other's thoughts took on a deeper meaning. It became clear to each of them that the baked soil on which they stood might prove to be the threshold of the land of enchantment. Each looked into the depths of the other's eyes so long that they lost all track of time. Finally, with an undeclared assent, they smiled.

Deborra sighed. "It was very exciting," she said.

"I shall always remember everything about it," declared Basil. "Everything we did and said."

Her mood became more serious. "But it has been a *very* great folly. Many people will suffer because of it. You, perhaps, and Grandfather. The people who followed my example and threw stones at the soldiers. The good Christians who helped us escape into the valley. Some of them may be punished. Why did I throw that stone!"

"You did it on an impulse."

Her mood underwent another change. Her eyes began to flame with the same passion he had seen in them when she urged the crowd to attempt the rescue of Paul. Gone was the quiet lady of the house with a jingling ring of keys on her wrist, the patient companion of the aged merchant. Here was the Deborra for whom she had been named, the Deborra who roused the people of Israel against Sisera and the hosts of Canaan many centuries before in the days of Shamgar. "I would do it again! Did you see them come marching in, those lords of creation? They were saying to themselves, 'We are Romans. Out of our way, Jewish scum!' Did you see the arrogance of their eyes? And the brutal way they cut through the crowds with their swords? I could not stand it. Yes, I would do the same thing!"

"I think all Jews must be Zealots at heart," said Basil.

"We are proud," she said. "And we have always been so few. We have been surrounded by powerful neighbors who have made war on us. Because we have been so proud, they have tried to break us, to make us forget our ways and to worship their gods. They have led us away into captivity, and burned our temples, and tumbled down the walls of our cities. But we have never changed; and because of this, we *are* Zealots at heart, all of us."

They turned back to the house then, but before they reached the door Basil came to an abrupt stop. He struck an angry hand to his forehead.

"I left everything behind!" he cried. "My tools. My materials. And— and the head of Paul! Now what am I to do?"

She became all contrition at once. "I am so sorry. It was my fault. My carelessness has done this to you." Her eyes seemed on the point of filling with tears. "Was the head finished?"

He nodded. "Yes. And I was pretty well satisfied with it. I must go back at once and find it."

Deborra gave her head a hasty shake. "That would not be safe. They may be on the watch for you to come back. No, Basil, we must wait and do nothing. I think it would be dangerous even to send anyone else to look."

CHAPTER VIII

B ASIL SET TO WORK as soon as he reached his room and had
made enough headway to arouse some confidence that a suitable copy of
Paul's head could be made when Benjie the Asker appeared in the doorway.

"A suspicious occupation," said the visitor, entering the room and closing the door after him. "Would it surprise you to know that a head in
clay, quite similar to what you are making there, has fallen into the hands
of Ananias, the High Priest? They are searching high and low for the
artist who ran away and left it."

Basil hastily draped a cloth over his work. "Have they been here?" he
asked.

Benjie shook his head. "The trail has not led this far. It is very fortunate
that the little lady of the house, who does not seem to have been behaving
herself today with her usual good sense, was not recognized. Of course,
if they succeed in tracing the artist, they may also lay their hands on the
more important figure in the case. How the worthy Ananias would enjoy
the chance to attack our master through his granddaughter!"

Basil had been cleansing his hands hurriedly at the laver. "What do you
want me to do? I presume I must leave."

The little man shook his head. "You will be safer here than anywhere
else. But you will have to go into hiding. I warn you that you must not
expect comfort."

"What about the—the other figure in the case?"

"The lady of the house," answered Benjie, "is already on her way to a
relative who lives some distance north of Jerusalem. She left—and most
unhappy she seemed at the need—with a guard of servants and Adam

ben Asher himself in charge." He went to the door and gave a quick glance up and down the corridor. "It will be safe to come now. Your belongings will be brought to you later. But bring the model with you. We want no other eyes to see *that.*"

The room in which Basil found himself ensconced within a few minutes was in the warehouse. It was reserved, clearly enough, for such use, as it could be reached only through a low opening behind a pile of meal sacks. It had no window and depended for light on a tongue of flame which Benjie set to burning in a pewter bowl filled with oil. The air was heavy but had a clean smell of grain about it.

Benjie looked around him and winked at Basil. "Everyone in the household will know you are here," he said. "All except Aaron. There is a continuous conspiracy to keep things from Aaron. He does not even know this hidden room exists."

"Can they be depended on to keep the secret now?" asked Basil anxiously.

The Asker interlocked his fingers and gripped his hands together tightly. "It will be kept as tight as that," he said. "Have no fear. You have many friends among the slaves. Ebenezer says you are like a young David with a chisel in your hands instead of a harp. But *that* is going too far." His errand was completed, but he delayed his departure to give some information about what had been happening. "Paul has been put under lock and key by the Romans. I am told that the High Priest and Rub Samuel are furious that he escaped the violent end they had planned for him. They are just as angry over the escape of a certain young lady and an artist who helped her get away."

"What will the Romans do with Paul?"

"The High Priest will demand that he be released for trial before the Sanhedrin. He will be murdered in cold blood if they can cajole or browbeat Lysias into turning him over to them. But the story is going around that, when they were going to scourge Paul, he told Lysias he was a Roman citizen. The captain will not dare now to hand him over."

It was impossible to keep track of the passing of the hours in the darkness of his sanctuary behind the meal sacks, but Basil had one means of guessing, the sounds that reached him faintly of warehouse activities. By this method of reckoning, the afternoon of the next day was well spent when the Asker paid him another call. The latter seemed in a satisfied frame of mind.

"Things have quieted down," he said. "Ananias—the High Priest—continues to demand the custody of Paul, but I have learned that Lysias will not give way. As Paul is a Roman citizen, he must be judged in a Roman court. It is certain that Lysias will keep his own toga clear by sending his prisoner to Caesarea and let Ananias scream himself into an apoplectic fit if he so desires. I may tell you also that the lady of the house reached her destination safely."

Basil sighed with relief. "Then we are over the worst."

"I hear," said Benjie, eying him closely, "that Ananias is taking a *very* great interest in the head of Paul. I am not sure we are over the worst." He paused at the door to say, "Simon the Magician will make an appearance in the city within a few days. Ananias has given his consent and has even agreed to let him use Herod's Gymnasium. These are indeed strange times, young artist."

2

After two days spent in the gloom of his sanctuary the spirits of the prisoner in that dark corner of the warehouse reached a low ebb. The air became heavy and the flicker of light in the pewter lamp made his eyes ache. He could not work and he could not sleep; nor after the second day could he any longer control his thoughts. He paced about in the darkness, his arms locked behind his back. Four steps would take him from one wall to the opposite one, and he began to understand the wild longings and the despair of a caged animal. His head throbbed continuously.

A plan for the silver framework had already taken shape in his mind. He would design an open scroll of grapevines into which the figures would be introduced, as well as small objects symbolic of the times and of the individual lives of the chosen twelve. The base would be a lotus blossom with two rows of petals. He could see this clearly in his mind and at intervals his fingers felt the urge to get started. To his dismay, however, he found himself unable to concentrate for any length of time. Other thoughts would come unbidden to fill his mind.

On the third night he had a dream. At the time he was not sure it was a dream because it seemed too real; the conviction of its unreality came to him later. He was lying on his couch and the light in the lamp had guttered down so low that most of the room was in shadow. He became aware with a start of surprise and fear that Ignatius was in the room and staring at him with hollow and sorrowful eyes.

"Father!" he cried, sitting up in his nakedness on the edge of the bed. He wanted to tell this visitor from beyond the grave that he had been despoiled, that the thieving Linus had robbed him of his inheritance. Something in the steady gaze with which his father was regarding him was proof, however, that this was not necessary.

"My son," said the spirit of the man who had been the great merchant prince of Antioch, "I have come to beg a favor of you."

Basil felt a cold chill pass over him. His midnight visitor seemed hazy of outline and lacking in substance. There was a weariness about him that carried no hint of everlasting content.

Ignatius continued speaking slowly and solemnly. "You must win back the fortune that you carelessly allowed my brother to steal from you, the fortune I made by a lifetime of toil and which he is now using to such corrupt purposes. It must come back to you so that it can be used as I intended." The visitor gave vent to a lugubrious sigh. "I am very unhappy, my son. I have not found favor because of the kind of life I lived. I am judged to have been grasping and unfair in my dealings with other men. It is held against me that I was a hard taskmaster to my slaves. There is one point in my favor, and one only, the purpose to which I desired my wealth put. Because of this I have not yet been wholly condemned. I am allowed to remain in the House of Suspended Judgment. The sheet they keep on Ignatius, oil merchant of Antioch, can be balanced in his favor only if you do as I bid you; if you get back what I left and spend it as I desired."

The eyes of the pale visitor were fixed on Basil with so much love mingled with supplication that the latter felt an eagerness to do what he could about the adverse balance sheet. "Father," he said, "I am going to see Kester of Zanthus as soon as I reach Rome."

The spirit nodded. "I know about your plans. I may tell you, my son, that Kester is an honest man. I can see into his mind and I know he remembers everything that happened on the day of your adoption. But he is an old man. I have been admitted to the house far beyond the skies above us where the sands run in the hourglasses, and there is little left in the one that bears the name of Kester of Zanthus. Basil, Basil, you must see him at once or it will be too late."

Basil was convinced now that it was not a dream, that it was really his father who had come into the room. He rose from his couch.

"Do not come too close!" exclaimed Ignatius. "It—it is not allowed."

"Father, I must explain," said Basil. "I want to do as you command me, but there is a difficulty. I have another task to perform and I am told I must attend to it first. It will take me to Rome, and there I shall see Kester. I shall then return to Antioch and use what he has told me to dispossess Linus. But all this will require much time."

Ignatius sighed deeply and gave his head a shake. "I know about the other task. It is allowed us in the House of Suspended Judgment to see and hear what goes on in the world. At this moment we are watching three wars, a king dying of poison administered by his favorite wife, an earthquake in Seen that is burying cities and changing the shape of an empire. But all of us know that what you are doing is of greater importance than everything else that is happening in the world. If you succeed, there will be great rewards for you. But will that help me? No, Basil, not if the sands run out in the hourglass of Kester before you get to Rome."

Basil had been aware from the first that they were not alone in the room, that someone else was present who could not be seen. At this point a voice joined in the conversation, a sharp and acid voice. It seemed to come from behind him, which was impossible because his couch was against the wall. It even seemed to him that the voice proceeded from the back of his own mind.

"Ignatius, you must not count on this ungrateful son," said the unfriendly voice. "He is a frail reed to lean upon. How do I know?" There was a laugh at this point, a bitter and scornful laugh. "I know because I live with him. I dwell inside him. I know everything that passes in his mind."

"Who are you and why do you speak in this way?" demanded Ignatius, looking about him to locate the owner of the voice, and failing to do so.

"Who am I? I am nothing now, no more than an evil spirit. Once I was a man of substance and wealth as you were, Ignatius of Antioch. My name was Claudius and I traded in naval stores at Joppa. I was not honest in my dealings and sometimes I sent ships out with bad food and inadequate supplies. Because of this I, too, failed to find favor when I reached the house where you stay. But now I want to explain to you that this son you adopted is a weakling and that he has no stomach for the kind of revenge a proper man would seek. He does not believe that an eye must be demanded for an eye, a tooth for a tooth. This is because he is becoming a Christian. He does not know this himself, not yet. But I, who dwell in his brain, know it."

"A Christian?" Ignatius seemed to have doubts on this point.

"Yes. They are all Christian in this house. They are followers of the Nazarene—and they are striving to win your son over. He has been so far persuaded that now his thoughts are full of tenderness and love instead of plans for his revenge on Linus. If you were to slap him on one cheek, what would he do? He would turn the other cheek.

"You asked who I am and so I must tell you more about myself. Mine is the kind of voice you will hear coming out of clouds and thickets and from mouths such as this. I go about doing evil. It is not that I always enjoy this duty that has been imposed upon me. It is a hard thing for a soul, which has lived in the physical comfort of a body, to find itself condemned to wander in the winds and the cold of space. There are many of us and sometimes, because of our mutual need, we flock together. I cannot explain why it is, but we gather in the most dolorous of places. At the dumps, where we cluster over heaps of fish scales and rotting bones and we are shoved about by snarling, sniffling dogs. Or we congregate outside the city walls after the gates have been closed for the night. There is no place more mournful than this; with the wailing of lepers and the complaining of travelers who have not arrived in time to be admitted as they shiver in their cloaks, and with the donkeys staked out where there is no grass to crop, and the wind whipping back and forth with the whimper of the lost souls on it."

The face of Ignatius wore a puzzled frown. "There is so little time for us to talk," he complained. "And this voice goes on and on. Will it never stop?"

The voice of the lost soul had no intention of stopping. "Even when we succeed in getting inside a living body, we are not very content. We are all people who have sinned greatly and we have no patience with the incitements of little minds to poor little wrongdoings. How would that magnificently wicked queen Jezebel enjoy living in the sour mind of a tattling, nagging woman? How would Herod, the greatest sinner of all, bear the stupidities of a dull, grasping merchant with no thought beside the price of dried fish?"

The evil spirit proceeded then to talk of its own experiences with the relish of one who has long been denied the sweetness of an audience. "I took possession of this young man when he was sold as a slave. His mind was then of the kind one could enjoy sharing. It was filled with dark thoughts of revenge. I fed these thoughts. *Aiy,* it was exhilarating! "But when we reached Jerusalem I was conscious of an immediate change. He stopped listening to me. Instead he was listening to the little granddaughter. His mind became soft and almost involved in the sickening throes of young love. How could I, a thoroughly bitter spirit, be contented in a mind filled with the honey of sweet thoughts?"

"Is there to be no end to this?" asked Ignatius in a despairing voice.

"I have said my say," declared the voice.

Basil fell back into sounder sleep at this point. When he wakened in the morning he remembered everything that had been said and he was certain it had been a dream. Later he began to wonder. He felt depressed in mood and irritable. He criticized without just cause the servant who brought him his morning meal, and when he fell to his pacing back and forth his mind was filled with an unaccustomed bitterness toward those who had abandoned him to such discomfort. He had never been like this before, and at one point he checked himself in his stride and asked aloud, "Can it be that there *was* a Claudius of Joppa and that he has taken possession of my mind?"

Later in the day something happened that convinced him it had not been a dream. He had seated himself at his table for the purpose of putting some finishing touches to a bust of Luke that he had been making from memory. It had been a labor of love and he felt he had been more successful with it than with any of the others. Every facial characteristic of the kindly physician had been faithfully recorded, every hollow and fullness, every wrinkle. He looked at it now, however, with a critical viewpoint and decided that it had one fault.

"The eyes are a shade too small," he said to himself.

In these lands where men's eyes narrowed to slits in the fierce light of the sun and were subject to many serious ailments as a result of exposure to light and heat and dust, the Greek people enjoyed a degree of immunity not granted to any other race. They were sometimes called Those Who See Much. Luke had eyes of a particularly generous size. Convinced that he had not done justice to his benefactor in this respect, Basil set to work to make the eyes larger. It was a difficult correction, but he began to feel as the work progressed that he was succeeding.

His mind in the meantime began to wander. It went back to the dream of the night before and finally came to rest on Linus. A picture of the usurper drove everything else out; Linus in rich robes, fat of body and smug of face, sitting in the offices of the white palace and issuing orders to the men who had once worked for Ignatius. A black hatred boiled up inside Basil. The voice that had spoken last night was right. An eye for an eye, a tooth for a tooth! What joy there would be in taking the throat of his father's brother in his hands and squeezing the life out of him!

In response to this inner impulse, his fingers dug deeply into the damp clay. The face of Luke vanished under the savage pressure. In the fraction of a second the loving labor of days was reduced to a formless mass.

Seeing what he had done, Basil placed the clay on the table in front of him and gazed in horrified silence at the hands that had committed this act of vandalism.

"It was not a dream after all!" he said to himself. "It was real. This happened. There is a spirit inside me. I heard it speak last night. And now it has done this! It took control of my hands and caused me to destroy my own work."

A cold tremor of fear passed over him. He got to his feet with an instinctive desire to run away. Then he realized that this was impossible; he could not run away from himself.

"What am I to do?" he asked aloud. "How am I to go on working since I can no longer control my hands?"

A sense of impending failure took possession of him. He would not be able to make the silver Chalice. Getting to his feet, he began to pace about the restricted space of the room in a spirit of desperation.

"I am sure of it," he said to himself again and again. "An evil spirit has taken possession of me! How am I to get rid of this demon inside my mind?"

3

Summoned by special messenger, Luke arrived at the house of Joseph early the next morning. It was apparent at once that a crisis had arisen. The hall before Joseph's room was filled with his people, the men silent and depressed, the women with drawn faces and eyes red from weeping.

"Did you hear the dogs in the outer court baying last night?" asked one man of those about him.

"Mine was crawling on his belly," contributed another. "It is a sign."

Aaron emerged at this moment from the door of his father's room. He was followed by the three most prominent medical men of Jerusalem, all wearing expressions which gave little promise or hope. They were greeted by a respectful clamor of questions. How was the master now? Would he survive this new attack? He had survived so many in the past, the good old master, that surely the dread hand would be stayed another time!

Aaron inclined his head toward the medical attendants. "It is in their hands," he said.

The oldest of the trio of doctors took it on himself to act as spokesman. He was a gray-bearded veteran named Isaac ben Hilkiah, whose reputation was based on a tumor he had opened on the head of Herod Agrippa thirty years before and who had done more than anyone to fill the family sepulchers of Jerusalem. "The Lord's will be done," he intoned. "Your master is old and filled with honors. It is our opinion that Joseph of Arimathea will be gathered this day to his fathers." He raised a hand in solemn admonition. "Pray for him. It is a matter of hours."

There was a moment of stunned silence, and then a woman whimpered. "God be kind to him, the old master!" cried another hysterically. A wave of distress passed over the watchers and spread rapidly throughout the house. In less than a minute a sound of loud wailing reached them from the quarters of the slaves. A young woman in an expectant condition cried out in shrill grief: "Bitter is the day that takes the master from us! My son will not be born in time to look on his kind face!"

Abraham, the waiter, his broad face as white as the marble on Solomon's Porch, plucked Luke respectfully by the arm. "The master asks for you," he said.

They left the main hall, which now resounded with loud wailing and lamentation, and took a side passage leading to the back door of the sick chamber.

"He has eaten nothing for two days," whispered Abraham. "There was this morning a melon from the hot lands beyond the Dead Sea. He has always been partial to it, but it is still beside his bed untouched."

As soon as he entered the room and caught a glimpse of the head of the household, Luke knew that Joseph was indeed a sick man. He lay without motion and looked very small and wasted in the wide expanse of his great bed. His eyes were fixed on the ceiling. The fan above was creating enough breeze to stir the linen hangings, but his face remained flushed and hot.

"Is it you, Luke?" asked Joseph in a tired voice, without moving his eyes.

"Yes, Joseph."

"Come closer. I have things to tell you."

Luke seated himself beside the bed. He laid a hand on the brow of the sick man and then pressed a finger on a vein in his neck where the blood throbbed sluggishly.

"Luke," whispered Joseph, "I have no illusions. This is the end."

The physician laid both hands on those of the head of the household. "My good old friend," he said.

"I am not going to ask you," went on Joseph in a low voice, "if you agree with those—those black crows. *Ahay!* I know I am going to die, but they are sure I have only a few more hours to live. How wrong they are! I cannot let myself die as soon as that."

"No, Joseph, no. We cannot spare you yet."

"I have been a good Christian." The sick man was speaking with great difficulty and had to pause often between words to catch his breath. But the urge to tell what was on his mind was lending him the strength to go on. "To a Christian there is no moment in all eternity to compare with the first vision of Jehovah seated on His throne with the beloved Son at His right hand. I know this, but—Luke, I stand on the threshold and I must confess to you my innermost thoughts. I am loath to leave this life! It has been pleasant to live with so much wealth and power. It is still pleasant to wake of a morning and see the sun shining on the Temple, to feel capable of attending to my affairs, to know that my granddaughter, who has always been like a butterfly in my house, is here to tend lovingly to my comfort. I have been a great man in the life of Jerusalem and of my own people. Luke, there will be more concern here over my death than in paradise over my arrival."

Abraham had been busying himself in the room, doing small things and keeping an ear tuned to the low murmur of his master's voice. Luke turned now and motioned him to leave. The servant frowned in dissent but, after adjusting the hangings to admit more air, left the room on reluctant tiptoe.

"If I had my way," whispered Joseph, "I would elect to tarry a while longer. I would like to see my granddaughter married and settled down. *Ahay,* there are so many things I should like to see! But it is not to be. I must resign myself to the end of all my earthly blessings." There was a long pause. It continued so long that Luke wondered if the dying man had reached the end of his strength. Finally, however, the whispering was resumed on a note of almost passionate intensity. "I must go on living still. My granddaughter cannot return yet. There would be too much danger in it, and I must not send for her. But I cannot die without seeing her again. She is all in all to me, my little Deborra. I must find the strength to go on living so that when I die it will be with my hand in hers."

Luke leaned closer to the recumbent figure on the bed. "The Lord is listening, my good old friend. Perhaps He will grant you this strength you beg."

"Make me a promise. That you will come to me every day. I shall need your help if I am to fend off the hand of the angel of death who beckons me even now." There was another long pause. Then he regained his breath sufficiently to voice a passionate wish that there be no more medical ministration. "Tell my son I will not see those prophets of doom again, those wailing Jeremiahs he brings to my bedside! My resolution wanes when I see their long faces and listen to their lamentations. They can be of no further help, save perhaps to speed my parting."

"It shall be as you wish. Aaron will be told they must not return."

The tired eyes, which had been fixed steadily on the ceiling, turned now and rested on the face of his friend. "I can find more strength in your smile, O Luke, than in the tamarisk leaves steeped in vinegar and left under the stars, in the hydromel and hyssop they force on me. I believe I can find the resolution I shall need if you will promise to sit thus by my side. I know this is—not going to be easy. No, it is going to be the hardest struggle of my whole life."

4

Basil was pacing up and down with furious strides when Luke, bending double, came through the aperture that served as an entrance. Basil came to an immediate stop.

"I have been hoping you would come," he said in an excited voice. "I need your help! I am possessed of an evil spirit!"

The physician raised the lamp the better to see his face. "It would indeed be strange," he said, "if you did not have some such wild fancy in a fetid hole like this."

"It is not a fancy," responded Basil in a somber tone of voice.

Luke smiled reassuringly as he replaced the lamp on the table. "All my life I have been hearing this talk of evil spirits and the need to have them cast out. My boy, it is a foolish and evil fiction. This much, of course, is true: there are evil spirits in all of us. But it is no more than the baser side of our natures taking the upper hand. There is no need for incantations and the burning of candles and the ringing of bells to get rid of these personal devils. All we have to do is to keep the better side of our natures in control."

Basil was not convinced. "It is said that Jesus cast out devils," he declared.

Luke touched a finger to his forehead. "What Jesus cured was the madness," he said. "What prompts you to these fears, my son? Have you been having strange dreams?"

"At first I thought them dreams. Now I think they were not dreams at all. That they were real."

"Tell me about them."

Basil recounted the story of the visit he had received from the spirit of his father and of the voice that had spoken up, seemingly from the depth of his own mind. Luke listened attentively.

"I have given some study to dreams, believing them an indication of the state of one's mind," he said. "There was a Roman who wrote seriously about them and who propounded the belief that dreams are the work of one's soul. If this is true—and I incline to think so—then indeed dreams are of the utmost importance, because through them we may read of the state of the soul.

"Every dream has a meaning," he went on. "You saw your father, and that may be good or it may be the opposite. It means, at least, that he thinks of you with affection in the place to which he has been sent. On the other hand, to dream of him, now that he is dead, is a sign of trouble to come, of afflictions to be visited upon you.

"But let us consider first what it means to see a ghost, for you most certainly have been visited by one, perhaps by two. To see a ghost in your dreams is a sign of disaster. It means that evil influences hedge you about, that the fingers of malignancy are reaching out of the darkness. But first, tell me this: did you see them vanish? Did they betake themselves elsewhere?"

"My father was still talking when I dropped back into sleep, but I am sure that the evil spirit had gone."

Luke shook his head with satisfaction. "Then we may consider that the worst consequences have been averted. The evil spirit had sensed defeat and had left. The comforting spirit of your father remained."

"But I do not think I was dreaming!" cried Basil. "I have had proofs since to the contrary. The evil spirit prompted my fingers to destroy something I prized most highly. I did not know what I was doing—but suddenly my hands mashed it to nothing! I did not will them to do it."

Luke placed a hand on his forehead. "You have a touch of fever," he declared. "At least I am able to cure *that*."

He proceeded to take some herbs from a bag attached to his belt. These he mixed with a sure and skilled hand, stirring them afterward in a cup of wine. The finished potion he handed to Basil, saying: "Drink this. It will take some of the disturbance out of your mind, my son."

Basil drank the medicine, which had a bitter but not unpleasant taste. He felt better almost immediately.

"That will make you forget your evil spirit, I trust. Has the headache gone?"

"Yes," said Basil, shaking his head with a sense of deep relief. "The ache has gone. But not what caused it in the first place. No, my benefactor, I cannot dismiss the conviction from my mind. I have had proofs. I tell you, it has been shown to me that something evil is lurking in my mind. I am so sure of it that I am no longer certain it will be possible for me to finish the Chalice." There was a moment's pause, and then he asked, "Would it be allowed me to watch Simon the Magician tonight?"

Luke regarded him thoughtfully. "It will be dark and there will be a great crowd at the Gymnasium." He nodded his head. "I am sure it would do you good. You would get some fresh air, and that is what you need above everything. You will have a chance to stretch your legs and you will acquire some new interests to occupy your mind. If you see this trickster perform, you may even forget this idea that seems to weigh so heavily on your mind."

CHAPTER IX

I

THE PEOPLE OF JERUSALEM had always gone unwillingly to the Gymnasium because it had been built by the hated Herod. On this occasion they went with no reluctance and in great numbers. The open space where the youth of the city were supposed to be trained in sports and acrobatics (in point of fact, they seldom went there) was densely filled, and it seemed to stir and ripple like a pool of water. When Luke and Basil arrived they had to stand so far in the rear that they could not see the platform on which the Cuthean magician would perform.

"It cannot be denied," said Luke unhappily, "that evil appeals more directly to the human mind than good. Peter and Paul speak to small groups in side streets. This man Simon is a Samaritan, but because he has a reputation for evil everyone wants to watch him."

Benjie the Asker, circulating busily, materialized beside them for a moment to say: "They are all frightened of the devils he brings with him. That rustling sound you hear is the quaking of a thousand unwashed hides in flea-infested garments. But nothing could make them stay at home."

A moment later the magician appeared on the platform. The hum of voices ceased. No one moved. The Bad Samaritan gazed about him for a moment and then raised an arm in the air.

"I, Simon of Gitta, called by men the Magician, give you greetings, citizens of Jerusalem." He spoke in a voice that carried easily and naturally to the far corners. "You have come to witness with your own eyes the feats I have been performing up and down the land and of which you have heard much. You are going to ask yourselves, when I am through, were they miracles or merely magic tricks? The answer I shall leave to you."

He was well advanced in years, but his age had not given him a stoop; in fact, he carried his cadaverous frame with some of the spirit and resiliency of youth. There was nothing ot the usual about him: he was curiously ugly; his nose was so bulbous at the end that his nostrils seemed to be hiding away like a camel's, and his skin was not dark but inclined to gray, as though years of poring over strange books and searching at midnight tombs had given it an unnatural hue. His eyes were intensely alive.

He was attired in a white tunic with crossed bars of other colors, a garment that seemed unseasonably padded; as well it might, because a maker of magic must carry the instruments of his trade concealed about his person. The tall cylindrical hat, rising to a peak, which was accepted as the badge of the trade, was missing, however. Above the closely muffled robe, his head was as bald as the egg of the mythical roc.

He was carrying a wand, one of unusual length and with an excess of carving. This he placed on a table in the center of the platform and over it threw a length of scarlet cloth extracted carelessly from a voluminous sleeve. The cloth writhed and shook. When it was snatched away there lay on the table, not the wand, but a copper snake that raised its head and emitted a hiss. The cloth was replaced and fell immediately into folds of emptiness. When removed a second time, the snake had vanished and there was nothing on the table but the wand.

"A simple trick," said Simon Magus, his lips curling in an ugly smile. "You have seen it performed many times, no doubt. Any trickster living in a sun-drenched villayet on the Red Sea can juggle thus with wand and snake. I offer it first so that ye may judge better of what follows, the strange things I shall show you that are not at all a matter of deftness of hand or of the props of illusion." He paused, and his glittering eye swept the gathering. "Hear me, O men of Jerusalem. There is a magic of the spirit which has been given to me and which I shall now employ."

Luke had not been much impressed with all this proud chatter. "Would you believe, my son," he whispered, "that there are people credulous enough to think this man is the Messiah? It is the truth. A cult was started in Samaria, where they profess to believe he works with divine aid. It is spreading quite rapidly. Many Greeks have joined and even a few, but a very few, Jews. I fear that this demonstration has been allowed in the hope that doubt may be thrown on the miracles of Jesus. The High Priest is willing to traffic with a Samaritan in his determination to destroy us."

Simon again raised his arm in the air. "I shall take no more of your time with simple legerdemain. I shall not try to befuddle you with appeals to Pehadron, the angel of terror, or to Duma, the prince of dreams. I shall now proceed to show you that I possess a power that is shared by no other man born of woman. There is a light within me that turns the external world to darkness but lights the world of dreams to the singing splendor of the stars. Because of these strange conditions under which I work, I must now call my chief assistant to my aid." He raised his voice still higher. "Come, my child. Is this not the hour for great secrets to be bared? The one moment of the day when hidden truths may be revealed?"

In answer to this summons, a young woman joined him on the platform. She was beautiful in a remarkable degree. Her hair, held on the nape of her neck in a curious web of golden thread that a Roman matron would have called a chignon, was as lustrously black as her large and expressive eyes. Her features had such purity of outline that she seemed the product of a great Greek artist. She was dressed in the finest simplicity, the *palla* she wore being of silk; and not the coarse bombycimon which was being made on the Isles of Greece, but the purest variety which came in over the camel trains from Tartary.

To appear unveiled in public was to break the great law of the East, but she seemed quite oblivious to the sensation she was creating. Standing perfectly still, her shapely bare arms crossed on her breast, she allowed her eyes to rove with no trace of confusion over the sea of brown faces turned up to her. The first hint of a concerted protest died away, and fists that had been raised in the air were lowered. Curiosity seemed to have conquered, for the time being at least.

"To what lengths will this man go?" demanded Luke. "He seems capable of doing anything for a sensation."

Basil had no comment to make. He had recognized the dark beauty standing with such unconcern under the still hostile eyes of the multitude. It was Helena, the slave who had run away from the white palace of Ignatius.

2

The face of the magician had been that of an old man when he first appeared on the platform. Excitement had now removed some of the evidence of the years. There was in his eyes an almost impish delight in the audacity he was displaying. His body seemed to take on a greater agility, his step was spry, he snorted triumphantly through his camel-like nose.

A seed was planted in a small earthenware bowl and grew into a tall plant before their eyes. Fruit sprouted on the branches and grew to ripeness. The girl picked a pomegranate from its branches and then glanced impudently about until her eyes caught those of a young sheik from the desert with a proud high hook to his nose. She threw the pomegranate to him, calling, "If you find it sweet, O Chief, think of me."

A sickle, which had been lying on the table, flew into the air. It hovered unsupported and then proceeded to cut the plant down close to the earth in the bowl, without the aid of any hand.

"No man that ever lived," boasted Simon, "could harvest a field of grain as quickly as this magic sickle."

With a sudden loud screech the magician bounded high into the air and in what had seemed empty space above him found a scimitar with a brightly burnished blade. Taking his assistant's throat in his other hand, he forced her to a kneeling position. With one clean, quick stroke he severed her head from her body and held it up for all in the audience to see.

"O Guardian Angel Shamriel!" he chanted. "Listen to me, Shamriel, hear my command. Restore this bleeding head to its proper place so that life may return to the body of my beloved Helena. Yah, yah, Zebart, Shamriel!"

The head and the trunk drew together. Simon ran his hands around the point of juncture, intoning a chant in a high singsong. All trace of fission disappeared, and a moment later the eyes opened, the girl smiled and nodded her head.

"O Shamriel, praise to thee!" chanted the magician. "My Helena lives again."

The horror and shock of the audience exploded in a deep murmur of wonder. The magician held out the scimitar for all to see that there was blood on the blade. Then he dropped it on the table and bowed to his watchers.

"Saw you ever the like before?" he asked. Then he turned to the girl. "My Helena, you are well again?"

"Quite well, master," she answered.

"Was it painful when my lethal blade separated your head from your body?"

"I do not know, master. I remember nothing."

Simon took her by the hand, helped her to her feet, and then led her to the front of the platform. She dropped a curtsy and smiled again at the amazed audience.

A moment of silence followed. It was the deliberate pause that comes when something of extreme importance is to follow. Then a cultivated voice spoke from the audience, and it was as though the curtain had risen at last on the play of the evening after an elaborate prologue.

The speaker used Aramaic, but his voice carried such a scholarly note that it was apparent he was more accustomed to speaking in Hebrew.

"O Simon, are you not bold," he asked, "to display your magic in the land where Jesus the Nazarene performed His miracles?"

The voice contained more than a hint of scoffing. Luke stiffened into immediate attention.

"I have heard of Jesus the Nazarene and His miracles," answered the magician. "Who indeed has not?"

The questioner in the audience now propounded another query, his tone still more suave. "Were these miracles manifestations of divine power, or could they have been wrought by the tricks of the magic trade?"

"I do not like your choice of words," said Simon. "Trade? It is more, much more, than that." He paused before adding, "Who am I to answer such a question?"

Luke spoke in Basil's ear. "All this has been carefully prepared in advance. I am sure this questioner comes from the Temple, that he is an agent of the High Priest."

"It is said," went on the suave and mocking voice, "that on one occasion this Jesus the Nazarene caused tongues of flame to appear above the heads of various men he called his disciples. It is told, moreover, that these common men of the people, these untutored fishermen and shepherds, spoke in many languages thereafter and also performed miracles. Could you, with your mastery of magic, perform such things again?"

Night had been falling rapidly. No steps had yet been taken to illuminate the platform, and the figures of Simon and his lovely assistant had become no more than shadowy outlines. Out of the darkness the voice of Simon was raised.

"My friend, whoever you may be, I tell you that it can be done again."

"Then indeed I consider that my time this evening is being well spent. Do I understand that you declare your ability to make a tongue of flame appear above the head of anyone selected from this audience even as Jesus the Nazarene did?"

"Yes." There was a long moment of silence before the magician asked, "Is it desired that I, Simon of Gitta, demonstrate my powers by repeating this miracle of which there has been so much talk?"

A chorus of voices rose from all parts of the crowd, cultivated voices that spoke in the common Aramaic but with the rich intonations of the ancient Hebrew. "Yes, yes!" they cried, and "Show us, Simon of Gitta."

Luke sensed more than before the smack of preparation in this and he shook his head in a sudden anger. "Is there nothing they will stop at?" he whispered to his young companion. "Ah, what hatred they still have for the Master!"

"In order to do as you wish, I must ask some assistance of you," declared Simon. "Three citizens will be needed on the platform. To silence in advance any criticism of my methods or any hint of collusion on the part of those selected to aid me, I ask that they be men of established reputation and so well known to all of you that it will be clear they have not been coached to play parts in a deception."

The cressets raised on poles at each corner of the platform had not yet been lighted, and by this time the Gymnasium was wrapped in almost complete darkness. There were sounds of discussion in one section of the closely packed audience, followed by that of feet ascending the steps. There was some uncertainty and stumbling in the dark.

"I cannot see," declared Simon. "My eyes are losing some of their power with the fast passing of the years. Are there three of you?"

"There are three of us, Simon of Gitta."

"Good! We may now proceed. I ask of you, most worthy sirs and citizens, who are at this moment no more to me than faint figures in the dark, that you follow my instructions closely. You must do what I ask. Nothing more and nothing less. You will first bind my arms with cords you will find beside you on the table."

Several moments passed with no sounds save an exchange of whispers between the three witnesses and the scuffling of their feet on the planks. Then the magician asked, "Are you satisfied that I now lack the power to use my arms? If you have any doubts, give the ropes another twist to tighten them further. I can stand the pain. Now bind my assistant also, but be gentler with her, for her arms are lovely and fragile and must not suffer." There was a pause. "Are you convinced she is powerless to take any part in the drama which is about to unfold? Helena, my child, are you suffering pain?"

"Yes!" gasped the girl. "Proceed quickly, my master!"

"Stand in line in front of the table, my friends," instructed Simon. "Do not touch one another. Do not touch the table. Banish all thought from your minds. Be receptive to the power I shall send you. O Shamriel, hear my plea! I beg your aid."

A complete silence had fallen over the Gymnasium. The figures on the platform were no more than dark shadows.

"One!" cried Simon the Magician.

A small flame appeared above the head of the first witness in the line, a Roman officer, judging from the fact that he wore over his shoulder a red cloak of the type known as an *abolla*.

Far back in the throng of watchers Luke drew in his breath sharply. "What sorcery is this man using?" he asked in a tense whisper. He laid a trembling hand on Basil's shoulder and began to quote from a story of the activities of the apostles of Jesus on which he had been engaged for many years:

"And suddenly there came a sound from heaven as of a rushing mighty wind, and it filled all the house where they were sitting. And there appeared unto them cloven tongues as of fire, and it sat upon each of them."

Then he whispered to himself: "This evil man! What harm will he do? Will he turn people's minds away from the truth?"

The "cloven tongue" had illuminated the stern features of the Roman officer for a few moments only and then had died out.

"Two!" cried the magician.

A second light appeared, this time above the head of the next witness in the line, a well-known rug merchant. He was an ancient man named Abraham ben Heleb and was counted among the wealthiest residents of the city. He seemed a little discomfited at the nature of the service being exacted of him. The shades settled down about him again.

"Three!" cried Simon, his voice shrill and triumphant.

This time the flame gave a brief glimpse of Ali, the beggar who sat every day at the Gate of Ephraim and demanded with arrogance charity of all who came and went. The mendicant, who was supposed to have accumulated much gold in his day, had time only to wink at the assembled audience before the light flickered out and the darkness closed in for the third time.

Then from all parts of the packed space there rose loud laughter and mocking voices. Even in the disturbed condition of mind to which he had fallen, Luke recognized still the scholarly note in all of them. "So that was the great miracle!" shouted one.

"Have they been given the gift of tongues?" demanded another. "Speak to us, O Ali from the Ephraim Gate. Speak to us in the tongue of Seen."

It became apparent now that there were few Christians in the Gymnasium, for the laughter was general. Gibes were heard from all parts of the darkened space in voices that were now rough and uncultured, the words from the most colloquial form of Aramaic.

A scurry of feet could be heard as assistants carrying burning torches mounted the steps of the platform. They set the oil in the cressets to burning. The three witnesses paused uncertainly and then began to file down.

Simon, panting with pain, cried to the dark-skinned assistants: "First, remove the cords from the arms of my helper. Be quick about it! She is suffering tortures."

"Yes!" cried Helena. "I cannot stand it longer."

When the cords had been removed she sighed audibly in relief. Simon, released in his turn, stepped forward to the edge of the platform.

"You have seen what you have seen," he called in a voice edged with malice.

The voice that had spoken in the first place was raised again. "You have shown us, Simon of Gitta, that it may be done. Now you must answer a question. How was it done? Had you divine aid? Or was it no more than a magic trick?"

If there had been a careful preparation of this act, as Luke believed, the magician now elected to deviate from the course decided upon. The answer he gave, it was clear, was not what the questioner expected to hear. "O friend, I have heard your question," he said. He paused then and allowed his eyes to take in for a second time the packed sea of expectant faces below him. He savored the anxiety with which they awaited his reply. "To that question you must find your own answer. Go now to your homes and give thought to what Simon, called the Magician but who perhaps is more than that, has shown you this night."

3

Luke, leaning on the shoulder of Basil, was silent as they made their way out to the street with the rest of the audience. Mindful of the danger of being seen and recognized, they did not linger but moved away with brisk steps. It was not until they had outdistanced the other spectators, who showed a desire to loiter and exchange views on the strange things they had seen, that the physician allowed himself to speak.

"It was trickery," he said. "A very clever piece of magic and nothing more. But how it could have been done passes my comprehension." He gave his head a sad and puzzled shake. "What ideas will those people carry away to their homes? Whatever they think about it, we have been done a great deal of harm. They will either believe that Jesus was a magician like Simon or that he, Simon, shares His divine powers."

Basil made no comment, but for the first time he was not in agreement with Luke. What he had witnessed had made a deep impression on him. When the scimitar in the hands of the magician had cut its way, seemingly, through the neck of Helena, he had been so stricken with horror that he could neither speak nor move. He could not understand how life had been taken away from her and then restored so easily unless it had been by the exercise of godlike powers.

Simon the Magician, it was only too clear, was a great as well as an evil man.

CHAPTER X

I

THERE WAS NOTHING but bad blood between the Jews and the Samaritans, but trade relations had to be maintained in spite of this. The tiny country of Samaria, lying high in the hills below the Plain of Esdraelon, was extremely fertile and justly noted for its fine cattle and the richness of its fruit crops; and Jerusalem, where the community of the Temple lived in luxury and demanded the best of everything, was the finest market for these products. Practically all trade between the two countries flowed through one needle-eye, the House of Kaukben. He was a shrewd Samaritan who had taken a woman of Galilee as his wife and was willing to live in an unfriendly city because of the fat profits.

His house was large and so continuously busy that six helpers were needed. They were all Samaritans, young men with narrow foreheads, long jutting noses, and calculating eyes. The clerks, three in number, seldom ventured out on the streets, knowing from bitter experience that every Jew they encountered would spit at them and taunt them and that shrill urchins would follow and pelt them with offal. They were disposed on that account to keep to the shelter of the tall and narrow House of Kaukben, just off the Street of the Oil Merchants, their pens scratching busily all day long in a hot room behind the sign that Kaukben, who was inclined to make capital of all things, had raised beside the front entrance, with the word *Samaritan* boldly displayed. Boys of the right spirit made a practice of passing the establishment once a day and throwing a stone at the sign. The clerks, therefore, pursued their duties to the sound of a steady rattle of missiles on the painted board and of loud shouts: "Cutheans! Sons of pariah dogs, fathers of hyenas, brothers of pigs!" Occasionally the one who sat nearest the one window, a post of danger because sometimes a stone would find this mark instead, would demonstrate that the spot possessed a compensating advantage. He would smirk and say, "Another of them just passed, a girl of rarely fine proportions, my friends, and such a fine swing to her!"

It was in the House of Kaukben that Simon the Magician was staying during his triumphant visit to Jerusalem, and it was on the rooftop that he rested from his labors that night.

He had thrown aside his conjurer's cloak, and it lay on a couch in such a position that its secret mechanisms were clearly visible; the pockets containing the articles that had appeared as he needed them and then vanished again, the linen "pulls" that made it possible to transfer things from one sleeve to another and from pocket to pocket, even the large receptacles containing the paper replica of Helena's head and the bloody scimitar used in the decapitation scene. Without the cloak Simon was dressed in a single garment, the *bracae* introduced into the East by Roman soldiers after campaigning in Gaul and Britain, which were cold countries. This consisted of a close-fitting set of drawers covering the body from waist to knees. Thus scantily attired, he looked old and thin and as brittle as a sun-dried bone.

The sorcerer was in a jubilant mood. He had been a great success and had astounded an audience of Jews. Now he had supped well on a slice of cold Samaritan beef and a rich dish made up of Samaritan dates, figs, and pomegranates mixed in wine. His bodily needs satisfied, he sprawled on a couch and watched Helena over the pewter drinking cup he was holding in his hands.

The girl had supped with him; lightly, for she was mindful of the danger to the feminine figure in rich food. She was equally disposed to relax after the strain of the evening. Having cast aside her sandals, she was taking great delight in wriggling the toes of her small and well-tended feet. Her dusky hair had fallen into some disorder, and her eyes, which were fixed on the lights of the city below, had a dreamy look. Her thoughts, clearly, were far away, so far away that she was completely unconscious of the presence of Simon.

"The High Priest was there tonight," said the magician proudly. Samaritans, suffering under the superior attitude of the Jews, made an outward pretense of equal antagonism but suffered underneath from a sense of inferiority. There was a great satisfaction for Simon in having brought Ananias out to watch him perform. "No one knew it. He was on one of the housetops where he could see everything. Did I tell you there were priests and Levites scattered throughout the audience to carry out his orders? They were all taking the greatest delight in what I, Simon of Gitta, was doing to break the Nazarene myth."

If the girl heard this, she gave no sign. She sighed and ran her fingers testingly over her crisp black curls.

"Why did I wait so long to make an appearance in Jerusalem?" demanded Simon. Although the question was addressed to himself rather than to his companion, he spoke in a loud voice. "I could have done this long ago. I could have done it after talking in Samaria to Peter, that stubborn and quarrelsome man. Have I told you how he answered me when I offered to pay well for the gift of tongues and the power to perform miracles?"

"Yes," answered Helena. "Many times. I am weary of the subject."

"He said to me, 'Thy money perish with thee, because thou hast thought that the gift of God may be purchased with money.' He said I would have to give up everything and become a mere follower. I laughed him to scorn. I, Simon of Gitta, was not like the ignorant shepherds and fishermen who were flocking to join the ranks. I was a famous magician even then. I had thought of a way of producing the tongues of flame, but I had not made the properties. I was a man of wealth and influence. If they had taken me in, I would have become the leader. Well they knew it, Philip looking so coldly at me and Peter with his great round head and strong hands. They did not want me and they were glad I did not join."

"Yes," repeated the girl. "That is the way you have always told me the story."

Simon raised himself to a sitting position and stared intently at her. Seen thus, he gave an impression of sinister strength and purpose. His deep-sunken eyes were filled with pride in himself.

"Perhaps it is well I waited after all," he went on. "Today I am supreme. The Emperor Nero has heard of me and wants me to appear before him. But before I go to Rome I must make other appearances, performing the feat of the tongues of flame. In Caesarea, Antioch, Damascus, Troas, Philippi. It has been so arranged with Ananias. I am to show the world that I, Simon called the Magician, can do everything that Jesus of Nazareth did."

Helena raised herself from the nest of cushions in which she had been relaxing. She looked at him accusingly. "You were too rough tonight in the decapitation trick," she said.

"Trick? I have no liking for the word, my child. I have often told you so."

"Much too often. But I go on using it because it is the only word I know."

"I am not a trickster," declared Simon proudly. "I am not a mere magician. As I stood on the platform tonight, with hundreds of Jewish eyes fixed on me admiringly, the eyes of all the great men from the Temple, I realized that as never before."

"So," said the girl, taking a grape from a platter of fruit beside her, "you are not a mere magician. What are you then?"

There was a long moment of silence, and then a change came over Simon. His mouth set in a new line and his eyes opened wider until a circle of white showed around them.

"When I appear before Nero," he said, "I shall not wear my conjurer's cloak."

Helena sat up abruptly, allowing her feet to touch the floor. Her eyes, which could be so soft and seductive, had turned hard.

"Are you mad?" she asked. "Appear without your cloak? Tell me, pray tell me, what you could do without it."

The magician leaned toward her. "Listen to me, my little Helena. Tonight I was aware of a strange power in my veins. I said to myself, 'Why should I depend on strings under my cloak and trinkets hidden away in pockets? Why should I have this beautiful girl to attract attention when it is desirable for no eyes to be watching me?' I knew that something had been given to me, the astral light that would enable me to perform miracles as Jesus of Nazareth did."

Helena pushed the platter of fruit away from her with an impatient hand. "I have seen this insane notion growing in you," she declared. "Listen to me, you dreamer of silly dreams! It will be a sad day for you if you ever rely on this new power and not on the trinkets in your cloak. You will go out on the platform and there will be no tricks you can do. And what will happen then, O Simon with the new power in your veins? I will tell you. Your audience will laugh at you. They will jeer and say among themselves, 'This man is too old to do tricks any more.' And once an audience has laughed at you, you will cease to be the greatest magician in the world. They will never again pay as much as a *lipta* to see you perform."

"My child, my little *zadeeda!*" protested Simon.

"Try once to perform without your conjurer's cloak," declared the girl, "and I will no longer be your little *zadeeda!*"

Simon's tone now carried a note of supplication. "What do you know of this change I feel in myself? Of the new magic in my fingertips? You know nothing of the visions I see. I tell you, something strange is stirring in my blood."

Helena answered angrily. "You have the greatest chance of your life and you are ready to throw it away because there is a crack in your skull. You say I do not understand. I do—I understand you too well." To herself she added, "You boastful old crow." "All this attention from the men at the Temple has gone to your head. You strut and puff and preen yourself—you, a Samaritan, with the High Priest of Jerusalem talking to you and planning things with you. And let me tell you this also: you know in your heart that Jesus of Nazareth performed real miracles and that all you can do is imitate them with magic tricks."

"I am as great as Jesus!" cried Simon. "Do you forget that people are beginning to say I am the Messiah? My following grows more numerous all the time. There are twenty thousand of them today. Well, ten, perhaps. There will be millions before I am through. They know that I, Simon of Gitta, have divine power also. I must go on, my Helena, I must follow my destiny."

Helena yawned. "I am tired," she said. "I have listened to a hot wind blowing from Samaria." She added with a sudden fury, "And what of your promises to me?"

Simon got to his feet. He walked to her and put a hand on her shoulder. "I shall keep all my promises to you, my child, my sweet *zadeeda*. Will you not in return be a little kinder to me?"

The girl shrugged his hand away from her. A manservant was coming up the stairs to the rooftop, looking apprehensively about him as though he expected to find a congregation of evil spirits there. Without daring to look in the direction of the magician, he addressed Helena.

"There is a young man below. He wishes to see you."

"What is his name?" she asked.

"He gave no name. All he would tell me was that he came from Antioch."

Simon looked up quickly. He had found Helena in Antioch under circumstances that made the place eternally suspect. "Send him away," he ordered.

"This is my concern," declared the girl sharply. "We cannot send him away without learning anything about him or what his errand may be. He may have a message for me." To the servant she said, "Tell him to come up."

The latter disappeared promptly down the stairway, glad to take himself out of such dangerous company.

Helena rose to her feet, her mind occupied with her appearance. "I shall see him alone," she said.

"The hour is late." The end of Simon's nose began to quiver with resentment. "I intend to remain."

The girl fitted her feet back into the sandals. She crossed to the couch where the conjurer's cloak lay and reached into one of the pockets for a mirror. Immediately she drew back from it with an exclamation of fear and disgust.

"That snake!" she cried. "It is still in the coat. You promised me the last time——"

"I am sorry. I forgot about him again. But why are you frightened of a snake without fangs? He is the most obedient and humble snake I have ever used."

"You know how much I dread them. Get me the mirror. I won't go near it again." When the glass had been handed to her, she proceeded to comb her hair with hasty strokes. "It is my wish that you take your snake and go away at once."

2

The scene had changed when Basil reached the rooftop. Simon the Magician had gone, taking all the tools of his trade with him. A single light flickered rather feebly under a canopy. Helena was reclining on her couch, the merest tip of a sandaled foot showing under the graceful folds of her skirt, her eyes soft and luminous.

She sat up in surprise when she recognized Basil. "You!" she cried. "It never occurred to me that it could be you. I heard you had been sold as a slave by your father's brother."

"My freedom was purchased for me."

Basil found himself with a sudden distaste for his errand. He advanced slowly, conscious of the steady regard of her disturbing eyes. Seen thus at close range, she was much more lovely than he had thought.

Helena had a sudden flash of comprehension. "You are the artist!" she exclaimed. "The one who left the statue in the Temple. I have heard much talk about it."

He regretted that he had come. He had broken his promises in doing so and, now that the magician's lovely assistant had connected him with the events in the Temple, there might be serious complications. He did not take the easy way, however, of entering a denial.

Helena gave him a reassuring smile. "Your secret is safe with me," she said. "If Simon knew, he would run with it at once to the High Priest, so I shall keep it to myself." After a moment she added, "It was wise of you not to give your name."

"I had that much discretion at least." He paused, finding himself reluctant to proceed with his explanation. "You are wondering why I came," he said finally. "And why I came at such an hour. I have heard that Simon casts out evil spirits and I—I seem to be possessed of one."

She was watching him with the liveliest personal interest, saying to herself that she would have recognized him under any circumstance. The sensitive features of the boy she had known had lengthened with maturity, but they had the same distinct line. His eyes were unmistakable.

"Simon casts out evil spirits," she said. "His fee is very high. Is that a consideration?"

Basil conceded that it was indeed a consideration. He had not yet been paid for any of the work he had done, and his pocket was empty.

"Why do you think you need the aid of Simon?"

He hesitated over the explanation. "I have ceased to act in a normal way," he began. "My mind is filled with dark thoughts. I do things suddenly without realizing that I am going to do them. I am sure these actions are prompted by this—this evil spirit."

"What kind of dark thoughts?" she asked.

"I think constantly of revenge for the wrongs done me. I try to stop but find that I have no control over my mind. The thoughts keep coming back. I am sure I have been placed under some kind of spell."

"The desire for revenge is the most natural thing in the world," declared Helena. The softness had deserted her eyes, leaving them hard and speculative. "I never forget a wrong or forgive an enemy. Is there a devil in me also that should be cast out?" She laughed. "If there is, it is a different kind of devil. My thoughts are my own and I am not ashamed of them."

Then she began to ask questions. "Did your master treat you badly? Did he beat you as Castor used to beat me?"

"No. But I was allowed no freedom. I did not leave the house once in two years. I gave all my time to work."

"Was your mistress—well, partial to you?"

Basil shook his head. "She thought only of the money they were making out of me."

She smiled knowingly. "It is certain then that your mistress was quite old. It is customary for wives to be *very* partial to young and handsome slaves. And you are quite handsome, my Basil. Do you remember I told you that first night that you were a pretty boy?" Without waiting for an answer, she went on with her questions. "What happened to Castor and the other slaves when Linus became the master?"

"They were all sold or sent to the warehouses. Linus wanted servants of his own choosing. The only member of the staff he kept was Quintus Annius. That was because Quintus knew so much about my father's affairs."

"I hope Castor was sold to a cruel master."

"He was sent to the warehouses, and one day his skull was crushed by a falling mast. Some thought it was by design and not by accident."

A deep satisfaction showed itself in the girl's eyes. "I am sure he was killed on purpose. How I hated him!"

Helena had been careful up to this point to appear impersonal. She had seen to it that the skirt of her *palla* remained in graceful folds across her knees. No more than the tip of the toe had been allowed to show itself. Except for brief reactions to mood, her eyes had been cool and unruffled, and darkly lovely. Now she held out a hand to him for assistance in rising, and the pressure of her fingers remained on his for a fraction of time longer than was necessary. She smiled at him as they stood close together. Being taller than most women, her eyes were almost on a level with his.

"You were kind to me," she said in a voice little above a whisper. "When you came into the house that first night you smiled at me. It was the first time I had been noticed by anyone I waited upon. It is not an easy thing to wait on people who never look at you, who try to make it seem you do not exist. Perhaps you learned that for yourself. And now I am going to pay you for that smile. Simon will do what he can for you. He will recite his incantations over you and perhaps he will succeed so well that the evil spirit will leave you and kick over the pan of water as he goes. Do you know about that? Well, you will find out later. And, Basil, it will cost you nothing. If you ever learn the fee that Simon charges, you will realize how much I value that smile you gave me."

"When shall I come?"

There was warmth now in her eyes, a personal note in her smile, which said that they were friends and that she was glad. "Soon," she said in the low tone of an established confidence. "I will speak to Simon about it at once. But it will be necessary to take the greatest care. He must not find out who you are." She placed a finger to her lips, and he noticed that it was white and well tended. "We will say you are a student from Antioch, your name—Alexander? You are the son of a rich trader in Eastern goods. You are moody and quarrelsome and you have seriously injured a slave in a moment of passion. Yes, we must draw a rather black picture of you, my Basil. It is because of this passion that you desire to have the demon in you exorcised."

"But will he not know that all this is a fiction? A man with his strange powers——"

"Simon is not a reader of minds," said Helena. "He will have no reason to disbelieve the story. You had better come the day after tomorrow. I am not sure how long we remain in Jerusalem, and so it will be wise not to waste any time." She touched his arm with her hand. It was for a moment only, but the blood in his veins responded to the brief contact. "To see you again and to find that she can be of help means a great deal to the poor little slave girl who was so very bold."

"Will I see you when I come again?"

"Oh yes. I assist Simon in everything and I shall be present when he labors to rid you of this demon of yours. And now you must go. The suspicion must not be allowed to enter Simon's mind that I have known you before and that—that we are friends."

3

They were early risers at the House of Kaukben. The porters broke their fast as the first light of dawn appeared in the sky. An hour later the three clerks brushed sleep from their eyes. They would be through with their frugal repast and ready for the labors of the day by the time Kaukben himself would summon them to prayers. He was a man of small originality and always began his exhortation in the same way. "O Lord, for thou art our Lord as well as theirs, teach us to be patient, show our feet the path of prudence——"

Simon and Helena enjoyed their breakfast a full hour after Kaukben and his family. Simon, smacking his lips over a dish of fresh fruit, said: "There is nothing to compare with the plums of Samaria. When you get a tough pomegranate or a dried fig, you can be sure it was grown on the rocky slopes of Judea or in the steaming country around Jericho."

The first rock of the day rattled against the sign and a clear, boyish voice cried: "Samaritans! May all the beads of sweat on your bodies turn to boils! May you pass stones when you cover your feet!"

Helena was eating bread and honey. "There are some magic powers in which I still believe," she said. "There is, for instance, the love potion."

"It is the most potent of all," said Simon, giving his head an affirming wag.

"Can you make one?"

Simon drew deeply on his powers of exaggeration. "I can make a love potion," he declared, "that would cause the Sphinx to raise its head in a mating call," and then threw back his own head with an approving roar of laughter.

Without raising her eyes she said, "I desire that you prepare one for me."

Simon's exuberance faded at once. He squinted across the table at her. "I know you too well," he said, "to think it is my affections you aim to stimulate."

"That is right. It has nothing to do with you."

The magician's face flamed with sudden anger. "You ask me to accomplish my own undoing? To place in your hands—your cruel, white hands, my fair *zadeeda*—the power to win the love of someone else?"

"Take any meaning from it you will." Helena spoke in a completely matter-of-fact tone. "But understand this, Simon of Gitta. I want the potion. I want it for use within twenty-four hours. And it must be properly concocted so it will have the desired effect. If you wish me to remain with you and to assist in your work, you will see to this."

Simon wrestled with this problem for several moments in brooding silence. "Do you want the effect of this potion to last?" he asked finally. "Or is it a temporary conquest you have in mind?"

Helena did not give him an immediate response. "I am not sure," she said.

After another long period of sullen consideration the magician threw both hands in the air. "So be it."

He left the room and returned in a short time with a box of new white wood in his hands. It contained a powder of grayish color. This he held out to her with an ungracious air.

"Listen to my instructions closely," he said. "Certain words are to be written in honey on the inside of the cup. These I shall write myself, as I will not trust the knowledge of them to anyone, least of all to you, my *zadeeda*. The cup will then be filled to the brim with a sweet wine, and in it you will sprinkle the dust. Enough to cover the eyelid of a newborn child, no more and no less. I shall measure it out for you myself. This powder is ground-up bone from the left side of the red toad that lives under briars and brambles, and it has been buried for seven days. I have treated it to a sweet fumigation by burning a mixture of saffron, ambergris, fruit of the laurel and musk, saying as I did so, *It blazes on the hilltops, it sweeps the valleys, it burns in the blood, thy blood, O beloved one!*"

It was quite apparent that he was doing her bidding with the utmost reluctance. His manner was impatient and he watched her with a look that said he would enjoy taking her handsome throat in his hands and squeezing it until she cried out.

"Now attend, my Helena, my gentle and unselfish little one," he went on. "Dress yourself in linen only, even to your shoes. There must be no knots in your clothing. Loose your hair so that no two threads may be tangled together, and allow it to hang down your back. Then you will wave a wand over the cup—this one which I give you, it is made of virgin hazel—and you will say seven times some words which I shall teach you."

Helena looked curiously at the gray powder. A question rose to her lips. "How much of the potion must he drink?"

Simon gestured impatiently. "If he takes no more than a sip, he will still fly to you like metal parings to a magnet. A full swallow and his heart will be in your hands. If he swallows the complete contents of the cup, he will be willing to kiss the dirty hem of your skirt when you are hobbling on crutches." He then added in an angry grumble: "Is this not like loading a camel with salt on a journey to the salt sea? What manner of man is he that a glance at you will not suffice? You are a love potion yourself, my Helena."

She smiled at this. "I am vain enough to enjoy hearing you say so. But"—she became sober of mood again and gave her head a determined shake—"in this case I must be sure."

"Who is it you wish to captivate? Is it Ananias, that prime example of impotence? Lysias, that stolid soldier with muscles of leather and heart of ice?" Then he added, as though he had come to a reluctant acceptance of her wish, "You should understand that this potion has one special quality. It acts with great speed."

4

Basil was received on his second visit to the House of Kaukben in a low-ceilinged room directly under the roof. Helena came in to greet him immediately, wearing a plain linen gown that covered her from throat to feet. Her hair was no longer massed on her head but flowed like black satin over her shoulders. She nodded to him with an impersonal gravity.

"The master will see you in a few minutes," she said. "May I offer you a cup of wine? It is a hot morning and you have had a long walk."

She lifted a silver cup from the table and carried it to him. She did not raise her eyes as she did so, and her long lashes traced semicircles on the white of her cheeks.

The wine was sweet and heady. The first sip had a curious effect on him, making him feel happy and exhilarated. He became acutely conscious of her charms. It *was* a hot day and his walk *had* made him thirsty. He drained the cup to the last drop.

"She is the loveliest woman in the world!" he thought, watching Helena, who had withdrawn to the other side of the room and was striking a gong. What grace there was in her walk! How lustrous were her eyes, how enticing the raven cascade that fell almost to her waist!

Simon appeared soon thereafter, followed by two servants. He also was dressed in garments of linen, but with a difference: the breast of his tunic was embroidered with scarlet figures and his white shoes were inscribed with scarlet crowns on the instep. He gave the visitor the benefit of a belligerent stare.

"So this is the young man who believes himself possessed of an evil spirit," he said. "What is your name?"

"Alexander."

Basil stared back at the magician. He found himself disliking this old man most intensely and at first he thought it must be due to the wine. On second thought, however, he decided that his antagonism could not be ascribed to the potion he had imbibed so readily. The wine had been making him look at things through a rosy mist. There must be another reason.

"Your occupation?"

"I am a student."

"That is bad. Evil spirits prefer to enter the mind of a scholar. Even the mind of a raw student, such as I judge you to be, has an attraction for them. It may prove difficult to force this demon in you to leave, but I shall exert all my powers. Are you ready?"

It was on the tip of Basil's tongue to say, "No, I have changed my mind. You are evil and I desire no help from you." Catching Helena's eye at that moment, he realized that she had arranged this meeting at his request and that he could not withdraw now. There was the possibility also that Simon, evil though he might be, would be able to give him freedom of mind.

"I am ready."

Watching the preparations for the experiment, Basil realized that he was now filled with doubts. Nothing would come of this. It had been a mistake, he was sure. Because of Deborra's earnest admonitions he had subjected himself to an influence that was causing her image to recede in his mind; and this, he told himself with a sudden sense of alarm, he did not want.

A chair was placed at one end of the room with a door behind it, and he was directed to sit there. A servant carried in a Persian rug and spread it out on the floor beside the chair. A tin vessel, about two feet high and shaped like a tub, was placed on the rug after being filled with water to the brim.

Helena's voice at his shoulder said: "Have patience. Do everything he says. It will take a very short time."

She had left the room a few minutes before and had returned by way of the door behind him. Although he did not turn to look at her, he was conscious of every movement of her linen skirts and of the unusual perfume she used. The image of Deborra receded still farther.

"What will he do?"

"He will tell you to look into his eyes and he will endeavor to exert sufficient force to reach the evil spirit inside you, commanding it to leave. If the power he exerts is strong enough, he will compel the spirit to give a sign on departing. It must spill the water from this vessel as it leaves your body. Only in that way can we be sure it has departed."

"Have you seen it happen?"

"Oh yes. Many times." Her voice fell to a whisper. "Banish all doubts if you can; for my sake, as well as for your own."

He turned to look at her over his shoulder. She was close behind him and she smiled down at him, a warm and intimate smile which seemed to say: "You and I, Basil, you and I. We are in this together." Her hand brushed his shoulder briefly as she stepped back, and he felt a tremor of delight.

"I am ready," declared Simon.

The magician raised a hand to his forehead and stared at his subject from under it. The whites of his eyes were clearly visible. Basil was so completely held by the intent gaze of this strange old man that he forgot everything else, even the presence of Helena behind his chair.

"The evil spirit usually makes its way into the human body through the mouth," said Simon, "but as you are a student, it may have gained entrance through your eyes. Open them wide. Wide, wide, as wide as you can. Keep them fixed on mine. Listen to the words I am saying."

There was a moment of silence, and then the sorcerer began to speak. Basil tried to follow but found the glib sentences long and involved, made up of pompous phrases without meaning or coherence. This did not matter. It was the voice that counted. Simon was speaking in a singsong, the volume rising and falling, endlessly, it seemed. Basil realized that he was on the point of losing himself in it. He was finding it hard to keep his eyes from closing. He thought of sleep with a deep sense of longing.

He could see nothing but the eyes of the sorcerer. They had become enormous, so huge, in fact, that they filled all of space. They seemed like those of a gigantic owl, an owl as large as a feathered mountain. They were demanding his obedience, and he knew that he was losing all power to resist.

He had enough will left to feel alarm. He must not give in, he must find the power within himself to resist. With his last vestige of mental control he realized that he must break by physical action the spell fastening on him. With the most painful effort he succeeded in raising himself from the slumped position into which he had fallen and even in turning his body sideways.

The spell seemed to have been broken. The voice of the magician stopped. Basil opened his weary lids and looked about him.

And then the tub of water toppled over and the water spilled out on the rug. It began to spread in hurried streams on the tiled floor. He raised his feet instinctively to escape it.

He heard Simon say in a normal voice, "It seems that we have had a success." The latter rubbed his hands together and nodded his head with satisfaction. "I did not think any demon that ever dropped from a tree at the full of the moon could resist that final exhortation I gave it. Your demon, my young student, was in such a hurry to get away that he left us no reason to doubt his going. Every drop of water has been spilled. He is already on his way back, and in a very great hurry, to the lazar-cote or the sewage trench where he belongs."

Still oozing content, Simon instructed the servants to remove the empty vessel and the water-soaked rug. "There is no man living today who knows more about demons than I," he declared. "There has been this knowledge in Samaria for many centuries, but I have carried things far beyond the previous limits. The demons know the power I hold over them."

When he had left the room Helena stepped close to Basil. "It has gone," she said. "I hope you are content."

Basil was silent for a moment. Then he gave his head a shake. "No," he said. "I am beginning to think that Luke was right. He said that the only evil spirit that can take possession of you is the bad side of your own nature. I can see now that I have been letting my own evil instincts have full rein and pretending to myself that I was not responsible. I was sure I had become possessed, but it was no more than a sop to my conscience. I have learned that much today."

"I do not understand," said Helena with a frown.

"I came to my senses just in time," he explained. "In another moment I would have been completely under his influence. But I roused myself and turned in the chair. As I did so, I saw the rug move. There was a cord under it that was attached in some way to the vessel with the water. At any rate, the vessel tipped and the water was spilled out. That destroyed the illusion with which I came. I believed that Simon was a man of strange powers. Now I know he is a trickster."

Her face expressed both surprise and dismay. For a moment she made no comment. Then apparently she gave up all thought of denial or defense. "You are right," she said. "*I* pulled the cord. Your eyes were too quick for us."

"When I realized what had happened I began to think. It was clear to me that all magic was accomplished by a hoax of this kind."

"No, no," she objected. "What you see on a stage is trickery. But do not make the mistake of thinking that there is no real magic in the world. There are forces that cannot be explained or understood—dark and sinister forces. I know this to be true. I have seen strange things happen."

"As to that, I do not know. But my eyes have been opened. From now on I shall try to find the cure myself for the dark moods into which I fall. If I succeed"—he paused and then indulged in a broad smile—"I won't need to have a vessel of water spilled to tell me. I shall know by the peace of my own mind."

"Then we have done that much for you." Helena had been indulging in some disturbed thought. "We shall have to be more careful. I must talk to Simon about our methods and the props we use. We may find others with eyes as sharp as yours." She gave him a quick glance. "You will not tell?"

He smiled and shook his head. "I give you my most solemn promise not to tell what I have seen."

Her eyes were serious, even pensive, and filled with regret. "I am sorry that what I have tried to do for you has been such a failure. Do you think ill of me?"

"No," he answered, speaking with some difficulty. For the second time he was feeling the fascination of a pair of eyes. He was well aware that this second experience in subjugation carried a greater menace than the first. "No, I do not think ill of you. I—I am afraid I think much too well of you. I came to have a spirit expelled, but it seems to have worked the opposite way. A second spirit has taken possession of me."

"And do you think it magic? Ah, Basil, do not believe it to be the black kind."

5

Before they parted it had been agreed that they would meet again. Helena had said: "There is all of life—all the years that count—ahead of us. We must not part like travelers who pass on the desert. Besides, I have things to tell you."

Three nights later, therefore, Basil waited until after midnight and then started out, leaving with infinite caution by one of the rear doors. A moon close to the full was casting enough light into the narrow streets to make progress easy. He continued to exercise the most intense care, however, realizing that in the first place he had no right to be out at all, and in the second that anyone who ventured into the streets alone at such an hour carried a passage to eternity in his hands.

He reached the entrance to the Gymnasium without any troublesome encounters on the way. The street here had been widened to allow of the passage in and out of large crowds, and he hesitated at the edge of the cleared space thus provided. There was no one in sight. Not a sound disturbed the stillness of the night. He allowed his indecision to stretch into minutes, nevertheless, watching and listening intently; then, with sudden resolution, darting across the square to the main gate. It was not locked, and he had no difficulty in making his way inside. The closing of the great door behind him had an ominous sound, like the triumphant clamping shut of a trap, and he stood still for several more moments in the darkness of the interior passage. Thinking that he heard a step behind him, a light and stealthy step, his hand went to the handle of the knife at his belt. Then the sound of his own name came to him in a cautious whisper.

"Basil!"

"Helena?"

A cool hand was slipped into his. Helena's voice, still in a low whisper, conveyed the fear from which she had been suffering that he had forgotten his promise to come. "But you *have* come!" she added.

Their hands still clasped, they traversed the passage with extreme caution, for it offered no light to guide their steps. They came then to a turn and proceeded up a flight of broad stairs. At the top it was lighter, and they discovered an open door. It was clear that Helena knew her way about the building. She stepped through the door without hesitation, and they found themselves in the open, the arena stretching below and the seats in a great empty circle about them.

"Do you think I selected a curious place to meet you?" asked Helena, keeping her voice still at a low pitch.

This thought had been in his mind, for certainly it seemed a strange place for a tryst. They had the stadium to themselves. There was something ghostly about the empty space beneath them; this famed meeting place where Simon the Magician had labored so hard to fix doubts on the memory of the martyred Jesus of Nazareth.

"I could think of no other place that would be safe," she continued as they found seats in the front row and huddled back against the high wooden back. "And it is easy for me to get here. The House of Kaukben is only a few streets away."

"I am beginning to see," said Basil, "that a better place could not have been chosen. Here we can talk without any danger of being overheard or interrupted."

She had been wearing a veil that concealed her face. Now she thrust it back and turned her head toward him with a smile. In the moonlight her eyes seemed enormous. They were darker and more mysterious than they had seemed to him before. Her nearness affected him as it had on the day when he sat under the ministrations of Simon; he was conscious of every move she made, the faintest rustle of her robe. When she reached out a hand and touched his sleeve, he was completely entranced and sat very still, fearing that any response he made would be too indicative of the state of his feelings.

"I can only stay a short time," she said, still in the lowest of tones. "You must have seen how jealous Simon is. He watches me all the time. If I had tried to leave the house earlier, he would have known. When I go out in the daytime, he has me followed. And that is not all. Those long-nosed clerks watch me. I am conscious all the time that their eyes are on me. They are sly and dangerous, one of them in particular. This one has a nose longer than the others and his eyes have more daring in them. I am so frightened of him that I had a lock put on the door of my room. Last night I heard steps outside and hands pawing at the lock. It was the daring one, I am sure. It would not have surprised me if he had been lurking about when I left my room to come here, but fortunately he wasn't. I think I got away without being seen. But I must not expect too much good fortune, I must return very soon. . . . I came to tell you that we are leaving Jerusalem in two days."

"So soon!" Basil found himself dismayed at the prospect of her early departure.

"Simon has made arrangements to appear in many cities. We go to Joppa first and then to Caesarea. I am not sure where else, but I expect we shall go to Antioch again and then to Tarsus and Ephesus. Finally we shall go to Rome."

"I am going to Rome."

"How very fortunate it would be," she said, "if we could be in Rome at the same time! Can it not be arranged that way? Our stay there will be a long one, because Simon thinks it will be the pinnacle of his career. He is to appear before Nero."

Basil indulged in some calculations. "I think it certain that I shall reach Rome before you leave," he said.

"And you will come to see me?"

He turned and found himself looking at close range into the deep pools of her eyes. "Yes," he said in a tense whisper. "Yes, I will see you when I am there."

She was the first to withdraw her eyes from such close and dangerous contact and, after a moment, she began to speak in a more normal tone of voice. "You are going to be a great artist, Basil. Simon thought well of the work you were doing in Antioch. He knew about you and he went out of his way to examine some of the pieces you made. Simon is more than a magician, he is a very clever and discerning man. He saw the promise of genius in you." She indulged in a light laugh. "How would it affect his opinion, I wonder, if he knew that the young man who came to have an evil spirit cast out was none other than the dispossessed son of Ignatius?"

"He has no suspicions?"

"None at all." Her manner changed again and became even more matter-of-fact. "I am ambitious, Basil. And so are you. Does it not seem to you that we could be helpful to each other? That we could even—do some of our climbing together? Simon is only a steppingstone to me. I want to go much higher, to climb, climb, climb!"

She began then to ask questions and to discuss the future in a way that indicated she had been giving much thought to the possibilities of an alliance between them. Did he remember very clearly when she ran away from the house of Ignatius? Had he followed her movements afterward? There seemed to be considerable relief in her manner when he replied that he had tried to get news of her but had failed. There had been a year, she explained then, before she attracted the notice of Simon, and it had been a most difficult time for her. Life had become much easier since meeting him. They had been in Antioch most of the time, and he had both friends and influence there.

"I was in the courtroom," she said, "when your case was heard. I did not dare speak to you because Simon would have heard of it, and that would have been most unwise. All I could do was to sit in a back seat and suffer for you. Ah, Basil, Basil, you were so badly treated! I knew from the very first what the verdict would be."

"I was unprepared," he said. "Linus acted so suddenly."

"Basil," she asked, "did you receive a note later, when you had been sold as a slave, warning you of Linus?"

The question was so unexpected that he studied her for several moments in a surprised silence. "Yes, I received a note," he said finally. "How is it that you happen to know?"

"I sent it."

"You! Helena, I had no idea it came from you. All I could do was guess, of course, but I was quite sure an old friend in the household had sent it."

"Simon knew Linus very well. One night when he was drunk Linus dropped a hint about his feelings toward you. Simon repeated it to me. It was then I sent you the note. I had learned to read and write by that time, being so very ambitious, as I have told you. When I heard a little later that you had left Antioch, I was so happy about it! I wanted to see you, but that, of course, was impossible. I was happy because I knew that the danger you faced there was very great indeed."

"If I had not received your note," declared Basil fervently, "I would never have been able to get away. I shall always be in your debt."

They were sitting very close together, and at this point she allowed her head to rest against his arm. "Basil, Basil, need there be any talk of debts between us? I sent you the note because you were in danger. Perhaps you face another danger now; of quite a different kind. You may fail to live the kind of life you should, to climb up where you belong. I might be of help again." Her head was still pressed against his shoulder, but her voice had become less dreamy and more assured. "Let us talk sensibly about the future. Your future. What do you know about Nero?"

"All I have heard is that he tries to act and sing in public and that the people of Rome are beginning to think him a fool and a buffoon."

Her head moved in a positive shake of dissent. "I have never been in Rome, but I am certain of one thing: the Emperor has a more serious side to him. He may be a buffoon, but he is not a fool; he is dangerous. But what should interest us is that he takes a great interest in all the arts. He looks to Greece and dreams of creating the same glory in Rome. You would be in the best position to win his favor, being neither a poet nor an actor and so not a competitor. You, a maker of beautiful things in gold and silver, might capture Nero's good will easily. If that should happen, every rich man in Rome would be running to your door. You would become rich yourself and famous."

It was an alluring prospect she was holding out. While he kept it in his mind, turning it over and over and liking it more all the time, Helena went on to tell him what she had heard about the court of the Roman Emperor, its magnificence and extravagance, its absurdities, its dangers. "You spoke of repaying me," she said at the finish. "There will be opportunities in Rome. Go and try your fortune at the court of Nero. At first there could not be any open alliance between us. But later—who knows?

I am not talking this way because I have become moon-struck sitting out here with you. I thought of this years ago—when I first saw the little figures you used to make out of wood at your father's house. That will make you think me a most calculating woman. Perhaps I am. At any rate, I can see that only a man may climb in this world and that a woman's calculations must be built around a man."

They sat in silence then for several moments, looking out over the torn sod of the arena and the ghostly emptiness of the rows of seats. Basil's mind was in a turmoil. What was happening to him? How far could he commit himself to this bright future she was painting for him? Did he want to continue this relationship, which had begun under such curious circumstances and which threatened now to disturb what had seemed to him his certain future, one of a happier and more serene kind? What disturbed him most was his concern for Deborra. She had been first in his mind, and now Helena seemed certain to usurp a large part of his thoughts.

Helena sighed. She pressed his arm and looked up into his eyes with a final smile before dropping the veil over her face. She rose to her feet. "Simon may have discovered I have left the house. Or that snooping clerk who makes my blood run cold." She raised a hand in warning. "No, you cannot go with me. I shall return as I came and I must return alone. Stay here until I have had time to cross the square. And, Basil, remember everything I have said."

She began to make her way back along the echoing emptiness of the seats, her dark robe drawn closely about her slender figure. A whisper came back to him:

"We will meet in Rome."

CHAPTER XI

I

AARON WORE A DEEP FURROW of preoccupation between his eyes when he arrived at the house of Ananias. Compared to the great palace of Joseph, the home of the High Priest seemed small, a white structure of two stories. He was too concerned with his thoughts to notice that two men standing near the entrance nodded to each other as he passed.

The house might seem small, but it had taken on distinction since the induction of Ananias into the high office. A servant with a deep band of blue on his robe motioned Aaron toward the stairs. Above him as he climbed was the life-sized figure of a golden angel on the landing wall. Another servant with the identical blue band stood outside the door of the room where the High Priest received his visitors. Back as far as the memories of men went, this room had been maintained in a traditional austerity, as sparsely furnished as a prison cell and dedicated to the hard labors of Temple administration. Ananias had been a sybarite in his earlier years, before unlimited indulgence had coarsened him, and this stage was reflected in the artistic appointments with which he had surrounded himself. There were fine old tapestries on the walls and in a corner a cabinet containing many beautiful figurines in Parian marble. There was much brown leather and gold leaf on the table and a beautiful pen with a jeweled handle.

"You are prompt," said Ananias, looking up with a quick and not too cordial nod.

"I came as soon as your messenger conveyed your invitation."

The High Priest was a sensual figure, his stomach grossly rounded, his face harsh and cruel. He was, it was clear, a vain man. Not content with the plain blue tunic of everyday wear, he had donned the ephod, an elaborately embroidered robe that was generally reserved for ceremonial use. The ephod was rarely seen except with the priestly breastplate on which Urim and Thummin and the accompanying precious stones were mounted, but his vanity had not led him to this breach of established custom. On his fingers, white and cruel, were many rings.

"It is reported," said Ananias, "that your father is in a seriously weakened condition."

"The physicians gave him a few hours to live on their last visit," answered Aaron. "That was three days ago. He is still alive. It begins to verge on the miraculous."

"We are not sentimentalists, you and I," said the High Priest, his close-set eyes studying the face of his visitor. "And we are alone. May I speak, then, with full candor and say that it will be a good thing for all of us when the venerable Joseph is laid away in the grave of his fathers?"

A glimpse into the cold recesses of Aaron's mind would have made it clear that he shared this view. The passing of the years had raised an ever-increasing impatience for the day when he would have full control over the great trade empire his father had created. It was not in his nature, however, to meet such a challenge as this with equal frankness.

"I must reconcile myself," he said, "to the separation that faces us."

The thick lips of Ananias parted in a scornful smile. "It seems I assumed too much," he said. The disease that had fastened itself on his bloated body had thinned his beard. He began to run his fingers through the unhealthy gray scraggle that was left and his eyes twinkled maliciously. "We have some decisions to make that call for frankness of approach, but in deference to the hypocrisy that so often obscures the relationship between father and son—and of which you seem to have a full share—we shall choose our words with regard to these little niceties and reservations."

He lifted a bell and shook it. A soft and silvery note was given forth, in keeping with the sacred nature of the duties performed in this room.

Aaron had watched Ananias in the Sanhedrin several days before when Paul had been brought in by a guard of Roman soldiers for a hearing before that stern tribunal. It had been with a sense of shock that he had observed the violence of the High Priest's methods. As soon as the apostle had started to speak with his accustomed vigor, Ananias had ordered a guard to strike him in the face. With blood streaming down his cheeks, Paul had retorted with a verbal blast that had chilled and frightened the members of the Sanhedrin because addressed to the head of the Temple.

They had been carried away later, however, by the eloquence of the plea he had proceeded to make. They had wrangled for hours, in fact, after he was taken back to Castle Antonia, although it had been clear to all of them that the fate of the outspoken apostle no longer lay with them but would have to be decided in Rome.

A sense of dissatisfaction with the High Priest now filled Aaron's mind. "A man like this," he said to himself, "does more to drive people to the Christian faith than all the gold my father has wasted on it."

In answer to the summons of the bell a servant brought in the clay head of Paul that Basil had left in the Court of the Gentiles. It was deposited on a corner of the table at which Ananias sat, and by chance it faced him with the same air of defiance that the original had displayed before the Sanhedrin. The High Priest reached out and turned it around with a flourish. He was proud of his hands and used them always with a certain ostentation, as though anxious to demonstrate that some part of him retained a degree of fleshly elegance.

"You sat with us when this man," motioning toward the head, "was brought in for a hearing."

Aaron nodded. "Yes, *rabbani.*"

The High Priest glowered reminiscently. "You heard him call me 'a whited wall.' I have been called more scurrilous things, but nothing has ever been said of me that sits more ill on my stomach. I shall never forgive Saul of Tarsus. My enmity will follow him to the end of his days." Then he nodded briskly. "But I did not bring you here, Aaron ben Joseph, to talk about this persistent advocate of heresy. I want to speak instead of the talented artist who made this. You are aware, of course, that it was this artist who rescued the girl after she threw a stone at the Romans."

"I have heard it said."

"You must be aware that it is the same man who was brought from Antioch by your father."

Aaron, not to be caught in any such trap, answered warily, "I doubt if it is the same man. There are many artists and silversmiths in Jerusalem."

"But only one capable of doing such fine work. You are aware, of course, that this man continues to live under your father's roof?"

Aaron was caught off guard. "I am certain," he exclaimed, "that the young artist left our roof some time ago, having completed what he came to do."

"Apparently I am better informed than you are of what goes on in that great warren of stone your father calls his house. I can even tell you in what well-concealed corner of the house the young man is lodged." He had been keeping his eyes fixed on his hands, but now he looked up suddenly and stared hard at Aaron. "I can even tell you the nature of the work on which he is now engaged."

"I shall have him routed out!" cried Aaron with an air of outrage.

"The time has not come for that," said the High Priest. "This is something that must be kept from the ears of the Romans. Much as I might like to humble the pride of Joseph of Arimathea, I do not want it done at a high cost. The Romans would take any excuse to step in and confiscate all his property—and I assure you that I desire that almost as little as you. We must be sensible and bury away the incident of the riot and never stir it up again. In any event, I do not want this young man disturbed. There is a touch of genius in him. I am almost disposed to think that the spirit of Scopas has come back and is expressing itself through the tips of his fingers. Do you understand much of Scopas and his work?"

Aaron shook his head in denial of such knowledge. It was clear he considered the matter of small importance.

"Scopas," explained the High Priest, "was the first artist to inject human emotions into the sheer perfection of Grecian sculpture. The men and women he created in everlasting marble were filled with loves and hates and fears. He did it in unmistakable ways. The heavy overhang of the brows lent emotional strength, even though the eyes were deeply shadowed. The flare of the nostrils lent excitement. He was a little rough and rugged and perhaps lacking in the perfection of those who went before him. But he brought a new note into the most enduring of all forms of art." He was beginning to wheeze from so much talking and found it necessary to pause in order to catch his breath. "I am getting as long-winded as that strutting little jackass Jorim who directs the cantillation of the prayers in the Temple, Jehovah forbid! But I must point out that there is much of the Scopas touch in this remarkable head of Paul. I do not want this young man treated roughly in any way. I want him to go on creating things as fine as this.

"But, Aaron, this artist is being made an instrument in a very dangerous plan," he went on. "I said before that the time has come for frankness between us. I shall keep nothing back. A member of your household staff has been in my pay for some time. Last night he brought me word that a certain cup is concealed in your father's house. It is plain and it is cheap, but any Christian would be willing to die for the privilege of touching it. It is the cup the Nazarene used when He broke bread for the last time with His followers. Your father has employed this young Greek to fashion a silver frame for it."

"I assure you I had no knowledge of this."

"That I know. Your father kept his possession of the Cup a secret, and it was not until recently that he shared his knowledge with anyone. That such a cup was in existence has been known to us for many years, and we have realized the importance of it. We have searched for it high and low." His hands drew so tightly together that they seemed an expression of the ruthlessness of their owner. "I shall not know a moment's peace of mind until it has been brought to me and I have seen it *broken into pieces and ground to dust before my own eyes!* I lay this command on you, Aaron ben Joseph, that you find this Cup at once, today, and bring it to me."

This demand created an unexpected change in the son of Joseph of Arimathea. His thin face flushed with resentment.

"My father is dying," he said. "Do you think me so lacking in feeling that I would disturb his last moments?"

"Let me explain the situation," said Ananias. "The preaching of Paul is splitting the Christian ranks. All Jews, even those who believe in the Nazarene, resent his insistence that Gentiles be admitted on an equality. They feel so strongly that from this time forward it will be among the Gentiles that new recruits will be won. And now we have this pestilential magician, this rancid Samaritan, stirring doubts in all minds by the miracles he is performing," A flush of excitement mounted to the brow of the High Priest. "With two such potent weapons in our hands, we may succeed in stamping out this dangerous heresy for all time! Can you not see how inconvenient it might be to let their leaders produce the Cup at this moment and use it as a new rallying point?"

"How long has my father been in possession of the Cup?"

"For some years——"

"Then"—with a satisfied wave of the hand—"a few days more will not hurt."

"A few days!" cried the High Priest. "Even a few hours may prove our undoing. Do you not realize, Aaron ben Joseph, that I have the power to compel your obedience?"

But Aaron had taken his stand and he was of too set a turn of mind to be easily dissuaded. "You are the High Priest," he said, "and so you have great power. You have the power of the Temple, the allegiance of the priests and Levites, of the sons of Zadok, of the singers and porters. It may be that the daggers of the Zealots are at your command."

The High Priest's nostrils were twitching angrily. "That may be true," he said.

"But," went on Aaron, "we also have power. A different kind, but one to be reckoned with nonetheless. The power of wealth, the power of the mighty shekel. Our influence spreads far beyond the limits of the Diaspora. No trading house in Jerusalem could continue if we ordered otherwise. In considering our strength, think not only of what we could do; think also of what we could undo."

Ananias was now thoroughly angry. He had withdrawn his hands from the table and dropped them in his lap, but not before his visitor had seen that they trembled with the rage that possessed him. "An hour ago, Aaron ben Joseph," he said, "I instructed Rub Samuel to have your house surrounded by his most zealous and willing men. They are at their stations now. No one will be allowed to enter or leave without being questioned and, if it seems necessary, searched. Even you, the son and future head of the house, will be stopped. We spoke of power. This is a demonstration of it."

"A ship from Troas is expected to dock at Joppa within the next few days," countered Aaron. "It carries a valuable cargo. If Joseph of Arimathea decided that nothing was to be purchased here, there would be no buyers. The shipowners would suffer a grievous loss. They are all men of Jerusalem, and I recall that on the list is a man *high in the Temple.*" Having thus thrown down the gage of battle, Aaron seemed to be enjoying his role. "We spoke of power. This is another demonstration of it."

The furious temper that had caused the High Priest to order the assault on Paul in court flamed up in him again. He pounded on the table with both fists.

"Thou stubborn son of an unregenerate father!" he cried.

Aaron, recalling the scene in the Sanhedrin, rose and leaned over the table. "Thou whited wall!" he exclaimed.

There was a moment of silence, and then Ananias threw himself back in his chair. He began to laugh. He laughed with so much gusto that his great mound of a stomach shook under the silver-fringed blue girdle about his waist. The bells on his tunic jingled loudly. "I have never liked you," he said. "You seemed to me as poor in spirit as a tinker's mule. But now

I find myself conceiving an admiration for you. I have changed my opinion so much that I shall make a bargain with you. Listen."

He wiped away the tears that laughter had brought to his eyes. "The man who brought me the information about the Cup, for which I paid handsomely, had something else of importance for my ears. It concerns you, my friend with the temper that kindles slowly, you and the money you are to inherit. I shall tell you what it is if you, on the other hand, will make me this promise: that you will not in any way interfere with Rub Samuel's men and that the instant your father's eyes close in death you will call them in to guard the house while you search for the Cup. That you will promise, moreover, to tear down every partition in the house, if necessary, and raise every foot of flooring until you find it; and that you will then bring it to me." The vigor with which he had spoken had brought a purple tinge to the High Priest's cheeks. He stopped for several moments while struggling to regain his breath. "Is that a fair exchange between the stubborn son of an unregenerate father and a high priest who has twice been called to his face a whited wall? Is it a bargain? Is it agreed?"

Aaron, somewhat aghast at the lengths to which he had allowed himself to go, had sunk back into his chair. Now, however, he discovered a sense of pride in having bandied insults and threats with the head of the Temple. He nodded his head.

"It is agreed," he said.

"Listen, then. Your father is diverting a large share of your inheritance from you. He is too good a Jew to do this in his testamentary instructions, but for many years he has been depositing a portion of his profits with the banker Jabez in Antioch. These funds, which now amount to a very considerable sum, pass to your daughter on Joseph's death. Your daughter is a convert to the Christian teachings and she understands that she is to serve in a sense as custodian of the money, and that some part of it at least is to be for the use of the Nazarene leaders. By this means your father will continue his support of the heresy after his death."

For perhaps the first time in his life Aaron's face was a mirror of all the emotions that filled him. In his distended eyes, in the flush of his face, in the spasmodic opening and closing of his fingers could be read the anger aroused in him and the determination he had already conceived that no part of his inheritance would be taken from him.

"Has your daughter passed the age of thirteen years and one day?" asked the High Priest.

Aaron nodded. "She has had her fifteenth birthday."

"Then she is legally of age. I hoped she was still a minor and barred from receiving this inheritance, except in trust." The priest looked somberly at his visitor. "I have some advice to give you. Your daughter, although of age, is still unmarried, and so she is under your guardianship. Have a trusted agent ready to leave as soon as your father dies. Send him to Antioch on the fastest ship you own or can charter. Give him written authority to claim the money in your name as father of the girl. Once you get the funds into your own hands, you will be in a position to control them so that not one half shekel will ever find its way into a Christian purse! You know what the law says, that a guardian may 'buy, sell, build, demolish, hire out, plant, sow——' You know what it says as well as I do." Ananias leaned across the table and regarded his visitor with an insistent frown. "You must realize the importance of this. Above everything, see that the girl does not marry. Once she takes a husband, your rights come to an end and she passes under his tutelage. Aaron, she must not marry!"

Aaron spoke through tightly locked lips. "I put no trust in agents," he said. "I shall go to Antioch myself!"

2

Basil had no appetite that day for the meal brought to him at five o'clock. It was an unusually good one. There was even a slice of hot meat and a batter as rich as the *keroshitha,* that wonderful dish made of dates, raisins, figs, and almonds that was served once a year with the paschal lamb. He said to the servant who came to remove the dishes, "Eat it yourself, Eschol the Toad." The servant, his eyes fixed greedily on the batter, answered, "I will cut off at the wrist any hand that tries to take as much as a mouthful from me!"

Basil had been existing in a state of mounting discomfort and tension. The air in the room behind the meal sacks had grown more fetid with each day of his occupancy. The throbbing of his head made the light of the oil lamp intolerable, and he spent most of his time in darkness. This left him with his thoughts for company, and it disturbed him that the picture of Helena filled his mind continuously. He would envision her as she had appeared on the morning of his second visit to the House of Kaukben, looking so cool and lovely in her severe linen gown, with her feet bare and her luxuriant black tresses hanging down her back, or as she sat beside him in the empty Gymnasium, her head pressed against his shoulder.

Although he allowed her to monopolize his thoughts, he was aware that his interest in her was both unwise and unhealthy. He had not failed to detect that her eyes, which were dark and soft and lovely, could also be hard and calculating. Her voice, gentle and enticing for the most part, had at times a different note. She had displayed an interest in him that caused his blood to tingle in recollection, but he was not convinced it went any deeper than self-concern. Yes, she could be cold and hard; but this, instead of leading him to a more sensible frame of mind, had the effect of stimulating his feeling for her.

"It is a good thing that I am tied here so closely," he said to himself many times. "If I dared venture out again, I would have gone at once to see her; and nothing but evil could have come of that."

As soon as silence settled down over the house, he ventured out from his place of concealment. His first visit was to the slave baths, where he laved himself thoroughly. The dull ache in his head left him with the first touch of the cold water on his brow. He felt so much stimulated that he said to himself, "Tomorrow I must work." He wondered when Deborra would return, and for the moment her image left no room in his mind for the dusky enchantress. After completing his ablutions he decided to risk a visit to the Court of the Packers in order to get some exercise. In the daytime this open space was the scene of much activity, of sweating porters who came and went, of carpenters breaking open cases that had come from afar or nailing up goods to be sent out. He had gone there often in the still of night because it afforded a larger space for pacing and still more because he could always look up and see the stars, and find much comfort and satisfaction in that.

His visit there this night suffered an interruption. As he paced up and down in the court, picking his way carefully among the wooden cases and the wicker hampers, giving the tool racks a wide berth, and setting his bare feet down with full regard for the danger of fallen nails, he became convinced that he was not alone. He heard sounds in the darkness, an occasional indrawing of breath, a stealthy rustling. He remained still, poising himself beside a tall basket that had come from the Far East and still had about it an exciting odor of spices and strange fruits.

It became clear finally that the sounds came from the east side of the court. Here, he knew, there was a long room that had two doors giving on the court, doors that gaped open and were never used. Although this room seemed to lack occupancy, the hint of an earlier importance still clung about it. There were large pieces of furniture made of black and brown wood against the walls, and everywhere piles of moldering papers. Of all the apartments in the great house, this seemed to offer the least attraction for a midnight visitation. Nevertheless, after a long wait, Basil heard a scratching sound from that direction and then a light flared in an oil lamp. To his intense surprise he saw the intent face of Aaron above the flame.

The son of the house was conducting a search. He moved stealthily about the room, holding the lamp up in front of him, his eyes darting nervously this way and that. Finally he approached the open door nearest the silent witness, and Basil then became aware that a bed had been placed immediately inside it and that the bed, moreover, had someone sleeping in it. The son of the house stood beside the bed for a long moment, looking down. Unable to see the face of the sleeper, Basil watched that of Aaron instead, reading a curious conflict of emotions there, anger and cupidity and, struggling feebly against the stronger feelings, pity and a hint of kindness.

The cover of the bed stirred and a voice, the voice of Joseph of Arimathea, said, "Is it you, my son?"

"Yes, Father."

"What do you want?"

Aaron responded by asking a question of his own. "What strange whim is this that has caused you to have your bed moved down here?"

The dying man did not answer at once and, when he did, it was in a voice so thin that the trapped listener in the darkness of the court could hear only an occasional word. He heard enough, however, to learn that Joseph had been convinced he might live longer if he found some way to keep his mind occupied. This room he had used through all the years of his active life. He had been moved here to escape the torpor into which he had been falling in his quarters above.

Aaron interrupted with a touch of impatience in his voice. "You have not set foot here for more than ten years. Not since you gave up full supervision."

"That is true. It was a—a grievous mistake to give things up as I did. I see now that ever since I have been doing little but—wait for death to come."

"Death is coming now. You must realize it, Father. What good can it do you to move to this hot corner? There is not a breath of air here. To stay will only hasten the end."

"No, my son. If I can keep my mind active, I can still live. A little longer; a week or two, perhaps. Long enough, I think, for the things I want to do."

"I hear," declared Aaron, his tone cold and accusing, all trace of kindness banished from his eyes, "that you have been summoning members of the staff here. You are asking them questions, giving them orders. I hear also you have been demanding to see statements."

"I tell you that I am striving to keep my mind occupied."

"You must be losing your mind."

Basil was so much occupied now in this encounter between the great merchant and his son that he allowed himself to peer out from behind the empty spice basket. He noticed that Joseph had shifted his position in the bed and that it was now possible to see his face. It was shocking to discover how thin it had become. The eyes had fallen far back under the noble arch of the brow.

There was a long pause before the sick man answered. "I am ill in body and in spirit," he said. "But my mind is as clear as it ever was."

Basil could see that the eyes of the son of the house were never at rest. They darted about, peering into all parts of the room, always coming back to a furtive inspection of the pillows on which his father's head rested.

"In the morning," declared Aaron, "I shall give orders to have you moved back."

Joseph answered immediately, his voice stronger and more alive. "Here I shall remain. Any orders you take it on yourself to give, my son, will be disregarded. Bear this in mind. Master I have always been in my own house, and master I shall remain until I have drawn my last breath."

"I think not. You are doing insane things, things I will not permit. I know about the steps you are taking, the base tricks you propose to play on your only son! Is it any wonder you cannot die in peace with such dishonesty on your conscience!"

"I have much on my conscience, Aaron, my son. I am aware that I have sinned in the eyes of God and His beloved Son. I have failed in so many things! But where you are concerned, my conscience is clear. You will get your full due, perhaps more. You will be the most powerful merchant in the world. Does not that suffice?"

Aaron was on the point of bursting out with direct accusations, but a sense of caution laid hold of his tongue in time. To let his father see that he knew of the cup in the house would serve only to put the aged man on his guard. It would be even more unwise to avow knowledge of the funds deposited in Antioch. He contented himself, therefore, with saying, "I have always known, Father, that you placed little confidence in me."

"Aaron, my son," said Joseph sadly, "if I have sinned against you, it has been in failing to do anything for your immortal soul."

"My soul is my own concern. You must know that I incline to the Sadducees and have no faith in this existence after death of which you speak so much."

"My son, my son! Must I die and leave you in such utter darkness!"

"There is one thing I must tell you," said Aaron, drawing cautiously on the knowledge he had brought away from the house of the High Priest. "The men in the Temple have been buying information from a member of our staff. What it is they have learned, I leave you to guess. Today the result was seen. The Mar, as they are beginning to call Rub Samuel, has set men about the house, and no one may enter or leave without being stopped."

The wasted body on the bed stirred with agitation. "It is only because I am dying that he dares do this!"

"Father," said Aaron, "there have been great changes in this world since you withdrew yourself from it. If you were still young and at the height of your power, you would be unable to fight against this man and his organization. I am telling you this by way of warning. Do not attempt anything that will give them an excuse to take possession of the house." His voice had ceased to carry any hint of compassion. "If you persist in your wrongdoing—if you attempt to rob me, your son and rightful heir— you will find me ready to fight with them in defense of my rights!"

"I have lived too long!" There was a piteous note in the voice of Joseph. "I have lived to hear my own son threaten to join with my enemies!"

Had Basil been forced into playing eavesdropper when Aaron talked to the High Priest instead of perching behind his wicker basket at this moment, he would have been spared much unnecessary agitation of mind. As it was, he reached the conclusion immediately that the Zealots had one purpose in watching the house, and that was to lay their hands on him. He fell into such a panic of speculation and the making of such hasty plans for escape that he did not hear anything more that was said between father and son. He was aware that they continued to talk, that Aaron's voice was bitter and menacing, and that it was not until exhaustion made it impossible for Joseph to respond to the accusations of his son that the latter withdrew.

Basil waited until the lamp in Aaron's hands had receded down the passage leading to the residential wing. Then he made his way out of the Court of the Packers and slipped back through the darkness to his place of sanctuary. He was sure that it would remain sanctuary for a very few hours only. There was no way to leave the house; and if he did accomplish the seemingly impossible, where, then, could he go?

For the first time since he had last seen Helena that disturbing figure played no part in his thoughts for the balance of a sleepless night.

3

Luke was surprised the next morning to find himself stopped on reaching the house of Joseph. At one moment the space in front of the entrance was empty; the next, two men were between him and the door. They had materialized from nothing, or so it seemed; and they were dark and unfriendly and fiercely terse.

"Who are you?" demanded one, a man of short stature with the shoulders and arms of a gorilla. He spoke in Hebrew instead of Aramaic, and from this Luke judged him a Zealot. Most of the nationalist party had reverted to the use of the pure tongue of their forefathers, scorning what they called the mongrel language now used as the common means of communication throughout the East.

Luke understood Hebrew but could not speak it. He responded in Aramaic, "I see no reason for answering."

"There is a good reason." The short man glowered as he said this and produced a dagger of the kind known as a *conchar* from under his robe. After allowing the sunlight to glisten momentarily on the bright blade, he dropped it back out of sight. "That is the reason. A good one, my ancient friend, the very best of all. You will not be allowed to enter unless you convince us you have the right."

Luke was showing the effects of his long stay in the heat of Jerusalem. Much of his life had been spent in the open, on the sea and on the camel trains, in Greek towns that perched on lofty promontories and looked far down on the parched land along the coast; wherever, in fact, the beckoning finger of Jehovah had summoned Paul. Since coming to the Holy City, the suspicions and the constant tug of bitter wills had galled and

fretted his generous mind. His eyes were shadowed with care, his brow
had become endowed with a mass of new wrinkles, even his beard covered his chest in limpness and discouragement.

He answered in an impatient tone, "I am a physician."

"So." The guard studied him closely from head to foot. "The old man
inside is close to death. You can do nothing for him. Not all the medicines
in the world can give him an additional day of life." After a moment of
sultry silence he added, "And a good thing it is."

Nothing more was said for a moment, and then the guard burst out
with an abruptness which startled the visitor, "My name is Mijamin. Have
you heard of me? I think perhaps you have, old man." He seemed proud
of his identity and prepared to proclaim it to the whole world despite the
illegality of the part he was playing at the house of Joseph. "And you, my
bearded friend, are a Christian. I am so sure of it that I should send you
away with a clump on the ear and a warning never to show your face
hereabouts again. You are a poor-spirited lot, you Christians; ready to
bow the knee to Rome, to accept chains with a weak, slavering smile. That
is not the worst part of it. You are telling others that it is wrong to resist
the slavery of Rome. It is because of your teachings that we have failed to
bring the children of Israel into a solid and united body to resist the enemy
of our race."

His eyes had become red and angry. He flourished a dagger within a
few feet of Luke's face. "This fellow Paul is no better than an agent of
Rome, a spy, for all we know. He surely must die. And you, my sly gray-
beard, are one of those who walk behind Paul and do his bidding. Now
that I have had a chance to look you over thoroughly, I recognize you as
one of them. I am sorely tempted to take that old throat in my hands and
bring your existence to a fitting end."

"Leave be, Mijamin," said the other guard. "This one is a mild and
harmless creature. And his errand is to see the sick man inside. It is not in
our instructions to stop the likes of him."

The second guard, who was tall and thin to the point of emaciation, ran
a hand over the visitor's frame, finding nothing to create suspicion. "Be
quick about your errand," he grumbled. "And don't try to bring anything
away with you. If we see a bulge under your robe, we will let sunshine
between your ribs!"

It was with surprise that Luke found himself escorted to the room
opening off the Court of the Packers. It was hot and noisy there, the air

filled with the loud shouts of overseers, the screech of saws, the staccato rap of hammers. He sensed the reason behind the change, however, when his eyes lighted on the sheets covered with columns of figures that were strewn over the bed. Joseph was paying no attention to these reports now. The mound he raised under the one thin covering was pitifully small, and his eyes seemed enormous in the bony mask of his face.

"My good friend," said the sick man in a reedy whisper, "I am happy to see you once more. It may be I shall not see you again."

Luke did not follow any of the usual routine of medical ministration. No purpose could be served, he knew, in that way. As he took a seat beside the bed he said to himself, "Nothing but his will is keeping him alive."

The sick man made a gesture with one hand as though to draw something from under his pillow, but found his strength unequal to it.

"My son knows about the Cup," he whispered. "He was asking questions last night. And making threats. It must not be left in this house or they will get it when I die. I am no longer able to plan how it may be saved. In your hands, Luke, I place this sacred trust." The voice fell to such a low note that the physician had to hold his ear close to the moving lips to distinguish the words. "It is under the pillows. Take it—and God grant you find a way to keep it safe."

Luke ran an exploring hand under the pillow and encountered many objects: a roll of accounts, a bag of gold, a carved piece of ivory in the form of a cross, the phylactery that had been removed from the dying man's brow. Finally his fingers encountered the Cup and he drew it forth. The urgency that showed in Joseph's eyes caused him to drop it immediately out of sight in the folds of his robe.

Joseph's eyes then closed as though glad to rest. "I have kept my trust," he whispered.

Adam ben Asher had been told of Luke's presence in the house. He was waiting outside the door, his brows drawn into a deep furrow. "Well?" he demanded brusquely.

"I see no change," answered Luke. "No other man could continue to keep himself alive this way."

Adam nodded his head in pride. "Joseph of Arimathea has always been different from other men. And now he is different in his dying." He proceeded reluctantly with an explanation: "I took it upon myself yesterday to send word to his granddaughter and now I am afraid I made a mistake. Will she be delivered over to the Romans by these men outside? Because, of course, she will return at once."

"Yes," said Luke, "she will return."

"She cannot get here before tomorrow morning. Will my poor master live that long?"

"It is as God wills," said the physician.

4

Luke made his way at once to the dark hole where Basil was in hiding. He found the latter wrapping all his belongings and his tools together in a piece of cloth. The lamp had guttered down to a low point, but it was possible to see that his face wore a look of grave resolution.

"I am giving myself up," said Basil. "It is the only way."

"You are giving yourself up? Do you mean to the men who stand outside the house?"

Basil nodded his head slowly. "They are here to find me, to make sure I do not get away. I broke my promise. I went out, and I am sure I was seen and followed here. It is better now to end it at once. There is enough trouble in this house without having me here any longer." He knotted the top of the cloth with hands that were unsteady. "This is all my fault. I did not have the good sense to see that what you told me was true, that I was letting the evil side of me get the upper hand. No, it did not suit me to believe that. I was sure an evil spirit had taken possession of me. I was so sure of it that I—I went to Simon the Magician and asked to have it cast out."

Luke seated himself beside the table and watched him with eyes that had become deeply intent.

"You went to see Simon the Magician! When did you do that?"

"I am ashamed now of how I acted. I went to see him first the night of his performance. You thought I was returning here when we parted company. But I went back and made inquiries. I found he was staying with a Samaritan, one Kaukben, who is in trade here. I went to his house, but I did not see Simon then. I asked for his assistant, the girl who appeared on the platform with him. You see, I knew who she was. She had been a slave in my father's house in Antioch."

"You did not tell me at the time that you recognized the girl."

"No, I did not want you to know what I planned to do. I can see now that I behaved very badly."

"I wish, my son, you had consulted me before you took such a step. When did you see Simon?"

"Two days later. Helena had promised to arrange things for me."

"And what was the result?"

"I found he was no better than you had said." Basil spoke with a bitterness that was directed entirely at himself. "I believed at first he had great powers. But he is a trickster."

Luke regarded him with a smile that was sympathetic and kindly. "I know something of their methods," he said. "Was the vessel of water spilled?"

"Yes," answered Basil. "But I saw how it was done. There was a cord under the rug."

"So that is it! I have often wondered. I am glad, my boy, that your eyes have been opened in time. Perhaps it was well that you had to be convinced the man was a fraud. Now, I can see, you are most sincerely convinced of the truth. You know that the state of your mind is always due to how much you give in to the evil in you—the evil that is in all of us."

"The consequences of what I have done seem to be falling on others," said Basil. He proceeded to tell of the conversation he had overheard between Joseph and his son, putting special emphasis on the fact that the High Priest had been paying a member of the household staff for information. "Aaron is working against his father. The house is surrounded by armed men. And this has been brought about by my blindness and selfishness."

Luke listened with a frown, his hands busy replenishing the oil in the lamp. When the task was completed, he raised it close to Basil's face. "I can see you are quite serious about this," he said. "You are willing to assume the blame and the punishment, and that counts very strongly in your favor. Yes, I am sure all this will be set down fairly and fully by the angels up there beyond the clouds who keep the everlasting records in books of gold and ivory. But, my son, I am disposed to think you are magnifying the faults of which you have been guilty. The clash between Joseph and his son was part of a quarrel of long standing. I have been talking to Joseph, and he is convinced that Rub Samuel's men have been placed about the house for a different reason. He is sure they want to get their bloodstained hands on something very much more important than a young artist from Antioch." He reached into the umber-colored robe he was wearing over his tunic and produced the Cup. "He believes this is what they want."

With the utmost reverence Luke placed the Cup on the table, his eyes filled with awe and wonder.

"See!" he said, reaching out and touching Basil's shoulder. "There is a light about it! It is like a celestial beam from above. A beam sent by the Lord, Whose beloved Son lifted this Cup and Whose lips touched its rim."

It was true. In the semidarkness the Cup could be seen clearly, its outline plain to the eye, even the indentations and irregularities of the lip easily distinguishable. There was something strange about it, something unearthly, which made Basil feel that he stood on the threshold of another world.

His feet must have carried him over the threshold, for he knew immediately that he had gone a long way from this close and dark corner in the house of Joseph where he had existed so long. He found himself looking into a room with an open window facing the east. The sun had set and the early stars could be seen in the sky. A group of men sat about a long table, partaking of the paschal supper. Why he knew all this would have puzzled him ordinarily, but now he did not give the matter as much as a single thought. There were certain things about this scene that were as clear to him as though he had been able to see into their minds. A cup, this same Cup, because the light playing about it now had illuminated it then, stood in the center of the board. One of the things he knew was that the room was part of a humble little dwelling at the Wall of David.

"These men," he said to himself, "are the disciples of Jesus."

It was strange that there should be one spot over which a curtain had been drawn. He could not see the figure in the center of the group. That someone sat there was clear enough, for all eyes were turned that way and all talk was directed to the One who occupied this shrouded part of the scene. Basil said to himself in wonder: "Deborra told me that the face of Jesus would be hidden from me. And here is the proof of what she said. But why am I allowed to see so much, and to see it so clearly, if that which is most important of all is to be withheld from me?"

Luke reached out and gave his shoulder a shake. "Come!" he said. "It is to be expected that you would be bemused, but—have you any idea how long you have been looking? Many minutes, my son. And there is so much for us to do."

Basil brought himself back with an effort. His eyes remained fixed on the Cup, and he became aware of a new quality in it. "It looks lonely!" he whispered.

"Yes," agreed the physician sadly. "And that is not strange. There was a divine moment when it was clasped in His hands. It was passed about the circle and consecrated by the touch of those brave men. Thereafter it was kept for many years in a darkness where no eyes, friendly or hostile, could look upon it. And now it is released into a mad world where the memory of the Son of Man is spat upon, a world torn and unhappy and ripe for a harvest of blood. This Cup, which Jesus blessed, finds itself in a cruel place that has not yet taught itself to accept His gentle teachings. Yes, my son, it looks lonely; and well it might."

The light did not fade away as they talked. Instead it continued to glow about the Cup, a glow as beneficent as the laws Jesus had preached. They watched in silence for several moments longer, Luke more than half convinced that a heavenly hand, like the one that wrote words of doom on the walls of Belshazzar's palace, would materialize out of the darkness and snatch it away.

"Joseph is getting very close to the end," said Luke. "Perhaps the Lord will allow him to live until tomorrow, when the little granddaughter will return, but it is beyond nature for his flesh to keep any longer from dissolving back into clay. I have just left him, and he gave the Cup into my keeping, charging me to find the way of saving it from hostile hands. But how am I to do it? He was convinced that the hidden niche he had built for it was no longer safe. Where can I find a place that will serve better? It cannot be taken away from here. Everyone who leaves is searched."

They sat and discussed the problem for a long time, their eyes never leaving the Cup, their minds filled with the gravity of their responsibility and the fear that they would not prove equal to it.

"We cannot walk blindly to the one place within these walls where it could rest safely," declared Luke. "Not unless the Lord directs us; and I do not yet hear the inner Voice that sometimes tells me what I am to say or do. Must we find the solution ourselves?" He went down on his knees and began to pray. "O Lord, look down upon us. We do not know which way to turn in this difficulty. Tell us how we may keep this sacred Cup from falling into wicked hands."

After a moment of silence he rose from his knees. "If the Voice does not speak to me now," he said, "we will know that for some reason we are expected to find the answer ourselves."

If the Voice answered, it was in Basil's mind that it gave the much-desired response. The reason for this was clear enough; he was familiar with the interior of the house in a way that Luke was not.

"There is a way," he said doubtfully. "I hesitate to suggest it, for it may seem to you wrong and perhaps even sacrilegious."

"Tell me," urged Luke. "The precious minutes are being consumed while we sit here in doubt."

"In the room where the slaves have their meals," said Basil, "there are a number of cups similar to this. They are kept on an open shelf together. I cannot remember how many—half a dozen, I think. Who would notice if there was one more than usual?"

Luke sprang to his feet. "The Voice has spoken!" he exclaimed. "This, of course, is the way: the safest hiding place is one that is not a hiding place at all. Place the Cup in full view, and it will be as free from notice as a chameleon against a tree trunk."

A doubt had come into Basil's mind. "The other cups are quite similar to this. How could we be sure of picking it out later from the rest on the shelf?" Then a solution of this difficulty came into his mind. "The lip is irregular. It was carelessly turned in the making and it is possible that since—since it was last used pieces have been cut away. Would you allow me to place a mark on it by which it could always be told from the others?"

Luke had no doubts. "I am sure the Lord would regard anything you did with a lenient eye."

Basil reached out a hand to raise the Cup, then drew back and looked doubtfully at his companion. "Am I worthy to touch it?" he asked. "I had a strange feeling in my arm, as though something was holding me back."

Luke's face lighted up with a warm smile. "It may have been a test. That you think yourself unworthy is enough to make it right for you to touch it. Do not hesitate, my son."

Thus reassured, the young artist lifted it in his hands and studied the lip. It seemed now no different from any other drinking vessel of the same kind. It had been shaped in great haste and it was entirely without decoration. The light that had radiated from it before had departed.

Basil touched a broken section of the lip with one finger. "I think a mark could be placed here. Could it be a symbol; a small fish, perhaps? I have been told that Christians are called the Order of the Fish."

"The term was used for a time after the death of Jesus." Luke seemed disposed to pass this over quickly, as though he disapproved. "It has not been used much of recent years. Still, it might serve as you suggest."

"I shall do no more than hint at it."

Basil placed the bundle of his tools back on the table and selected from it a small chisel and a hammer. Placing the drinking vessel on the table, he set to work and in a very few minutes had succeeded in raising a small figure that had a suggestion of a fish about it.

"The Lord has guided your hand," declared Luke. "It looks like the flat fish of Galilee." He collected the shavings of the metal that had accumulated on the table. "These I shall keep. I shall treasure them as long as I live."

All doubt had left his face. His eyes had lighted up with a sense of confidence. The weariness that had been so noticeable when he arrived at the house of Joseph had gone; and this was not strange, for he was certain that he and his companion had been selected for a proof of divine guidance. "Tell me where this room is and I shall take it there. Without any hesitation I shall place it out where all eyes may see it, where any hand may reach out and touch it. I know that what we are doing is right."

CHAPTER XII

I

At noon on the following day Basil was roused from his uneasy musings by an outburst of shouting in the house. It came first from the slave quarters and then spread to other parts, increasing in volume all the time. His first thought was that the men of Rub Samuel had broken in, but on second consideration he discarded this explanation. There was a note to the tumult that had nothing to do with conflict; a triumphant note like the song of warriors returning from victory.

After it had continued for several minutes without showing any signs of abating, he found himself unable to remain any longer in concealment. Venturing out cautiously, he discovered that the warehouse wing was completely deserted. The shouting now came from the front section of the house. He proceeded in that direction along deserted corridors, becoming aware as he did so of a miracle that had been happening that morning. Into the heat and the haze and the dust of the city had come a breeze. It was not a great wind, it blew lightly and fitfully from the hills of the north; but small though it was, it was like a cool hand placed on a fevered brow. To the people of Jerusalem it would seem a benediction straight from Jehovah. The wide stone halls in the house of Joseph, raised high on their black pillars of basalt, had been opened to receive it. The hangings on the walls and the patterned curtains that masked the heavy doors swayed and billowed at its touch.

Finally he found himself in the close proximity of the main courtyard, and here a strange spectacle greeted his eye. The slaves were parading about the court and the adjacent halls. They marched three abreast and they were singing loudly, their heads thrown back as they sang, their eyes filled with exultation. Ebenezer was in the lead, capering the steps of the Dance of David, his arms crossed behind his bent back and his fingers twitching in imitation of the orders he received from his master.

Basil recognized the song they were singing. It was known as the Unchaining.

"No more of labor in the fields, no swish of whip, no awl-pierced ears;
No longer need to wait in pain the coming year of Jubilee;
No weeping for the wife long lost, the children wrested from one's arms;
We are free, O Lord above us, we are free!"

Basil had been told that this was the oldest of all chants, that it had been sung for the first time when the children of Israel crossed the sands of the Red Sea. Having heard the story of the Crossing from Deborra, he realized that the Unchaining could not have been sung at that early day. The Israelites had been held in Egypt in a state of perpetual slavery, and it had not been necessary then, as it was now, for a life slave to have awl-pierced ears; nor had the year of Jubilee been conceived, the recurring seventh year when all slaves of Jewish birth received their freedom. Ancient the song was, however, and Basil found himself humming in concert as he watched the marchers. He could appreciate how they felt.

"This is what Deborra promised them that day," he said to himself. "Joseph has freed his slaves!"

He became aware then of the face of Aaron staring down into the court from an upper window. It did not require more than one glance at the bleak and antagonistic expression of the latter to realize that the son of the house was bitterly opposed to the step his father had taken.

Among the spectators was Adam ben Asher. He stood beside Luke and seemed almost as much out of sympathy with the spectacle as Aaron himself. He glowered at the antics of Ebenezer and said in an impatient mutter: "And now what will they do? Will they expect to find work in a city where half the people starve for bread? Soon they will come back, begging for their chains, offering their ears to the piercing of the awl."

And then something occurred that seemed to Basil a second miracle. Deborra appeared in the front entrance, which had been opened to catch the vagrant breeze. She was accompanied by a train of dusty, weary servants. Some had arms filled with bundles of clothing. One, a brawny black boy with a good-natured face under a red turban, was carrying the *kinnor* of his young mistress, an instrument of many strings made of beautifully carved *algum* wood. Another held over her head a cover made of woven reeds as a protection against the fierce assault of the midday sun. Hovering on the edge of the group were an intent pair who, clearly, were there on Rub Samuel's orders.

Over a white linen tunic Deborra was wearing an outer garment of yellow silk with black embroidered bands. Her turban, puffed out on both sides to provide protection against the heat, was of a somewhat deeper shade of yellow with a rich tinge of the orange. The effect was completely becoming and, in spite of the weariness of the long journey that manifested itself in shadows about her eyes, she suggested the freshness of a daffodil. There was no consciousness of this in her manner. She was looking about her with the most intense anxiety. When her eyes rested on Luke and Adam advancing to greet her she questioned them in a whisper of passionate supplication.

"Am I in time? Is my grandfather still alive?"

Luke answered with a grave nod. "He is alive. But you must be reconciled to this: that he has clung to existence only in the hope of seeing you again and that now his hold is weak. We must be honest with you, my child. It is—a matter of hours."

"Let me go to him at once."

Basil watched her as she followed Luke down the hall toward the room where Joseph had elected to spend his last days. She looked neither to right nor left, and it was clear that she had one thought only in her mind. He followed at a safe distance when she had passed and saw her pause at the door to ask, "Why is he here?"

"It was his wish."

It became apparent then that the clarity of mind that Joseph had exacted of himself had now deserted him. Through the open door they could hear him talking in a feverish monotone. He had slipped away from the safe moorings of the present and had reached the choppy waters of the past. " 'Behold, Lord, the half of my goods I give to the poor.' Even as I, Zaccheus, even as I; though truly not to the extent of half, for I have been wise in trade and much profit have I made. Generously have I given of what I earned, even though I *followed afar off*. Did I err in not coming to the fire and sitting myself down there as Peter, Peter of the high heart, did?" The voice fell off into more incoherence at this, and they could hear him muttering of Peter and John and Paul and Andrew. He kept coming back to the thought that seemed to weigh on his mind, the part he had played in the great drama. "It was not fear. I did not hold back because of that. Is it not known to all men that I went to Pontius Pilate and asked of him the body of Jesus? What hands were they that touched the holes in His feet and the great wound in His side? Mine, for I took the body down from the cross. It was in my sepulcher that the body lay. It was from my sepulcher, which was hewn in stone, that Jesus came forth. It was stone of mine that was rolled away, and it was there that the two men in shining garments stood. It was not vouchsafed me to see Him, but truly I wrought so that what He had prophesied might come to pass."

"Grandfather!" said Deborra.

The sick voice stopped. There was a moment of silence and then Joseph said: "Deborra! It is you! You have come back."

"Yes, Grandfather."

"I thank thee, O Lord, for granting me this wish of my heart. Now I am happy and at peace. I knew you would come, my child, if I—if I did not give in. It has been hard. I had to be firm with this angel who sits beside me and keeps saying that I have been expected long since. But now you are here, my Deborra, and I may say to the angel, 'Have your way at last. Lead on, I am ready.'"

2

Adam ben Asher dropped a hand on the shoulder of Benjie the Asker, who had been a witness to Deborra's return. "You will come with me," he said.

He led the way to a small room not far from the Court of the Packers that served him as a personal office. It was filled with a curious collection of articles. In addition to many dusty rolls on which trade records were kept, there were maps of the camel trails and the routes of sea navigation, enough of them to fill all the wall space. The floor was so littered with camel equipment that it was hard for Benjie to find standing room.

"I heard today," said Adam, "that someone had been selling information to Ananias, and then I remembered passing the house of the High Priest and seeing one of our men come out. This happened a few days ago, and I thought at the time it was strange. Now I think it highly suspicious. Who was it I saw, Benjie the Asker? It was you."

"I was there," declared Benjie easily. "I was making a call on some of the servants of Ananias. In quest of information."

He was wearing a shirt of black linen and over this a rust-colored garment. Adam made a sudden pounce at him and raised the shirt from around his waist. This revealed a hairy expanse of body and a wide belt to which a flat leather purse was attached. Despite squeals of protest from its owner, Adam opened the purse and found it well stuffed with coins.

"Gold!" he cried. "It is as I thought. The gold of Ananias the High Priest. *Heu-heu!* Benjie the Asker has become Benjie the Babbler, Benjie the Teller, Benjie the Two-faced!" He thumped with both fists on the puny shoulders of the Asker. "This is the traitor. This is the base-born one who sells everything he knows to the man in the Temple! You have received much more than thirty pieces of silver, thou betrayer of friends, thou seller of secrets not thy own."

Benjie tried to wriggle free of the hold on his shoulders. "I have taken pay in both hands instead of one," he acknowledged sulkily. "Can a poor man earn enough with one hand in Jerusalem to feed a large family? Joseph has paid me in one, Ananias in the other. Is it a crime?"

Adam proceeded to manhandle the unrepentant seller of information. He slapped him on each cheek, he poked knuckles into his eyes, he beat him vigorously on the chest with a sound like the strident rat-tat of the *tof,* the frame drum of the Jews. Then he took him by both shoulders and shook him until the knees of the miscreant went limp and his teeth chattered.

"Is it a crime?" cried Adam. "It is the worst of crimes. You, the jackal with twenty pairs of ears and a hundred eyes, told the High Priest that it was Deborra who threw the stone at the Roman——"

"No, no!" exclaimed Benjie. "I told him nothing about the little lady of the house. I could never do anything to hurt her. That I swear to you by the feet of all the prophets, by the ashes of the Red Heifer!"

Adam's grip on his shoulders loosened a trifle. "If I could believe that, I might be persuaded to spare your life. But I declare to you now that I shall squeeze your throat until your face turns black and your breath stops if any harm comes to her."

"Adam, have pity on me!" cried Benjie. "I cannot resist the feel of gold on the palms of my hands. It has such a sweet touch. I have broken faith because of it. I have sold my friends. I shall never see the face of my Master. Adam, Adam, I cannot sleep at night through thinking of it!"

Adam looked at him with a hint of understanding in his flat gray eyes. "There can be no excuse for what you have done, but I can feel sorry for you, O Benjamin who deserves to wear a coat of one color only, the deep scarlet of shame." As he spoke he continued to administer sharp physical attentions, a vigorous rumpling of the hair, a kneading of knuckles in the hollow of the neck, a succession of slaps with the flat of the hand. "Yes, I feel a great deal of compassion for you." The ribs of his victim resounded to the tattoo he proceeded to play on them.

Benjie cried breathlessly: "I do not wish to die because of your pity."

"I must have from you," declared Adam, "a full record of the information you have sold to Ananias. If you will do this, and so make it possible for us to protect ourselves, I shall spare you the full punishment I had intended for you. Are you prepared to tell me everything?"

"Yes!" affirmed the Asker eagerly. "I am ready to tell you every piece of news I took to that man in the Temple with the big belly and the frog eyes." He cringed away from the great callused hands of the caravan leader. "I will do more than that. I will tell you something that you should know at once if you are to avert a great calamity."

"Heu-heu!" exclaimed Adam. "Now we have cracked the shell and come to the rich kernel of the nut."

"The instant my old master dies," said Benjie, dropping his voice, "Aaron will give a signal from the window of his room and the men of the Mar will break into the house. They will let no one leave until they have found the Cup! Aaron did not agree to this at first. He made other promises, but Ananias was not satisfied, so Aaron has given in and they will have a free hand."

Adam gave him a final shake and let him go. He said, walking to the door with such vigorous strides that he scattered the accumulations of equipment that stood in his way, "You may have redeemed yourself for the harm you did before."

"And now," said Benjie, "there is another matter of which I shall tell you, the matter of an inheritance——"

3

An hour passed after Deborra entered her grandfather's room and closed the door behind her. Adam ben Asher, having made certain necessary arrangements, paced about the hall, keeping his eyes fixed on the heavy oak barrier behind which his old master was spending his last moments. Luke went to the sanctuary and there found Basil hard at work on the design of the frame for the Chalice. The excitements of the morning had proven a stimulus, and he was making progress by the flickering light of the lamp.

The physician proceeded to tell him of the situation that had developed as a result of the funds held by the Antioch banker. "Aaron will sail for Antioch to claim the money as soon as his father's body has been laid in the sepulcher," he said. "Adam is to take Deborra by land. It will be a race, a camel train against the sails of the ship. The camels they will use belong to Adam. Knowing that Aaron will not keep him a single hour after Joseph's death, he has been secretly buying them for the house he will set up in opposition. I am told he has acquired the strongest and fastest camels in the whole world. In spite of his bark, which I allow is sharp and loud, Adam has a great heart. He is prepared to drive this fine fleet to the utmost in the race."

Basil had suspended work to listen. He asked now when Adam would start.

"Within an hour of Joseph's death. So much depends on getting to Antioch first that Deborra will not stay for the burial. It will almost break her heart not to follow her grandfather to the grave, but she understands the urgency and she is ready. You, my son," went on Luke after a moment, "will not be left to the mercies of the dagger men. You are to leave the house with the camel train."

"But how will I get by the guards around the house?"

"There is a plan. I cannot explain it now."

Basil motioned to the clay model on which he was working. "Am I to go on with this?"

"Of course. Joseph has spoken to me several times of his confidence in you and his desire to have you finish the Chalice. He has been so concerned about it that he has kept a bag of gold under his pillow for the purpose. Deborra will bring it with her."

Basil laid his work aside and threw a damp cloth over it. "And what of you?" he asked. "Do you go with us? The thought of separation from you is one I cannot abide. You have been to me everything my father was before he died. Nay, you have been much more, for you have given me spiritual guidance. I feel the future will be blank without you—without your kindness, your help and encouragement."

The celebration of the slaves had ended with the arrival of Deborra, but for a time thereafter sounds of activity had been noticeable about the house. Now a complete silence reigned over the great establishment, a silence filled with the intensity of grief. His people waited in sorrow for the word that Joseph of Arimathea had come to the end of his long days. There was consciousness of this in the low tone of voice Luke employed in answering.

"What you have said makes me very happy, my son. I am going with you. Paul is to be sent to Caesarea to be tried before Felix. My place is by his side, but it will be a long time before he is led out from his cell for the hearing. A year at least, we are told."

"What is to be done about the Cup?" asked Basil anxiously.

"It has been put in my charge and I shall make it my only care until we have taken it to a place where no hostile hands may touch it." Luke continued to speak with sudden emphasis. "Paul is the voice of Christianity. He is carrying the teachings of Jesus to the whole world. He has always had his own group of helpers about him, but he could have done it all himself. We who have followed the trails of conversion with him have always known that he did not need us—Matthew or Mark or Luke, or any of the others. He can stand alone, that man of iron and fire. I, Luke, of my own free choice, shall stand beside him when his moment of trial comes. I earnestly hope to share in whatever his fate may be. But first there is the Cup to be taken care of, this one great reminder that Jesus came to us in the guise of a man, this sublime relic that someday may be so important to the faith. If we can get it out of this house, and out of Jerusalem, I shall go on with it to Antioch, where it may be kept in full safety."

Luke then nodded his head at Basil and smiled warmly. "You have been behaving with discretion and courage. You saved Deborra from the consequences of her rashness, and since then you have been enduring great hardships without complaint. The one slip you made can easily be forgiven in the light of what you have done. I am not acquiring in my old age the prophetic vision, but this I do perceive—that your prospects are pleasant and bright. There is something back of what I am saying; something that I have no right to divulge."

Basil looked at his hands, which were black and callused from the work he had been doing. "If I am to go with them, I must prepare myself. Would it be safe for me to go now to the washroom? I have fallen into the habit of waiting until after midnight, when no one could see me." He shook his head in despair. "Living in this dark hole has made it impossible to keep myself clean. Could I have something better than the rough soap in the slave quarters? It makes little impression on my skin."

The long confinement had done more than blacken his hands. It had put hollows under his cheekbones. There was the hint of a stoop in his shoulders owing to the low ceiling of the room. He looked weary of body and depressed in spirits. Luke studied him thoughtfully.

"There seems small need for concealment now," said the latter after a moment. "It will be safe for you to return to the room you used before, and I will see there is plenty of hot water for you. While you bathe I will find what can be done about suitable clothes."

"I have only the *colobium* in addition to what I wear. I should not speak of it with disrespect, for it is the badge of my freedom."

"But a somewhat meager garment," amended Luke, measuring him with his eyes. "And the material is of the plainest. I think we shall have to get something better."

CHAPTER XIII

I

LUKE AND HIS YOUNG PROTÉGÉ, on their way to the room the latter had occupied before, visited the dining hall of the servants. They found it, to their surprise, the scene of considerable activity. The former slaves, who seemed content to remain in the house in the capacity of free servants, were decorating the walls with midsummer flowers, the red of poppies, the yellow of the ranunculus, the white of the earliest wild cyclamen that were being found around the edges of the Mount of Olives and in the Valley of Hinnom. Candelabra of many branches had been placed in the corners and were being stocked with the fat candles of beeswax which the Romans had introduced into the country. At one end the women were erecting a canopy with rolls of white ribbon and were achieving something that bore a resemblance to a pond lily.

The two men did not pause to speculate on the meaning of these preparations. Their eyes went anxiously to the wall where the drinking cups were kept in full view.

"It is there," said Luke. "In the exact position where I placed it. No one has touched it. Is it not strange that now it looks no different from the others?"

Half an hour later Basil emerged from a steaming bath. He was refreshed in body and somewhat more composed in spirit. His hands were white from vigorous and sustained scrubbing. He looked at them with satisfaction and said to himself, "Now I may feel some pride in myself again."

Slipping the thin *colobium* over his shoulders, he walked to a window and looked out into the glare of early afternoon. Immediately beneath him he could see the spot where he had stood with Deborra after their mad scramble through the Valley of the Cheesemakers.

"I knew I was falling in love with her," he said to himself. "From the moment she threw the stone I began to see her in a new light. She was no longer just a young girl in the house with a ring of keys in her hands. She had shown a high spirit. No wood sprite ever ran with more grace. As we faced each other, her eyes were shining, her cheeks were flushed, she was lovely and eager and very sweet." A conviction took form in his mind. "If I had declared myself then, she would have said yes to me."

But almost immediately after that had come his meetings with Helena, and now he was utterly confused and unhappy. Why could he not banish the dark eyes of the magician's assistant from his mind as thoroughly as he had rid himself of his belief that the evil in him was due to the presence of an alien spirit? It should not be difficult, because he saw matters in a clear enough light to realize that there was something furtive in his concern for the slave girl who had run away from the house of Ignatius. He was ashamed of the desires she roused in him, but they persisted nevertheless.

"It's as though I had been drugged with a love potion," he thought. This brought up a memory of the cup of wine he had imbibed so freely before Simon appeared on the scene and which had affected him in curious ways; but he dismissed immediately the possibility that it had any connection with the present state of his feelings. "I must not pamper my conscience a second time. The evil in me is not due to outside influences. I must be honest; it is a part of myself."

Perhaps Deborra had found reason to forget that memorable moment when they had paused on the lip of the valley. She had thought only of her grandfather on her return an hour before. That, however, was natural enough; for grief is a consuming emotion, great enough to banish all others, because it is concerned with the irrevocable. Not a single glance had she cast about her in search of him as she came through the open door and traversed the long hall.

Luke returned to the room with a bundle of clothing, which he placed on the bed.

"I hope they will fit you," he said. "Try them at once, for time presses on us. There is much to be done while Joseph still lives."

Basil lifted the clothing. "This is handsome," he said, feeling in his hands the cool linen of the tunic.

"I will explain about this raiment as you dress. There was a time when

Joseph was certain he would never be blessed with a child." In his youth Luke had been a teller of stories in the market places of Antioch, and he fell readily again into the tricks of his old trade. "He had no children, and the Lord Jehovah did not seem disposed to bless Gael, his wife, with fruitfulness. So he began to look about him for a son to adopt, even as your father did. His choice fell finally on Stephen, the son of Shaphat, a dealer in leather and a poor man. Stephen was fifteen, a tall youth with a light in his eye, a skilled finger on the strings of the harp, a voice sweet and full; a young David, as you see, with some of the promise of the shepherd boy Samuel selected from among the sons of Jesse. Joseph never acted on impulse, and he had seen much of the boy before he made his choice and he had come to love him. He began to lay away gifts against the day of the legal adoption. There was the *kinnor* that Deborra uses, thinking it her very own and not knowing it had been intended for someone else. The merchant who sold it to Joseph swore by all his heathen gods that the strings had known no touch save the fingers of a king long since dead, in the East. There were also clothes of a rare fineness.

"But Shaphat had known days of adversity and had found it necessary to raise his family in Beth-Jeshimoth, which is called the Place of the Desert. Here it is so hot that the sap of life burns out early. Stephen had never recovered from this, and there was always a flush in his cheeks and he was as taut of spirit as the strings of the *kinnor*. Before the day of the adoption he was dead. Joseph mourned for him sadly and long; and it was then that the Lord, Who is above everything a just God, relented and saw to it that a new life stirred in the womb of Gael. Aaron was born, and his coming brought peace of mind to Joseph. But he never forgot the tall Stephen who might have been his son, and he laid away the clothes in camphor and he saw to it that they were watched and kept in perfect preservation. He never spoke of Stephen thereafter, and I do not think that either Aaron or Deborra has known anything of him. But before his last illness closed on him Joseph told me that, inasmuch as you were a son by adoption also, and because you stirred in his mind some memories of the fine young Stephen, he wished you to have the clothes, so that finally they would serve some part at least of the purpose for which they had been made.

"And so," concluded Luke, "they are yours. I think it desirable that you wear them today."

Basil put on the white linen tunic and over that the middle garment, which was a marvelous garment indeed. It was made of the finest and heaviest of silk and it was in two parts. The upper part was a jacket that fitted snugly over the shoulders and arms and was embroidered on the breast in gold thread with an eagle clutching a serpent in its mouth, the sign of the tribe of Dan, to which Shaphat had belonged. The lower part was a skirt, bound tightly at the waist and falling just below the knees, and made of the rarest of all colors, blue. It was a color hard to obtain with the dyes in use, and so people had to content themselves with purples, reds, and yellows; but the skilled hands that had woven this piece of material had caught by some happy chance the very finest shade, a blue darker than the deepest tones of the sky and richer than the corn-flower or lupine. Along the hem was a fringe of golden thread.

The sandals were attached to long pads of leather that had been of the same shade of blue originally. These extended to the knee and were enriched with embossed threads of gold carrying in miniature the design of the eagle and serpent. The leather had mellowed to a soft haze of color throughout the years. Strapping the pads about his calves, Basil ran his fingers with a feeling almost of reverence over the soft leather, being strongly drawn always to things of beauty.

It might have been expected that, attired in such splendor, he would exhibit some traits of pride. But the cool of the linen on his skin and a consciousness of the fineness of the outer garments gave him instead a feeling of humility. In donning the clothes he seemed to have become a part of the family of Joseph and to have taken on obligations that would have belonged to the Stephen for whom they had been designed. He felt very clearly a responsibility in the matter of Deborra. Stephen would have protected her. He would have made himself a buckler between her and all evil.

"Now you see yourself with an open eye," he thought. "You are not worthy of her. You have evil in you that you seem incapable of con-trolling."

"The clothes fit you well," declared Luke, nodding his head with satis-faction.

"I wish," said Basil, "that they did not make me so well aware of my shortcomings."

On their way to the airy corner of the great house where Deborra's rooms were located, they passed a door before which Ebenezer was standing guard. He gave them a reassuring nod of his bald and yellowed head. "He is deep in documents and has no suspicions as yet. A few moments ago he did come to the door and say, 'Is not the house very quiet?' I answered him, 'All are mourning the inevitable.' 'Why are you here? Are you not a free man?' I answered, 'Yes, I am a free man, but I am also a man of habit. Have you commands for me?' He shook his head and frowned. 'I shall never have commands for *you.*' And then he went back and closed the door."

The main room in Deborra's quarters was filled with maidservants who were bustling about with great heaps of clothing in their arms and so much excitement in their minds that an elderly woman, clutching a piece of parchment importantly, had to keep admonishing them. "Sarah, come hither!" she would say. Or, "Marianne, have your feet gone to sleep? Hurry, child!"

To spare them the discomfort of all this confusion, the two visitors were shown into a smaller room, which contained the bed of the lady of the house. It was a small bed and it looked cool and virginal in the modesty of a corner. Basil, feeling that more than a single glance would be a profanation, turned his back and looked out a window that afforded him a full view of the white splendor of the Temple. He heard Luke leave, but he did not know that Deborra had entered until she spoke.

"Basil! I—I am back from the exile into which I was sent because of my folly."

He turned slowly. Deborra, he saw, had been yielding to her feelings, because there was a hint of redness about her eyes. She had striven to repair the ravages of grief, however, and she even had a smile for him as they faced each other.

She was in a snow-white simplicity of raiment that did not suggest readiness for immediate travel. This surprised him, particularly when he noticed that her hair was hanging freely on her shoulders. Although the dress was modest, it allowed her arms to show. They were white and rounded with the sweetness of youth. Her sandals were thin, with delicate bands of silk as white as the feet they clasped.

"You look well," she said when he failed to find the words of greeting he sought. "Such a beautiful blue you are wearing! I envy you. I have been told I look well in blue, but I have never worn anything so fine as that."

She was carrying a cloth bag in one hand, tied rather daintily with yellow ribbon. This she now held out to him. When he took it from her he knew from the feel and the weight of it that it was filled with money.

"Grandfather kept it under his pillow," she said. "It is to pay for the making of the Chalice."

He could tell that the bag contained enough to pay for his travels and leave him an ample reward as well. Such a feeling of exultation swept over him that he wanted to toss it into the air.

"This is the first money I have had in over two years," he said. "I cannot tell you what a new sense of freedom it gives me. I am indeed my own man now."

She seemed to forget her grief for a moment and even to share his mood. A smile lighted up her eyes. It was for a few moments only, however. A look of intense gravity succeeded. Yielding then to an emotion that could be nothing but panic, she covered her face with her hands.

"Basil, Basil, how am I to say it!"

"What is it you wish to say?"

She raised her eyes with a suggestion of almost desperate courage. "I think it would be kind if you—if you would turn your back. That would make it easier for me." When he had complied with her wish by turning around so completely that she could see nothing but the back of his head and the gold-fringed blue outer cloak, she still hesitated. "I cannot find the words. Have you any idea of what I must say to you? No, you could not know. It was promised that you would be given no hint." Then she caught her breath like a swimmer before plunging into cold water. "Basil, will you be my husband?"

For a moment he was incapable of any reaction save one of surprise. Then he was assailed by a feeling of alarm, of fear for the ambitious plans that had filled his head since his last talk with Helena. If he married Deborra and settled down in Jerusalem, or wherever she might prefer, what chance would he have to make a place for himself in the world of art? Would it be possible for him to develop still further the perceptiveness of his mind and the skill of his hands?

Following this hasty reaction came other thoughts. He was torn by conflicting loyalties. He owed so much to Deborra and her family that he could never pay the debt. To them he owed his liberty and his selection to make the Chalice. To Deborra he was indebted in less tangible ways; for her immediate sympathy, her understanding, her comradeship. He had liked her from the first moment, and this had been tending inevitably to love. When they stood together on the crest of the valley after their escape from the Roman officers, it had seemed to both of them that love had come, that thenceforward their feet would tread the same path.

Then he had seen Helena and had become aware of two things, that his feelings were not so far committed that he could be unaware of all other women, and that he was deeply obligated to her also. The service she had rendered him in sending the note of warning could not be overlooked, nor could he forget the picture she had spread before him of what life in Rome could be. She had conceived plans for him in which she expected to play some part. He had promised to meet her in Rome. Here, then, was another loyalty to be considered.

These thoughts, which take so long in setting down, consumed the briefest possible time in passing through his mind. They had caused him to pause, nonetheless; and in such a situation the shortest delay can be cause for doubt and distress. Basil was perhaps unaware that his decision was not an instant one, that he had delayed on the brink to look back. His decision, however, was the only thinkable one in view of his ties to the family of Joseph and the relationship that had grown up between himself and Deborra.

"May I turn now?" he asked.

"Yes." A change could be noted in Deborra's voice. Something had gone out of it. Some of the spontaneity. She had not failed to notice his hesitation and she was wondering, with a dismay that was frightening because unexpected, what had caused it. "Yes, Basil. I—I have managed to say it. And now we must talk."

He turned about. Her eyes had been fixed on the floor, but she raised them at once and studied his face. Why? they asked. Why did you hesitate? Have I been taking too much for granted?

"I am—I am deeply honored," he said. His voice was quiet, even formal. There was another pause, an almost imperceptible one. Was it because some of his doubts still persisted? "I have not been in a position to propose marriage to you. It is doubtful if I ever would be. And so I am happy that you have spoken."

She seemed to stand on tiptoe in her desire to look closely into his eyes. Her head was tilted upward and her hands were clasped tightly together. "Oh, Basil, Basil!" she said. "Are you sure? Are you quite sure?"

He took her closely interlocked fingers in his hands and smiled down at her. It was on the tip of his tongue to say, "Yes, I am quite sure." But the intensity of her eyes caused him to stop. Could he be anything but completely honest? His smile changed to a puzzled frown.

"We are deciding the whole course of our lives," she said. "We must be so very sure."

His frown deepened until a crease appeared between his dark brows. "I am at a loss," he declared. "The Christian code is very strict. I do not understand it fully. If I obeyed it, as I am desirous of doing, would it be necessary for me to tell you everything that is in my mind?"

Her eyes filled with troubled thought and she allowed them to fall. "Because what I have done is so unusual, so unnatural, I am doubly sensitive. And when you hesitated, I did not know what to think—— Are there things you should tell me?"

"Perhaps," he said unhappily. "But I am not sure. It is very strict, this code of yours. I think it is good, but I do not know what it demands of me."

Deborra began to speak slowly and with obvious reluctance. "I, too, am at a loss. Doubts that I do not understand have come up between us. Perhaps I should speak of something I had intended to keep locked up in my own heart." She drew back and clasped her hands tightly together again. "As soon as I arrived back, there was a meeting to decide what steps should be taken. The advisability of an immediate marriage for me was agreed upon. I said that I—would speak to you."

"I am an ex-slave, a freedman," said Basil.

Deborra flamed to his defense. "You were born a citizen of Rome and sold into slavery through a great injustice. You have been restored to your standing, and in Antioch they think well of you and have nothing but sympathy for you."

She seemed reluctant about telling the rest. "There were two with me, Grandfather being too ill to take any part. One of them approved my choice at once. That was Luke. The other had nothing to say, but after the meeting he came to me and said he did not approve. There was something, he said, that I should know. You had been kept under watch and so it was known you had left the house three times. He meant to continue and tell me everything he knew, but I would not let him." She looked up at him with stormy eyes. "I told him I would not listen to another word! That I would not believe any ill of you!"

"What he told you was true." Basil spoke in a low tone. "They had given me a dark hole in the warehouse as a hiding place. I was warned not to venture out, but I disobeyed them. Three times, as he said. Twice in the night and once during the day. I knew it would lead to serious trouble if I were caught, but I felt that I had to go." He paused and seemed at a loss as to what he must tell. "Each time it was to see Helena, the girl who assists Simon the Magician."

She looked incredulous. It was clear she had not expected to hear anything like this. There was a long moment of silence. "I have heard of her," said Deborra finally. "It is said she is—quite lovely to look at."

"She had been a slave in my father's house in Antioch. Soon after I was adopted she ran away and I heard nothing more of her until I saw her on the platform with Simon. I went to the Gymnasium with Luke and I recognized her as soon as she appeared." He found now that he had a deep reluctance to tell her the reason for the two visits he had paid to the House of Kaukben. "It is a long story, Deborra, and I will not take time to tell you about it now. I had good reason for going to see her, and this much I will say: it was not interest in her that took me there. She told me then that she had sent me the note of warning about the intentions of Linus. I felt deeply indebted to her. She urged me to make my plans for living in Rome because there would be such opportunities for me there. It was agreed between us that I would see her when I reached Rome." He paused again. "If I hesitated before answering you, it was because of this."

She asked in a voice that seemed drained of all feeling: "Are you in love with her? Is that what you are trying to tell me?"

Basil shook his head. "I am not in love with her. But I think now that I must tell you she has been much in my mind."

Neither of them seemed able to break the silence that fell between them. Deborra was thinking: "He says he does not love her. But—but I wonder. I can be sure of one thing now: he does not love me." Basil, thoroughly miserable and at the same time angry with himself, found nothing further to say.

The maidservant Sarah came into the room with a message on her lips. It had to do with the rapid passage of time and the need to hurry with the many things that remained to be done. Something in their attitude, however, served to warn her that they must not be interrupted. They stood near the open door opening on the balcony, their faces taut with emotion, their eyes so intent on each other that they were completely unaware of her arrival in the room. They were ignorant that the sun had climbed high enough into the sky to shine down directly on them with a furious intensity. The insects in the trees below were droning sleepily and incessantly.

Sarah asked herself, "What is disturbing them, these two pretty young ones?" She had no doubt that it was something most serious; and after a moment she turned silently and left the room, her message undelivered.

It was Deborra who broke the silence. "Basil, do you know how hard it was to ask you to marry me? And now I must say something more that will be—quite as hard for me."

She walked to the door that gave access to the balcony. For several moments she leaned against it, gazing out into the brilliant, glittering sunlight. When she turned back, her mood had changed. Her manner had become composed, her voice normal in tone. She even smiled. "My grandfather always said that I took after him in many ways. I think that I do. I knew how his mind worked and so I am sure what advice he would have given us at this moment. He would have said: 'My children, this money was saved and laid aside so that my assistance to the impoverished little church of our Lord Jesus could be continued after my death. It is necessary for you to see that my wishes are carried out.' Yes, he would have said that. And now, Basil, I find I must say the other thing that is going to be so hard. I cannot suggest marriage to anyone else. Not—not now. I cannot humble myself a second time. And we must hurry in making up our minds because there is so little time. I think that Grandfather would suggest as the only solution, since between us we have so many doubts, a marriage of—of form only. It is not at all unusual. With us many marriages begin that way. It may be"—she was watching him intently— "that you would find this a more acceptable way."

"Deborra," said Basil earnestly, "I will be proud to marry you. I will marry you on whatever terms you wish. Any conditions you make will be acceptable to me. I shall strive hard never to cause you trouble or pain."

"If we marry, will you think it necessary to keep your promise and see this—this woman when you are in Rome?"

He shook his head. "If it is your wish, I shall never see her again. That I promise."

"Then," she said after a moment and in a low tone, "it is settled."

With the decision made, Basil realized that he had found relief in promising not to see Helena again. He hoped this would make it possible for him to banish her from his mind completely. It might even be that he and Deborra would regain the mood they had shared as they stood together that day on the crest of the valley.

It became apparent to him at once, however, that any such happy development as that was impossible. Deborra's attitude had changed. She was no longer composed, as when she had spoken of the qualities she shared with her grandfather. She was pale and her eyes had a withdrawn look. There was no suggestion about her that she would welcome a return to a better understanding between them.

"I owe you thanks," she said in a voice as devoid of feeling as her eyes. "You have been honest with me—and very kind."

"No, I have not been kind," answered Basil unhappily.

After a moment she said: "It will be necessary for the ceremony to take place at once. You have noticed, no doubt, that I came dressed for it."

3

Adam ben Asher was standing at the entrance when Luke reached the dining hall of the servants. Under brows as black as a thunderstorm his eyes were as nervously active as a sparking fire.

"The people we sent for are beginning to arrive," he said in an undertone. "They are standing outside. The Mar's men are worried. They are buzzing about like horseflies." He paused and then burst out angrily: "What would you have to say about a man of Gaza who still expected the gates that Samson carried away on his shoulders to be returned at this late day? You would call him a fool, a credulous fool. I am as stupid as that, I think. I, Adam ben Asher!"

The informality of the wedding of Deborra and Basil was in keeping with the tradition of simplicity that governed the marriage rites. Only six members of the household were admitted as witnesses, and the rest were under the most stern injunction to remain in their rooms. The chosen six stood in a line facing the canopy when Deborra entered and took her stand there. She had added a long veil to her costume, and it was impossible for Basil, when he joined her, to see anything of her face.

Uzziel, the overseer, who was an elder of the church, stood with them under the canopy, his face damp with excitement and his fingers tightly locked about the silver vessel that was to serve as the Cup of the Blessing. They repeated in turn the *Berchath Nissuin,* Basil stumbling over the unfamiliar words and having to be prompted throughout. Deborra's reading of the lines was clear and steady, although her voice seemed toneless. Uzziel then invoked the benediction and frowned at the bridegroom when he did not proceed at once to the next step.

"It is customary," he said in a severe tone, "to raise the veil of the bride." Then he added in a whisper, "Must I explain also that you are expected to utter a cry of joy when your eyes rest on the face of the one who will henceforth share your joys and sorrows?"

Basil raised the veil, but the exclamation he gave was a poor imitation of the joyousness that tradition demanded. The pallor of the bride was startling and the unhappiness he saw in her eyes made such pretense impossible.

"At this point," said Uzziel, clearing his throat importantly, "it is usual for the marriage contract to be read aloud. As there has been no opportunity to prepare one, we proceed to the concluding rite, the sharing of all present in a cup of wine."

Adam ben Asher had not moved from his post near the door. If there had been any eyes to see it would have been clear that his dark face was reflecting openly all the emotions that consumed him. "I was never promised the hand of Deborra as Rachel was promised to Jacob," he was thinking. "But I labored long for my master in hopes that this reward would be mine. At the end of his seven years of servitude Jacob did not get his Rachel, but in her place he was given the older sister, Leah. The Word says that Leah was tender of eye, but I am not sure of that. I think she had hips like a chariot horse and that she was flabby and blotched and as yellow as the falling leaves. There is not even a Leah for me to be consoled with, and now I must ruin my fine camels in a mad chase on the desert. Why should I waste my hard-earned substance in this way? Truly, I am a credulous fool. I do this so that the bride, who prefers another man to me, may win an inheritance to share with him. I am like the ass on which Balaam rode when he issued out to join the princes of Moab and which was smitten by him three times when it warned him of danger." He gave an angry shake of the head. "But I shall do everything I can. There is nothing I would not do for the little Deborra."

The ceremony had been completed. Basil and Deborra were man and wife in the sight of the Lord and in the eyes of men. One of the flagons on the shelf was filled and passed around the small circle of witnesses. Everyone took a sip in turn; even Adam, although he frowned as he did so and muttered in a partly audible tone: "My ears must be growing out from my head like those of Balaam's ass. Soon they will be large enough to flap in every breeze."

"It is customary," said Uzziel, "to preserve the cup in which the happiness of the newly wedded couple has been pledged."

A sheet of rich white satin was brought out, and Deborra spread it on a table under the shelf. Basil, as was the custom, stood beside her.

"We must live in separate tents," said Deborra in a whisper. Her hands were busy and they trembled a little as she proceeded with her task. "I do not know how it may be explained, but I shall try to find some way."

Basil nodded his head in silent assent. He felt completely unhappy as he watched her fingers at work. Things could have been so different if he had exercised some restraint over his instincts. He had sought out Helena for a purpose that had seemed to him both necessary and laudable. There had been no desire on his part then to see her again. The fascination she had for him had begun with his second visit, when Simon had practiced his trickery to such small effect. He could not understand why his feelings for the ex-slave girl had become charged so suddenly with violent emotions. But that was how it had fallen out.

"We must try to act natural," continued Deborra, keeping her eyes down. "The truth must not be suspected; at least, not at first. It will not be possible to keep it a secret always. That I realize. But my pride—yes, I have pride, although I could not blame you if you doubted it—my pride demands it should not happen at once. I could not stand to have it known now. My grandfather is dying and I am doing something for which my father will never forgive me. He may even denounce me and cast me off. On top of this I do not want it said that I—I had to buy a husband."

"Deborra, Deborra!" he exclaimed. "You do not think of it that way!"

"That is what everyone would say." She stole a glance about the room. Luke had begun to speak, and the rest seemed to be listening intently and watching him. "Will it be hard for you to pretend? To make it seem we are truly man and wife, even though we do not share a tent?"

"You must see how deep my feeling for you is——" he began.

She gave her head a quick and passionate shake of denial. "It is not necessary to—to say such things to me. We both understand the relationship between us." To herself she added, "I do not want him to think he has to be kind to me, to—to throw me crusts!" There had been in her voice a suggestion of emotions that might suddenly break the control she was maintaining over them. It was in a calmer tone that she went on after a brief silence. "We have only a moment left; and so, please, listen to what I have to say. We must seem affectionate. We must talk together a great deal—alone, whenever possible. We must smile. No one must be allowed to see that all this will be on the surface. Are you willing to help me by keeping up this pretense?"

"I am willing to do everything you suggest."

"But," said Deborra in a tense whisper, "we must not carry it too far. There must be no embracing for appearance's sake. No touching of hands. We must practice our deceit in other ways."

"I understand. It shall be as you say."

Luke was still speaking. The wrinkles about his eyes smiled as he told stories of the bride: how Deborra had once said in his hearing, when she was a very small girl, that she would never marry anyone but a king of Israel like David and that she would have twelve sons and name them after the twelve tribes. Later she had said that the husband she sought must be as wise as Solomon but that only in his wisdom must he be like that great king, he must never have more than one wife; and she had reduced the number of sons she desired to four, their names to be Peter, John, James, and Andrew.

"I am a sorry substitute for what you wanted in a husband," said Basil in a contrite tone.

She said to herself, "You could have been all that I ever wanted, all I ever dreamed."

The rest of the company in the room were so interested in what Luke was saying that no one noticed what was happening where the newly wedded couple stood. They did not see that the bride, with hands that now trembled noticeably, had wrapped in the sheet of handsome white satin, not the cup that had been passed around, but one that had remained untouched on the shelf. It was a plain old cup with a battered rim under which there was a mark somewhat like the flat fish of Galilee.

CHAPTER XIV

Luke and adam accompanied the bride to the door of her grandfather's room but did not go in with her. A small group had been waiting quietly in the hall, and to each of these Adam took a document for signature. "It may be necessary later," he explained, "to prove that the marriage of the daughter of the house took place before the death of the master."

Having observed this precaution, he began to pace up and down and to talk of the greatness of the life that was coming to an end. He spoke for the most part in a rumbling undertone but occasionally allowed his feelings to show in an outburst of words.

"There has never been his equal," he declaimed. "Abraham was a poor man, Job in the days of his affluence a mere seeker after wealth. Pharaoh did not lavish on Joseph a tithe of the gold that came into the possession of Joseph of Arimathea. His glory will be sung in the records of his day, but no one has known him as I did. His word was as good as the bond of a king. His heart was as clean as the morning sky. His mind was like unto a blade fresh from the firing. He was always right. And now this goodness and wisdom must end in the tomb! Open your minds to sorrow, all ye who knew him and benefited at his hands. Prepare to lament his passing——"

He stopped abruptly and allowed his eyes to dart hurriedly from one face to another. "What folly have I spoken? There must be no lamentation. Not a single note of grief must be raised to let it be known when our master and friend has closed his eyes. The sorrow we feel must be expressed for a time in silence."

It was a very few minutes later that the door opened and Deborra appeared. She was composed, but her cheeks were white and she did not raise her eyes.

"He is dead.'

Every head was lowered at once. The silence was so complete that it seemed unnatural, for grief in a Jewish house is loudly expressed. After some time had passed eyes were turned to Adam for a hint as to what was now expected. He was holding his eyes down and his lips moved in prayer. No one moved or spoke. Finally Adam looked up and motioned to Ebenezer, who stood on the edge of the group.

"Much will depend on your vigilance," he said in a low tone.

Ebenezer stole away silently. He took up his station outside the door of Aaron. Until other arrangements had been completed, no one was to be allowed to carry to the new master of the house the word that Joseph of Arimathea had been gathered to his fathers.

2

The two *conchar* men who stood guard at the main entrance had been keeping their eyes on the windows above them where Aaron had his quarters. At the same time they were conscious of something else that was going on about them, which had the effect of putting them on their guard. Men and women in rather considerable numbers were arriving and standing about in silent groups. They came chiefly from the valley and they were people of humble dress and mien.

"What does this mean?" demanded Mijamin of his fellow. He had, apparently, a temper as short as himself, for his hand played irritably with the dagger at his belt. "Why are these poverty-stricken laglags coming here and hanging around like this?"

"They are Christians," declared the tall *conchar* man. "They have faces like sheep. They smell like sheep. That is always the way with these Christians. I am sure they have come to mourn the death of the old man within." He nodded his head, which was bald and covered with huge yellow freckles. "When is this old moneybags going to give in and die as any decent man would do? I am tired of standing at his door."

The neighing of horses reached their ears from a piece of open ground some distance down the street. It was the start of a crevasse that cut its way down into the valley, and it had become overrun with scrub trees and tall weeds. As it had always been used for thievery, dicing, and lust, it had become known as the Bellows of Beelzebub.

"The old man will die within the hour," said the short one, paying no attention to the sound of the horses. "It stands to reason that he cannot cheat the angel of death any longer."

He proceeded then to order the assembled watchers about with an unnecessary violence. They were compelled to retire to the far side of the open space in front of Joseph's door and to stand in line. They were told, moreover, that they were not to open their mouths nor to shuffle their feet; that they were not, in fact, to make any noise whatever. They must expect quick and sharp punishment if they did. A pat on the dagger could be construed as a hint at the nature of the punishment that would be meted out to them.

An interruption occurred almost immediately thereafter. It did not come, however, in the form of a summons from the window of Aaron, as they had expected. It took the form instead of an exodus of people in some numbers from the front door. The two guards forgot everything else and hurried over.

First came two young men carrying hymeneal lamps above their heads, and this could mean one thing only, that a wedding had taken place. Usually there were friends of the groom who danced ahead of the happy couple and sang songs in praise of the beauty of the bride. That this element was missing did not raise any doubts as to the nature of what was taking place. A young couple followed immediately after, and it was quite clear that they had been standing together under the nuptial canopy. The bride was in white and looked quite as lovely as brides are supposed to, and the bridegroom was in the splendor of an embroidered cloak.

"A wedding," said the Mijamin. "Were we told what to do in the case of a wedding?"

"No," answered the tall one. "The Mar told us everything else, but he had nothing to say about weddings."

The bride was carrying a round vessel in one hand and dipping into it with the other for small coins, which she tossed to the spectators. The vessel, which was not large, was elaborately swathed with white satin. The bride called greetings as she distributed the largess and, whenever she remembered that it was customary for brides to smile, she smiled.

Mijamin rubbed his jaw with an undecided hand. "Now what are we to do?" he asked. "We have only two pairs of hands and we cannot search all these people. Do you agree that we should order them back into the

house and then scatter these watchers and send them home? If they refuse to obey, there will be trouble. We will have to slit throats. I confess
to you, Eleazar, that I do not like slitting throats at a wedding."

"No," agreed Eleazar, "I do not mind at a funeral, because there you
are dealing with death. I do not think I would mind at a christening, because all the troubles in the world start with births. Too many people are
being born. But it is not fitting that there should be slitting of throats at
a wedding." He had been watching the hymeneal procession as he
spoke. "This bride has a nice round eye and in other ways she is pleasantly round. But wait, wait! Look at her closely, Mijamin! Is she not the
granddaughter of the old man?"

"What is that?" cried Mijamin. He rushed in closer to the marching
celebrants, shoving those nearest him aside in his haste. Then he turned
back in a furious concern. "You are right. It is the granddaughter. What
strange proceedings are these? Is this all a mummery to throw us off our
guard? Eleazar, run to each of the other entrances and tell our men to
come here at once. We are going to need all the help we can get. No,
have one man left at each gate and bring the rest back with you. This
may be a ruse again to draw us away from the other doors. Quick! There
is not a moment to be lost!"

But by the time the tall man returned at a frantic lope, stretching his
thin legs like those of a crane, and with three helpers at his heels, it was
too late to take any effective action. The watchers, the sheep who had
roused the scorn of the two men at the front entrance, had broken their
lines and surged forward to join the marchers. Scores of others, men and
women who had remained unseen up to this point, now poured out from
the narrow entrances of streets and from doorways. From the house came
more of the staff, all of the ex-slaves who had not been present at the
marriage rites. Raising their voices in a hymn, they fell into line solidly
about the bride and bridegroom. It was to be expected that Aaron, whose
face appeared suddenly at his window, found it hard to believe his eyes.
It was clear he thought that a band of maniacs had collected suddenly at
his door. Many of the marchers were now dancing, and all were singing
at the tops of their voices.

The *conchar* men hovered on the edge of the crowd like angry killer
sharks swimming beside a solid school of fish. All they could see to do was
to plunge into the crowd and strike right and left with their weapons.
Adam ben Asher, finding Mijamin in a furious conference with several
of his men, proceeded to make clear the futility of such a course.

"Half a dozen men cannot make any impression on a crowd as large as this," he declared, shouting to make himself heard over the din. "Oh, you could kill a few of us, of course. But see! They are well on their way, and you can neither stop them nor drive them back. Would the killing of a few stragglers help the cause to which you are sworn?"

"By the eighteen benedictions, we have been caught napping," said Mijamin bitterly. "What will the Mar have to say about this?"

It was clear that what the Mar might have to say later was a matter of small consequence. The singing, shouting, dancing crowd had already debouched from the square in front of the house of Joseph. They were now close to the open space down the street where the neighing of horses had been heard at the Bellows of Beelzebub.

Mijamin collected his fellows about him. There was a crestfallen look on all their faces.

"It has not been our fault," he declared in a tone of disputation. "How could we know they would have the help of all the Christians in Jerusalem? But since it has happened, we must try to correct the mistake. You, Eleazar, see to it that a man remains at each door and that no one is allowed to enter or leave under any circumstances. You go into the house yourself and tell Aaron the search for the Cup is to be made at once. We must not delay because the old man refuses to die. Make it clear to Adam that the bed of Joseph will be searched if necessary and that the pillow will be dragged from under his head and opened."

"It is more likely," said Eleazar, glancing after the noisy procession, "that they took the Cup with them."

"I think it almost certain that they did." A disturbing thought took possession of Mijamin's mind. "Did you notice that the bride carried a cup or a basket, covered with white, in her hand? Do you suppose she was flaunting *the* Cup in our faces?"

Eleazar did not think so. "They would not carry it openly. Christians lack the daring for that."

"They have shown more daring today than I have any stomach for," grumbled Mijamin. "But I agree, it is more likely that someone carried it out under a cloak." His manner became peremptory. "You, Amashsai, seek out Rub Samuel and inform him of what has happened. Tell him I shall follow these people and report to him on their movements. Make it clear to the Mar that if they have taken the Cup I will come back with it—or not come back at all."

BOOK TWO

CHAPTER XV

I

THEY TRAVELED for six hours, for the most part on narrow roads that sloped continuously upward. The stately camels Adam had provided went at a slow gait, putting their broad, padded feet down with care. The midday heat was stifling and cruel. The country had taken on some of the aspects of the desert that stretched interminably eastward from the Jordan; it had become brown and yellow; the vines on the straight orderly ledges of the hills were wilted almost to blackness; the fruit trees, having yielded their harvest, were finishing the summer in a state of drooping coma. The flocks of sheep were finding little to crop and they greeted the travelers with bleats of discouragement.

The first night was spent at a khan within sound of the sluggish ripple of the Jordan. It had looked imposing at a distance, a high huddle of roofs in a wooden wall twenty feet high, but at close range it proved to be an unclean hurly-burly of a place. They rode in under the arched gateway with much jingling of bells and waving of bannerets and feather plumes, much glistening of cowries and sequins. Adam took one look around the crowded courtyard; at the fiercely dignified men in huge turbans, chaffering and debating in noisy groups, watchful of everything that went on, each arrival and departure; at the sun-baked faces of their wives, in robes of the color of raw liver, who were busily engaged at the entrances to the alcoves along the walls in preparing the evening meal with the smallest of copper saucepans over the tiniest of fires; at the little leather tables already set out with dates and dried raisins and coconut strips. He had not expected to find the place so crowded at this season of the year, and he entered into negotiations rather grudgingly for the use of the porter's lodge over the entrance. The owner of the khan, an Armenian of ancient vintage, decided that the circumstances warranted a demand for a figure higher than usual.

"Such fine camels!" he cried. "Such leather! Such tassels of gold! Is it that Joseph of Arimathea is dead and has left you a great fortune?"

"Joseph of Arimathea is dead," answered Adam, "but I have no expectation that he has left me anything. These camels are my own. They have been selected with great care and I have paid for them out of my savings, which, by all the benedictions, are small. I am in no mood to be robbed, Hasoud."

The argument went on so long that Deborra said "Kharr!" in a weary voice. When the camel obeyed the command by sinking to one knee, she stepped down stiffly from the canvas cover of the *tola* under which she had been riding. Because of the haste of their departure from Jerusalem, she was still wearing her white wedding dress, which looked rather rumpled and dusty. She glanced about her and saw that Luke, looking old and very tired, was following her example. Basil had already dismounted and was rambling about the courtyard, a conspicuous note of color in the midst of the general brown shoddiness.

The bitter contest over price came to a conclusion, and Deborra followed Adam up a twisting and insecure flight of wooden stairs to the single room over the entrance. It was not large and was as hot as an oven; but it was comparatively clean and would suffice for the whole party with the exception of the camel men, who would curl up in the courtyard close to their charges. Deborra was relieved by this arrangement, which delayed the need for an explanation. She seated herself near one of the windows on a rug spread for her by Sarah, her maid. Adam came over and squatted himself down tailor-fashion beside her.

"Our little bride is tired," he said. Like one who cannot resist probing at a sore spot, he proceeded to speak of the wedding. "Such a beautiful bride, such a faithful little Rachel, glad to give her hand to her eager Jacob! But the Jacob in this case has not been compelled to labor seven years for his bride." When Deborra made no response, he went on: "Is it not an ideal match? And here the bridegroom cometh, this luckiest of men. How well favored he is! How handsomely he is attired! Could any maiden resist that blue cloak?"

Basil crossed the room to where they were sitting. He wore an uneasy look.

"There is a man in the crowd below who stood outside the house of Joseph today," he said.

Adam looked up quickly. "How can you be sure?"

"He was standing at one side when we came out of the house. There was another man talking to him with a dagger in his hands. I looked at them with some care, being sure they had been there on guard."

"Is he tall or short?"

"Short. There was a mark at one corner of his mouth. A scar, perhaps."

Adam nodded his head. "Mijamin. One of Rub Samuel's men. He would cut all our throats with ease and thoroughness and eat a hearty supper immediately after. He will try to get his hands on this Cup." When Deborra and Basil regarded him with startled looks, he indulged in a scornful snort. "Did you think I did not know about it? I have a good pair of ears and a useful pair of eyes. There is very little that I miss. I was certain you would have it with you, and I am not surprised that our handsome and alert bridegroom catches a glimpse of the dreaded Mijamin below. We shall have the men of Rub Samuel on our heels the whole distance, and their daggers, perhaps, in our backs." He glanced at their anxious faces and indulged in another snort. "Where is it now?"

A small interior window looked out over the courtyard. Deborra walked to it and from this point of vantage scanned the scene below. The crowd seemed to have become louder and noisier. Caravan men, with faces the color of cocoa and eyes that were never still, were arguing in groups. Traders with shrewd eyes, slatternly servants, emaciated beggars who had been forced out to the edges like flotsam in a whirlpool; everyone talking at once, every eye on fire, every hand in action.

Deborra's servants stood in an aloof group. The women had dropped veils over their faces, but in spite of this precaution they were being watched with an avid curiosity. They were standing closely about an elaborately carved chest that had been painted a warm carnelian shade. The rest of the party's belongings had been heaped up in a careless pile with a very old and plain chest as the base.

Her eyes did no more than dart across the servants guarding the ornate chest and then came to rest on the dilapidated specimen under the rugs and assorted utensils of travel. She gave a sigh of relief when she saw that Luke had stationed himself close thereby and was watching with zealous eyes.

She turned back from the window and said to Adam, "The Cup is being carefully guarded."

The latter took his turn at the window. After a moment's scrutiny of the noisy scene he clapped his hands and shouted an order to his men below. In a matter of seconds all of the belongings of the party had been carried up and deposited in a corner. Luke followed in the wake of the old chest.

"Everything we own will be stolen if we give those thieves below a chance to set their clever fingers to work," Adam said. "And now, if you three innocents will listen to me carefully, I shall endeavor to make clear to you the nature of the troubles which lie ahead of us."

He walked to each window in turn, glancing out to make sure they could not be reached from below. Then he visited the head of the stairs and listened carefully.

"Throw a potsherd through any village in Palestine and you will hit at least three Zealots," he said. "Open your mouth with an opinion in any public place and a Zealot will answer you, probably with a blow. In other words, my three unworldlings, the men of Rub Samuel are to be found everywhere, and Mijamin can summon them to his aid at any time and in any place. He will wait until he thinks the circumstances most favorable and then he will strike. Our best plan will be to provide him with the opportunity—and have a warm reception planned. I think I begin to see my way clearly."

He seemed reluctant to reveal the nature of the plan he had evolved, glancing anxiously at Luke and suspiciously at Basil. Realizing, however, that they must be taken into his confidence, he continued with his explanation. "Tonight I shall circulate below—where I know most of them and where, of course, they all know me—and I shall let it be known that tomorrow we will progress as far as En-Gannim and pitch our tents outside the town. The mention of En-Gannim will set the mind of Mijamin to work at once. As you all know, it lies in a shallow valley at the southern tip of the Plain of Esdraelon. Now it happens that Mijamin was born and raised on the Plain, and he knows that the Zealots are strong in all the towns there. All he will have to do is to start ahead of us—I expect he will steal away from here in the middle of the night—and gather about him the men he will need. I shall let it be known that, to save time, we intend to raise our tents on the crest of the valley. Mijamin will rub his hands and whistle through his teeth with delight when he hears this, for the crest of the valley does not afford any cover for defense and there is, for good measure, a wadi running along it in which an attacking force may approach without being seen. He will think that Adam has become as blind as a bat in daylight when he hears where I shall pitch the tents.

"It so happens," he went on, with open relish of his own craft, "that En-Gannim has an advantage for us of which he knows nothing. Just above it, in a green spot scooped out from the Plain, lives a very good friend of mine. His name is Catorius, and he is a Roman. He was serving in this country when his term ran out and he was allowed to remain here, having married a woman of Emek-Keziz, a fine big woman with thick limbs and a heart as warm as the sun-baked town where she was born. They took land on the Plain and there they have been successful in raising two commodities: sheep, which have made them prosperous, and sons who are the bulwark of their old age. When we have pitched our tents outside En-Gannim and darkness has fallen, I shall steal over to the house of Catorius in the little dip in the hills and beg the aid of these three sons of his."

"Are they Christians?" asked Luke.

"Christians?" cried Adam. "No, Luke the Physician, they are as simple and natural as the sheep they tend, and as pagan as Astarte."

"Is it then right to involve them in our troubles? Moreover, can we put full trust in them?"

Adam burst into a roar of delighted laughter. "If your gentle heart, O Luke, must overflow with compassion for someone, save it for the unsuspecting men Mijamin will bring against us and who will find themselves confronted by these Sons of Anak from the Plain! They are sometimes called the Giants of Slador."

Having thus settled the most pressing of their problems to his own complete satisfaction, Adam proceeded to issue orders for the night. It would be necessary for one of them to sleep with the Cup under his pillow, and for this he selected Luke. The rest would take turns at standing watch during the hours of darkness. Basil was given the first turn, with Deborra to follow and Adam to watch last.

"We must set out at break of dawn," decided Adam briskly. "And now for supper."

Basil took his station at the head of the stairs. The courtyard had lapsed into a silence broken only by an occasional whimper from one of the camels or the chatter of a hyena on the prowl. He was conscious every moment that the sacred Cup was in the room and that he was guarding it. He had expected it would shine through the wood of the broken chest with the strange glow that had radiated from it in the gloom of his sanctuary in the house of Joseph. Each time he turned to look he was surprised at the darkness. He could see nothing but the white of Deborra's dress where she lay in a corner. Her breathing was so light that he could not tell whether she was awake or sleeping.

Once he heard the stairs creak and his hand closed on the hilt of his dagger. For several minutes he waited tensely, but the sound was not repeated. Nothing happened; a rat, he decided. He was realizing how deep was his concern for the safety of the Cup. His brow was bathed in perspiration and the palms of his hands were damp.

As time passed he became certain that Deborra was sleeping and he hesitated to rouse her when the time came for her to take his place. She stirred, however, and sat up in the darkness.

"Basil!" she whispered.

"Yes, Deborra?"

"Is it not time for me to begin?"

"Not yet. Go back to sleep again for a while."

"I have not been able to sleep. I have been lying here and thinking."

"All the more reason then for getting to sleep now. We have a hard day ahead of us."

"But you need the rest as much as I do."

He heard her move. When he turned and looked in her direction, she was already on her feet.

"Where are you?" she whispered.

"Here. At the head of the stairs."

She crossed the room on naked feet and seated herself beside him on the top step. After a moment she began to speak in a low tone.

"Let us talk for a while. There will never be a better chance. I want to say, Basil, that I begin to see I was wrong in doing this. It is unfair to you to be tied to a wife you do not love."

"But, Deborra——"

"It is the truth, Basil. There is no need to spare my feelings by protesting. The only excuse I have is the need to help the leaders of the church." The tone of her voice suggested now that she was drawing a rueful amusement out of the situation in which they were placed. "I have, at any rate, shown how much I trust you. Has it occurred to you that as my husband you could take my inheritance and use it in any way you see fit?"

This aspect had not occurred to him. "No. I have given it no thought."

"It is true. We are wedded on the terms of Baal and Beulah. To keep the money out of my father's hands, I have put it into yours."

"Are you afraid of what I may do?"

"No, Basil. You are good. You are unselfish; too unselfish, perhaps. No, I have no fear at all." She leaned her head against the wall and sighed deeply. "We must strive to be kind to each other. We must remain friends in spite of everything. I was not kind to you today. I said hard things, and my mind was filled with hard thoughts. There was no reason for me to feel that way, or none that I can see now. You had done nothing wrong. But my pride had been hurt and so I—I found bitterness on my tongue. Such pride is an evil thing, Basil, and I am sure that I have been guilty of much wickedness."

"If there has been any kind of wickedness, I am the guilty one," declared Basil.

She indulged in a long and deep sigh. "Do you remember the bargain we made between us? That we would always smile when we were together? And ever since we have done nothing but feel unhappy and draw long faces. I have even lost my pet, my poor, solemn little Habakkuk. Ebenezer is keeping him until I can take him again."

"Ebenezer will be a kind master to him."

"As I lay in the dark back there I was thinking about this sad pass to which we have come. I could see how easy it would be for us to become bitter and angry with each other."

"I am sure I could never be angry with you."

Basil discovered that his feeling for her had taken on a deep tenderness. The mood of that rare moment when they had paused after their scramble through the valley came back to him. He was acutely aware that she was very close to him in the darkness and that they were man and wife. He thought, "Why should I not take her in my arms as any other husband would do, even those who see their wives for the first time when they raise the veil?" Perhaps love would develop through such abruptness. Perhaps the image of Helena would then pass out of his mind and never return.

There was tensity in the air between them. Deborra had raised her head from its anchorage against the wall and was looking at him in the dark. Had the same thoughts entered her mind? How slender she was in her fine white raiment!

Then came recollection of the way she had looked after he had first spoken of Helena; cold, hurt, eternally aloof, unforgiving. He had agreed to her conditions and he must not attempt to break his promises

at the first opportunity. She would feel nothing but contempt for him
if he did.

The golden moment passed, if indeed it had been such. He became
aware that Deborra's mood had changed. She drew a deep sigh and then
began to sob gently in the dark. "My poor grandfather!" she said. "Please,
Basil, I must sit here alone for a time with my grief. I must reconcile
myself to living in a world which he has left."

He went back to his own corner. Adam was snoring vigorously, Luke
with dignity and serenity, the servants like a full orchestra of *kinnor,
shofar, hozazra,* and *tof.* Not a sound came from the courtyard below.
Mijamin, no doubt, had left long before this to recruit the Zealots of the
Plain. Basil realized suddenly that he was tired from the continuous
excitements and the efforts of the day. He fell off quickly to sleep.

2

Since dawn they had been passing the high circle of hills that was
called Samaria and was marked on the south by Mount Gerizim and
on the north by Mount Ebal. The country of the Samaritans had looked
cool and inviting; the slopes were green and there was a promise of
sweet content and abundance in the valleys lying between the tree-
fringed peaks. Adam could not keep his eyes away from this fortunate
land where so much of the history of his race had been made. He kept
up a continuous tirade in audible tones.

"Why is it," he demanded of the world at large and even perhaps of
the Jehovah who had been responsible for the way things had fallen
out, "that the cursed Cutheans have this most favored land for their
own? Why do we, the children of Israel, who have been chosen by the
one and only God, have to subsist on slopes of bare limestone or on
desert lands where men faint of the heat in midday? Why must we
raise our crops on baking plains? Perhaps," with a grumbling acquiescence, "it is done as a test. As we must live harder, we have become
keen and practical and as bright as burnished metal. We are tempered
in the heat of the sun, and the blood runs passionately in our veins.
If we had these green hills for our own, we might in time become as
soft and worthless as the Samaritans." He concluded with a sigh, "But
it would be pleasant to live in such ease and comfort."

It was late in the afternoon, and the peak of Mount Ebal had receded so far into the distance that the traditional cursing from its slopes could never have reached them even if relayed by a thousand trumpets. The steady pace of Adam's carefully selected camels brought them abreast of a much smaller party. A wrinkled face peered out at them from the curtains of a curiously shaped conveyance that had curtains of the brightest scarlet embroidered with dragons. In a high and thin voice that suggested the twittering of birds at the first dawn, the owner of the wrinkled face said, "Peace be with you, honored sirs, and may abounding prosperity be your lot."

"Peace be with you," responded Luke, who rode on the right wing of the cavalcade.

"Like the barnacles that cling to the tail of a sea leviathan," said the ancient traveler, "we shall, with your beneficent compliance, follow in your dust for the rest of the day."

"If it is security you seek, honorable friend," said Adam, who was riding with no cover from the blaze of the sun, "my advice would be to avoid us as you would a band of lepers. We ride in the shadow of constant danger."

"May you raise a large family of sons with the same honesty," declared the stranger. "But the dangers which surround you cannot be greater than the unknown terrors that threaten the solitary traveler. I have been much on the trails in my day, and this lesson I have learned, that there is safety only in company."

Adam nodded his head. "That is true. For our part, O friend from the East, we are glad to welcome you. We are happy for any increase in our ranks."

"We are men of peace," warned the ancient traveler.

"I had already judged you to be such. But your presence swells the size of our caravan and gives a hint of great strength. Go you to Aleppo?"

The weazened head peering out from the dragon ambush nodded in response. "To Aleppo, honored captain. Then we turn on to the Bagdad trail. I come from Seen, and it is to that land of countless blessings that we return."

"Seen!" cried Adam. "It is the land of enchantments and of the dreams of all men with restless heels. All my life I have longed to go there, to test its wonders with my own eyes." With a sense of pride he added, "I have been as far as Samarkand."

"Samarkand is a city of much honor. A busy city where even the teeth of the keenest traders are in constant jeopardy. Will I seem to boast if I say that the traders of Samarkand have been sitting for ages at the feet of men from Seen?"

Adam asked with an almost wistful interest, "Does Seen lie far beyond Samarkand?"

"Men follow the Pe Lu for many changes of the moon between Samarkand and Seen, my son. There are thirty days of travel in sight of the Snowy Mountains, and after that the Wall and the great plains and the winding course of the mighty river." The enumeration of such distances gave a hint of weariness to the nodding of the ancient head. "I am a prince of the royal house and my name is P'ing-li. It has been a trial to everyone, and most particularly to myself, that I possess those restless heels to which you have referred. We have, no doubt, much in common, honored captain, and many tales to repeat back and forth. I shall be forever honored if you and such of your company as you deem meet will join me for the evening repast. I shall be proud to lay before you foods of Seen of which you have never heard."

"To sup with you, Illustrious Prince, will be an honor of which my grandsons will boast," declared Adam. "It is certain, however, that the dangers of which I spoke will take me early from the delights of your table."

The old man nodded in acceptance of the condition. "You and those you bring to my tent may sup with daggers loosed in the belt and eyes turned back over the shoulder. It is my earnest hope that the flavor of the foods I shall set before you will for a brief moment seduce you from the contemplation of danger."

The site Adam chose for his camp was on a flat piece of ground well above the valley in which En-Gannim nestled, its flat white roofs like eggs in the nest of some monster bird. It was exposed on all sides except the north, where a shallow wadi wound its way down from the hills. "We are open to attack," said Adam to Luke, grinning with pleasure in his own astuteness. "Let us hope that Mijamin is already aware of the full extent of our folly."

Basil watched the servants of the Chinese traveler erect a fabulous pavilion for his use. First they brought forth a pole three feet in length and from inside it produced length after length of diminishing circumference, each length having been contained inside a larger one, until they had a center pole of full fifteen feet. Rods were attached to the top and stretched out to carry the first layer of the cloth cover. Side panels fell from there to the ground and were firmly anchored with metal pegs. All this was accomplished with quick and deft movements and took a surprisingly few minutes to finish.

›   Then miracles began to happen inside. A gorgeous carpet was spread on the sand, and on it rugs and cushions were heaped. Small sections of gilded wood became an elaborate chair with carved back and arms. A tiny ivory taboret sprouted up beside it as though by magic. Drinking cups appeared seemingly out of the air. The head servant, who had directed the work, glanced about him with a critical eye and said: "It is well enough. Now, O sons of sloth, the cooking tent."

On entering the pavilion, which was as vividly carmine as the setting sun, the four guests found that a space in the rear had been closed off behind a heavy curtain. A yellow hand swung it back almost immediately and their host emerged, revealing himself to their eyes as a small and bent figure in a gorgeous blue-and-black robe with a silk skullcap fitted down closely over his bald old head. Two servants teetered along on each side of him, holding cushions on which his forearms rested. The reason for this became apparent when they had seated themselves on the carpet about a low table. The fingernails of the prince were so long that they were held in guards of gold. The guards were three inches long and curved at the ends to allow for the tendency of the nails to curl under. As the nails lengthened with the years, these gold casings were worn lower all the time, and had now reached the stage where they threatened to lose all contact with the flesh. They were elaborately decorated with precious stones.

He kept his hands in front of him on the table and at intervals studied them with conscious pride.

"I am deeply honored by the presence of such illustrious guests," he said, bowing to each in turn.

Deborra had remained standing in the background, knowing that custom forbade her to be seated. The prince chirped to the servant who stood behind him, and the latter set up a small table under the slope of the side. "It is our wish," said the old man, "that daughter of honorable guest be seated in our presence and partake of food at seemly distance." This concession gave much pleasure to all of them, for it meant that she would share their dishes while they were still warm and would, moreover, be able to listen to their discourse.

The servant then handed around tiny cups containing a delightfully delicate and hot liquid.

"I beg you will overlook the sad deficiencies imposed on your much-honored host by the difficulties of travel," said the old man, who had not moved his hands. He gave a second chirp, and the servant raised the host's cup and placed it in his right hand. The prince curled his fingers around it and raised it to his lips with a gratified sigh. Deborra turned her eyes away, for it made her think of the talons of a bird of prey gripping the white-plumed neck of some feathered victim.

"I am the grandson of an emperor," explained the prince. "He was much given to marriage, and there were two hundred and forty-eight known grandchildren. The honor, though still great, was, as you see, somewhat diluted." He added after a moment: "I was not allowed to use my hands, and my nails have never been pared. For as long back as my memory goes, I have never been able to pick anything up with my fingers. My servants are my hands." He indulged in a reminiscent sigh. "This conceit of my class made me rebellious as a youth. I conceived a desire to employ my hands in the painting of pictures. It was sternly forbidden me to do so, and for the entertaining of such thoughts I was severely disciplined."

The main dish proved to be a hot and succulent one. It was composed (no other word could describe the preparing of such an ambrosial dish) with shreds of coconut, an assortment of curious nuts and hot spiced sauces nestling in snow-white rice. There were other dishes, including transparent bean curds and cold slices of pork that had been cooked with ginger.

Their host ate little and talked much. He had come this great distance west—yea, here to the very rim of the world—because of rumors that had reached his country of the teachings of one Jesus. Being of a race that counted peace the greatest of boons, he had found that this hint of a wonderful new philosophy had plucked at his heart like the fingers of a harpist. (What a musician had been lost, he interrupted himself to say, when the gold coverings had been attached to his fingertips!) So concerned had he become by the whispers that reached his ears that he had even learned the language of the far west, this Aramaic of strange sounds that warred with his tongue. An Arab scholar had been found to act as his tutor, and in due course he had set forth to visit the lands where the man Jesus had lived and preached and died. He had been a month in Jerusalem. He had talked to the priests of the

Temple, including the High Priest, whose appearance and manners had astounded him, and the pedagogues with their minds as sharp as gimlets. He had visited as well the leaders of those who professed to believe in Jesus; and now he was returning to his home, hopeful of reaching his palace in the City of the Thousand Bridges before his eyes closed in the long sleep.

Luke listened with so much interest that the food before him remained almost untouched.

"Do you care to tell us, Most Illustrious Prince P'ing-li, what conclusions you carry back with you?" he asked. Thinking an explanation necessary, he informed the royal visitor that he himself was a Greek.

"We have heard in Seen of your Grecian culture," said the old man with a kindly nod of the head.

Luke went on to say that he had been a Christian for many years and it had been his great privilege to accompany the apostle of Jesus, who was known as Paul of Tarsus, on most of his travels.

"I heard much talk of Paul, but it was not permitted me to speak to him in his prison cell. It was a matter of much regret to this insignificant seeker after the truth who has heard that the tongue of the apostle is like a blade of the sharpest edge."

Adam had been keeping an eye on the sinking rim of the sun through the raised curtains at the entrance of the pavilion. He rose at this point and said that the errand of which he had spoken earlier called him away and he must beg the permission of his host to withdraw. A nod of the birdlike head of the old man conveyed his consent, and a twittering summons brought his servant to raise his limp right arm in a gesture of farewell.

The prince turned back immediately to Luke and the talk between them was renewed. He was returning home, it developed, with many reservations. Jesus had preached charity and peace and yet his teachings had made bad blood among men of his own race and had led to much cruelty in the world. Why was this? Why had the coming of the great preacher Paul led to hate and bloodshed? It was the way of all worship throughout the world for men to sacrifice to the gods, not the gods to men. Why, then, had Jesus, Who was known to be a god, been taken out and crucified?

"It is a matter of the deepest regret, Most Learned and Illustrious Prince, that Paul is not here to speak with you and clear your mind of such doubts," said Luke. "He sees the truth with great clarity. I am a very poor substitute, but this much I can do for you: I can tell you everything that is known of Jesus. For over twenty years I have sought information about Him and I have gathered a complete story of His stay on this earth. Would it be of interest to you to hear what I may tell of Him?"

The prince called, "It grows chill, most unobservant of servants." The man brought rests of velvet and laid his master's hands on them before binding them carefully in wrappings of wool. With a sigh of relief the tiny figure sank back against the huge scarlet cushions that had been piled up behind him. His eyes glistened with anticipation in the yellow of his face. "This is what I followed the Pe Lu to hear!" he cried. "Tell me everything about the man Jesus. Leave nothing out, I beseech you."

Luke began to speak, choosing his words with great care at first but gradually allowing his feelings to take the reins. His eyes lighted up as he told the story from the first night at Bethlehem when the stars had massed in the heavens to send their light down directly on the manger where the holy child lay. Basil listened with as much eagerness as the little man from the East. He had long desired to hear the story of this new God whose face must be revealed to him before he could complete his mission. He had heard bits of it, mere fragments that had aroused a desire for the whole story. The heads of the three men drew closer together as the vibrant voice of the old physician recited. They seemed to lose all consciousness of time.

Deborra, sitting patiently under the slope of the canvas wall, watched them intently. Her eyes, naturally enough, rested most often on the face of Basil. It was a good thing that the recital engaged their attention, because otherwise they might have perceived how the sweet gravity of her eyes dissolved into mists of unhappiness. Why, she was asking herself for the hundredth time, had this terrible thing happened to keep them apart? What kind of lure had the magician's assistant used to disturb his mind? What cure could there be for such an infatuation?

The sun disappeared and darkness settled down. An hour passed. There was silence outside save for the uneasy rustling of the camels, the occasional unhappy yelp of a dog, or the high laugh of a hyena from the distance. Luke's voice went on, telling the magic story, his listeners as attentive as at the start. A second hour passed. Deborra realized that Adam ben Asher should have returned before this. Had an accident befallen him? Had he found it impossible to enlist the assistance of his old friend's sons and was now seeking help elsewhere? She became so anxious, and finally so desperate, that she was not able to follow the concluding stages of Luke's recital. Her ears strained for every sound, dreading to hear the rush of Mijamin's men from the cover of the wadi. Every sound from the darkness outside became to her the first indication of an attack.

Then a high-pitched and vibrant call sounded from a distance. It came unquestionably from a human throat. Luke stopped speaking and turned in the direction from which the cry had come. Basil sprang to his feet and ran to the entrance of the pavilion, from which he looked out anxiously into the blackness of the night. Deborra followed him there.

"It is the signal," she said. "Adam is returning. I must let him know that all is well."

She placed the fingers of both hands on her neck and tightened them about the vocal cords. The call that issued from her throat was identical with the hail that had reached them from the dark, a high, strained note. Basil knew that the women of Israel used this method of attaining high notes in tribal singing and he watched her curiously. The call was sustained for many seconds and could have been heard for a long distance.

It became evident almost immediately that Adam was approaching the camp along the upper edge of the wadi. He was not returning alone, for in a very few minutes they could hear the steady tramp of several pairs of feet.

Basil, looking up at the stars, had forgotten everything but the wondrous story to which he had listened. He was thinking how the stars had guided the Three Wise Men to the manger at Bethlehem. It seemed to him that they were unusually bright again and that a particularly luminous group hovered over the cluster of tents. Was this to show that the most sacred reminder of the life on earth of the man, into whom the child had grown, was hidden here? A sense of expectation took possession of him. He was almost convinced that the footsteps approaching were those of people coming eagerly to gaze on the humble cup.

Deborra seemed to understand what was passing through his mind. She smiled up at him and laid a hand on his wrist. "Basil," she whispered, "I think it is Adam returning, but we must be prepared in case I have been mistaken."

He still remained under the spell. "Herodotus on the forum in Athens," he declared fervently, "never told a story to equal what I have heard tonight."

3

Three young men, wearing the rough sheepskin cloak of the shepherd, followed Adam into the circle of tents. They towered over him. They had wide shoulders and necks like marble columns and great, muscular arms. There was nothing arrogant about them in spite of their obvious might; instead they wore gentle smiles, as though they were abashed at being in such company. They were so much alike, moreover, that it was hard to believe that even their parents would be able to tell them apart.

"These are my good friends, the sons of Catorius," said Adam by way of introduction. "Their father is a student of Roman history and an ardent admirer of the Gracchii, and so he named them Sempronius, Tiberius, and Gaius. I confess I cannot tell them apart, although I am almost sure that this one beside me is Tiberius."

"No," said the member of the trio thus indicated, speaking in a high and amiable voice. "I am Gaius. The youngest. This is Tiberius beside me. Sempronius is on his other side."

"I shall try no more!" exclaimed Adam. "I have been miscalling them all the way down from the Plain. Of this only am I certain, that no one save Samson of immortal memory could prevail against these three mighty men."

"I gave orders for a supper to be prepared," said Deborra. "It is ready in my tent."

Three pairs of eyes lighted up in approval as the sons of Catorius wheeled in unison and followed her. The appetites of the trio would, it was clear, be sharply applied to the supper that had been spread out for them. Adam walked behind, dropping an admiring hand on the rippling muscles of the back nearest him.

"It was on shoulders such as these that the gates of Gaza were carried, Sempronius!" he exclaimed.

The recipient of the compliment was pleased enough to smile modestly, although he disclaimed the power to equal the feat of the great Samson. "My brothers and I are strong. There is no denying it. But in the Jewish book it is said that no man had the strength of Samson." After a moment he added, "And I am not Sempronius. I am Tiberius."

Lights had been extinguished for an hour. Adam ben Asher sat inside his tent with the men of the camp squatting silently about him.

All were armed and in a state of nervous alertness. The moon had broken through the clouds and it was now possible to see the shapes of the tents and the tops of the trees that lined the wadi. Sitting on the edge of the group, Basil found the attentions of the night insects almost unbearable and kept up a continuous beating of his arms to drive them away. The three young shepherds seemingly were impervious to such attacks. They sat together in the open and never moved a muscle. The only sounds came from Adam himself. Fearful that Mijamin was not going to take advantage after all of the opportunity that had been provided for him, he emitted an occasional grumble of discontent.

Basil's thoughts were still on the story of Jesus and His sojourn on earth. He no longer had any doubts that the gentle man of Nazareth was the Son of this one God to Whom the people of Israel prayed, and that someday He would return to the earth. This conviction was one of the mind rather than of the spirit, for it had not brought him any of the exaltation he had seen among the brave and humble people whose greeting to each other was, "Christ has risen." That might come later. In the meantime he was happy to be able to accept the story without any reservations. The words of Luke had brought into his mind the picture of a slender figure moving among the people who came out in such multitudes to see Him. He had seen the ill rise from their beds and walk at a quiet word of command and the lame throw away their crutches. He had seen the form of the Great Teacher ride into Jerusalem for the last time; he had observed again that touching scene in the upper chamber of the house at the Wall of David. There had been one disappointment for him, however; the face of Jesus had always been turned away from him.

"Listen!" said Adam suddenly.

The group around him stiffened to attention. At first they could hear nothing, then slowly it became apparent to all of them that there were sounds on the night air that could only be man-made, the pressure of an indiscreet sandal on the pebbly earth, a stealthy breathing close at hand.

"Wait!" whispered Adam, sensing a tendency on the part of those about him to get hastily to their feet.

And then a voice came out of the darkness, a loud and commanding voice. "Adam ben Asher!"

When there was no response, the summons was repeated in a still louder tone. Once again: "Adam ben Asher!"

Adam rose then to his feet. He walked to the entrance of his tent. "Who is it?" he demanded. "And what do you want of me?"

"An attentive ear, first of all," said a voice which was that of Mijamin. "Understand this, Adam, my friend. I have men surrounding your camp. I prefer to finish what I have come to do without trouble or bloodshed. But if any attempt is made to interfere, my men will not hesitate to kill. I give you warning now not to make a move of any kind. Stay where you are, Adam ben Asher. Your people must remain in their tents. Is that clear?"

"It is clear."

"They must not obstruct my men in any way. They must make no commotion and they must not speak. Is that also clear?"

"That also is clear."

"My men are coming in now. Remember, all of you, what I have said. I want you to realize that you will pay ten times over for any hurt that may come to them."

Adam began to laugh at this point. "Yes, Mijamin," he called. "Come in, you and your men. I have been expecting you."

The men about him rose silently to their feet. Weapons were raised in readiness.

"Remember, my brothers," said Sempronius. "I am the eldest and so I speak for our good father. The Lord has said, 'Thou shalt not kill.' I lay this command on you, Tiberius, and on you, Gaius. Do not strike with all your strength. We must drive these intruders away, but also we must show them compassion."

4

Basil followed one of the three brothers—he did not know which— into action, marveling at the size of the club the latter carried. He said to himself, "It is more dangerous than the jawbone of an ass." It was light enough to see that the invaders on this side of the camp were numerous and well armed. Fortunately it was light enough for the followers of Mijamin to make a discovery themselves. A voice from their midst cried out, "It is one of the Giants of Slador!" The effect of this discovery was to discourage any effort to charge in for the easy success that had been promised them. They hung back and waited to be attacked.

The son of Catorius obliged them by going into action at once. He called in his high voice, "Follow me!" and then proceeded to cut a wide swath with his club. The invaders had so little stomach for this kind of fighting that his flailing blows fell, for the most part, on empty space. The Zealots fell back with such willingness, in fact, that in a matter of very few minutes the struggle had come to an end.

Basil had no opportunity to share in the exultant chase that followed. Someone sprang at him from a clump of underbrush and he found himself involved in a furious tussle. His opponent fought like a wildcat, and Basil would have been worsted quickly if he had not been lucky enough to drive a knee into the man's groin. The Zealot sank to the ground with a gasp, and Basil took advantage of his momentary helplessness to plant himself squarely on his back and pinion his arms. Lacking the strength to force his prisoner into camp, he did the next best thing; he retained his position and waited until it would be possible to summon assistance.

The victory was as quick and complete in the other areas, an equal reluctance being shown on each flank to stand up to the furious onslaught of the Giants of Slador. Although the initial clash was accompanied by an uproar of clanging metal and an angry babel of voices, this soon subsided into sounds of retreating feet and the triumphant shouts of the defenders.

As soon as the outcome of the struggle was assured and the enemy had betaken themselves off down the course of the wadi with much more speed than they had shown in their approach, lights flared up in the camp. Strutting in high triumph, Adam went from tent to tent and saw to it that torches were lighted and placed on high poles. He said to everyone he met: "It is all my doing! I trapped them. I brought them here. I had the blow ready that turned their blood to water and their bones to flabbiness. I, Adam ben Asher."

The illumination of the camp revealed a number of things. Deborra, dagger in hand, had seated herself on the broken chest, which had been placed in her tent, prepared quite apparently to defend to the last the precious object contained therein. Luke had improvised a platform for the care of the wounded by spreading blankets over a mound of tamarisk boughs. The Chinese prince had issued out from his pavilion with attendants on each side to support his forearms. He had been hastily muffled up in warm woolen garments and was demanding to know in a querulous squeak, "Are you engaged, honorable sirs, in one of your disputes over points of belief?"

Basil called urgently from the shadows, "I have a prisoner here and need help to bring him in."

There was general jubilation when it was discovered that the prisoner was none other than the organizer of the attack.

"*Heu-heu!*" said Adam, planting himself in front of the captive Mijamin with a gleam of delight in his eyes. "This is most fortunate. This makes my triumph complete. Now we shall be able to make sure, Brother Mijamin, that you cause us no more little inconveniences of this kind." With obvious reluctance he added, "It seems we must give some credit also to our worthy bridegroom."

When the three brothers came back into camp, wearing cheerful but modest smiles, Adam pointed to the figure of Mijamin seated in chagrin on the ground with his arms trussed behind him. "What are we to do with this fellow?" he asked.

One of the three scratched his head with a bloodstained finger. "I am Sempronius and so I speak for our father. This wicked man has earned death, but our father has taught us to look on violence as sinful. Our wish is that you do not slit his throat, as he deserves, but find some other way of preventing him from harming you further."

"Then tell me, Sempronius, is there in the hills where you tend your flocks some place to keep this troublemaker until we have passed on and can be sure of reaching our destination safely?"

The oldest brother had a deep cut on his forehead and blood had been flowing freely over his face. This had robbed him of his habitual mildness of expression and had given him instead a villainous scowl. His voice, however, was as gentle as ever. "There is a place in the hills where we could hold him for as long as you desire. It is a cave and it is dry and more comfortable than this bad man deserves. I am sure our father would agree to keeping him there."

"A week will be long enough," declared Adam, savoring his victory with a hearty smacking of lips. "By that time we will be so far along that we cannot be overtaken. But I am compelled to mention another point. Is it right to drag you further into our quarrels? If the Zealots of the Plain know that you are holding this fellow a prisoner, will they not try to get him away from you?"

"No," said Sempronius. He glanced at each of his brothers and received from them in turn a nod of the head and an answering "No." "It is this way, O Adam ben Asher," he went on. "We live quietly and we keep to ourselves. No one comes near us, and so they will not know that we hold this man of blood our prisoner."

"But after he is released? Will they not then seek to revenge themselves on you?"

Sempronius gave his head another shake. "No," he affirmed in his high, quiet voice. "We are very much feared. All they ask of us is to leave them alone. Oh no, Brother Adam. They will not make war on us of their own accord."

"Then it is settled!" exclaimed Adam. "You will, if you please, take this adder, this devil in the guise of a man, and keep him in that fine dry cave of which you speak. You will, I am sure, treat him more kindly than he deserves. But if he attempts to run away, I trust you will break every bone in his troublemaking body."

The oldest brother nodded. "Kindness should never be carried too far. The time comes when soft words must be replaced by the breaking of bones."

"Are you listening, O Mijamin?" demanded Adam.

"I am doing more than listening," said the Zealot leader. "I have been thinking deeply and I am still in a state of wonder as to what has happened this night. It is true that our immortal Samson killed a thousand men with the jawbone of an ass and that he slew a lion in the land of Timnath with his bare hands and then drew strength by eating of the honey he found in its carcass later. It is true that, after he had been shorn of his locks like an uncleansed Nazarite and then blinded, the strength came back slowly into his stunted muscles and he pulled down the pillars of the temple where the Philistines had gathered in their thousands to mock him. But Samson was a servant of God and was given his strength for a purpose. It was not by the power of his human arm alone that he slew the thousand men; the anger of Jehovah had chilled the hearts of the Philistines, and they were like lambs led to the sacrifice."

He stirred uneasily on the ground and strove to ease the pressure of the cords on his arms.

"Now these three young men from Slador are tall and strong and they are mighty in conflict. But they are not like Samson, who could prevail against any odds. There was no reason for my men to lose heart at once and refuse to fight. They came with me in sufficient numbers to overcome a dozen such as these. Why, then, did they turn and run away? Can it be"—he paused and gave his head a puzzled shake—"can it be that Jehovah is concerned about the safekeeping of this Cup? Does He place about it the veil of His inflexible will so that what seem to be miracles are wrought in its defense? Are we, then, in the wrong? I am deep in a pondering as to the truth, Adam ben Asher, and so far I have not seen the light. Perhaps in this dry and comfortable cave of which these three tall young men have spoken I shall have the time to reach a conclusion.

"But," he cried in a concluding word of fierce determination, "do not make the mistake of thinking you have seen the last of me. I do not know what I shall do or where I shall go. I dare not return to Jerusalem at once and face the Mar with another failure to explain. Watch, rather, for me in Antioch. I shall undoubtedly appear there in course of time; though for what purpose I cannot say."

Luke had taken off his outer garment of brown wool and had stripped his tunic down to his waist in preparation for the work ahead. No one had been killed, fortunately, but there had been much letting of blood. There were broken heads aplenty and deep cuts and painful contusions. Among the assailants who had been too badly hurt to get away was one who lay outside the circle of light and moaned piteously for help. It developed later that he had suffered a dislocated hip as a result of being tossed over the heads of his fellows by one of the three brothers.

The physician washed all cuts in a solution of wine and water, working with sure and gentle hands. His face, which showed deep lines of weariness, was filled with compassion for the sufferers. It was a firm conviction with him that wounds should be kept moist, and he strove to accomplish this by a special method of bandaging. He would moisten a piece of sponge and place it over the wound, covering it then with leaves of delicate texture before putting on the final bandage of linen.

All three of the brothers had suffered injury, but nothing of a serious nature. Luke said in an admiring tone as he bound the gash in the head of Sempronius: "Never have I encountered such perfect physical specimens as you and your brothers. Have any of you ever been ill?"

The oldest of the trio smiled and shook his head. "No, Master Luke, we are never ill. Why should we be? We eat simple food, we live in the open, we sleep well under the stars. We do not see other people and so we do not catch their complaints. It is a good life we have, my brothers and I." He nodded to lend added emphasis. "We heal quickly. In a week there will be no trace of this cut on me."

The Zealot with the dislocated hip was brought in last. The Chinese prince, who had caused a seat to be arranged for him beside the bed of tamarisk boughs and had watched everything with an avid interest, now licked his lips. "This will be good to watch," he declared, his head nodding with excitement on his thin neck. "He will be a loud sufferer, this one. He will make most lusty outcries."

He was not disappointed. The injured man, who had been beseeching help so loudly, began to entreat that he be left alone when Luke proceeded to lash his arms to his sides. His protestations rose to a still higher pitch when his legs were bound together above the knees with a stout strap of leather. When one of Luke's assistants attached an iron hook to the limb of a tree hanging over the improvised bed and the wounded man realized that this was part of his treatment, he let out a loud screech and called on Jehovah to save him. Paying no heed to his cries, two of the assistants lifted him up high and then suspended him head downward on the hook like a quarter of beef. He swung back and forth for several moments, moaning, "O Great Father above, save Thy humble servant who will be butchered like a stalled ox!"

"This reduces the dislocation," explained Luke, who saw that the watchers were sharing the horror of the patient. "It is always a hard matter to get the joint back into place. It is a serious dislocation and so, much as I deplore the necessity, we must proceed to the most extreme of methods." He felt the hip and then nodded to one of the assistants. "Now, Tabeel, if you please."

The man Tabeel placed his arms about the waist of the sufferer and allowed his own feet to swing off the ground so that the whole of his weight was added to that of the patient. The patient cried out loudly to Jehovah and then fainted. Luke, his face tense, seized the man's thigh and gave it a skillful twist. There was a loud, cracking sound and the bone slipped back into its socket.

"Let him down!" cried the physician.

The assistants lowered the body to the bed of boughs. Luke ran an exploring hand over the hip and then nodded with satisfaction. The operation had been successfully carried out.

"Most excellently done," said the prince, bobbing his head. "I enjoyed it very much. How horribly he screamed!"

Luke was washing his hands in a bowl of hot water. "That one is the last," he said, "and I am happy there are no more. As I grow older I find in myself an increasing reluctance to cause pain."

The first light of dawn was showing in the sky. Adam, who had a quick eye for any chance to save, shouted to extinguish the torches. The three brothers exchanged glances and then nodded in unison.

"Our mother has been tending the flocks," said one. "It is time we returned to relieve her."

"There will be breakfast in a very short time," protested Deborra. "I will tell the servants to hurry their preparations."

"Our mother will have food for us," said the one who had spoken before. "It is kind of you, good lady, but we must not delay longer."

"But are you strong enough to walk so far?" she asked. "You all have wounds. Surely it would be wiser to rest before setting out."

The spokesman smiled quietly as he raised his club over his shoulder. "Our hurts are small."

Two of them took Mijamin between them and set off with vigorous strides, a compelling arm through each of his. His short legs seemed to be moving with some of the speed of a mockingbird's wings in keeping pace with them. The third looked back over his shoulder and gave Deborra a shy smile of parting.

"Thank you! Thank you all so much!" she cried, waving a hand to them. "The Lord will bless you for the splendid thing you have done tonight." She waved again for the benefit of the one who had lingered. "I know which one you are. You are Gaius."

The smile on his face broadened with gratification at being thus identified. "Yes, lady," he said. "I am Gaius. The youngest."

Adam watched them stride off along the crooked path that followed the winding course of the wadi. Then he turned and gazed intently into the west.

"The ship on which your father sails to Antioch," he said to Deborra, "has had no delays. None of which we know. It may be that it has made a great gain on us already. There will be no chance for sleep now. We must have the camels loaded and be on our way." He glanced along the northern trail, which was wrapped in a white morning mist. "It is going to be a very hot day."

CHAPTER XVI

I

THE THIRD DAY saw them toiling along the high paths between the Plain and the Sea of Galilee. By night they were well beyond the uppermost tip of the sea and within sight of the three peaks of Hermon, which is called the Snowy Mountain. All this was country sacred to the memory of Jesus, and so Deborra had not drawn the curtains, fearing that something would escape her. It was a sore blow to her that they could not spare the time to visit Nazareth. She looked longingly up the rocky road that led off to the west and the little village where the young Carpenter had spent His youth, and then she sighed and said, "I would be happy with seeing no more than the roof of the little house of Joseph."

Sometimes the road had climbed so high up along the crest of the hills that they would catch glimpses of the water of Galilee. The water was green and still and overhung with clouds as white as the inner walls of paradise. Memories clustered about this sacred sea, and at times Deborra was unable to contain herself. "Perhaps," she would cry out aloud, "it was here that Jesus walked upon the waters!" or, "Could it have been here that He wrought the miracle of the loaves and fishes?" Once, her grief flooding back into her mind, she burst into tears. "My grandfather and I often talked of the time when we would come here and follow in Christ's footsteps; and now he is dead and I must do it alone!"

At a point where the road turned sharply northeast, a ruddy-faced man in a patched woolen garment of russet color came out in front of them and raised a detaining arm.

"Are ye Christians?" he asked. "Do ye seek to see the country where Jesus lived and first taught? If such ye be, then Theudas is your man. I, Theudas, son of Javan, know the country of the Christ better than anyone living. I can show ye——" He stopped abruptly, his eye having traveled as far along the line of the caravan as the camel on which Luke was perched. His confidence slumped like the drooping of the tail of a reproved dog. "So! We have Luke with us. Luke the Scribbler, Luke the Skeptic. Luke who will not agree that Theudas knows about what he tells. Out with it, then, Luke the Faultfinder! Tell them that Theudas knows nothing, that he is a fraud!"

Luke looked sternly down at the man. "You know nothing, Theudas," he said. "And you *are* a fraud. You make a living by cheating people with false information. This much I promise you: that some day retribution will overtake you. You will raise an arm to point your lies and your body will turn to stone, and you will stand there forever after like the pillar of salt."

A spasm of fear shook the frame of Theudas. "Look not at me!" he cried. "I will not be put under one of your spells! I am too wise to be caught in any such net. I am a friend of Simon the Magician. I will go to Simon and I will say to him, 'Something must be done about this pious old healer of bodies, this Luke from Antioch.' And Simon will do my bidding and turn you into a snake to crawl for all time on your belly and hiss at men!"

They rode on without paying any further attention to him. He remained in the middle of the dusty highway, shaking his fists in the air and screeching after them, "Luke, Luke, Luke! May you get the camel's itch! May you waste away with a running of the reins! I spit on you, Luke the Letter of Blood. Luke the Leech!"

Luke was compelled to smile. "He is a vituperative rascal," he said to Deborra, who rode beside him. "The danger with such beggars is the harm they can do to the credulous and to earnest seekers after the truth. Do you know that there are merchants already in Jerusalem who are prepared to sell pieces of the cross on which Jesus died? The cross is in existence and in safe hands, but it will never be divided up for sale among a lot of greedy dealers. There will be more of this traffic as the years pass and the memories of men grow dim. For that reason we should be severe with impostors like Theudas, even though they sometimes cause us to smile."

They made camp for the night on the crest of a hill that seemed no more than a mile from the foot of Mount Hermon. The next morning that mile would keep stretching out and multiplying and would turn into many miles indeed, but at this quiet hour of the evening it seemed to the weary travelers that they could see every scar on the face of the mountain and that no more than a foot forward would take them into the evening mists which, as usual, had gathered about the peaks, and that they would feel the cool moisture like a benediction after the heat of the day.

2

Adam ben Asher saw to it that the tents were raised with more than the usual expedition and then summoned a council. It met inside the circle of tents, from which rose the tantalizing odors of the supper that was being prepared. The drivers and guards squatted about Adam. As he was acting as his own overseer, he occupied the center, facing the white-capped peaks of Mount Hermon. Luke, Deborra, and Basil, being no more than travelers, were relegated to places outside the circle, and it was understood that they might not take any part in the discussion without the unanimous consent of the caravan men. Deborra, finding herself seated beside Basil, gave him a long and careful smile before drawing her purple *palla* about her shoulders and lapsing into an attentive silence. Seated directly across from them, Luke watched with a frown. It was clear that he was puzzled by their attitude toward one another.

Adam began by informing the council that it was highly necessary to reach Antioch before a certain ship could get to that city. The ship in question, which had sailed from Joppa soon after their departure from Jerusalem, was a fast sailing vessel and capable of doing the equivalent of sixty miles a day or even better. Glancing about the circle of absorbed brown faces, he propounded the question, What chance did they have of winning the race to Antioch?

There followed one of the long silences to which men of the East, and particularly those who passed their lives on the desert trails, were much addicted. Then one of the guards caught Adam's eye.

"Master!"

"I am listening, Shammai."

"These are good camels," said the guard. "Their feet will never linger enough to suffer from sand burns. It is true that some of them are old, but is it not said with great truth that a strong old camel carries the hides of many young ones?"

"It is a wise saying, Shammai."

"The pace must on that account be set by what these older ones are capable of doing. They can do fifty miles a day. But, master, they can do fifty for no more than five days at a stretch. If you try to keep them longer at this fast pace they will grumble and complain. Then they will groan and whimper; and very soon, master, they will drop down to their knees and their heads will sink forward slowly, and they will die of the efforts they have made. I am young, but this I say without hesitation, even in this company of men who are older and wiser than I am, that it would be wrong to do more than thirty-five or forty a day. That gait can be maintained for the whole distance, and none of them will be any the worse for it."

"We have listened to the words of Shammai," said Adam. "If we follow his advice, what chance have we of getting first to Antioch?"

"May one speak who knows little of such matters but has sailed much on the seas?" asked Luke.

Adam waited for the nod of acquiescence from the brown heads of the caravan men before saying, "We shall be glad to listen."

Luke bowed to the company and expressed his appreciation in the customary phrase, "I thank those who are wiser than I." Then he bowed to Adam alone. "It is true that a ship may make sixty miles a day, but this is only the case when conditions of wind and sun are perfect. It is to be expected that on some days at this season there will be no wind at all and that ships will float idly on a sea without any swell and with sails hanging as limply as vines after a frost. On such days no progress may be made at all, or at the most a few miles. On the other hand, if the winds are strong, it may be impossible to venture out from the harbor, or at best to creep from island to island. Even when the winds are not heavy they may blow from the north or west, and then it becomes necessary to take slanting tacks so that a ship may seem to be accomplishing a full day's journey and yet be no more than a few miles farther at the end of the twenty-four hours."

"What does Luke the Physician advise us to do?" asked Adam.

"I have no advice to give. My sole purpose was to make it clear that there will be difficulties at sea as great as any we may encounter."

Seated cross-legged at a point of the circle opposite Adam was a young driver with dark, eager eyes and a ready smile. Basil had liked him from the start and had made occasions to talk with him. He sang a great deal and his name was Chimham.

"Since there is need to reach Antioch first," said this young camel man, "we should take every risk to win this race."

Basil leaned forward excitedly. "Chimham is right!" he cried. "We cannot afford to be cautious. We must take risks."

Adam turned toward him with a hostile eye. "You are an outsider," he said, "and may not address the council without the consent of the members."

A slow fury that had been aroused in Basil by the open antagonism of Adam was on the point of breaking into a blaze. He was so angry at this stage that for a long moment he did not dare risk speaking. Finally he said in a suppressed tone, "Have I the permission of the council to speak?"

The white-swathed heads bowed their willingness. Basil edged forward and began: "Yes, we must take risks. What will it benefit us if we spare the camels and arrive in Antioch too late to accomplish the purpose that takes us there?"

"They are my camels," asserted Adam.

"You have kept us well aware of that."

"If they are driven beyond their powers and die, it will be my loss."

"That is clear to all of us."

"The point," declared Adam angrily, "is worth raising, I think."

"It is worth raising." Basil stared at the caravan owner with no attempt to conceal his feelings. "It is a point I wish to discuss with you alone after this council is over."

"I cannot conceive of anything *you* may say that will have any bearing on the decision that faces us."

"Perhaps," declared Basil, "you will change your mind. In the meantime I have a plan to propose. It is not necessary to drive the whole fleet to the limit of their powers. Select instead the two strongest and fastest and give them no more than a rider to carry and a small supply of food. I am told that under these circumstances a good camel can do more than fifty miles and keep it up indefinitely."

"That is true," said Chimham. It was clear that he had sensed what Basil had to propose and was in full agreement. "We have several in this fleet that could keep up that gait as far at least as Antioch."

"The riders," went on Basil, "should set out at once and carry the word ahead to Antioch that nothing should be done about a certain matter until the full caravan arrives. I believe they could be counted upon to arrive three or four days ahead of the caravan and that they could get there ahead of the ship."

Chimham had been doing some intensive reckoning. "Give the riders a free hand and they might arrive five days ahead of the rest," he declared.

"May I speak?" asked Luke.

There was a solemn bobbing of heads. Adam, rubbing his nose in concentrated thought, paid no attention to the request.

"I think we have listened to words of good sense," declared Luke. "We will have some advantage under this plan, and the possibilities of loss are reduced to the effect on two camels only."

Adam looked up to ask, "Who will volunteer to act if this plan is decided upon?"

"I will go!" cried Chimham eagerly. "Let me have old Bildad. He is as stubborn and mean as the Bildad for whom he is named, the comforter who sat so sour on the stomach of Job. He knows my ways and he likes me; that is, if a camel has enough sense to like anyone or anything. Some say they don't, but I think they do. I promise this much by the earth and my head: let me have Bildad and I will ride him down the four-columned Colonnade at Antioch before the sails of the ship can be sighted by the harbor lookouts."

"Fine words," grumbled Adam. "You blow so hard that you could stir up a wind strong enough to bring that ship into port ahead of the best camels that ever trod the trail." He looked unwillingly at the circle of camel men squatted about him. "Who else?"

Basil did not wait for permission to speak. "Let me be the other to go. I know nothing of the handling of camels, but I am willing to learn. I am so concerned with the need to complete the journey in the shortest possible time that I am prepared to place myself under Chimham's orders and to do everything that he may demand of me."

Deborra touched his shoulder with an anxious hand. "But, Basil, can you stand the fatigue?" she whispered. "Can you bear the exposure to the sun by riding without cover? Should this not be left to those who are accustomed to the life of the desert?"

He answered in a low voice, placing his head in close proximity to hers but keeping his eyes on the ground. "It is my duty to go. I could not make this journey in comfort while others took the risks for us. If I did that, I should never be able to hold my head up again. Surely you agree with me." Then, with some reluctance, he went on to give another reason. "By going I will, moreover, release you from the embarrassment of my presence. You will not be under the necessity of explaining why we do not share a tent. I confess that I also will be most happy to escape from my share in this embarrassment. The plan," he added after a moment, "will be to start tonight after a few hours' rest. We will be well ahead of the caravan by the time you set out in the morning, and so there will be no gossiping or whispering or rubbing of hands about us. It is a perfect way to escape the difficulties of our position."

While this went on Chimham had been addressing the council. He had expressed his willingness to have Basil as his companion and to undertake himself the care of both camels. He recommended that a younger camel than the morose veteran Bildad be selected. His choice, he said, would be Romamti-ezer. "Ezer," he declared, "is a glutton and a complainer. He is a snarler and a howler by night and he would rather snap at the kneecap of a rider than an acacia bough. But he is strong and he will keep right up with Bildad. They will be the best combination."

Adam looked up with a scowl and made a silent appraisal of the circle of his men. "Then it is settled," he said. "Chimham and the bridegroom. Bildad and Ezer. Youth and experience. Peace be with them."

3

Adam had dipped a hand in the dish of stewed lamb and was gnawing a knucklebone with relish. He sloshed his hand in hot water and gave his chin a hasty rubbing when Basil approached him.

"You expressed concern over the safety of your camels," said the latter. "I come to propose that you allow me to purchase from you the pair we shall put to the test of this fast journey to Antioch."

Adam indulged in a grunt. "Bildad and old Ezer will come high. Have you any idea *how* high?"

"I do not care." The smolder of Basil's resentment had now been fanned into an active blaze. "I have money. I have little knowledge of the value of camels—and little desire to know—but I think I have enough to pay for two. I want to make this clear. That I would rather be stripped of my last coin than be beholden further to you."

Adam studied him with a shrewd eye. "Speaking right up to me like a stout little man," he said. "This is a new face you are showing."

"I have stood as much from you as I can. When I leave camp tonight it will be with the hope that I never set eyes on you again."

"And I have stood as much of you as *I* can stomach," declared Adam. "The dangers you will encounter on this journey cannot be too great to satisfy me." He was silent for a moment and then threw restraint aside. "If the balance were cast up between us, who would come out ahead? If you have any doubts, I will tell you. *You!* I have said many bitter things about you, both to your face and behind your back. A favorite pastime with me for the rest of my life will be to speak of you with scorn and bitterness; but all you will have to complain of will be the rasp of my tongue. On the other hand, do you realize what you have done to me?"

Basil nodded his head. "Yes, I know."

"You have given me good reason to hate you." Adam made an expressive gesture with his hands. "Oh, I will sell you the camels, and I will put the price high because of the intensity of my dislike for you. There will be satisfaction for me if I can succeed in making you pay most handsomely through the nose."

Although he had said that he had no knowledge of the value of camels, it seemed to Basil that the price Adam then proceeded to state was fantastically high. He was slow at calculating, having little gift for figures, and it took him some time to decide that he could meet the price set and still have enough left to pay his expenses on the trips ahead of him. He did not then hesitate a moment longer.

"I accept," he said.

Adam snapped his fingers impatiently. "Will you not give me the satisfaction of bargaining with you, of overreaching you in the end?" he cried. "No, I see you have no such intention. You are too proud. It suits you better to look at me with a cold eye and say to yourself, 'I will not bandy words with this higgling dog.' Let us get it over then as quickly as we may. Count out the money and give it to me. You are not generous enough to let me be the winner in as small a matter as this. Hurry! I am anxious to see the last of you."

Basil took the purse from his belt and counted out the money. He tried to be quick about it as Adam had demanded, but his unfamiliarity with money made this impossible. Adam watched with no attempt to conceal his contempt and impatience.

"A word of advice," said the caravan owner as the counting went on. "Learn something about the ways of the world. You are the little Deborra's husband, and for her sake I do not want you to be cheated all your life as I am cheating you now. And another hint. Where did you get those clothes in which you were married?"

"They were a gift from Joseph of Arimathea."

"That is strange. My master must have realized that they carried the device of the eagle and serpent, which is the insignia of Dan. You are not a member of the tribe of Dan and you have no right to wear the device. My advice to you would be to have all the embroidery and the embossing removed."

"I will never wear the clothes again if that will suit you better."

Adam scowled. "I would be best suited if there had never been an occasion for you to wear them."

The count came to an end and the money was handed to Adam. He checked the amount carefully before putting it away in his own belt.

"I think it is even between us tonight," he said with belated satisfaction. "You have scorned to bargain with me. I have cheated you outrageously. Yes, it is even." He gave his head a slow nod. "And now for some more advice, which I give in full honesty. Sleep until midnight. You will need every minute of rest you can get. Chimham will see to it in the meantime that all necessary arrangements are made. This, I trust, is the last time I shall speak to you, but I am not a hypocrite and so I do not say, 'Peace be with you.' This much I do wish you, a fast and safe trip to Antioch. I wish it most earnestly for the sake of the little Deborra."

"Then," said Basil, "we are, for once, in accord."

4

When Basil sought out Luke in the small tent the latter occupied and said he would like the privilege of sleeping there until midnight, the physician regarded him with a questioning eye.

"This is strange behavior, my son," he said. "Can it be that you have quarreled with your wife?"

Basil shook his head. "There has been no quarrel. All I am free to tell you is that I am here at Deborra's wish." He added after a moment's pause, "If there is any fault in the matter, it is mine."

He stripped to his scanty linen tunic and stretched himself out on a blanket. There was an open space to admit air at the peak of the tent, and through it he could see a dense cluster of stars. He studied them for a moment and then closed his eyes.

"I think," said Luke, "that I shall have a talk with Deborra."

Basil opened his eyes at once and turned to look at him with an anxious frown. "You will not find her willing to talk. Would it not be kinder to spare her your questions?"

Luke hesitated for a moment only. "No, my son. I think it is necessary to speak to her before you go away. All human troubles can be disposed of when approached in the right way. You will tell me nothing. Have I your permission to ask your wife a few questions?"

Basil was unutterably weary. He had passed through three exacting days, physically and mentally, and he had not slept in that time. His eyes seemed incapable of turning in their sockets when he strove to raise them for a glance at his companion's face. He allowed them to close again.

"So be it," he said. "Ask her your questions. I leave this in your hands—and in hers." Having said this, he fell off soundly to sleep.

Deborra's maidservant was combing her mistress's hair when Luke appeared at the entrance of the tent. His "May I enter?" brought an affirmative response before the bride realized that her face was coated with a thick white substance. He looked so startled that, in spite of the troubles that weighed so heavily on her mind, she indulged in a brief smile.

"I should have told you to wait," she said, "until I had removed all the evidence of my guilty secret. Now you have discovered me in one of my wicked habits; of which, I confess, I have a number. A woman's skin becomes parched and dry when exposed to the sun of the desert. A cream like this helps it very much. This comes from the East—the very far East. Every caravan that comes in brings a small box for my use. It is delivered with the utmost secrecy." The maid had succeeded by this time in removing all traces of it from her cheeks. "I know it is considered wrong to use salves and lotions even though Solomon's Queen of Sheba brought them with her. I do not think it wrong. I think it sensible."

Luke's manner made it clear that he desired to speak with her alone, so Deborra dismissed the maid. With her face free of the cream, her weariness and distress of mind were clearly apparent.

"Your husband sleeps in my tent," said Luke.

Deborra flushed. "Did he make no explanation?"

"None."

Deborra allowed her hands to fall limply to her lap. She sighed. "It is in accordance with an arrangement we have made."

"Will you allow me to ask some questions?"

She hesitated and then said, "Yes."

"If it had not been necessary for Basil to ride ahead, would he have shared your tent?"

"No," she said with reluctance.

"The arrangement of which you speak was made before the wedding?" She nodded. "Yes, before. We decided it would be a marriage of form only."

Luke frowned as though he could neither understand nor condone such an arrangement. "Does he love you?"

"No, he does not love me."

"And what of you? Do you love him?" Before she could answer he went on: "You must forgive me for probing into your affairs in this way, but I am convinced this is wrong and that something should be done to alter it before it is too late."

She hesitated for a moment and then answered his question with simple dignity. "I love him truly and deeply, else I would not have married him."

"I am glad to hear you say that. But why was Basil willing to marry you if, as you say, he does not love you?"

She explained with an air of weariness, "It had been settled, as you know, that I should go to Antioch with the status of a married woman. It had been in my mind that he loved me, but when I found that it was not so, I suggested the marriage of form."

"With the intention of seeking a divorce later?"

"I do not believe in divorce. But if Basil desires to be free of me later, I will not stand in his way." She shook her head with an air of hopeless- ness. "If you please, I would rather not talk about it any more. It is very hard for me to discuss this with anyone."

"But, my poor child," said Luke, "I feel a responsibility for what has happened. It was I who pointed out to your grandfather the advisability of arranging a marriage for you before you went to claim your inheritance. I was convinced then that a genuine attraction had grown up between you and Basil. When you told me he was your choice, I was very happy about it. I was certain he was in love with you."

"So was I." Her voice quavered. "I would not have spoken to him if I had not felt sure. And then—and then he did not answer me at once and I knew I had taken too much for granted. When he told me about the other woman——"

Luke's brows drew together in a troubled frown. "Is he in love with another woman?"

"He says not. But he told me that she was—that she was much in his mind. He feels indebted to her because she sent him a warning when he was a slave in Antioch—a warning of the danger in which he stood. It was because of this that he began to offer up prayers and that you came to take him away."

"He told me of receiving a note. But he did not know at that time who sent it."

"She told him when he saw her in Jerusalem. It—it is the woman who assists Simon the Magician."

Luke had been running his hands through the soft strands of his beard, but at this point he stopped. He stared at Deborra with incredulous eyes. "That infamous woman!" he exclaimed. "It is hard to believe."

"I found it hard."

"I have never believed in love potions or spells, counting them no more than silly tricks of the magic trade. Now, for the first time in my life, I find myself inclined to think there are such things. No other explanation seems possible in this case."

A stern frown had driven all trace of benevolence from Luke's face. He remained for several moments in an absorbed consideration of the situation. Then, with apparent reluctance, he entered on an explanation. "The leaders of the church of our Master," he said, "have to be more than evangelical preachers. They have the welfare of the church in their hands and so they require to have some political sense as well. It was recognized that Simon the Magician's efforts to rob men of their belief in the divinity of Jesus would have to be met. Certain inquiries about him were made. As a result we have learned many things since Simon made his appearance in Jerusalem, things about him and about this woman Helena as well. After running away from her master in Antioch, she lived with a number of men before Simon. It may be that the need will never arise to use this—or any of the shoddy things that have been discovered in the record of Simon, that very bad Samaritan. I trust not. But"—the frown on the usually benign brow became still more pronounced—"something must be done to cure this foolish boy of his interest in the woman. Does he know you are in love with him?"

"No, no! I—I have tried to maintain some reticence about my feelings." Deborra's eyes filled with tears of weariness. "He is no happier than I am. I don't think he knows what we expect of him. We have told him he must not do things that had always seemed right and natural. We tried to make him change his way of thinking to ours. I am sure he is mixed up in his mind and that he made the confession to me because he thought it was the Christian way of acting."

After a moment's thought Luke nodded in agreement. "You are right, my child. The poor fellow is befuddled by our preaching at him." He laid a comforting hand on hers. "I came to suggest that you make an effort to bring him to his senses, even to the extent of letting him see the state of your feelings. Can it be done?"

She shook her head vehemently. "No, my kind friend. I can do nothing more until he comes to me and says—the things I must hear him say. To do anything else would be a sure way of losing him."

"But are you prepared to go on like this? To be a married woman without a husband? To make your life a sham? Surely, little Deborra, there is something you can do."

"Yes, there is something I can do." She achieved a smile, although it could not have been described as a cheerful one. "I can wait."

Basil came to the tent of Deborra in a woolen cloak that swathed him warmly from neck to ankles, for the air had turned sharply cold. In recognition perhaps of the biting proclivities of Ezer he had strapped the faded leather pads about his shins. A small bundle of clothing, a very small one, was slung over his shoulder.

"We are leaving now," he said.

Deborra had not been able to sleep. She had slept so little, in fact, since her return to Jerusalem that her eyes seemed to have grown in size until they dominated her face. Nothing had been requisitioned from the last of the little boxes to lend her color, and so her cheeks were pale.

As soon as the first sound of his approaching footsteps had reached her ears a thought had begun to throb in her mind: "I love him, I love him, I love him!" Now she asked herself, "Can I let him go like this? Should I not make one effort?" None of this inner struggle showed in her face, however, and she spoke in a quiet voice. "I dread to think of the hardships ahead of you. But I have been considering and I can understand why you feel it necessary to go. I will pray for your safety and well-being, Basil."

She was holding a pewter bowl in which a wick was floating in a bed of oil. By this rather feeble light he could see the paleness of her cheeks and the studied control of her expression. There were two beds on the ground. In the one that he, as her husband, might have occupied, the maidservant Sarah was lying. She had wakened and he could see that she was watching them through half-closed eyes.

"We have discussed our route with Adam," he explained. "As you will follow the same course, you will have word of us at every stop you make. I believe," he added, "that we will reach Antioch in time."

"Yes," she said in a low tone, "I am sure of that."

He touched the pouch at his belt. "I have the letter to the banker. It should serve to delay any decision until you arrive."

She voiced a fear that had been in her mind since he had decided to go. "Will there be any danger for you in Antioch?"

"My freedom was purchased legally and I carry the document that attests it. I have so little fear that I intend to make an effort to see my mother. Linus will probably refuse to let me in, but I shall try."

"Take every care," she urged. "You must remember that Linus has become a man of great power."

"I will take every care. That much I promise you most solemnly. I shall do nothing that might prevent me from finishing the Chalice."

"Basil——!" She did not continue with the words that had risen unbidden to her lips, but she said them to herself with a passionate intensity: "I cannot bear to let you go like this! Say you will put this foreign woman out of your mind! Say you will try to love me instead!"

All that she put aloud into words was a question: "Are you sufficiently rested?"

"I slept soundly for three hours and now I feel fresh and ready for our adventure."

They touched hands lightly and briefly. Basil adjusted the bundle over his shoulder. "Farewell," he said.

"Farewell. May Jehovah look down on you and give you His protection."

CHAPTER XVII

I

THAT FIRST NIGHT the two riders drove on steadily through the darkness, then through the glory of the dawn and on into the freshness of the hours of early morning. They desisted only when the sun reached a high place in the heavens and began to unlimber the full fury of its attack. Stretching themselves out on the sand, they slept with cloaks spread to shade their heads, while Bildad and Ezer contentedly munched capparis and sunt leaves and nebbuk bushes, snorting with pleasure over the salty flavor of an occasional leaf of salsola. In four hours, the bitterness of the solar assault having abated, they were up and off again.

Two episodes occurred during the second day that astonished Basil in his complete ignorance of the ways of the camel. Something had happened to cause a sense of grievance in the tiny brain of Bildad. His resentment showed itself in an unwillingness to be pressed, in much snorting and tossing of his muzzle, in an occasional backward snap in the hope of catching some portion of his rider's anatomy in his powerful, projecting teeth.

Chimham was puzzled. "What have I done to this old rascal?" he asked aloud. "I am not aware of any injury, but it is clear he is in one of his very worst fits." He was finding it necessary to keep his dagger out and to strike with the handle whenever the head of the camel swung around. "He must be placated or I shall come to some serious injury."

He called, "*Kharr!*" and the angry camel, through force of habit, came to a halt. With much snorting and whining it reached a kneeling position, and the rider sprang quickly to the ground. Removing his tunic, he tossed it in front of Bildad and then retreated in great haste.

Something happened then that roused Basil abruptly from the almost comatose condition to which he had been reduced by the heat. Bildad seized the garment in his fierce teeth and proceeded to tear it into shreds and tatters. The infuriated camel brought his forefeet into play to complete its destruction, stamping on it furiously. The tunic was soon reduced to pulp, but the animal continued to vent his anger on it with a high screeching.

"He thinks it is me," explained Chimham. "What a pity that the tunic was new. But it had to be sacrificed. Better to lose a piece of cloth than to have your face trampled to nothing. I have seen *that* happen."

He then walked toward the camel with an air of confidence, chirping and calling him by name. "Good Bildad! Brave Bildad! My fine Bildad!" he said. The camel, trembling a little, stood perfectly still.

"Keep away from him!" cried Basil, who had been appalled by the fury of the exhibition. "He will tear you to pieces!"

"No, it is quite safe now." Chimham spoke with confidence and continued to approach the camel. "He has vented his spite, and in that funny little lump of brain of his he is quite satisfied. He is sure he has paid off the score. I am someone different. He does not care about me at all."

Basil watched, nevertheless, with considerable apprehension and was prepared to rush to his new friend's assistance if the need rose. Chimham had been right, however. He stepped up into the *rakhala,* the concave saddle with elevated pommel that camel men used. Reaching out a foot, he touched the neck of the now quiet Bildad. The camel groaned, raised his muzzle to whine piteously, then began to rise from his kneeling position. "*Khikh!*" called Chimham, and the animal started off without any hesitation.

"My good fellow!" cried Chimham. He turned his head to look back. "What a strange old *buzzud* he is. I have no idea what fancied injuries he had been storing up, but I have never seen him in such a tantrum before. It is all over and forgotten now. We will be the best of friends, he and I."

The second incident concerned Basil and occurred some hours later. The sun had climbed higher and higher into the sky until it was directly overhead and its rays beat down with merciless intensity. Basil became dizzy with it. He was barely able to retain his seat in the saddle and had to cling to the high pommel with almost lifeless fingers. Chimham was in the lead and was impervious, seemingly, to the devastating heat.

Basil was on the point a dozen times of suggesting that they stop to rest, but pride held him back. He had said in volunteering that he could

withstand the physical hardships and he did not want to give in as quickly
as this. Once in desperation, as he felt himself reel sickly in the saddle, he
said: "Chimham, have mercy on a poor beginner! Is it not time to rest?"
When his companion did not respond or turn back to look, he realized
that he had formed the words with his lips but had not spoken them.

An eternity seemed to pass,. an eternity spent in a steaming caldron.
Basil clung to the pommel with his numb fingers and managed to keep
from falling. It was clear to him, however, that sooner or later he would
lose consciousness and drop from his high elevation to the ground. It
would be a dangerous fall, for Ezer was a lanky animal with legs of
unusual length. The sand, moreover, had been swept by winds and beaten
down by the passage of countless caravans. There were rocks by the side
of the trail, sticking jagged teeth out of the scanty underbrush. Nothing
could be done about it; he had lost all capacity to act, even to speak.
There was nothing to be done but cling to the saddle and wait for the
inevitable.

"Someone else will finish the Chalice," he thought. He had left with
the others the model he had made for the frame. He was not entirely
satisfied with it and intended to improve upon it in many ways before
casting it in silver; but it was beginning to take on substance and form
and sometimes, when he studied it with the enthusiasm that will swell up
inside a creator, he had been carried away with its beauty. With the frame
were the clay models of the figures. It should not be hard, he reflected,
for whomever they might select to complete it from the stage where he
was leaving it.

Then it seemed to him that he was aboard a ship. It was careening
ahead at a furious rate and he was hanging to the side. The rate of progress was so violent that he was jerked back and forth and collided with
objects of such fixity that he rebounded painfully from them. He heard
the voice of Chimham from somewhere in the far distance shouting desperate instructions, but his mind was unable to grasp them. Even if
he had been able to comprehend, he lacked the power to do anything
about it.

The ship came to an abrupt stop, and he realized that he had parted
company with it. He was hurtling through the air, and the thought flashed
through his mind that this would be the end, the end of everything. He
was reconciled to the idea of death. It would bring release from the
agonies of travel and escape from the pitiless sun.

When he landed, it was in a pool of water. It was not deep, and he plunged through to the bottom, striking the mud with a jolt that he felt through his whole body. For a moment he made no effort to move, taking a physical pleasure in the sudden coolness. Then the instinct of preservation caused him to struggle to a standing position. He discovered then that the water was only deep enough to reach his knees.

The shock of the immersion had cleared his brain. He looked about him and saw that the water into which he had been thrown was a small pool in a palm-fringed oasis. Ezer had already sunk to his knees at the edge and was drinking voraciously.

Chimham was riding up in furious haste and waving his arms. "Get him out!" he shouted. "He must not drink before eating. It will kill him!"

Basil dragged his feet out of the clinging mud and struggled to the shore. Ezer whimpered in protest when he was hauled away from this spot of great delight.

"Did you lose control of him?" asked Chimham, riding Bildad up to the line of the trees but no farther. "I shouted to you, but you paid no attention."

"I think I lost consciousness," said Basil humbly. "The heat was more than I could stand. I am afraid we shall have to make a stop here. I feel limp and useless."

Chimham looked up at the sun and then nodded his head. "We kept at it too long. My friend, when you feel yourself going this way, you must let me know. After all, you are new to this kind of thing; and better men than you have been unable to stand the heat of the midday sun. I can see you are all puffed up with foolish pride and do not like to give in. Let me tell you this: pride is the poorest kind of cloak against that devouring sun god up there above us." He looked around the oasis and nodded with satisfaction. "This is a perfect resting place. I am feeling the need of it myself."

Basil had enough strength left to walk to the shelter of the nearest tree. He sank down with a sigh of complete weariness. "I am afraid I can do nothing about pegging the camels out," he said.

"There is little to be done."

"Why did Ezer run away like that?" asked Basil, too tired to raise or turn his head.

"He smelled the water. Camels cannot resist it; they start off pell-mell for it at the first whiff. It takes a strong arm on the curb chain to hold them in. I should have warned you of that. Well, no harm seems to have been done. Get off to sleep now. You will waken up a new man."

2

"This life is terrible beyond all description," said Basil as he and his companion sat at supper beside the Antioch Road under the walls of Aleppo. It was a plain meal they were eating: a square cake of a doughy substance, which Chimham cut into wedges with his dagger, some dates and dried grapes and a moldy piece of cheese.

"It is indeed terrible," agreed Chimham, his mouth full. "And also it is beautiful."

"I am unable to see the beauty of it. Do you follow this life by choice?"

The other man nodded. "I ran away from my home as a boy to become a camel man. I shall never leave it. When my time comes, I shall be buried by the side of the trail under a single stone, and the howling of hyenas will be my requiem. I ask nothing better."

It was incomprehensible to Basil that anyone could live such a life by preference. He had become thin and his face was drawn and deeply lined. His skin was several shades darker.

"The sun strikes like the blow of a hammer," he said. "I can feel it beating down on my head all day long. Clang, clang, clang! It never stops. I sink into the saddle under the cruelty of it. It seems like a malignant god who has sworn to drive me mad. Every time we start out, I take a look at it blazing away so hatefully up there and I say, 'Today you will win. I can stand no more of you.' "

"You have never suggested a delay or an earlier halt," commented Chimham, raising a piece of cheese to his mouth on the point of the dagger.

"Not yet. But I have been close to doing it a thousand times."

"Well," said the camel man cheerfully, "we are getting to the end of it. By this time tomorrow night we will be within sight of the walls of Antioch. We must be at least four days ahead of the caravan."

Such a fierce longing took possession of Basil for the shelter of cool stone walls and the sanctuary of trees where his enemy could not reach him that tears came into his eyes. "What a blessed life it would be," he said with a deep sigh, "to live in a cave, a dark cave with moisture dripping from the walls and an underground pool. Or in a temple with stone walls and pillars. Or on top of Mount Hermon in a house covered with snow!"

"You are wrong," said Chimham. "The sun is the best friend man has. Every morning when I wake up I say a prayer to him. I say, 'When Joshua commanded you to stand still, why didn't you become stationary up there in the sky?' The moon is a sorry substitute, although I am compelled to say that I have enjoyed many pleasant hours by its pale light." He turned and motioned over his shoulder in the direction of the Aleppo gates. "I heard something back there. A band of Arab bandits have been on the prowl hereabouts. They have picked off some stragglers from caravans passing through. The guard on the gate said we should not venture out alone. Old Zimiscies, who owns the khan, said the same."

Basil frowned doubtfully. "If we attach ourselves to a large caravan we will lose a lot of time. Can we afford to do it?"

"Can we afford to lose our lives?"

"The danger of that would not be very great."

Chimham brushed a hand across his lips as a sign that he had finished his supper. With deft movements he wrapped up the remains of the meal and attached the bundle to his saddle. "I think we are likely to slip by them in the dark. I do not like to risk the loss of the reward I have been promised if we get to Antioch first. I am ready to take the chance if you are."

They discussed the matter at some length and found themselves agreeing that the danger was not great enough to warrant them in delaying their arrival at Antioch. "Bandits prefer to work in the early morning and again just before dark," said Chimham. "Sometimes they will see where a caravan has camped and attack it later, but generally they have a reluctance about the night hours. By dawn we should be far enough west to be well out of danger. I say, let us risk it." Basil nodded. "Then it is settled."

They sat in silence for several moments. "These camels belong to you," remarked Chimham.

Basil was startled. "It is true. I bought them from Adam ben Asher. But how did you find out?"

"He told me before we left that I need not consider myself responsible to him for them. I hope you drove a hard bargain with him."

"No," answered Basil. "I paid him what he asked."

A look of intense pain crossed the face of his companion. "By the earth and my head!" he cried. "That was a great mistake. I am sure he cheated you."

"I know he did. He boasted of it to my face. I did not care. All I desired was to close the deal with as few words as possible."

"Do you know that Adam hates you?"

"I am sure he does. And I hate him. My dislike of him equals my hatred of the sun. I link them together in my mind; the great, burning face of the sun and the sneering countenance of this vain, loudmouthed Adam."

Chimham studied him intently for several moments. Then he nodded in a sudden decision and reached for the small bundle of his clothing, which lay on the ground beside him. It proved to be a single cloth wrapped around a collection of articles of such great value and variety that Basil sat up straight and looked at them with amazed eyes.

"What loot is this?" he asked, staring at the sparkle of precious stones on the white of the cloth. "Have you robbed a temple?"

"When I was a boy I saw a conjurer put his head in the mouth of a lion," declared Chimham. "That is what I am doing now: I am placing myself in your power. No, my friend, this is not loot. I do some trading myself. All these articles I expect to sell to merchants in Antioch."

Basil reached out a finger and touched the smooth surface of a ruby as though doubting its reality. "I do not understand," he said with a frown. "Why do you work as a mere camel driver when you carry such wealth as this?"

"To engage in trade a man must go from place to place. Could I afford to fit out a caravan myself? Let me explain the situation to you. The only safe way to transport goods is by caravans of such size that raiders do not dare risk an attack. This puts trade in the hands of a very few men. Joseph of Arimathea was the richest of them all, although your father in Antioch was one to reckon with. A little man, desiring to have his share, must do as I do. I hire myself as a driver and I carry goods secretly from one place to another, trading with merchants of the East who themselves lack the resources of the great caravan owners. They trust me with goods to offer dealers of their own size in Jerusalem and Caesarea and Antioch. I am paid a share of the profits on all sales I make. As I have no difficulty in finding buyers, I do very well.

"I break a rule of the road in doing this," he went on. "No camel man is allowed to do any trading on his own account. If Adam knew what I am doing, he would seize everything I have and then he would have me beaten out of the caravan. After that I would be on a list and I would be as much of an outcast as a leper with a bell around his neck." He indulged in a broad grin of self-congratulation. "Yes, I do very well. Some time ago I decided that, as I was taking such risks anyway, I might as well take more. I buy some goods myself now and take the chance of selling them. My profit on these sales is—well, it is quite colossal."

There was a moment of silence and then Basil asked, "Why do you tell me this?"

Chimham did not answer at once. He held up a square-cut sardonyx of remarkable size and fineness. "The High Priest may have finer stones than this in his Breastplate of Judgment, but still it is a good one. I already have a buyer for it." A small knife with an ivory handle was next displayed. "Look at this blade. You could cut right through the proud gizzard of a Roman with it. And have you ever seen sweeter jade than this cup, which was carved out of a single block? I bought it, knowing where I could find a buyer for it." He smacked his lips. "The profit I make will be even sweeter than the jade itself."

"At this rate you will become a rich man quickly."

The enthusiasm of the illicit trader showed immediate signs of abating. He gave his head a shake. "I am a close buyer. I am a remarkably fine seller. But in spite of everything my savings are small. You could cover them with the napkin in which the single talent was wrapped." He indulged in a rueful smile that still held some remnant of self-pride. "There is a reason, and I can give it to you in one word. The word is 'Wives.'"

"Wives?" repeated Basil. He looked at the smooth face of his companion, its lack of lines, the clear and youthful color of the flesh. "You look no more than a few years older than I. How many wives have you?"

"Four. One in Jerusalem, one in Caesarea, another in Bagdad, and one —the youngest and my favorite, although I love them all—in Antioch. You see, my young friend, I differ from other camel men, who are content to make love to women and then leave them, or who go to the little houses on the walls. When I see a woman who takes my fancy, I want to keep her for my own. I want to marry her. Yes, four times I have been unable to resist this desire. Twice I have been stopped by parental interference." He drew a deep sigh. "I love them all very much, but there is no denying that they are costly. They keep me poor, particularly my little Irene in Antioch, who has a weakness for presents." He pointed to the jade cup. "I find it necessary to make many deals as good as this one to keep my four families in comfort."

Each statement that his companion made had increased Basil's astonishment. "How many children have you?" he asked.

"Eleven," answered Chimham with open pride. "Seven of them are girls, which is a tragedy. But my four sons are all bright little fellows with sharp tongues and eyes like big black currants from Corinth. They will make fine traders when they grow up. The sons of Chimham will form a partnership and set themselves to gobble up all the trade with the East."

"Do each of your wives know about the others?"

The eyes of the camel man opened wide in horror. "By the earth and my head, no! I love my plump little quails so much that I tell each one she is the only woman in my life. It is the one safe way. You will find that out when *you* have more wives."

A silence followed. Chimham wrapped up his stock in trade and knotted the bundle with strong, sure fingers. "And now I shall answer your question," he said.

He looked up at Basil and gave him a knowing wink. "I took you into my confidence because it seemed to me that we might become partners. I know all the twists and quirks of the Eastern trade. I know all the merchants there and along the Mediterranean as well. You own these two fine camels. You are married to a rich wife and might be able to get into the palms of your hands a little meestak. You know what I mean? Meestak, money.

"Now let us consider how things might work out. We would begin with the two camels, and I would trail along at the rear of the big caravans for a time with one helper. Pretty soon, my friend, we would have four camels and two helpers; then more camels and more cheating rascals of helpers. In time we would have great caravans of our own and men would say, 'Once there was Joseph of Arimathea and Ignatius of Antioch. Now there is Chimham and his partner, Basil, son of Ignatius.' When that time comes my eight or ten wives—oh yes, I shall go on marrying, I feel it in my bones—and my droves of handsome children will live in fine white houses with servants to swing fans over them at their meals. And you, by the earth and my head, will be the richest man in the world."

Basil shook his head slowly. "No, my friend. I am not intended by nature to be a trader. I would be of no use to you at all. What has happened has been between you and the men who employed you, and it is no concern of mine. Save for this: I was so indebted to Joseph of Arimathea that I could not profit by anything earned at his expense. On the other hand, my friend Chimham, I am deeply indebted to you. As a token of how conscious I am of my debt, I shall give you these camels when we reach Antioch. My suggestion to you is that you attach yourself to this old prince of Seen and accompany him back to his own land. You could then return with one of the silk trains and bring with you enough rare goods to make the beginnings of an honest fortune."

Chimham's dark eyes lighted up with enthusiasm. "By the earth and my head, you are right! This is the true road to everlasting riches." A doubt clouded his face. "But will the prince come as far as Antioch? The road to the East turns off at Aleppo."

"It was his intention to leave the caravan at Aleppo, but I heard him say he would accompany them to Antioch. He desires so much to learn about Jesus of Nazareth that he clings to the side of Luke and plies him with questions. I will be surprised if he is not converted to full belief before he turns homeward."

The illicit dealer in the goods of the East got briskly to his feet. He chirped to the camels, "Come, Bildad, come, Ezer. You have had four hours of rest. Your bellies are filled with good dried beans. All of your stomachs have water in them. Why, then, this sloth? We must be on our way, O Bildad, thou bag of bitter gall, and thou also, O Ezer, thou indolent youth. There is not another moment to be wasted."

3

The first stage of their evening ride proved to be unsatisfactory. The camels grumbled and whined and could not be persuaded to the steady rhythmic pace by which the miles were slowly but surely consumed. Old Bildad screamed continuously to the rising moon in protest.

"The fear grows on me," called Basil to Chimham, who rode in the lead, "that we will not arrive in time after all. It is my fault. I have been a drag on you. And now these accursed beasts are going to give us trouble. We will never reach Antioch at the rate they are going."

Chimham did not seem much disturbed. "Bildad is in a complaining mood," he said, "and I cannot find it in my heart to blame him. We have driven them hard and they are tired. They think they are entitled to a full night's rest."

"It is true they have done well so far. But we might as well be camping as loafing on the road like this. Chimham, my friend, I am serious about this. I am deadly afraid we are not going to get there in time. This afternoon as we slept I dreamed of the ship. I do a great deal of dreaming. No sooner do I close my eyes than strange fancies come to me. This ship was sailing into the harbor with the wind at its back, its large square sail stretched tight. Aaron was standing on the deck with a smirk of triumph on his face. We were somewhere back on the trail, and so I knew we had lost." He gave his head a despairing shake. "Is there nothing we can do?"

His companion took a fatalistic view of the situation. "If we lose, it will be because it is not the Lord's will that we get there first. We have done our best. We are four days ahead of the rest. Can flesh and blood do better than that? You are as thin as a fasting priest, and the hollows around your eyes give you a close resemblance to that ill-disposed beast you are riding. No blame can be laid on us, so why repine?"

"It will be a great tragedy!" cried Basil. "I am not thinking of the fortune my wife may lose. It would be a serious matter, but, after all, other fortunes can be made. There is another reason that you know nothing about."

"Do not be too sure. There is always much talk around the campfires at night; and Adam ben Asher, though a man of great gifts, has a tongue that wags at both ends."

"Perhaps, then, you know why we must make every effort. Will they start to run if we beat them?"

"Beat them as much as you like. It will not help in the least. But if we had a camel singer with us, it would make a great difference."

Basil stared at his companion with a puzzled frown. "A camel singer? Do you mean they can be encouraged by music?"

Chimham's white turban nodded in the gloom ahead. "It is one of their most curious traits. Certain voices please their ears so much that they fall into a charmed state; like snakes attracted by playing on the flute or the strings. Their feet begin to move in perfect rhythm, and they keep it up as long as the singer can go on with his songs."

"Why, then, are you not singing? You have a fine voice."

"It is true that I have a fine voice," agreed Chimham. "I have always been proud of it. When songs are sung around the campfire at night I am called on first. Women have been known to swoon with delight when I sing of love by the light of the moon. I won two of my wives that way. But not camels! My voice does not please them at all. As soon as I start they raise their heads and shake them peevishly. It is as though they were saying, 'Why does this noisy laglag whose voice is like that of a jackdaw with a frog in its throat disturb our peace?' You do not believe? I shall give you the proof."

He began to sing in a high and melodious voice. It seemed to Basil a pleasant performance, but it was apparent at once that the camels did not agree with him. Ezer stopped in his tracks, planting his feet down stiffly in the sand. His attitude said, "I will not take another step as long as we must endure this unseemly uproar." Bildad emitted a whine that carried with it a note of derision.

The singer suspended his efforts and said in an exasperated tone: "You have seen. There are singers they do not like, and I am one of them. I am sure you agree that the stupid brutes show bad taste." He was silent for a moment and then asked in a tone of voice that made it clear that the idea had occurred to him for the first time: "Why do you not try it? Who knows? You may be the one to set them jogging again."

"I am not a singer," protested Basil.

"It is worth a trial. There is this to be considered. They are accustomed to the Aramaic and they might not take to your poetic Greek and the wild notes of your music. Do you know any Jewish songs?"

Basil gave the point some thought. "When I was a boy in the Ward of the Trades," he said, "there were some Jewish children who sang a great deal. I remember one of their songs, which they called *Little Issachar*. One of them would stand in the center and the rest would join hands and dance around him. There was no end to the verses."

"I know that one. We used to sing it when I was a boy, up in the hills around Galilee. I know all the verses. Try it, my young friend. It may be that you were designed by nature to charm camels with your voice."

Basil was doubtful of the result, but he decided to make the venture. Raising his voice, he sang the first of the verses that he remembered.

> *"Simple Little Issachar, son of Lot,*
> *The demons will get you when the winds blow hot:*
> *And when they do, you will wish they had not,*
> *Simple Little Issachar, son of Lot."*

The two riders were equally surprised at the result. The camels fell into a steady gait at once, raising their heads and emitting low grunts of satisfaction.

"Your voice is as thin as a reed," said Chimham. "But they like it! By the earth and my head, you are a born camel singer. If you can sing all night, we shall be in Antioch before you know it. Keep on! And that smirk you saw in your dream on the face of Aaron will turn into a scowl of defeat."

So Basil went on singing. He sang for hours, or so it seemed to him. The stars came out and the moon climbed up high into the heavens. His voice grew hoarse. When he ran out of verses his companion prompted him. The camels made it clear that they wanted nothing else. As long as he regaled their ears with the adventures of Issachar, they continued to forge ahead with a long easy lope that consumed the miles as surely as hungry men empty the evening kettles. The shells on their harness jingled and the bells kept up a steady accompaniment to the music.

As he sang, Basil's thoughts took a more optimistic turn. Perhaps they would be in time, after all, and Deborra would be able to claim her inheritance. It would be, or so he had been told, a very great fortune; so great that there would be plenty of gold to send the preachers of Christ's word out to new and strange lands. He took a great satisfaction in the thought that he was being helpful in bringing to all the people of the world that magic story he had heard himself from the inspired lips of Luke. It would be carried to the Far East, to Bagdad and Samarkand and the Indies, even in time to Seen, that distant and fabulous land. It would travel also in the other direction, to the colder countries of the West, to Gaul and Spain and beyond the Pillars of Hercules, even across the narrow strait to the island of the white cliffs and the singing barbarians.

Wherever it was told people would come to see the light and to believe in Jesus. This vision took such hold of his imagination that new strength came into his throat and he sang on, knowing that if he stopped, the smooth pacing of Bildad and Ezer, those severe critics, would cease also, and the chance to spread the gospel might be hindered.

Finally he could sing no longer. Such weariness overtook him that he fell asleep in his saddle. It has been noted before that there was a lifelike quality to the visions that occupied his mind in slumber. He could see those who came into his dreams as clearly as though they were real. Voices were distinct and everything that was done and said seemed natural and believable. Two such visions came to him as he lay sprawled between the camel's hump and the pommel of his saddle.

In the first his father paid him another visit. Ignatius looked a little sad, which was natural enough because he found it necessary to explain that he was still being detained in the House of Suspended Judgment. There did not seem to be any disposition to press his case, however, and he had even been given certain duties to perform. In company with large numbers of other souls—the number ran into the thousands, he was inclined to think—he was employed in tending the gold bindings of the Great Books of Record. It was, he explained in a discouraged voice, rather menial work for a man who had been such a prominent figure on earth, but, after all, what was to be expected? It was not certain yet that the final decision in his case would be a favorable one.

The House of Suspended Judgment was so large that no one there had any conception of its limits. Those who inhabited it seemed no different from human beings. They were of all shapes and sizes and they wore normal clothes, being allowed complete latitude in that respect. All the colors known on earth were to be seen, and rumors had reached his ears that in the regions beyond, about which there was continual awe-struck speculation, there were other wonderful colors on which human eyes had never rested, glorious shades that would blind any mortal.

But, declared Ignatius, one was conscious always of great forces, of strange and wonderful regions that might be reached later, of the grinding about them of the mills of fate. There was, in particular, the Wing of the Future, in which no denizen of the House of Suspended Judgment was allowed. He himself, by an error that had been corrected almost immediately, had been permitted to get inside. His stay had been for no more than the time consumed in the winking of an eye, but he had seen this much: a huge panorama of space through which gray clouds raced. On the face of the moving clouds the scroll of the future was being shown. There had been a multitude of souls, whose duty called them there, studying the pictures with intent eyes.

This brought Ignatius to the reason for his second entry into the dream-world of his adopted son. He, Basil, was behaving with neither good sense nor sound judgment. He had a wife with all the best virtues and who, moreover, loved him as a wife should. Was it his purpose to throw away a second fortune? There was still time for him to redeem himself and settle down to a normal and happy life. Whatever he did, he must make his home in Antioch and under no circumstances was he to return to Jerusalem.

At this point Ignatius began to draw on what he had seen during the winking of an eye while he stood in the Wing of the Future. He became incoherent. Words poured from his lips: blood, fire, struggle, death. If the words seemed to lack form, they left one impression, that he had glimpsed on the racing clouds a picture of war and destruction in the city of David.

This dream faded away suddenly and another took its place. This time a very definite warning was delivered and it came from Zimiscies, the aged owner of the khan outside Aleppo. Basil, who had seen him on two occasions, had no difficulty in recognizing him now. He seemed a perfect symbol of impending tragedy, a stooped figure and a huge hooked nose in a face with wasted cheeks. "Come back!" he kept repeating, beckoning with his arms. "Did I not give you warning of the Arab raiders? You will ride into danger if you keep on. Turn your camels back east if you set any value on your lives!"

The message was conveyed with such conviction that Basil came back to consciousness charged with a sense of urgency. He returned to a clear, still night; so clear that the eye could see as far as in daylight, and so still that it seemed certain they would hear any sound made in the world, from the delving of a mole to the clomp of a gold-shod heel on Parnassus.

Basil told hurriedly of his second dream but elicited no comment from Chimham other than the conviction that Zimiscies was a chronic spreader of rumors. "Never have I been to Aleppo without having that old weeping Jeremiah tell me it would be unsafe to continue. He wants all travelers to stay and pay him rent for space in that flea-infested inn of his."

Basil was peering ahead and listening. "Do you hear a sound coming from up there in the north?" he asked. "It seems to me like the hoofbeat of horses."

Chimham turned his head in that direction and listened also. After a moment he shook his head. "I hear nothing. I think we are the only people awake tonight."

CHAPTER XVIII

I

THE MAIN CARAVAN had been proceeding in the meantime at a more normal gait, traveling at night and camping during the heat of the day. Although they had fallen far behind, they had done as well as could have been expected of a train of such size (the old prince being still with them and more satellites having been acquired as they went along), and it was a tired company that set up its tents beside a small stream a day's journey south of Aleppo.

Adam ben Asher paused at the entrance of Deborra's tent to say: "Three more days of this. You look tired, but that is to be expected. It has been a hard journey. Never before have I ridden through such heat!"

She had been leaning against the tent pole with closed eyes and she opened them now with every evidence of extreme weariness. From where she stood, she could see the eastern horizon flooded with the warm lights of dawn.

"What word is there of Basil and his companion?" she asked.

Adam said, "None," and made a sweeping gesture of his arm to call attention to the emptiness of the space where they had chosen to camp. "No human eye seems to have rested on them since we got that report south of Hamath. When they are as far ahead of us as three days, it is harder to get definite word. We shall hear nothing of them today unless the birds bring us news." He stopped and gazed intently into the west. "This I did not expect. Someone is coming our way."

A mere dot on a side path turned into a man afoot, and the man afoot became in a very few minutes a shepherd, a young shepherd walking to brisk good purpose. He turned aside to pay them a visit, swinging his long gnarled crook by way of greeting. In spite of his obvious youth, he had a matted beard that covered all of his throat and much of his chest. It seemed likely that he had been tending his flock in the cluster of low hills to the west and was now on his way home.

"Peace be with you, friend, and may your flocks increase and multiply," said Adam when the visitor had entered the circle of their tents.

"Peace be with you, strangers."

"Saw you aught of two men traveling north and alone by camel some days ago?"

"There has been much traffic to Aleppo." The young shepherd's eyes studied the trail reflectively and then came back to rest first on his interrogator and then on Deborra. "As it chanced, I spoke to two such men at this same hour and very nearly this exact spot. They had ridden all night and they were pausing here to feed their camels and replenish the water bags. We spoke a few words only and then they were off."

"What do you recall of them?"

"One was very knowing in the life of the trails. He was thickset and he had a wagging tongue. The other was younger. He was beardless and he had little to say."

Luke had joined them, walking stiffly after the long hours they had spent in the saddle. He nodded to the shepherd. "It is clear that it was our friends you saw. When was it you met them?"

The shepherd began to calculate by a backward method. "Yesterday there came to the hills the Roman collectors of the tax"—he paused and spat his contempt of them—"and found Horgan the Hittite and Diklah the Moabite, who had hidden themselves in the hope to escape paying. The collectors took them away, and I fear it will go hard with them because it is getting to be a habit to run away. Horgan and Diklah had been no more than a day in hiding. They told me when they arrived that the Romans had reached their village the day previous to that, with their clerks and their staves and their accursed lists. Now I am on sure ground in this matter of time because I recall it was still a day earlier that I saw the two men of whom you ask. They told me the tax collectors were at work in Emesa when they passed through. This came back into my mind when I learned that the filthy locusts had settled on this district. Let us then count the days which had elapsed." He began to do so with the help of his fingers. "Four. Yes, it was four days ago that I spoke to them."

"Four days!" Luke's eyes lighted up with pride. "They have done nobly. They have truly ridden as hard as Joshua's men in pursuit of the army of the five kings!"

It was contrary to custom for a woman to speak in a company of men that included a stranger, but Deborra could not contain herself any longer. "How were they?" she asked. "Did they seem to you very weary?"

The shepherd bent over and picked up a dried faggot of wood that lay in the dust. He snapped it into two pieces with a loud cracking sound. "The younger of them, the beardless one, was just like that. A touch, a word, and he would fly into pieces. They told me they were on their way to Antioch. The young one will be lucky if he gets that far." The shaggy head nodded briskly by way of emphasis. "Even the other one, who seemed to me as tough as old leather, was doubled over in his saddle and his face was as gray as the dust of this road."

Adam led the visitor away to share the meal that was in course of preparation. Luke seated himself at the entrance of Deborra's tent.

"You are consumed with fears," he said. "Come, my child, there is no reason to feel that way. They are in Antioch now. At this very moment, when I read in your eyes the anxiety that is feeding on you, they are sleeping on soft couches while about them the great city is beginning to awaken. Yes, they have completed their journey and are resting from their efforts."

"But you heard what the shepherd said."

Luke nodded reassuringly. "They are not only in Antioch but the decision has, perhaps, already been made. I am sure they have seen the banker and have told him their story. He has in his hands the documents they carried to identify themselves to him."

Deborra became more calm. "I have prayed to Jehovah a hundred times a day," she declared, "to watch over them and show forbearance."

"Such faith will bring its own reward. I am sure that Jehovah has listened."

The three sat down to supper together in the cool of the evening. Work on the dismantling of the camp had been begun and in another half hour they would be on their way.

They were rested and relaxed. The kind, strong fingers of Sarah had kneaded the tired flesh of her mistress's face and throat and had applied sparingly a little color from the contents of the toilet box. The young bride had regained her spirits and was disposed once more to look on the bright side.

"Antioch is a beautiful city, I have been told," she said. "It will be a pleasure to see it."

"I am a prejudiced witness to its many merits," declared Luke. "It is my home. I love it and regard it as the greatest city in the world. Of course," he felt impelled to add, "I have not seen Rome."

"But you have seen Jerusalem!" cried Adam. "How, then, can you call Antioch the greatest city?" He paused and then went on in almost breathless partisanship: "There is no place to be compared with Jerusalem. The Temple is there, and all the true grandeur and glory of the world are in the Temple."

Luke nodded in understanding. "It is true that God gave Jerusalem to His people. But, Adam, I was thinking of material things; of wealth and population, of beautiful buildings, of wide streets and spacious gardens, and of fair breezes blowing across harbors filled with tall ships. And there is something I must tell you, something that disturbs me very much. I had a most strange feeling about Jerusalem this time. It seemed to me old and weighed down by a sense of tragic destiny. I almost believed that its end was near at hand—that it was waiting as Jesus waited on the Mount of Olives. I would not have been surprised when we left if we had found a great stone rolled against the Damascus Gate, and angels with flaming swords on guard."

"You are letting your imagination lead you, Luke the Scribe!" cried Adam indignantly. "Do you mean that Jerusalem seems to you like a city of the dead? Let me tell you this: the city of David will stand in all its greatness after the memory of Rome has been lost and Antioch has been buried under an avalanche of rock from the hills about it."

"My hope is that you are right," said Luke. "It is dreadful to feel that destruction hovers over those ancient stone walls and broods above Mount Moriah. Your opinion is as good as mine, Adam. I spoke only as a man— a man of faulty vision. I am not a prophet."

The resentment Adam felt over what had been said manifested itself first in a long silence and then in an outburst because of what seemed to him a personal slight.

"I am the one who has made it possible to get the Cup—this Cup by which you set so much store—safely out of the hands of the High Priest and the Zealots. I have done much of the planning and I am risking my savings in this journey—not to mention my skin, which I value. Yet I was not taken into your confidence about the Cup, and it was only by accident that I learned of its existence in the first place. I do not like being disregarded, Luke the Physician, and I am speaking out to let you know."

Luke looked distressed. "There is justice in your reproaches. We have accepted your aid. We have benefited by your courage and farsightedness as well as by your generosity. I can see now, though we have always appreciated what you are doing, that we have not made you aware of it." He paused to give his head a shake of self-reproach. "The fault is mine, my good friend Adam, and I am truly contrite."

"I have not seen this Cup for which all of us have risked so much," grumbled Adam.

Luke glanced over his shoulder at the work going on about them. All the tents were down save that of Deborra. He raised a hand and called, "Let it stand for a few minutes." Then he nodded to Adam. "Come, our brave and generous friend, let us repair this oversight at once. Let us show you the Cup that Jesus held and then passed to His disciples on that night so many years ago."

They got to their feet and walked to the tent. Sarah, who was busily packing, left at a word from her mistress. The old chest stood at one side, almost hidden under bundles of clothing. Deborra raised the lid, and Luke drew out the Cup from its resting place.

The canvas flap had been drawn over the entrance, so there was almost complete darkness inside the tent. No one spoke or moved. It was Adam who broke the silence finally.

"I can see nothing," he said. "Can we not have some light?"

Luke threw back enough of the canvas to admit light. It was then possible to see the tent pole and the chest and the bundles piled up above it. The Cup was visible against this background, a battered drinking vessel lacking in beauty of design.

All three studied it in a silence that lasted the better part of a minute. Adam was again the first to speak.

"It is very plain," he said.

"Yes, it is plain," agreed Luke. "It would bring a small price if offered for sale as a drinking cup."

"I expected it to be different, though I cannot tell you in what way. I must have thought there would be something remarkable about it." Adam's voice suggested that he was not only surprised but a little resentful. "I have seen cups just like this in the huts of shepherds. And in the poorest of inns."

"Yes. In the huts of shepherds and the poorest of inns."

"Well," said Adam after a final pause, "I have seen it. You had better put it away now so the packing can be finished. We must be on our way."

When they emerged from the tent into the surrounding dusk and Adam proceeded to busy himself with the details of moving, Deborra looked up at Luke with eyes that were misted in wonder.

"I saw it!" she whispered. "When the tent was so dark. I could see the Cup as clearly as I could later. I think there was a light shining from it and yet I could see nothing else. It was very strange. It was so strange that I wondered if it was all my imagination."

"No, my child. There was a light shining from it. You saw the Cup and so did I. I saw it once before. When it was first entrusted to me by your grandfather and I took it in great fear to the room in the warehouse where Basil was hiding. It shone then with the same strange and holy light."

"But Adam saw nothing at all."

"Adam is lacking in faith. He is a man of great honesty and integrity, but he does not believe in Jesus and there is in him a tendency to scoff. I am sure, my child, that the radiance of the Cup is only in the eye that looks upon it. If you have faith, it glows for you with this serene light. If you lack faith, it is—well, as Adam said, it is then a very plain cup."

They proceeded to pace up and down together while the preparations for departure went on about them. "This is something I have often discussed," said Luke, "with the others. Those who were with the Master in His wanderings saw many miraculous things. I have been close to Paul and I have no doubt that great powers have been conferred on him and on Peter. But this I may tell you: there have been few miracles."

The stars were beginning to show in the sky. Luke paused and gazed up at them. "We know so little about the God Who made the world and the heavens and Who rules our destinies. Men have seen Him, but He always appeared to them in the guise of a man like themselves. We cannot conceive how He will look when He sits on His judgment seat. We do not know where He abides, although it seems certain that it is somewhere up above us. It must be far above the clouds and the stars. There He sits and everything moves at His nod. Do you find it hard to believe that the great and omnipotent God, in His might and sometimes in His wrath, can spread out a hand and bring a miracle to pass?

"And yet I am sure He would never have found it necessary to have miracles happen except for one thing. The children of Israel expected their Messiah to come like a king, another David. It is hard for them to accept a humble carpenter instead. And so perhaps the wise and all-seeing Jehovah thought He would assist their stumbling faith with proofs that would be startling.

"But, my child," he went on, "we cannot expect Jehovah to give so much time to our weaknesses and our puny needs that He will keep His hand stretched out to lend us aid. Instead of ruling us by miracles, He has infused in us certain qualities that enable us to accomplish the divine purposes by ourselves—faith, loyalty, courage, tolerance. It is by the faith in us that we become Christians, and it is because of our faith that we are sometimes rewarded with proof that God watches us and is pleased. I am sure that was why we were allowed to see the holy Cup in the darkness of the tent. It was not fancy, not a trick of the imagination. We saw it—clearly, unmistakably, wonderfully! But Adam's eyes, which had no faith to open them, saw nothing until light was admitted into the tent; and then all he perceived was an old cup that was very plain.

"Those with whom I have worked," he continued after a pause, "have realized that we must not stand by and wait for God to accomplish by a miracle what we should do by applying the powers He has stored inside us. Power for good has been in men all through the ages, but the coming of Jesus was needed to release these qualities in us. Because of this, men and women are enduring all things for their faith, even the cruelest of deaths. As belief in Jesus grows and spreads, the faith of men will become the greatest force in the world."

"Do you mean," she asked, "that faith gives us all, even the humblest of us, a share of the divine?"

Luke nodded his head gravely. "That is what I believe, my child. But our mortal minds will always remain incapable of comprehending the purpose of God. The truth has been revealed in some part to Peter and Paul and we must, therefore, follow them in all humility, listening to what they say, believing what they believe. We must be happy that it is in us to use this faith and to accept these great truths."

There was a moment's pause. "What of Basil?" asked Deborra. "I mean, what happened when you first saw the light of the Cup?"

It was so dark now that they had to walk slowly and take each step with caution. Deborra could not see the look of satisfaction which lighted up the face of her companion. "Basil perceived it," he affirmed. "He had not reached any belief in Jesus at the time. He was still groping in the dark. But he saw the light as clearly as I did. His mind is like a rich loam. The seed has been planted, and it will not be long before the power of faith will sprout, and grow, and blossom."

Adam took his stand at the head of the line of camels. With a flourish he raised the *hozazra* to his lips and sounded an urgent call. "Hurry!"

the trumpet said. "The cool hours are here for our use. The long trail stretches ahead. To your saddles! Hurry! Hurry!"

2

A man with intense black eyes and a voice like a trumpet was talking to a circle of listeners in a corner of the courtyard of the great khan outside Aleppo. "The hour draws near!" he cried. "The shackles with which Rome binds the world will soon be broken. Jerusalem is ready. The daggers are being forged for Israel's freedom——"

Adam ben Asher turned away with a disturbed shake of the head. "How can this loud-mouth make such promises?" he said to himself. "Can the children of Israel resist the might of Rome alone? It is not hard to foresee what will happen to this man. He will die with nails through his hands and feet."

He lingered for a moment in another corner, where a whirling dervish was displaying his weird skill to the beat of a drum and the whine of a flute-like instrument. He passed a snake charmer without a second glance and he refused to be drawn into any of the groups of eager talkers who thronged the yard. Finally he sighted the bent head of Zimiscies, the proprietor, and hurried in that direction.

Luke had remained at the entrance. He saw Adam fall into talk with the owner and then allowed his glance to take in the confusion of the yard with the warm interest of one who loves his fellow man. He also heaved a sigh of regret when some of the phrases of the impassioned orator reached his ears. It was some minutes before his eyes returned to Adam, and he was surprised to find that the latter was still talking with old Zimiscies. Adam's face suggested that his apprehensions had been roused by what he was learning.

"Does he bear bad tidings?" Luke asked himself. He waited with mounting fear until Adam concluded his talk and made his way back through the crowded courtyard.

Adam for once was at a loss for words when he reached the entrance. He gave Luke a quick glance and then dropped his eyes.

"It seems," he said, "that our two young men have been unfortunate."

"What has happened?" Luke laid a supplicating hand on Adam's arm. "What evil has befallen them?"

"Zimiscies tells me that a party of Arab bandits has been raiding hereabouts." Adam kept his eyes on his feet, which he shuffled about uneasily. "For a fortnight all travelers have been warned to be on the watch. Chimham was told it would be dangerous to start out at night with only one companion. But it seems they decided they could not afford to wait. They agreed to take the risk."

There was a long pause between them. "And they were attacked by the raiders?" asked Luke finally.

"Yes. It is not known what the outcome was—whether they were made prisoners or killed. One of the Arabs was caught in Aleppo today."

Luke's grip on his companion's arm tightened. "Do you think it likely that the Arabs would hold them as prisoners?"

"Only if they saw a chance to collect ransom money." Adam paused and gave his head a dubious shake. "The Arabs are a violent lot. We must face the truth. They are more likely to kill those they rob than make prisoners of them."

Luke lowered his eyes and began to pray under his breath. "O Jehovah, we bow to Thy will, knowing Thou art all-seeing and wise and that Thou hast a reason for everything. If these brave young men have been killed"—he choked with the emotion he was feeling and could not continue for a moment—"if they have been killed, then, O Lord, give us strength to bear our loss. We know Thou wilt have a reward for them. Look down on those who have been bereaved——"

Adam spoke unwillingly. "There is a confession I must make to you. You have seen that I have no love for this man who supplanted me. For that I offer no excuse, nor is any needed. Any other man would have felt as I did. But there is something else. I cheated him. He came to me and said he wanted to buy the two camels, and I set a very high price, thinking it would serve as a starting point and that we would arrive at a fairer price before we got through. It is true that I baited him; and when he became angry and refused to bicker with me over the price, I took his money—the full amount. There is this much to be said for me: I told him to his face that I was robbing him." He paused and then added in a grumbling tone: "Now that *this* has happened, it weighs on my mind."

"It is a matter of no consequence now. But I beg of you, Adam, my friend, cleanse your mind of this hate you had for him. To let any of this feeling remain in your heart will weigh against you."

Zimiscies came hobbling across the courtyard, his head bobbing with each step. "The Arab they caught had Jewish coins in his purse," he volunteered. "He is being questioned before the *duoviri* now. They will use the smallest of canes, of course. The blows will be gentle—oh, very gentle indeed—but they will fall on the soles of his feet as steadily as the drip of water in an autumn shower. *Tap, tap, tap!* And after a few minutes of it a terrible agony will flow through his body. His feet will swell and become purple and he will not be able to stop himself from crying out." The old man shook his head with relish. "I have watched them use the cane, and it is always the same. No victim of it can resist crying out to his gods to be allowed to die quickly. But this one will not tell them anything. No, they are tough and proud men, these Arabs, as proud as the gods of evil. He will die under the torture without confessing."

"Then we cannot expect to hear anything more?" asked Luke.

Zimiscies motioned in the air with one of his far from clean hands. "The rest of them are gone with the winds. We shall hear no more. It will remain, O Venerable Teacher, one of the mysteries of the trail."

Luke and Adam walked back slowly to where they had camped outside the walls of the khan. "One thing is clear," said the latter. "They did not get to Antioch. By this time Aaron may have arrived to make his claim. I think it certain now that we will get nothing out of all our mad racing and scrambling."

He was so concerned with the train of thought aroused by these speculations that he paid no attention when Zimiscies came out through the gate and called after them. It was Luke who returned to hear what the old man had to say.

"I neglected to tell you this," said Zimiscies. "The man they caught was riding one of the stolen camels. Can you conceive of such daring and arrogance? It is said to be a valuable beast, a big brown fellow with very long legs. And it was most handsomely bedecked with shells and bells of jade."

"Was it one of the camels belonging to our two young men?" asked Luke with a heart so heavy that he could barely formulate the words.

The old man nodded. "There can be no doubt of that."

Adam continued to discuss the situation when Luke overtook him on reluctant feet. "We must do whatever we can. There can be no sleep tonight; let us strike camp at once and ride on. There can be no stop until we reach the city."

"Yes, we must make a last effort," said Luke. "And, Adam, let us keep our tongues still about this. There is no definite proof yet. It would be cruel to—to disturb her unnecessarily."

Adam agreed with a nod of the head. The depth of emotion that

Luke's voice had betrayed caused him, however, to study his companion with some curiosity. Luke, he saw, was pale and obviously quite shaken. "You seem to feel this deeply," he said.

Luke made no immediate response. He continued to walk slowly, his head lowered, his hands clenched at his sides. "I had come to love him like a son," he said finally.

CHAPTER XIX

I

THE CITY OF ANTIOCH, viewed from the approaches to the Iron Gate, was as magnificent as Luke had promised. Behind the seemingly endless wall with its four hundred towers it was the embodiment of all the legends of the East. Here, it seemed, turbaned potentates must rule in resplendent despotism, here princes wander in disguise to find adventure and romance, here behind ivory walls the veiled houris must abound and dread demons exercise their evil powers. Deborra felt a stirring of interest as her eyes rested on the marble grandeur of the city, but the mood was of brief duration; no more, in fact, than a single moment, for she sighed immediately and fell back into the unhappy speculations that had occupied her since they turned west at Aleppo.

Adam, who was riding beside her and striving to divert her attention by reciting a story, noticed her lack of interest. This ruffled his pride. He had fallen into the habit of telling anecdotes from the holy writings with his own interpretations and in his own words, assisting the narrative with intervals of furious piping on the *ugab* he carried by his saddle, and even lapsing at times into song. He was accustomed to attentive audiences.

He was giving his own particular version of the story of Jonah and had reached the point where the self-willed prophet found himself in the belly of the whale.

"Now this Jonah," he said, "was surprised to find that the belly of a whale was not a large place after all. He had always believed it must be able to accommodate a fishing boat or two and a whole company of men like himself, but now he discovered he could not stand up straight. He could see quite well because this soft *ganoofa* of a whale had sludged up a lot of weeds from the bottom of the ocean that gave off a kind of light.

He saw that there were small porpoises around him that would never sport around again on the surface of the water, and large jellyfish that had once been red but were now dead white from fear, and shrimps that were making a great noise by clicking their claws together. Jonah did not like the look of the place, nor the smell of it for that matter, and he began to jump around and shout: 'I am a man and a prophet and I have still a lot of prophesying to do for the Lord. It is not meet that I should perish in the belly of a whale.' At this all the fishes raised their heads and began to chant together:

> " 'To finish all his prophecies,
> He surely should not fail.
> It is not meet that he should perish
> In the belly of a whale.' "

Adam came to an abrupt stop and looked accusingly at her. "You are not listening," he charged.

Deborra shook her head. "You are holding something back from me," she said. "I have been sure of it ever since we left Aleppo. What is it? If you have bad news, I should be told. I am not a child."

Luke was riding on the other side. The journey from Aleppo, which had been accomplished without a stop for sleep, had left him in an exhausted state. Weariness showed in the tones of his voice.

"It is true," he said. "We have been keeping something from you. It did not seem either wise or fair, dear child, to disturb you with—with the rumors we had heard."

She turned and looked at him beseechingly. "What is it? Tell me, I beg you. I cannot stand this uncertainty any longer."

Luke looked ahead down the road and could see the Roman eagles above the Iron Gate. The telling could not be put off any longer. Adam, strapping the *ugab* in place with a somewhat sulky air, gave him a nod of assent.

"It is considered kind," began Luke, "to tell of bad fortune by indirection and by slow degrees. I am not sure this is a kindness. In any event, I am lacking in the art of dissimulation. Deborra, my dear child, we have reason to fear that there will be sad word waiting for us when we reach that—that forbidding gate ahead of us. It may take the form of the absence of those who should be there to greet us."

Deborra did not speak. She kept her eyes down. Her hands, grasping the pommel of the saddle, were white with strain.

"There was trouble on the road from Aleppo. Arab raiders attacked a small party riding through the night from Aleppo. Later one of the bandits rode into Aleppo and boasted openly of their success. He was captured, and it was found that he had Jewish coins in his purse. Also, he was riding one of the stolen camels, a rangy brown male with jade bells——"

Adam looked up with sudden intensity. "Where did you hear that?" he demanded.

"I was so depressed that I neglected to say anything. Zimiscies followed us out from the khan and told me about the stolen camel."

Adam astonished them by beginning to laugh. He not only indulged in a loud burst of mirth, but he gave his thigh a resounding slap. "'A rangy brown male,' he says, 'with jade bells.' It is true that the camels I sold him had jade bells. But—a *brown* one? Luke, my good friend, the ones I sold were not brown. They were white! As white as the belly of an underbaked fish, as white as the wattles of old Zimiscies himself, as white even as that small bit of fleece up there above us in the sky!"

Deborra's eyes caught fire. "Adam, Adam, what are you telling us? That—that they are safe, after all?"

"That is what I am telling you. It must have been another pair of travelers who were attacked at night and robbed by the bandits."

Deborra stretched out her arms on either side and pressed her fingers into their proffered hands. They rode thus linked for several moments in the silence of an intense relief.

"My friends!" she breathed. "My kind, good friends! I shall love you all the days of my life."

The contentment that Adam shared with the others was of short duration. He began quickly to frown, to mutter and shake his head. When they reached the stage of the road where all the different routes converged in front of the Iron Gate, he brought his camel to a stop.

"What right have we to be so confident?" he demanded to know, staring unhappily at his two companions. "We should have been met before this. I have no liking for this lack of attention. It is the advance rider of misfortune."

Deborra's confidence was easily shaken, perhaps because her previous despair had been so deep. She looked at him with worried eyes. "Adam!" she exclaimed. "You are rolling the stone back against my heart. Do you think we jumped too easily to a conclusion?"

"Perhaps," he muttered. "But that is not all."

Adam brought his whole caravan to a halt, and the dense traffic had to divide back of them and roll by on each side of the road. This interruption was not well received. The sun-browned men, compelled to execute this maneuver, shouted insults at them as they passed. They were moving slowly because the way here became, under the best conditions, like the neck of a bottle; and now the cork had become wedged in the neck. They passed at a snail's pace, a thicket of colored turbans nodding high above the plumed heads of the camels. Their eyes expressed anger and contempt, their lips gave forth the picturesque abuse of the East; camel men, merchants, priests, soldiers, beggars, thieves.

"Speak to no one," counseled Adam, leaning over toward Deborra. "Keep your hand on your purse and your eyes open, even as you listen to me. I am afraid I have been guilty of a great carelessness. I assumed we would be allowed to enter the city without any question. I never gave a thought to the possibility that your father might arrive first and win over the police. We should have halted outside and sent someone to spy out the land. It would have meant a delay, but we would have been spared any danger.

"Your grandfather has arranged everything according to the letter of the law," went on Adam. "Of that we can be sure. He had the profits deposited in Antioch because that removed the transaction from the control of Jewish law. Here Roman law prevails, the code of the Twelve Tables. I think we can be equally certain that the provisions of the bequest are as sound and ironbound as a centurion's breastplate. If no one else had known of the funds stored here, Jabez could have turned the money over to Deborra without taking any other steps. But as the bequest is being contested, he will have to go into court and obtain an *addictio*. We know that magistrates can be bribed. There has been one recent case of *that*. Suppose your father has already arrived and has found that he is being forestalled. It is reasonable that he would try to enter into an arrangement—a conspiracy, rather—with Jabez and the magistrate by which he would pay them to give the decision to him. It would turn his soul inside out to do it, he would suffer, he would cry out in his anguish; but he would come to the necessity in the end. And then what would happen to us?"

"There is sense in what you say," declared Deborra with a serious nod of the head. "I have had an uneasy feeling about what may happen."

"It is a simple matter to bribe officials in Antioch," said Adam. "Particularly the police. I have done it myself. With a little silver and a friendly smile. Now, if your father has been spreading a little baksheesh, the police will be waiting to pick us off one by one like grapes from a bunch. It seems probable that our two young men got through safely, but they are not here to meet us. Why? I think it likely they are watching rats scamper across their feet in a city prison. If that is where they are, the rest of us may join them. The easiest way to win a decision in court is to prevent your opponents from appearing."

Adam continued to shake his head doubtfully. "And why is no one here from the banker to meet us? It is a courtesy he would not overlook if he still had an open mind. I do not like the smell of this at all. We shall be scooped in as we pass the gate. You, my little Deborra, may never see as much as a dinar of all that great fortune, and I may lose my camels and equipment. Nothing that the police of Antioch get into their fists is ever given up. It is an amiable trait of theirs. I know of it from long experience."

There was much confusion and noise ahead of them at the gate, where a squad of custodians sweated over the task of inspecting the long files of anxious travelers. They were reversing the practice of Cerberus by paying small heed to those who were leaving but regarding with suspicion all who sought to get in.

The confusion caused by the stopping of the caravan brought one argus-eyed official down the road. He planted himself in front of Adam and barked at him furiously. "Why do you stand here? Have your brains a palsy as well as your legs, you morsel of fresh dung blown in on the hot wind of the desert?"

Adam glowered back. "It could be," he said, "that the great lady who rides with us has changed her mind and does not desire to enter this thrice-accursed city."

The custodian squinted sharply at Deborra. "Great lady?" he said. "Is it the great lady we have been watching for? Comes she from Jerusalem?"

"It is as I feared," whispered Adam to Deborra. "There is trouble ahead for us."

"Great lady or not, move on inside the gate!" cried the guard with renewed exasperation. "We will ask our questions within. You cannot stand here."

"We have a prince with us, a very powerful and wealthy prince who comes from Seen. Do you treat princes as you would one of your own flap-gutted olive merchants?"

"A prince?" The official laughed scornfully. "If Sargon, king of kings, were alive today and riding in to Antioch, we would not allow him to squat on his royal behind at this part of the road. A mere prince, say you? Don't prate to me of princes. Get your prince, and your great lady too, inside that gate as fast as you can."

Adam did not need any further evidence. "The word has been passed down the line," he muttered. "It has even reached this mangy user of puny power and has turned him unfriendly. We may as well prepare ourselves for the worst."

2

They fell into the slow pace of the ingoing stream and in the course of minutes drew close to the imposing arch of the Iron Gate. A man with a face as round as a melon stood just outside the arch and called something in a monotonous singsong. As they approached closer they realized that he was repeating perfunctorily: "Adam ben Asher! Adam ben Asher!"

Adam swung his camel off to that side and stopped in front of the caller. "I am Adam ben Asher," he said.

"Good!" cried the man in a tone of intense relief. "My voice was on the point of giving out. It may be ruined beyond all hope of repair."

"Am I interested in the condition to which your voice has been reduced?" snorted Adam impatiently.

"I have messages for you," said the stranger with offended dignity. "And greetings from my master, Jabez. I have stood here for three days and called out your name. Never have I left my post from the moment the gate opened in the morning until it was closed at night. My voice——"

Adam interrupted with a violent gesture. "Did your master instruct you not to stir from the cool shadows of the gate? Is it not known to you that the custom is to ride out and convey greetings some considerable distance down the road? That the newcomers are then pleasantly regaled with wine and told what they should know of what is transpiring inside the walls? Did it enter that great head of yours, which I suspect is filled with seeds rather than brains, that your failure to appear in the appointed way might give rise to serious misapprehensions?" Having thus vented his displeasure, Adam gave the stranger a sound buffet on the shoulder by way of compensation. "There! It shall be reported to your master that you labored at your appointed task with a diligence that merits reward. And now for the messages."

The rest of the party had passed in under the arch and had been motioned into a compound to the right. They were told they might as well dismount as there would be delay in the questioning. Deborra, having obeyed these instructions, glanced about her in great distress of mind, thinking of what Adam had said. Whether or not Basil and his companion had escaped the attention of the bandits or whether, having emerged safely from this danger, they had been seized by the Antioch police, the fact remained that they were not here to greet her. This was proof enough that things had gone wrong. She stared unseeingly over the whitewashed walls of the compound and gave not a single thought to the other problems that faced them. It was stiflingly hot in this airless corner packed with anxious humanity, and she was barely aware that her maid had come to her side and was vigorously plying a fan over her head.

Then she saw Chimham. He was standing at the entrance and smiling broadly. He was alone, but her heart jumped with instinctive relief. That he was here, and felt free to smile, was proof that all was well. Basil had not come, but there would be reasons for this, which she would learn in good time.

Chimham, she then perceived, was arrayed in the greatest magnificence. He was wearing a towering sky-blue headdress with a cyclopean crystal glittering on its front. His tunic was of the same shade of blue and his sash was russet. There were beads as large as duck eggs around his neck, and the straps of his sandals were of several shades, all glaringly bright.

"If you had been a day later, gentle lady," he said to Deborra when she motioned him to break through to her, "*he* would have been here to greet you. This morning he was judged as still too unsteady of limb to venture this far."

"Then he has been very ill," she said, anxiety taking possession of her again.

"By the earth and my head, he has been a sick man! If we had ridden one hour less it would have been all right. Or if, say, the road had been a league or two shorter. It was only in that last hour that the sun conquered him. One moment he was sitting high in his saddle and singing to the camels, and the next he was sprawled out and in his mind a hot wind was blowing through the bulrushes. He was delirious when we rode in. The guards began to question us, and he told them his name was Little Issachar, son of Lot. For two days he did not know who he was."

Deborra's eyes showed how deeply this picture had affected her. "He must have suffered very much!" she exclaimed.

"Lady, I have lived on the trails all my life, but never have I gone through the equal of this. There were times when I could feel the bulrushes starting to stir in *my* mind." Then he gave his head a confident nod. "But it is all over and he is getting well fast. He even talks about setting out for Ephesus at once. I do not think that would be wise."

"No," she agreed, "I do not think that would be wise at all."

Adam appeared at her shoulder at this moment and whispered that he had much to tell her. He kept his news to himself, however, for his eyes had lighted on the resplendent camel man.

"Why all this mummery?" he demanded. "Why are you dressed up like a second-rate Solomon?"

Chimham protested indignantly, "These are my wedding clothes. Today I am taking unto myself another wife."

Adam walked over to him and sank both hands into the voluminous blue folds of the tunic. He gave the camel man a furious shake. "I have been doing some thinking about you," he said. "I have heard of your marrying habit, and I have been wondering. How does a man support a string of wives on what I pay you? And now I am starting to believe there is truth in something else I have been told. Yes, the conviction grows in my mind every time I look at you, my fine bridegroom. Do you remember what Samson did when he found that the young men of Timnath had been plowing with his heifer?"

"You will take your hands off me," said Chimham, trying to carry off the situation with dignity.

"The mighty Samson," said Adam, shaking him harder than ever, "went out and slew thirty of their kinsmen. I begin to detect about you, O Chimham, taker of wives, a stench of the same kind of husbandry. I am not another Samson, but I have it in my power to exact a sharp punishment."

"You speak with a double tongue. Your words mean nothing to me." Chimham shook himself free. "This I may say to you, Adam ben Asher: I am no longer your man."

Adam indulged in a snort. "We are in accord there. You are no longer my man."

Chimham faded into the background, and Adam began to impart the information he had gleaned in his talk with the banker's emissary. "Your father reached the city yesterday," he said. "They were becalmed for three days, which was a fortunate thing for us. He has seen Jabez, he has talked to the city authorities, he has been closeted with magistrates. Now that you have arrived, there will be a meeting tomorrow before a magistrate."

Deborra looked up with intense anxiety. "Adam, what do you expect will happen?"

"I have no definite opinion yet. I think it will depend on Jabez. If he decides to be honest about it, we will win. This man of his gave me some information that will be useful in dealing with him. He is a small man and sensitive about it. He would regard any reference to the thick sandals he wears as a personal insult. On the other hand, he is always gratified when the beauty of his wife is mentioned. She is a statuesque creature and rules Jabez with a rod of iron—inside the house. No one unwilling to declare her the most beautiful woman in the world has ever done well in this city. These are points, little Deborra, that you must bear in mind.

"Now that I have told you that," he went on, "I shall add the things I knew about him before. He began as a money-changer and, as you know, they are the sharpest and hardest men in the world. As Jabez is very small, his nose was always closer to his stacks of money and so he did better than anyone else. At that stage of his career he was very sharp and very hard, willing to starve an orphan or strip a widow for the sake of a copper coin. Then a change came over him. As soon as he became rich and powerful he began to allow himself the great and rewarding luxury of being honest. It is said that he could not be tempted now by an offer of Nero's throne. It is often this way; early peccadilloes become steppingstones to a sterling middle age. And because of this curious new habit of his, I think we may have a chance to win."

His turn having been reached, Adam left to face the questioning of the guards. As soon as his back was turned, Chimham came sidling up again. "Gentle lady," he whispered, "I have something to tell you. He was right about it. I *have* been plowing in his field." Deborra had no idea what he meant and she was still further mystified by the winks and nods he was indulging in. "Gentle lady, you can help me. With the old one; you know, the sharp-clawed monkey from the East. Tell him I am smart and can spot a bargain with the back of my head. Tell him I want to go East with him. You could tell him, if you think it would help, that the wife I take today will be the last one, that I will be like a bachelor for the rest of my life. Make him any promise you like, great lady, and I will strive to live up to it."

Deborra stretched out a hand to him. "I do not understand what all this is about. Perhaps you will make it clear later. But I *do* want to help you. I shall speak well of you to the prince, if that is what you mean." She nodded to him and smiled. "I want to thank you now for what you have done. I am sure you helped my husband in many ways and made things easier for him. For this I am very grateful." Then she added with a burst of unrestrained feeling, "Thank you, thank you, many times!"

The emissary of the banker approached her, bowing so low that she could see little but the bald top of his head. "Great lady, I am to tell you," he said, "that a house has been secured for your use while you remain in the city. I am ready to take you there now."

3

The house that had been reserved for Deborra's use was situated in a thinly settled section between the green and mysterious glades of Daphne and the Bridge Gate on the racing Orontes. It stood behind a stone wall of comforting height, a white building with thick parapets around its flat roof. The previous occupant had been, obviously, a man of wealth and discrimination and a collector of beautiful things. The rooms were filled with rare specimens of the best things from all parts of the world: tapestries from Rome depicting the heroic figures of poetry and mythology, tall vases of bronze and porcelain, sculptured figures of the breath-taking beauty that only the fingers of Grecian genius had produced.

In the center of the entrance hall, on a tall pedestal of marble, stood a vessel of glazed pottery, a squat object with the round belly of a complacent heathen god and handles like the talons of a mythical bird of prey. There was a long funnel on the top that suggested it had been used for religious rites. Luke, regarding it with aversion, reflected that in this ominous kettle, perhaps, the hearts of sinless virgins had simmered to appease a Jovian appetite.

The old prince from Seen, who had accompanied them, set up his tents in a grove of trees outside the wall. He inspected the works of art in the house with a somewhat supercilious eye. "Does it seem to my most kind and honored new friends," he asked, "that there is a slight hint of coldness in the figures? That there is a certain lack of the light and color found in the art of my country, so far away, alas? It is not for one as humble and unlearned as I to make criticism in the face of so much beauty. These suggestions are put forward with a proper humility."

Deborra whispered in reply, "I would not dare say it aloud, Honorable Prince, but there *is* a coldness about all this. And too much display and nakedness." Then she added, "It is most kind of you to come so far out of your way with us."

P'ing-li nodded his head so vigorously that he found it hard to recover control over it. "As the years mount, so does my unworthy sense of curiosity," he acknowledged. "Could I turn east at Aleppo and never know if my gentle little lady succeeded in getting her inheritance? I could not have died in peace without knowing. And I wanted also to see when the romance, which has flowered so slowly, came at last into full bloom. Will diminutive and very lovely lady forgive an arrantly curious old man if he asks, is this tardiness due to Christian teachings?"

Deborra shook her head slowly and ruefully. "No, Honorable Prince, the tardiness is due to difficulties that we have created for ourselves."

The venerable head began to bob again in an ecstasy of conviction. "It will be all the sweeter," he asserted, "when the difficulties have melted away like snows in spring."

Luke's inspection of the house led to the selection of a room on the second floor for the temporary housing of the Cup. The room was approached by a steep and narrow stair and had one obvious advantage: it could be defended more easily than any other part of the house. The battered chest was carried at once to this haven and hidden in a corner under a pile of rugs and mats. In the course of a few hours two young men of serious mein put in an appearance. Luke, knowing them both to be earnest believers, with strength in their arms as well as resolution in their hearts, expressed an immediate approval of their selection.

He told them guardedly of the nature of the trust to which they must dedicate themselves. "Until the princes of the church in Antioch can decide on a permanent place for this sacred relic," he said, "it must be kept here. Its safety is in your hands. Neither of you must ever leave the room. You must never eat or sleep at the same time. Your daggers must never be far from your hands. One of the leaders of the Zealots, a most determined man named Mijamin, will come to Antioch very soon. His purpose will be to learn of the whereabouts of the Cup and wrest it from us."

The two young men placed their hands on their hearts and pledged themselves solemnly to defend the cup as long as breath was in their bodies.

These arrangements had been completed when Adam ben Asher arrived. He looked unnaturally repressed and at first had very little to say.

"I shall leave," he announced to Luke, "as soon as the hearing tomorrow is over. I won't be needed any longer. I have done my part."

"You have done it well," said Luke. "I know that Deborra feels most deeply in your debt."

The grin on Adam's face took on a rueful tinge. "That will be my reward," he said. "It is all I expect."

They were standing on a terrace with a mosaic floor in fine colorings. A shallow parapet along the edge contained many curious figures of gnome-like proportions and with square and unnatural faces, the kind of thing that men found when they took to digging around ancient ruins with mattock and pick. Adam looked along the row and scowled.

"There is nothing finer in the world than stone," he said. "The mountains are made of it and they stand up against the sky as timeless almost as the air itself. Stone is hard and clean and pure. But artists with twisted souls take stone into their hands and turn it into hideous things like these. What are they supposed to be? Are they graven images for men to worship instead of the One and Only God?"

Adam withdrew his eyes from the ghoulish figures and stared up at the sky. "I leave her in your hands," he said. "I am never taken into anyone's confidence, but it seems to me that things have not been going well with her. What kind of marriage is it she has made? The eyes of a bride should be filled with happiness; hers are full of shadows instead. You may know why this is so."

"I think I understand." Luke nodded his head with a grave air. "It is something that time will cure."

Adam did not share this confidence. "I hope you are right, Luke the Scribe," he said in a bitter voice. "The happiness of the little Deborra means so much to me that I would come back from the borders of Seen to help her."

The caravan owner fumbled at his belt and produced a small bag tied with a careless knot. This he held out to Luke. "I beg you to do me a favor. Give this to our not too devoted bridegroom. I told you that I cheated him when we dickered for the two camels. This contains what I received in excess of their real value."

Luke accepted the bag, realizing from its weight that the profit Adam was surrendering had been a handsome one. His eyes lost some of their weariness and he smiled warmly at his companion.

"This is another evidence of your good heart. You are excelling yourself in generosity."

"Not at all." Adam's tone was sharp. "I am being thoroughly selfish. I am taking away from him the satisfaction he has been getting from a feeling of moral superiority. I do not think he will be pleased to have this money back. He would prefer to go on believing that I had behaved badly, that I am no better than a grasping and vulgar trader. Well, there is the money. See that he receives it at once." His manner changed and became friendly again. "What are your plans?"

"I received a message from Paul before I left Jerusalem. He gave me instructions, and I shall be busy carrying them out. They have to do largely with the state of the church here in Antioch. It has been a target for the Judaizers and has suffered some losses in strength." Luke's eyes began to glow with awakened zeal. "It was here that the resolve to carry the Word to all the peoples of the world was fostered. It was here that the name 'Christian' was conceived and first used. The welfare of the Antioch church concerns us all deeply."

"Do you still believe that some kind of doom hangs over Jerusalem?" There was a hint of amused tolerance in Adam's voice.

"I dream about it continuously," answered Luke. "It will come soon, Adam. There will be fighting and destruction, and the streets of the Holy City will run with blood. Paul has the same fear. He believes the Zealots will bring about the razing of Jerusalem by preaching armed resistance to Rome. That is another reason why he urges the strengthening of our foothold here. The teachings of Jesus must not be forgotten in the flaming walls of the city of David."

The earnestness of the old physician began to have an effect on Adam. He became somewhat uneasy. "Then you do not expect to go there again?" he asked.

"I return very soon. If it is decided that Paul is to be sent to Rome for trial, I shall make the journey with him. If, on the other hand, the issue is to be decided in Caesarea, I shall take my place at his side."

Adam gave him a curious look. "You have changed. I always thought of you as gentle and human, the one disciple of the Nazarene with a twinkle in the eye. Now you are getting like the rest of them. You talk of death and destruction. You keep preaching at me that the city of

David will be destroyed. I am disappointed in you, Luke the Physician. I prefer you as you were before you wrapped yourself up in the toga of prophecy."

"Must I tell you again that I am not a prophet? I am an old man who sees that things are going wrong in the world. I have always thought that the truths of Jesus could be taught best by spreading the doctrine of charity and pity. Now my heart is cold because I am beginning to see that the seed must be planted in the soil of tragedy. Only if watered by the blood of martyrdom can the tree grow to greatness." He sighed and spread out his hands in a gesture of disillusionment. "The habits of men cannot be changed easily. It seems that the human mind can't be reached by kindness alone. Man understands violence better. Perhaps the church of Jesus will gain strength from the flames of Jerusalem. Perhaps faith must be continuously renewed by persecution and cruelty."

Adam had regained his normal mood. He grinned and waved to Luke airily as he turned to enter the house. "I will see you then in Jerusalem, my venerable friend," he said. "The city will be busy and it will be filled with peace, and wherever we go the dome of the Temple will be in our eyes. The only lamentations we hear will come from the Wailing Wall."

4

Deborra had thrown herself with zest into the preparations for occupying her new house. When Adam found her she was in a spacious room on the ground floor, surrounded by her servants, and she was busily instructing them in the arrangement of the belongings they had brought with them. Her cheeks showed a slight flush of excitement, and it was clear that, for the time being, she was happy.

The weather was providing something in the nature of a miracle. A breeze was blowing off the sea and had already dissipated the murky heat of the city. The tops of the green trees in the first of the two interior gardens swayed pleasantly and seductively. Deborra had donned a silk tunic and, in the fashion of the day, had bound her right arm inside it, leaving only one arm free. It was a graceful arrangement, if somewhat cramping, and showed to advantage the slender lines of her shoulder and waist. In her left hand she carried a small fan shaped like a palm leaf. This again was in accord with the dictates of fashion.

Adam's manner was brusque as he repeated his intention of leaving on the conclusion of the hearing.

Deborra stepped clear of the circle of domestics and came over to him. She looked both shocked and sorry.

"Why must you go so soon?" she asked. "Surely you are in need of rest."

"I am not needed here," he answered in a grumbling tone. "And my own affairs are pressing. I go back to Aleppo and strike directly for the East from there. I shall return in a few months with great loads of valuable goods."

"I shall miss you so much." She was on the point of tears. "How can I repay you for all you have done for me?"

Adam brushed this aside and asked a question of his own. When did she plan to return to Jerusalem? He was hoping, it was clear, that she would be there when he returned from the East bearing the sheaves of his industry.

Her brows drew into a thoughtful frown before she replied, "I am not sure. I may never go back. This city is my husband's home, and my place is with him. I do not think"—she flushed unhappily—"I do not think my father will ever want to see me again. He may disown me and cast me off. Why, then, should I return to Jerusalem?"

Adam had been holding his feelings under a close check. Now he allowed a trace of temper to show. "How can you live so far away from the altars of your own people?" he demanded. "Is it not clear to you already that this is a city of pagan abominations? The people of Antioch bow down before graven images. They are lewd and wicked. You will be unhappy."

"Adam, it is beautiful here! And there is a large Christian colony. I do not see why I should be unhappy."

"Look at this house!" Adam swept an arm impatiently about him. "It is full of obscene figures and heathen decorations. Even the walls are made of tile from the devil-worshiping desert and not of the clean limestone of our native hills. Everything is so wrong here that my flesh crawls with repugnance."

"But," cried Deborra, "there is so much real beauty. I have been reveling in it. This wonderful breeze from the sea, the beautiful gardens, the green of the trees, and the flowers I see blooming behind the white stone walls. Adam, this is a city of enchantment. I think I can be happy here."

"Will you be happy when the paschal moon is in the sky and you cannot see the Temple in the fading light?"

Adam turned and stamped to the door, striking a hand angrily against a linen tapestry hanging on the wall beside it. "Heathen gods, heathen conceits, all this artistic emptiness!" he cried. He paused and threw back to her over his shoulder: "I shall return directly to Jerusalem from my travels in the East. It seems improbable that I shall ever see you again."

"Adam!" she cried. "Of course we shall see each other. I would be most unhappy to think otherwise."

"*Sahumah,*" he said. He hesitated and then added with a shrug of his shoulders, "I suppose now I shall have to look around for a Leah."

CHAPTER XX

I

SITTING ON A HARD STONE BENCH in the court, with the eagles of Rome embossed in black marble on the wall above her, Deborra was aware that her father had never once looked in her direction. He had already taken his seat when she entered, and beside him sat a doctor of the law who had accompanied him from Jerusalem. They had been sharing an uneasy silence, but as soon as she came in the lawyer began whispering to her father with an intense earnestness. Aaron had said nothing but had nodded his head at several points.

She watched them with saddened intentness. "My poor father!" she thought. "He has always been an unhappy man. He complained so many times that I thought more of Grandfather than I did of him. And he was right: I loved Grandfather above everyone."

She remembered then the name of the man with her father. He was called Ohad, and he stood high in legal councils and was heard often in the Sanhedrin. That Aaron had brought him all the way to Antioch was proof of the extent of his determination to acquire the funds that his father had accumulated with Jabez. The nose of Ohad protruded from his long and narrow face like the beak of a bird of prey. He filled her with dislike and distrust.

"What are they whispering about?" she wondered. It was about her, of course. The somber look in her father's eyes made her certain he would never forgive her.

Adam and Luke shared the bench with her, but Basil had not been well enough to come. Her two companions were saying little and keeping their eyes fixed on Jabez. The latter, who was seated in front of the raised dais of the magistrate, was as small as the reports of him had indicated; a neat man in a spotless toga with deep purple bands. He had a well-trimmed beard and a rather fine mane of pomaded black hair. There was a pile of parchments in front of him, and his trim hands riffled through them at intervals with swift dispatch.

"Everything depends on this banker," whispered Adam. "The rest of them are no more than shadows; Aaron himself, that voracious pelican he has brought with him as a lawyer, the magistrate, all of them. It is what Jabez is going to say and do that counts. I wish I knew what was in his mind."

Deborra looked at the dapper little man again and decided that no one could do more than guess what was going on in his mind. He was completely self-composed.

"As we cannot know what he is thinking," went on Adam, "I wish we had Benjie the Asker here to find out what the lesser men are saying. Perhaps," getting quietly to his feet, "I may be able to pick up some information myself."

The few spectators in the courtroom were paying little attention to the main characters in the drama. They had no eyes for anyone save Prince P'ing-li, who had come in with a retinue of servants and was sitting at one side. They whispered excitedly about the costliness of his carmine robe that was thickly encrusted with precious stones. As his chair lacked side supports he had called upon two of his servingmen to hold his forearms on the usual cushions, and this both puzzled and amused them. Stories were being whispered back and forth. He was a famous conjurer from the East who rode on the back of a fire-spitting dragon and who, moreover, could summon demons to fly in through the window and set the earthly pomp and majesty of Rome at naught; he was a man of such wealth that Jabez would have to bow and scrape before him; he was the ruler of a great foreign country who had come in person to study the workings of Roman law.

The one who deserved the most attention, and was getting the least, was the magistrate, sitting high up above them in a silence that seemed sullen. Deborra had taken one look at him and had fallen into a state of panic, fearing that justice could not be obtained from one who wore the stamp of corruption so openly. He was a squat old man with bloodshot eyes and cheeks as flabbily dewlapped as a hunting dog's. He wheezed and groaned whenever it became necessary to change his position. His toga was carelessly draped over his grossly fat shoulders and showed unmistakable stains of perspiration. A thin man with red hair who resembled a ferret sat at his shoulder with a bundle of documents in his hands.

When this most unpleasant-appearing old man spoke, his voice created a measure of surprise. It was clear, concise, well modulated.

"The document," he said, "seems to be drawn in accordance with the Twelve Tables." He glanced down at Aaron and his legal supporter. "What points do you wish to raise for my consideration?"

Ohad rose slowly to his feet. He had long and spindly legs and created the illusion of a crane watching by the side of a stream for unwary fish. "'The passionate man cannot be a teacher,'" he quoted. "I shall strive, Learned Judge, to discuss the points involved without any trace of passion. Moreover, I shall speak with a proper brevity. Permit me first to make a statement from the Laws, 'A man cannot disinherit his legal heir.'"

"You quote from the Laws? It is not from the Twelve Tables that you draw this pronouncement. What laws, then?"

Ohad, speaking with a mellow and unctuous roll, could not keep a hint of superiority from showing in his voice. "The laws of the Hebrew people, O Learned Judge."

"This is a Roman court," said the magistrate in a dry tone.

"I use the Hebrew words only because I am most familiar with them. For this I crave your indulgence. But, Learned Judge, the principle stated is the same in all laws. It is to be found in the Twelve Tables. A man may not disinherit his rightful heir."

Several men sprang to their feet and contended for places in front of the bench with the obvious intention of speaking. The magistrate commanded silence by a noiseless twiddling of his fingers. "I, Fabius Marius, will state the answer on this point. The Twelve Tables permit a man to exclude his son from inheritance, provided the name of the son is stated specifically."

One of those clamoring for the right to speak exclaimed: "May I call to the attention of the learned judge that the documents Joseph of Arimathea drew up for the guidance of Jabez declared specifically that his son Aaron was not to receive any of the moneys? The instructions are clear and not open to misconstruction."

It became apparent at once that no set rules were in use for the presentation of evidence or the hearing of witnesses. Men crowded below the magistrate's bench and expressed their opinions or endeavored to call his attention to documents in their possession. These eager disputants, who were from both sides, were without exception elderly men and learned in the law. Their heads shook and their long beards waggled with the vehemence that possessed them.

Ohad became convinced quickly that there could be no advantage in disputing the exclusion of Aaron from the inheritance. He lowered himself into his seat and began to speak in earnest tones to his principal. It was apparent that the latter was not in immediate agreement. He seemed to be fighting back in a state of sullen fury, and it was not until the weight of the arguments the man of the law brought to bear became too heavy that he gave in. He twitched his shoulders in bitterness rather than resignation. When Ohad rose to discuss the second of their claims he turned to stare bleakly at the nearest window.

"O Judge," said the lawyer, "there is nothing in the instructions to deny Aaron the right to act as his daughter's guardian. Nay, it is an established fact that he may continue to exercise all duties and responsibilities as long as she remains in his tutelage."

"Is she a minor?" The magistrate's voice carried a strong note of skepticism. His shortsighted eyes darted about the courtroom. "I believe she is present. Will Deborra, daughter of Aaron and a principal in this case, stand up?"

Deborra rose to her feet. She flushed when she realized that every pair of eyes in the room had turned to stare at her save those of her father, who continued to gaze out of the window. She was dressed quietly in a white *palla* with gold and blue bands, and her hair was bound with a gold ribbon. The judge leaned out over his bench, the better to see her, and then gave his head an approving bob.

"Women cannot be called as witnesses," he said, "and so I may not ask you any questions. I desire to state, nevertheless, that I have already reached two conclusions. The first—and I am sure that all will agree with me here—is that the daughter of Aaron is a most handsome young woman indeed." The courtroom tittered and the magistrate beamed and nodded his head like an ancient but pranksome faun. "The second is that she has come of age legally, it being my understanding that the age fixed under Hebrew law is thirteen years and one day."

Luke rose to his feet and advanced to the bench. "I have documents to offer," he said, "in proof of the fact that Deborra, daughter of Aaron, is in her sixteenth year."

Fabius squinted down at Luke suspiciously. "Who are you?"

"I am called Luke the Physician. I was for many years a close acquaintance—nay, a close friend—of the deceased Joseph of Arimathea. I was

present in his house and witnessed the marriage of his granddaughter.
I accompanied her from Jerusalem to Antioch."

The magistrate consulted a list in front of him. "You have not been
summoned," he complained.

"This man is a leader among the Christians," declared Ohad bitterly.
"For many years he has accompanied one Paul of Tarsus on his journeyings about the land."

The eyes of Fabius turned slowly from Ohad to Luke. "You are a
companion of Paul of Tarsus," he said to the latter. "In spite of this I
am prepared to accept the documents you bear. But you will not be permitted to offer oral evidence."

Fabius ran a quick and practiced eye over the parchment. "The statements contained here," he said, nodding his head, "bear out the conclusions I had already reached. The daughter has come of age legally."
He inclined his head in her direction. "You may now sit down."

When Deborra had resumed her seat, Adam tiptoed up behind her and
began to whisper in her ear. "I have learned one thing. Your father paid
a visit to Jabez this morning and they quarreled, noisily and unmistakably. The banker's face was red with anger when he escorted your father
to the door. Has he been taking any part in the proceedings?"

"None," answered Deborra. "He has not raised his eyes once."

Adam frowned uneasily. "I do not understand this," he said. "Does
Jabez intend to stand aside and play a neutral part? If he does, it will
weigh against us."

"I think," whispered Deborra, "that we were wise not to entrust our
documents to him."

Adam lowered his head still further. "I have also gleaned some facts
about the judge. He was a slave in Rome but secured his freedom and
later became a Roman citizen. This may be a fortunate thing for us. It is
said there was some opposition to having him hear this case."

Deborra looked at the magistrate with new eyes. It seemed to her
now that she could detect the faintest hint of kindliness in the purple-
veined expanse of his face.

"He became a political force in Rome but made enemies by speaking
his mind freely about men above him in rank. He was sent here as a
measure of exile. It has been the same; he continues to make ill-wishers
by his persistent candor. In spite of this he is liked by the common
people, and it is generally believed he is honest." After a moment
Adam added: "He has had little education and depends on that red-

headed shadow back of him; and *he* is as venal as a professional beggar."

Fabius raised a hand to still the bickering voices beneath him. "It is contended by the learned man from Jerusalem," he said, "that the heiress in this case is under the guardianship of her father. This does not apply, because she comes into court a married woman. She is now under the tutelage of her husband."

Ohad had declared his intention to conduct himself without giving way to passion, but at this point his face became contorted with feeling and his voice shook with an anger he made no effort to conceal. "The man she married is an ex-slave!" he cried. "He has had his freedom for a few weeks only. I assert without any fear of contradiction that a freedman may not usurp the authority of the head of a family. This is a point we are prepared to fight, if necessary, in the highest tribunal in the world."

A murmur of voices filled the courtroom, and it was apparent that some approval of what the doctor of laws had said was helping to swell the volume of sound.

"Less than an hour ago," said the magistrate, "another court passed on an application by the man who stands in the relationship of husband to the heiress in this case. The application was for reinstatement as a citizen of Rome. It has been affirmed."

For a moment the people in the room were too surprised by this announcement to make a sound. Deborra found herself on her feet, with no consciousness of having changed her position, an exultation in her veins that she had never before experienced. It was hard to keep from shouting out aloud. All about her people had risen also, and she saw that on most of the faces there was excited approval. Then the silence was broken by a loud outburst of enthusiasm, in which she joined.

The judge made no effort at first to still the uproar. He seemed willing to have the fact of public assent established before making an effort a second time to command silence. The response when he did raise his arm was not as immediate; it was many seconds before his order was obeyed.

Ohad remained standing throughout the demonstration. His eyes, which encroached closely on his long expanse of nose, darted about the room with quite apparent surprise. When silence had been restored, he began to speak in a voice that lacked some of the ease of delivery he had displayed before.

"The action of the court comes," he declared, "as a complete surprise.

And, I may add, it gives much cause for amazement. In view of this it becomes necessary for me to make a statement on behalf of my principal, Aaron, son of Joseph. As soon as he returns to Jerusalem, it is his intention to move to have the marriage set aside. His daughter did not have his consent. In fact, he knew nothing of her intentions until after the wedding had taken place. The ceremony occurred, moreover, after the death of Joseph of Arimathea. It is established in our laws that a marriage may not take place within the thirty days of mourning prescribed."

The man at the magistrate's shoulder spread out seven fingers on the table. Fabius grasped what he meant at once and raised his head to speak. "Is not the term of mourning seven days instead of thirty?"

"It is seven days after the death of a woman," declared Ohad, "but thirty in the case of a man."

"A distinction," cried the old magistrate, "with which I am in disagreement. There is at least equal reason for mourning the passing of a good woman as for any man who strutted in the toga of high office. And my enemies and detractors, of whom there are many, may make the most of what I have said." He paused then as the man behind him thrust a document into his hand. After making a pretense of reading it, he nodded his head and handed it back. "A statement has been placed in evidence to the effect that the wedding took place half an hour before the death of Joseph of Arimathea. More than fifty persons who were in the house at the time have either signed it or affixed their marks to the document."

The doctor of law continued his argument in a spate of glib words, and other voices joined in. It became a jumble of sound finally, with the opinions of the participants becoming more heated each moment. The magistrate allowed the discussion to continue for some considerable time. Finally he employed a sharp twiddle of his fingers to signify that the end of his patience had been reached.

"But we deal with an accomplished fact," he declared. "The young woman *is* married. No matter what the circumstances of his past, her husband is today a Roman citizen. The law places her under his tutelage. Can I disregard this in the mere expectation that a court in a foreign land may declare the marriage void? In a suit, moreover, which has not yet been entered for hearing?"

The eyes of Deborra and Luke met, hers wide open with delight. "We are going to win!" she said in an exultant whisper. "My good friend, I can feel it. I can see it in the eyes of that strange old man. We are going to win!"

Luke's eyes indulged themselves in a pleased twinkle. "I feel the same way," he said. "Jabez has done nothing to assist us, but the magistrate is not allowing anything to stand in the way of an honest view of the facts. Yes, my child, we have every reason to be satisfied so far."

Adam did not share their optimistic mood. He stared across the room at his old enemy and the man of the law who had turned to consult with him. "They will have something more to say," he muttered. "Ohad is as cunning as a fox. He is not beaten yet. Don't let yourself get too certain until the verdict has been given."

Aaron and Ohad became involved in an argument, and it was apparent that the great doctor of laws was finding his client stubborn and intractable. At first Aaron gave his head a frigid shake at everything the other man said. Once he exclaimed in an audible voice: "No, no! I do not agree. I do not, I tell you." The lawyer continued to press him, and after a time Aaron began to weaken. His protests became petulant rather than violent. He still shook his head, but the earlier heat had left his denials. Finally he threw both hands in the air, and so gave in.

Ohad turned and addressed the magistrate. "O Learned Judge," he said, "it is my purpose to propose a compromise. It is a measure in which I lack the full approval of my client, who feels he has rights and privileges which should be recognized. In the interests of a quicker settlement, however, he has agreed to let me make the suggestion I have urged upon him. It is this, Learned Judge." The lawyer placed a judicial finger on the tip of his nose and squinted down at it in deep concentration. "Delay the making of any decision until after the legality of this marriage has been tested. In the meantime let the funds remain in the hands of Jabez. He has handled them for many years with a skill and foresight that we all recognize. It will not be a hardship for the ultimate winner to have him continue his stewardship for such longer time as is necessary to allow the court in Jerusalem to reach a decision."

"I knew it," muttered Adam. "I was sure Ohad would have something of the kind to propose. This is a shrewd move. If they win before the Sanhedrin and get the marriage set aside—and they may, if only because Aaron's consent was not obtained or even on influence alone—then the court here will not continue to regard Deborra as a married woman. They have nothing to lose by this and a great deal to gain. Yes, Ohad is as sharp as a new pick."

Deborra had lost her exultant mood. She glanced with apprehension at Luke and found that he was listening to Adam with a disturbed pucker between his eyes.

"Look at the judge," said Adam. "He sees this as a means to escape responsibility. Do you recall that Pontius Pilate tried every way to avoid making a decision in the case of Jesus? This magistrate has a mind of his own, but he is not averse to shuffling off the load." He gave his head a discouraged shake. "I do not like it. Any delay is in their favor. If the court postpones a decision as he is suggesting, they will have many months in which to work. In that time the sun of influence might climb high enough into the sky to scorch and destroy all the green shoots of justice. I tell you, I do not like it at all. We have everything to lose by this proposal."

At this moment a disturbance was heard at the entrance to the courtroom. In spite of a negative order from an official at the door, Linus came striding in, his eyes glistening in full consciousness of his importance. One hand held his toga in place; in the other he carried a chariot whip. He walked with a loud clomp of leather to the front of the room and stationed himself before the magistrate.

"It has been brought to my attention," he asserted loudly, "that a case is being tried here that concerns a former slave of mine."

Adam twisted excitedly on the bench. "Look at Jabez!" he said in a whisper. "I swear he was expecting something of this kind to happen. His eyes are like sparks from a wood fire."

At this stage the face of Jabez, which had been as expressionless as a marble wall, was turned toward the bench where Deborra and her allies sat. He smiled at them. Then, to their amazement, he allowed his left eyelid to droop. It was no more than a momentary flicker, but none of them had any doubts as to what had happened. The great banker had winked at them.

"He arranged this," whispered Adam. "He saw there would be some advantage for us in having this man stalk in like a conquering general."

The old magistrate was looking down from his high perch at Linus, his eyes reflecting a sudden frostiness.

"You have not been summoned to appear."

"I have not been summoned to appear." Linus indulged in a laugh that said such details did not concern him. "It happens, O Fabius, that I have information to give you. And so I am here."

"This information concerns the character of one of the parties in this hearing?"

"It concerns the character of one Basil, son of Theron, seller of pens. It concerns also the rights of slaves and ex-slaves."

"And you consider your views on these points to be worth the attention of the court?"

Linus began to scowl. "I do. It is your duty to hear what I have to say."

The magistrate continued to speak in fully controlled tones. "The courts nevertheless are not open to any citizen who desires to express his opinions. Your ideas on the subject of slavery are well known, and in many circles they are not highly regarded. It is well known also"—his manner became suddenly glacial—"that Linus has small regard for the workings of the law. He believes, perhaps, that all judges are open to corrupt persuasion. Certainly he makes it clear that he considers himself above the rules that apply to lesser men." He leaned out across the bench and scowled at the spluttering Linus. "If you had information that you considered pertinent, why did you not advise the court in advance?"

"I am here," declared Linus.

Fabius snuffled angrily and let himself sink back into his chair. He continued to glare at the unbidden witness.

"Your information can have no bearing on the issues before this court. A decision given out in another court has settled all questions with reference to the status of the man Basil." He pointed a finger suddenly at the figure in front of him. "Stand down! You will not be heard!"

Then the magistrate proceeded to make it clear that the incident had jolted him out of the indecision with which he had listened to the persuasive arguments of Ohad. He brought his fist down sharply on the surface of the bench.

"I now declare that no evidence has been introduced into these proceedings to justify me in disregarding the clear and precise instructions that the deceased Joseph of Arimathea drew up for the disposal of these funds. What he desired done with the moneys was made evident, in full accord with the spirit and letter of the Twelve Tables. The will of the testator, if in any degree reasonable, must always be the main consideration. I shall draw up an *addictio* at once, authorizing Jabez to distribute the funds as set forth in the instructions."

The old prince, his parchment-like face wreathed in smiles, sought out Deborra as soon as the signal to rise was given.

"It was not possible to hear what was said because of inadequate knowledge," he stated. "But it must be, from the sunshine of your faces, that this judge, whose wisdom is greater than his appearance hints, has been fair and judicious in his decision. This humble witness of your triumph is very happy indeed."

Deborra looked about the court for Adam but failed to see him. He had already bidden Luke farewell and left the court. In the door he had turned for a final look at the radiant young woman who had served so long as the Rachel on whom his fancy had been fixed. "Farewell!" he muttered. "For over twenty years I have flouted the law that says a man must marry by the time he is eighteen. I must continue to disregard it because I can see now that I shall carry your image in my heart always, little Deborra. But I shall never see you again."

2

A minor official of the court bowed before Deborra as she prepared to leave. "Your presence," he said, "is desired in the Chamber of the Petitioners."

She looked at Luke for guidance. "I think you will find it is your father," he said. "I will go with you as far as the door to make sure."

It was Aaron who had sent for her. He was alone in the Chamber of the Petitioners, and it was clear from the spots of color visible in the region of his eyes and cheekbones that he had taken the decision in a bitter spirit. Without glancing up he continued to turn over the documents spread out in front of him.

"It is you?"

"Yes, Father."

"You are satisfied, no doubt, with what you have done. You have subjected me to suffering and humiliation. I have had to stand in a foreign court before a hostile judge and see my only child range herself with my enemies. I must now return to Jerusalem, leaving you with the ex-slave you married without seeking my consent."

"Father, I am filled with regrets." Deborra was feeling so much compassion for him that she found it hard not to break into tears. "If there had been any other course open to me, I would have taken it. But there was no way."

"You were acting, I am sure, on advice that came from my father. I have been aware for many years that he held me in small regard. All his affection was given to you. I had none of it."

Deborra said in a low tone: "No, no, Father, you are wrong. It was always very clear to me that Grandfather yearned for a closer understanding with you and would have done anything to bring it about."

Aaron raised his voice in angry denial. "He built a wall between us that could not be crossed. It was all because I refused to share his religious beliefs. He stole your affections from me and then turned you into a Christian."

He was attired in plain white robes, which accentuated the slope of his narrow shoulders. This made him look so thin and insignificant that his daughter felt her heart fill with pity for him.

Aaron raised his head and stared into her eyes for the first time. He spoke in a furious haste. "I do not hold the memory of my father in honor or respect. He forfeited his right to any filial feeling on my part. I never want to hear his name spoken again." He picked up one of the documents in front of him and shook it at her. "Here! If you will sign this, we may still avoid the consequences of what you have done today."

Deborra looked at the document with trepidation. "What is it?"

"Your acquiescence to certain conditions. If you sign this, you will be agreeing to return with me to Jerusalem and to become a party to the action I shall bring to have your marriage set aside. You will be consenting also to have me assume control of this inheritance until such time as you marry with my consent. Sign this document, my erring and misguided child, and I will restore you to all your rights. You and your children after you will inherit everything I possess. You shall be in the meantime the mistress of my home, the sole object of my love and solicitude."

Deborra began to sob. "You know full well, Father, that I cannot do this."

"And why not?"

"Because"—the flow of her tears made it difficult for her to speak—"it would be throwing aside everything that Grandfather desired. And it would mean leaving the husband I love with all my heart. Surely you must see that what you ask is impossible."

Aaron tossed the document down in front of him. "Think well, child. Your chance for serenity and happiness, for a secure future, depends on the decision you make."

"I cannot do what you demand."

"Is this your final word?"

"Yes, Father."

Aaron rose to his feet. The color had ebbed from his cheeks and left them white. He stripped the linen tunic from his shoulders and tore it into two pieces.

"Then hear what I have to say, stubborn and unfeeling child. Even as I cast this garment from me, I cast you out of my life. You cease to be my daughter from this moment. Your name will never be spoken in my hearing. This is my decision, and I shall never change."

When Deborra told Luke what had occurred, he nodded to her gravely. "It is what could be expected. Your father is a bitterly disappointed man. He has taken the only form of retaliation open to him."

"Surely his heart will soften. Do you not think he will change his mind in time?"

"It is always best to be honest, my child. No, I think there is little chance that he will relent. Once he has chosen a path, it is impossible to divert him."

Deborra's tears began to flow again. After several moments of unrestrained weeping she began to laugh hysterically. "He will never mend the breach between us, but I am sure the first thing he will do is to take the pieces of his tunic and have *them* mended," she said.

CHAPTER XXI

I

JABEZ SAT at a long table in a huge room when they were ushered
in to see him the next day. Nowhere in this quiet establishment was there
any hint of the turmoil and chaffering of the court of the money-changers
where denarii were changed into didrachmas and half shekels and men
haggled over the lepton, which was usually called a mite. A silence as
complete as could be found on a high hill during a windless day filled the
pillared room. Jabez looked up from the small pile of documents in front
of him and invited them to be seated.

"Everything is settled," said the banker, tapping the marble top with
his small white knuckles. "Here are the documents to be signed. May I
say I am happy to have this matter concluded so satisfactorily—and in
accordance with the wishes of my very dear old friend?" He looked inquiringly at Deborra. "Your husband is not with you?"

Luke took it on himself to explain. "I am in agreement with his physician, who considered it unwise for him to come out yet. He will be able
to come tomorrow."

"Then the signing must be delayed another day." Jabez lifted one of
the documents on the table. "This contains the terms of the settlement.
You are to receive on signing one half of the moneys due you. There is
some inconvenience in this for me, as the amount is large, very large
indeed. But I can manage to pay. You are to receive, in addition, the ownership of the house in which you are now living and which seems to please
you. There are other purchases to be made for you—of jewelry, of household appointments, of horses, an Assyrian dog, an Egyptian cat. There are
appointments of gold for a religious shrine, the location and nature of
which are not indicated. Whatever is left after these matters are attended

to is to be held here and to be subject to your demands later. I may tell you there will be a substantial balance."

Deborra asked anxiously: "You have not forgotten the sword with the jeweled handle for my husband? And the cloak with a gold clasp and all the new tools with silver handles?"

The banker nodded. "They are on the list. I did not enumerate all the items here." He added in a severe tone, "I do not approve of many of them, as I have already told you."

"There is to be a gold chain for Adam ben Asher and a fine emerald for the wife he will marry someday. And presents for all the men in the train and the servants who came with me. And there must be gold bracelets for the three sons of Catorius on the Plain of Esdraelon, Sempronius, Tiberius, and Gaius."

Jabez nodded again. "A jeweler waits in another room with samples for your inspection."

Deborra turned to smile at Luke. "Best of friends, what am I to do for you? You have no personal wants. To give you anything similar to the—the most inadequate gifts with which I am expressing my gratitude to all my other friends would be lacking in suitability and in care on my part. Perhaps there is some wish you have."

Luke laid a hand affectionately on hers. "It can be stated at once. A purse, my child, a very plain purse, but one filled with small coins, so that when I walk in the Ward of the Trades I shall be able to provide some relief for the poverty there. Make me a dispenser of your bounty."

"Yes!" cried Deborra eagerly. "It must be like the magic purse that never became empty."

"Your coming to Antioch," said Luke, "will be a memorable event for the poor, hungry old men in the ward and the undernourished children."

"Have a care!" exclaimed the banker. "This magic purse might deplete a fortune as large even as yours, generous lady." His lips drew tightly together. "I do not believe in magic purses."

He made a move to get to his feet but changed his mind. After a brief hesitation he reached for a jeweled box that lay on the table close to his hand. This he opened, revealing that it contained a sticky paste of a shade that defied identification, except that it bore a faint resemblance to violet. Dipping a forefinger into it with the utmost care, he drew out an infinitesimal quantity of the paste. This he placed on the tip of his tongue. His eyes closed and a sigh, which could be induced only by a pleasurable sensation, escaped from him. His lips closed tight, and it was several moments before he opened his eyes. They seemed to have acquired a completely new brilliance, and his manner had become more brisk and animated.

"Cannabis," he said. "It comes from the Far East, from India. I do not offer it to anyone. It is strictly forbidden to all members of my household to touch the box; although I make no secret of my addiction to it, having the strength of will to use it in the smallest quantities. I cannot be sure that anyone else would exercise the same restraint and so I allow it to myself alone. When I have labored a long time and a weariness has possession of me, I take a little of it. It restores all of my powers at once.

"And now," he said, shoving the box to one side and turning to Deborra, "there are perhaps some questions you would like to ask."

"Yes," she answered eagerly. "I would like to know how it happened that my husband's citizenship was restored. You know all about it, I am sure."

"It was not easy," said the banker. "The deposing of your husband was much talked about at the time and almost everyone was convinced he had been unjustly treated, that the magistrate had been bribed. When it became known that his freedom had been purchased and that he had applied for reinstatement, it seemed to a number of citizens, including myself, that the chance had come to compensate him in some small degree. We met and decided to exercise such pressure as might be needed to have it put through the court quickly—and quietly. Needless to state, perhaps, all of us were antagonistic to Linus and what he represents."

He smiled at Deborra and gave his head a vigorous shake as though to clear it. "We were in agreement that the confirmation should come at the moment when it could do him the most good. It was not entirely a coincidence that it came when it did.

"It would not have been possible to get him his citizenship if it had been in Rome," he proceeded to explain. "The slaves and freedmen greatly outnumber the citizens there, and so the slavery laws are strictly enforced. But in the provinces, and most particularly here in Antioch, we are disposed to wink at the regulations. We do things our own way. The plan was carried through neatly and with the greatest secrecy. Linus did not know anything about it. He would have moved all earth and the nether regions to upset us, had he known."

"We are disposed to think," said Luke, "that the appearance of Linus in court was another little conspiracy of the same kind."

"It was not a coincidence. Linus, actually, is a stupid ox; it did not occur to him that the idea of going to court had been insinuated into his mind for a purpose. He saw only that the chance had come to be harmful. That he had crossed weapons with Fabius on several occasions added to his willingness to interfere, and so he came striding in, expecting to sweep everything before him."

The drug was beginning to act and the banker's eyes had narrowed to slits. His reserve of manner had left him and an almost theatrical tendency had supplanted it.

"It was, as you observed, a great success. Fabius, angered by the confident manner of Linus, espoused our point of view." His tongue had now ceased to be on its guard and showed a tendency to loquacity. He talked in grandiloquent terms. "He is always in need of a bath, our good friend Fabius; a sot, a glutton, a leering satyr, a moldy wineskin washed up by an overflowing sewer. But as I listened to him it seemed to me that a great white light played about him and that he had sprouted a pair of the spotless wings of your Hebrew angels."

"Will my husband be in any danger if he remains in Antioch?" asked Deborra.

The exuberance of manner departed and Jabez gave the situation some careful thought, drumming on the table with the tips of his slender fingers. "Linus may be counted upon to show enmity," he said. "Fortunately he has been shrinking in stature. He began with a great flourish and a sounding of trumpets, but recently it has become apparent that he has made serious mistakes. He has proven himself somewhat rash in speculation and he has made some political alliances that are not well advised. The results are now being felt. Linus at the moment is on the defensive."

The great money-changer slid down from his chair. All the lightness of mood that the drug had induced seemed to have deserted him. There was coldness and menace in his eye. No one looking at him in this mood would have given a thought to his lack of stature.

"We have plans about this fellow," he said. "We do not like him at all. Before long we shall take some steps to put him back where he belongs."

The coldness left his eyes as suddenly as it had come. He even smiled. "And now for a much pleasanter matter. We shall go upstairs and pay a visit to my wife."

2

Like the fair and virtuous Lucretia when visited by the false Sextus, the lady Antonia was seated with her handmaidens when they reached her apartments. The parallel ended there. Some of the servants were busy with•distaff and needle, it is true, but Antonia herself was not taking any part in their labors. She was reclining on a couch while one of her maids burnished and colored her fingernails, and she was gazing idly out of an open window through which the last manifestations of the previous day's breeze were stirring the curtains. It seemed certain enough that on her feet she would be somewhat taller than her attentive husband, and she was unmistakably beautiful in a pronounced and dusky way.

It became clear to Deborra at once that she had been laboring under delusions in the matter of feminine dress. The whole matter had seemed very simple; there was a narrow range of colors to select from and few established designs. Antonia, quite clearly, had never acknowledged such limitations. Her robe was bewilderingly novel: of a rich plum brown with panels of yellow on the shoulders, laced with the richest of blues, and a star of the same shades on the breast. From her waist, which was close-fitting instead of blousing loosely to obscure the girdle, there radiated small pointed shafts of gold, pointing both up and down and edged with a more delicate tone of blue. Each movement of her arms revealed the quite amazing fact that the sleeves were lined with gold silk. Deborra was so fascinated with this originality and audacity that she could not take her eyes from the figure of the matron.

Perhaps the effects of the drug had already worn off. Perhaps it was habitual with Jabez to show restraint in the presence of his rather formidable wife. At any rate, he addressed her in a subdued tone.

"My sweet wife, my delicate little fuchsia bud, I have brought guests. This is Luke the Physician and this is Deborra, the granddaughter of my once very good friend, Joseph of Arimathea. You have been hearing a great deal about them."

His wife paid no attention at all to Luke but fixed her decidedly handsome, if rather bold, black eyes on Deborra with an interest she made no effort to conceal.

"I have been hearing a very great deal," she said. "So much that I am afraid I shall be intrusive and ask many questions."

"In that case," said Jabez in a playful tone, "we shall leave you two lovely children together to chatter and gossip. Perhaps you will permit us to return later for such refreshments as you may care to offer us."

The banker's wife lost no time, as soon as the two men had withdrawn, in probing into the state of Deborra's mind.

"You are very young," she said. "But somehow I feel that you are not enjoying the ecstatic happiness that is supposed to be found in an early marriage with the man you love. It was a love match, was it not?"

"My husband," said Deborra hesitantly, "is the man of my choice."

The lady Antonia seemed to find food for reflection in this reply. "Forgive what may seem rude curiosity on my part," she said. "But I am sure you need the advice of someone who is older and more experienced than you. Is it not so?"

Deborra decided to confide in this new acquaintance. "Yes, it is so," she replied.

The dark eyes of the matron studied her with the interest a scientist might display in some new specimen. "Can it be that this young husband of yours has—shall we say—other interests?"

Deborra, embarrassed by the presence of the maids, made no reply. The matron took instant note of her hesitation and realized the reason for it. "Never mind my girls," she said. "I always have them about me. They amuse and stimulate me. I am lost without them."

"But—but anything I might want to say would be for your ears only."

"They never repeat what they hear or tell what they see. I have trained my little pets to be absolutely silent and discreet. If you wish me to be helpful, you will have to conform to my ways. This may seem strange to you, but I promise that you can talk with perfect freedom in front of them." She sat up on her couch in order to reach out a hand to pat her visitor reassuringly on the arm. "My dear child, there is nothing easier in the world than to solve your difficulties with a husband. Is that not so, my girls?"

The handmaidens seemed unanimously convinced that the need to worry over the behavior of husbands was slight.

"If it happened to be a matter involving a suitor or—shall we say?—a lover," went on Antonia, "you might expect to find it difficult. Suitors are always jealous, moody, ready to take offense. A lover is always a source of trouble and grief to a married woman. Take my testimony for what you like; a lover is never worth the pain and embarrassment he is certain to cause you. But a husband! My dear child, husbands were made to be twisted around fingers. You live in such intimacy with them. You can resort to tears; you can sulk, scream, threaten, refuse his wishes. When a man becomes a husband, he surrenders all his advantages."

"I thought it was the other way round," said Deborra timidly.

"Only when a wife does not appreciate *her* advantages," declared the matron. "Husbands are lordly creatures. But it is only on the surface."

It was clear that the maidservants were all very fond of her. They followed every word she said and laughed delightedly over what she did. They were kept busy saying, "Yes, mistress," but there seemed to be sincerity in their affirmatives.

"I think perhaps you have been raised in a household of men," said Antonia, studying Deborra with an eye that was as shrewd as it was bright. "You have not seen much of other women. That is bad. Your enemies through life will be other women, and so you should understand them and know what to expect."

When Deborra looked both puzzled and startled, the matron proceeded to expound the point further. "It will always be women who stand in your way and contend for the things you want," she declared. "They will try to outdo you in looks. They will try to win the attention of men from you. When your sons become men, they will take them away from you; and sometimes they will treat them badly and return them to you in shabby condition. Now let us consider this woman who is making you unhappy. I have no idea who she is or what her station in life may be——"

"She was once a slave."

"It is a curious thing, dear child, that a woman slave has a particular appeal for men. She can be beaten and put in chains, and her virtue is like a tag that he can tear from her at his own sweet will. It is clear this ex-slave knows how to attract men. More, perhaps, than you do."

Deborra nodded her head unhappily. "I do not think I know anything about it at all."

"You had, of course, many suitors."

"No. I did not know any young men. My grandfather lived a most secluded life and he wanted me with him all the time."

"No suitors! This is worse than I suspected. My child, my child! We must indeed take you in hand. Let us see what my little girls can show you."

Two of the little girls, whose names were Saida and Zenobia, proceeded to demonstrate how feminine charms could best be displayed, by a sinuous way of walking, by the use of a fan, by a careless dropping of the *palla* to reveal a generous portion of the neck and shoulder, by allowing glimpses of the foot beneath the skirt.

Antonia asked Deborra, "Have you employed such simple little artifices as these?" and the latter answered that she had not. The large, arched eyes of the matron studied her figure intently. "You are exactly right for it," she said. "You are small and nicely put together. Your shoulders, I can see from here, are quite lovely. Now let's have a look at your foot. My dear, my dear! Why have you so neglected your opportunities? Your foot is a shade on the chubby side, but it is white and pretty. So few women have nice feet, and it is a shame not to make use of ones as lovely as yours. Do you believe in cosmetics?"

The young wife, who was feeling hopelessly old-fashioned and on the defensive, was glad to be able to say that she used cosmetics. When she had enumerated the various aids to beauty she employed, however, Antonia gave her head a despairing shake.

"It is clear," she said, "that the little boxes that were brought you from the East were filled with articles selected by men. They know nothing of such things. Women haven't used such simple aids since the Queen of Sheba visited Solomon. And how many centuries ago was that? Zenobia, bring *my* box."

It proved to be a very large box, made of an Eastern wood that filled the room with an aromatic odor. From inside it the matron, who clearly owed some of her beauty to the use of its contents, produced a great variety of jade and silver bottles. She drew them out one at a time and explained their use as she did so. Deborra listened with mounting awe as salve and lotion and chemical mixture of one kind and another were brought out and commented upon. "Never worry about your complexion," said Antonia. "It is good enough, as it happens. Most women do worry and it is very silly. A complexion can be put on and off at will. I change mine to suit each robe." Observing a look of amazement on Deborra's face, she added, "And so will you, my child, when your education has been completed."

The box contained also a half dozen or more perfume sprinklers, all of them tall bottles with slender necks about five inches high. Deborra, invited to investigate them, was amazed at their strangeness and piquancy.

One was reserved for the last, a bottle taller than the others. Antonia did not touch it. She gave it instead an almost timid look and said, "It is called Circe's Secret, and there is a story about it."

"Please, mistress, tell us," clamored the young maidservants in chorus.

Still regarding the tall bottle askance, the mistress of the house proceeded to tell the story. "Do you know about Circe's Palace and how sailors were lured ashore to visit it? Well, it seems that a sailor went there once who was more interested in the fine wines Circe provided than in Circe herself. Because of this, the foolish fellow was able to get away from the palace without being turned into a wild beast or a snake or a mythical bird. Thinking this bottle contained wine, he took it with him and went rolling down the road to the harbor. He succeeded in getting off the island and was picked up by a passing ship. When he found the bottle contained perfume instead of wine, he fell into a savage mood and threw it into the scuppers. The contents would have been lost if the captain had not been curious about the shape of the bottle and picked it up. That is how it happens to be in existence." She gave the bottle a close look and then shuddered. "There is a penalty that goes with it. For every drop you use, a month is taken off your life. I stopped using it long ago."

The maids uttered many exclamations (although they had heard the story many times, without a doubt) and refused to look at the bottle that could cause so much evil. Deborra was bold enough to express her skepticism. "It is contrary to the holy teachings," she said, "to believe in stories of magic."

"I do," declared Antonia. "One *must* believe. I saw Simon the Magician once and I could not sleep for two nights because of the strange things he did."

Deborra asked quickly, "When did you see him perform?"

"More than a year ago. I thought him fearsome but very fascinating."

"Did he have a woman with him then?"

"No, not then. I have heard much about her since. It was here in Antioch that he found her. She had been a slave in the house of——" She stopped abruptly and looked at Deborra with redoubled interest. "So, that is it." She reached out a cautious finger and touched the perfume bottle. "My child, I give it to you. I can see you may find yourself in need of an aid as strong as this. I must tell you candidly that I shall be glad to see the last of it."

"Is this the very bottle that the sailor took with him?"

The matron nodded. "My husband paid a high price for it on the assumption that it *was* the bottle. He is never deceived about anything he buys."

Deborra looked at the sprinkler with doubtful eyes. She was certain it would be wicked to make use of it, even to accept it as a gift. Did she want to fall into step with evil? What would happen if she put a drop of this potent mixture on her robe?

Abruptly she reached out and lifted the bottle in her hands. "Thank you," she said. "I shall take it."

Antonia gave her an approving tap on the shoulder. "I see you have a will of your own. And you have daring. You need not have any fear, dear child. You will accomplish your desire.

"And now," she went on, "we shall have some refreshments all by ourselves. My husband and his friend shall have theirs downstairs. I think we must have some of that delicious mixture that I am told I should not eat; the one with the dates and peaches and ground almonds, and that wonderful batter. And a nice sweet wine. It will improve your chances to win husbands, my girls, if you get a little more flesh on your bones."

3

Sarah labored with loving care over the appearance of her mistress, dressing her hair in tight curls by the use of an iron resembling a reed. This had the effect of making Deborra seem even younger and rather gay and happy. Having accomplished this, however, the maidservant crushed down on her head a Grecian *sakkos,* a covering that resembled a cap. It was effective enough in itself, being of blue silk, but it hid all the carefully contrived curls save a narrow fringe above the forehead. The *palla* in which she had robed her mistress had been selected on the advice of the lady Antonia. It was of the same shade of blue, carefully draped about the neck and with divided sleeves that came to the elbow only and were held together at intervals by twisted ribbon of a deeper shade of blue. The *stola,* as the upper garment was called, fell almost to the ground and had a wide band around the bottom embroidered with gold silk.

When the robe had finally been adjusted and the last brush of an anxious hand had been given the dusky curls, Sarah held up before her mistress a bronze mirror. Her own face was wreathed with smiling pride in her handiwork.

Deborra, studying her face with concentrated care, said to herself: "He will like me now. Surely, surely he will like me now!" To make this desired result more certain, she practiced the casual shrug of shoulder and arm that caused the *palla* to drop from one shoulder. The expanse of flesh thus placed on display was white and delicately rounded.

"Do not fear to show your feet," counseled the maid. She gave her head a scornful toss. "They must think themselves great beauties, flouncing and prancing around. You have a better foot than any of *them*. They all have such thick toes."

"The master is below," announced one of the other servants, appearing in the doorway.

Deborra remained perfectly still for a moment. Basil had arrived, to share with her the new home that was theirs by virtue of the agreement made with the banker. Her heart fluttered and then seemed to cease beating. What would he think of these beautiful new clothes? What would he think of her?

What attitude was she to take? Should she show herself cool and detached? Should she be friendly and indifferent? Should she make use of the feminine wiles she had been practicing so carefully?

"You are ready, mistress," said Sarah after a final glance of inspection.

When the maid had left the room Deborra walked to the tripod table that held her toilet articles. The house had provided many discoveries during the relatively few hours she had occupied it and none that pleased her more than the luxury of her bedroom. The tripod was made of silver and stood on beautifully carved supports. On its burnished top was a silver laver, a brush with a carved back, and a dainty drinking goblet.

The chair in front of the table was of the *cathedra* variety, with a circular back. It was piled high with cushions, into which she had nestled comfortably while Sarah labored over her hair. The sprinkler that Antonia had given her stood on the tripod, and she reached for it with an uncertain hand. She would use it sparingly, she decided, no more than a single drop; not because she thought of the month of time it might cut from her life but because of a sudden sense of reluctance and shame.

She paused with the sprinkler held in one hand above her shoulder. Did she want to win him by such methods? Could she descend to appealing to his senses in this way?

She lowered the hand that held the sprinkler. The *palla* had slipped again, revealing generously the white of her throat and shoulder. She pulled it back into place instinctively with her other hand. At the same time she drew her heels together so that no part of her foot would show beneath the rich hem.

"I cannot!" she said to herself. "I cannot attract him in such tawdry ways. I must not throw myself at his head like a woman of the wall. I must leave it to him. If his attitude does not change, I must do nothing about it. Not even though it means that I shall be lonely and unhappy for the rest of my life."

Having reached her decision, she carried the sprinkler to the laver and emptied out the contents. An exotic odor filled the air.

"I leave it to Antonia and her maids to captivate men by such means," she said aloud, and turned slowly to walk downstairs.

She was cool and self-possessed when she reached the entrance hall. Her robe remained steadfastly in place about her throat. Not so much as the tip of a toe had she displayed in coming down the stairs. Basil was studying the designs on the glazed brick walls with so much interest that he did not become aware immediately of her presence.

All the careful thought she had given to the words she would use went for nothing when she saw him.

"How thin you are!" she cried. "Basil, Basil, how you must have suffered!"

His first impression of her was one of surprise. He said to himself: "She has changed. She looks older; her eyes show a difference. And she has become quite lovely." A feeling of humility took possession of him. It was hard to believe that one who had so much to offer was his wife.

"It seems," he explained, speaking with some reluctance, for he felt that his share in the exploit did him small credit, "that I lacked the strength for such an adventure. If there had been any more distance to go, Chimham would have been compelled to ride on without me. I was a drag from the beginning, I am afraid. But I am recovering now. I am feeling so much better that my fingers itch to be at work. That, it is now clear, is where I belong; in a workshop with tools in my hands, and not out adventuring." Then he looked more closely at her and smiled. "You have come through the experience much better than I. It seems actually to have done you good."

Deborra's cheeks colored at his praise. "I am glad you think so." She hurried then to safer ground. "Have you heard that the settlement was made yesterday? At least we agreed on some of the details. It cannot be final until you have signed. Jabez wants you to see him today." Her anxiety returned as she studied the contours of his face, which had sharpened noticeably. "Will you feel able to see him?"

"I am strong enough for that." Curiosity prompted him then to the asking of a question. "I have been looking about and studying the decorations. What house is this?"

"It is yours."

"Mine? I don't understand."

"My father," explained Deborra with a feeling of reluctance to open a subject so painful to her, "has cast me off. He has disowned me for all time. I have no desire to return to Jerusalem and so, if you feel as I do, we could make our home here in Antioch. The terms of the agreement include ownership of this house."

"But you said it was mine. I did not realize that the agreement between us went as far as that." Basil was puzzled and his pride had taken alarm. "Could we not have things arranged on some more—more sensible basis?"

Deborra shook her head. "It is the law. Nothing can be done to change it. You are the head of the household, and everything that was mine is now yours." Then suddenly she began to laugh. "How strange we must look! We are standing here and talking like a pair of strangers, and yet we are man and wife. I am sure we are a great disappointment to everyone. I can feel the eyes of P'ing-li on me even now. He must be watching us from somewhere beyond the wall. Do you know, he has come to me three times in the last two days and asked questions about us."

"I was surprised to find his tents outside the walls," said Basil. "Is he proving difficult with his curiosity?"

Deborra shook her head with a smile. "Oh no, no. We are very good friends, the prince and I."

Her heart was getting out of control. She said to herself: "Why do I bother about my pride? Why do I not suggest that the time has come to—to break the agreement? It may be that he is waiting for me to speak. Why not use the old prince as my excuse? I could say that the time has come to—to pretend. Then I could walk out into the garden with him and let him put his arm around me. I could rest my head on his shoulder. I could smile up into his eyes as a bride should. Then the kind old man, who would be watching us, would be satisfied." Her thoughts went on tumultuously from that point. "It is not of the prince I am thinking. It is of us, my husband. I am thinking that perhaps then you would find it pleasant to be with me, that you could forget everything else."

But her pride, which had been bludgeoned into the taking of so many difficult steps, was not prepared yet for this. She had no way of knowing that Basil was thinking: "Can I tell her how much my feelings have changed? No, my tongue is chained." She hesitated, and that was fatal; her willingness to surrender took wings and could not be summoned back.

She recovered her self-possession slowly. "But we must do something to keep up appearances," she said. "Here we are, with a large and new establishment. It seems to be filled with people. I do not know yet why they are all here. The first step, don't you think, would be for us to go together on a tour of inspection?"

"Yes," responded Basil. "I have been looking at the walls. The art is strange and rather barbaric, but it has great power. I am anxious to see the rest of the house."

They made their way accordingly to the inside door, which opened on to the first of the two inner courtyards. Here stood a tall figure carved out of dark stone. It had huge limbs and a terrifying face.

"What is this?" she asked. "I saw it yesterday when we arrived. I could hardly sleep last night for thinking of it."

"It is Zeus Herkeios," answered Basil, studying the figure that towered high above him. "He is the protector of households."

Deborra looked up at the stone face of the god and shuddered. "I think we need someone to protect us from him," she said. "Is he as cruel as he looks?"

"He is not supposed to be cruel at all. But now that you raise the point, I agree that he has a villainous look about him."

"Is he one of the gods of the Grecian people?"

"He is the first of them, the great god. But I think we should have him removed as soon as possible. Quite apart from the effect he has on you, I consider the statue a very poor one."

Deborra led the way then across the first court and into an *aula* leading off to the right. Through this narrow and rather dark hall they reached a room of generous dimensions that was light and cheerful and had one drawback only, another statue. This time the figure was neither large nor terrifying, and it represented a goddess.

"It is Hestia," said Basil. He pointed to a marble hearth in front of the figure where, if they could judge from its blackened condition, a continuous fire had once been kept burning. "She is the goddess of fire and of the kitchen and hearth. A rather gentle and humble lady. There is nothing to be feared from her, but, still, she is as pagan as Zeus. If we are to be consistent, we must condemn poor Hestia to the same fate."

All sense of restraint and awkwardness had left Deborra's manner. She walked lightly about the room, inspecting everything and finding much to interest and amuse her. She called several times, "See, Basil!" or "Come, tell me what this is for." Finally she asked, "What was the function of this very curious room?"

"It was used for religious observances having to do with family life—

births, marriages, christenings. And also it was a place of sanctuary. Slaves who were to be punished could come here and ask aid of Hestia. Then they could not be whipped until their guilt had been proven. A husband could come here to avoid a nagging wife, and a wife to escape a cruel husband. It has always been a most useful room in a Greek household." Then he added: "Hestia is the least regarded, poor lady, of all the sacred tribe on Parnassus. She is generally depicted as dull, self-effacing, and lumpish of figure. Even in view of that, the sculptor in this case did her something less than justice. Her charms do not overwhelm you, do they?"

"Such as they are, they are not well enough concealed," declared Deborra. "Please, get rid of her too. But I think, Basil, that we should retain the character of the room. We could call it the Room of Kindness."

"I think it a very happy suggestion."

Deborra had regained her good spirits completely now. "Which of us," she asked, "will find it necessary most often to come here? You, escaping from a nagging wife, or I, from a hectoring husband?"

They continued their tour then and came in due course to the high room before which stood one of the two young men. The door was open, and through it they could see the other guard, sitting cross-legged on the floor beside the chest. He had cast off his outer robe and a dagger could be seen at his belt.

"They are to remain on watch day and night," commented Deborra.

"They are not like the Giants of Slador," commented Basil in an equally low tone. "But there is a fine air of resolution about them."

Deborah turned toward the guard on the door. "Elidad."

"Yes, gentle lady," responded the guard, stepping forward.

"I think my husband would be interested in what happened last evening. When Harhas, the presbyter of the church in Antioch, came to discuss the situation."

Elidad flushed bitterly. "He came to raise the point as to whether we should defend the Cup if an attempt were made to seize it. He said it was wicked to shed blood and that if Irijah and I should kill a man, even in so good a cause, we would be condemned forever to the outer darkness."

"Would you mind repeating what you said in answer to Harhas?"

Elidad looked at them with the hesitation of a man of few words. "I said to Harhas that I could not stand by and see this precious Cup, which the lips of Jesus touched and which has been confided to our care, taken from us by those who do not believe in Him. I said I was prepared to spend eternity in the outer darkness without repining if I had to be sent there for fighting against those who would steal it from us."

"And what did Irijah say?"

The second guard, who had continued to sit beside the chest, sprang to his feet. "I will answer that myself!" he cried.

Coming to the doorway, he leaned against the stone frame and twirled the dagger in his hand.

"Yes, Irijah," said Deborra. "It is your own report we would like to hear."

The second guard's eyes began to burn. "I am a man of peace!" he cried. He raised a finger and pointed to his right cheek, which had a shallow scar running from the corner of his eye to the hinge of his jaw. "Observe. It was the knife of a Zealot that did this. I said to myself, 'And unto him that smiteth thee on the one cheek offer also the other.' They were the words that Jesus had spoken, the command He had laid on us. I obeyed that command. I turned the other cheek." He swung his head around and revealed a somewhat similar scar on the left side of his face. "You see now that I am, as I have said, a man of peace.

"But"—and his eyes began to burn even more brightly—"I remember what Moses, our inspired leader, said. *'I will make mine arrows drunk with blood.'* It was not the will of the Lord that we who believe in Him should be cowards. There comes a time when evil men, who have smitten you on both cheeks, will demand of you your soul. They will take liberty away from you and put shackles on you so that you may no longer worship the Lord in your own way nor tell other men of His teachings; and when that time comes, we must fight! What we may submit to as individuals we must not suffer as members of the church of the Lord Jehovah and of His son Jesus. If any men of ill intent come here to take away the sacred Cup, we must shed their blood and ease their souls from their bodies. And we must fight until not a breath of life is left in either of us!

"And that," he concluded, "was what we told Harhas, the presbyter of the church."

Deborra and Basil walked away in a different mood from the lightness of spirit with which they had concluded their survey of the house. The talk with the two earnest guards had taken their minds back to the Cup and the great responsibilities they shared. "I have been shown," Basil was thinking, "what true faith should be, the kind of faith I lack, even though

I have come to believe in Jesus as a prophet and a divine teacher. Someday, perhaps, I shall feel as they do."

"My grandfather, who was wise in all things," said Deborra, "used to say that the future of Christianity would not rest with the old men. He said they were hairsplitters and quiddlers. The cause, he was sure, would be won by the young men who were ready to fight and die for their faith."

4

The new house was like a conjurer's bag because it had many surprises to offer, and the most surprising of all was Deborra's bed. In the first place, it was quite enormous, being large enough to accommodate several people of her size. It stood high off the floor and had to be climbed into with some care. It was embellished with ivory decorations and had sheets that were elaborately embroidered. Most important of all, it was made of citrus wood, which came from Africa and was so much valued that wealthy men in Rome paid huge prices for a single piece. It was told of Petronius, a courtier whose opinion was much valued by Nero, that he had sold fifty slaves in order to purchase a plank of the best citrus wood and that, moreover, he was in the habit of pointing it out to guests and running an affectionate hand over its beautifully grained surface. He was reported to have said that it was well worth the price he had paid. All in all, therefore, Deborra's bed was a very grand one indeed.

She sat on one side of it while Sarah made her ready for the night. First of all, the maidservant released her hair and allowed it to fall in unrestrained abundance over her shoulders, leaving no more than a few curls on the forehead and a quite small one in front of each ear.

"I think, mistress," said Sarah, her fingers busy at undoing the loops of bound silk that fastened the tunic in the back, "that this is a house made for happiness and peace. I hope the mistress's husband will be happy here too."

"We must see that he is comfortable," said Deborra, keeping her tone entirely matter-of-fact. "His windows must be kept open so the cool breezes from the sea will reach him. We must learn about his likes in food and his favorite wines." She nodded her head and smiled. "He is still much of a stranger to all of us, Sarah."

When the serving-maid had retired, the young bride settled herself in bed. It was infinitely soft, for the mattress was stuffed with sheep's wool, and she sighed with pleasure. Then she reached out an arm and extinguished the light. This did not leave the room in darkness, for the moon was well up over the horizon. It was flooding the groves with a silvery glow, as though curious to discover what might be happening in those mysterious thickets, and it still had enough curiosity left over to reach into every corner of the airy bedchamber.

This invasion of her privacy was not the reason that she failed to get to sleep. She raised herself on one elbow. "Tonight," she thought, "he may come and say to me the things I must hear from him. Surely he will come tonight!"

It was evident that Basil had not yet sought the comfort of his couch. His footsteps could be heard at intervals in the adjoining room and occasionally the scraping of a chair. "Can it be," she wondered, "that he has gone back to his work?" For the first time she was prepared to believe that there were things as important as the completion of the Chalice.

An hour passed. An occasional sound reached her from the other room to let her know that he was still awake. Her hopes dwindled slowly, but by the end of the hour she had been convinced that he had no intention of paying her a visit. A lump came into her throat.

"At the least," she thought, "he might have come to the door to bid me good night."

It occurred to her then that he might as readily have expected this of her. She had laid down the conditions of their marriage. If they were to be relaxed, should she not be the one to take the first step? She rose and slipped into a wrap of green velvety material that Sarah had left on a chair near the bed. It had a scarf at the neck that could be wound around the throat once and then tied in front. Her fingers were unsteady as they performed this task.

The opening of the door between the two rooms revealed Basil at a worktable under one of the windows. His head was bent and he had tools in each hand, a hammer and a chisel. Two oil lamps had been lighted and placed on each side of him.

She stood silently in the doorway, one hand nervously grasping the knob. "I am beginning to believe," she said to herself, "that he thinks of nothing but his work."

Conscious finally that he was being watched, Basil dropped the chisel on the table and turned to look over his shoulder.

"I have come," said Deborra, "to wish you good night. And to warn you that you should not be working so late."

Basil shifted his position, and the light from one of the lamps made it possible for her to see that his face was deeply lined with fatigue.

"Have I worked long?" he asked. "It seemed to me a few moments only. There is so much to be done!"

She walked slowly into the room, the hem of the green garment sweeping the floor, one hand holding the scarf in place at her neck.

"I hoped——" she began. Then she became aware that he had not fully withdrawn his attention from his work, that he was only partly conscious of what she was saying. She checked the words of guarded invitation that had been on the tip of her tongue. Instead she asked, "Would it disturb you if I sat here for a while and watched you?"

He turned completely around then and ran a hand across his eyes. "No," he answered. "But I am sure you will find it dull. You see, I have made a clay replica of the Cup and I am fitting the framework around it. It is slow work and not at all interesting to watch."

"I cannot get to sleep." She drew up a chair and perched herself on top of it, with her knees drawn up under her chin, her hands clasping her bare ankles. "I like to know everything you do about the Chalice. Please do not shut me out. Can you talk about it while you work?" She studied the frame that already covered the replica of the Cup. "You have done a great deal to it since I saw it last."

"Yes, a great deal. I have introduced symbols into the pattern—doves and lambs and helix shells. Right now I am soldering it together." He turned to her and smiled. "Does your interest extend that far? If I talk about it, your eyelids will become as heavy as the lead I am using and you will fall asleep in your chair. You see, I consider it necessary to use the very finest solder. I make it with one ounce of pure silver, two ounces of purified copper, and three ounces of lead. Then I pour in a little finely ground sulphur—— Are you still listening?"

"Yes, I am still listening. And I understand what you are saying." To herself she added: "Oh, Basil, Basil, do you not see that every word you toss me so carelessly thrills me to the core of my being? Do you not understand that everything you do, even to the mixing of solder, excites me? But of course you do not see these things because you do not know how much I love you; and because you, my husband, do not love me."

Basil went on with his explanations: "The figures are going to be so very small that I must surround them with devices to assist in identifying them. Around the figure of Jesus I will show the Holy Ghost in the form of a dove. Above Him will be the Star of the Nativity."

He was speaking in a reflective tone and, after the first few minutes, he kept his eyes exclusively on his work. Once he broke out into a bitter tirade at himself because his fingers had fallen into error. This made her certain that he had forgotten she was there.

"Will he never see how much I love him?" she asked herself. "Must I go on like this, keeping all my thoughts to myself, making no effort to win him to me? Oh, Basil, Basil, look at me once again as you did that day when I threw the stone at the Romans!"

Inevitably the need for sleep overtook her. Her eyelids became heavy and several times she caught herself nodding. She sighed then and lowered her feet to the floor, the nicely shaped white feet she had refused to use as a means of winning his interest. It did not occur to her, because the action had been so natural, that he could have seen her whole foot and even more had he been noticing.

"It is very late," she said. "You should stop now. You must be very tired."

His eyes were still preoccupied when he turned to look at her. "I must finish what I am doing while the solder remains fluid." He studied the frame that was now solidly clamped around the clay model. "There is still a full hour's work. You had better not stay up any longer, Deborra. Your voice tells me that you are tired."

"Solder!" she said. "We seem to have talked more about solder than anything else. It is, of course, a subject of deep interest."

She stood up. Her feet vanished from sight as the folds of the green wrap fell into place. The scarf was gathered so closely about her that very little of her throat was visible. This did not matter because he had already turned to his work. Her eyes, fixed on the back of his head, were rebellious. "The smallest detail of what he is doing is more important to him than I am," she thought.

She asked as she turned toward the door, "Can I get you some food or a cup of wine?"

He shook his head. He was too absorbed to take any interest in food or wine, let alone to understand the emotional strain that showed in her voice.

"There is nothing I want," he said.

Deborra walked slowly to her room. "He looked at me but he did not see me. He has no interest in me at all. If I asked him to accept my love, he would say the same thing, 'There is nothing I want.'"

"Good night, Basil," she said at the door.

There was a barely perceptible pause before he answered. "Good night, Deborra."

She closed the door softly behind her and climbed into the stately bed of scented citrus wood. She began to sob passionately. "There is nothing more I can do," she said to herself in the darkness.

CHAPTER XXII

I

For two weeks Basil worked with unabated concentration. The sense of urgency that had filled him during the ride from Jerusalem had not entirely subsided and, in addition, he was thinking constantly of the need to reach Rome. He sat at his worktable all through the day and sometimes far into the night. At meals he had little to say, being absorbed in his thoughts. His appetite was small and he had to be urged to partake of the fine dishes spread before him.

Only once in the two weeks did he venture from the house, and that was to pay a visit to his former home on the Colonnade in the hope of seeing his mother. He was refused admittance.

Understanding the fever that possessed him, Deborra made few efforts to break through the wall of his silence. Sometimes she sat beside him and watched his hands at work, not disturbing him with talk. Many times a day she would pause in the doorway of his room, to watch for a few moments and then pass on with an air of unhappiness.

Once, when she was playing in the second court with her newly acquired dog, she looked up and saw to her surprise that he had left his bench and was watching from the upper balustrade. She walked over and raised her head.

"Why am I so honored?" she asked.

"I am in great trouble," he said with a sigh of weariness. "It is hard to transfer a likeness when you must work in such minute proportions. I wish the Chalice could be twice the size. The head of Luke gave me great difficulty, perhaps because I was anxious to do him well. And now Paul is being stubborn. He seems almost to take a pleasure in eluding me."

His eyes moved to the dog, which had squatted down beside his mistress. "That is an odd-looking fellow. He has the clumsiest feet I have ever seen."

"What you need is rest," said Deborra. "Forget about your difficulties with Luke and the stubbornness of Paul. Come down here with me. We will sit in the shade and talk. I have so much to tell you." She added after a moment's pause, "He is a very fine dog."

"I cannot spare the time yet." Basil lifted his hands from the stone railing and disappeared inside.

The frame for the Chalice began finally to reach the stage of completion. There were still empty spaces, and these would be filled in due course with the heads of Jesus, John, and Peter. Basil looked at his work and knew that it was good, that the Chalice when finished would be a thing of great beauty. This gave him no sense of satisfaction and no happiness, because the feeling of urgency refused him any peace.

One morning he went out for a stroll and found himself by accident among the tents of P'ing-li. The latter was seated in a folding chair and was gazing straight into the east with a suggestion of longing on his wrinkled face and in the stoop of his back. He looked up when he heard Basil's step.

"This is happy meeting, honorable young artist," he said. "I have questions which I make bold to ask. Why must the feet of connubial bliss travel with leaden soles? Why do not these difficulties become settled?" He paused and then chirped an order to a servant who hovered in the background. The latter vanished, to return later with a satin-wrapped bundle, which he placed in his master's lap. "These are gifts. They are to be left with my good friend, Luke the Healer, and presented to the pretty bride and her honorable young husband as soon as the imminence of an heir is announced. Pretty bride knows of this but has not seen gifts, which are to be kept a secret. It is the earnest hope of humble giver that they will please both parents of forthcoming child."

"We are unworthy of such very great kindness," said Basil.

The old man gave his head a brisk shake. "But keep the condition firmly in mind, honorable young husband. Is it an incentive to a more romantic attitude that at your age this now ancient sojourner had three wives and four male children?"

"The comparison is not entirely fair, Illustrious Prince," Basil pointed out. "In the Christian following one wife is deemed sufficient."

"A wise rule in many respects. It does not seem likely that any of my wives would have made me sufficiently happy and content, but it must be borne in mind that our standards are different. No, none of the eight would have sufficed." The eyes of P'ing-li took on a reminiscent gleam. "It is my belief, honorable young friend, that I might have found among my concubines some capable of keeping me happy."

There was something incongruous about talk of this kind falling from the lips of such a tiny rack of skin and bones, and Basil found it hard to keep a sober countenance when he asked, "Did Illustrious Prince have many concubines?"

The old man broke into a pleased cackle. "A very great many. A long time would be needed to recall and count them all." His mood became severe and he scrutinized his visitor's face with shrewd attention. "It is my humble wish that honorable young artist will prove quick to accept a hint."

The next morning Basil's feet took him in that direction again and he found the prince sitting in the same location and with the same absorbed interest in the eastern horizon. The old man gave his head a nod of dignified pride. "The total, honorable young artist," he stated, "was fifty-nine."

Basil looked puzzled at first, having forgotten the point on which their conversation had reached its conclusion the previous day. Then his memory returned and he smiled. "Fifty-nine concubines?" he asked. "It seems a goodly number."

P'ing-li nodded with a reminiscent relish. "I counted them last night before I fell asleep. It took several hours, but I enjoyed it very much. Some of them were lovely. They came from all parts of my country; almond-eyed beauties from the south, plump little chicks from the north, girls brought all the way from Tartary——" He broke off and then resumed with many enthusiastic nods. "Those who came from Tartary were always favorites."

He checked his rhapsodies at this point and fell into a more reflective mood. "Yes, honorable young artist, I had much happiness with all my bustling little hen pheasants. But now, when I look at pretty wife of honorable friend, I think perhaps it better to have one wife only and no concubines at all. It is one of many lessons I have learned." His eyes acquired a calculating light. "Honorable artist and pretty wife will find the presents much to their taste."

2

When visitors began to come to the house, Deborra stood between them and the hard-pressed artist. She attended to them with a coolness and dispatch which demonstrated how very much she took after her grandfather.

The first of the visitors arrived with a great deal of noise and con-fusion. Half a dozen or more chariots clattered up the steep incline from the city road, a trumpeter in the first one blowing furiously for the way to be cleared. A swarm of boys followed them, shouting with excitement.

The chariots halted along the wall. Linus stepped down from one of them, throwing an order over his shoulder that the juvenile element should be driven off with whips. He swung open the front door without waiting to announce himself. A reluctant Quintus Annius, with docu-ments under his arm, followed a few steps behind.

If the purpose of the usurper had been to impress the household, he had achieved a complete success, for the crunch of wheels and the stamp-ing of the horses had brought the face of a domestic to every window.

"I desire speech with the head of the house," said Linus to the servant who met him inside the front door.

It was Deborra, however, who came to receive him in the first court-yard. It was an affront to meet him there, for guests of importance were taken to the second court, which was reserved for the use of the family.

Linus recognized this, and the scowl on his brow grew deeper. He was looking hot and dusty, to begin with. His neck was as thick and red as a butcher's, and the long leggings of leather that covered his shins could not conceal the hairiness and crooked contour of his limbs. He stared at her with every evidence of ill will.

"I came to see Basil, once a slave in my household," he said.

"I am his wife."

"I already know that. But I have nothing to say to you."

"My husband is busy. He cannot see you today. If you prefer me to speak with full candor, I must tell you that I hope he will never see you. I will deliver to him any message you may care to leave."

"I am a direct man. I do not like dealing with go-betweens, even when they are wives." Linus was becoming angry. "I came to give a warning to this man whose wife you have become."

Deborra remained perfectly cool and self-possessed. "Your likes in the matter do not count. Tell me about this warning and I will convey it to my husband. May I add that we have been expecting a visit from you, with no feeling of pleasure but also with no sense of apprehension?"

"Some days ago," declared Linus, his small eyes sultry with resentment, "he called at my house. He was refused admittance. I want him to understand once and for all that he must never try this again. A second attempt will bring a violent reprisal."

"He went to see his mother. He is very fond of her, and it had come to his ears that she was not in good health."

Linus snorted loudly. "She is no kin of his. The courts so decided."

"No matter what a corrupt and well-paid magistrate may have decided," said Deborra, "my husband considers her his mother. It is his intention to make another call." She looked at him with a steadiness that caused him to drop his eyes. "You will not close your doors on him a second time."

"I have plenty to say to him," declared Linus. "Since you insist on it, I will tell you. He has been at his tricks again. Worming his way into the household of a rich man and insinuating himself into the good graces of the women. He did it here with my brother's wife, persuading her to support him in his claim to being an adopted son."

"That is a lie."

The usurper went on with increased truculence: "He failed here. So he went to Jerusalem and had better success. He seems to have talked himself into your affections. I saw your father before he returned to Jerusalem, and he told me the whole story. This ex-slave seems to have been clever and completely unscrupulous. It will avail him nothing in the end. Your father will take the matter into the courts when he gets back. You lacked his consent, and that will cost you dear. This most persistent of conspirators——"

"Have you said what you came to say?"

"Not all. I hear the pair of you are planning to make your home here. I will not tolerate it. His presence would be an affront. I am giving warning that you must leave."

"We will stay here in spite of you."

Linus waved a hand in the direction of Quintus Annius, who had remained some distance in the rear. "Do you see those documents he holds? They are notes of the story your father told me. How this man played on the senility of your grandfather and then took advantage of you, a girl of tender years. It is not a pretty story at all. I shall know how to use it." He scowled directly at Deborra for the first time. "You will do well to heed my warning. I have power in Antioch. Great power, if I care to make use of it. If you stay, you and your ex-slave, you will receive a second proof of the power I hold."

"You seem to have delivered your message, so I will see that the servants show you to the door."

Linus, his face an angry red, turned on his heel. "I shall lose no time," he threatened. "You and your upstart husband shall feel the full weight of the influence I can bring against you."

"Permit me to correct you. You *had* power and influence in Antioch. You no longer have. At some time in the near future my husband will pay another visit to the house on the Colonnade; *his* house, if you please. And when he does, the power will be in his hands."

The usurper turned and left the courtyard without another word. The chariots departed with less ostentation than they had displayed on arriving.

Deborra had kept up a bold front, but secretly her confidence had been somewhat shaken. She gave her head a shake. "I do not care about the property. But can Father succeed in having our marriage annulled? That is the only thing that counts."

3

More visitors put in an appearance on the following day, first a man with thin shoulders and a stooped back and a woman who gazed about her with truculence and who tossed her head angrily when the servant at the door demanded to know who they were. It was the woman who answered.

"Never mind who we are," she said, her hands on her hips. "We will give our names to the magistrate if it is necessary. We have come to claim a runaway slave."

"There is none such here," said the servant.

The woman brushed past him and stalked into the first court. She threw back her head and began to screech. "Come down, you Basil! Come down, slave! We are your owners and we have come to claim you!"

Deborra came hastily into the court when this clamor began. She had been engaged in household duties and was wearing a plain red robe with her hair bound in a light turban known as a *tsaniph*. She looked disturbed, as well she might, having no idea who they were or the reason for their coming.

"What is it?" she demanded. "Why are you here?"

The woman drew herself up with an attempt at dignity, although her eyes were already beginning to glitter furiously.

"You must be the woman he married," she said. "If you are, I feel sorry for you; but I have nothing to say to you. I am here to claim my property." She threw back her head again and allowed her voice to rise to a shrill pitch. "Come down, slave! We have found you out and it will do no good to hide, wherever you are."

The man took it on himself to explain at this point: "I am the owner of a slave who ran away from my house some months ago. We know that he is here."

Deborra turned to look at him. He was very dark and so small that there was something almost comic about his attempt to assert himself. "I begin to understand," she said. "Are you Sosthene of Tarsus?"

"Yes, I am Sosthene." He had intended to say more, for his mouth remained open. His wife intervened, however, giving him an impatient shove with one of her skinny arms.

"Keep out of this," she warned. "They will get the better of you if you do not keep that idle mouth shut. I know them. I know *you*. It was decided between us that I would do all the talking."

"There is no more talking to do," declared Deborra. "My husband's freedom was purchased from you——"

"It is a lie!" cried the woman. "He ran away. Not a single coin did we receive for him. He will be soundly whipped when we get him back."

Deborra, whose face had become white and tense, had to retreat a step to avoid the arms Eulalia was waving about in a kind of frenzy.

"My husband has the documents," she said. "Are you aware that he has been restored to full citizenship? How dare you bring such an absurd charge as this?"

"Lies!" cried Eulalia. "We signed no documents. If you have documents, they are forged. We will go to the court and say so. You had better talk no more about documents."

Deborra disregarded the man, who stood silently and gaped about him, and looked steadily at the woman. She said in low and unhurried tones: "I can see that you are as base as you appear. How fortunate it is that we can settle this matter easily. Luke is here. You will remember that it was

Luke who arranged the terms with you. He will soon make it clear that this is all a wicked pretense on your part. You have been sent here by Linus."

"Lies! Lies and deception! Linus did not send us. I know nothing of this Luke."

Sosthene shuffled his feet uneasily when Luke entered the court, but his wife was prepared for it. She stared at the newcomer and then turned back to Deborra.

"I have never seen this old man before. I will not listen to any lies the two of you have made up."

"You speak of lies." Luke walked to the center of the court where the pair were standing. He looked steadily into the woman's eyes for several moments. His manner reflected a deep sadness. "Of how much evil the human heart is capable! Think, woman, before you persist in these pretenses."

"Look not at me, old man!" cried Eulalia. "I do not know who you are. Never before have I seen you."

Luke's eyes had become deeply reflective. When he spoke again, it was apparent that the voice that sometimes spoke in his mind and told him what to say or do had been prompting him. "You are saying to yourself, 'He came, this soft-spoken but hard old man, in the hours of darkness and no one saw him. This makes it safe to claim we know him not.'"

"Now you are trying to put lies into my mind."

"You are thinking this also, 'We have acted poor and our neighbors will swear we have not the money to buy another slave.'"

The woman's jaw went slack and she stared at him with nothing to say. Sosthene elected at this point to speak. "It is true," he declared, nodding his head, "that we have not been able to buy a new slave to assist me in my work."

"Keep your loose mouth closed!" cried Eulalia. "They will get the better of you. You are as soft as dough."

Deborra interrupted to ask, "Was not the money paid to them by Jabez?"

Eulalia began then to cackle with scorn and triumph. "If we *had* sold him, would we have been simple enough to leave such proof as that?"

"They refused payment through Jabez," affirmed Luke. "I had to go to his house and get them gold. The woman would hear of nothing else."

"It will be our word," asserted Eulalia, "against that of a wandering

Christian and a runaway slave. We are known as honest citizens. We pay our taxes. The best people buy from us. You know what the verdict would be in any court in the land."

There was silence for a moment, and then Luke began to speak, looking directly into the woman's eyes. "I will tell you the thought that fills your mind at this moment. You are thinking, bearer of false witness that you are, that it is a good thing we do not know you bought land after all. It was not the farm of the Three Pear Trees. It was a somewhat smaller one and closer to the city walls. There you have a keeper whose name is Maniteles and who is stiff in one leg and cannot expect much pay. He gets, poor fellow, very little from you. Shall I tell you the exact amount?"

"Lies," said the woman in a tone so low that it was almost humble.

"You bought this land the day after you disposed of Basil and—*you paid the exact amount you received for him.*"

Eulalia was staring at Luke in openmouthed unease. Sosthene was unable to cover up the alarm that had taken possession of him.

Luke's eyes still held Eulalia an unwilling victim. "It is possible sometimes to read what is passing through the mind of another. I may tell you that yours is wide open to me. It has been telling me everything that happened."

"Lies!" she exclaimed; but all of the certainty and most of the venom had gone out of her voice.

"You denied being sent here by Linus. That is false. You saw him last evening. You demanded one hundred dinars for the service he asked of you—to come here with this story—and it was finally agreed you were to receive eighty. Half of that amount was paid you in advance."

"Let us go!" cried Sosthene. He looked pale and abject.

"When the slave girl Agnes was purchased, you told neighbors that you had received a good figure for the man and that now you had sold a dying girl for the price of a healthy one. Your neighbors have little love for you and they have repeated the remark widely."

"Enough!" exclaimed Sosthene. "We will go from here and we will never come back."

He took one of Eulalia's arms and began to drag her from the court. She tried to hold back, casting angry looks over her shoulder but being careful to avoid the eyes of Luke.

When the outer door had clanged behind them, Luke nodded slowly to Deborra. "We will hear nothing more from them. The woman has already made up her mind not to return the forty dinars to Linus. She has gone away hating us but afraid of what more we may learn. She is afraid of her past."

Deborra was looking pale and tired. "I was in a panic!" she acknowledged. "That evil woman! What would we have done if she had been able to establish her claim?"

4

A third visitor arrived within an hour after the departure of the discomfited silversmith and his shrewish wife. Deborra, in the meantime, had finished her household duties and had arrayed herself in cool white. She was sitting in a shaded corner of the second court and strumming idly on her *kinnor* when a tall man with a wicker tray on his head was ushered in by the custodian of the door. If Basil had been there he would have recognized at once the fine brow and widely spaced eyes under the tray and so have identified the visitor as the vendor of sweetmeats who had paused once under the *aliyyah* of the house of Ignatius to deliver a surreptitious message to a customer.

The tall man bowed without disturbing the position of the tray or dislodging its contents, a feat possible only through long practice. "I have messages," he said, "for those who dwell in this house."

"My husband is engaged," said Deborra. "But Luke the Physician is here. Shall I have him join us?"

The man bowed again. When Luke arrived, his eyes heavy with the afternoon sleep from which he had been roused, he recognized the visitor at once.

"It is Hananiah," he said, smiling in welcome. "It is gratifying to see that you continue in good health. This is Deborra, the granddaughter of Joseph of Arimathea and wife of Basil. What have you learned on your journeyings back and forth through the streets of the city?"

"That God is good," answered Hananiah, "and that His Son has brought much happiness into the hearts of men. I have learned of things that matter much less, Luke the Physician." He dropped his voice to a low pitch. "Tobias, who watches at the Iron Gate, reports the arrival of Mijamin, the Zealot from Jerusalem. He came alone, looking very tired, as though he had seldom stopped for sleep. Having in mind what you told us of the activities of this man, we have seen to it that his movements are watched. What I am particularly charged to tell you is that a meeting of the Zealots is to be held tonight. They will no doubt discuss the news that Mijamin brings. We have not been able to learn where the meeting is to be held."

"The coming of Mijamin," said Luke, "has to do with that which is being guarded in this house."

Hananiah nodded his head. "There is this much in our favor. The authorities watch the Zealots closely. It has been forbidden them to hold meetings or to gather in force. They will have to act with great caution. Jehovah be praised for all His mercies."

Luke watched the tall figure on its way to the door. "Hananiah was once a man of great wealth. When he came into the fold he gave his olive groves to the men who had worked for him and turned all his gold to the church to be distributed among the poor. For years he and his wife have lived under a strip of canvas in the back yard of a tannery. His wife makes the sweetmeats and he sells them, and they live happily on the meager proceeds."

"He has a wonderful face," commented Deborra.

Luke was giving thought to the situation they faced. "Basil must not be told of this," he said. "If he knew, he would think it his duty to remain with us. It is more important to have the Chalice finished so we can give it into the hands of the church leaders, here or in Jerusalem. I confess it will be a weight off my mind when it will no longer be necessary to keep it hidden this way. To have it finished should be our first consideration, and so we must not keep him here."

"Yes, we must see that he goes at once to Ephesus."

Luke smiled at her with affectionate confidence. "To let him go will put a heavy load on your shoulders, my child. I know you can carry it." He considered the situation with frowning absorption. "There are a thousand Christian homes in Antioch. We can find in one of them a safe place for the Cup. Perhaps we should see to its removal at once. Mijamin will not waste any time."

Basil made his way down to the court, coming straight from his worktable. His hands were discolored from his labors and there were beads of solder on the folds of his acid-stained tunic. He looked very tired.

"I have finished," he said. He sank down on a bench close to the chair where she was sitting. "There are still the heads to be done after I have been to Ephesus and Rome. Do you not agree that I should take the first ship sailing north?"

Deborra had laid the *kinnor* to one side and was engaged in some sewing. She looked up at him and smiled.

"I am delighted that you are through. Are you pleased with it?"

"I don't know." He shook his head doubtfully. "The design is good. But have I carried it out as well as I should? Sometimes I look at it and think to myself that Scopas could not have done better. Sometimes I feel that a green apprentice would crush it under his heel rather than acknowledge it as his own. At this moment I am too tired to have any feeling about it at all." He leaned against the stone back of the bench and gazed up at the patch of sky above the green tiling of the roof. "I thought I heard voices down here. They sounded loud, as though there was some dispute."

Deborra had lowered her eyes over her work. She continued calmly with her sewing. "It was nothing," she said. "Nothing, at least, for you to be concerned about."

5

The days had fallen into a pattern. Deborra and Basil began them at an early hour, rising while the freshness of the dawn was still in the air and breakfasting together in the second court while the sky in the east was filled with shifting fingers of light. Basil was an easy and even enthusiastic riser and he always came to the meal in the best of spirits. He talked, he laughed, he even sang. His appetite was good. Deborra was an unwilling riser. Left to herself, she would have remained in bed to a much later hour, and so she came to the table on laggard feet. She would yawn, and she never had much to say. She would sip a cup of milk without any pleasure and nibble at some bread and fruit.

As the day progressed, this state of affairs reversed itself. His optimism gradually lessening, Basil would hear his wife's voice raised about the house and gardens and he would trace how it became more animated as the hours passed. She supervised the work of the domestics with thoroughness but still had time for music and for romping with her clumsy, heavy-footed dog. The cat from the Nile, having conceived an intense distrust of the dog, could not be persuaded to join them. He did a great deal of morose sitting on walls and would not come down.

Basil could chart the rise in her spirits by the fall of his own. He grew less buoyant as time flitted by and more disposed to look on the dark side of things.

At the end of the day an elaborate supper would be served and the young wife always tried to make an occasion of it. She dressed herself carefully. Her spirits then reached a peak; she laughed easily and recounted with animation the events of the day. Basil would listen in a mood of mild melancholy. "And now it is you," she would say, "who look as though the end of the world is near at hand."

Basil was to sail for Ephesus on a vessel that left at dawn. It had been Deborra's hope that they could have their last meal alone together, but she came to realize that this would be selfish. She prepared a very special supper, therefore, and had Luke, Prince P'ing-li, and Chimham sit down with him. She contented herself, as a good wife should, with seeing that they were served tender slices of the roast young kid, that the bread was crisp and hot from the oven and the wine well cooled. The same food was being sent up to Elidad and Irijah at their posts above, and once she went to visit them and make sure they had everything they desired, pausing to sit for a few minutes beside them and talk of their homes and families.

As she moved about her tasks she caught scraps of the conversation at the table where the head of the household sat with his guests. P'ing-li, as usual, was plying Luke with questions about the life and teachings of Jesus. Basil was in a silent mood. He was eating little and seemed to be taking small interest in his guests. Chimham, who had secured the consent of the old prince to follow the train of the latter into the East, was in an exultant frame of mind and ate and drank a great deal.

Once, when the talk had died down momentarily, Chimham began to talk about himself, declaring that he was a failure as a husband. "When I supped for the first time with my new wife," he declared over the rim of his wine cup, "we were very close and affectionate. We ate from the same dish and used the same spoon, turn and turn about. But before we were through she came around to the question of presents. What would I bring her from the East? I should have given her the rough of my hand there and then. It is the only safe present for a begging wife." He indulged in a gusty sigh. "Yes, I am a failure. It has always been this way. I have never given any of them the rough of my hand. When I married the first of them—I am not sure at this moment which was the first—I should have whittled a stick and made the surface hard and smooth, and I should have placed it inside the door of my house. I should have said to her, this first wife: 'Observe! This is a stick. It is a heavy stick. If you displeasure me, I shall beat you well on your full-of-the-moon.'" He sighed again.

"By the earth and my head, that is what I shall do when I marry my next wife."

Basil kept his eyes on Deborra as she moved about her tasks. She had not allowed Sarah to cover her head with a *sakkos,* and so the dark curls clustering about her brow made her look very young and a little gay and impudent. Her dress was the color of an unripe peach and very simple in line, and for the first time since her grandfather's death she was wearing jewelry. There was a heavy gold chain wound half a dozen times or more around her neck and a ring on her left hand with an emerald as large as a camel's eye.

The sky began to darken with the coming of night. Deborra seated herself at a small table under the arched walk that surrounded the court, and a servant brought out a lighted lamp and placed it beside her. The Egyptian cat, attracted by the light, emerged from some high perch and rubbed against her ankles. She reached down a hand and smoothed his ears. "You might really get to be fond of me," she said, "if you were willing to try."

The analogy this suggested caused her to look at the table where Basil sat with his guests. His eyes met hers and, sensing an invitation, he rose to his feet and crossed the court. He seated himself on the opposite side of the table from her.

"You seem low in spirits," said Deborra. "I expected you to be happy tonight. You are setting out to finish the Chalice. While you are away you may find the evidence to use in ousting that wicked man. Your going, then, should not be an occasion for the drawing of a long face."

"I am happy that the time has come to set out on my travels, and yet I am also sad at the need to go," he said. It was so dark now that the lamp did not make it possible for either to read what was written on the face of the other. He began to speak of something that had been in his mind. "I cannot understand why things have been so easy. I expected trouble from several sources. In fact, I was reconciled to postponing my journey until we had settled some of the problems hanging over us. But everyone seems to have left us alone."

Deborra responded with a grave nod. "Yes, we have been most fortunate."

"I suspect it has been a lull. I shall hurry back in expectation of the breaking of the storm about us." He checked himself abruptly. "It may be that you do not want me to return."

She said "Basil!" in a tone that suggested reproach. Then she fell into a thoughtful mood, and it was some moments before she began to speak of what she was thinking. "I want you to return. I would be—yes, I must say it—I would be quite unhappy if you did not. But it depends on so many things, doesn't it? On whether you want to return. And on whether we can get some matters settled between us."

"It must be as clear to you as it is to me," he said in a low tone, "that we cannot go on as we are doing."

"No," she answered. "That is true. It was agreed between us at the start that our marriage would be on the terms I had suggested. I want to say now that you have been very kind, Basil. You have kept to the terms with—with the greatest strictness."

"I knew it was your wish."

"Yes, it was my wish. I cannot find fault with anything you have said or done. And now that you are going away, I want to thank you for being so fair always, and so very kind."

"If there is to be any change, it must be in accordance with your wishes."

She cried out vehemently: "No, no! What we are to do with our lives depends entirely on you. On what you have to tell me when you come back. Basil, don't you see that—that from this moment on I cannot speak another word? That I must wait for you to say whatever is to be said?"

He reached a hand across the table in the dark and touched hers. "I have been on the defensive and have not felt free to speak. But now I can see that I have been lacking in understanding," he said. After a moment of silence he rose to his feet. "Let us stroll in the garden while we finish our talk. Do you realize as much as I do that we owe something to these friends who are so deeply concerned about us?"

"Yes, I know that we do."

She rose in turn and walked slowly out into the garden with him, a hand on his arm. They might have been a devoted pair of lovers, because her dark head was a scant inch from his white linen sleeve; but this explanation was too good to be true to the trio watching them at the supper table.

"They wonder what is going to happen to us," said Basil. "The prince has spoken of it several times."

"He has also spoken to me," said Deborra. "I have become very fond of him, even if he is such a funny little man. He giggled so delightedly when he told me about the presents he is leaving. I can hardly wait to know what they are." It was a good thing that the darkness hid her face, because it flamed with color when she realized what she had said. In an effort to cover up the slip of her tongue she hurried on: "He leaves in a few days. I shall miss him very much. It is going to be quiet here."

They had reached a spot where it was possible to see the moon rising over the upper portions of the house, and they stood in silence for several moments watching it. Their minds were so filled with what the future might hold for them that the old prince was for a moment banished completely from their thoughts.

"Basil," said Deborra, "I exacted a promise of you. That you would not see Helena when you were in Rome. Now I withdraw it. I want you to promise that you *will* see her."

Basil was taken by surprise. He frowned in the darkness, wondering what reason she could have for changing her mind. "I intended to abide by the promise I made you," he said. "There is no desire on my part to see her."

Deborra spoke slowly. "I think it would be a wise thing to do. Don't ask me for my reasons. I am not sure I could explain. Perhaps this one reason will be enough; that it might be helpful to both of us later—when it comes to deciding what we are to do."

He hesitated and then said, "It shall be as you wish."

It came to Basil suddenly that everything that now counted in life could be found here: peace and the chance for great love, his friends seated about his table, the Chalice in the room above, his workbench and tools, the belief that he shared with those who meant the most, Deborra and Luke, and that filled all their minds with a clear white light, the girl by his side who was becoming again infinitely precious to him. It was Deborra, he knew, who counted most of all. He said to himself: "Her eyes are brighter than I thought Helena's to be. Her hair is softer and more lustrous. She is very young and sweet and desirable."

Aloud he said: "There will be many ships sailing for Ephesus. I could take a later one."

"Yes, Basil," she said breathlessly. Then she summoned the resolution to add: "I want you to stay. I do! It would make me very happy. But it is so important to finish the Chalice. It is a sacred duty."

His arm went about her. He drew her closer. It might have been counted a minor miracle that in the darkness his lips found hers unerringly, except that her willingness had been such a great help. For a moment she clung to him, standing eagerly on tiptoe. Then with a deep sigh she drew away.

"The prince will be glad," she whispered. "Was it for his sake that you kissed me?"

"I did not give him a thought," declared Basil.

There was a pause, and then she began to whisper again. "I will be less unhappy now to see you go. But, Basil, we must face it. It is your duty to go, and mine to let you. You must see her, as you promised, when you get to Rome. This I am going to ask of you: see her with new eyes. Only if you can forget her completely, after seeing her, will it be possible for us to plan a different kind of life to share."

BOOK THREE

BOOK THREE

CHAPTER XXIII

I

RAGUEL, the dyer, said: "You desire to see John, son of Zebedee? John, the disciple beloved of Jesus?" He read again the letter Luke had given Basil, but his manner did not lose the edge of suspicion it had taken on at the first mention of the latter's errand. "Do you not know, youth, that you might as well expect to look into the sky and see the face of Jehovah?"

Raguel was a man of substance. He had a large establishment: large, at least, for the section where it was located, at the fringe of the Greek portion of Ephesus. It was all in one room: an elevated space where the family lived and that reflected the cheerful red of earthenware and the rich tones of brass and bronze, and even the luxury of a carpet from the desert, and a lower section where the domestic animals were kept. There was, however, a second building, connected with the house by a latticed passage. Here the vats were kept and no fewer than three assistants worked with their arms in highly colored juices.

"John," he went on to say, "is a fugitive in the sense that the authorities would like to get their hands on him; to put him out of the way or exile him to one of the prison islands. The Asiarchs do not love him at all. He has taken to preaching the end of the world. He tells the people of death and fire and destruction, and so they fear him. They think, these poor, blind oxen, that if they can destroy the one who preaches danger they will destroy the danger itself. So John must remain in seclusion. It is not wise to trust strangers who come seeking him out."

"But is not this letter sufficient proof of my purpose?"

"Far from it," declared Raguel bluntly. "Luke is a kindly man. He sees the good and he has a blind eye for evil. It is not in his nature to scent treachery. And, moreover, he has no conception of the difficulties we have in keeping John out of the clutches of the Asiarchs." He stared at Basil with the bold eyes that hinted at a nomadic strain in him. "What is this Chalice that is mentioned in the letter?"

Basil explained briefly, but it was apparent from the first word that Raguel's mind had been made up. The latter frowned at the end of the brief recital.

"Simon the Magician was here last week," he stated. "He was so diabolically clever that many people went away convinced the miracles wrought by the Son of God were no more than tricks. He caused tongues of fire to appear above the heads of his assistants. He scoffed and railed at the truth. But that was not all. There was a man in his train who came from Jerusalem and was named Loddeus. This Loddeus mingled with the people and told them, among other things, that the Cup Jesus blessed at the Last Supper and passed to His disciples is no longer in existence."

"I have seen it!" cried Basil. "I have seen it four times. I was present when Joseph of Arimathea produced it first from the hiding place and showed it to Paul and Luke. I saw them go down on their knees, with tears in their eyes, and kiss the rim of the little Cup. I know where it is today."

"Listen to what Loddeus told." Raguel's manner still showed no signs of relenting. "He swears that the Zealots took it away from the Christians in Jerusalem and carried it to the High Priest. Ananias had a servant bring in a hammer and pound it into dust. Then he himself, unwilling to trust the task to other hands, went in his ceremonial robes to the shore of the Dead Sea where the holy river flows into it. It was in the early morning, and he waited until the ridge of white foam appeared at the mouth of the river and then into it he tossed the dust of the Cup. It was carried away on that strange wave and so found its way to the bottom and was lost in the salt of the sea. Then he raised an arm and cried out, 'Never more shall this reminder of unrest rise up to plague us!' Loddeus said that many people witnessed the ceremony and that he was there himself."

"It is a pack of falsehoods!"

Raguel gestured with both hands. "People are accepting it as the truth. And so when a beardless boy comes and says that the Cup was not destroyed, are we to believe him? Are we to accept him on faith and let him know our most closely held secret, the whereabouts of John?"

At first Basil had nothing to propose for the unraveling of this unforeseen difficulty. If the letter from Luke did not suffice, what more could he do? Finally, however, he said to the dyer: "It may be I could convince you by telling the whole story; how I came to be in the household of Joseph of Arimathea, and everything that has transpired since. It is a long story."

Raguel was dressed in a purple robe to anticipate the stains that his garments were certain to suffer in the course of his work. His neck and arms and ankles were discolored with splotches of this shade. He dried his hands on the skirt and then held the letter up to his eyes for a final appraisal.

"I go on an errand on the Lord's Day," he said finally. "It will mean a seven-mile walk and the same distance back. If you care to go with me, there will be time for the telling of this story." He gave his head a warning shake. "It will be a hot and dusty walk. It leads into one of the most desolate spots on the face of the earth. Think twice before you decide to accompany me."

Basil felt his heart sink at the need to face once more the malice of his great enemy, the sun, but he did not hesitate in answering. "Have I come all the way to Ephesus to see John, only to be sent away without an effort? I will go with you. I am sure the story I have to tell will banish from your mind the lies this Loddeus is spreading."

Raguel let his eyes range to the raised portion of the room where a plump woman with warm brown eyes was working among the cooking utensils. She nodded her head to him and he smiled and nodded back. "You will stay with us. My Elisheba is a good provider and she will not mind another mouth to fill because my assistants have their meals with us anyway. We will start at dawn. *Maran-atha!* It will be a hard walk!"

2

Segub, who was called the Zebra, emerged from the dyeing room, where he and the other assistants slept on rolls of bedding behind the vats. His nickname rose out of his unwillingness to wash the dye stains from his person. His neck was red, his chest purple, his bony ankles a weak blue. He rubbed the sleep from his eyes with a slow hand.

"It will be hot," he said, staring into the east. "Jehovah have pity on all flint-heads like my master who will walk to the mines this day."

"If you were a good Christian," said Raguel, "you would be going with us."

"I am a good Christian," retorted Segub. "I believe in the words of Paul, who said to us, 'The Lord's Day is made for man, not man for the Lord's Day.' I shall pass the hours in the shade of a tree and I shall think of you, master, toiling over the sands to those thrice-accursed mines."

Raguel began the long walk with a pucker between his eyes. "I was converted to the teachings of Jesus seven years ago," he said. "Do you see what that means? All my life I have lived under the Laws, and I am now too old to change. Many Christians disregard the strictest of the Laws. They lean on the utterances of Paul and say, 'Is it not true that Paul says this or that?' They are becoming very lax. But I—I cannot change my ways." He sighed deeply. "Have you noticed any difference in me?"

Basil saw now that his cheeks looked sunken and that new lines had sprouted around his mouth.

"I lack teeth," explained the master dyer, "and on the Lord's Day I dare not use the substitutes that have been made for me. Why, do you ask? Because when they fall out—as they do a dozen times a day—I could not put them back in; that would be work, and all work is forbidden. Nor could I carry them, because that also would be work."

Basil pointed an accusing finger at a brass plate with a spoon tied on top of it that his companion had tucked under one arm.

"But is it not work to carry that?"

"No, my young friend. Do you not see the distinction? A spoon is helpful to support life, and so it is allowed to carry one wherever you go. If the spoon happens to be on something else, then it is permitted to take the other object as well. Yes, it is a subterfuge. I grant it. But such subterfuges make it possible to exist under the strictest laws, and so all good Jews do as I am doing. I carry this plate with a clear conscience."

The freshness of dawn had been driven from the air already by the conquering sun. Segub the Zebra had not overstated things; it was going to be a very hot day. Raguel sighed and looked up into the sky. "I am no longer young, and it becomes increasingly hard to walk to the mines. Now, young stranger, you will tell me your story."

Basil slung the blue cloth that contained his supply of clay from one shoulder to the other. He was finding it a little hard to breathe. "I was a slave in Antioch," he began.

It took quite a time to finish the story, but there must have been conviction in the narrative. At the finish the master dyer nodded his head with a hint of belief.

"I do not think you could make up such a tale," he said. "To believe what you have told would make me very happy. We who depend on the word which reaches us from other places need a symbol on which to fix our eyes. What better one could there be than the Cup of the Last Supper? But it is true that Loddeus also told a story of convincing detail." Raguel studied the face of his companion, which was looking flushed and feverish under the solar onslaught. "Somehow I am disposed to put my trust in you rather than him. There was a glibness about him that sat ill on my stomach."

They were walking over baked roads that were hard and rough to the foot. There was not so much as a single palm to lend them shade. The mountains that sheltered the city were now close at hand, their peaks starkly outlined against the thin blue of the sky. The few stragglers they passed were like white wraiths, their feet plodding slowly, their heads sinking despondently forward. Even the cry of birds overhead was muted and seemed to come from a great distance.

Raguel raised his staff and pointed. "The mines are over there, at the base of the hills. Those who work in them are all Christians—poor, patient fellows, any one of whom would die willingly for a single glimpse of the Cup. Young man, young man, you would not trifle with anything as sacred as this? Are you telling me the truth?"

"I have spoken the truth," declared Basil, laying a hand on his heart.

Raguel looked at him intently for a moment. Then he smiled and nodded his head; he was convinced at last. He touched a hand to the brass plate under his arm. "I am taking this," he said, "to one of those gentle, tired men who work so hard in the mines. His brother was crucified two days ago with this plate nailed to the cross and on it no more than a number. Last night, after darkness had fallen, I went to the Knoll of the Dead Men under the shadow of the Rock of Vultures and I stole the plate because I thought my poor friend Abishalom would want it.

"Can you believe," said Raguel as they continued to plod on through the intense heat, "that my friend Abishalom has never been more than a mile away from the place where he was born? Will you accept my word for it that he does not know what is done with the ore he carries in sacks on his back from the mine shaft to the mill, limping all the way because he is lame? That he has never seen a piece of the burnished brass they make in the mill? All these things are true.

"He is married, my poor friend, and he has seven children. His wife is a bitter woman who tells him he is a weakling, a failure. She has thrown it into his face always that he is not good enough to work on making the brass in the mill instead of carrying ore on his back. That is why he has never set foot in the mill. In his way he is proud, my friend.

"He had an older brother, Hobab, who was strong and upstanding and a leader among the miners. As a boy Hobab always helped the lame Abishalom over the rough places, sometimes carrying him on his back. He was always gentle and loving as an older brother should be, and as a man he continued to help and cherish him, sometimes sparing a coin or two when the tax collectors came and Abishalom had nothing to give them. But Hobab had a great temper, and when the Zealots began to make trouble with the miners he incited his peace-loving fellows to strike back. There was fighting and a man was killed. The Roman soldiers came and took Hobab away, saying he was the ringleader. They crucified him on the Knoll of the Dead Men." His face had fallen into lines of sadness. "I am told that Abishalom has not spoken since they took his brother away. He lies on his bed and stares at the wall with eyes that see nothing. It may be that he will never get up again."

They had come in sight of a cluster of small huts. Raguel raised his staff and pointed at one of them. "That is where he lives," he said. "I will go in alone, if you do not mind."

It was a long time before he came out. Saying nothing, he seated himself beside Basil, who had found a spot that was in shadow from the sun. He lifted a handful of the sandy soil and let it trickle through his fingers, his head bent over to watch. He repeated this several times and then he began to speak.

"It is no wonder," he said in a reflective tone, "that men like Abishalom have such barren lives. It is hard to live where the earth is so lacking in fertility. It is a struggle to survive. But," he added with a sigh, "he will not have to struggle longer. My poor friend has very few hours left."

Neither of them broke the silence for several moments. Then the master dyer again raised his voice. "When Christians gather together for talk, it is the question of life after death that concerns them most. It is a new thought, strange and wonderful, and it lights their minds like a thousand suns. They play with it as a beggar child might play with a precious stone he has found in a dustbin. They believe, but at the same time they marvel at their own audacity. They con over the evidence. 'Did not Jesus say this?' and 'What did He mean when He told His disciples that?' They quote the words of Peter and Paul and sometimes they reflect that the Grecian people also believe in a future existence. But always it is vague and they long to have their minds set at rights." He lifted his head proudly. "I have no doubts. I am one of the few. I am never troubled in my mind. Ever since I accepted Jesus I have been sure that I would see Him in all His glory. I am happy in my faith. And now, praise to Jehovah and His only begotten Son, my poor friend Abishalom is able to share my faith!"

He turned to Basil a face that glowed with light. "He lay there in the stifling heat of a corner, his face like a mask of death. I do not think he knew me when I bent over him. I placed the brass plate in his hands and told him what it was. Do you remember what I said, that he had never seen a mirror? He looked at the bright brass of the plate, and a face looked back at him. They were much alike, the two brothers, and he cried out at once that it was his brother he saw. 'O Blessed Father in heaven,' he said. 'There is a life after death! See, my brother has not gone down into the darkness of the grave. He looks at me from the plate under which his body died. His eyes smile at me, they weep, they try to tell me things.' It was hard for him to hold the plate so that he could continue to watch the face in it. After a long time, while he gathered his strength for more words, he said: 'I know what he is trying to tell me, my fine, tall brother who died so bravely. He says he will be there to meet me when I die and that he will take me up on his back and carry me far out over the clouds and through the stars on the path to paradise!' "

A doubt drifted across the dyer's face for a brief moment. "It may seem to you that my friend has been cheated, that he has been brought to a belief in the future life by a trick. It is not so, young stranger. The Lord must have put it into my head to steal the plate from the cross on which Hobab died and take it to his brother. It was Jehovah's way of showing the truth to this humble man with his simple, clouded mind. *Aiy*, you should have seen Abishalom's face! It glowed with the happiness that had come to him. And"—he gestured quietly with his hands— "who knows? Can we be sure it was not Hobab who looked back at him from the plate of brass? Stranger things have happened, my boy."

The sun had stolen up on them, determined to deny them the shelter that a sparse and mournful tree had been affording. It was now peering straight around the tree and directing its rays at them like arrows of fire. Raguel said: "We must be on our way. But first I shall tell you one thing more. I saw that my friend's wife was eying the plate with a speculative gleam, and I knew she was wondering how much she could sell it for. So I called the older of the two sons aside. He is a boy of thirteen, and I think he must be a good eater and sleeper and that his bowels are regular because he already has much of the great strength of Hobab. His name is David, but all his life he has been called Young Waxy Nose. I said to him: 'From now on you must never allow anyone to call you Young Waxy Nose, but always it must be David because very soon you will be the head of the family.' And I looked him hard in the eye and said to him sternly: 'David, do not allow the plate to be taken from your father's hands. Stand by him, and when he dies—for he is going to die, David, and you must be brave and not give way to the tears I see in your eyes—you must see to it that he is buried with the plate clasped as tightly as he holds it now.' And the boy choked back his tears and he stood up very straight and said: 'It will be as you say, Uncle Raguel. I am now the head of the family and I shall give the orders.'"

There was no longer any hope of comfort where they sat. Raguel sighed and rose to his feet. "Come," he said. "There is more for us to do."

They turned, and Raguel led the way toward the base of the nearest mountain. The heat here was even harder to endure. It was reflected back from the rocky surfaces of the hills and seemed to settle down about them like a sullen and angry cloud.

"Have you heard, my young friend," asked Raguel, "that there are miles of subterranean galleries under the city? We are not certain today of the purpose for which they were designed, although it is thought they may have been intended as a means of escape if the city should fall to an invading army. They run out under the walls. One line of galleries has an exit under the base of this mountain ahead of us. No one knows this save the men who go down into the mines with their picks, all of whom are Christians. It was they who discovered the steps that connect their shaft with the last of the underground chambers, and they have kept the secret of it closely." He paused, and his eyes, half closed in the glare of the sun, looked up at Basil with a smile. "I am going to take you to see John," he said.

"When?" cried Basil with relief and delight.

"Now," said Raguel. "He will attend the services that begin"—he turned to stare up at the position of the sun—"in about half an hour."

3

The chamber in which they found themselves after the descent of a sloping passage through dark rock was dimly lighted by torches fixed at intervals in the walls. After his eyes became accustomed to the gloom Basil saw that the space below was already well filled. The people sat for the most part on the natural flooring of stone, but a few, who seemed to be on watch, stood along the walls; men of serious mien, intent, resolute, even fanatical. They seemed less predominantly Semitic than at the other Christian gatherings Basil had witnessed, and he commented on this in a whisper.

"Nearly all here today are converts of Paul's," answered Raguel. "He has been much in Ephesus and, whenever he comes to expound the truth to us, we grow and multiply. There has been whispering of late among the Jewish people that Paul is trying to lead them away from the Laws of Moses. They do not like it. They resent his efforts to carry the Word to Gentiles. Many have recanted and become the strictest of Judaizers, casting Jesus out of their hearts. They are the most bitter against us. They give encouragement and aid to the Men with the Daggers." Basil could see an apologetic expression spread across his face. "Was it any wonder, my young friend, that I was suspicious of you and not prepared at once to lead you to John? Next to Paul, he is the one the backsliders would like most to deliver over to the Asiarchs."

More people continued to arrive, weary men who walked stiffly and paused before entering to shake the dust from their robes.

"Where do they come from?" asked Basil.

"Many are miners and live hereabouts. The rest are from the city. It is the rule to start during the hours of darkness to avoid notice, for it is above everything necessary to conceal the secret of where we meet. They will go back by twos and threes, being very leisurely about it and making it seem that they have spent the day walking in the fields. They, the bitter turncoats and the men who carry daggers, know better, of course; but so far they have failed to discover anything about us. We change the places of meeting every few weeks. I don't know where we shall go next."

Raguel fell silent at this point and laid a restraining hand on Basil's arm. The services were beginning with a reading from early writings. The member who did the reading stood on a ledge of rock at one end of the chamber. Knowing that most of them came from the poorest part of the population, Basil was surprised at the scholarly note in the speaker's voice and the fine intelligence in his face. The reading was followed by singing in which all joined. There was a pause then, and Basil took advantage of it to look about him more closely at the earnest men and women who made up the gathering. His eyes, having completed the circle of the chamber, came back again to the stone ledge, and he was surprised to find that it now had a new occupant.

The newcomer was of undistinguished stature, being under the average in height and thin to the point of emaciation, a stooped and somehow pathetic figure in a plain white robe. He looked about him and raised an arm in the air; and the rustling and the whispers ceased and the figures seated in the semi-gloom became as motionless as the warriors and gods that were traced crudely on the walls above them.

Basil turned to his companion with an inquiring uplift of eyebrow, and Raguel answered by shaping noiselessly with his lips the single word, "John."

"I come to you, mayhap, for the last time," said John, speaking in a thin, high voice. "It is written that soon I shall be taken and sent to the islands, to be held there in captivity by men who are filled with hatred and fear. They fear and hate me, but even more the vision that has come to me. My eyes have been lifted to the heights and I have seen the writing on the heavenly walls beyond the clouds and the stars. The voice of the Lord has spoken in my ear and has told me that I must preach to men of what I have seen and heard."

His voice rose suddenly to a high pitch, filled with conviction and passion. "Ye that walk in the truth, who have been born of God because ye believe that Jesus is the Christ, ye need have no fear. He that came by blood and water will come again soon, and it is not strange that these others are filled with a fear of His coming. The time is close at hand! I shall speak to the seven churches before the time comes, and what I have to tell will turn the blood of the kings of earth to water, and the blood of the great men as well as the little men and the scoffers. And they will seek to hide themselves in the depths of the forests and under the waters and in the bowels of the earth under the high tombs of the mountains."

Basil was listening intently, but even as his ears were filled with the strange words of the passionate little man his fingers were pulling excitedly at the blue strings of the cloth. He did not want to miss a single word that fell from the almost bloodless lips of the apostle, but he knew he must not lose this opportunity to imprison in the damp clay the unusual countenance of this favorite follower of Jesus. It was not a difficult task in one sense, for the leonine head of John was different in ways that set him sharply apart. His protruding forehead of a thinker and dreamer was like a broad penthouse. The straight nose was long enough to balance the width between eye and ear, but it made the mouth and chin seem small by comparison. The mouth, Basil perceived, was sensitive and the chin courageous, but it was only with a second glance that he noticed them at all, so immediately did his eye absorb the grandeur of the brow and the banked fires that smoldered beneath it.

"Will I be able to capture his mighty spirit?" thought the young artist, his fingers furiously busy. "Can I make it clear that this is a man who walks and talks with God?"

The apostle was telling of his vision in words that were sometimes vague and sometimes even incoherent but always touched with a power that transcended human use. Basil became so carried away finally that he lost concern with the task that had brought him there. His hands ceased their efforts while he watched and listened. At least it seemed to him that this was so; but at a moment when the apostle paused, he realized that, without any prompting of his will, they had resumed the work of molding and manipulating the clay.

He was filled at once with a sense of horror. It had happened again! He remembered how his fingers had dug so passionately into the clay when his thoughts had turned to Linus and the revenge he craved, and how completely they had destroyed the first model he had made of Luke. Was this a repetition? Had the clay in his hands been turned into another formless mass? He was afraid to look.

John's voice ceased its fervid outpouring. After the customary breaking of bread, he lifted an arm in blessing. A moment of silent prayer followed, and then he stepped down from the ledge of rock. Basil felt the hand of Raguel on his shoulder.

"The meeting is over," said the dyer, getting to his feet. "You have seen John, young stranger. You have heard him speak. Has it not been a wonderful experience?"

"I shall always be grateful to you," replied Basil, following him out into the ascending passage to the mine. He continued to carry the clay in both hands, but he had not yet mastered his feeling sufficiently to risk a glance at it.

When they reached the open air he raised it to a level with his eyes and immediately felt his spirits bound out of control. He wanted to shout aloud in delight and surprise. His hands had not betrayed him a second time. Laboring on of their own accord, they had achieved more than they might have done if his will had been directing them. The accurate modeling that he had begun consciously had been carried on to a finish, even to the matter of details, the lines so deeply marked on the forehead and about the somber eyes, the sunken contour of the cheeks, the sensitive lips. It was, he realized, a finished effort; to go on with it further would be to strain for something beyond perfection.

"A spirit took possession of me today," he thought exultantly. "But it was not an evil one."

The men and women who had been sitting at the feet of John were not lingering or standing about in groups to exchange opinions and experiences as they would have done under any other circumstances. With quiet resolution they were setting off for their homes. Never more than two went together, and they were scattering to different roads as quickly as possible.

Raguel was staring with astonishment at the clay head in his companion's hands. "You made that?" he asked in an incredulous whisper. "You made it while we were inside? It is hard to believe, and yet there is the proof of it." He gave his head an emphatic nod. "Now I no longer have any doubts. The story you told me was true. The Cup is safe. Someday your efforts will make for it a frame of fitting beauty. I am happy that I trusted you and brought you with me today."

CHAPTER XXIV

1

IT W A S L A T E in the evening, but a stifling heat still gripped the city on the Tiber. One of the travelers, who had come on the same ship from Ephesus and who had a house near the Fabricius Bridge, had agreed to show Basil the way to the small inn where he was to stay. They had been much in each other's company, and the young Roman had finally divulged that he was a Christian.

"It will be so dark that we will see little," said the Roman, whose name was Crassus. "That is a pity. One should see Rome first in the middle of the day, when it is the most exciting spectacle in the world. It passes all belief then." He indulged in a sigh that was only faintly regretful. "It is the most wicked of all cities, but you cannot help loving it. Life seems empty when you are away."

"Were you born here?" asked Basil.

The other nodded. "I was born in the house where I now live. I took over the house and the trade in Eastern goods when my father died. I am different from most of the Christians in Rome. I am patrician. Although I do not believe in squandering money"—this was easy to understand, for he had been the one to suggest that they make their way through the city on foot—"I am a rather rich man. I do not give the church all my profits, but I give a large share."

They passed the Aventine Hill and the tufa quarries. There was nothing here of the glory of Rome at midday. The streets were dark and empty. They skirted the Circus Maximus and came rather wearily, for the grades had been steep, into the Forum Romanorum. The young patrician said proudly, "We now stand in the exact center of the world."

The Forum was crowded and noisy even at this hour. They stopped in front of the Temple of Janus, and Crassus pointed out that the bronze door was open. "It is never closed when Rome is at war," he said. "Indeed, one might say it is never closed."

Most of the people in the Forum were sight-seers, staring at the monuments and looking in the clear moonlight at the temples that hedged the square in on all sides. All of them had been drinking freely, for Rome was a convivial city. Their voices were shrill and loud.

An occasional train of chariots would come galloping down from the Palatium, where Nero and his court feasted and roistered, or directly from the Capitol, where affairs of state kept the imperial officers in uninterrupted bondage. They invariably slowed down to an easy clopping gait through the Forum and then wheeled in various directions, to go clattering with furious haste through the streets that radiated from it. The people scattered to get out of their way and then stopped to jeer angrily after them.

"There seems to be much freedom here," commented Basil. "I see no signs of a police watch."

His companion went into an explanation. "There are fire guards. They will pass back and forth through the Forum several times in the course of a night. But the city has no police. The Praetorian Guards are supposed to keep peace in the city, but they are never seen around at night. There are always companies of the Guards at the Palatium, of course, and up on Capitoline Hill."

"Can it be," asked Basil, "that the people are given a free hand so they will forget their poverty and the political freedom that has been taken away from them?"

It was clear that Crassus did not allow his religious beliefs to affect his political views. He looked at Basil with a critical air. "Many think there is too much political freedom in Rome," he said.

Knowing that there were thieves everywhere, they never let their hands get far away from the dagger hilts under their tunics. This constant threat led Basil to ask a question, "What kind of an establishment is this I am going to?"

Crassus did not seem to think well of it. "It is called an inn, but it is really a boarding home, an *insula,* kept by an elderly fellow who is called Old Hannibal. The place is well known because Old Hannibal has a son who is a famous gladiator."

Basil indulged in a puzzled frown. "It seems a strange place for them to have picked out for me."

"Not at all," said Crassus. "There are no Christians in the place and so it is the safest for you." He proceeded to demonstrate that, for a Christian, his interests went far afield. "The son is called Sisinnes the Unbeaten. I never lay wagers now, but when I was younger I made money all the time by betting on Sisinnes. He is a Samnite; that means he fights in the Arena with the traditional sword and shield of Rome. That makes him popular with the people and they come out roaring for action whenever he is matched. He has never lost a fight. They say he has made himself a fortune by placing wagers on himself. He could have retired long ago but he prefers to go on fighting to add to his wealth."

Their tired feet had led them toward the foot of the eastern cliff where the grim Mamertine Prison stood under the Capitoline Hill. Crassus did not like this neighborhood, and his steps picked up speed in his haste to get away.

"There are underground cells," he whispered, "where all people condemned to death are kept. There are always some Christians in them. The Emperor hates us. He is willing to see a Christian sentenced to death on the flimsiest grounds, even on suspicion. No one knows why, but it is true that he would like to get rid of all the Christians in Rome." He indulged in a shudder. "It may be that friends of mine are down there now. Waiting—waiting to be beheaded or crucified. Perhaps they are sitting in those damp horrible cells this very minute, knowing that they will die at dawn. It makes my stomach turn over to think of it."

Basil was saying to himself that it would be a relief when he had seen the last of his companion. On board ship Crassus had been a pleasant fellow traveler, but since setting foot in Rome his attitude had changed. He had become superior, rather supercilious, and very conscious of his status as a patrician. Luke had said often that wealth and Christianity did not go well together. "Joseph of Arimathea was one of the few exceptions," he pointed out. "Both Peter and Paul have found it necessary to stop visiting Christians of high social rank."

They came shortly after to a part of the city that lay between the converging Quirinal and the Esquiline hills like the smear of a greasy finger on fair parchment. It was called the Subura, a narrow region of vice and poverty, where the shops bulged so far out into the streets that passers-by had to walk through them, where the goods offered for sale were cheap and tawdry and had the stamp of suspicion on them, where sellers of illicit and stolen articles flourished and the sly individuals who catered to ignorance and superstition and greed. Thieves and escaped slaves existed in the dark recesses of Subura and ventured out only at night. As the edict forbidding the entry of vehicles into the city by day was being strictly enforced, all conveying of food supplies had to be done during the hours of darkness, and the streets of Subura already rumbled with the gritting wheels of country carts loaded with provender and squealing pigs and clacking geese, and the air was filled with the bicker of trade.

Beyond this belt of infamy and suffering and tears the hill rose sharply, and in a small triangle of sloping ground there was an oasis of comparative peace. Here were dwelling houses of mean size, crammed in as tightly as hens in a huckster's crate, the homes of small incomes and mediocrity.

Crassus led the way up into this triangle, his nose wrinkling with disapproval, although it was likely that he had a business interest in some of the questionable enterprises of the malodorous belt; all Roman citizens of wealth drew much of their revenue from Subura. There was the hint of a sniff in his voice as he entered on an explanation. "You have just passed through the worst part of Rome. It is said that Julius Caesar had a house here once, but that was a long time ago. One cannot conceive of the fastidious Caesar existing in such a pigsty."

As the long walk over the paved roads of the city had stolen the resiliency from their leg muscles, they went at a plodding gait.

"Here it is," said Crassus finally. "This is the inn of Old Hannibal. I will leave you here, my friend. Forget everything you know about me now that you are in Rome. I have no desire to find myself in the Mamertine; and I recommend caution to you for your own well-being." He raised a hand in a gesture of farewell. "May your affairs in Rome prosper so that you may quickly return to your beautiful wife."

The inn was a small structure of stucco in bad repair. The stillness was so intense that Basil was afraid the knock he gave would be heard all over the neighborhood. It was not heard inside the house, however, and he had to repeat it. The door opened then and a man peered out at him.

"You knock late," he said in a kindly tone. "What is it you want?"

He spoke in Aramaic, which was a relief to Basil, whose ears had been assailed from the moment he entered the city with a babel of unfamiliar talk.

"I desire accommodation for the night," Basil answered, depositing his bundle of belongings at his feet. "I have a letter to the keeper of this inn."

"Then I will rouse him."

Basil could hear him fumbling in the darkness of the interior, and in a few moments he emerged with a lighted lamp in one hand. By the light thus afforded he was seen to be a man of quite advanced years who yet retained some hint of energy. His thick, unruly hair and beard were white.

"Come in, stranger," he said. "You journeyed to Rome by sea?"

Basil nodded. "I came from Antioch. By way of Ephesus."

He found that he was standing in the common room of the inn. It contained a long table with benches on each side and a collection of dishes at one end. The room had about it all the commonplaceness of poverty. The table was plain and cheap, the benches would creak with little weight, the lamp in the old man's hands was of the everyday kind that could be found along desert trails and on city dump heaps.

"If you will give me the letter," said the old man, "I will take it to him."

He was gone for a few minutes and then returned with a man who was very old and very small, with something birdlike in the brightness of his eye and the high, thin tones of his voice. He held the letter open in one hand.

He spoke first to the other old man, who was standing outside the circle of light cast by the tiny lamp in his hand. "Cephas," he said, "the letter is from Luke."

"From Luke? That makes it different. We may take it for granted that the young man is to be trusted."

"I thought so from the first."

"Where is Luke?"

"I left him in Antioch," said Basil. "He was in good health. He was expecting to be bidden to Jerusalem."

"It is written in this letter," said the inn owner, "that you come on an errand in which *we will be glad to assist*. Nothing more is said, save this: *that the nature of the errand is such that you will be slow to disclose it.*"

Cephas indulged in a laugh at this point. It was a vigorous laugh to issue from a frame so much bent with the years. There were both courage and optimism in it.

"I think the cautious Luke was putting in a hint for the guidance of the young man," he said.

"He read me the letter," declared Basil, smiling. "And he looked at me most solemnly when he came to those last words."

The proprietor seated himself at the head of the table and motioned to Basil to take a place on one of the benches.

"We will ask no questions," he said. "Do you agree, Cephas?"

"We will wait," said Cephas, "until our young friend feels that the time has come when the nature of his errand may safely be disclosed."

"He will ask none of us."

Basil nodded with a smile. "None."

"It will be difficult to give you a room by yourself." Old Hannibal considered the problem with a frown. "Let me see. There is the east room above. I could move the Armenian out and put him in with the brothers from Bithynia. But what could I do with the trader from Syracuse who shares it with him?"

"Put the trader from Syracuse out with me," suggested Cephas.

"He might refuse to pay me my full fee if I did that to him."

Cephas smiled, as though he understood his weakness fully and was amused by it. "You like to have your full fee, Hannibal. Perhaps it is well that you do. I judge it is not an easy matter to run an inn like this and keep things on an even keel."

Old Hannibal sighed. "It is not at all easy." He pondered his problem with many nervous nods of his head. "He must have the east room. I will get him food, Cephas, while you see that the chamber is made ready for him."

While the proprietor set food on the table Basil turned over in his mind what he would tell them. He decided at once that any reference to Simon the Magician or Helena would be a mistake. He would make every effort to see the latter, having promised his wife so solemnly that he would do so, but he would ask no aid in finding them nor display any interest in what they were doing. When a platter with cheese and bread had been placed in front of him and a cup of rather thin wine, he realized that he was hungry. Hannibal, watching him with quick dartings of his eyes, became friendly and confidential.

"I can be of help to you, young man," he said. "Because I have had this house for so many years and because of my son, I am well known in Rome. Many people come here—to see my son, it is true, but then they talk to me. I hear things. There are people you would like to see? I could tell you where to find them."

"Yes," said Basil. "I was going to ask your help."

Cephas returned and seated himself at the table although he did not help himself to the food. "The room is yours," he said, smiling. "They grumbled a little, but they gave it up."

"There is a matter of personal business to which I must give immediate attention," said Basil. "I must see an army contractor who is called Kester of Zanthus. Perhaps you can tell me how I should go about finding him."

Old Hannibal gave his head a pleased nod. "My son will tell you what to do. He knows all the great men in Rome. He will send you to the right place. He, my son, is great himself." His eyes sought those of Cephas with a hint of appeal in them. "It is hard to accept what—what he is. My son, young man, is a gladiator. He fights in the Arena and kills other men. He has never been beaten. He"—he hesitated and then added with a kind of fascinated pride—"he has killed thirty-seven men."

Cephas said in a quiet tone: "The world is full of great men. Of men who are great in one thing. Hannibal's son is one of these. He is supreme in his trade. He is the greatest killer of other men."

"My son will know this Kester. I am sure he will. I am sure he will be able to tell the young man all about him. We will speak of it in the morning."

Basil's spirits rose. One hurdle had been passed, he felt. A more difficult one remained. He pondered the matter and decided he should give them some intimation of his main purpose in coming to Rome.

"I must see Peter," he said, letting his voice fall. "I know it is going to be hard to find him. He is here in Rome, but he is in constant peril and he must have buried himself away among the Christian families." His eyes traveled from one to the other. "I know that you are to be trusted, else Luke would not have directed me here."

The two old men had looked at each other at the first mention of Peter's name. They seemed startled and afraid. He could read in the quick meeting of their eyes that they had acquired a slight suspicion of him that they had not held before.

"I am certain," said Cephas after a moment, "that it will be possible to take you to Peter. But, my young friend, you will have to abide yourself in patience. You must not expect to waken in the morning and find Peter seated by your bedside. It will be necessary first for you to confide in us in the matter of the duties that take you to him." He smiled across the board at the newcomer. "We cannot expect you to do so at once. There must be a mutual confidence established between us. And now you are tired. I can see weariness in your eyes. I am sure you are ready to seek the couch that I have emptied, with some difficulty, for your use. Come, I will show the way."

2

Basil was up early the next morning. It was soon after dawn, in fact, when he wakened from his heavy slumbers in the east room. After such ablutions as the facilities of the inn made possible, he put in an appearance in the common room, expecting to find it unoccupied at such an hour. To his surprise he found Cephas preparing the table for the first meal of the day. Old Hannibal's twittering voice could be heard in the kitchen, where, obviously, the food was being prepared.

"Must you rise so early?" asked Basil of the old man, noticing how heavily he moved about his tasks.

Cephas smiled cheerfully. "It is part of my work," he said. "Hannibal and I rise with the sun."

"It is a long day for both of you."

Cephas began to wash and dry spoons in a basin of warm water. "I do not mind. As you grow older, my young friend, you have less need of sleep. I am satisfied with a few hours and then I rouse and lie in the darkness. I think of all the things I have done in life that I should not have done. I think"—he hesitated and sighed—"of the times when I failed, when my courage did not rise to meet an occasion. I find myself longing for the dawn. I do not find the need to rise early a hardship." His eyes took on a faraway look. "My son, it is a compensation of age that you can be sure the dawn is near at hand."

The other guests began to appear, their noses having detected the imminence of food. They seemed listless and had very little to say. A dozen in all gathered in the long room and stood about, conversing in small groups, their eyes fixed expectantly on the door through which, as they knew from experience, the food would arrive.

Standing in the front entrance, where the door had been thrown wide open to admit the freshness of the early morning air, Basil caught snatches of their low-pitched talk. He heard the name "Simon" repeated several times, but as they spoke in a language foreign to his ears, he could not tell at first whether or not the reference was to the magician. Once only a voice was raised in Aramaic, and this gave him a clue. "The woman is not human," said the voice. "He has created her by his magic power. He has stated this to be so." Clearly it was Helena and Simon Magus who were under discussion. Basil said to himself: "I will go to her first. Then I shall be able to do the rest with a freer will."

The same voice spoke a few minutes later. "Where is Sisinnes the Unbeaten? Has he chosen this morning to oversleep?"

Cephas had been hurrying back and forth between kitchen and dining room. He paused for a moment to say: "No, Vardish. The man of might is awake. I heard him heave and groan some minutes ago and then the floor shook as his feet descended on it. He will be down at once, and so it will not be necessary to delay the serving of the meal."

A few moments later a heavy tread sounded on the creaking stairs and an apparition appeared in the room that caused Basil to gape with surprise. The newcomer was tall and proportionately broad for his inches. As he wore nothing but a loincloth, it could be seen that his arms and legs were magnificently thewed and that his chest was like that of the god who held the heavens suspended above the earth on pillars. He paused and gave his limbs a luxurious stretch.

"I have decided to do no exercising until I have broken bread," he announced. His voice was curiously high and thin. It ascended suddenly in a screech of command. "Cephas! Cephas!"

The old man came running through the dirty linen curtains that screened the entrance to the kitchen. "Yes, Brother Sisinnes? What is it you wish?"

"Food," said the gladiator. "I am famished."

Cephas disappeared behind the curtains and returned in several minutes with the first dish, which he placed at the head of the table. It steamed deliciously, and Sisinnes the Unbeaten lost no time in applying himself to it. "Good, very good," he said, looking at the others, who had remained where they were. Basil had risen with a sharp appetite and he was preparing to take a seat at the other end of the table when the man Vardish laid a restraining hand on his shoulder.

"We do not sit down until the last dish is on the table," he explained. "It is a rule of the house."

"But," said Basil, motioning toward the gladiator, who was already deep in the dish, "he has started his meal."

The other man shook his head. "The rules never apply to Sisinnes."

Cephas, his face red with his exertions, ran back and forth, bringing in dish after dish. He grouped them around the first one. Sisinnes examined each as it arrived, tasted it, and either nodded his head in approval or grunted in criticism. Finally the array was complete and Cephas raised his voice to announce the fact.

"You may sit down," he said.

There was a rush to the table and a scramble to get seats as close to the head as possible. Sisinnes scowled at them. "Mind your manners," he grumbled. "This haste is unseemly." He suspended his eating long enough to begin passing the dishes to those closest to him, for none had dared to reach out a hand. He raised a platter of fish and looked at it. "There is one fine fat fellow here," he said. His eye went up and down the line. "I allot it to Vardish. He is looking even more puny than usual this morning."

"What of me?" cried one of the others. "I also am undernourished and in need of every scrap of food I can get."

"You?" snorted the gladiator. "You remain thin through sheer gluttony. I have been watching you and seeing what tremendous quantities of food you waste on that miserable body of yours. You will have nothing but a head or a tail this morning." He scowled at the spectacle of the many heads bent over plates. "You will bring ruin to my poor father by your gourmandizing."

Sitting at the far end, Basil did not understand any of this talk. He was not faring very well. The dishes were practically empty when they reached him. Cephas paused behind him to whisper: "Do not despair. A fine fish has been kept on the fire for you. You will have it out there. It will be hot, and the cook is making one of her best sauces for it."

The low conversation at the foot of the table drew the gladiator's attention to them. "Whispering?" he said. "Is it something you are keeping from me? And who is this underfed youth? Is he a night traveler, a bat who comes in the hours of darkness?" He indulged in another scowl. "Why is it that every traveler whose stomach has fallen in through starvation finds his way here?"

"The young man is from Antioch," explained Cephas. "His ship arrived last night."

Sisinnes studied Basil with a critical eye. "Is he a Greek?"

"Yes, Brother Sisinnes."

"I have fought a few Greeks in my time. They are graceful and fast on their feet, but I had no difficulty with any of them. I soon finish off these dancing masters. The spectators always turned their thumbs down on them, and so death it had to be. They like a man who goes in and fights it out, blow for blow." He was holding a huge slice of melon to his face, and nothing could be seen of him but his eyes. "Only once have I found it necessary to fight for my life. It was a hulking Goth who used a weapon he called a pike. He was as strong as a brass bull."

"Did you kill him?" asked one of the guests.

The gladiator shook his head. "He fought so stubbornly that they did not turn down their thumbs. But he never fought again. His injuries were too great. I heard not so long ago that he died." He reached out and pinioned the questing wrist of the man opposite him. "Keep your greedy hands off the grapes. I have not made my selection yet."

A few minutes later, his hands filled with fruit, the gladiator got to his feet and left the table. "Come now, the lot of you. There has been enough of this stuffing. You will all get up from the table."

The guests obeyed without a word of protest. The benches were shoved back as they got up, their eyes fixed longingly on the dishes where some scraps of food were left.

"I shall now get to work," announced Sisinnes the Unbeaten. "I must be in condition for next week. I am to fight a Scythian. He is a retiarius and fights with the net. I shall have to chase him all over the Arena. It will be the worse for him."

One of the guests had seemed more filled with curiosity than appetite. He had eaten very little, and when most of the guests trooped out to the yard to watch Sisinnes at his delayed exercises, this man engaged those who remained in whispered conversations. Basil saw that Hannibal had parted the linen curtains and was looking in, his face wearing an expression of unease.

"Who is it?" he asked Cephas in a whisper.

"He is asking questions," answered the old man. "They never stop. Always it is someone new who does the questioning, but always the questions are the same. He will be asking about our young man from Antioch."

Seated in the kitchen and eating with relish the fish that had been reserved for him, Basil was told that the low-voiced questioner was one of the men of Tigellinus, the head of the policing force that Nero was instituting. "They are getting the names of all the Christians in Rome," whispered Cephas. "We do not know what he means to do, this wicked young Emperor who has killed his evil mother and his wife. But this much we can be sure of: his plans are evil plans."

"What will he do about the Christians?" asked Basil.

Cephas had begun work on the scrubbing of the dishes. "The days of persecution are drawing nigh," he said. "We are sure that the hour will soon strike."

"Is that why Peter has come to Rome?"

The old man did not pause in his labors. "I think it is one of his reasons."

"It is a good thing that my son is here," said Hannibal, who was keeping pace with Cephas in his work, his thin and heavily veined hands moving ceaselessly. "It puts us above suspicion."

"But the questioners still come," said the old man.

3

Basil had decided to rest for the first day. He did not, however, join the others in the yard to watch the mighty Sisinnes at work. Instead he decided to satisfy the curiosity that had been roused in him by the position of Cephas in the household. During the first few hours he kept a close eye on the activities of the old man, noting how continuously he worked, and with what zest, as though he felt an urgency to serve. He slept, Basil discovered, under a metal lean-to at the rear of the house. His bundle of bedclothing, most scrupulously clean, had already been spread out in the sun. He seemed completely absorbed in the trivial but wearisome tasks that fell to his share and completely content in carrying them out. His face was serene, if not entirely happy; and only occasionally would he fall into a sort of reverie, when his gaze would become fixed on the sky or on the parched leaves of the lone tree in the yard and his thoughts would go to something far off.

Studying him at these odd moments when the old man allowed himself the privilege of dreaming, Basil realized that his face had an unusual quality. It was round, with a broad brow and eyes widely spaced, a somewhat aggressive nose, a strong mouth that reflected all his emotions openly.

The fingers of the young artist had been idle for weeks. It was time they were put to work, he decided, and accordingly he brought out his tools and clay and set himself the task of reproducing the features of the inn drudge. It had to be done with the benefit of no more than occasional glimpses of the subject, for the old man hurried from room to room on his broad bare feet and seemed unaware of what was being done.

It may have been that the face of Cephas lent itself particularly well to the purpose; it proved to be, at any rate, the easiest portrait Basil had ever attempted. The likeness came into the clay at once: the broad brow, the intent deep eyes, the big-boned nose that seemed to have suffered the flattening effect of a blow; above all, the air of resolution, the kindly forthrightness. In an hour the portrait had been completed. Instinct as well as training told its creator that anything more would be superfluous. An additional pressure of finger on clay would detract rather than add.

He carried it out to the kitchen, where Cephas was scrubbing the brick floor with decisive movements of his still strong arms. The old man straightened up with an effort, pressing one hand to his back in doing so. He stared at the clay model in bewilderment.

"Young man, who are you?" he asked. "To very few is such a gift as this given."

"Do you think it a likeness?"

Cephas smiled. "I have not inspected myself in a mirror in many years. But you have me; there can be no doubt of that. I am quite astounded. Is it to do work of this kind that you have come to Rome?"

Basil seated himself in a corner of the kitchen, which was shaded from the sun and so retained still some share of the coolness of the early morning. He placed the model on a corner of the table with the satisfaction an artist takes in praise.

"Have you ever heard of one Joseph of Arimathea?" he asked.

Cephas had gone back to his work. He nodded without looking up. "I have heard of him. The great merchant of Jerusalem."

"He is dead."

The busy hands stopped. For several moments Cephas remained in silence, a sudden sadness on his face and his strong frame showing a tendency to droop. "Joseph of Arimathea is dead!" he said in a whisper. "That splendid old man, that strong right arm of the true faith, that prop in times of stress and trouble! He was very old, but—he had come to seem immortal. Now that you have told me this distressing news, I realize that I have never considered the possibility of Joseph's death."

"There is something I must tell you that concerns him. It is a strange story and it is because of it that I have come to Rome." Basil paused. "Because Luke sent me here, and from things I have heard you say, I am sure you are a Christian. And perhaps Hannibal also. Do you want to tell me if this is so?"

The old man rose to his feet and seated himself at the table, facing Basil. "In Rome one no longer says openly and freely for all to hear, 'I am a Christian.' It might lead to punishment, perhaps to death. A Christian must not fear death, but one must be ready to live and work for the purposes of the Lord as well as die for them. It is wrong to rush blindly to martyrdom. It is for Him to decide when the service of living no longer suffices and the time has come to look into the face of the angel of death."

Through the open door of the kitchen they could hear the grunting of Sisinnes as he still continued with his muscular preparations for the bout ahead of him. Cephas leaned his head across the table and began to whisper. "I speak to you in full candor because you have come to us with the hand of Luke. If you need this assurance before telling anything more, then speak on. We are both Christians, Hannibal and I. There are no others in the house, nor is there any suspicion in the minds of those out there that we belong."

Basil, accordingly, told of Joseph's plan for the making of the Chalice and of his own part in it. The old man's manner changed as he listened. He seemed to lose the stoop of age, he held his head erect, his eyes became watchful and intent. Had Basil observed closely he would undoubtedly have seen that Cephas had taken on authority, but his interest was in the narration, and the only impression he gained was of the deep interest of his auditor.

At the finish of the story Cephas remained silent for several minutes, his eyes fixed on the clay model that stood at his side. It was a convincing proof that there was truth in the story he had heard.

Finally Cephas began to speak. "There has been among us much anxiety about the Cup and so there will be rejoicing when what you have told me becomes generally known." He nodded his head with an intensity of satisfaction. "Your story has brought me much happiness. How grateful we will all be to the good Joseph—and to you for the part you have played. But, my young friend, a word of warning: do not tell your story to anyone else. Keep it locked away. There would be danger for you in such a telling. This, however, I may say to you: at the proper time you will be taken to Peter. He is in Rome, and it is in his mind that he will finish his days here. But he has to be very careful and so he is seen little, and he also waits."

"I had hoped to return to Antioch quickly," said Basil. "I will have much work to do in finishing the Chalice. And my wife waits for me there."

Cephas smiled warmly. "A month, a week, a few days. Does it matter much? I have lived so many years that I have ceased to count the days as important. But with you, I see, it is different. You are young and impatient. You have a loving wife waiting your return. Every day to you is like a year. And so I shall use what influence I may have to make it possible for you to finish what you have come to Rome to do."

He had started to pace up and down the room. His plain brown tunic, which was ragged along the lower hem, had been drawn up above his knees to give his limbs more freedom of movement. He paused beside Basil at one point and said in a whisper that did not carry even to the open door: "You asked me a question and received the answer. Now I ask you the same. I think I know what you will say, else Luke would not have sent you here; but I should like to hear it from your own lips."

Basil had difficulty in finding a response that would convey the truest clue to the state of his mind. "I believe in Jesus," he said. "I believe Him to be the Son of the one and only God. I believe He will return to this earth and I hope His coming will not be long delayed. But because I do not share the ecstasy which these beliefs have brought to others, I think there must be a higher point of conviction that I have not reached."

Cephas nodded his head. "Sometime soon it will come. It may be that you will suffer a severe blow or that you will be called upon to make a sacrifice. In the strain of such a moment your eyes will be opened. The tinder in your heart will take fire. You will feel a great happiness gain possession of you. The world will light up and the sun will shine in all the dark places where before you saw nothing but shadows. You will cry out what you believe and you will want everyone to hear."

CHAPTER XXV

I

Below the Atrium Vestae, where the Via Nova swings in an arc to join the Via Sacra, there stood here and there, in odd corners, a few houses that had been left behind when the district ceased to be residential. They were crowded in between governmental buildings or they occupied irregular plots of ground created by the confusion of the streets. They had once been occupied by citizens of the first importance, but now they had ceased to be desirable in any way.

One of these survivals of a better era was a tall and narrow house with an entrance framed in marble that had become yellowed by time and blackened by the grime of years. This gloomy abode had been rented by Simon the Magician for the period of his stay in Rome and it suited his purposes well. Visitors could come and go without attracting any attention, because in all reason it would be assumed that official errands took them there. Ever since his first appearance before the Emperor Nero (which had been an amazing success, sending chills down every spine), these visitors had been coming, seeking assistance in matters of a devious nature and paying handsomely for such things as charms and love potions. Most of them were women who were carried to the neighborhood in covered chairs on the shoulders of sweating slaves and who glanced about them before emerging from behind the curtains and slipping in under the dirty marble lintel.

One morning the room on the ground floor that served as an office was occupied by an industrious Helena, who pored over a sheaf of documents and frowned at the difficulties they presented. She was startled when a hand was laid with the pressure of familiarity on her bare shoulder. Her face flushed when she found that it belonged to Idbash, the boldest of the three clerks who had served Kaukben in Jerusalem.

"Never do that again!" she said, shaking his hand off quickly. "Never. Do you understand?"

Idbash looked down at her with smoldering eyes. He had come up a long step in the world when Simon had decided that he would be useful to take along, having been promoted to the post of major-domo. It was a large establishment now in view of the magician's new prominence, and Idbash was fully conscious of his importance.

"You have allowed me greater privileges than touching your shoulder, my beautiful Helena," he said.

She regarded him with cold detachment. "Are you forgetting that you take orders from me?" she asked. "Remember this always: I have never allowed you a privilege of any kind."

Idbash said in a voice of the deepest intensity, "My beautiful Helena lies."

She was surprised to find that his face had become pale and that his very long and very thin nose was twitching violently. "The past is the past," she declared, as though saying so sponged out everything that had happened. "That is a lesson that quite apparently you must still learn. Clerks can be made into major-domos, but I remind you that major-domos can be changed back into clerks even more quickly."

"If I should go to Simon," said the young Samaritan, "it would not be to tell him of what there has been between us. No, no, my sweet and beautiful Helena, even a simple Samaritan can see far enough from the end of his nose to avoid any such mistake as that."

Her voice was deceptively low and free of feeling. "You have thought, then, of going to Simon?"

"Yes! By the rocks and falls of Ebal, yes! But when I do go, I will tell him other things. Perhaps I will tell him of the visits that have been paid by a certain great senator. Of the notes he has sent. Of the flowers and melons and sweetmeats. Of his even more substantial presents."

Helena laughed scornfully. "You have my permission, Long-ears, to tell your master anything you care about the great senator. You will not be telling him anything he does not already know."

"It must not be the senator, then," said Idbash, his beady eyes bristling with malice. "I might tell him instead of someone who is not rich or well known. A certain young officer in the Praetorian Guard, perhaps?"

Helena had continued to turn the documents over with a pretense of industry. At this point her hand stopped. "And now, Long-ears, it is you who lie."

"I speak the truth," said the major-domo with sudden roughness. "I have followed you. Three times I have followed you when you slipped out at night. I have hidden myself among the statues on the Forum Romanorum. I have seen him come out of the shadows to join you. Once I was standing behind the open door of the Temple of Janus when it happened. I have followed him to his barracks and so I know who he is. I have made inquiries and I know a great deal about him. I have made acquaintances among the servants of the Guards and I have been told many things. I could weave a pretty story about the lady who says I have never before laid a hand on her shoulder." The venom died out of his voice and he looked at her beseechingly. "I would die for you!"

Her anger conquered her. "You are a liar and a thief of reputations! You are a Samaritan! If you dare to speak to me again like this, or if you speak to anyone else, you will be sent back to your post behind that sign where the stones strike all day long."

She gathered up the documents and left the room without another glance at him.

Servants and porters passed her respectfully as she pursued her way to her own rooms on the floor above. The screech of saws and the clang of hammers came from the rear of the house, where carpenters were constructing an ingenious device with hidden wires; a most curious contraption, indeed, which Simon the Magician intended to employ soon in his efforts to shake belief in Christianity. An individual in a rumpled toga raised an unwashed arm carelessly in greeting to her and said in an off-hand tone, "Blackbirds roosting in a philosopher's hat." This salutation marked him as a member of the fraternity of magicians in Rome. He was, obviously, down on his luck and had been hired to act as one of the corps of assistants Simon would use in dazzling Rome; in the manipulation of invisible wires and whispering tubes and in creating interruptions at exactly the right moments.

Helena paid no attention to the greetings of these supernumeraries. She hurried to her bedroom and began to cool her burning face in the scented water spouting from a mechanical laver. She was thus engaged when a maidservant came to the door.

"A visitor for you, gentle lady," said the girl. She proceeded then to demonstrate the thoroughness of the training to which even the domestics were subjected in this unusual establishment. "He is young. Rather handsome. A Greek, I think. His robe is plain but of the best material. I suspect there is little money in his purse. He seems to be uneasy."

"You tell me everything but his name."

"I did not tell you his name, but he has not been truthful about it. He says he came to see you in Jerusalem and that his name is Alexander."

Helena dried her face quickly. "Take him to the small reception room off the *aula* downstairs. Do not offer him wine or refreshments. Tell him there will be some delay. But," with an admonitory frown, "do not let him go away."

The frenzied existence into which he had been plunged by his sudden great success had created curious moods in Simon the Magician. He was disposed to wander about in a kind of daze, his mind filled with triumphant speculations that he did not share with anyone. He had left the management of the household in Helena's capable hands. His interest was intermittent even in the work going on about the place. What made things still more difficult for Helena, who was doing most of the planning, was his tendency to drink.

There was a wine cup in his hand when she found him on the rooftop. He had placed a yellow robe inscribed with the words SIMON MAGUS over a comfortable couch and was reclining on it at his ease. She snatched the wine cup away with a furious gesture.

"Sit up and pay heed to what I say!" she cried fiercely. "What is more useless than a bird with a broken wing? I will tell you, my arbob of fools: a magician with an unsteady hand."

Simon was sufficiently mellowed by the wine to accept this reproof in an amiable mood. "Does it matter that my hand may become unsteady," he asked, "if my spirit waxes in resolution and a divine strength surges through my being?"

"You are drunk already," she said with disgust. "I have no time to deal with you now as you deserve. Gather your wits sufficiently to tell me if the potion is ready for the rich widow who was here yesterday."

"Ah, yes, the fat and oily widow from the provinces. The love potion is prepared. How much good will it do that waddling specimen of middle-aged folly?"

Helena made no response, being already halfway down the stairs to the floor below.

"She is in a vile mood, my *zadeeda*," said Simon aloud.

He got to his feet and walked unsteadily to the parapet. Here he stood for several minutes, looking up at the tall temples on the crest of the

Palatine Hill above him. He began to talk to himself in a mumbling torrent of words.

"Twenty thousand, fifty thousand, one hundred thousand. They are beginning to see, to believe in me. Soon I will have more followers than this meek Jesus. I am not meek! How Nero watched me! I could see out of one eye that he was frightened and fascinated. He talked to me so eagerly afterward. It was hard to answer his questions without giving too much away. He did not think all of them tricks. *That* I could see; he was sure I had magic powers and he was afraid of me. Perhaps he will write a song about me and sing it to the people."

He threw back his bony shoulders and stared about him triumphantly. His eyes wandered to the left of the Palatine crest where white parapets stood up above the fringe of trees. He raised a hand in salute.

"If you were alive today and could stand up there on the roof of your grand house, O Cicero," he cried, "we could exchange greetings! Two great men could wave one to the other. As it is, the great maker of magic, who is alive and reaching his peak of divinity, sends his salutations to you, who have been dead and moldering in your grave a hundred years, O Cicero, greatest of orators!"

He retraced his wavering steps to his couch. "I will convince them. I will hold them spellbound even as Cicero did. I will convince *her*. She laughs at me now, but I will prove to her that I have the same power as this man Jesus!"

2

When Helena entered the small reception room where Basil waited, she was attired once more in a straight and loose linen robe. Her feet were bare and her black hair fell freely over her shoulders. It had been brushed until it shone. She stood in the doorway for a moment and looked at him reproachfully.

"I know all about you," she said. "The story reached us at Ephesus. You are married. To the granddaughter of Joseph of Arimathea. I never expected to see you again. I was sure what had happened would change everything." Then she smiled, raising her eyes gravely to his. "But you have come after all. You haven't forgotten the promise you made that— that night when we had the Gymnasium all to ourselves but still whispered as low as though there were thousands of ears about us to listen. For that, Basil, I am very grateful."

She was more beautiful than before, he said to himself. Her eyes were soft and inviting. The severity of her garb did not succeed in concealing the enticing grace of her figure.

Uneasily he said: "I do not know what our permanent plans will be. At present we have a house in Antioch, and it may be that we will stay there."

She looked at him with instantly aroused interest. "In Antioch?" Her eyes became shrewdly reflective. After a moment she nodded her head. "After all, it was to be expected. Your wife's father was not likely to approve."

"We are in Antioch because Joseph had accumulated funds there for my wife's use."

Helena's eyes narrowed in speculation. "Her father must have been very angry. Simon, who knows him well, says he is the most grasping man in Jerusalem. Do I offend you by speaking so freely of your affairs?"

Basil denied any feeling of offense by a shake of his head. "I have seen little of Deborra's father. It is unlikely I shall ever see him again."

"Then it is as I thought." Helena's mind had gone busily to work. "Have you ever spoken of me to your wife?"

"I told her of meeting you in Jerusalem."

"Do you think that was wise?" She did not wait for an answer. "It is always the way. Men cannot keep anything from their wives. I am sure she was not pleased. Of this I am certain: you must not speak of coming to see me here."

"She wanted me to see you. She made me promise I would do so."

Helena looked surprised. "Your wife is wiser than most would have been. She is wiser than I expected."

She had seated herself near the one window in the room and had arranged the linen folds of her robe gracefully over her crossed knees. He could see her bare feet. They were small and white and shapely. She asked, "Does this mean you will give up your ambitions?"

"No, no!" cried Basil. "I am more determined than ever."

"I am glad you have no intention of living on your wife's bounty." Helena gave him the benefit of an open scrutiny. "I have already made some moves in the hope you would remember your promise. We have important connections at the imperial court. You see, Simon's appearance before Nero was a great success, and at this moment he is the most talked-of man in Rome." She paused and looked at him with a smile that said, How happy it will make me if I can be of help to you. "The Emperor has been told about you. If you still desire it, you can be taken to him." Basil hesitated and then shook his head. "I have every intention of striving for a career. But not by the favor of the Emperor. I have other matters to attend to while I am here, and there will not be time to seek favor at the court of Nero. Things press at home, at Antioch. My stay here must be a brief one."

"I was afraid of this." Helena sat in deep thought for several moments and then clapped her hands together. "I have been very thoughtless. You must have a cup of wine." She gave instructions to the maidservant who answered the summons. "As soon as you have quenched your thirst, I shall have more to say."

When the servant returned with a flagon that awakened memories in his mind, Helena insisted that he bring a chair and sit near her while he quaffed it. Her eyes had achieved a soft and dreamy look. "Is the wine to your taste?" she asked.

Basil, in a defensive mood, was thinking: "This will be a test. Will it have the same effect on me as that other time? Luke laughs at love potions and says it is the good or bad in one that counts. Well, now we shall see."

He took a deep draught. It was cool and refreshing and it sent a tingle through his veins. He kept his eyes fixed on his companion. Helena had turned and was gazing out of the window at the inner court, where many activities were in progress if they could judge by the sounds that reached them. Her profile seemed more delicate than he had remembered it to be. She brought her head back and leaned close toward him.

"You will make a great mistake if you let this chance slip. The Emperor is the vainest man in the world: If you did a model of him that he liked, he would shower you with favors."

She sat in silence for a moment, studying him closely. She was making it clear that her emotions had been stirred. Her eyes had acquired a suggestion of moisture and she was breathing hard. She reached out her hands to him impulsively.

"Basil! Are you not glad to see me? It makes me happy to sit here so close to you." Then she began to whisper. "Oh, I understand. I can see it has been made hard for you. You will forget your ambition. You will forget—me."

When he gave no indication of responding she allowed her hands to drop to her lap. Her eyes told him that his coldness had hurt her.

"The forgetfulness is starting, Basil. What else could I expect? But I wish you would believe me when I say I put your interests above everything. It is the truth. I want you to become a great man. Whether it is with my help or not does not matter. Basil, that much you must believe."

"I know your generosity. You have given me proof of it."

"You are not drinking your wine. Can you not wait long enough for that before rushing away on your other concerns?"

Basil raised the familiar flagon to his lips again. "It is good wine. I hope, Helena, that what I have said will not make you think me ungrateful."

There was a knock on the door, and then it swung in to reveal the tall figure of Idbash. He looked at them with an interest he made no effort to conceal.

"Clients are arriving," he said to Helena. "The widow from the provinces is here. A poet who needs some stimulation of his muse is coming. A senator is on his way; *the* senator, mistress. I can get no response from —from the one who sits on the rooftop. He waved me away angrily and said you would see them."

"They will not like it," declared Helena. "They want to see Simon himself. Our trade will fall off if he keeps this up."

"The senator will be pleased," commented Idbash with an ugly curl of the lips that was meant for a smile.

"I will attend to them. Get a cup of wine for the widow. Plain wine with a dash of some drug to make it taste strange. She will never know the difference."

When the long nose of Idbash had seemed to fold up and disappear and the door had closed on his narrow, arched back, Helena rose slowly to her feet. "You *must* return. It is so important. Where are you staying?"

"With an old man who keeps a sort of inn."

She asked in a tone that contained a trace of sharpness, "Are the people there Christians?" Not waiting for an answer, she went on: "Keep away from all of them! They are falling into the ill will of the Emperor. One of the reasons that Simon is in such high favor is because he is throwing doubts on the miracles of Jesus. This delights Nero. Basil, this is most important. It would not be safe for you to be associated with them in any way."

He rose to his feet, and they faced each other for a moment. A hurt look had come into her eyes. Then she yielded again to impulse and, taking one of his hands, pressed the palm of it against her face.

"The pretty little boy who came to the house of my master will not forget the poor little slave girl?" Her voice seemed choked with emotion.

"Oh, Basil, Basil, do not forget me! Do not put me out of your mind!"

She turned so suddenly then that the linen skirt twirled about her, allowing him a brief glimpse of white ankles. The door closed after her.

On leaving the room Helena sought Idbash. "That man I have left," she said in low and urgent tones. "Have him followed. I must know where he is living."

The young Samaritan's lips curled up in another unpleasant suggestion of a smile. Seeing his hesitation, she caught him by the sleeve.

"Listen to me, Long-ears!" she cried. "You will do as I say. I want you to send the most reliable man in the house. Attend to it at once unless you want me to have you driven out on the streets! You would not like it, my Idbash. The streets of Rome hold out no welcome to a man who has quarreled with his master."

3

After her departure from the room Basil lifted the flagon and drank the wine to the last drop. Then he began to laugh.

"Luke was right. To believe in love potions is an absurdity. I have finished this one and it has had no effect on me at all. She gave it to me with a purpose; I am certain of that, but I am equally certain that the purpose has failed. I shall never see her again and I have no regrets about it. I never want to see her."

He replaced the flagon and made his way to the door. "That other time it was my own evil instincts that made her attractive to me," he thought. "I must face the truth. There is evil in me and I allowed it to come out. But thanks to the wisdom of my wife, I am now cured of that particular evil."

He left the busy house of Simon on jubilant feet. He was happy, so very happy over the discovery he had made that he wanted to shout out to the world about it. He had come to the realization that he was in love with his wife!

"How could I have been so blind?" he demanded of himself with a feeling of chagrin for what now seemed to him a monumental lack of discernment. "My Deborra is sweet and loyal and brave. Each time I saw her I grew more conscious of her loveliness. But I allowed myself to look at someone else. I allowed this other one to stay in my mind and so I could not enter with a whole heart into my marriage with Deborra." He stood still and looked up earnestly at the blue sky above him. "I thank Thee, O Lord, that my eyes have been opened at last."

It was a beautiful day. A touch of fall was in the air, and he stepped out briskly, conscious of a new sense of well-being as well as jubilation over the change that had come about inside himself. How wonderful it would be, he thought, if Deborra were here with him! They would join hands, perhaps, as they had done that day when she threw the stone at the Roman soldiers and they had raced for their lives through the Valley of the Cheesemakers. He wished so much to have her with him for his first clear look at the great city of the Caesars that it was like a physical pain.

"How wise you were, my Deborra," he said aloud. People passing in the street turned to stare at him. A solid citizen, wearing his toga with an air of importance, stopped and said in a bitter voice: "These crazy foreigners! Our great city is filled with them. It is being ruined."

Basil continued his train of thought, but he was careful to keep it to himself. "My sweet and wise Deborra asked me to see Helena with new eyes," he thought. "I have done so, and she has become a shadow of the past. But that is not all. I am seeing everything with new eyes. Myself, my future, my work. And Rome! I am able to look at this city and see things that were hidden from me before. The whole world is new and the life we shall live in it, my wife and I, will be full of happiness and, I hope, achievement. And all this comes to me as I make use of these new eyes.

"But most of all I see you, my Deborra, with new eyes. I see your fine white brow; your own eyes, which are so understanding and so very bright and lovely; your mouth, which I have kissed once, and once only, and that a fleeting one that we allowed ourselves to please an old prince from Seen. I shall hurry back to you on feet burning with impatience, my wife, and I shall spend the rest of my life making up to you for my blindness in the past!"

He had reached the entrance to the Forum Romanorum. It was filled with people and pulsing with the continuous drama that the life of Rome generated. He came to a stop and said to himself, "I don't care if they think I am mad. I cannot keep all this inside myself any longer." Raising his voice, he shouted, "Deborra, I love you, I love you, I love you!"

CHAPTER XXVI

I

BASIL WAS USHERED into an anteroom that had something of the appearance of a temple because of its high ceiling supported on pillars of the darkest variety of tufa. What caught his eye at once, however, was a display of shields propped at intervals along the walls. They were uniform in size, but each one was painted a different color. Despite the resplendent newness of them, they looked what they were: war shields for legion soldiers to carry into battle, being very long and obviously of great strength and weight.

A bald-headed man with a parrot nose and a hint of the rodent in his eyes planted himself flat-footed in the path of the visitor.

"What do you come for?" he demanded. "To ask a favor?"

Basil nodded his head. "I come to ask a favor of Christopher who is called Kester of Zanthus. He has granted me a hearing at this hour."

"I granted you the hearing, young man," said the assistant. "I granted it on my own authority, which is considerable, I may tell you. You see me here with a pen in my hand, but if you think I am a mere clerk you are wrong. As wrong as Pompey. But now I must tell you this: seeing that you ask favors, you may as well turn on your heels and walk out again."

"But——"

The assistant interrupted him with a wave of his hand. "I am as hard as these shields," he said with an air of satisfaction. "It is my inclination always to refuse things, to say no to callers, to knock down rather than to help up. But compared to the man in there"—he motioned over his shoulder with his thumb in the direction of an inner door—"I am as soft as pulp, I am a weak giver-in, I am a fair mark for beggars."

"But," said Basil in a tone of distress, "but, surely, I am to be allowed to state my request."

The clerk considered the point with a judicial squint. "Well," he said finally, "I will go this far. I will ask the man in there."

He left the room, closing the inside door after him. On his almost immediate return, he gave his knobby head a reluctant bob of assent. "You are to go in when he calls. But I must give you warning. The man in there is in a very bad humor. He will be short and ugly with you. Do not expect anything else."

Basil had employed the interval by examining the shields and had made a discovery that puzzled him. He looked inquiringly at the assistant. "May I ask a question?"

"I do not promise to answer it. No information can be given out about army supplies."

"I have noticed that each shield in the room has a name painted on it, a different name for each one. I cannot help wondering why."

The assistant's eyes began to glow with mingled feelings of importance and gratification. Although there was no one else in the long high room, and no echo of footsteps from the stone-flagged hall, he glanced about him with an extravagant air of caution. Then he put the tip of a forefinger to his lips and winked at Basil.

"The man in there thought of it," he whispered. "It was given out that new shields were needed for the legions in Britain after the terrible time they had fighting those painted barbarians and the wild women who dressed themselves in black and fought harder than the men. Contractors buzzed about these buildings like flies. He"—motioning again with his thumb—"sat in there alone for two days and thought about it. No one was allowed to see him. He roared at me with rage if I put my head inside the door. And then"—the clerk's eyes began to gleam—"he came forth with an idea. Young man, it was nothing short of genius. He said to the government buyers, 'What you must do is make these new shields a means of adding to the pride of the troops.'"

Basil looked his surprise. "I thought that Roman soldiers were superior in every way to all others."

The bald-headed man shook an accusatory finger in his face. "They are! Make no mistake about that. But do you know that they are always fighting against odds? That they are always outnumbered? It is the rule to have no more than two legions in any one theater of war. Twelve thousand men, and sometimes they face armies of one hundred thousand.

They have to be the greatest soldiers in the world, but also they must have confidence in themselves. Is that clear to you?"

"You have made it very clear."

The assistant nodded his head several times. "The man in there came forth with two ideas, in fact. The first was that the shields should be given a more rounded form so that loaded javelins could be carried in the hollow. Do you know about this new loaded javelin? No, I was certain you would not know. Well, they were first tried in the Illyricum campaigns and were so successful that it was decided to make them stock equipment. They weigh ten pounds and are sure death to an opponent at any distance within thirty yards. Five of them can be carried in the hollow of these new shields.

"But," he went on excitedly, "his second idea was even better. Build up the pride of the individual soldier by having a different color for each company of a hundred and have the name of each man printed on the shield he will carry."

"A remarkable idea indeed."

Basil's tone had carried enough sincerity to satisfy the pride of the assistant. The forefinger the latter speared at the visitor expressed triumph. "The result of these ideas hatched in the mind of the man in there," he cried, "was that we received the whole order. Twelve thousand shields to be delivered within three months. The colors have already been selected for each century. One hundred and twenty different shades, think of that! The names are to be lettered as fast as the lists can be sent to us. More orders will come to us later because they are bound to want the same results in all the theaters of war."

"Send him in," called a deep and reverberating voice from behind the inner door.

2

The owner of the deep and reverberating voice proved to be a man of no particular size at all, except for his head, which was very large. If the head of Kester of Zanthus had been used as a boulder and shot out from one of the siege machines that he had on occasion sold for use by Roman armies, it would, without any doubt, have made a crack in any wall. It was, moreover, equipped with a broad and intelligent brow and it was surrounded with a thatch of reddish hair peppered with gray. On one side of the table behind which he sat was a platter with broken bits of bread and meat, on the other side a huge charger with every kind of fruit.

"Who are you?" he demanded in a tone that suggested the rumble of an approaching storm.

"My name is Basil, son of the deceased Ignatius of Antioch."

"Basil, son of Ignatius," repeated the contractor. "Ignatius was once my best friend. I was a witness at your adoption, young man. But wait a moment; there was a story I heard about that." He paused and then burst out with a roar like a beating of cymbals and drums. "That sniveling, slavering Hiram of Silenus, for whom I never had anything but contempt, lied about your adoption in court after Ignatius died. His testimony was accepted by a magistrate of the same base caliber, and you were denied your rightful inheritance."

Basil nodded to confirm this. "I was declared a slave and sold to a silversmith."

"That, too, I heard. I intended to take some action at the time. But"—his voice died down to a low bass mutter, as though the storm were receding—"I was very busy and it happened so far away. The result was that I did nothing. And so you are the young man who was treated so badly."

"Yes, worthy Christopher. My freedom was purchased three months ago and I have been reinstated as a citizen. My freedom I owed to Joseph of Arimathea, and I am now married to his granddaughter."

A look of keen interest had taken possession of the face of Kester of Zanthus. His burdensomely large head gave a nod. "It is gratifying to learn that your fortunes have taken a turn for the better. You have come to me, perhaps, with the thought of getting evidence for a new hearing?"

"That is my purpose in coming."

The triangular-shaped eyes of the contractor studied him still more intently. After several moments of this he suddenly threw back his head and cried out "Maximus! Maximus! I know you are listening with your ear to the door. Come in at once, Pry-eye. I have need of you."

When the bald-headed man obeyed the summons by coming in breathlessly as testimony to his haste, the contractor instructed him to get parchment and pen.

"Set down what I am going to say," he ordered. "I shall want four copies. One for myself. One for this youth. One to be sent to the military commander in Antioch, who is a very close friend of mine. The fourth is to be for use here in Rome. Perhaps to be laid before the Senate. Are you ready?

"I was one of five witnesses [dictated Kester of Zanthus] when Ignatius of Antioch purchased the son of Theron, a seller of pens, and adopted him as his son. The ceremony was carried out in accordance with the regulations as set forth in the Twelve Tables. Three times, in a clearly audible voice, the man Theron announced his willingness to sell his son. He did it with dignity and with such regret as might be expected; for a man who sells his son for adoption publicly proclaims that he himself has been a failure. The scales of brass were struck three times by the ingot of lead, wielded by one of the other witnesses, Hiram of Silenus by name. When the scales had been struck for the third time, Ignatius declared in the hearing of all that he accepted the boy as his son and his heir and that he would name him Basil after his own father. He gave us each a buckle of silver with five points and his own name and the boy's inscribed on the back, as has become usual in adoptions. I am wearing my buckle as I set this down.

"We then shared in a magnificent meal of five courses and drank of the five finest wines. There was much talk of the intentions of Ignatius for his new son. Ignatius said that he did not desire his son to follow him in his trading. He desired instead that the boy should devote himself to his great talent. Theron, who impressed me as a man of fine feelings, talked wisely and well, but at the end wept into his wine cup because he would never see his son again.

"I give these details to demonstrate how full and clear is my recollection of the events of the day. It has been brought to my attention that, after the death of Ignatius, his sole surviving brother brought suit, claiming that the boy had been sold to Ignatius as a slave. The only witness who survives besides myself, the afore-mentioned Hiram, swore at the hearing that the ceremony had not been one of adoption. Against this perjured evidence I set forth my own testimony and hereby declare Hiram of Silenus to have deliberately perverted the truth.

"To all whom this concerns, Greetings."

When the bald-headed man had withdrawn to make the copies of the statement, Kester of Zanthus interested himself in the food in front of him, helping himself to a luscious pear.

"You were not at your own ceremony of adoption," he remarked. "Nothing was said about it at the time, but I wondered."

"I ran away," explained Basil. "I loved my real father and did not want to leave him, even to become the son of a rich man. Of course I soon came to love my adopted father also."

"It does you credit," declared Kester, engulfing the pulpy side of the pear with one bite. "Your real father was a man of intelligence. It was not his fault that the selling of pens was such an unrewarding occupation. Where did you go when you ran away?"

"I went to the waterfront and hid myself in a warehouse cellar under a pile of coal."

"I think," said the contractor, "that under the circumstances I might have done the same."

3

Basil returned to Subura in a mood of great jubilation. His copy of the statement crackled under his tunic, and this was all the assurance he needed that he would soon be restored to his proper station in life. His head was packed with rosy-tinted dreams. He would persuade Deborra to move to the white palace on the Colonnade where he had been raised. He would summon back Chimham and make a place for him, a post befitting so able a trader and the husband of so many wives. He might form an alliance of some kind with Adam ben Asher.

"How pleased Deborra will be!" he thought. "I will no longer be an ex-slave. It will be legally established that I never was a slave. Not"—with an affectionate smile—"that she ever showed any concern about my standing."

After he had passed through the confusion and noise and stenches of Subura and had turned into the winding road that led up toward the inn, he became aware that Cephas was climbing the steep grade ahead of him, leaning on the arm of a younger man than himself.

Cephas had not been seen about the inn for two days. When Basil had asked Old Hannibal about him the latter had been, he thought, somewhat evasive. "He comes. He goes. He is not here now."

"You say he goes. Where does he go? I do not understand this."

The proprietor had seemed very much disturbed at being thus pressed for information. "Do you not see that there is always danger?" he asked. "There has been another man here. Asking questions. Looking around. It seems that even we are under suspicion now and we thought we would be free of it. Steps must be taken because it is the same all over the city. The Christians know that danger hangs over them." His wrinkled face reflected a state almost of panic. "This I may tell you. Cephas should not have gone away at this time because it is best for those who ask questions to think he is here all the time. But he felt it his duty." His eyes met Basil's and he nodded vigorously. "You do not know what a wonderful man he is. He wants to serve those about him. Sometimes I have risen before dawn and found him sleeping against the wall, and in his bed someone who had come asking for shelter. Half of the time he gives his food to beggars and goes without himself. He says he does not need food. Whenever he goes away I am filled with fear because sometime he will go away and not come back." The proprietor looked about him anxiously to be sure that no one was within hearing distance. "Cephas is not what he seems. That much I may tell you. He is here for—a purpose. I do not like to see him work so hard, but he insists. He likes to serve; and also he believes that he should play his part here naturally."

Basil hurried his steps and came abreast of Cephas and his companion. "I have just seen my missing witness," he said. "It was a most satisfactory talk I had with him."

Cephas knew enough of his story to understand what he meant. He stopped and smiled. "That is good, my son. You will tell me about it later." He turned to his companion. "Mark," he said, "this is the artist from Antioch of whom I have spoken. He is the one who took a lump of clay and in an hour turned it into such a likeness of old Cephas that you might have expected it to open its mouth and speak in the dialect of the Galilee."

Basil's interest had been aroused by the mention of the stranger's name. "Mark!" he said to himself. "This must be the Mark I have already put into the Chalice." Luke had given him a description that had seemed adequate.

The companion of Cephas was a short and powerfully built man of middle years, and there was about him a distinct hint of rusticity. This may have been due to the roundness of his head and face and the shortness of his creased and pugnacious nose. He walked with a slight stoop of the back, and one shoulder was so much higher than the other that Basil recalled something he had been told by Luke, that Mark had been a water carrier.

Basil said to himself, "There can be no mistake. Now that I see him I can tell what a discerning report of him I had from Luke. But there are things I must change. His face is shorter than I made it, and I gave his beard too much length. I got his nose perfectly, but the eyes, no. I must give him that slight droop of the lid. It is a good face; I could make it from memory."

"I sometimes speak of Mark as my son," said Cephas. "He has been with me much of recent years and I have found him a sturdy staff on which to lean."

When they reached the *insula* Cephas bade farewell to Mark with an affectionate warmth. "God go with you, my son. We shall see each other again soon."

After the old man had vanished within, Mark turned a troubled pair of eyes on Basil. It was clear that he felt some apprehension about Cephas and that he wanted to speak of it. If such had been his intention, however, he changed his mind. Giving his peasant-like head a nod that seemed abrupt and almost unfriendly, he turned on his heel and walked briskly down the hill. Basil recalled what Luke had told him of Mark. "He is much as Peter was in his younger years, a fighter with the heart of a lion. But he lacks Peter's affability and great ease in winning the good will of men."

As he turned to follow Cephas inside, Basil found himself wondering about the old man. "He is regarded as a leader. That much is clear enough. Can it be that he is Peter?" He pondered this possibility but finally dismissed it with a shake of the head. "Why would Peter, who is the recognized leader of the Christians and the vicar of Jesus, be staying in this poor inn? Why would he be acting as servant to travelers who come and go? No, it cannot be Peter." He gave his head another shake. "I promised not to ask questions. But I would like to learn more of this strange old man."

The atmosphere inside the lodginghouse carried a slight note of strain when he entered. Sisinnes, eating an enormous supper, was in a grumbling mood.

"We are headed for more wars," he declared, laying a slice of warm meat dripping with juice on a piece of bread and crunching it in his strong white teeth. "It will be very upsetting. I am against wars. My opinion is this: let us confine our fighting to its proper place, the Arena."

The guests had gathered closely around him. "But, Sisinnes," said one of them, "the might and power of Rome are based on war. We must go on extending. There are still a few bits of the world that do not belong to us."

"Leave them alone!" growled the gladiator. "What happens when we conquer a new country? We bring back more captives. Droves of them. Great hulking beasts with no brains in their heads. We make gladiators out of them. There will be so many of them that the arenas will be glutted."

He cut himself another slice of meat with as much heat as though it were the throat of an imported gladiator.

"What makes it worse," he declared, nearly emptying his tankard, "is that these captives are always adept at some strange and barbaric kind of fighting. They fight with spears or slings or they take to the *jaculum* and fight with stinking fish nets. Some of them will be used for chariot fighting, which"—he looked about the circle of his listeners with mounting heat—"is fit only for such mad savages."

"But the spectators clamor for chariot fighting," interjected one of the guests.

"Spectators!" Sisinnes spoke with heavy scorn. "Spectators have no rights and should hold no opinions. We hate them, these greedy beasts clamoring for blood and turning their thumbs down for brave fellows to be killed."

"If there were no spectators, there would be no bouts," commented the man Vardish.

Sisinnes immediately changed his front. "They have their place. I do not deny that."

Basil had no appetite. He drank a cup of wine, and then another, without feeling any effect. He rose from the table and strolled out to the street. There was a hint of clouds back of the Pincian Hill.

"Father," he said, looking up at the sun, which was sinking behind the Palatine, and at the western sky, which was still shot with streaks of lavender and red, "are you up there and can you still hear me? Do you know what has happened today? I have the statement of Kester of Zanthus and I am going back to Antioch with it at once. It should set things right for both of us. I hope you are listening, Father, and that my news has brought ease of mind to you."

Yes, he said to himself, he must find Peter as quickly as possible and then start on his return journey. "Deborra, Deborra!" he thought. "Have you any idea of how well things have gone for me? Have you any way of knowing what is in my mind this minute? Do you know how much I have come to love you?"

A man in a purple livery came toiling up the slope, followed by two soldiers with the plumed helmets and bright scarves of the Praetorian Guard. They stopped in front of the inn.

"I seek one Basil," said the official in the imperial trappings. "He is a worker in gold and silver who comes from Antioch."

"I am the one you seek."

The official looked him over carefully. "You answer to the description. You are to come with me. Your presence is required in the palace of the Emperor."

Basil was both surprised and alarmed. How could his presence in Rome have become known to the officers of the court, and why should he be summoned there? Was Kester of Zanthus responsible? That seemed highly improbable because he had left the contractor no more than a few hours before. It must be due, he decided, to the efforts of Helena.

Perceiving his hesitation, the imperial messenger said in a reproving tone: "Caesar does not invite. He commands. You are to come with me at once."

"I will need to change my attire."

"Be speedy about it. You are to bring your belongings with you." The officer looked about him with the same distaste Crassus had shown. "*Faugh!* I have no desire to stay longer than is necessary."

When Basil re-entered the inn, the opening of the door gave Sisinnes a glimpse of the uniforms outside. He sallied out to investigate. The court officer's attitude changed at once. He approached the gladiator with deference.

"I have made wagers on you often," he said. "And I have always won."

"Naturally," said Sisinnes. He glanced at the two young guards with an eye of scorn that said, How I would enjoy getting these monkeys in the death enclosure with me! "My next appearance may be my last. I wish to retire without a defeat, but also I have no stomach for what is being done nowadays. Soon they will be sending boys with slingshots into the Arena, and cooks with sharp spits, and miserable little apothecaries who will fight by throwing acids in the eyes of proper fighters. I like the old ways."

Basil gathered his few clothes and his tools. He carried the clay models of John and Cephas to the kitchen and confided them to the care of the latter. The old man looked startled when told what had happened.

"There is no way of knowing the reason for this summons," he said. "It is clear that Nero has become interested in you. Always remember this, even if you bask in the imperial favor: Nero is as changeable as the weather. The thunderbolts of his wrath fall out of a cloudless sky. If you ever find yourself in need of help, bear in mind that there are many Christians at the court. They will be ready to help you."

"How would I know who they are?"

Cephas gave the matter some thought and then mentioned the name of Selech. "He is the head cook and a man of very great influence. He is an imaginative man as well as a brave one. Seek him out as soon as you reach the palace. Tell him of the Cup if you think it advisable. Say to him, 'Cephas says, "Peace be with you today, for tomorrow the storm cometh."' You will find him a bold and a true friend and always ready to risk his own head for one who is in trouble."

CHAPTER XXVII

I

THERE WERE CHARIOTS waiting at the foot of the slope. Basil took his stand in one of them, his blue cloth bag over one shoulder, his bundle of belongings at his feet. They set off with much cracking of whips and loud hallooing to the horses and they cut across Subura like cleavers through moldy cheese. The wheels creaked and groaned, the sparks flew. Dogs raced after them, barking madly, and the populace scattered as they went clattering by. They skirted the base of the Capitoline Hill and slowed down to a more sedate pace when the sprawling palace of the Caesars showed above them, a glitter of lights in the darkness of the evening.

A cohort of the Praetorian Guard was marching down the road ahead of them, destined for the Palatium to take over the duty of protecting the ruler of the world. The chariots were brought to a halt, for the Guard must never be interfered with, and no attempt was made to approach the entrance until the last of the imperial soldiers had disappeared within. Then they drove with due decorum up the steep slope of the winding road.

They came to a halt under a marble portico, and Basil was both astonished and horrified to find that the attendants who stood on duty there were attached by chains to the stone walls. A brisk young man appeared on the scene. He studied Basil closely and then accorded him a welcoming wave of the hand.

"I have instructions to look after you and convey to you the orders of Caesar. It is because I speak Greek that I have been selected. My name is Q. Septimus Rullianus. Do I not speak your language well?"

"I am better acquainted with Koine than the classic tongue," said Basil.

"So am I." The court official, who had spoken in halting classroom Greek, lapsed into the common tongue with relief. "We shall get along well. Now for the orders. First you are to be shown to your room, and then I am to take you where the whole court sits in worshipful adoration at the feet of Caesar. You will not be called to his attention. You are to sit within close range of his almost blinding magnificence and you are to make a model of him, head and shoulders only, in clay. If what you do pleases him, you will be summoned into the Presence later. If not, I expect you will be required to slink away into the darkness, unnoticed, unrewarded, unsung. It is reasonable, is it not? Caesar cannot waste time on mediocrity."

"It is both reasonable and fair. Do I begin tonight?"

"You begin tonight. It is an impatient Caesar under whom we sit." The curious eyes of the young official took in the details of his attire. "My advice is to go just as you are. Your garb is unobtrusive and will make it easy for you to escape notice in this apiary of gay-plumaged birds."

They had been proceeding through lofty halls tenanted by busy people. Now they turned into the fainter illumination of a wing of the palace. A mustiness was easily to be detected on the air. The walls were discolored, the hangings were in tatters, the scanty furnishings were decrepit and unashamedly shabby.

The friendliness of Q. Septimus Rullianus had been genuine enough to make Basil feel at ease with him. "It has been suggested to me," he said, "that I make the acquaintance of Selech. Would you take me to see him?"

"Those who made that suggestion were people of discernment," declared the court officer. "Selech is one of the great personalities of the court. For the fact that I am an inch thicker around my belly than when I came, I give him my respectful thanks. He is Greek, as you perhaps know."

Basil shook his head. "I know nothing at all about him."

"I have forgotten his real name, but I know why he decided to call himself Selech when he was put in charge of the tables of Caesar. I shall tell you the story."

They had reached the room that had been assigned to the newcomer. It was small and it was quite shabby. The bed had broken down at some stage and had been propped up with blocks of wood. The curtains at the one window were in holes and had been made of flimsy material in the first place and in tawdry colors. The court officer waved an apologetic hand as they stood in the doorway and surveyed this poor domain. "The palace of the Caesars is a filthy old barracks," he said. "When Agrippina decided to make her son Nero an emperor, the first thing she did was to make people think she was economical. She was the wife, the second wife, of her own uncle, the Emperor Claudius, and she would not let anything be spent on the palace. All Rome marveled and said, 'What a splendid empress is this!' She won the succession for Nero by shoving aside the Emperor's own son after serving a dish of mushrooms to old Claudius. Mushrooms, my new friend, have never been served in the palace since, and you will be wise never to use the word. The great Nero has an understandable dislike for it. Now that Agrippina is dead and Caesar has his beloved Poppaea as his empress, the palace will be overhauled one of these days. They have plans between them. I think they would like to get rid of this drafty old ruin and start all over again. Have you seen the Empress?"

Basil shook his head. The court officer pursed his lips while seeking words that might do justice to her. "Have you ever studied the lovely pinkish red of a peach that has ripened on a marble wall and has become soft and warm to the touch? That is Poppaea." He returned then to his starting point. "About Selech. What I am going to say will probably offend you. Take all the great men of Greece, Solon, Pericles, Phidias, Socrates, Demosthenes. Roll them all into one, add all their reputations together, and the total will fall a long way short of the greatness of the original Selech. Hail, Selech, greatest of human benefactors!"

"I think you are making fun of me," said Basil. "Who was this man you praise with so much exaggeration?"

"The original Selech was a Phoenician and probably a cook. He was a man of no known attainments and certainly of no fame. But one day this humble maker of soups and baker of meats placed some salt on the tip of his tongue and said to himself, 'Would it not be a good idea to put salt into all foods that are being prepared?' He tried it and knew at once that he had stumbled on a great discovery. All cooked foods had been flat and insipid on the tongue, but from that time forward man began to enjoy his food. The secret of seasoning had been revealed. It was, therefore, entirely fitting that this man should assume the name of Selech when elevated to the post of head cook in the palace of the Caesars."

Septimus waggled a thumb over his shoulder, and the servant who had carried Basil's scanty belongings to the room turned on his heel and left. The young Roman motioned Basil to follow him to the window.

"There is time for a talk," he said in a confidential tone. "I want to give you some advice before you become embroiled in this madhouse that is called the court of Nero. It is not only your chance for success that is at stake but perhaps your life as well. I am young, but I have kept my eyes and ears open. I am rather shrewd. I am shrewd enough for this: I shall never try to climb while Nero is Emperor. It is too dangerous. It is safer to bide one's time. Nero will not live long; a quick ending to this madness is written in the stars. Perhaps under the man who succeeds him there will be opportunities to get ahead without putting your head in jeopardy."

They seated themselves on chairs before the window. It was a sultry evening, and the young Roman wriggled his limbs free of the folds of his outer garments and gave a sigh of gratification. The moon had not yet appeared, and the palace gardens were wrapped in blackness. Bats swirled and circled on silent wings, and the sounds of cautious wild life in the thickets reached their ears.

"This is the situation," began the young Roman. "There are two parties bitterly opposed to each other, each bent on ousting and extinguishing the other. The first is the party of Tigellinus, who was once nothing but a riding master but is now captain of the Praetorian Guard and the director of police. Tigellinus is no more complex than a butcher's thumb. He is a toady and a killer combined. He tells Nero that he is a god, that everything he does is right and perfect. Tigellinus knows only one way to succeed, to kill off competition. He lies about them first and weaves webs of false evidence about them. He strikes suddenly and ferociously. He is a stabber in the back, a worker in darkness, a foul and angry bird of prey.

"The other lot," went on Septimus, stretching out his legs in the rare luxury of coolness, "are a party of sophisticates headed by one Petronius. They are men and women of refinement. Their minds are subtle. They approach Nero from the other extreme. They do not praise everything he does; in fact, they are more likely to criticize him. They tell him he possesses genius but has not yet reached his full power of creation. When they do praise him, they use such engaging reasons and speak with so much discernment that Caesar appreciates it more than the fulsomeness of Tigellinus. He expands with gratification and prances with joy, like a faun who has been patted on the back by a visiting god. This is very clever. So far, it seems, they have had the better of it."

"Has the Emperor any real gift?" asked Basil.

Septimus nodded his head emphatically. "Actually he *has* a touch of genius in him. It is not great and it is hidden away in the rock of his follies like a precious stone in a matrix. But it is there. He is a strange combination. He's interested in nothing but art. The details of administration drive him into screaming fits. But," he added, "another word about the party of Petronius. They do not believe in force as a weapon. They would not use a dagger from behind, but they are not above dropping poison in a wine cup. But they prefer to kill with ridicule, to triumph with their minds rather than their muscles.

"Tigellinus will win in the end. His is the elementary method. Brute force will always prevail over finesse. But the struggle will be a long one. My advice to you, Basil of Antioch, is this: have none of either party. Plow a straight and narrow furrow. Speak to these others as little as possible. Form your own opinions but do not be free in expressing them. You may succeed that way. Certainly you will live longer."

"To what do I owe my summons here?" asked Basil.

"I know the whole story," answered Septimus with a self-satisfied wag of the head. "You owe it to a lady. A lady with beautiful, melting eyes and a straight slim back. In other words, to the mysterious Helena who assists Simon the Magician so beguilingly."

"That is what I suspected."

"She has the ear of a man rather high in the Senate. It was not the best way to reach the favor of Caesar, because he is disposed to look on politics with scorn. But this particular senator is sufficiently loudmouthed to make himself felt. He it was who called the imperial attention to the fact that a promising sculptor had arrived in Rome. Nero listened to him with as much, perhaps, as one half of an ear and decided to give you a trial. A somewhat grudging trial, as you realize. It is because he thinks so ill of politicians that you have been sent to this wing of the palace, the most dilapidated part of the whole shabby establishment. Perhaps it is just as well, however. You don't belong to either party, and so they may leave you alone."

"You speak," said Basil admiringly, "with all the wisdom of a senator yourself."

"I concede that I am clever. I was born to be a politician and a courtier. My chance to climb will come someday, but I prefer to wait until the odds of survival are healthier."

The young Roman leaned forward and pointed into the shadows of the garden. "Do you see a glimmer down there? A suggestion of light striking on water?"

Basil looked in the direction indicated and nodded his head. "I see it." "It is a swimming pool. A small and most exclusive one. It is dedicated, in fact, to the rounded thighs and dimpled hips of one bather only, the lovely Poppaea herself. It is not easy to locate, being well screened with trees and shrubs, but it can be identified by a semicircle of statues on high pedestals that surround it. I point this out to you, not with the idea that you should penetrate into this most sacred spot, but because the pool is the starting point of a long row of trees. Follow the trees and you come to a strategic part of the palace wall. Here the water conduit enters the grounds, and by some fault of engineering, which I chanced to discover one day, the pipe has been sinking and the earth with it. There is now a hole under the wall, one just large enough for a man to crawl through. As far as I know, I am the sole possessor of this valuable piece of information, because the wall at that point is well screened with underbrush.

"Sometime, my young friend," he went on, "go out there and find the hole under the wall yourself. It may be a very handy thing to know. If you should climb into the favor of Caesar and then tumble out of it, it would be useful to know of a way of escaping quickly."

"Is it impossible to remain permanently in the favor of the Emperor?"

"As unlikely as to see the sun cross the skies twice in one day. Nero, you see, is mad. His is the most dangerous form of madness; he always turns and destroys the things he has valued most highly. He is like a wild boar, striking first at those nearest him. If you should happen to be near him when he gets into one of his butchering sprees, get out of the palace quickly. Get out at the first hint of red in the imperial eye and the first weaving and clashing of the tusks, and run as fast as your legs will carry you to the hole in the wall."

Basil turned over in his mind this advice, which his new friend had given him so freely and generously. He realized that he had listened to an honest picture of conditions at court and that he would be wise to remember every word that had been said.

"If I come through this ordeal with a whole skin," he said, "I shall have you to thank for it."

"We must be good friends," declared the young Roman. "I like you. I admired the cut of your jib at the first glance and I said.to myself, 'Here is a fellow after your own heart, Q. Septimus Rullianus. He must not be allowed to go blindly to his ruin for lack of a word from you to set him right.' Yes, that is what I thought and that is why I have done so much frank talking to a stranger. I knew right away that I could depend on your discretion. And now"—getting to his feet—"there will be just enough time to pay a visit to the great Selech. I think you will find it interesting to see an imperial banquet in the making. I myself find it more edifying to watch the cook who prepares the wonderful dishes than the gluttons who consume them."

2

"The moment has arrived to test the new brewing of garum," announced Selech, the Archimagirus of the imperial household. He looked down at Demetrius, the Obsonator, who sat on a platform several feet below him. "Will you have them bring in the cask? I confess, Demetrius, that I am anxious about it. It is an experiment this time."

The Obsonator assumed a worried air at once. He was in a state of jangled nerves to begin with, having been up at dawn to visit the markets at the Treminga Gate, where he had found it hard to bid in the supplies he needed. This had been followed by a contentious morning spent along the Subura Way, buying capons and ducks and country sausage and peacocks' eggs. There had been a particularly bitter bout with the only provision merchant in Rome who had thrushes fed on crushed figs and who knew the full value of his merchandise. He had been fidgeting about and biting his nails and wondering if he had neglected any of the thousand details that filled the daily life of the head buyer for the imperial table.

He looked up at Selech on his imposing platform and frowned. "An experiment, master? I do not understand."

"I have allowed no one to know. Not even you, Demetrius," declared the head cook. "I thought it would be unfair to make you share my anxiety. I decided to use"—he paused a moment for effect—"nothing but the liver of the red mullet this time. Will it have the flavor I expected? That has lost me some sleep. All the usual flavorings were put in, of course—the Falernian, the vinegar, the garlic, the sweet herbs. I have kept it now a full week beyond the two months to be sure it would ferment down to pure liquid. Well, we shall now know the result. The cask, Demetrius."

The vessel, carried in by a slave a few minutes later, was of well-seasoned wood and capable of holding five or six gallons. Unwilling to have hands less skilled than his own perform the task, Selech took a bit and drove it into the wood of the side. A pungent odor assailed their nostrils as a dark brown liquid began to bubble out of the small hole thus made. The head cook sniffed nervously and then dipped a spoon into the liquid that was being caught in a small dish. At the first sip an ecstatic smile took possession of his face.

"It is perfect!" he announced. "Never, Demetrius, has there been anything to equal it. With such a seasoner as this, all meals will be banquets."

Selech settled back into his chair and allowed his eyes to roam over the domain where he ruled supreme. He saw that the huge brass caldrons in the exact center of the kitchens were steaming and bubbling with promise of plenty of hot water for all purposes. A dozen slaves hovered about the caldrons, their faces red from the steam, their white caps already limp. This part of the scene was repeated wherever he looked: hot and harried slaves who went about their work with the constant fear that something would go wrong and they would be blamed and punished. There were literally hundreds of men and women at work under the vigilant eye of the Archimagirus: pastry cooks, seasoners, bakers and basters, and the less skilled workers who made fires and carried burdens, who picked the poultry and toiled in the treadmills and turned the spits.

His eyes kept turning back to the long table where the pastry cooks were sifting flour through Spanish sieves of linen thread. This, a difficult operation at all times, was particularly important tonight. The Emperor had sent down word that he wanted *oublies,* and the flour used for this delicacy had to be as minutely fine as the unseen dust that blows between the worlds. Other cooks were macerating honey to be mixed with the flour, which would then be twisted into spirals and dropped into deep fat. The Emperor had been known to eat a dozen *oublies* at one meal, dipping them in wine with his own hands and shaking sugar over them from a gold cruet; but they had to be just exactly as he liked them or the royal temper would flare.

Q. Septimus Rullianus led Basil through the kitchens and up to the platform where the Archimagirus sat. "A new guest of Caesar's, O Selech," he said. "His name is Basil; he comes from Antioch and he desires a moment of private conversation with you."

Having made this explanation, the young Roman retreated down the steps to the platform where Demetrius was still shifting his feet about nervously and running his hands through his hair. "A young Greek," he whispered. "He is a sculptor."

"Caesar has never been satisfied with the sculptors who come to him," said the head buyer, looking more disturbed than before. "I trust this one will be better than the others. If not, the Divine One is certain to complain about the food. It is his way."

Selech had turned his head no more than an inch to look at his visitor. "What do you wish of me?" he asked. His voice was precise and rather severe.

"I have been staying at the inn of Old Hannibal," said Basil. "When the summons from the palace came, Cephas advised me to seek you out as soon as I arrived."

The expression on the face of the chief cook did not change. "Cephas?" he said, raising his eyebrows. "Cephas? Oh yes, I recall now. The old man who works at the lodginghouse." His eyes had gone back to their scrutiny of the busy scene beneath him. "Is it curiosity about the imperial kitchens which brings you to me, young sir?"

"No, it is not curiosity," said Basil. The lack of cordiality he was encountering caused him to hesitate about going any farther. "I came to Rome with a letter from Luke. That may make things clearer to you."

At this the attitude of Selech changed. He looked directly at Basil for the first time, and there was friendliness in his previously austere eyes. He rubbed a hand along his high-bridged nose, which would have been a truly majestic feature if it had not been slightly pinched. After a moment he smiled.

"A letter from Luke!" he said. "You have seen Luke, then? With your own eyes?" The tone he used would have been fitting if he had asked, Have you ridden across the sky with Phoebus Apollo?

"I have seen much of Luke. He is my benefactor, and I owe everything worth while in life to him." Basil paused before adding, "Cephas sent a message for you, 'Peace be with you today, for tomorrow the storm cometh.'"

A troubled look took possession of the head cook's eyes. "How wise of Cephas to warn us of the dangers ahead. It is so easy to forget, to fall into relaxed ways of living and thinking, with no thought for the bitternesses of the morrow." He indulged in a deep sigh. "Will you be a guest of Caesar's for long?"

"I do not know. I am to make a model of the Emperor's head in clay. Septimus Rullianus says the length of my stay will depend on how much favor my work finds."

The head cook allowed the severity of his face to relax into a welcoming smile. "You will forgive me, I hope, for my caution at the first. We have to be so very careful. I think it was in the mind of Cephas that you might find yourself in need of advice, perhaps of help. You know, do you not, that there are some of us here who are always willing to do what we can? Do not hesitate to call on me if the need arises. But remember, I beg of you, to use the utmost care. There are eyes everywhere, and ears, and minds filled with malice. The Emperor himself has a continual fear of conspiracies, and someone has distilled poison into his mind about Christians and the teachings of Jesus."

There was an interruption at this point. Selech's eyes had focused on something at a distant table. He called down to the buyer of food: "Demetrius, betake yourself to the capon table. Warn them most solemnly about the stuffing. There must be plenty of ginger and a somewhat less heavy hand with the pepper and allisander. Our master complained about the stuffing last night. He thinks us deficient in such niceties."

Demetrius turned almost purple with resentment. He walked up beside Selech and said in his ear: "He thinks us deficient in the niceties of seasoning, does he? What does he know about such things, except perhaps"—his voice fell almost to nothing—"the niceties of *seasoning mushrooms!*"

Selech turned back then to Basil. "I have not been as fortunate as you. I have never seen Peter. He is in Rome, as you doubtless know, and I have heard from him, but never have my eyes rested on that divine old man. Someday, I trust, it will be my privilege to see him and talk with him. You, my young friend, have been highly privileged. You have seen Luke."

"When I was in Jerusalem I saw Paul and James and Jude. On the way here from Antioch I stopped at Ephesus and heard John preach."

Excitement grew beneath the calm surface of Selech's eyes. "You have seen Paul and James and Jude! Young man, young man, how great your privileges have been. And you have heard John preach! Was it like seeing the heavens roll back and hearing a great voice come to you from beyond the stars?"

"It was indeed like hearing the voice of Jehovah. It was clear to us who heard him that he had talked with God."

"And what word have you of Paul?"

"He is still in prison. The last word we received was that he had appealed to Caesar."

A strained look appeared on Selech's face. "This means that sooner or later he will be sent here. There is no fault in Paul, but he will be condemned to death if he is tried in Rome. Public opinion is being stirred up against us." After a moment given to anxious thought he said: "They seem to be drawn here, the leaders of the church, by an influence and a force that may be that of God. I very much fear they come here to die." He lowered his voice to a cautious whisper. "There are many hundred Christians in the palace. More than half of my people belong. You see, they are slaves, and the teachings of Christ give them hope and a life everlasting to look forward to. But a word of advice, young man: never let it be known that you are one of us. There are perhaps three men in the palace whose discretion could be counted upon. I will tell you who they are; have no confidences with anyone else. People talk, even the kindest and the best-intentioned."

On a table just below the raised platform of supreme authority the winedrawers were preparing to open a leather bottle of such extreme antiquity that it seemed capable of falling to pieces at the touch of a careless finger. Selech found it necessary to give them all his attention. His fine high forehead gathered itself up into a nervous and somewhat irritable frown.

"Have a care!" he cried. "You are not handling a pig's bladder filled with mashed pompion. That bottle has been lying in the cellar for two hundred years, waiting for the moment when the voice of a Caesar would demand it." He indulged in a fretful sigh and said for Basil's ear alone: "They will find in it nothing but a residue as thick as honey. This will have to be taken out with the greatest care and then thinned slowly in water. There must be the smallest conceivable tincture of rose in the water, no more than a single leaf to a quart. The water must be heated just so much and no more. If it should be allowed to come to a boil, that priceless wine would be ruined. It is a gift to us from ages past, and we must treat it with due reverence. When it comes to straining the wine, I shall do it with my own hands."

"Will this old wine be very potent?"

Selech shook his head. "There will be about it a richness and a delicacy. When Caesar touches this ambrosial wine to his lips, he will know that all the refinements, all the gathered wisdom and light of two centuries have come to him in a single sip."

Selech seemed too concerned with his responsibilities for further talk, so Basil got to his feet. The head cook nodded his approval. "See, they are getting ready to take up the first course," he said. "If you are to sup with Caesar, you had better make your way at once to the banqueting hall and find yourself a place. You will not want to miss anything of this." He nodded with pride. "It will be a spectacle worth seeing. And I promise you it is a feast you will remember until you are laid out in cerements."

A procession was forming on one side of the room. In the van were the musicians, robed in gold and red and with bay leaves in their hair. There were players on the lyre, the cithara, the trigonon. Some had their nine-reeded pipes of Pan ready at their lips, some were prepared with the double clarionet, some had trumpets of Galatian bronze slung over their shoulders, their lungs filled for the first triumphant blast. The cymbal players had their half globes strapped to their wrists, the drummers had their sticks poised for the first rumbling beat on the gut stretched tautly across the tympanon.

Behind the musicians there was a long train of servants in immaculate white with trays on their heads. On each tray was a saucepan of Corinthian brass, smoke seeping out from the false bottoms that held fires to keep the foods warm. These saucepans held the amazing variety of dishes that made up the first course: the dormice prepared with poppy juice; the many varieties of sea food, encircled with damson plums and sprinkled with cummin and benzoin root; sausages made with eggs and breast of pheasant; eggs made of paste and colored blue and filled with the yolks in which nestled a fine fat little ortolan roasted to a turn; grasshoppers fried to a light golden brown and sweetened with honey; lettuce and large black olives; pomegranates cut open and garnished with rosebuds.

Selech, his chin raised high and his finely chiseled features tense, rose to his feet. He raised a baton in the air, and his eyes went up and down the procession to make sure that no detail had been neglected. He waved the baton once and then brought it down.

Immediately the drummers went to work, the cymbals clashed, the bronze trumpets sounded a fierce, harsh note. Everywhere the slaves stood at attention beside their tables and fires, their eyes rolling with excitement. Each one had something to wave, a poker, a cleaver, a basting spoon. Demetrius, in a frenzy, jumped up and down on his platform and waved his hands, with their closely bitten nails, above his head. He shouted in a high voice: "The first course is going up! Great of the earth, prepare yourselves for it! Open thy mouth, O Caesar, the first course is ready for you!"

3

When Basil reached the banqueting hall of the Caesars, the guests of Nero were already stretched out on their couches. Their hands and feet had been laved with perfumed snow water, which slaves had carried about among the tables. A short prayer had been said to Jupiter and a pledge had been drunk from crystal wine cups, each drinker~spilling a drop or two on the floor for the invisible lares.

Basil was escorted by Septimus to a small table that, clearly, had been reserved for him. Although within twenty feet of the couch where Nero reclined, it was well off to one side and partially screened by a high bank of flowers. From this point of vantage he could see everything. He stole one glance at the Emperor, surprised to see how young he looked in spite of an early corpulence, and then found his eyes drawn to Poppaea beside the ruler. The new Empress was a vision of snow-white skin and delicate tintings of pink, of reddish hair that glinted and crinkled under the lights in the tall candelabra above her, of shoulders slender and milky in a white silk *palla* edged with blue.

He opened the blue cloth bag on the table and fumbled at the strings, his eyes still fixed on this rose-leaf beauty who was already being called the Wicked Empress.

"Am I to begin at once?" he whispered. There was no answer. Turning, he found that Septimus had already withdrawn.

The second course was being brought in with as much fanfare as the first one. Acrobats capered ahead of the procession, turning handsprings and somersaults. The musicians were piping and sawing, the drummers drumming madly. A table stretched its full length of forty feet in front of the Emperor's couch, covered with gold cloth and piled high with flowers at intervals. One of the marching chefs deposited a wild boar's head in the center of the table and started flames crackling about it while his fellows paraded before the ruler of the world with dishes for his inspection and selection: capons and ducks and peacocks (with their tails spread out in full glory), wild game, rare fishes highly seasoned, young pigs roasted whole, great loins of beef with pink flanks and rib bones dripping with fat, quarters of stag and roebuck.

Nero took no interest in the food. Some remains from the first course were still about him on platters, but he had eaten little. Occasionally he cracked off the head of a paste egg and scooped out the contents, but it was done with no enthusiasm. Caesar lacked appetite and, as those about him noted with distress, he most clearly was suffering from boredom.

Basil, at his solitary table behind the banked flowers, satisfied his hunger with a slice of beef, on which a few drops of the new and pungent garum had been sprinkled, and a concoction of preserved figs served with damson plums. He did not linger over the meal and, at the finish, laved his hands in a dish of scented water brought to him by a slave whose eyes were never raised from the floor. After a deep pull at his wine cup (how could any wine be so wonderful!) he instructed the slave to remove all the dishes, and then spread out the contents of the blue cloth in the space thus provided.

A sense of satisfaction took possession of him. He hummed softly to himself as he set to work.

The head of Caesar was an immediate challenge. Under a mass of coarse red curls the protuberant eyes of the world's master stared out, avid for admiration, watchful, as though underneath he lacked any sense of assurance. His nose was ill-formed and bulbous. The auburn beard had recently been shaved off (and the strands saved for posterity in a golden box embossed with pearls and precious stones), thus revealing the thick and puffy lips and the cruel but weak mouth. It was a face in which perplexity vied with savagery and the instincts of a mild youth were being submerged in the urgings of lust and ambition.

Basil took no more than a moment of study of this rather frightening face in reaching a decision as to what he would do. A head such as this was not to be presented in the conventional Roman fashion, with blank eyes and stiffly formal hair. Instead he would show Caesar as a human being; exactly as he saw him, in fact, a clumsy hobbledehoy who was still capering like a wood sprite but was changing rapidly into an evil satyr. The imperial eyes, he decided, must be made to look out at life with uncontrollable eagerness; the nose and mouth must reveal the appetites that were growing in him. This might not be what Caesar wanted of him, but he must risk it. If the likeness already coming to life with the first pressure of his fingers proved displeasing to Nero's pride, then he would betake himself away as quickly and unobtrusively as he could. No harm, he hoped, would have been done.

It was not until he was well along with his work that he caught sight of Simon Magus. The great magician was sitting bolt upright in the center of the great banqueting hall and eating with an air almost of condescension. He had robed himself in black, and above this funereal garb his bony face looked sinister and withdrawn. The other guests had shunned the seats and couches immediately about him, and so he sat in an isolation that added to the effect he was creating.

Watching him, while he allowed his hands to become idle momentarily, Basil recalled the scene in the House of Kaukben when the cord beneath the rug had been tugged and the vessel of water spilled. "He is crooked," he thought, finding it hard not to laugh. The sinister quality of Simon was no more than a pose, but it happened to be a pose that was deceiving all of Rome.

Up to this moment he had taken no interest in the company, but now he found himself glancing about in the hope of finding Helena. She was not to be seen, and this was not surprising, for there were several hundred people in the hall. He assumed that all the great of Rome had assembled to do honor to their young Emperor, having no way of knowing that the company was a peculiarly mixed one, that with the members of the old Roman families were the new rich who had risen through political activities and the manipulation of state contracts, as well as the younger group who were running after false gods, a gay and sophisticated set under the leadership of Petronius.

It was not an edifying scene. The guests of Caesar were eating and drinking to excess, and license had been given full rein. They talked in shrill voices and laughed loudly and foolishly; they flirted and ogled. The men went prowling on feet that were unsteady and visited the couches where the youngest and prettiest of the ladies were ensconced, seating themselves beside the languid occupants and serving them solicitously. They offered wine cups to lips that were held up invitingly for more than the caress of the golden wine.

Helena must be somewhere in the room. She would not have neglected the chance to be present on such an occasion, but Basil failed to see her. There was, he thought, a resentment of her absence in the stiff attitude of Simon. Was she languishing somewhere in the hall with a new admirer?

Basil said to himself, "I am here to record the features of Caesar, not to watch the antics of his guests." He turned his back with relief on the bacchanalian scene and kept resolutely at his task.

4

Nero was not drinking and he was doing no more than trifling with the luscious fruits and the rich tarts and cakes of the dessert. It was clear that he was finding the evening a dull one. His lips were gathered up in a pout, his low forehead wore a scowl, and his eyes found no pleasure even in the unruffled beauty of Poppaea. He looked about him with an air that said plainly, "These shallow worldlings, satisfying their gross appetites while divinity watches in disgust!"

Finally the smoldering imperial eye came to rest on the oasis where Simon the Magician sat in silent solitude. An idea took possession of him.

"Simon Magus!" he called.

Simon rose from his seat and bowed slowly three times from the waist.

The company that filled the central part of the banqueting hall had lapsed at once into silence, but to overcome the sounds of revelry from the far parts the royal voice had to be raised to make itself heard.

"Have you any more tricks to show us, O man of dark wiles and diabolic skills?"

The days of study and consultation in the house on the Nova Via, the steady practicing with new assistants, the making of mysterious props had all been in preparation for two occasions; and this was one of them, a preliminary to the great display with which the Bad Samaritan planned to astound the world. Conscious of the hovering of destiny above him, the great magician took a few steps forward.

"O Caesar," he said, "I have words in mind rather than deeds. There is a discourse that should be addressed to your learned ear and to all these who sit about you. I desire to demolish certain misconceptions that are held on the subject of what is called magic. If I have your august permission to speak, I shall strive to say what must be said in a few words. And as I talk perhaps my hands will not forget their trade but will perform certain new and ingenious feats and conceits for your amusement."

His right hand had been extended in front of him in a rhetorical gesture. It was empty, as all those who sat close about him were in a position to know. But at this moment they saw a lighted candle suddenly appear on his open palm. Simon lowered his arm and looked at the flickering flame as though he himself was as much surprised as any of them. He glanced about him until his eyes settled on a corpulent senator who was in the act of lifting a wine cup to his mouth. With a gesture of unconcern the magician dropped the candle into the wine, where it was extinguished with a single flutter and hiss of sound.

He had chosen his victim well. The senator spluttered at the indignity he had suffered but subsided when the whole room broke into laughter. Nero, startled, indulged in a slight chortle. Then he coughed and chortled again, this time on a higher note. His enjoyment continued to mount and expressed itself in a crescendo of sounds. Finally he threw back his head and gave way entirely to relish of the trick, exploding into a high neighing hysteria.

Simon took a few more steps forward. "O Caesar," he said, "it is believed that magic is all a matter of dexterity of the hand and of certain aids that the magician conceals about his person. What I shall speak of is a far different kind of magic, the dread powers that fall into the hands of any who dare break the seals of the sable books. I would speak of secrets that can be learned by probing into the high vaults of the unknown and of the strange divinity that enters the veins of the initiate."

He raised his arm in a gesture, and again a lighted candle appeared on the extended palm. A second time he simulated surprise and then crushed out the flame on the bare back of a female slave who was passing with empty dishes. The startled girl emitted a scream and dropped her burden on the floor. Again Nero went through the preliminary starts of choking sound and stammers of delight, rising into another outburst of uncontrolled laughter.

"I spare her the hundred lashes she deserves for her clumsiness," he said when speech was possible to him, "because she has made me laugh on an evening that has been barren of amusement."

Six times the lighted candles appeared from nowhere while the voice of the magician continued its discourse. He found ways to dispose of them that caused laughter. Between the outbursts the hall possessed itself in silence, all eyes fixed on the thin fingers of the Samaritan where the candles sprouted so mysteriously.

A middle-aged man sat at Nero's right hand. The top of his head was bald and as white as newly quarried marble. He had an intelligent dark eye in a plump face and he was attired with fastidious care.

"He is a vile fellow, this Simon," said the middle-aged man at this point, leaning closer to Nero, who was still nursing his amusement. "He is so very ugly that he makes my flesh creep. But this must be said for him: he is an artist."

"An artist?" The Emperor's voice showed that this point of view came to him as a surprise. "Come, Petronius, you are leading up to one of your quips. A paradox, perhaps. You do not believe this fellow to be an artist. Can there be artistry in as low a trade as the making of magic?"

"There is artistry," declared Petronius, watching the thin streak of light in the green cymophane ring he was wearing, "in the building of a dry wall, in the flexing of a bow, in the concoction of a double-faced tart to tickle the palate of a Caesar and smear the cheeks of his greedy henchmen." The leader of the party of sybarites raised his eyes to look across the floor at the magician. "Observe, O Caesar! Have you ever seen anything more like the black birds of death than this creature from the East in his severe robe and his face powdered to look like the bare bones of a skull? Everything he does, every movement of his body, has been carefully planned and timed. Consider how deftly he leads you first to wonder and then to laughter."

While Petronius whispered Simon continued to talk, but he had lost the attention of the Emperor. "He can put dread in your heart by the way he walks. His feet move like the feet of cruel, mythical birds, stalking, slinking, stealing up on you. There is a suggestion of evil in the way he curls up his toes. And see how he moves his arms. They are like shafts of tempered metal, and his hands are like the heads of serpents, poised and ready to strike."

"Yes, yes, Petronius," said Nero, who was now watching Simon with eyes that had discovered in him new fascination. "As always, my Petronius, you are right. It amazes me how infallibly you detect these things."

What followed immediately made it seem possible that Simon had heard what they were saying. He changed his tactics and ceased to startle and amuse them with lighted candles. His hands, which had seemed to Petronius like the heads of serpents, justified the comparison by reaching out with the speed of a fang and whisking away the flowers that stood in the center of one of the tables. A snake with a coral band bound round its neck had been coiled beneath the bouquet. It raised itself and hissed at the startled occupants of the table. Simon pointed a finger at it, and the snake shriveled and disappeared. A moment later he stopped a waiter who was hurrying by with a covered dish. With a quick movement of his arm the Samaritan drew off the cover, and it was found that the dish contained not a Janus tart of rich plums or a cluster of sweetmeats, but the same snake with its identifying coral band and its flattened head darting viciously over the rim.

Continuing his discourse, Simon paced about the floor, throwing guests into paroxysms of terror by discovering the snake in the folds of robes, under chairs, and once in the horn of a musician. Finally he came to the climax of the evening's amusement by raising his eyes to a pillar, at the base of which sat a self-important politician and his fat wife. Following the direction of his glance, the company saw that the snake was beginning to slither down the pillar, its head thrusting out this way and that as it slowly writhed its way down.

The pair below were unaware of what was going on and continued with what they had been doing, the husband drinking wine and the wife eating a bunch of grapes with exaggerated good manners. Every eye in the room was fixed on them by this time in delighted anticipation.

Hearing a rustling sound finally, the wife looked up to find the head of the serpent directly above her. Her lips opened and she emitted a sound like a cork being drawn from a bottle. Then she toppled over, sprawling on the floor in a dead faint.

Each time the snake had appeared Nero had gone through the process of mounting hysteria, culminating in wild peals of laughter, but at this point his sides heaved and he rolled on his couch in a perfect orgy of delight.

Simon waited for the laughter to subside. After a glance at the figure of the woman lying unnoticed on the floor, her face pressed into the squashed grapes, he raised both hands in the air to compel the giggling, guffawing revelers to silence. Then he walked forward until he stood directly in front of the breathless Emperor.

"O Caesar," he said, "I offer a suggestion for your august consideration, in due humility but with a conviction that much good would come of it. There is a test I desire to make."

"What is this test, Simon Magus?" asked Nero.

The magician raised both of his arms in a passionate gesture. His face, carefully powdered as the observant eyes of Petronius had detected, turned even whiter. There was a fanatical gleam in his eyes.

"A test of power, O Caesar!" he cried. "Match me against the Christians like gladiators in the Arena. I, Simon of Gitta, called the Magician, against these men who prate of humility but who say they can perform even as Jesus of Nazareth."

Nero leaned forward, his interest sharply aroused. "A match against the Christians?" he cried. "But how, how? What would be the nature of this match?"

"Summon us before you to show what we can do. I have certain wonders to perform. Let them do these miracles of which we hear so much. You, O Caesar, to be the judge between us. I am weary of the din they raise. Wherever I go they say to me, 'You, Simon, you are bold to stand up and make magic where Jesus of Nazareth performed His miracles. What great conceit is this you have of yourself,' they ask. They call me the Bad Samaritan and they make mock of me. I shall not rest until I have proven to all mankind that Simon of Samaria can perform greater miracles even than their master who died on a cross at Jerusalem."

The Emperor's fingers plucked at his chin as though he missed the auburn beard he had sacrificed to the shears of tradition a short time before. He turned an eye in the direction of Petronius.

"What do you think?" he asked. "Do you favor, my Petronius, this contest he desires so fiercely?"

The sybarite did not seem much impressed. "It might prove amusing, O Caesar," he said indifferently.

A squat, black-browed man, even more vainly attired than Petronius and loaded with jewelry, appeared at the Emperor's left side and began to speak in his ear.

"We can make good use of this plan, O Caesar," he whispered. "It may drag the leaders of this troublesome sect out of their holes. You know how numerous they are becoming and how secretly they spread their nets."

"You are right, Tigellinus." Nero continued to press his nervous fingers on the bare expanse of his chin. "They are all around us. They delve in the ground like moles. They frighten me because I do not know what they want. Yes, let us bring them out of their holes. Question this fellow, Tigellinus, as to how he wants to have his test."

The captain of the Praetorian Guard stepped forward and faced the magician. "Simon of Gitta," he said in a tone of authority, "tell us who these leaders of the Christians are."

"Their acknowledged leader is here, a man of Galilee, a poor fisherman. His name is Simon, but he is called Peter. It is said of him that wherever his shadow falls the sick become well and the lame walk. They say he raised a woman named Dorcas from the grave at Lydda. He is a humble man, but he has a bold plan in his head: to make Rome the center of the Christian church. Summon this Simon called Peter to appear before Caesar and give proof of these powers he claims to have. Challenge him to raise the dead."

The close-set eyes of Tigellinus were fixed on him with deep calculation. "And what can you do, Simon of Gitta? Can you also raise the dead?"

Simon lifted his arms again. "This I declare before Caesar and all those who sit at his feet. No man can bring the dead back to life. I, Simon of Gitta, cannot do it. I defy this boastful man Peter to come forward and perform this feat."

"What, then, do you propose to do?"

Simon made his answer directly to the Emperor. "Can men fly like the birds of the air? The Jews have belief in a band of spirits they call angels. These angels are of great strength and they appear and disappear in the sky. They have wings more powerful than those of the strongest eagle. It may be that there are angels and that they can fly. But can men fly?"

Nero turned to Petronius on his left. "Tell me, Petronius, have men ever flown?"

The leader of the party of sophistication seemed to take small interest in the matter. "Stories have been told of men flying, but I don't believe them to be true. It is certain that no one has ever seen them fly."

"I will fly!" cried Simon. "This is what I propose. I shall build a tower, a tower higher than any building in Rome. I will build it wherever is deemed best. If Caesar gives his august consent, I should like to place it in the imperial gardens so that the ruler of all the world could watch what I shall do without any trouble. From the top of this high tower I shall launch my body into space and fly out over Rome." He paused and looked about him with glittering eyes. "I defy Simon called Peter to fly as I shall fly, in the sight of all Rome, high up in the sky with no wings to support me and naught but the divine spirit that animates my body."

The young Emperor had listened to this discussion with every evidence of excitement. He was leaning forward to watch Simon, his eyes seeming to protrude from his face more than ever, his hands gripping his knees tightly.

"Build your tower, Simon Magus!" he cried. "Build it here in the gardens of my palace and do it quickly. I shall wait for this contest with the greatest impatience."

5

Still busy at his task, Basil became aware that the behavior of Caesar's guests was getting progressively worse. Incredible things were happening throughout the banqueting hall, actions and caresses that none save the most hardened could contemplate without shame. It became impossible for him to concentrate on his work in such an unhealthy atmosphere. Collecting everything into the blue cloth, he made his way out. After several false starts he found his way back to the hall that led to his room.

He discovered, to his surprise, that a light was burning in the bedroom. Pausing in the doorway, he looked about him. A small degree of illumination was supplied by an oil lamp on a bronze stand, and the corners of the apartment were in shadow. Back in the shadows he saw Helena watching him intently.

"I have been waiting for you," she said.

Basil walked slowly into the room, a sense of extreme uneasiness tugging at him. He had hoped he would not have to see her again. Nothing but embarrassment and ill feeling could result, he was sure, from this seemingly clandestine encounter.

Helena's eyes were full of mystery and enticement. She raised an arm in a gesture of invitation, and the sleeve of her *palla* slipped back to the shoulder. It was a beautiful arm she thus displayed, although it seemed perhaps a shade less slender than when he first met her in Jerusalem.

"Did you see me below?" she asked.

He answered that he had not. Simon had been always in his range of vision, but he had caught no glimpse of her.

"I could see you," she said. "You were very diligent. I watched you all the time. My companion charged me with a lack of interest in him. It was quite true. I took no interest in him at all."

"I stayed as long as I could." Basil placed the cloth on the table and drew out the still damp model of the Emperor's head. This he placed beside the lamp. Helena came closer to the light and studied it.

"Do you realize," she said, "that this is the first time I have seen any of your work?" She seemed to draw in her breath. "The likeness is startling. You almost expect him to speak. Or sing." A further moment of intent examination followed. "I wonder if he will like it. There is never any predicting what he will think. Or do—or say."

The sense of uneasiness had been growing in Basil's mind each moment. Every sound in the hall made him start and look about him. He did not want it said that he had taken this beautiful and dangerous woman to his room.

Helena noticed his distress. "It must not be thought we are keeping a tryst here. See, my apprehensive one? I shall remove the danger."

She reached out an arm to the lamp. It was a covered lamp, made of clay, and the wick was tightly enclosed. Her fingers snuffed out the flame expertly, and darkness descended on the room.

"It will be better this way, dear Basil." Her voice sounded farther away, although he had not heard her move. "I am sitting over here. On the couch, your virgin couch. Come, there is room for you. We can sit at our ease and talk in such very low tones that no one will hear us."

He remained where he was. "There are things I must say. Will you listen and make an effort to understand?"

There was a long moment of silence. Then she said, in a quite different tone, one that seemed to have divorced itself from personal feeling for the moment: "Before we talk—about ourselves—there is something I want to discuss with you. Did you hear what Simon said to Caesar?"

As Simon had spoken in the Latin tongue, Basil had not understood a word of the discussion. There had been no one near him to whom he could turn for enlightenment, and so he had continued to work through the episode. This he explained to her, and she told him briefly of the nature of Simon's proposal.

"I think Simon has gone mad," she said in conclusion. "There was a purpose in what he said tonight; an insane purpose, I am afraid. You understand, I am sure, that there is no doubt about his ability to fly from the top of the tower. We have seen to that. There are ways." She paused, and he could hear her draw in her breath as though she were excited and angry. "But does he intend to make use of what we have made? I have doubts, and it disturbs me so much that I think I shall go mad too. I am afraid he thinks he can fly without any help."

"None save Jesus and the holy angels can fly," declared Basil.

Helena was even more emphatic in her opinion on this point. "No one can fly. If this insanity grows on him I must be prepared to take steps. I have no intention of standing by and seeing him throw everything away. He can make a great fortune here, for himself and for me. But what disturbs me even more is the fear of being involved in a failure. If he is going to have this test with the Christians, he must win—or face the anger of Caesar. I do not want to be within close distance of the imperial temper if Simon loses."

"He will lose!" declared Basil urgently. "God will see to that. Jehovah will not allow this wicked purpose to succeed. You must leave at once. Get away while there is time."

"There is another course I can take. If Simon does not come to his senses, he can be exposed. I am prepared to do this if necessary, to go to the Emperor and tell him that Simon will lose if he is allowed his own way. Or I could go to the Christian leaders and tell them everything— about the device we have finished."

Basil found it hard to believe that she was prepared to betray her master in this way. Simon had raised her from the lowest level, he had educated her, he had provided her with the chance to cultivate her capacities of mind as well as her beauty.

"Helena!" he protested. "You cannot be serious. You must not think of betraying your benefactor."

"My benefactor?" She indulged in a bitter laugh. "You are innocent in the ways of the world. Do you not suppose I have paid a heavy price for everything this scheming Samaritan has done for me? I owe him nothing. Nothing at all. But that is not the point. I am convinced he is going mad. He talks strangely, and there is a glitter in his eyes that makes me shiver. Why should I have to share in the consequences of his folly?"

"Why do you tell me this?"

"Because I want you to understand. Also, I may need your assistance. The time may come when I shall want the Christian leaders to be told. But," she went on quickly, "I do not want to make any move yet. There's still a chance he can be brought to his senses. There *is* a suggestion I would feel safe in taking to the Emperor, that I do the flying instead of Simon. Oh yes, I could do it. I understand how to use this device we have made. Better than he does, perhaps. Why should there not be a great woman magician?"

"Now I suspect *you* of being mad."

"My mind has never been clearer or more sure. There are things, of course, that I could not do but that are easy for Simon because of the strength in his arms and his power of endurance; but there are others I could do much better. I could fly better. Basil, I could fly as beautifully as these curious creatures called angels in which, I suspect, you hold belief. And yet I am afraid of heights. My flesh cringes when I think of plunging off the top of that tower. It would be like dying a hundred deaths, but—I would do it!"

"Put such thoughts out of your head!"

"Do you not see," she said, "that I would have something to offer the public that no magician has ever had? Beauty and seductiveness. I could put romance and glamor into magic instead of dread and terror alone. Oh, there would be something of terror also."

"Helena, you frighten me. They would take you out and stone you to death as a witch."

"Has a beautiful witch ever been stoned to death?" He heard her catch her breath in a light laugh. "They reserve that for the old ones and the ugly ones."

Then her voice changed and he could tell she was disturbed and less sure. "But perhaps you do not think me beautiful. I do not believe you do because you are still standing over there. And here is a place waiting for you beside me in the darkness. Basil, listen to me. Carefully, if you please. Because you are acting so strange and cold, I am compelled to make a confession. I have given you love potions. Twice. Did you have any suspicion of it?"

"I wondered about it."

"I wanted so much to win your devotion. I am going to tell you everything. They were the most powerful potions ever made. It was all in accordance with the secrets that Simon possesses. The ingredients were carefully prepared and they were mixed with the wine in the most exact proportions. The words were intoned over them to start the spell. I observed every care. Not a strand of hair on my head was tangled with another. I wore nothing but linen that fell in straight lines without any twisting or knotting. I wore no shoes. I carried both flagons to you myself, clasped tightly in my hands because I hoped the love I had for you would flow from the tips of my fingers into the wine and that you would come to feel the same way about me.

"Are you saying to yourself that the potions failed? No, Basil, they did not fail. It is becoming clearer to me every moment while you stand over there alone that they failed with you but—I am afraid the spell worked, even though it was in a different way. It recoiled and made me the victim. I became the captive myself."

She had forgotten the need for caution and was using a tone that suggested hysteria. "Basil, I have told you everything because I long for—for at least a share of your devotion. Has it made no difference? Are you determined to be cold and aloof and to stay so far away from me? Has not my humble confession made you want to come closer? There is just enough room for us to sit side by side." She said nothing more for a moment. "It seems I have marked my power of attraction for you too high. You do not move. You have nothing to say. Does this mean you want me to leave?"

"Yes. I want you to leave."

He struggled with the words he had been rehearsing in his mind. "Helena, I want you to understand this: that a lifetime of striving would not pay back what I owe to my wife and to the memory of her grandfather, who did so much for me. My release from slavery, my chance to succeed, my peace of mind, my opportunity for love and happiness; all this I owe to them. Even if I did not love my wife, I would rest under an obligation to her for the rest of my life. But I do love her. I love her so much that her image will fill my heart as long as I live. I love her so much that I do not want to be responsible for bringing any shadow of doubt or suffering into her sweet eyes."

No sound came from Helena. He reached out in the darkness, and his hands encountered the lamp. Beside it stood a lighter. It was a rather complicated device, but he succeeded in fitting the laurel rod into the soft column of ivywood and in giving a spin to the bow. There was a quick spark, which fell into the receptacle for the tinder, a mixture of dried mushrooms and charred canvas. The tinder caught fire at once and he raised it to the wick of the lamp.

Helena had left, he found. He did not know whether she had waited long enough to hear what he had said.

CHAPTER XXVIII

I

SEPTIMUS RULLIANUS looked at the bust of Nero on which Basil had worked unremittingly for three days and then repeated the comment Helena had made. "I wonder if he will be pleased with it. It is remarkable, I think, but it has a squint of villainy about it. You have given him the exact suggestion of animal cunning that animates the august countenance. Still, there's a hint of genius about the face as well, and the Caesarian eyes may detect it; he is sharp that way. Well, I shall take it for his inspection, and then we'll know. My advice to you is to go outside in the meantime and enjoy the only good thing about this smelly, run-down, hagridden rabbit hutch—the beauty of the gardens."

Before following this advice Basil sought out Darius, who had been one of the few recommended to him by Selech the Great. Darius was the director of palace amusements, and Basil located him in a large and airy room on the ground floor which, he concluded, had once served as a state apartment. It was now tenanted by active young men with the arms of gorillas and the legs of race horses. They were swinging on ropes from the ceiling and hurtling through the air from one rung to another or were throwing double flip-flops and tossing each other about with abandon. There were jugglers keeping swords and metal disks and porcelain plates in the air, and dancers going through complicated gyrations.

Darius, who was as bald as a roc's egg, talked to Basil of his troubles. "Caesar is hard to please," he said. "He wants something new all the time. The last time I used acrobats he said to me: 'By Tiberius'—he always calls on his ancestors, by Augustus, by Claudius, by Caligula, and this time it was Tiberius—'by Tiberius, I hate acrobats. They have faces like pigs. I would rather watch wrestlers who have great bellies of suet. Take these acrobats out and crack their empty skulls against the nearest wall.' Fortunately he still likes jugglers, and I happen to have a fine corps of them. He likes dancing, and that is a great difficulty, for the art of the dance has fallen on evil days in Rome since Cicero said, 'No sober person dances.' It is all professional and it is very dull and sober. They act out scenes from history in pantomime. Look at them over there in that corner. Did you ever see anything more stilted and stupid?"

Basil looked in the direction indicated and said: "There is one dancer who isn't stilted and stupid. That girl." She had attracted his attention at once, because in a group of dusky companions her hair was like moonlight. Her eyes were blue, he thought, and she was dancing with a gaiety the others lacked.

"That is Juli-Juli," said the director. "I grant you that she is different, and I have great hopes for her. No Roman-born woman dances professionally, and we have to depend on men entirely, but it happens that Juli-Juli has foreign blood and is allowed to—to demean herself in this way. How fortunate it is! She will be a great success when she is introduced." He raised his voice. "Juli-Juli, come here!"

The girl came to a stop, poised herself for a moment on her naked toes, and then floated over to where they stood. She smiled at Darius (Basil had been right about her eyes; they were a startling blue) and said something in soft slurring tones. The director of entertainment regarded her with an affectionate twinkle in his eyes.

"I want you to dance for this young man. He won't be able to speak to you because he does not know our language."

The girl gave Basil an intent glance. "I am sorry I cannot talk with the young man, master. He looks very nice."

"He is very nice. But he is married to a beautiful wife and, moreover, he is a very serious young man. There is only one fault I have to find in you, Juli-Juli: you are not as serious as you ought to be. I even suspect you are quite a flirt."

"Yes, master, I am a flirt. Is it wrong?"

"There will be no flirting in heaven," declared the master of entertainment with sudden gravity.

Juli-Juli looked downcast for a moment. Then she nodded her head and smiled. "Then if one is to do any flirting at all, it must be in this life." She became sober again. "Master, I am young and I am a slave. One must get some pleasure out of life."

Darius resumed his conversation with Basil, dropping back into Koine. "She had a Gothic father. Her mother was Roman and a very sweet and gentle lady. The girl belongs."

Basil dropped his voice to a whisper. "Do you mean that she is a Christian?"

"Yes. And a most devout one. She's a slave, of course, and as she belongs to the royal household she can never hope for her freedom. But she does not let her lack of prospects affect her spirits. She is always gay and as proud of her dancing as a tiny dog with a big bone in its mouth." He turned and nodded to the girl. "I can see that the young man thinks you are very pretty, Juli-Juli. Now for that dance. Show him you have nimble toes as well as bright eyes."

The girl seated herself on the floor and tucked up the skirt of her tunic with the unconcern of a child, showing a very neat and white pair of legs in doing so. Over her small and equally white feet she began to draw coverings of oiled skin. They fitted so tightly that it took much tugging and smoothing to get them properly adjusted. Basil looked down at the fair nimbus that had won his attention first and asked, "How old is she?"

"Fifteen. They will insist on marrying her soon. In fact, there has been some talk of offering her as a prize in a gladiatorial contest. I hope to save her from that by making them see she is too valuable as a dancer to be handicapped by childbearing."

The girl sprang to her feet, shuffled them to make sure the coverings were in proper place, and said to Darius, "I am happy to dance for him, master." She looked up at Basil in farewell. "*Vale!*" she said, and then sprang into the steps of a dance.

There was nothing sedate or stilted about her conception of dancing. She was like a shadow and she seemed almost to float without touching the floor. The sun, pouring through one of the windows, caught the golden lights in her hair and caused Basil to say, "She is like a primula tossed about on the wind."

Darius threw a kiss at the air. "She dances," he declaimed, "like a moonbeam, like a wood nymph. You are seeing her now in her serious mood. She is trying to impress you because she thinks you are nice. When she wants to, she has a knack of drollery about her and she does rowdy little dances. She is irresistible then!" He paused and beamed excitedly on the visitor. "Selech and I are planning an entrance for her when she makes her first appearance. No, she had not danced for the court yet;

I have been saving her. When she does, my young friend, you must be there."

The gardens were ablaze with the bright reds of early fall: the mighty canna, tall and scarlet and majestic like a true floral symbol of the empire; the wild ranunculus blooming behind walls or in the shade of trees where the fierce sun could not reach them; the glowing landamun bushes. It seemed to Basil as he wandered up and down the shaded paths that there was a slave at work on every shrub, a spade available for every square yard of ground. These silent laborers, with the imperial disk about their necks, looked at him with a smolder of hatred, as though he belonged to the cruel keepers who held them in chains; but never for a moment did they pause in their work.

He went casting about for the line of trees that Septimus had pointed out to him. After following many false leads down green paths lined with oleander and bright with the scarlet bloom of salvia, and through spiny mazes, he finally came upon it. It began, as Septimus had said, at the massed shrubs that screened the pool of Poppaea (which was even more effectively closed off by parading eunuchs with drawn swords) and led off to the east in almost a straight line. He walked slowly in the shade of these tall trees and came, after what seemed a full mile of tramping, within sight of the wall. It was of crumbling dark stone and had a fortress-like height and sentries pacing along the top with spears on their shoulders. There was a dense mass of shrubbery where the line of trees ended, and behind this, he was sure, would be found the hole in the wall that the young Roman had described. Basil waited until the back of the nearest sentry was turned and then plunged into the cover of the brush.

There was a hole at the base of the wall, almost completely hidden by the accumulation of many seasons of leaves and by graceful fronds of fern. Kneeling down, he brushed the leaves away and put his head and shoulders in the hole. It proved a close fit, and he said to himself that, if the need to make a hasty exit brought him to this tunnel, it would be a fortunate thing for him that his stomach was still flat. At the other side he could see more ferns and the brown of the leaves and the merest hint of daylight.

He emerged cautiously from the cover of shrubs with a certain sense of satisfaction. Like a good general, he had his line of retreat ready. He indulged in a slight shiver. "I wonder if that tunnel is full of snakes!"

2

Septimus was in the bedroom when Basil returned from his rambles in the garden. The Roman held out a new tunic to him and said, "A gift from Caesar."

It was, Basil thought, the finest garment he had ever seen. It was made of a stiffly rich material of the nature of brocade; amethyst in color and embroidered thickly and magnificently with light blue and silver-gray. It developed that there was a belt of embossed silver to go with it and a silvery scarf for the shoulders. There were also leg pads of gray leather that fitted the shins with the ease and tenacity of silk.

"Why am I so honored?" asked Basil.

Septimus grinned at him. "I suspect he likes what you did. He did not confide in me, but I can put two and two together. My orders were to get you into these gay plumes and then escort you to the Presence. There's a bracelet for your arm as well." He produced the object in question and looked at it with a wondering shake of the head. "It is three inches wide and solid silver! It goes on the upper arm. And do you see that band of amethysts on it?"

When Basil had arrayed himself in the gifts of Caesar, Septimus looked him over with a rueful smile. "This poor moldy crow will now lead the way to the august Presence. Will it annoy you, O Artist of the Rising Star, to walk in the company of such a dingy specimen?"

He continued to talk as they traversed the echoing halls of the drafty palace. "What will the fair Poppaea think of her husband's new protégé? They say she responds to masculine attraction like a panther springing from a tree. Walk warily, my friend, these halls are full of man-traps.

"And remember this, O Lucky One," he continued with a severe frown. "Never address a remark to the Splendor of the World. Wait for him to speak and then answer; and, my good little Basil, choose your words with the sagacity of a Seneca. The fewer you use, the fewer your chances to make mistakes."

He led Basil into a small room that opened off one of the more magnificent of the state chambers. The few furnishings were old and there were holes in the carpet. The only occupant of the room, as far as he could see, was a lean old man in a plain toga who stood stiffly near the window and seemed very much preoccupied. Where, then, was Caesar?

He had the answer the next moment; the Emperor was lying flat on his back with his arms and legs spread-eagled on the floor. There were two large flat stones on his chest, but he was breathing, nevertheless, deeply and easily.

"Another weight, Terpnus," said the recumbent ruler of the world.

Terpnus, the singing master who now took up so much of Nero's time, looked at his pupil with a line of worry deepening in his tight-skinned brow. "I doubt the wisdom of more pressure, O August Master," he said. He stepped forward toward the figure on the floor with the intention of removing the weights, but an impatient motion of a fat bare arm forbade it.

"Another stone, Terpnus."

A stone was added. The weights continued to rise and fall with the imperial breathing. "Still another!" The voice in which Nero had spoken was rather less robust and steady. The singing master knew when it was incumbent on him to act. Instead of obeying his pupil's demand and adding a fourth stone to the chest of divinity, he removed those that were already there.

"The perfection to which your voice is attaining," he said with a prim severity, "must not be spoiled by going too far."

Nero sat up on the floor, looking winded and even a little shaken. He paid no attention to Basil standing uneasily at one side of the room; rather, he seemed to be striving studiously to create the impression that he was unaware of an audience. He was carrying on the conversation with the old teacher, nevertheless, in Koine.

"You are right, Terpnus," he said. "I am inclined to carry things to extremes. It is a weakness of mine. Oh yes, I have weaknesses, Terpnus: I have indeed. I must learn to obey without question."

In a few moments he was so far recovered that he got to his feet and began slowly to perform some exercises of the arms. Puffing a little, he said, "I feel certain, Terpnus, that no one in the world can show the equal of my chest expansion."

The singing master replied testily, "It is not wise to talk while doing the exercises. May I point out, O Caesar, that I have mentioned this often before?" Then he gave the desired answer. "It would be interesting to measure the chests of some of the strongest gladiators. I am disposed to think, master, that your expansion would excel any of them, even Sisinnes the Unbeaten."

The pair of them, master and royal pupil, proceeded then to another phase of the daily ritual. Terpnus, with quick and nervous movements like a mother hen, took a sprinkler and sprayed the august throat with an aromatic liquid. Then he produced an ointment and massaged the throat and chest with quick and skillful strokes of his fingers. A clap of the hands brought a trio of musicians and a drummer into the room. Terpnus hummed until he struck the right pitch and then listened with his head on one side while the flutes and the cithara collaborated with the royal voice in running up and down the scales, the drum coming in with a regular rat-tat.

Basil, accepting the role of watcher that had been thrust upon him, was surprised at the range and quality of the voice of Nero. It had become the custom on the outside to laugh at this Emperor who wanted to be a public performer and to say that all he could produce was an amateurish squawk. It was evident that he had a voice that warranted the efforts he was making to develop it. A robust tenor, it was full-throated and clear on the top notes, and of a blandishing sweetness.

As he followed the directing arm of Terpnus up and down the scales, Nero made it clear that at last he had become aware of his audience of one. Out of the corners of his small and avid eyes he was watching Basil and noting his reactions. After striking a particularly high note, his eyes would glint and it was clear that he would have liked to say, "What do you think of that, artist fellow?" His awareness of the silent witness resulted also in a tendency to act, to strike poses as he sang, to gesture floridly with his arms. His voice kept pace by straining for effect. Once it flattened and went off the key. He reached vigorously to regain it and emitted a note ending in an almost ludicrous screech.

"Enough!" cried Terpnus. The old teacher was all apologies and contrition. "It was my fault. I kept you at work too long. But, Caesar, you were in such rare form that I could not bear to bring the lesson to an end. I made you go on and on. I should be punished for my selfishness."

"Part of the fault was mine," conceded Nero. "I am too willing. I expect too many miracles of my voice. Master, I acknowledge it; I have been showing off."

Another clap of the Terpnusian hands resulted in the arrival of a steaming dish, a big silver spoon, and a scented towel. The odor of fried onions filled the room.

"Must I, Terpnus, must I?" cried Nero in piteous tones. "You know

how much I despise onions. It requires such an effort of the will to get
them down. Cruel taskmaster, do you insist that I eat this vile mess
because it is good for my voice?"

"I insist, O Caesar."

"Very well." Accepting the command with sudden and complete good
nature, the royal pupil seated himself before the dish of onions and
proceeded to eat them with a suggestion, even, of secret enjoyment. When
the last oily sliver had gone its way down the royal throat, Nero rose to
his feet and daintily wiped his lips and fingers on the perfumed towel.

Then he turned and shook an accusing finger in Basil's direction.

"There is a lesson in this for you!" he cried.

There was something studied about him, as though he had rehearsed
in his mind what he was going to say. "If I, Caesar," he went on, "must
subject myself to the tyranny of training, I, with the voice the gods
have been good enough to give me, and with cares and responsibilities
weighing as heavily on my back as the weights they heap upon my chest;
if I make sacrifices like this, what, then, should you be ready to do?
You too have a gift. Yes, you have a good gift. You too may contribute
something to the advancement of the arts if you are prepared to pay the
price. Benefit, therefore, by what you have seen today."

"It has been a lesson indeed, O Caesar," said Basil. "One I shall never
forget."

"And now," cried the Emperor, "summon Petronius. There is something I am going to say and I want him to hear it."

The entry of Petronius was preceded by the bringing in of the bust
that Basil had made of the Emperor. It was placed on a small table in
one corner of the room. Nero looked at it and then waved a triumphant
hand.

"My friend Petronius," he said to the new arrival, "on you I rely in
matters that are close to my heart. You are my never-failing mentor and
my patient guide. I have something now to say to you. It has been my rule
to defer to your judgment, to wait for you to speak. Now for once,
Petronius, I shall speak first. Observe! I proclaim this likeness of me,
which this young artist from the East has made, a masterpiece! It has
power and fidelity. It shows me, not as a divinity on a high pedestal, but
as a man—a living man, Petronius, who loves and hates and strives and
suffers. Look at it well. I defy you to think otherwise of it."

Petronius stationed himself in front of the bust and studied it from
every angle. After several moments of silent absorption, during which

the outwardly confident Nero fidgeted behind him and gave every indication of being secretly nervous, the mentor and guide turned.

"You are right," he declared. "Your eyes, O Caesar, have picked out all the admirable qualities in this work. It is not perfect. It has flaws both in conception and execution. But it is remarkable for a reason that has swayed my judgment as much as it did yours." He took another look, his lips pursed reflectively. "I consider this important because it may be the start of a new trend. It has a novelty of approach as well as fidelity to life, as you so astutely said. These qualities are not to be found in the conventional efforts of other sculptors. Yes, O Caesar, we may have before us the first example of a new school of sculpture."

"I knew it!" cried the Emperor. He was delighted beyond bounds to have his judgment endorsed. In fact, he seemed almost ready to dance in the exhilaration this caused him. "I saw all these things in it from the start. I, with my own eyes. I knew it to be real, new, worth while." He waved an excited arm at Basil, who had thus been the means of earning him so much gratification. "Artist, you are to remain near me. This gift of yours must be developed. You must be given every chance. Your work will help me to show the world that Rome is becoming the real center of culture, the capital of artistic achievement. You shall have rooms in the household wing. Also, you must have a pension." He burst into loud laughter. "That would have been a sad thing to overlook. Even artists must live. You must begin at once on more studies of me. I want to see myself in many aspects. I want to become acquainted with myself." He nodded his head excitedly. "I am going to make you work hard. Ah, yes, Artist, I shall prove myself a strict but a fair taskmaster."

"The whip is needed on the back of the race horse," remarked Petronius, "and an insistent hand on the shoulder of the artist."

"He shall have the insistent hand." Nero beamed at his protégé. "My own personal discovery! My little genius! I am fond of you already."

3

For three weeks Basil rode on the crest of the wave. He was conscious all the time, nevertheless, that each additional day he was kept at court might mean he would be absent from his wife's side when she would need his aid. He fretted and fumed but kept his concern in the privacy of his own mind, for it was quite obvious that the Emperor was not only delighted with his work but took pleasure in his company and had no thought of parting with him.

He did four more studies of Nero, two of them full-length, and the Emperor was lavish in his praise of them all. A high and airy room had been given him for his work, with plenty of light from the north. His new master proved so exacting that Basil had no time for anything but work. Twice a day the royal train would come for sittings, Nero beaming with anticipation and followed by a motley company of special favorites, servants, musicians, and drummers.

"My little genius," he said once, "it is my desire to encourage you in every way. You must repay me by doing such great things that the whole world will say, 'Nero was right. He found this obscure artist. He saw the elements of greatness in him.'"

Another time he said: "We are both young, we are artists, we have aspirations, we suffer, we strive; and we need all the encouragement we can get. We must help each other. I shall draw inspiration from these likenesses you are making of me. And I shall inspire you by singing to you with my golden voice while you work."

The studio was filled as a result of this with noise and confusion all the time. Picking with skilled fingers at the strings of a lute, the ruler of the world would sing in his high sweet voice while Basil's hands labored with the damp clay. The musicians never ceased their efforts; the drummers pounded out their rhythms unremittingly. Jugglers would be summoned to perform for Caesar while he sat. Food would be brought in and wine served. The flutists would lay aside their pipes for brief moments to enjoy a morsel of the food or to pull thirstily at a flagon of wine, but the drummers seemed able to eat and drink without suspending their efforts at all. Once Nero summoned a corps of dancers to amuse him, and they did in pantomime the *Bellicrepa Saltatio,* which was based on the rape of the Sabine women. Basil found it hard to concentrate while hairy dancers panted and sweated and postured.

On one occasion Tigellinus came to the room, followed by a decayed specimen of a man with a furtive eye. He engaged Nero in a whispered conversation and, when the Emperor disputed with him rather violently, he called upon his creature to supply evidence on the point at issue. The man did so without daring to raise his glance above the level of the royal knees, and Nero listened with an impatience that began finally to subside. At the finish of the colloquy he said to Tigellinus in an audible voice: "So be it. I give in to you. But it is hard, Tigellinus. The man was a friend. I liked him."

Coming back to the bench on which he had been posing, the Emperor showed signs of some perturbation of spirit. He frowned and changed his position constantly and seemed thoroughly unhappy. Finally he burst out with an explanation: "Pity the lot of one born to rule! It has been reported to me that a friend of mine, one in whom I had reposed every confidence, has been secretly working against me. I have been compelled to agree to what Tigellinus proposes. My friend must die." He paused and suddenly clapped his hands together with a suggestion of satisfaction. "I must forestall the too zealous Tigellinus. I shall send word to my friend to open his veins and so bring things to an ending before Tigellinus can seize him. Yes, that is the proper solution of this difficulty. I feel better about it already."

Secretaries would run in and out at all times, and the Emperor would groan over the documents they brought and bewail the hardness of his lot. Sometimes he would wave the documents aside and refuse to read them. Basil found himself wondering how the ship of state continued to sail its course with so many delays. At the end of each sitting Caesar would depart with much shaking of his head and many groans over the hardness of the life of those who wear crowns. "How can I go on?" he would cry. "Ah, my little genius, pity me! I am an unhappy man!"

Basil did not realize how enamored he had become of his own success until the evening when a general named Flavius, who had returned from a successful campaign in the East, was the guest of honor at Caesar's table. The victor proved to be a spare soldier of middle years with a face completely lacking in imagination and urbanity. He partook of little food but drank with practiced steadiness, and it was clear that he was astounded at the magnificence of the banquet.

Basil and Septimus were sitting together this evening, and the latter shook his head over the attitude of the returned warrior. "What they say about Flavius must be true," he muttered. "They say he is a dull fellow, a disciplinarian and a martinet, and nothing else. It is even being said that he had simpletons fighting against him and so could not help winning."

As soon as the long and elaborate meal was over Nero sang for his guests without much urging, accompanying himself on a small lute. He was in good form, with a control that never failed him. There was, it is perhaps needless to state, a thunder of applause at the finish. The royal troubadour accepted this loud tribute with a pleased nod of his oversized head and even condescended to the use of the phrase that paid singers employed. "My lords," he said with a low bow, "the artist thanks you for your attention."

He laid aside his lute then and began to talk in a voice that gained excitement as he went on, his remarks being addressed directly to the victorious general. Flavius listened with no trace of expression on his face, which the suns of the East had baked to the color of earthenware.

Basil could not tell what was being said. He was beginning to have the first smatterings of knowledge of the Latin tongue, but his mastery of it was not equal to the rapidity of the words that came from the royal lips. After a while he turned to Septimus and asked what it was all about.

"The Emperor is telling Flavius that Rome must now achieve a new kind of greatness. He says that the world has been conquered and so there is no longer any chance for generals to add to the glory of the empire. It remains for him, the Emperor no less, to lead the way to a new kind of conquest; the subjugation of the arts and the centering of all creative efforts here in Rome. It is all a lot of weak pap and rancid onion oil. That poor Flavius, with his stupid little mind, cannot make head or tail of all the fine phrases our Caesar is spinning about him."

"The general looks puzzled," commented Basil.

"I too am puzzled," acknowledged Septimus. "Should ideas like this be advanced in public by the ruler of the world? What will the armies in the field think?"

The Emperor's fervor mounted as his discourse went on and on. Once he turned to the corner where Basil and his companion sat and pointed a finger. For a few moments all eyes in the place were fixed upon them.

"What did he say?" asked Basil when the flurry of interest in them had come to an end.

"I am not sure I should tell you," answered Septimus. "I suspect you of a weakness for flattery. Still, you might as well hear it from me as from others. It seems that our Caesar conceives himself the source of inspiration that will raise up in Rome a galaxy—his own word—a galaxy of great artists who will excel the achievements of the early Greeks. He says you are his first discovery. He pointed you out to the company and predicted that someday you would be ranked with the great men of the past."

Basil said nothing. The praise that had been lavished on his work was, he acknowledged to himself, most gratifying. For several moments he sat in an exultant glow. "Why should not Caesar be right?" he thought. He had been demonstrating to them that there was in his hands a touch, at least, of genius. Why should it not bring him recognition and acclaim?

Then he brought himself up with a sharp tug on the reins of his common sense. He was allowing himself to be carried away by the first words of public praise. Even if it were his intention to continue indefinitely at the imperial court, it would be dangerous to swallow good opinions so avidly; and it had never been his purpose to consider this more than a brief interlude. He had other work to do. "Now that I know how susceptible I am to praise," he thought, "I must be on my guard. And it is very clear that I should get away from here before my vanity plays me worse tricks. I must be on my way."

He nudged the elbow of Septimus. "I can see that I have been here too long," he whispered. "What can I do about leaving? Must I have Nero's consent?"

Septimus had been looking rather grim, but at this he brightened up. "I thought for a moment you were lost," he said. "I could see a gleam in your eye and I said to myself, 'He is not going to be able to resist this bait and he will be drawn into all this tug of war and seesawing for the royal favor.' But now I see you have a stiffer spine than that." He gave his head a shake of warning. "It would be folly to let the Emperor know what you are planning. He is so heated up himself with his visions of a new glory that he would think you guilty of treachery, if not of treason."

"Does that mean I must stay here indefinitely?" asked Basil. "Am I a prisoner?"

"In a sense. A prisoner of your own success. Still," whispered his companion, "there is always the hole under the palace wall. That is your only hope of getting away now. But I would not advise using it unless you are sure you can leave Rome immediately."

4

While Basil labored and Nero sang, the timbers of Simon's tower were rising in a section of the palace gardens that faced the main portico. The few odd moments the former had to himself were spent watching the upspringing of these ominous walls.

His first impression was one of amazement at the speed and efficiency with which everything was done. The engineer in charge, a cool young

Roman, seemed to know everything. He spoke very seldom, but when he did, things happened rapidly. Basil liked to watch the bringing in of the stout tree trunks for the base of the structure. They were dragged by four or six horses harnessed side by side, raising a cloud of dust like a charge of chariots. This would be followed by a speedy unhooking operation, and the claws of the compound pulleys would seize the logs and toss them up like straws to the places designed for them. It was exciting to see all this accomplished without raising a bead of sweat on the brow of a single slave, how the stays were swung aloft, and the rails and the oblique struts that were known as dragon-beams.

He became so much interested that he inspected the tools the workmen used and found them new and infinitely superior to anything he had ever known. The great saws had crossed teeth to prevent binding in the wood, and this was something very new indeed. The simple boxes called planes, with straps for the hand, could be run across a plank with great ease and leave the surface as smooth as marble. He doubted if Jesus had worked in Nazareth with tools as fine as these.

"It is no wonder," he thought many times, "that Rome rules the world." He graduated from this feeling of interest to one of alarm as the tower kept rising higher and higher into the sky. It had become now a threat, a tangible threat, to Christianity. He would stand and stare up at it and say to himself, "If Simon flies off from the top, the world will believe him capable of doing anything that Jesus did." He knew that nothing had been heard from the leaders of the Christian church in Rome. If the challenge of Simon had reached their ears, they had refused to respond. Nero railed bitterly about the silence of the detested Christians. "Simon Magus will do what he can," he said one day to Basil. "If these sly dogs do not then come forward to face him, they will receive the punishment they deserve."

Basil had no doubt that Simon would succeed. He remembered what Helena had told him of the new device that would be carried, in great secrecy no doubt, and installed at the summit of the tower. Simon would fly high up in the air, and no one below would be able to see how it was done. They would raise their voices and cry out that a miracle had been wrought.

One day Basil stumbled on a confirmation of what Helena had told him. Walking close to the foundations of the high wooden walls, he caught a word of Aramaic spoken by a workman who was operating a bow drill with a strap like the leash of a top. He was addressing a fellow worker who was operating a drill that scooped out wood with ease and precision.

"He will do it by wires," said the first carpenter. "Bronze wires. Do you know what they are?"

"By the adz of Atlas, yes!" answered the second. "I have seen them, great, heavy ropes of bronze that could rip the bowels from a mountain of copper."

"But this is different. It is called—*drawn wire*. I am not sure what that means, but I suppose the stuff is drawn out, by some magic Simon knows, until it becomes very thin. This much I have been told, that it keeps all its strength no matter how thin they make it. Do you believe that, Jacob?"

"I do not believe it, Ziphah. It stands to reason that when you reduce the size of anything you take away from its strength."

"But this is said to be different, I am telling you, my Jacob. It can be made as thin as a cobweb, but it never loses strength. It is a kind of miracle. I hear this pestilential magician has strips of this wire as long as fifteen feet."

There was the explanation, said Basil to himself as he walked away in a state of great alarm. These wires like cobwebs would be painted so they would not glisten in the sun and no human eye would be able to see them from the ground. There would be a wheel concealed at the top of the tower that would swing Simon around the narrow apex, allowing him to rise and dip in the air like a swallow about the parapets of houses.

"That is how it will be done," he said to himself. "Should I go to Nero and tell him about it? Would he believe me if I did?" He decided after much earnest thought that nothing would be accomplished by going to the Emperor. Nero wanted Simon to succeed, by hook or by crook, because he desired to see the Christians confounded in the eyes of the world. He did not care what means the magician used. In any event, what proof did Basil have to offer? He had nothing but suppositions.

When he turned back to the palace he encountered Helena in the gardens. He had not seen her since the night of his arrival at the palace, and it was apparent to him at once that her attitude had changed. There was no mistaking the coldness in her eyes.

"What do you think of it?" she asked, gesturing toward the tower. "It is to go still higher. Simon does not believe in doing things by halves. He says he is going to fly and so he wants the upper reaches of heaven for his flight."

"The higher up it goes," said Basil, "the less chance there will be for the wires to be seen."

"Wires?" Helena gave him a level glance that was nothing less than glacial. "What are they?"

Basil did not attempt to answer. The girl regarded him with no evidence of a rise in the temperature of her eyes. Then she changed the subject.

"You are flying high yourself," she said. "You are soaring in the heavens of Nero's favor. Has it been pleasant to climb so rapidly, even though you know you owe your chance to someone else?"

At this Basil's attitude became as chilly as her own. "I did not want this to happen. You arranged it, I know, but it was against my wish. I was summoned to appear and I had no alternative but to obey. I had no desire to do any of this climbing you hold against me."

"You had no desire to climb? That I do not believe. My shoulders are bruised by the stamp of your heels." Her feelings became more hostile with every word she spoke. "I talked to you about Simon and his delusions. Have you mentioned this to others?"

"I have not repeated a word to anyone."

"Put what I said out of your mind!" Her tone was sharp. "I must have been out of my own mind when I spoke to you. It was very foolish of me." For several moments she kept her eyes on the ground, and it was clear that she was seeking her way to a decision. Then she looked up suddenly. "The palace rings with your praises. Everyone says your models of Nero are true to life. You have looked into his eyes and read his soul. I wonder, O Basil, if you have any desire to look into my eyes and read what is in *my* mind? You might find it very disturbing if you did. Very disturbing indeed, my little Basil!"

CHAPTER XXIX

I

ON THE EVENING following his conversation with Helena, Basil visited the domain of Selech on his way to the banqueting hall. There was an air of expectancy in the kitchens, which he attributed at once to a curious object standing in front of Selech's platform, a structure about six feet high and resembling a closed chair. There were handles on each side, front and back, by which it could be carried. On examining it with some curiosity, Basil discovered that the base was of wood but that the rest was made of pastry. It had a delicious aroma, as though it had come fresh from the ovens, and it was coated over with sugar to make it a warm and inviting brown. On the top there was a bird's cage, also made of pastry and filled with canaries. The birds, twittering among themselves, were perched on swings of hard candy. The top was fringed with candy bells that jingled lightly.

"What is this?" asked Basil when Selech joined him near the pastry chair.

"It is to be used for a surprise tonight," explained the Archimagirus. "Observe, there is a door, and no one will be able to see inside when it is closed. The chair will be carried in with great ceremony; music and drums and acrobats. The canaries will be singing like mad, and then—the door will fly open and someone will come out."

It was clear who the someone would be, for at this moment the little dancer Juli-Juli arrived in the kitchens and began to weave her way across to them. She was dressed in green and her arms were filled with a mass of fluffy yellow plumes. It was clear that she was very much excited, because she smiled and waved to them and began to dance her way around the ovens and tables.

"Is it ready?" she asked. "How wonderful! I am ready, O Selech. I can hardly wait. It smells so good that I am afraid I shall bite holes out of it when they are carrying me in." She smiled at Basil over the burden of plumes. "Please, Selech, tell this young man all about it. He is a very nice young man and he has a beautiful wife. But he is very serious, and I think we could get him to smile if you told him."

"He will be there to see for himself," protested the great cook. "Should we rob him of the surprise?"

The girl smiled at Basil again and held out the plumes for his inspection. He could see they consisted of two large wings and a cap shaped like a cock's comb. She put the cap on her golden hair, pulling it down tightly over her ears, and then made motions with her arms to indicate that the wings would be attached to her shoulders.

"Tell him my first number will be a bird dance."

Selech translated this and then added an explanation. "There is a spring under the chair. When it is released, she will shoot out through the door like a bird in flight."

Juli-Juli was fairly dancing with excitement. "Tell him about my second number, Selech. Ah, that second number. I want him to know about it. Then he will be sure to wait for it."

"Do not fear, Juli-Juli. The young man will wait."

"She will make a very lovely bird," declared Basil.

Juli-Juli did not need to have this translated. She sensed his admiration from the smile that accompanied the remark and smiled back at him, nodding her head delightedly. "Do not repeat this, if you please, Selech, but it is a pity he is married," she said.

"She will appear with the dessert," explained the cook. He turned to the little dancer. "Caesar will think you a real bird when the door opens and you fly out. You must do your teacher credit tonight. You must dance, Juli-Juli, as you have never danced before. But now I think you had better return to your own quarters. Darius will be wondering where you are."

Another surprise awaited Basil when he reached the banqueting hall. A table had been placed behind the couch of Nero, and on it were the five models he had made of the Emperor. It was the first time they had been put on display, and he wondered about the reason for showing them on this particular evening. He was conscious also of a stirring of pride. Perhaps he was to be singled out for some kind of honor.

He felt a lift of spirits as he glanced about the lofty, resounding hall with its enormous pillars that had been raised to the glory of Augustus, the first of the emperors. For three weeks he had lived in this atmosphere of greatness, a greatness that had dwindled and become tarnished and tawdry. He had been a success. The Emperor still babbled about him with undiminished confidence. People were talking about him, he knew, quoting the things Nero said, calling him the little genius. No matter what the future might bring, this was something he would always remember, that he had won respect for his capacity in the bitter jealousies of the halls of Nero.

Having won the full approval of the Emperor and the sophisticates about him, Basil felt he could afford to rest on his laurels. It was time for him to be going. He had other work to do that pressed on his consciousness. He wanted to be back with Deborra, making up to her for his past blindness. He wondered if this might not be the right occasion to ask the consent of Nero to his withdrawal from court. He decided that, should the Emperor prove in an amiable mood, he would take the risk of asking.

For the first time he indulged in the general practice of wandering about the long hall with its many levels and its constant interruption of steps, where the guests were already reclining on their couches. The company was more brilliant than usual. The women seemed to have known that the amber-haired Poppaea, reclining in a sulky, silken boredom beside her imperial mate, would take this occasion to set off her warm brown eyes with her fabulous jeweled earrings. At any rate, they had arrayed themselves brilliantly. Their arms were covered with bracelets and their fingers were stiff with rings. They were proving quite careless with their lower draperies, for at this season they still wore their garters on bare flesh and were anxious to show the rubies and opals that nestled in the bands of black velour or silk.

Basil noticed also that there were amethyst drinking cups at nearly all places, which meant that the guests had brought their own with them. The table appointments at the palace had fallen into an eclipse of shoddiness during the reign of Claudius, and from this there had been no revival. Amethyst cups protected the users from intoxication and so were considered essential.

Simon the Magician, occupying his usual place in a sardonic silence, was one to be avoided; Basil did not want to be recognized as the youth who had gone to him to have an evil spirit cast out. He saw the victorious general, Flavius, in the relative obscurity of a side couch, the penalty for proving dull and unresponsive. Helena was beside a handsome young man with dull eyes, attired in the rich trappings of the Praetorian Guard. She carefully avoided meeting his glance as he strolled by.

Nero, it became evident at once, was in an amiable mood. He sang with great restraint after the serving of the first course. He sang again, with less restraint and a tendency to overact, after the second course. Everyone applauded madly, and he beamed with gratification and puffed out his great thick chest. There was a feeling of easiness and satisfaction in the air because of this, but at the same time there was also an undercurrent of fear. The place reserved for Tigellinus was empty. Basil asked himself the question that all others in the hall were raising: What dark matters kept the police head away?

The dessert had been brought in, consisting of huge platters of fruit and nuts and dishes of gold heaped with luscious honey cakes and trays on which were spread out tarts of such flakiness that the mouths of the nearly satiated diners opened again in greedy anticipation. There was a pause. Two gladiators had come into the hall and were standing in the open space beneath the flight of twenty marble steps that led up to where Nero sat. They had their short blunt swords in their hands and were ready to set about the business of slashing and cutting at each other. Darius, as master of ceremonies, did not raise his baton, however, for the carnage to begin. He was standing at the foot of the stairs, his eyes turned to the high arch where swinging doors closed off the passage leading to the kitchens.

Without warning these doors were flung back and a blare of sound was heard, the high whine of the pipes, the mad thrumming of strings, the beating of drums, voices raised in a rolling chant. A procession began to unwind itself into the hall. Acrobats were in the lead, turning handsprings and leaping high into the air and shouting, "Hup! Hup!" in excited voices. After them came dancers, one at a time, each attired to represent a great figure from the Roman past or a god straying from Olympus; each with a set pantomime to heighten the illusion. The musicians followed, and the drummers. Then four slaves in red and white, with red leather straps across their shoulders, carried in the pastry cage. Tall candles had been lighted at the corners, the canaries in the upper cage were singing ecstatically, and the candy bells jingled with each move.

The cage was carried to the space below Nero and there deposited on the floor. As soon as it touched the marble the pastry door swung open and a green-and-yellow Juli-Juli flew out. She wafted her wings up and down with quick movements to simulate flight. When the force that had launched the gay figure from the cage was exhausted, she came to rest on her small bare feet at the base of the ascending stairs.

The dance that followed was far removed from the stiff pantomiming of the professional dancers. Using her canary wings gracefully, her chin held high, Juli-Juli drifted about like thistledown, while the musicians played a soft air and the drummers came in with no more than an occasional soft beat. She was so light in her movements that she came close to flying indeed, and some of the guests raised the query among themselves as to whether Simon the Magician would do better. The dancer came to a breathless stop beside Darius, who had remained at the foot of the steps.

The applause was loud and sustained and counterpointed with demands for an encore. Nero had risen to a sitting position, the better to see, causing an ominous creaking in the frame that was as dilapidated as all the other furnishings of the palace. He said in a gratified voice, "It has been a great pleasure." Even the languid Poppaea had joined in the applause.

Darius placed a hand on the little dancer's shoulder and waited. When the noise had subsided, he addressed the Emperor.

"O Caesar, this young performer who has appeared before you for the first time has another dance that would be different. It would be quite different indeed, O Caesar. It is such a departure from the accepted ways that it could only be introduced to your attention as an innovation, even as an experiment."

"A departure from the accepted ways?" Nero's bare feet had touched the floor and he seemed on the point of rising. "There is nothing I like better. Let us watch this experiment, Master Darius."

"The dancer would require——" The hand of the master of entertainment on Juli-Juli's shoulder conveyed a message. She stooped, took the skirt of her flowing green tunic in one hand and raised it a few inches to display the bareness of her feet. "It would require, O Caesar, the use of sandals."

Nero looked down at his own sandals, which had been placed by the side of the royal couch when one of the slaves had laved his feet in the perfumed snow water. They were plain, perhaps the plainest in the hall, for he had never conformed to the custom in Rome to walk on soles of gold and silver, sometimes inlaid with precious stones. He looked down at his broad wooden footwear, and a gratified grin spread over his face at the originality of the conception that had come to him.

"She needs sandals?" The royal voice was pitched high so that everyone in the room could share in the airy flight of his fancy. "Would her feet feel unworthy and falter in their steps if they were fitted into the sandals that have protected the feet of Caesar? Or would they be inspired to an even greater nimbleness? It is an interesting point." He looked in the direction of his mentor. "What do you think, Petronius?"

"It is an amusing conceit, O Caesar," responded the suave voice of Petronius. "I am certain that the sandals, having known the touch of divinity, would infuse the dancer's feet with some of the divine fire."

"Take them to her!" cried Nero.

A servant appeared at once to obey this order. Juli-Juli sat herself down on the bottom of the marble steps and proceeded to strap the sandals to her feet. People rose from their couches and pressed forward to watch. She looked very small at the base of the imposing stair, so small that it was almost as though they were watching a pretty kitten at play. Her yellow cock's-comb cap had fallen from her head and lay beside her on the floor.

The sandals of Nero were very large and the feet of Juli-Juli were very small. It took a great deal of tugging and pulling to make the straps secure. When she stood up and took a tentative step, they clattered alarmingly.

"Can you dance in them?" asked Darius in an anxious whisper, fearing that this daring move he had planned out in his mind was due to fail.

"Yes, master," she whispered back. "The looser they are, the more they will clatter. That is what we want."

She stood still for a moment, and her glance went up to the raised floor where the great Nero sat. A sudden panic swept over her. What would the ruler of the world think of this new dance she was to perform? Would it seem to him undignified, perhaps even cheap and common?

"Master," she whispered, her cornflower-blue eyes turning to him in alarm, "I am afraid. I do not think I can move my feet."

"Come, child!" Darius was seriously concerned. "Dance as you do in the practice hall, forgetting everything. Smile. Sing, if necessary. Just be natural, Juli-Juli."

She made an effort, and her feet achieved a first step. She looked up at the master of entertainment with a plaintive smile. "Here I go! The slave who may shock the guests of Caesar. Pray, master."

All public dancing was performed with bare feet or with the oiled-skin coverings Juli-Juli had used in practice. The first *clip, clip, clop* of her sandaled feet on the hard floor, therefore, roused the company to startled attention. It was new, it was strange, but there was something infectious about the rhythmic regularity of the sound. People began to nod their heads to the even clatter of the loose sandals and to beat time with their own feet. It was so infectious that Caesar could be seen tapping on the table at his side to the beat of the wooden soles. Even the dignified head of Petronius nodded in unison.

The control and precision of the diminutive dancer were shown to best advantage when she began to climb the marble steps at the top of which divinity sat. Her feet touched each step in perfect time, *clip, clip, clop, clippety, clip, clop,* but when she reached the one immediately below the top, she hesitated as though conscious of her unworthiness, and then danced backward to the lower level, never missing a beat. This had such an effect on the audience, who were telling each other that there had never been anything like it before, that they began to encourage her loudly to go all the way up, Nero joining in.

But Juli-Juli had other plans. Dancing with gay and impish gestures, she drifted about among the tables and couches. Male guests reached out inebriated arms to capture her, but she always succeeded in eluding them and never once missed in the accurate beating of the wooden soles. Once she seized a cap from a matron that contained a brilliant jeweled pin and put it on her own head, then threw it to the owner on the next time past. She reached for a scarf from a dusky beauty and waved it about her head as she danced before tossing it back. A fatuous senator, smiling like the full moon, took the wreath of laurel from his brow and offered it to her. She put it on her golden hair at a rakish angle and did a circuit of the hall before returning it to him.

Finally she came to the climax of her dance. She paused almost imperceptibly beside Darius and whispered: "I am going to sing. I am going to sing to the high gods of the earth up there above us!"

She began then to repeat her performance on the stairs, dancing up hesitantly, retreating hurriedly; and as she danced she intoned in a voice audible to those above:

"Pe-tron-i-us! Pe-tron-i-us! Will you say I am guilty of a breach of etiquette?" *Clip, clip, clop.* "Tig-ell-i-nus! Tig-ell-i-nus! Will you put me in a prison cell if to the top I get?" *Clip, clip, clop.* "Nero Caesar; Nero Caesar! Sitting there above us like the sun up in the sky. Nero Caesar! Nero Caesar! Will you feel too much affronted if a new and awe-struck dancer dares to reach an elevation quite so high?" *Clip, clip, clop.*

Then she dashed suddenly toward the stairs and mounted them to double time, *clippety, clippety, clippety, clippety—clop!* She stood at last on the highest level, her head held down, her yellow wings drooping, as though she were made of wax and had begun to melt already in the great light of the divinity that blazed up there.

Nero did not need the shouts of approval of his guests, nor the slightly amused smile on the face of Petronius, before expressing his own reactions to her performance. His face quite pink with excitement, his broad bare feet spread far apart, he called out, "Never have I been more entertained." Then he glanced about him, his eyes coming to rest on the baldness and waxiness of Petronius. "This kind of dancing," he declared, "is as new as the children who are being born in Rome this very minute. Listen, Petronius. Listen, all of you. Listen, the world! I have coined a name for it. The Dance of the Sandals of Caesar!"

The applause broke out anew, being directed now at the Emperor in loud admiration for the aptness of his phrasemaking. This led him on to indulge in another gesture. "I desire," he announced, "that these sandals be dipped in gold and hung up in a place of honor. As a reminder," he added, "that it was with them that this venture into a new phase of the art of dancing was made in the presence of Caesar."

An interruption occurred at this point. The missing Tigellinus came into the hall, followed by one of his officials. He strode up the twenty marble steps without any hesitation and stationed himself before the royal couch.

"There has been trouble of which you should be informed, O Caesar," he said. "Quintus Clarius has been murdered. His body was found early this evening in his own private bath. He had been strangled to death with a knotted towel."

"Has the assassin been caught?" asked the Emperor.

"We have not yet succeeded in identifying the murderer," answered Tigellinus. "It seems certain that the deed was committed by one of his slaves. They are all being held in chains for questioning. It will not be hard to get at the truth. It may be that the guilty slave was paid to do away with his master. There are stories being circulated"—he gave a significant glance in the direction of Petronius—"that bear this out."

If such stories were being circulated, it was more than likely that Tigellinus himself had been responsible for starting them. Quintus Clarius was one of the wealthiest men in Rome and an active supporter of the Praetorian captain in the struggle between the two factions. The hostile dark eyes of the captain darted again at Petronius.

The latter, fully aware of the implication in what his rival had said, did not show any concern. In a voice that carried a faintly veiled note of amused scorn at the hint of his involvement he said: "Quintus Clarius was known to be a hard master. Does that not offer a hint as to the motive for this vile crime?"

"The truth will be brought to light," declared Tigellinus. "And the motive, without a doubt. The slaves are being put to the torture." He added with a contemptuous gesture of his hands: "They are a miserable lot. It is hard to believe the reports I have of them. It is said that they are Christians without a single exception."

"You say they are all Christians?" Nero, whose interest had been somewhat perfunctory up to this point, blazed into a passion. "Is it not true that he had upward of a hundred slaves? Can it be that in a single household there are one hundred converts to this insidious, this unclean belief! Tigellinus, this is indeed serious. Are we like to be suffocated in this rising wave that comes up like the poisonous gases from the swamps?" His face had turned a furious red, his eyes were distended. "Have all of these slaves killed!" he commanded. "It is the only thing to do. We shall then be certain that the guilty one has suffered for his crime; and as for the rest, we will be well rid of them."

It was clear at once that this pronouncement had not found favor with the company. Some of the guests were too intoxicated to do more than stare up at him with blank faces, but with all the rest there was evidence that they had heard the imperial dictum with surprise and a sense of horror.

Tigellinus was too insensitive, or too indifferent, to understand or care. "It is true, O Caesar, that something must be done to stop the spread of this faith," he said. "You have given me an order that may seem drastic. But there is this to be considered: the execution of these slaves would serve as a notice to the world, and to the people of Rome in particular, that they must not accept this heresy."

Petronius had been more observant. He decided to make himself the spokesman of protest. "Your desire to check the spread of this curious religion is natural and commendable, O Caesar," he said. "I am not well versed in the laws and so my opinion may not carry any weight with you. This, nevertheless, I feel quite strongly, and there will be many in Rome to feel as I do that this particular crime does not warrant such a sweeping measure of retribution. People will say that the execution of one hundred people, slaves though they are, is not in accord with the principles of Roman justice. They are not criminals, they are suspects only. There is this to be considered also. The slaves are valuable. They constitute, no doubt, a considerable part of the estate of the deceased man. What of his heirs? Are they to be the losers, or will they be compensated for their loss from the public funds?"

Tigellinus needed no further prompting to throw his influence on the side of severity. "Unusual situations call for unusual measures," he declared. "This was in the mind of Caesar when he ordered the execution of all the suspects. He has a gift for cutting straight to the roots of a problem and making the wise and proper decision. I am convinced that in this case he is right."

Petronius was not prepared to give way. He approached Nero and said to him in a low tone of voice: "What you propose will be extremely unpopular with the people. Your leniency in the past has made you much loved, and those who admire you for it will not understand. They will be shocked and horrified and they will say, 'What has come over the master we have loved so well?' Think carefully before you commit yourself to this course."

"O Caesar!"

A woman's voice had been raised from the body of the hall. When all eyes were turned in the direction from which the sound had come, it was seen that Helena had left her couch and was approaching the open space at the foot of the steps. Her face was pale and wore a look of inflexible determination.

"Caesar may well be disturbed over the spread of this religion," she declared, coming to a stop where the two forgotten gladiators still stood with their drawn swords. "Does he know the extent to which it has penetrated into his own household? Is he aware that it is growing all the time, that converts are added almost every day? This much he should know, that many of the high officers of his household are Christians and that they stand together in everything."

"What proofs have you of what you are saying?" demanded Nero.

"The truth of what I say is known to every guest who sits here tonight," declared Helena. "I have dared to speak. Perhaps now there are others who will come forward and say that they know the situation to be a serious one."

"Are you charging that there is a conspiracy in my household?" Caesar's voice showed how seriously disturbed he was. "Do you think they plan to—to use violence as in the case of Quintus Clarius? Is this what you are trying to tell me? Speak up, woman. You need not have any fear of consequences."

"There is plotting going on, Caesar. To what end I cannot say."

Nero had been taken by surprise. His face, after turning an angry red, had become pale, and there was a suggestion of panic in his protuberant eyes. He looked at the faces about him as though fearing to find in them confirmation of the alarming hint that a conspiracy was being hatched against him in his own household.

"Tigellinus!" he cried. "Tigellinus, can this be true? If such desperate things are afoot, I should be told, I should be protected! Why have you not placed guards about me? Why is an attack on my person made so easy for these conniving traitors?"

"Caesar need feel no alarm," said Tigellinus, who was watching Helena as though gauging her value as an instrument. "The necessary steps are taken at all times to protect your sacred person, O master. I am well aware that there are many Christians among your servants. A few may hold posts of responsibility, but most of them are slaves; it seems to be a faith best suited to those who exist in slavery. As to this talk of a conspiracy, it shall be investigated, quickly and thoroughly, but I am not prepared to believe yet that there has been any actual plotting against the person of our beloved ruler."

"We must be sure, we must not be overconfident!" cried Nero. He turned and pointed a finger in the direction of Helena. "We must have names. You have brought a serious charge and now you must support it by giving the names of those involved. I insist on knowing everything."

"It is not hard to give you names, O Caesar."

Helena glanced about her, and her eyes came deliberately to rest on Juli-Juli, who had betaken herself to one side and was now seated on the floor.

"Question this slave who has just danced for your amusement."

Juli-Juli had been unbuckling the straps of the sandals. When she heard this, her fingers became stiff and cold and could not continue with their task.

The assurances of Tigellinus had not served to dispel Nero's alarm. He seized upon this first piece of tangible information. "Tigellinus!" he cried. "Question this girl. We must get at the truth. We must not wait. A moment's delay may defeat us."

The captain of the Guard looked down gruffly at the small figure in yellow and green sitting on the floor. "You have heard what has been said," he declared. "Stand up and answer. Be quick about it. I want you facing me."

Septimus, sitting beside Basil, had been giving him a whispered report of what was happening. The latter watched Juli-Juli with the deepest apprehension. He found himself shaping a desperate appeal in his mind. "O Jehovah!" he prayed silently. "Do not let this brave little child suffer. Look down on her, O Lord, and protect her from this evil."

The dancer rose slowly to her feet and stood facing her questioner, a sandal in each hand. All the brightness with which she had danced had gone out of her, but she showed no signs of fear. She looked steadily into the eyes of Tigellinus.

"You heard me ask if you are a member of the Christian sect. Is it true?"

The girl answered in a clear high voice that carried no suggestion of hesitation or unwillingness. "I am a Christian. I believe that Jesus died on the cross that men might be saved. I believe in the everlasting life."

A blaze of red took possession again of the broad face of Nero. He pointed at the royal sandals with a finger that trembled in fury. "Take them from her!" he cried. "They have been profaned. Everything this girl touched has been profaned. Tigellinus, see that it is all destroyed. Have a fire here in the full sight of everyone." His voice rose to as high a note as any he achieved in his singing. "The dignity of the throne must be protected. Do as I bid you, Tigellinus."

The captain of the Guard proceeded to carry out this order. He yanked the sandals from her without ceremony, then he turned her about and tore the wings from her shoulders. An order in the meantime had sent his morose assistant to collecting the articles the guests had loaned, unwillingly in some cases, for the dance. The matron flinched when her cap was demanded, crying: "You must not take my pin. It is very valuable. It cost many thousand sesterces. Take your hands from it, do you hear!" Her husband said between gritted teeth, "Make no scene, you fool; let them have the cap, stick and all." The gauzy scarf and the senator's wreath caught fire as soon as a light was applied to the heap on the marble floor. The citrus wood of the sandals began to burn, and an aromatic odor filled the room. Everyone knew that from this moment forward it would be highly unsafe to make any reference to the Dance of the Sandals of Caesar.

"May the taint in my household be removed as easily and as thoroughly!" cried Nero. He turned again to Tigellinus. "Have this girl put into the wall bracelets. A night spent in them——" He faced about, and it could be seen that his nose was twitching and that the grip of his anger had brought out splotches of purple on his brow and cheeks. "A whole night of it will prepare her to talk in the morning. She will be only too glad to tell you all she knows about this conspiracy then, this secret plotting and conniving. Remember this, Tigellinus. We must have names. Do you hear me? We must have them all. None of the guilty is to escape us."

Tigellinus summoned two officers to take Juli-Juli in charge. They bound her arms behind her back with rough hands and then led her down the marble steps she had climbed in her dance with so much gaiety and abandon. It was not until she was seen between the two burly guards that the company realized how small she was. She walked with her head raised, her eyes fixed on the lofty arch of the ceiling. Where the rest of the company saw nothing but the dark shadows, the blackness of the dusty stone, she was aware of a great light breaking through, and of music, high and clear and celestial.

"She will tell us all we need to know after a night in the bracelets," promised Tigellinus. "If she does not talk willingly, we will know how to make her."

"Yes!" cried Nero. "We must have names, Tigellinus. All the names."

"O Caesar!"

It was Helena again. She had remained where she was and now she took a step forward and rested one foot on the lowest of the steps.

"As you desire names, I have one more to offer. Ask the artist who did these models of you, O Caesar; this sculptor who has come from Antioch on an undisclosed mission. Ask him why he is here. Ask him if he is a Christian."

There was a long pause. Nero looked startled and thoroughly dismayed. Then he said in a hurt tone: "No, no! Not this man for whom I have done so much! Not my own discovery, my little genius!"

"Question him, O Caesar."

Septimus explained to his companion in a desperate whisper, "She has named you!" When he heard this Basil was certain that his heart had stopped beating. He was conscious at first of nothing but a great fear, a panic that took possession of him and urged that he run from the hall, that he never stop until he had put the court of Nero far behind him. Then he became afraid of his own lack of resolution and he said to himself: "I am going to play the coward. I am going to lie to save my life. I lack the courage of that poor little dancer."

Nero was staring into the corner where the man he had discovered and honored was sitting. He pointed a forefinger.

"You have heard!" he cried. "Stand forth and give us your answer!"

A miracle happened then in the heart of the young sculptor. A sudden surge of exultation swept over him, carrying away all his fears and uncertainties. He knew then that his belief in the teachings of Jesus had ceased to be a detached conviction, as cold and considered as a mathematical problem. He believed with his heart, and he was happy in his belief. He now felt the same ecstatic joy that he had seen so often in the eyes of others.

It seemed to him that his spirit had moved far away to a place where he heard calm voices speak, and there was a consciousness all about him of the forces that ruled destiny. The life he was living and the world in which he lived it shrank to the smallness of the vanished hours of a single futile day; and the fears growing out of this transitory existence were emotional phases that dissolved as easily as the scurrying minutes.

When he brought his mind back, it seemed to him that the hall was flooded with a great light, a brighter illumination than the sun had ever supplied.

He rose to his feet and, as he did so, he could hear the words of Cephas: *"In the stress of such a moment your eyes will be opened. The tinder in your heart will take fire. . . . You will cry out what you believe and you will want everyone to hear!"*

It had come about as Cephas had promised. His heart had taken fire. He wanted to cry out before the court of Nero so that everyone would hear.

He heard himself saying in a voice that was calm in spite of the spiritual excitement that filled him: "I am a Christian, O Caesar. I believe in the teachings of Jesus of Nazareth."

Few people in the hall understood the words, but the meaning was clear to them all. There was a moment of silence. Then Nero coughed and gave the familiar nervous catch of his breath that grew until it had become a torrent of almost insane laughter. At the peak of this outburst, however, he checked himself with startling abruptness. Silence again fell on the room. He turned his eyes to the row of clay models.

"I have made a grievous error!" he cried. "I have deceived myself and in doing so have deceived the world. I thought this man had genius in him. I praised his work. But now my eyes are opened and I see that all this"—he pointed an angry hand at the row of models—"is part of a conspiracy. Observe! He has made me less than a divinity; he has made me no more than a man. I can see his purpose clearly now. Ah, how sly he has been, how cleverly he has shown weaknesses in me, making me look covetous and angry and—and *weak!* It has been deliberately done, a scheme to belittle me in the eyes of my subjects, to destroy me for posterity!"

He turned with sudden ferocity and seized the nearest of the models. Raising it above his head, he dashed it to the ground, where it broke into small fragments.

Basil said to himself: "This is the end. I will be sent down to stand in the bracelets with the little dancer. Tomorrow we will both die." He was not conscious of any fear. Before him stretched a few of the scurrying hours that would so quickly become a part of the past. They would be hard hours, filled with agony perhaps, but after them would come eternity, and the peace and joy he had glimpsed.

No one was looking at him. Every eye was fixed with a fascinated interest on the gesticulating figure of Nero. Septimus touched his arm and pointed down the marble steps behind them. There, back of a row of pillars, the four slaves had stationed themselves with the pastry cage.

"Get into the cage!" whispered Septimus.

Basil glanced about him. No one yet had eyes for anything but the scene being enacted at the royal table. He stole down the steps on cautious feet and ensconced himself in the cage. There was a moment's hesitation, and then one of the slaves closed the pastry door. He found himself in darkness. There was another hesitation, a sound of whispering among the carriers. Then he felt them raise the conveyance. They moved slowly, casually.

Basil could hear Nero pouring forth his anger and bafflement in a continuing torrent of words. There was a crashing sound that meant that another of the models had been dashed to the ground. A third crash followed. Caesar did not intend to leave anything tangible as a reminder of his grievous error.

The easy, unhurried progress of the carriers continued unchecked. Basil heard the swinging doors move as he was carried through. And then the four slaves picked up their heels and ran as fast as their legs would carry them along the halls, the crust of the cage flaking down on the tense occupant and threatening a collapse of the pastry walls, the canaries too frightened to make a sound, the candles snuffing out in the rush of air, the candy bells breaking off and rolling in all directions on the dirty marble floor.

CHAPTER XXX

I

Destroy it!" ordered Selech the Great with an urgency in his voice that came close to panic. "Throw every morsel of the pastry down the drains. Chop up the wooden base and burn it. There must not be a trace of this cage left. And no one here is to have any clear idea as to how or when it was brought back. Now, where is the young man?"

One of the four slaves, in a thick accent that marked him as coming from the country at the foot of the boot, answered, "In the spicery, O Selech."

Basil was sitting on a bag of salt when the head cook entered the low-vaulted room where the spices were stored. There were bins on all sides containing cummin and sassafras and marjoram and galingale, and the air was filled with the pleasant odors of rosemary and rue and thyme. He looked pale and unhappy.

Selech observed the pallor and the unhappiness, but he saw no trace of fear. This was surprising, for he himself was deeply perturbed, and the four slaves who had carried out the cage were in a state of understandable palpitation.

"We cannot let them get their hands on you," said Selech. "It is tragedy enough that our little Juli-Juli had run foul of the Emperor's madness."

"What will happen to her?"

"What happens when a baby lamb is caught in the folds of a python?" Selech made a despairing gesture. "We must get you out of here, but my wits are not equal to seeing how it is to be done. It is certain that Tigellinus will have the guards on the alert. They are already patrolling the top of the wall with lanterns, I am sure."

"There is a hole under the wall," said Basil. "I know where it is. But where could I go then?"

Selech thought for a moment and then turned to Demetrius, who had accompanied him.

"Elishama ben Sheshbazzar?" he said in a questioning tone. "Elishama's house is close to the wall under the hill. Do you think we could ask such a dangerous favor of him?"

Demetrius bit his nails in an agony of indecision. "The dealer in gems? We would be asking him to risk his life, the lives of his family, his fortune, everything. And his fortune is a very large one, you must remember."

"Elishama is one of the most devout of Christians," declared Selech. "I think we must try him. But, Demetrius, go with the young man. Go in first to Elishama, leaving the young man outside. Tell him everything. If the dealer in gems says no, we will try someone else. But I think he will say yes. He is gentle and a man of peace, but as brave as a lion down deep in his heart."

Selech then addressed Basil in a worried tone. "Much depends on your ability to keep out of their clutches. Walk in discretion, my young friend, and take heed in everything you do. The lives of many people hang in the balance tonight."

Basil had found himself little concerned over the problem with which the two officers of Nero's household were struggling. His personal safety seemed a small matter. Above all the thoughts that filled his mind and the emotions they engendered was a sense of relief and joy. He had emerged from the valley of indecision. It had needed a crisis, a threat, to bring him to realization of the fullness of his faith. His mind was now so clear that it seemed to him like a room into which sunshine poured and through which comforting breezes blew; no dark corners, no forbidding shadows, nothing but light and happiness and this new security of the spirit.

Selech looked at him with a nod of approval. "You do not seem to have any fear. That is a very good sign."

"I am filled with fears!" exclaimed Basil. "There is Juli-Juli. What will they do with her? Can we not help her? Would Nero let her go free if I offered myself instead?"

"No," answered Selech with decision. "That would be a useless gesture. The Emperor would send you down to stand beside her in the bracelets and to face the questioning later."

"I am not afraid for myself," said Basil. This was quite true. Since taking his stand openly, the prospect of being punished for what he believed held no dread for him. "But I am possessed of a desire not to die now. If I do, my wife will never know how much I love her."

A puzzled look came over Selech's face, so Basil saw that further explanation was necessary. "There were circumstances that sealed my lips," he said. "And I did not realize how truly and deeply I love her until I came to Rome. Now I am filled with my devotion and I do, not want to die before I can tell her how blind I was and how wide my eyes have been opened."

"I am sure," said Selech, "that the Lord will lead you back to her. I wish I could be as sure that all the Christians who live under Nero's roof have as good a chance of escaping his wrath." He turned to his assistant. "You must start, Demetrius. Go out through the vaults. Take the shaded paths where the light of the moon does not reach. And do not forget my instructions when you come to the house of Elishama ben Sheshbazzar."

2

After crawling through the hole under the wall and discovering that it was filled with living things that slithered away from them, Basil and Demetrius came down to the house of Elishama ben Sheshbazzar, which hugged the base of the Palatine Hill. The grade was so steep at this point that they seemed to stand directly above the tall home of the gem merchant. With one false step they would land directly on its flat rooftop. They were much disturbed by the lights that gleamed from every window, for this meant that the establishment was astir and more than normally active for the hour.

When they reached the level of the street below, Demetrius stopped and shook his head. "It must be filled with people," he muttered. "Elishama will not be able to take you in. Still, I shall go in as Selech ordered. Stay until I return and stand back in the shadows. Make no noise. We may be preparing a place in the Mamertine for ourselves, you and I."

He was gone so long that Basil became convinced he did not intend to come back. This visit to the house of the gem merchant was no more than an easy way of taking leave. Perhaps Selech had wanted to get him off his hands as quickly and easily as possible and so had sent him out with

Demetrius with instructions that he was to be left to his own resources. Well, he was free of the palace, at any rate, and that was a first stride to freedom.

But how could he now proceed? What method was open to him for making his escape from the city? The harbor would be closely watched, and he dared not show himself there. It would be equally impossible to get away by land when he had no knowledge of the country, of the people or the language. It became clear to him as he stood in the shadow of a clump of eucalyptus trees that his position was a hopeless one. He could not turn back. The inn of Old Hannibal would be closely watched. He would not dare show himself in the anteroom of Kester of Zanthus. Instead of waiting to be captured, would it not be better to return to the palace and yield himself up to the wrath of Nero?

He was still debating the point when the lights of the house began to go out, one at a time, until the place was in darkness. A few moments later he heard a step approaching.

"Where are you?" whispered Demetrius.

"I am here."

The food buyer came up beside him and said in a relieved tone that they were to go in. "Elishama agreed at once," he said, "but it took some time to get everyone out of the way. The road is clear now. I will take you in and then I shall have to leave. I still have work to do before I go to visit the markets."

"You have risked a great deal for me," said Basil gratefully. "Everyone has been most unselfish, you and Selech and those four carriers who got me out of the banqueting hall."

"Repay us by not letting them catch you," whispered Demetrius. "I will be frank with you. We want nothing so much as to have you vanish. After all, we have our own skins to think of."

They entered the house by a rear door. Basil could not see anything and he followed his companion with arms outstretched in the dark. From the sound they made, he concluded they were in a large hall, and this was confirmed when a light burst suddenly out of the darkness some distance from them. A lamp had been lighted, and back of it Basil saw the head and shoulders of a man; a magnificent old man with flowing white hair and beard, a noble brow, and a pair of eyes filled with kindness and resolution. The lamp cast so small a light that it was as though a window had been opened and the head of the old man was on the outside looking in at them. Basil felt an immediate relief, for it was plain to be seen that this face, which seemed divorced from its body, was filled with compassion as well as courage.

"I am Elishama ben Sheshbazzar," said the owner of the house when they had come close to him. His voice was as warm and friendly as his eyes. He looked straight at Basil then and said, "Christ has risen."

The young sculptor felt a wave of pride as his lips formed the customary response. He had a right to use it now, for he believed in Jesus and had declared himself openly. By so doing he had thrown away all chance for reward at court and had placed his life in jeopardy. At last he belonged.

"He sits at the right hand of God," he said.

The words brought a sympathetic smile into the eyes back of the lamp, and Basil felt that a bond had been established. He said to himself, "Wherever I go, I find myself needing the help of unselfish men like this; but I have done nothing to deserve it."

"Follow me," whispered the gem merchant. "It will be wise, young stranger, to step lightly, for I do not want the sound of a new foot to be heard in the house. My people are not yet settled down for the night."

"I can do nothing more," said Demetrius at this point. There was an unmistakable note of relief in his voice. "And so I shall bid you good night and farewell."

Before any response could be made he turned from them and they could hear him stepping with great care to the door at the rear. Basil heard him go with regret. Another friend had come briefly into his life, had helped him, and now had departed.

The owner of the house led the way then into a room off the hall and closed the door after them. The lamp gave enough light for Basil to conclude that it was here the gem merchant conducted his affairs, although no stock was in sight; a spare room of no particular size, with cabinets on all sides, a table that served as a desk, and two chairs. His eyes fastened at once on a replica of the Temple that stood on the table. It was probably two feet high and made solidly of gold and burnished to such a degree that it shone richly in the small light cast upon it.

"Sit down," said the merchant.

He placed the lamp he was carrying on the table and from it drew a light, which he applied to the wick of a much larger one. The room sprang into new life then, and Basil could see that his host was tall and with the stoop of advanced years in his back. He was gentle, but it was clear he was also proud. There was compassion in his face, but an alert intelligence as well. A robe of immaculate white linen formed the base of his costume, and over it he wore an outer tunic of an amethyst shade that was magnificently embroidered and embellished. He wore a black skullcap, and around his neck there was a gold chain that was long enough to stretch from one end of the room to the other. A large carbuncle glittered on one of his fingers.

"I offer my regrets for the circumstances under which it is necessary to welcome you into my house," said Elishama ben Sheshbazzar. "My helpers were all at work when Demetrius came to me. The house servants had not finished their labors for the day. My wife, who is in delicate health and must not be subjected to any disturbance or alarm, had not retired for the night. All my people are Christians and, I believe, completely dependable, but it must be as clear to you as it is to me that the fewer who know of your presence in the house, the less chance there will be of mistakes or slips; and so a better chance of helping you out of your difficulties. I shall endeavor to confine all knowledge of you to one servant and myself. Not even my wife is to know, or my fine sons, of whom I have three."

He had seated himself at the table, and his arms in their ample amethyst sleeves rested on its top. Although he was watching his guest, the model of the Temple was always in his line of vision.

"The report I have had from my good friend Demetrius is very disturbing," he said gravely. "There will be much suffering because of the wild charges this woman has made. But it is clear that you behaved with great courage. Men do this when the fire of conviction burns warmly in their hearts, but I never get over my wonder when I encounter evidences of it. Ah well, ah well, there is in each of us a little of our Lord in heaven. More in some than in others." His eyes had been glowing warmly, but at this point they lost their fine content and became apprehensive. "Yes, my young friend, trouble and fear hang over the palace of Nero tonight like a black cloud. Everything she said, this wicked siren who parades herself on the public platforms with Simon, is false. There has been no conspiring. But because of her evil inventions there is danger that all of our people will be driven from their posts. The Emperor may treat them far worse than that."

"Let us pray that no great harm will come to Juli-Juli," said Basil fervently. "I did no more than follow her brave example tonight, but she was not as lucky as I. It weighs bitterly on me that I made my escape in the cage in which she had been carried into the hall and in which she was to have been left."

"It is asking much, I am afraid." A look of the deepest gravity took possession of the noble countenance of Elishama ben Sheshbazzar. "The wrath of Nero will not spend itself at once. There will be some victims. She may be the first."

"Is there no way of getting her free?"

"Nothing short of a palace revolution would do it." The old merchant sighed deeply and glanced down at his hands, which were lying on the table in front of him. They were remarkable hands, delicately shaped, the fingers long and tapered and sensitive. After indulging in a moment of concentrated thought he looked up again. "The Jews who live in the Diaspora have much to contend with. We must endure the envy that our successes bring us, and a dislike because we are the chosen of the one living God. These feelings seem to have grown deeper since the coming of Jesus, Who was of the seed of David and Whose gentle teachings are too new and strange for them. And"—he reached out to touch a reverent finger briefly to the golden replica—"we live with a longing that burns in our hearts for the sight so dear to all the children of Israel, the sun glistening on that great roof of gold under which—under which the spirit of God comes to commune with His people." He looked up then. "I say this because so many of the servants at the palace, on whom the wrath of Nero may fall, are Jews who have seen the light and believe in the teachings of God's only begotten Son."

There was silence for a moment before Elishama reached out one of his beautiful hands to touch a circular object that lay on the table in front of him. "We must give my young men a chance to fall asleep before we venture into any other part of the house. In the meantime, to take your mind from the troubles that hang over us, I will explain to you about this."

He lifted the object so that Basil could see it was a clay model of a tiara and then replaced it on the desk.

"Being a sculptor and a worker in silver, you will be interested in this model. Do you think it good?"

"Yes, it is beautiful indeed. I have been admiring the design."

"I appreciate such praise from you because I designed it myself and I am doing the most intricate part of the work. The telling will serve a double purpose because it will be at the same time an explanation of why my young men were working so late tonight. I am not a hard taskmaster. I ask of them no more than seven hours of labor each day although in Jerusalem we worked much longer. It is becoming the custom in Rome to so arrange the working hours that they have most of the afternoon free. At the moment we are engaged in a race against time. This is the model of a tiara we are making for the Empress. A few days ago the Emperor became most insistent that it be finished in a much shorter time than he had stipulated at first. He is a man of small patience, and nothing will satisfy him short of a miracle on our part. He can hardly wait to place this remarkable gift on the head of his wife, who—ah well, ah well, we must concede that she is beautiful—who will wear it to great advantage. Because of this my young men and I have been working day and night."

Basil had been studying the model as its originator spoke, admiring its proportions and the delicacy of the design. Certainly it would be beautiful on the amber locks of Poppaea.

"As you perhaps know, there is in Rome at the moment a great liking for the opal," went on the gem merchant. "It is placed above all other hyaline stones. It is not a first favorite with me. I place the ruby and the sapphire above it, and someday, when we learn how to cut it, the diamond will be the greatest stone of all. But the men who buy the jewels and the women who wear them will be content with nothing but the opal. I bend to this popular demand, and so there will be many fine black ones from Egypt used in the design, set off with one truly magnificent specimen of the fire opal. The black ones are remarkably good." He hesitated and then drew from a drawer under the table a stone of considerable size, which he held up for his visitor's inspection. "Yes, there is much to be said for it. The opal has such warmth and variety of color."

The stone was dark and luminous with green lights against a background as black as a thundercloud. It was, Basil said to himself, like a glimpse of the green flames of the nether regions, a little terrifying and yet with a fascination that could not be denied.

"There will be rubies as well," explained the gem merchant. "I decided against the use of turquoise, but I am using many sapphires." His eyes began to glow with enthusiasm. This was natural, for all Jews had a deep love for the sapphire. They believed that it restored failing sight and could even check the flow of blood from a wound. "Yes, I am setting some magnificent sapphires into the design. There will be a few olivines and, of course, some amethysts."

"It will be costly."

"Add the value of Pompey's chessboard, which was made of gold, and that of the men, which were cut from precious stones, to the cost of the golden vine of Aristobulus and the fabulous necklace of Lollia Paulina, and you will still not equal the cost of this tiara that is to rest on the head of our new Empress." The merchant looked earnestly across the table at his guest. "Were you long enough at court to learn that Nero is unhappy about the city of Rome? He finds it crowded and ugly and with too many offensive smells. He dreams of a cleaner and finer capital. Young stranger, he could sweep the Subura out of existence with the money he is putting into this tiara, and build wide streets and clean houses instead. Ah well, ah well, there will be a handsome profit in it. Much of the profit will go to some more commendable use than the adornment of the body of the fair Poppaea."

The black opal was replaced in the drawer and the model was moved to one side. The merchant rose, walked to the door, and opened it with great caution. The house had fallen into slumber; no sounds, at any rate, reached their ears. After a moment he returned and began speaking in a low voice. "I have been talking to fill in time. Now it seems safe to take you to the room where you will spend the night. I think all my young men are asleep, but it will be wise to remove your sandals. Permit me to make suggestions for our mutual good. Bolt your door on the inside and do not open it unless you hear someone rap twice slowly and then twice rapidly. That will be the servant I have selected to share the secret. When you open the door, stand well behind it, and under no circumstances go near a window. The name of the servant is Joseph. He was born in the Valley of the Cheesemakers. He is very deaf and very faithful."

"I will take every precaution," promised Basil. "That is the least I can do when you are risking so much."

The gem merchant pressed a reassuring hand on his shoulder. "You stood up before Nero and proclaimed yourself a Christian. I, who must conceal my beliefs, can surely do this much. I do it gladly." He placed a brass cover over the lamp so it would not give a wide reflection in passing through the halls. "I will visit you in the morning and we will discuss plans for your escape from Rome."

3

The bedroom was large and airy and furnished with a degree of luxury that came as a surprise after the Spartan quality of the room below. There was a large bed and a sunken bath in one corner. A detailed map of Jerusalem had been sketched in colors on one wall. He caught glimpses of such aids to comfort as a laver, a wine container, and an assortment of bottles and drinking cups. The air was delicately perfumed, and a cool breeze blew in through the windows.

He found it impossible at first to sleep. The events of the evening kept running through his mind. He paced up and down the room on bare feet, his hands clenched, his whole body taut. The vision of Juli-Juli chained to a wall would not leave him. There must be something they could do to help her. But what, what? His thoughts kept running into this mental cul-de-sac.

He spent some time in front of the map, lamp in hand. With the fore-finger of the other hand he traced the course he and Deborra had followed when they fled from the Court of the Gentiles and led pursuit through the domain of the poor cheesemakers. He lowered himself with great care into the water that filled his bath and lay there without moving, hoping that slumber could be induced in that way. It did him no good. He was as wakeful as before when he emerged from the tepid water. As he dried himself he kept asking the same question. What could be done to help the little dancer?

It was strange that he could not get to sleep, for physically he seemed very tired. His legs balked when he started back at his pacing. He seated himself with a deep sigh in a chair facing the windows.

Immediately, as though he had come to witness a play, the wall seemed to recede and dissolve, and he found himself looking at a familiar scene. It was familiar because he had seen it before, the gathering of twelve men about a long table in the Wall of David. He knew it was not a dream this time. He could not have fallen off in the winking of an eye, and the scene was much too vivid, too clear. Every detail was as clear as though he himself sat in this room in the Wall of David. It was the same as before in the matter that concerned him most: the space in the center was still vacant.

His eye was taken immediately by the man who sat on the left of the open space, and he said to himself with elated excitement that it was John. There was no mistaking the Beloved Disciple. The protruding brow and the widely spaced eyes, the sensitive and eloquent mouth were the same. This young John had a bodily vigor that the wasted figure preaching in the mine near Ephesus had lacked, and his face was that of a young man; a young man of great courage and sweetness.

"Peter will be on the other side," Basil said aloud, turning his eyes in that direction. He broke at once into an excited laugh of recognition, for the figure to the right of the space was none other than Cephas!

So the old servant at the inn was the acknowledged leader of the Christians, as he had half suspected, the disciple who had been chosen by Jesus. This explained the deference paid him by Hannibal and by the man Mark. It explained his absences also, for the responsibilities of leadership would call him away at times.

The Peter who sat at the right was far different from the gentle old man of the inn. He was having nothing to say and his eyes were stormy and unreconciled to the nature of the separation that Christ had said was soon to take place.

But Basil had not time to study more closely the face of the moody Peter. Something was happening to the scene; something far different from anything he had witnessed before. It caused him at first a shiver of dread and then, taking him to the other extreme, a sense of blissful anticipation. The space that had been empty was no longer entirely bare. Someone, still no more than a shadow, was sitting there!

He strained his eyes to see, and gradually the form became clearer, as though a process of materialization were taking place. Slowly the shadows turned to substance, and out of the merging of surfaces and colors a face appeared. It was the face of a man in his early prime, a face delicate, gentle, but wonderfully strong and wise, although at that moment it was tortured with a tragic duty and sad beyond all human comprehension.

"I am seeing Jesus!" whispered Basil. "I can see His eyes, as Deborra said I would."

At that point the eyes seemed to look directly at him and to smile. They were wonderful eyes, set wide apart under a broad brow; wise, discerning, compassionate eyes that could express humor and sweetness even though a great sorrow possessed them.

Basil lowered his head, saying to himself, "I am not worthy to look any longer." He had never felt so humble, so full of human faults, so conscious of his sins. What right had he to pry further, to continue watching this holy scene?

As he sat with his brow in his hands, however, it came to him that there was reason behind this vision, that it had been allowed him so that he could finish the Chalice. He must conquer his sense of humility and take advantage of the sublime opportunity that had been offered him. Convinced of this, he opened his eyes and studied the face of Jesus with the keen intentness of the artist.

With new eagerness he took account of details. The nose of Jesus was neither long nor prominent. It was straight and with a delicacy of modeling that gave it beauty. The mouth expressed all the qualities that showed themselves in the eyes. The chin, which was bare of beard, showed strength as well as gentleness.

"I have been allowed this vision," said Basil to himself with a sense of urgency and excitement, "so that I may finish the Chalice. I must get to work. Now, at once."

At this point he realized that he was asleep, after all, for he could not bring himself back to consciousness. Knowing that he must set his fingers to their task while the vision of that incomparable face was clear in his mind, he strove harder to free himself of the shackles of slumber. He struggled and groaned. Realizing finally that he held something of weight in his right hand, he struck his leg a blow with it. He felt a sharp pain and, with the mists of sleep dissolving at once, he sat up straight in his chair. He was staring into the blackness of empty space, in which the outline of the curtained window was barely discernible.

He was weak with excitement and his brow was covered with perspiration.

"Jesus, Master!" he said in a tone under a whisper. "You have given your servant this great privilege. I have seen You, I have looked into Your eyes, I have seen You smile. Put now into my fingers the power to perpetuate for all time what I have been shown, so that other men may see also."

All lassitude left him at once, and he felt strong and capable of achieving the task ahead of him. He fumbled at the table for the lighter and finally created a flame that flickered uncertainly before taking a steady hold on the wick. It was going to be a very inadequate light for the work he had to do, but he would make the most of it. Fortunately he had carried the blue cloth bag with him as usual that evening and it had been on his shoulder when he fled from the police. The clay was damp and ready for use, and he spread his tools out in front of him with fingers trembling with eagerness to begin and fear that he might fail.

He worked with intense concentration, repeating over and over that he had gazed on the face of the Son of God and that it would remain fixed in his mind forever, even though his hands might fail to bring it to life in the clay. He had no conception of time, save that he was sure the hours were speeding away. The insufficient light hampered him, but he did not dare seek to better it. Even when a gray light showed faintly through the window, he did not venture to draw back the curtain, remembering the explicitness of the restrictions his host had placed upon him.

He knew that if he did not achieve at once what was demanded of his hands it would be useless to attempt change or revision later. With this thought driving him on, he never ceased in his feverish manipulation of the clay until the light stealing in around the curtains had a clearness and vitality that warned him that day had come.

He looked at what he had accomplished and said aloud, "This is all I can do." He knew it was good. The face that had gazed at him in his dream now looked out from the gray clay. It was lacking in many respects; some of the mystery of the face was gone, and still more of the light in the eyes; but his fingers, he said to himself, were human. He would leave it as it was.

He turned toward the window and said, "Day has broken," rising at the same time to draw the curtains more securely. The action made him conscious again of a pain in his knee. Glancing down, he saw that his leg was streaked with blood. It had been one of his knives he had found in his hand when the need to rouse himself had caused him to strike the knee. There was blood on the floor where he had been sitting.

4

Joseph brought up the midday meal. A few moments after he left, four raps were repeated on the door to announce the arrival of Elishama ben Sheshbazzar. The gem merchant looked a little more stately in his person and a great deal easier in his mind. He seated himself near the table while Basil continued with his meal of kidneys stewed in wine and dressed with African figs.

"The turmoil at the palace has subsided somewhat," reported Elishama. "No evidence of a conspiracy has been uncovered, and the Emperor is beginning to quiet down. It seems that no one came forward to support the charges of this infamous woman. A whisper did reach Nero's ears about Selech, but at that point the Empress put her foot down. It is said that she spoke quite violently to her royal spouse. 'These drafty halls in which we have to live are bare and shabby,' she told him. 'I shudder at the ugliness of everything and at the smells about the place. All we have to make life supportable is the best cook in the world. Are you going to get rid of him on suspicions?' Petronius, who knows the real value of Selech better than anyone, supported Poppaea. And so, after much grumbling and many loud outcries that he stood alone while assassins sharpened their daggers for him, Nero gave in."

Basil sighed in an intensity of relief. "What happy news you have brought!" he exclaimed. "I was afraid that all who had helped me would be hopelessly entangled."

"No one seems to know how you escaped from the hall," said the merchant. "All eyes were on Nero. When he came to the end of his tantrum, they looked for you, and you were gone. The possibility that you were carried out in the pastry cage does not seem to have occurred to anyone." He was silent for a moment as he offered Basil a dish containing pheasant sausages prepared with garum. "Selech was not called up for questioning. Darius was examined and he showed himself of small resolution, protesting loudly that he was not a Christian. I hear that Nero came around to speaking of you with regret. 'I shall miss my little genius,' he said. 'Unhappy man that I am, compelled to sacrifice friendships in the interests of the state!' If he continues to feel this way, you might regain your standing with him in time. But he is as capricious of temper as a panther with a thorn in its paw, and I would not advise any effort to return until he gives more certain indications of forgiveness."

"I must leave Rome at the first possible moment," declared Basil. "I had little taste for court life at any time, and now I am completely cured of it."

"Wisely spoken," said the merchant, nodding his head approvingly. He gave vent to a sigh. "You speak of having no taste for the life of the court. I lack taste for any part of the life I live here. I think it is the same with all the Jews of the Diaspora. They exist in a state of melancholy, quite unreconciled to life so far from the Temple. It is inevitable that we must continue to leave Jerusalem, for the genius of the children of Israel is too strong to be confined to that small strip of land between the Jordan and the sea. It needs the whole world for its expression, and so we move about and set up colonies. We become successful and prosperous, but we are unhappy all the days of our lives. I do as many do who have become rich men; I surround myself with luxury and try to find compensation in that. The doors of my house are made of tortoise shell, the handles are of silver. I partake of food off plates of gold and silver. But it is a small recompense for what I have given up. I sometimes think that I would be happier living in Jerusalem in poverty and obscurity; but if I returned I would soon find myself longing for the fruits of my labors here. There is, in other words, a devil with a pitchfork on each side of me. I can never be happy." He remained sunk in thought for some moments. Then he began speaking of other matters. "There will be a meeting of the leaders of the church here tonight to confer with Peter. It had been arranged before you came. Much as I dislike bringing more curious eyes into the house while your safety hangs in the balance, it is too late to think of postponement. There is this also, that the meeting was called to discuss the challenge of Simon the Magician. Further delay is impossible."

"I saw Peter in a dream last night," said Basil. "What I was shown confirmed a suspicion that has been in my mind." Observing a look of apprehension in his host's eye, he went on to make an explanation. "I know where he is living. I stayed at the inn where he works for a week before being summoned to the palace. I am still at a loss to understand why he chooses to exist under such difficulties."

"It is easy to understand when you know how bitterly the tide of opinion has been running against us in Rome." Elishama gave his head a shake of great gravity. "Peter lived at first in the Trans-Tiber, where there is a large Jewish colony. But some months ago Tigellinus adopted a more severe attitude. He began to send his officers throughout the city to ask questions and make lists. It was clear that he wanted the names of all the Christians in Rome. We felt it was unwise, under these circumstances, for Peter to remain openly where he was. It was agreed that he would either have to go into hiding or establish a new identity where he would be free of suspicion. He went to serve with Old Hannibal, whose connection with the faith had never been suspected. He has remained there ever since, content to serve in a menial capacity and to do the bidding of the guests who come and go. The authorities have no idea that this old man who works so patiently is the Peter who is our leader." He filled his guest's cup with wine, which was fragrant and well cooled. "You spoke of a dream. I am very much interested, having devoted some time to the study of dreams and trances. Did you see others in this dream?"

"I saw all the disciples who broke bread with Jesus on the last night," declared Basil. "John was there. I heard him preach at Ephesus and so I was able to recognize him at once. At first there was one vacant place, but as I watched it gradually filled and I—I saw Jesus! I beg of you, O Elishama, not to think I am inventing a tale. I saw the room in the Wall of David and I saw the face of Jesus as clearly as I see yours now. He smiled at me. I looked into His eyes, His grave and understanding eyes." Basil came to a stop. He must convince his host of the need to see and speak to Peter. "I hesitate to put such an idea into words, but it is necessary for me to see Cephas when he comes. I have things to tell him. Things that are very important."

Elishama ben Sheshbazzar considered the matter carefully. "This much I can promise," he said finally. "That you will see him. The meeting is to be held in my showroom, which is the largest in the house. It has a watching gallery. You see, human nature is frail. Women of wealth and high station are particularly frail when they see beautiful things spread out before them in great profusion. Some of them are certain to become what we call light-fingered. And so it has been the rule with merchants who have large stocks of jewels to have a hidden gallery where watchers can keep an eye on these fashionable customers. My showroom has its gallery, and it will be your privilege to stand there and watch when Peter sits down in consultation with the princes of the church in Rome. I shall whisper in his ear that you are a witness and so you can feel guiltless of eavesdropping." He paused. "As to speaking with him, that will be for Peter to decide."

A question had been on the tip of Basil's tongue from the moment the merchant entered. He had feared to ask it, but now he forced himself to the risk of hearing what he dreaded. "What of Juli-Juli?"

The face of the gem merchant became grave. "The dancer displayed a courage and fortitude in contrast to the weakness of her instructor," he said. "She refused to give any information. They got nothing from her at all, not a name, not a hint."

"But——" began Basil, and then stopped. He found it almost impossible to articulate a further question. "But—did she come through the ordeal safely?"

Elishama shook his head. "No," he answered. "No. That was not to be expected. She refused to yield—and so she died under the torture."

"Dead!" cried Basil. A feeling of horror had taken possession of him. "How can there be such cruelty in the world?"

"She has been the first to suffer martyrdom. There will be many more as time goes on. We are preparing ourselves for it."

When he was alone Basil took a few steps blindly in the direction of the window. With unseeing eyes he gazed out over the rooftops shimmering in the midday heat. Everything seemed black and hopeless. Juli-Juli had died to save others from the fate that had overtaken her. That brave little spirit was no more. The light feet that had performed with such gaiety the Dance of the Sandals of Caesar were still.

"O Lord Jehovah," he whispered in a choked voice, "I hope You did not let her suffer too much, that brave little girl." Then he raised an arm in a gesture of farewell and called, *"Vale!"*

5

Peering down through the narrow slot in the stone wall, Basil saw Peter seated at the head of the room. The space about the apostle was crowded with people who had eyes for no one else. Since his dream he had known that Cephas was Peter, but in the appearance of the leader of the church there was some room for surprise. The hair and beard of the apostle were snow-white and most benevolently tended and curled. He was dressed in linen of a matching whiteness. But it was a change in his attitude that was most to be remarked. This was not the self-effacing old man of the inn; it was an acknowledged leader, a man who knew how to command, how to make his will accepted. The earnest-faced people who filled the room waited on his words and listened to him as though the departed Jesus spoke with his tongue.

It became apparent that they had been discussing the challenge of Simon Magus, for Peter now said: "We have been too much concerned with this wicked man. He and his knavish tricks will soon cease to be of any consequence."

"But, Peter," protested a voice from the end of the room, "you must agree that he has been doing us much harm. People have been wondering, whispering, asking questions. Some have been won away. If we let him do his flying from the high tower he has built without anything being heard from us, men will indeed begin to ask if he has greater powers than those whom Jesus named to act in His stead."

Another voice spoke earnestly. "It was you, Peter, who said to the lame beggar sitting for alms at the Beautiful Gate, 'Rise up and walk.' It was you who raised Tabitha from the dead. Can you not find it in your heart to perform a miracle for the confounding of this persistent gadfly, this wicked Simon? We know that with the mere stretching out of a hand——"

"My brothers," said Peter, "do you think it the will of the Lord that I so demean the power that has been given to me, among others, that I would use it to put a mere trickster out of countenance before Caesar?"

"All the world will be watching!" cried a third voice. "Watching and listening and drawing conclusions."

There was a brief silence before Peter spoke again. "Know this, my brethren, that I have never attempted to use the power unless the Lord spoke in my ear and commanded me to do so. Since that night when Simon stood before Nero and said, 'Pit me against these Christians,' I have listened. But the Lord has not spoken. I have not heard Him say to me, 'Arise, Peter, and do that which I command thee, that this man from Samaria shall no longer utter his boasts.' And, my friends, I have been happy that the Voice has not spoken. I see clearly that it would be wrong to match ourselves against a man who utters abominations and deals in the wicked use of charms and potions."

"But," protested one of the listeners, "should he be allowed to fly out from his tower for all Rome to see and marvel at?"

"I do not believe, my good friends," answered Peter in a voice of sudden finality, "that we should question the will of God in advance. Our faith should be equal to believing this, that He will be watching when Simon Magus steps out on his new Tower of Babel. We should be ready to believe that, whatever happens, it will come about because He willed it."

Basil, watching and listening eagerly, felt a glow of satisfaction. This was the answer he had expected to hear. It would make no difference if Peter knew that Simon relied on tangible aids and that it would be easy to expose him before the world. The answer would still be the same: The Lord will be watching.

The voice of Elishama ben Sheshbazzar made itself heard. "Peter is right, my friends. Should the lion turn his head to the channering of the hyena?"

Basil began to move along the dark and cramped passage in which he stood, feeling his way from one slit of light to another, and so getting a complete view of the gathering below. He saw the ascetic face of Selech, the nervous and unhappy visage of Demetrius, the beautifully modeled head of Elishama. Beside the latter sat a delicate lady with a face of great sweetness who undoubtedly was his wife. He saw also the round head and uneven shoulders of Mark, who looked a little out of place in a gathering of such gentility and whose frown testified that he was aware of it. On all of the many faces he studied there was the same look of reverence, the same willingness to abide finally by the decisions of the ancient fisherman.

Basil was not aware when the topic of discussion was changed below because at this point he found himself thinking of the tragedy that had occurred. He clenched his hands angrily and said to himself: "Why do I not return and wheedle myself back into the good graces of Nero? Someday, perhaps, I would find myself alone with him and I would say, 'Caesar, do you remember the girl Juli-Juli, who used your sandals in a dance, and whom you had killed?' And then I would cut his base, thick throat from one side to the other, and the voice he thinks so golden would be as still as her light feet." As soon as this thought went through his mind he was conscious of a feeling of guilt. "My conversion cannot yet be complete," he said to himself in a panic, "since I can still have violence in my heart." It was not until he reached the slit at the far end of the room and could look down across the assembled company to where Peter sat in his fine white linen that he felt any comfort. "It was Peter," he said to himself, then, "who drew a sword on the Mount of Olives and smote off the ear of Malchus. It cannot be the will of the Lord that His people should always abstain from anger."

These thoughts distracted his attention until he heard a voice below him asking, "Is nothing to be done for the slaves of Quintus Clarius who are to die in the morning?"

The silence in this room, where the princes of the church in Rome sat with backs pressed against the cabinets in which Elishama kept his stores of precious stones, was so complete that Basil could hear the faintest rustle of a tunic on the wooden benches.

"This is in all of your minds," said Peter in a voice to which compassion and sorrow had given an edge of intensity. "You are asking, 'Is it the will of God that these hundred men and women, all of whom believe in Jesus and strive to walk in His steps, shall be put to death for a crime of which they are innocent?' You are thinking, 'Surely the Hand of the Lord will be stretched out to save them.' "

"Yes, Peter," said Elishama, "these thoughts are in all of our minds."

"My brethren," said Peter earnestly, "I can give you no answer save the one you have already heard. The Lord has not said, 'Arise, Peter, and save them.' And truly, brothers and sisters in the faith, should we expect Him to speak? Listen, listen in patience and understanding. It is always known on the eve of a great battle that on the day following thousands of fine young men will be cut down ruthlessly. Does the Lord feel it incumbent on Him to interfere in these tragic butcheries? When the forces of nature gather for the flooding of a mighty river or there is an agitation in the bowels of the earth and it is known in heaven that an earthquake will follow, the Lord does not reach down to remove the people who stand in the path of destruction. When a pestilence begins in the slums of a city, the Lord does not intervene to save the thousands who will die miserably of the plague. Life on this earth is made cruel by the barbarities of nature and the wickedness of men, and thus it has been from the beginning.

"Hearken to me still," he went on after a pause. "The words I am going to say to you have been in my mind for a very long time. I give utterance to my thoughts now because I am sure the Lord is putting the words in my mouth so that ye may know His will. There must be a testing of the faith of man if the teachings of Jesus are to prevail. It becomes ever clearer that the test will be here, in Rome, on which the eyes of the world rest and where a strange and cruel man sits on a temporal throne. The fate of these poor slaves who now lie in prison will be no more than a beginning. Rome will know such persecution as the world has never seen before. Many of us who sit here tonight will be among those who perish. Verily, it is the will of God that many shall die so that a great faith will rise triumphant out of martyrdom."

Peter rested for a moment and then spoke in a voice that had risen to an exultant pitch. "It is my hope that I, who denied Jesus on that blackest of nights, will be among those chosen to suffer, so that I may see the glory of the new dawn. And this I say to you, that the Christians of Rome will display such an unshakable faith in the face of the sufferings to come that all will wonder and say, 'What of this man Jesus, what is His secret that men and women will die at His beck?' And all over the world the true faith will spread and all men will bow down before the living God."

Basil watched the face of the inspired fisherman and he knew that everything Peter was saying would come to pass. Luke had prepared him to believe that a greater miracle than the delivery of slaves from a jail was the creation of such faith in the frail hearts of men.

"This I shall do tonight," concluded Peter. "When we have ended our deliberations, I shall go to the Mamertine, where these sad men and women are held. It may be that the Lord will not permit the walls of that cruel prison to remain a barrier and that I shall be able to enter into the cells where they wait. And I shall strive to bring to them such assurance of the peace and happiness into which they will be released by the cruel hand of Nero that they will face the morrow with the courage we must all summon to support us when the testing comes. Tomorrow," he cried, "is the beginning! Let us turn our faces ahead with belief that out of our sufferings will come a spreading of the gospel over all the world."

6

It was late when Peter entered Basil's room. He joined the young sculptor on a carved bench against the wall.

"The eyes of God have been upon you, my son," he said. "He has plucked you out of the clutches of the wicked Emperor as our friends below desired to see Him pluck the condemned people from the walls of the Mamertine."

"I escaped in the cage that brought the little dancer into the hall," said Basil with self-bitterness. "Knowing that she died, I find it hard to rejoice in my good fortune."

"Grieve not for those who go to a sure reward."

There was a moment's silence and then Peter said, "It is certain that you are destined for special labors in the vineyard." The merest hint of a twinkle developed in the deep-set eyes. "Were you much surprised when you saw me below and knew that old Cephas of the little inn was Simon called Peter from Galilee?"

Basil shook his head. "No, Father Peter. I was prepared. I had been shown you in a dream."

He proceeded then to tell of the scene he had witnessed in his sleep. Peter listened with the most intense concentration and, when the point was reached where the face of Jesus grew out of the blackness, he reached out both hands and grasped those of his young companion. His eyes were glowing with fervor.

"My son, you have seen Jesus!" he exclaimed. "How few are those living today who have gazed on His face! Even though you stood up boldly before Nero and pledged your faith, as I knew you would when the time came, it was not to be expected that this reward would be given you. Most clearly," he added, "it is the will of the Lord that this Chalice should be finished."

Basil got up from the bench and trimmed the wick of the oil lamp so that it gave out a better light. He carried it then to the table where the last of his efforts stood under the covering of a damp cloth. He raised the cover and stepped back.

Peter gazed on the head that had been revealed; and then his hands drew together, his mouth quivered with overwhelming emotion, and he sank down before the table on his knees.

"It is the face of Jesus," he whispered. "Truly, my son, you have been inspired. Thus have I seen Him look often; His eyes so clear, so penetrating, so full of pity and understanding; His mouth so gentle and tender. It was thus He looked on that night when we broke bread in the Wall of David. It was thus He looked when He came to us for the last time." He began to say a prayer in a low and passionate tone. "O Jesus, my Master, may I look upon Your face soon as this young man has looked upon it for a moment in his dreams? As You have deigned to come to him, come Thou to me so that I may have Your guidance in the dark days that stretch ahead. I am old and tired and I need Your comfort and aid, O Jesus, my Master, my Saviour!"

A moment later he rose from his knees. "Replace the cloth, my son," he said. "Until you have made it into permanent form and the chalice is completed, you must guard this as the High Priest guards the secrets of the Holy of Holies. This is a gift for the generations of believers who will follow us." His voice became more normal as the necessities of the situation intruded themselves on his mind. "A ship sails from Rome for the East in a few days whose captain is a Christian and will take you with him. I have spoken to Elishama, and he agrees that you should take advantage of such a good chance to get away." He inclined his head again to look at the face of Christ. "Guard it well, my son, guard it with your life if necessary."

CHAPTER XXXI

I

HELENA WOULD HAVE BEEN seriously concerned if she had known that Simon rose at dawn on the day of the test. The first streamers of light in the eastern sky saw him on the rooftop, watching the marble parapets come into view along the crest of the Palatine as the sun picked them out one by one. As usual, his eyes came to rest on the house where Cicero had lived.

"O most eloquent of men," he intoned, stretching out his arms. "If only you were alive today to recount with your silver tongue the astonishment I shall cause the world!"

His gaze turned then toward a mere glimmer of white where the walls of the Palatium showed through the trees. "Verily, Nero," he cried, "I shall gratify today your hatred of these sanctimonious people. In a few hours we will both be able to sit back and pat our bellies with pride and say, 'Come up, Peter, come up, Paul, what have you to say for your puny miracles now?' "

As soon as it became light enough, he immersed himself in an Eastern manuscript on magic and the occult. He had purchased it many years before at a very considerable price but had never been able to reach an understanding of what it contained. Now he seemed to be reading with great absorption, as though the power had suddenly been given him to assimilate its strange knowledge. As he turned the parchment with eager fingers, he muttered to himself: "Yes, this is the truth. I have always known that these forces existed and could be summoned to the aid of anyone with the audacity to try. No one has more audacity than I."

He was still poring over the manuscript when one of his helpers put his head through the trap door that gave access to the roof. It was an impudent head, with a slack mouth and a leering eye, and there was a complete lack of respect in the greeting he gave with a jaunty wave of his hand: "Blackbirds roosting in a philosopher's hat!"

"Balchis!" cried Simon. "What do you mean by disturbing my studies? Betake yourself and your stupid expressions of the magic trade out of my sight and hearing."

The assistant's grin changed from an expression of impudent amusement to one of contempt. "What I came to tell you is this, O man of mighty learning! One hour ago we finished our task of installing the little device under the top of the tower. There was not a prying eye to see what we were doing. There it is, as snug as a louse in a beggar's shirt. And it works, O wise Simon. Set your great mind at rest. You will be able to fly out and back as easy and safe as a twittering little lovebird."

"Yes, I shall fly," declared the great magician. "But I shall have no need for this device that you have set up in the tower. A great force has been infused into my veins, and I shall ascend into the sky without any other aid."

"The belch of an Apulian mule driver for that, O bold Simon!" said Balchis. He proceeded to let the trap door down after him as he descended the stairs, and so vanished from sight.

Within a very short time Helena raised the door and stepped up to the stone roof with an impatient tap of sandals. She carried a robe of yellow and black over one arm.

"Here it is," she said. "The seamstress finished it late last night. You will recall—if you recall anything I say or do, which I sometimes doubt—that we made tests and decided that this combination of colors would show most conspicuously against the blue of the sky. See! It will be a becoming costume for you."

Simon looked up from his manuscript with little interest. "It is excellent."

Helena spread the robe out on the table beside him. She seated herself on the stone ledge that ran around beneath the lip of the parapet and looked with rising indignation at the partly empty leather bottle at his elbow. "You have been drinking!" she charged. "And on the day of the test."

"Yes, my *zadeeda,*" he answered. "I was so fully aware of its being the day of the test that I was up at the break of dawn."

"And you have kept yourself busy drinking ever since!" she cried. "Simon, you have been behaving like a fool. Do you not realize that it will take all your strength to perform this feat?"

Simon was very proud of his physical strength. He stretched out an arm and flexed his muscles. "Look at that! I am as strong as a gladiator."

"Your arm is thin. You have not been eating enough and you have been drinking too much." She turned on him in a sudden fury. "Has it entered your head that you dare not fail? The Emperor wants the Christians humiliated. He expects this of you, and so you must succeed. You think you stand high in the favor of this young Emperor, but make no mistake about what will happen if you fail!"

The magician raised his head proudly, as though he felt the eyes of Cicero on him from the heights above. "I shall not fail," he declared. He picked up the manuscript and began to read, keeping the corner of one eye on his companion to discover what effect this had on her. "This is an amazing document, my Helena."

"You could not understand a sentence in it whenever you tried it before."

"The power to understand it has been granted to me." He looked at her with a burning eye. "The gift of tongues, my Helena. It has descended upon me."

"The gift of one tongue will descend upon you if you do any more drinking today. A sharp tongue, my Simon." Helena whisked the bottle up from the table. "I ought to remain and keep an eye on you, my little man. But I must visit the tower and make sure that—that *it* has been set up properly. They tell me everything is right, but I do not trust any of them. I must see with my own eyes." She cast some final remarks back over her shoulder as she descended the stairs. "The midday meal will be served in the tower, and the test comes immediately after. Can I be sure that you will arrive in good time and in good condition? I will not have a chance to return for you. Promise that you will do no more drinking. You must have a cool head today."

"You may count on me," declared Simon with a sudden accession of dignity. "Have you any conception of the great powers that accompany the gift of tongues?"

2

The lower floor of the wooden tower had been solidly walled so that the men in charge of the operations could use it as their headquarters. There were a long trestle table, on which the plans had been kept spread out for their convenience, and several camp chairs of the kind used by soldiers in the field. Against one wall there was a narrow flight of wooden steps leading to a trap door in the ceiling. Shavings were piled in heaps in all the corners, and the place was filled with the pleasant smell of new timber.

When Simon arrived, the trestle table had been cleared off and a repast spread out. He was carrying his head high, and the ancient manuscript was tucked under one arm. His robe was white and came only to his knees, revealing the fact that his legs were as crooked as a horn trumpet and covered with coarse reddish hair.

"Nero has made a gesture to the public in my honor," announced the magician with an air of pride. "He has thrown open the gates and allowed them into the grounds to see me fly. All Rome will soon be on the Palatine Hill. They will cluster around the walls like flies on a greasy skillet, and every tree will carry a heavy crop of them. It is going to be a day that men will remember."

Helena looked at him with dismay. "Simon!" she exclaimed. "Where is the black-and-yellow robe you are to use?"

"I decided against it." He swayed a little and had to balance himself by resting a hand on the table. "I shall fly just as I am. It is more fitting, my *zadeeda*. It is right for me to be robed in white when I am to fly like the angels." He looked at her with a flaring of nostrils. "The gift of tongues, remember, has descended upon me."

"Sit down and eat!" Helena's voice was grim. "There will be no time to send back for the robe. There are only twenty minutes left, and it will not do to keep such a large crowd waiting, to say nothing of the Emperor. You have been drinking after all, you perverse fool, and I am sorry I went to such pains to have your favorite dishes. There is mutton and a fine fillet of turbot, and fresh fruit from the markets."

The magician seated himself at the table, but after one mouthful of the mutton stew gave over the effort to eat. "My mind is on higher things than filling my stomach," he declared. "After it is over I shall eat. And drink. I demand, my kind Helena, that there be plenty of wine for me when I have emulated the angels of the Lord, for I shall have a thirst on me like a traveler from the desert."

Helena had seated herself across the table from him. At this she leaned over, the better to scrutinize the expression he wore.

"You keep speaking of flying like the angels. What do you mean by that?"

"I mean that I—that I will fly as they do, even though I lack their wings. I will fly"—he indulged in an inebriated gesture—"far out over Rome. Everyone in the city will see me and they will cry, 'There is Simon, to whom the gods have given invisible wings, the great Simon of Gitta!'"

"You will not fly farther from the top of the tower than fifteen feet," declared Helena.

"There will be astonished people in Rome today," said Simon with a sudden blaze in his eyes. "And none more than you, my *zadeeda.*"

There were two assistants at the table, Idbash sitting on her right, and the impudent trickster who had visited Simon that morning on her left. Helena withdrew her eyes from Simon's face and addressed herself to them.

"You see, he is drunk! But that is not a serious matter; I have seen him give a full performance with a belly rumbling of wine. What disturbs me is that—that I am becoming certain he is out of his mind. It may be necessary to keep him here by force. I could go up and fly in his place."

"You cannot be serious!" cried Idbash. His small eyes, which were so much like black currants, were filled with astonishment.

"I am serious about it. I am of a mind to go to the Emperor and tell him that this change of plan is necessary."

Simon had been listening with fire growing in his eyes. He stood up and glared across the table at them. His hands took a grip on the side of the trestle. Suddenly he jerked it up and thrust it against them, sending all three to the floor, together with the tureen of mutton, the platter of fish, and all the different varieties of fruit. Before they could extricate themselves and scramble to their feet, he had mounted the stairs. They heard him drop the trap door behind him with a loud crash and then drag lumber and other heavy objects upon it to prevent them from following. They could hear him laughing.

"I will go alone to the top of the tower," he called down to them. "I will have no assistants turning a wheel for me. I shall fly of my own efforts as the angels do; and all the world will wonder. Yes, my Helena, all the world will wonder at Simon of Gitta."

"He has gone completely mad!" cried Helena, getting to her feet and looking with a furious dismay at the food stains on the new robe of blue and gold in which she had arrayed herself for this momentous day. "I am going to the palace. He must be stopped. You must see to that."

The assistant had climbed the stairs and was endeavoring to force his way up through the trap. They could hear Simon piling more obstructions on top of it and laughing with a hint of maniacal delight.

"Get ladders!" she ordered in a breathless haste. "There are open spaces above. You can climb through and follow him to the top. Hurry, if you put any value on your skins! The punishment of Nero will fall on us if we don't stop this drunken fool in time."

Nero's gesture to the public had resulted in an immense influx of people. They were now packed tightly about the tower, and the palace grounds were filled all the way back to the walls. Every tree was black with spectators and every rooftop on the Palatine Hill was filled. The roads to the hill were crowded with disappointed people who could get no closer.

Helena, emerging from the door of the tower, saw that the path to the palace had been overrun in spite of the efforts of the Praetorian Guard to keep it clear. She plunged desperately into the mob, crying at the top of her voice: "Let me through! I must get to the palace. Let me through!"

As she struggled to open a path for herself, she heard someone cry, "There he is!" Other voices took it up. "Yes, there he is!" "He's climbing the stairs!" "Look, he's all in white."

3

Nero and his immediate circle sat in a small enclosed garden in front of the palace. This was a most suitable location, for it not only afforded them a clear view of the tower but it gave the throngs in the garden a chance to see the laurel-crowned head of the young Emperor. There were continuous cries of "Hail, Caesar!" At intervals Nero would respond by bowing.

Despite the gratification he took from this evidence that his popularity had not died, the Emperor was not in a happy mood. The uneasiness aroused in him by the charge of a conspiracy in his household still clung to him. His eyes darted suspiciously in all directions, and twice he gestured to the guards to come closer to his person.

"They have been dangerously silent, these Christians," he said to Tigellinus. "Why do you suppose we have heard nothing from them? What are they plotting against me now?"

"They are doing nothing at the moment," declared his political henchman. "The promptness with which we acted has had its effect. Even if they had designs before, they have none now. They are too frightened to raise their heads. The extermination of those slaves has been a lesson they will never forget."

Nero rubbed his plump white hands over his beardless chin. "I trust you are right, Tigellinus," he said. Then a different grievance took possession of his poorly balanced mind. He turned in the other direction and tugged at the plain linen sleeve of Petronius. "I am most unhappy, my friend," he whispered.

"Unhappiness, O Caesar," said Petronius, "is the penalty of genius. Only men of mediocre quality can enjoy peace of mind."

"Then I must be a great genius!" cried the Emperor. "My capacity for unhappiness has no bounds. I was too hasty in destroying all the busts he made of me, Petronius. I am realizing now that they were as good as I thought at first. It was mad of me to break them. It was a pleasure to look at them. I would sit and study them and say to myself, 'Here is Caesar, Caesar as he looked to those about him, Caesar preserved for posterity!' And now they are all broken and thrown out on rubbish heaps!"

"The man who made them is still alive," said Petronius. "I did not think quite as highly of his work as you did, O Caesar, but there is no denying his gift. He is meretricious, tricky perhaps; but unmistakably clever."

"Petronius, Petronius, there is genius in him! I become more certain of it all the time."

"Then pardon him publicly and summon him back," advised the arbiter in a tone that indicated he considered the matter of small importance. "He would be happy to return, having sampled once the sweetness of royal preference. I presume he is hiding somewhere in Rome and that he would emerge at once on your invitation."

But Nero shook his head. "No, Petronius, I cannot bring him back. I had a great liking for him. We were much of an age." His lips, which had a blubberly suggestion about them, quivered with unhappiness. "I was not allowed friends as a boy. In spite of his impudence in facing me with such an abominable confession, I still think of him at times with an affection I cannot forget."

"All you have to do is lift a finger to bring him back."

"No, Petronius, mentor and friend, I would fall into a rage if I saw him again and I would send him to the same death as the dancer. Besides, he affronted me publicly. He said to my face, 'I am a Christian.' I could not pardon him because it would shatter my dignity. No, no, I must not try to bring him back." He was silent for several moments, while conflicting emotions showed on his face. "Sometimes I hope Tigellinus will find him so I can decide on the tortures to which he is to be put before he dies. But sometimes I find myself hoping he will escape."

The crowds had been getting thicker in the imperial gardens as more people managed to squeeze past the sentries at the gates. There was more noise, more excited talk, more laughter. The cries of "Hail, Caesar!" were louder and were interspersed now with demands that the magician lose no more time in attempting his feat in the air.

Suddenly there were loud and excited shouts of "There he is!" Nero sat up straight in his ivory chair so that his head no longer lolled against the golden eagle on the back. He glanced in the direction of the tower, and then shouted as eagerly as anyone, "There he is!"

The sides of the tower were not cased in, and it was possible to see that upright ladders led from one platform to another. A figure in white was climbing with dignity and calm. A ladder had been placed against the side, and the impudent assistant was hurrying up it.

Helena had succeeded finally in fighting her way to the royal enclosure, where two guards stood like guardian angels with drawn swords. "I must see the Emperor," she said to them. "It is a matter of—of life and death! I implore you, let me through!"

"Stand back!" said one of the guards gruffly. "No one is allowed to see the Emperor today."

"I must see him!" she cried. "I must see him at once." As the guard's only response was to give her a far from gentle shove backward, she raised her voice. "Caesar! O Caesar! I must see you. I have a message for your ears."

"This is the woman who helps the magician," said the second guard uneasily.

Nero heard the outcry and took his eyes from the white figure progressing up the ladders long enough to look in her direction. He recognized her with a frown.

"It is that woman again," he said to Tigellinus. "Why is she making such a disturbance? Go to her, Tigellinus, and find what she desires to tell me."

The head of the police made his way to the garden entrance. The two guards stepped back a pace to allow him to face the insistent visitor.

"What is it this time? Have you more rumors to destroy the peace of the Emperor? Say what you have to say in a few words. I have small patience with you."

Helena told him what had happened, adding: "He has gone mad. If he is not stopped, it will be a great victory for the Christians."

The intimation of a Christian triumph persuaded Tigellinus that his master should be told. Nero's hands pawed nervously at his shaven chin as he listened.

"He must be stopped!" cried the Emperor. "He must not be allowed to die of his folly in the sight of all Rome."

Simon was now close to the top and was moving more slowly, as though the long climb had stiffened his muscles. Thousands of eyes watched in a silence that seemed strange after the turbulence with which his arrival had been awaited.

"It is too late to stop him," declared Tigellinus. "I could order the guards to shoot arrows at him when he reaches the top. But they might have to shoot many in trying to get him—and an arrow that goes up must come down. They would fall like hail on the good citizens of Rome on the other side of the gardens."

"I am tempted to give the order," declared Nero.

Petronius, who had been listening, said hurriedly: "You must not, O Caesar. Rome would not take well to such careless murder of her citizens."

The upper section of the tower had been closed in for the mysterious device. On reaching this point, Simon disappeared for a few moments and then stepped out calmly on the bare platform above. For a brief space he scanned the crowded gardens beneath him and then, folding his arms across his chest, gazed out over the myriad housetops of the city. This was done with dignity and ease, as though divinity were looking with tolerance on the tawdry handiwork of men.

"An artist to the end," commented Petronius.

Nero's doubts seemed to leave him as he looked up at the tall spare figure in white. "I think he is going to fly!" he exclaimed. "I feel it in my bones." He made it clear immediately, however, that he had not abandoned his doubts entirely, for he turned to Tigellinus and ordered him to see that the woman did not get away.

The feeling that had permeated the broad framework of the imperial bones had been at fault. There was to be no proof of superhuman qualities that day.

Simon the Magician, Simon of Gitta, the greatest performer of magic tricks the world had ever seen, stepped to the edge of the platform. He turned in the direction of the palace and raised both arms in the air as a salute to the majesty of the throne. A series of bows to the dense throngs followed. The raised arms made a final gesture as a signal that he was ready. For a moment he stood poised on the tips of his toes, then without any hint of hesitation Simon Magus cast himself forward into space.

For the briefest interval of time the white-robed body seemed to maintain itself, then there was a panicky agitation of the limbs and the figure jerked over in the air like an acrobat doing a somersault. Again it performed a complete turn, then began to fall. It gained momentum every second as it plunged down headfirst to the ground.

A great shout, combined of excitement and horror, rose from the crowd. Around the base of the tower people were struggling frantically to get away before the body could descend on them. It came hurtling down, and there was a dull thud as it struck the ground, an unmistakable thud that told all Rome that Simon the Magician had not fared well.

"He has broken his neck most thoroughly," said Petronius. Then he added, "And most artistically."

4

Nero listened to the bedlam of sound from the crowded gardens. He was frowning and there was a flush of anger on his cheeks.

"This has been a bad thing," he muttered. "What will the people of Rome say? Will they think better of the Christians?"

"They could be guided in their thinking," hinted Tigellinus. "It can be given out that the Christian leaders called on evil powers to paralyze his body when he sprang into space."

Nero had been looking into the wild confusion of the grounds where members of the Guard had formed a ring around the prone body and were forcing the sensation-mad people to stand back. He turned to Tigellinus on hearing this suggestion. "You think the Christians could be blamed? If they are said to be at fault, they can be punished. We must give it some thought, Tigellinus. Ways must be found to make them pay for the death of this fellow."

An officer of the Guard made his way into the enclosure and bowed before Nero. "The man is dead," he announced.

Tigellinus began to issue orders. "Remove the body at once. We will decide what is to be done with it later. Get it out of sight as quickly as possible." He turned to whisper in his master's ear. "It can be given out also that Simon was the victim of treachery among his own people. They had been quarreling. There was some kind of a struggle before he started to climb the tower."

"Are any of them Christians?"

"I do not think so. But it can be announced that they are."

The failure of Simon's effort to fly had been such a disappointment to Nero that he was left with a furious desire for some kind of retaliation. The words of Tigellinus offered him a way.

"Make prisoners of all of them," he commanded. "The people of Rome have been robbed of the spectacle they came out to see, and we must not let them go home in a grumbling mood. Give them something more to watch, Tigellinus. Take these ungrateful servants of the magician to the top of the tower and cast *them* off." He glanced about his immediate circle with wildly excited eyes. "It will be a just punishment. Lose no time, Tigellinus. It must be done while the excitement runs high."

"What of the woman?"

"Keep her until the last so the people can feast their eyes on her while she waits to die."

Helena had been standing at the entrance of the royal enclosure while Simon completed his climb and through the moments of horror that followed. Realizing her danger, she decided then that it would be wise to get as far away as possible from the royal eye. At the first move she made, however, the hand of one of the guards fell on her shoulder with a heavy finality.

"Stay where you are," he ordered gruffly. "How do I know what orders will be coming?"

Accordingly she was there when the order came. The two guards trussed her arms with violent speed and skill and placed her between them. She was taller than Juli-Juli, but there was a similarity of position that would have occurred to who had seen the dancer led from the banqueting hall. It might have occurred to some also that the finger of fate had intervened and a debt was being paid.

Helena accepted her lot with courage. She did not struggle or weep. She made no effort to appeal to the only power from which release could have come. Knowing the uselessness of an appeal, she did not look in Nero's direction.

"What will they do with me?" she asked in a low voice.

One of the tall soldiers made a gesture to indicate the top of the tower. "You are to be taken up there."

Helena shrank back. "No!" she cried. "No, not that! I am not afraid to die, but I—I have such a dread of heights!"

"It will be quick," said the soldier in a matter-of-fact tone.

Simon's assistants had sensed the probability of trouble as soon as the tragedy occurred, and so the officers sent by Tigellinus came back with one only. It was Idbash, who had fallen a victim to his own lack of expedition in getting himself out of harm's way; a thoroughly frightened Idbash who struggled and dragged his feet and proclaimed his innocence with piercing violence. They brought him only as far as the entrance to the enclosure and held him there while waiting for orders. His fears increased when he saw that Helena also was a prisoner.

"Mistress, gentle lady!" he cried. "I have done no wrong. Tell them I am just a servant. I did not know anything. Please, kind mistress, tell them this is a mistake, that I have done nothing."

Helena's face was white and her limbs were trembling, but she answered him in an even voice: "No one has done anything wrong. But we are going to be punished."

"What will they do to us?" asked Idbash frantically. "Mistress, kind mistress, do something for me. Tell them I am innocent. Tell them I know nothing."

"I cannot help you, Idbash. I cannot help myself." Helena's voice suggested a fatalistic resignation. "You said once you were ready to die for me. Now you will have part of your wish. You are going to die with me."

BOOK FOUR

CHAPTER XXXII

I

B<small>ASIL ARRIVED</small> in the port of Antioch without a coin in his purse. The money from Joseph of Arimathea had dwindled rapidly in Rome and more slowly during the long sea voyage. Now that it was gone he found it necessary to make his way home on foot and this was not an easy matter, for the Grove of Daphne lay fifteen miles from the water-side. In addition to his clothes and the tools that he carried in the blue cloth, he now had a large and very important bundle in which three life-sized busts were securely packed in straw; the most precious freight ever to travel on a pair of shoulders, he said to himself as he set off, the heads of Jesus, Peter, and John.

It was a trying walk, much of the way uphill, and the sun was begin-ning to settle behind the trees of the Grove when he came in sight of the house. He stopped and deposited all of his bundles on the ground while he took an ecstatic look at the white walls behind which he would find Deborra; waiting for him, he hoped and believed, with as much love in her heart as he was storing for her in his own.

The air had been filled all afternoon with a fall haze and now it was pleasantly cool. The white walls spelled love and comfort and peace, and the opportunity to begin a new life, a life of united purpose.

"I thank Thee, Lord," he said in a silent prayer, "for bringing me back safely from so many perils and with a new and clean heart."

As he stood and gazed so expectantly ahead, a tall old man with a tray of sweetmeats on his head came slowly up the road. Basil was not aware of his approach until he heard him say, "A fair prospect, young sir."

Basil turned and looked at the speaker with an immediate sense of familiarity. He was certain that he had seen this old man at some previous time.

"Could anything be lovelier," asked the sweetmeat vendor, raising an arm and pointing westward, "or carry so much promise of peace as that light over the trees?"

Basil said to himself, "I am sure the light in my Deborra's eyes will be even lovelier."

"When one becomes older," continued the vendor, "the autumn days are especially precious. They symbolize the passing of time and the approach of the goal to which one's weary feet have been climbing so long."

Basil was now convinced that this was the same vendor of sweetmeats who had paused under the entrance to his father's house on the Colonnade. "I saw you once," he said. "It was years ago, but I remember it very well because I saw something at the same time that I was not supposed to see." He proceeded to tell of the passing of the note, and Hananiah smiled as his own recollection went back to the episode. After a perceptible pause Basil plucked up his courage to say, "Christ has risen."

Hananiah turned to him so eagerly that the contents of the tray were in momentary peril. "Now I am sure," he said. "You are Basil, son of Ignatius, about whom I have been told so much. I am happy to see that you are back safely from your travels."

"It is through Luke that you have heard of me?"

"Yes, my young friend. I have seen Luke many times since his return to Antioch."

"Is he still here?"

Hananiah nodded his head. "He is still here. I am seeking him now, as I did once before when there was news to be handed on. I did not see you then."

"Was I here at the time?"

The old man inclined his head. "It was before you left."

"I was not told of your visit. Nor did I hear the news you brought."

"My visit was to bring the word that Mijamin had arrived in Antioch. I saw your wife, as well as Luke."

Basil felt a sense of fear take possession of him. "You say Mijamin reached Antioch before I left? I did not know." He clutched with sudden anxiety at the sleeve of the old man. "Has there been trouble? Are they all safe—my wife, Luke, my other friends? And what of the Cup?"

"There has been no trouble. I think you were not told about Mijamin because it was feared you would refuse to leave if you knew; and it was in their minds that the completion of the Chalice could not be delayed."

Basil considered this explanation and then nodded his head. "I am sure that was why. They also knew how necessary it was for me to go to Rome, for reasons other than the finishing of the Chalice." His voice rose. "My wife is the bravest woman in the world. She let me go and stayed behind to face the danger, and she did not say a word about it."

"You cannot sing her praises too high. As for Mijamin, his threat came to nothing at the time. The Zealots were being watched very closely and, as he was responsible for some disturbances, he was put in prison."

"Then the Cup is safe?"

"The Cup is safe." The sweetmeat vendor lowered his voice. "The trouble seems like to come to a head now. Mijamin will be released from prison in a few days. He is a most determined man, as you have reason to know. We shall have to be on our guard."

Basil reached down for his bundles and lifted them to his tired shoulders. "We must lose no more time in talk," he said.

The manservant who came to the door was new. He looked with justifiable suspicion at the dusty, burden-laden figure of Basil and the old man with the sweetmeat tray on his head.

"My mistress is at supper," he said. "This is no time to ask speech of her."

"Tell your mistress," said Basil, "that a tired traveler returning from Rome desires very much to see her at once."

Basil, waiting at the entrance, heard the patter of Deborra's sandals in the *aula*. She was walking quickly, but as she came nearer the speed of her footfalls diminished. She appeared to hesitate and, on reaching the threshold, she came to a halt and regarded him with grave and questioning eyes.

For the first time in his knowledge she was wearing the *instita*, the band around the bottom of the robe which women donned on being married. But this had not made her seem any older. "She does not look like a matron," thought the returned husband. "She looks like a little girl who has dressed herself for the part."

His mind was full of the things he wanted to say, but he did not say any of them. Words seemed not only unnecessary but impossible. Without being aware that he had changed his position, he found that she was in his arms, that he was holding her tightly and caressing her hair with one hand, and that her head was on his shoulder. She was weeping quietly, but he knew that her tears were the tears of happiness.

They stood thus for a long time, longer than they realized, for they were conscious of nothing but themselves. Basil placed a hand, then, under her chin and raised it so that he could look into her eyes, reading there a full confirmation of all his hopes. The tears had been like the briefest of showers and she was now smiling.

"I have so much to tell you," he whispered.

"Are you going to tell me all the things I said you must before—before we could put our misunderstandings behind us?" The small spat of rain was over completely; her eyes were bright and wide with content. "It is no longer necessary. You have told me everything I wanted to know. And without saying a word."

"But I have so many words!" he cried. "It will take days and weeks and years to say them all. And they will be very much alike. I will be saying the same things over and over again. That I love you, love you, love you. That you are the most beautiful and bravest woman in the world. That I treasure the little white lobe of your ear and the tip of your nose, which has such a pretty curl to it, and the light in your eyes. Nothing else will ever matter. I shall go on telling you these things as long as I live."

"You will have a willing listener," she whispered. "Oh, Basil, I shall be such a greedy listener! I am sure you will never say enough words like that to satisfy me."

Luke had followed her out from the supper table at a discreet distance and was standing in the shadows of the court. Sensing his presence, Deborra stepped back from her husband's embraces.

"Basil is back," she called to him. "And he is very brown and strong from his journeyings. He has not had a chance yet to tell me his news, but there is something in his eyes that makes me believe he has succeeded in everything he set out to do."

Luke came forward then. It was apparent at once that he had been existing under a heavy load of anxiety, for he looked older and very tired. His face seemed to carry as many fine lines as the palm of the hand.

"My son," he said, "I too suspect that the large bundle at your feet is filled with sheaves of your garnering. But as I stood back there in the court I could not help seeing something that pleased me quite as much. May I now rest content in my belief that you and my precious Deborra are—are as much in accord as your attitudes suggested?"

They said "Yes!" to that simultaneously and then smiled at each other. Deborra placed a hand under Basil's arm and pressed her head against his shoulder. "I think we are in a rather perfect accord, Father Luke," she said.

"There is much to be told about my visit to Rome," declared Basil. "It is true that I succeeded in doing all the things that took me there. But there are other things to tell you. The situation is very serious."

"The serious news must wait until you have had your supper," said Luke. He smiled at them with deep affection. "Bless you, my two children. You look so very happy together." He would have said more, but he had become aware of the sweetmeat vendor standing outside the door with the tray still on his head. "Why is Hananiah here?" he asked. "Has he come with information?"

The old man advanced a pace within the door. "You have, it is clear, much more pleasant things to discuss than the information I bring. Perhaps you will allow me, Luke, to speak a few words in your ear and then take my departure."

"I have been very neglectful," said Deborra. She ran a hand quickly over her dark locks to restore them to order. "Will you forgive me, Hananiah, for not seeing you there? It is an occasion when a husband comes back from a very long journey, and that must be my excuse. Come, we will all go in to supper."

"I have little appetite," said the old vendor, hesitating in the doorway.

He allowed himself, nevertheless, to be relieved of his tray. After he and Basil had bathed their faces and hands they went in to the table, where several leaders of the Antioch church were sitting.

"My husband has returned!" cried Deborra. "I am afraid I shall be an inattentive hostess for the rest of the evening. I want to sit beside him and listen to him and be very happy that he has come back safely and well." She added after a moment in a gay tone, "And now that I have made my apologies in advance, I hope you will forgive me and make yourselves at home."

There was an immediate demand for the news from Rome, and so Basil proceeded with his story, holding back one part only, his visit to Kester of Zanthus. Deborra, sitting close beside him, watched his face in the intensity of her interest, but she lowered her eyes when he began to speak about Simon the Magician and Helena, as though she did not want to spy on his thoughts. Her head came up with a startled abruptness when he told of the manner in which they had died.

"I did not see anything that happened that day," said Basil. "It was necessary for me to remain in hiding. I left the day after, and all Rome was filled with the story." His manner became subdued and he lowered his voice. "I was told that she died bravely. As bravely as the little dancer for whose death she had been responsible."

Deborra, pale and shaken with the story, whispered in his ear, "I am feeling very sorry for her." He nodded back. "Yes, I too had deep regrets. I warned her to leave, but she had become very antagonistic to me at that time and paid no attention."

The part of his story that won the closest attention from the serious group around the table was Peter's prediction of the persecution of the Christians in Rome and of the great impetus it would supply to the spread of Christ's teachings throughout the world. They discussed it with grave faces and in tones that expressed the fears it had aroused.

After the guests had gone, Deborra went to her room and returned quickly in a dark blue coat that was padded and tufted and most beautifully embroidered with gold thread. Her eyes showed signs of tears.

Basil was so dismayed at this seeming proof of a changed mood that he took her face in his hands and looked into her eyes with a puzzled frown. "Tears?" he said. "Have you been weeping, my love? Are you not happy?"

"Oh, Basil, yes!" she cried. "I am so happy that I cannot make up my mind which to do, whether to laugh or cry. So I do both. But the tears you see in my eyes now are for those two poor women who were killed in such cruel ways—and for all the women in Rome who are going to die." Then she blinked her eyes free and smiled. "I have bundled myself up warmly so that we can go out into the gardens. Do you remember, my husband, that at supper on the night when you left I sat at a table all by myself and that you came over and seated yourself beside me? We went into the garden later and you kissed me; and I knew that you were coming to love me after all. I have seen to it that the servants have not moved the chairs in which we sat. Everything is just as it was—like a shrine— and no one else has been allowed to sit there. Let us go out now and take the same chairs; and talk and talk and talk until the hunger that I have to hear your voice has been satisfied a little."

There was a chill in the air when they reached the court, and Deborra shuddered. She snuggled her chin down into the warm wrap.

"This is a gift," she said. "From that sweet old prince. He gave it to me before he left. You do not know that he died on reaching Bagdad and they took his body back to his own country to be buried. Chimham brought us the news when he returned."

"I am sorry he came to such a sudden end. His death must have upset all of Chimham's plans."

"Not seriously." Deborra began to laugh. "He amuses me so much, that funny Chimham. I don't think it possible to upset him seriously. He bought goods in Bagdad and loaded the two camels you gave him, and then he sold everything here in Antioch at a very good profit. You need never worry about him; he is going to be a rich man. The last time I saw him he was preparing to start back for the East with an extra camel and two helpers. He looked prosperous and rather fat, and very, *very* pompous. He brought back something else from Bagdad. Can you guess?"

"Another wife?" cried Basil.

Deborra laughed delightedly. "You have guessed it. Another wife. A very fat and cute little woman who giggles a great deal and rolls when she walks. She comes from a country much farther east and speaks a strange language. They cannot exchange a word and have to depend on signs still. When Chimham wants to tell her he is pleased, he kisses her. When he is annoyed, he boxes her ears. When he wants her to go anywhere, he points and gives her a pat on—well, on whatever part of her happens to be nearest. The last time I saw them together, he showed signs of being rather tired of all this—this pantomime."

"I am fond of Chimham," said Basil, "but I cannot understand why he is so determined to set himself up as another Solomon and fill houses with his wives."

Deborra laid a hand on his arm when they reached the arched enclosure. "We must take the same chairs," she said. "I have planted a shrub out in the garden at the exact spot where you kissed me. I water it every day and it is growing beautifully."

"Every evening at the same time I will lead you out there and kiss you again. It will be a ritual we will never forget."

Deborra cried excitedly: "How strange that you thought of saying that! It was what I was going to suggest. But I am so happy that you thought of it—and said it first!"

Basil took down Deborra's *kinnor,* which was hanging on the wall back of them, and began to strum on it. "There was a sailor on the ship coming back who was from the south of Gaul," he said. "It is a warm and gentle land and this man had a fine voice. He sang many songs of his country. This is one of them. I am playing it because the words went something like this: 'Envy the sailor, because he sees only the green waters and the scudding winds and the deep blue of the sky. Envy the maker of gems, because he gazes constantly into the beautiful souls that have been caught and preserved in transparent stone. Envy me, because

I come home to my little house at the edge of the woods and find Thee.'"

Deborra had tucked her feet under her skirt to keep warm and had muffled her hands in the ample sleeves of the oriental robe. "It is a lovely song," she said happily.

"I am going to write verses of my own to sing to the air," he declared. "The first will begin, "Envy me, because I have come home and seen Thee, my Deborra, with new eyes.' There will be a hundred verses to tell you what I see with these observant new eyes of mine. There will be one to the wave in your hair above your forehead, and one to the bold curl in front of your ear, and one to the shy curl that hides behind it. There will be verses to the sweetness of your smile and the smallness of your feet and the dimple in your elbow, which I would be happy to kiss this instant if you did not have your arms tucked so comfortably into your sleeves."

"I hope you will never stop writing new verses," said Deborra, stretching out her arm to him.

"I shall be writing them all through eternity."

When they retired finally into the house, she took him to his rooms on the floor above and pointed out where his bundles had been placed. "You need new clothes very badly," she said with a stern shake of her head. "You are quite shabby. It will be the first duty of your wife to see that you are made to look less like a beggar at the city gates."

They stood close together in a silence that lasted for several moments, looking gravely and intently into each other's eyes.

"You have much work to do still on the Chalice," she whispered. "Will you begin tonight?"

He gave a sober nod in answering. "It is true that I have much to do still. But——"

Deborra moved a little closer and smiled up at him. She needed none of the wiles which the lady Antonia's maids had taught her. Circe's Secret would have been superfluous at this moment. Her eyes were wide and shining, her color was high, her lips were slightly parted.

"Do you remember," he asked, "when there was the first hint of romance between us?"

She nodded eagerly. "It was when the Roman soldiers chased us. Listen, Basil. Do you hear it too? It is men's feet running after us and shields clashing and voices shouting. But they did not catch us, did they?"

She turned at that and began to run away across the room. Basil bounded after her. When they had raced together through Mount Moriah and down into the valley, he had found it hard to keep up with her, but he had no such difficulty now. In a few strides he had overtaken her and had gathered her up into his arms. He raised her high off the ground, with one arm encircling her waist, the other under her knees.

"Did you think I would let you get away?" he demanded.

"I do not think," she answered, pressing her face deeply into the hollow of his shoulder, "that I wanted to get away."

He paused when he reached the entrance to her rooms and then slowly and with due ceremony carried her across the threshold.

2

When Basil wakened he heard Deborra stirring about in her room. This was unusual, for she was generally tardy about getting up. He hesitated. "I should not go in," he said to himself. "And yet how can I wait to see her again?"

So he went in and found that she was standing beside the laver in the act of giving her face a very thorough scrubbing. A single garment had been wrapped about her, leaving her arms and shoulders bare and even displaying her ankles rather fully. She looked so young and slender, and so very desirable that he stood for several moments and considered her with awe and devotion.

"I should not have come in," he said finally. "Do you mind?"

She lowered her hands from her face to smile at him. "You are my husband and I love you," she said. "Why should I mind?"

At that he took her in his arms and kissed her. "I did not realize before," he murmured, "that the very best time for a husband to kiss his wife is when her cheeks are damp."

"I have been scrubbing and scrubbing and scrubbing my face in order to get myself thoroughly awake," said Deborra. "You know that I am never myself early in the morning. But *this* morning I must be bright. I must keep my husband interested and pleased."

"But was it necessary to rise so early?" he asked, smiling at the earnestness of her expression.

"Oh yes, it was necessary indeed. This is going to be a wonderful day and I do not want to miss a single minute of it."

The wonderful day began, however, with Basil laying out his tools and getting ready for work. Deborra had half expected this, but she made one effort to convert him to a better method of spending the day. "I had hoped," she said, "that you would do no work. We could go for a day in the woods and take my dog with us and have a thoroughly idle time. Do you not think it would be pleasant?"

Basil shook his head rather sadly. "I wasted so much time at the court of Nero. And the voyage coming home seemed to stretch out endlessly. This has given me a sense of urgency about the work. I feel that if I wasted a single day I would be punished by not being allowed to finish the Chalice."

Deborra gave up the effort. "I will not disturb you," she promised.

It became necessary for her to interrupt him, nevertheless, at a late hour of the morning. She paused in the doorway and reluctantly addressed his stooped back.

"Two friends are here," she said. "Elidad and Irijah."

He turned around at once. "The two strong young men? Is it going to be necessary for us to have guards?"

"You have heard that Mijamin is to be released from prison. Luke is afraid that the—the trouble will start now. The Cup, as you know, is not here. Luke took it away as soon as you left, but he has not told what he did with it. The Zealots tried hard to find it and searched through the homes of Christians all over Antioch. It was a very thorough raid; in one day and night they went from house to house and ransacked everything. They found nothing, but they did much damage."

"It is reasonable for them to think that it will be brought back here now that I have returned to work on it."

"Luke is certain that Mijamin will think so. But he does not want it returned until you have finished." Deborra turned her attention to the new arrivals. "They are nice young men. So quiet and gentle and so very humble. But you should see the bundles of clothing they brought with them; they are so pathetically small and cheap. I feel very sorry for them."

Basil laid down his chisel with a serious air. "I was talking to Hananiah last night. He and his wife gave everything away. Now she is old and frail, but they go on. They intend to go on living as they do as long as they survive. Listening to him, I had some grave misgivings. Is it possible to serve Jesus if you are rich and live as the rich do?"

Deborra considered the point with a gravity to match his own. "I would like to repeat what I heard my grandfather say because I am sure it would relieve you of those misgivings," she said finally. "He said that the Christian church will become the same as any other religion in one respect, that it will have to be governed and controlled and supported. There have to be leaders, inspired leaders, and there have to be missionaries to spread the gospel, and there have to be martyrs to create traditions and build faith. And, he added most emphatically, there has to be money.

"Do you know," she went on, "that Hananiah and his wife, Dorcas, live all the year round under that strip of canvas? In winter they have a fire, but they do not possess a brazier and the fire has to be built on the ground. They use bits of wood and dried camel dung and anything else that Hananiah can pick up. They have one set of blankets and one plate and one drinking cup between them. They have no knives or spoons. Their bed is a pile of rocks stuffed with dried moss. They have an empty case in which hides had been packed as a table."

She came close enough to lean a hand on his worktable. "Basil," she said, looking down at him earnestly, "I am as anxious as you are to give myself to His service. But how can we, you and I, be most useful? By finding a tannery yard and living under another strip of canvas? Young people who expect to have children cannot do that. By going out as missionaries to far parts of the world? I am not at all sure we would do well as preachers. But we can continue of great use by helping to produce funds for the church. That was my grandfather's part, and I think we are best fitted to follow in his footsteps. While you have been away I have been thinking about it and planning. I have some ideas as to how we could go about it."

Basil looked up at her and smiled at the gravity of her expression. "I suppose you are right. I spoke without having given it any serious thought. You will have to be patient with me, my very capable little wife. I am a new convert and sometimes I find myself ready to explode with zeal." He paused and then gave his head a nod. "Yes, I can see now that you are right. We must find the way to be most useful."

It was drawing on toward the middle of the afternoon when Basil became aware that someone was watching him and turned around from his work to find his wife in the doorway.

"I have been here for quite a long time," she said, taking no more than a step into the room. "Are you very much displeased at being interrupted?"

He stretched his arms slowly and luxuriously. "I am tired," he said, "and it is a pleasure to be interrupted. By you."

"I did not intend to. I have been coming to the door and watching you off and on all day—and you were so interested in your work that you did not know. I came"—she began to count—"eleven times."

He rose to his feet, stretched again, and strolled to the laver in a corner of the room. "I shall do no more. Give me time to get myself clean and I'll be ready to join you. For the rest of the day we can be as idle as you wish."

"Wonderful!" cried Deborra. "This is what I hoped for. Perhaps it was because I was hoping so much that you turned finally and saw me."

He had stripped off his outer tunic and allowed the inner garment to fall to his waist. Deborra was too startled to move at first.

"I don't think," she said, "that I should stay."

He answered by quoting her own words. "You are my wife and I love you. Why should I mind?"

He finished his ablutions and stretched out a hand for the towel.

"No, no, that is not fair!" she cried. She took the towel away from him. "I must have a chance to test that discovery you made this morning." She stepped close and put her arms around his neck. "You were right! It is wonderful to kiss your husband when *his* face is damp."

But then everything was wonderful for the rest of the day. They went for the walk in the woods which she had suggested, taking the dog with them. They spent two hours in that part of the Grove which stretched down toward the house, and they found that there was magic in everything, particularly in the rich tints of the autumn foliage. They found a late pear tree, and it was apparent to them both at their first taste of the fruit that, although nature had been bringing forth crops of pears for untold centuries, there had never been any to equal these. The dog, wild with delight at being allowed to go with them, chased rabbits and treed other wild things and barked and succeeded finally in running himself into a state of complete exhaustion. "He is a wonderful fellow," declared Basil. A pebble became lodged in Deborra's sandal and Basil, stooping to dislodge it, remained in that position so long that she laughed and asked the reason. "I have made another discovery," he declared. "You have the most wonderful feet in the world."

They thought at first that this day of wonders reached its climax with the sunset. They had swung around the Grove of Daphne and had come to an elevated location where it was possible to look full into the west, and it was as though the Maker of sunsets had said to Himself, "I have fashioned millions of young couples who have fallen in love; but these two seem to be a little more in love than anyone has ever been and I shall have to do something unusual for them." It was indeed an unusual kind of sunset. The western horizon was as red as the fire opals the matrons of Rome prized so much, and there were coral and amethyst shades on the edges of the clouds, and under everything else a strong illumination, as though the day actually had been memorable enough to warrant a blaze of glory at its finish.

But the real climax, they found, came later: when they sat down alone to supper and Deborra was dressed in pink. He had never seen her in pink before. The robe was rather elaborate, having a Grecian triangular overdrape of white edged with black in front and sleeves with no fewer than five openings held together by straps of the same black material. It was exactly the kind of robe a bride should wear on such an occasion and he delighted in it, saying to her with pride that no color could more adequately set off the dusk of her hair and the subdued shadow of her eyes.

"I am not hungry tonight," she said, cupping her chin in her hands. "I have told the servants to go to bed, that I will clear the table and trim the lamps. We will be all alone, my husband, without a listening ear or a whispering tongue near us."

The cat came and sprang into her lap and purred. The dog came slinking in, knowing that this was forbidden territory, and crouched at her feet. Basil had reached down the *kinnor* from the wall, but he placed it on the floor beside him without striking a note.

"I don't want to talk or sing at this moment," he said. "I want only to sit here silently and feast my eyes on you."

3

A tempestuous wind, which sailors called Euroclydon, was blowing at sea and all Antioch was suffering in the freezing cold that had descended from the mountains. The beggars in the market places and at the gates had purple noses. Men who carried brick or tile on their backs had to stop often and flail their arms about them in order to keep warm. Even in the house on the edge of the Grove of Daphne, where connubial bliss might have been expected to make two of the occupants impervious to such small matters as an atmospheric change, everyone was unhappy. The menservants, with the red flannel of the *bracae* covering their chapped knees, carried braziers into all the rooms and lighted charcoal fires in them but did not relieve the discomforts to any extent. The maidservants, being young and therefore a little giddy, were glad that their winter robes were long enough to hide the ill-fitting *indusium* that clung about their limbs from waist to ankle.

Basil's work was nearly completed and he was driving himself hard to finish it, although at frequent intervals he had to stop and hold his numbed fingers over the smoldering fire in the brazier. Finally, with an air of great triumph, he picked up a hammer and gave the clay replica of the Cup a blow that shattered it into an infinitesimal number of pieces as a sign that he needed it no longer. Deborra chose this moment to enter the room, muffled up in a *palla* commodious enough to provide a hood for her head and to cover her feet completely. Basil, who had not hesitated about donning the *bracae,* did not know how greatly she was suffering from the cold. Later, when such exciting matters had ceased to be mysterious, he would realize that she never wore the ugly leggings the servants used. She had to content herself with a much less warm garment that hung from her shoulders by straps and came only to her knees, where it was rather loosely held in by garters.

"I am nearly frozen!" she said. "I would not have left my fire and come here to interrupt you unless I had something to tell you; something that is very important. So important that I could not wait."

Basil reached out a hand and tweaked the end of her nose, which was cold and, if the truth must be told, a trifle red. "My poor little rabbit from the warm South has not raised a coat of winter fur yet," he said. "We always have a few days like this in rugged Antioch, my shivery one. Are you regretting that you must go on living here?" Then his eyes lighted up and he raised his voice to an exultant pitch. "I am delighted you came because I have something to tell you. I have finished the Chalice! See, I have broken the clay model. There is not another stroke of work to be done on it."

Everything else went out of Deborra's mind. She clapped her hands and then threw her arms around his neck and hugged him ecstatically. "Have you really finished?" she cried. "I am so glad. It has taken you so long and you have worked so hard. Am I allowed to see it now? You have been so secretive about it and I have not had a single glimpse since you returned from Rome."

He placed an arm about her waist and turned her around to face his worktable, where the outer frame of silver was covered with a clean linen cloth. He removed the cloth and they stood in silence for several minutes, looking at his handiwork. It was finished to the last detail. The twelve small figures, all of which could be identified as minute copies of the life-sized clay models, occupied their places against the intricate background of vines. The lip had been turned and embellished with infinite and loving care. The base was mathematically perfect. The twelve models were grouped about the completed frame and seemed to constitute a guard. They had an air of vigilance about them.

"It is beautiful!" cried Deborra. "Oh, Basil, it is the most lovely thing in the world. I am sure if my grandfather could see it he would say you have done what he wanted—and more."

Basil studied his work with a brooding air. "I wish I could feel as sure of that as you do," he said. Then he remembered that she had come in the first place for a purpose that had nothing to do with the completion of the Chalice. "You said you had something to tell me."

"Yes," said his wife, removing her eyes from the silver reliquary. "It is not like this. It is not about something that is finished. It is—well, it is about something that has just begun."

"I don't understand——" began Basil. Then he stopped. He took her by both shoulders and pulled her around so that he could study her face. "What was it you said?"

"Yes." Deborra nodded her head and gave a short, breathless laugh. "Yes, we are going to have a child."

It was Basil's turn to forget everything else. He took her in his arms and pressed her cheek to his. They stood thus for a long time, too happy and awed with the magnificence of their good fortune to utter a word. Deborra had begun to weep quietly, and he could taste the salt of her tears on his lips.

It was Basil who broke the silence. "I am very proud," he said. "Very proud and very happy. I am sure that Prince P'ing-li, if his spirit is anywhere about, is almost as pleased as I am."

"Yes," she whispered. "The dear old man would be pleased. And think how happy Luke will be when he hears!"

Basil fell into another silence and then announced, "I shall name my son Joseph."

"I too would like him to be named Joseph. But if it should happen that a name had to be found for my daughter, what will you have in mind?"

"I have not given that possibility any thought."

Luke paid them a visit in the afternoon, and it was arranged that the completed Chalice would be shown to the leaders of the church the following day. The old physician was in a depressed mood. A letter had been received from Paul, who was still held in prison at Caesarea and was himself in a low state of mind as a result of his long incarceration.

"There is a new governor whose name is Festus," Luke told them. "This man Festus is as corrupt as all the rest of these officials who are sent out from Rome, and it is clear to Paul that he could secure his release at once if he cared to offer a suitable bribe. This he refuses to do. He will die in his cell before resorting to any such step. He is convinced that they are now so tired of him that he will soon be sent to Rome for trial and he wants me to join him." He looked at them with an air of the greatest gravity. "We are all old men and likely to hear the call at any time. It may be, my children, that I shall never see you again."

Basil felt his heart sink. The thought of separation was painful to him, particularly as he knew the hazards that a visitor to Rome would face.

"You have your lives before you," said the old man, the gravity of his face relaxing. "Your feet are set in the right path. You will see many changes and you will face dangers; but something tells me that you will have a long life together in which the happiness will outweigh the sorrow. You will raise fine sons and daughters and you will play your parts in the building of a great church." His manner changed and he placed an urgent hand on Basil's shoulder. "Do not return to Jerusalem. Passions are running high there, and nothing can prevent an outburst against Roman rule soon. It may not be this year, or next, or the year after that. But it is coming. The signs are in the sky, as plain to be seen as a black cloud. Jerusalem is going to suffer as she has done so often in the past. Remain here, my children, where there will be work for you to do."

He had brought a large bundle with him, and this he now proceeded to open. "As I must leave so soon," he said, "I see no reason for delaying any longer the delivery of the prince's gifts."

The eyes of the young couple met. Deborra blushed but did not protest when Basil began to explain. "We feel free to accept them now. It seems that—that the condition has been met."

"It becomes very clear," declared Luke, beaming at them, "that the Lord looks down upon you with great favor."

The gifts were so generous that all three fell into a state of astonishment. For Deborra there was a fan of jade and parchment with an emerald in the handle, a dragon ring with rubies serving as eyes, and a half dozen jade cups as delicately shaped as flower petals. For Basil there was a ring with a green cat's-eye and a belt of heavy leather with plates of bronze set off by myriad small precious stones.

There were two other gifts, wrapped with great care in doeskin. "For the first-born son," said Luke, removing the covering.

One was a suit of heavy black silk with a diminutive pair of trousers and a round black hat with a jaunty peacock's feather. The other was a hideous mask most ingeniously contrived out of a light material which none of them had ever seen before.

Deborra put the ring on her finger and admired it and then opened her fan with a flourish of pride. It was not long, however, before she laid her personal gifts aside and fell to examining those for the first-born son. She smoothed the soft material of the suit and then held it up with a delighted smile.

"How handsome he will be in this," she said. "He will look very odd but every inch a man! Ah, this lovely feather! I am sure he will be very proud of it and strut when he has it on. And think how he will delight in putting on this dreadful mask and frightening other little boys with it." She glanced at her husband, her eyes round with pride and expectancy. "I can hardly wait for him to grow big enough!"

CHAPTER XXXIII

I

W E S H A L L K N O W very soon where Luke concealed the Cup,"
said Basil.

The cold still gripped the city and there were braziers glowing and
hissing in each corner of the room. The three old men who stood with
Luke at the other end had come long distances across the city and they
looked as though they had been chilled to the bone. They were grouped
around one of the braziers, but there was still a suggestion of purple in
their faces and they kept their robes wrapped up closely around their
necks.

A table had been placed in the center of the room. At one end was
the newly finished silver frame for the sacred Cup, surrounded by the
twelve life-sized models from which Basil had worked. At the other end
were dishes and knives and spoons, in readiness for the meal that would
be served later. The two young guards stood at the door.

"The secret will be revealed at last," answered Deborra.

They were sitting together on a bench pushed back against one of the
walls. Deborra was wearing a plum-colored cloak over all the usual clothing, but even this did not serve to keep her warm. Politeness forbade the
tucking of her feet under the folds of the cloak, and so, exposed to the
heavy coldness of the room, they looked blue and pinched.

She called his attention to another man who had put in an appearance,
brushing past the two guards with a somewhat lordly air. "That is
Harhas, the head presbyter of Antioch." She studied the newcomer
closely. "He has the reputation of being very stern and unbending."

Harhas was a man of advanced years who wore severity on his face
like a badge of merit. He was lame and, as he hobbled across the room

with the help of a cane, his eyes darted actively in all directions, seeing everyone, noting the arrangements; clearing his throat the while with a belligerence that hinted at his willingness to batter down and destroy any suggestions that might be laid before him. He paused for a moment at the table to inspect Basil's handiwork. Without any comment, save a slight tightening of the frowning lines of his brow, he stumped rheumatically to where Luke stood with the other presbyters.

"It is said," commented Deborra in a whisper, "that Harhas is very hard to get along with. If he cannot have his own way he gets angry and says, 'I wash my hands of it.' Luke said once that he had washed his hands of so many things that he ought to have the whitest pair in the world. Of course," she added, "he is a very saintly old man."

"When it comes to deciding what is to be done with the Chalice, will we be allowed to express our opinions?"

"Oh no, no." Deborra looked rather shocked. "Harhas is very strict about things like that. He has told Luke that it is a matter for the presbyters to decide. Even Luke may not be allowed a voice. I am sure we will be expected to leave the room if they discuss it here." She looked at Basil as though doubtful of the wisdom of telling him anything more. "Luke had difficulty in persuading him that you and I should be allowed in the room at all, even for the placing of the Cup in the frame."

"This old man," said Basil, "must think he is as important as the High Priest and the King of Jerusalem and Caesar, all combined in one."

"Look!" exclaimed Deborra. She was staring at the door with an air of the most intense surprise. "Now what does this mean?"

Basil turned in that direction, and his astonishment equaled hers when he saw that Hananiah was standing there, dressed in his familiar brown robe (he possessed no other), which had been mended and patched so often that little of the original material remained. From force of habit, no doubt, he was carrying his tray on his head. A pace behind him was a small woman, wrinkled and gray with age, who carried a large bundle of old clothing on a stick across her shoulder. Still another pace behind her was a young man with a pleasant and open countenance, dressed in the plainest and simplest of gray cloth. This trio paused at the doorway and looked about them with some hesitation.

"Then it is true, and he is going!" exclaimed Deborra. She turned and whispered an explanation to Basil. "The young man is David, their grandson. There has been talk that he would go out as a missionary, but his grandmother did not want him to go so soon. This means that it has been decided. Just think, Basil, their only grandchild!"

"Where is he being sent?"

"It was intended to send him to the East. The very far East, perhaps as far as the prince's country. It will be a life mission. They will never see him again, those two poor, wonderful old people! They may never hear any word from him."

Luke had advanced to meet the newcomers. "Hananiah and Dorcas and David!" he said. "Come in, good friends. Come to one of the fires. I am afraid it has been a long walk for you, Dorcas. I told this stiff-necked husband of yours that we would arrange for a conveyance, but he seemed to think there would be something sinful in indulging yourselves to that extent."

"He knew my wishes," answered the old woman, smiling and nodding. Any estimate of her probable age grew with each glimpse of the almost transparent ivory of her face, but her eyes were bright with intelligence and high spirit. "I preferred to walk. This—this is a pilgrimage."

Luke took the bundle from her and placed it with great care on the table. Hananiah had already confided his tray to the custody of one of the servants. On Luke's insistence the three seated themselves near one of the braziers. Their eyes became fixed at once on what the table held, and they fell into a mood of the deepest absorption.

Luke looked about him and then, as a matter of form, addressed himself to the head presbyter.

"When it became necessary to find a sanctuary for the Cup," he said, "I gave the matter prayerful consideration and decided I could not do better than confide it to the care of Hananiah. It seemed to me entirely fitting that it should be given into the hands of one who has served the Master so splendidly although so very humbly."

"And how did Hananiah go about the keeping of this great trust?" asked Harhas in a sharp, demanding voice.

A wind came howling about the parapets of the house, thrusting down savagely into the inner court and causing the leaves to whirl up from the ground and dance and toss about. Cold came in gusts through the linen which had been stretched across the windows and caused the occupants of the room to shiver more than ever.

"Tell us, Hananiah," said Luke.

The old man seemed very conscious of his unworthiness. "The Cup was handed to us in many swathings of silk. I want you all to know that the coverings have not been removed. No eye has rested on it. No hand has touched it." He had been keeping his gaze on the floor, but now he looked up and smiled nervously. "I consulted with Luke," he went on. "Beside the brick oven where Dorcas makes the sweetmeats there is a tin box in which she keeps sugar. I—I took a very great liberty." His air had become abashed and apologetic. "I placed the Cup in the tin and covered it with the sugar."

One of the presbyters asked, "And did not those who came to search look in the tin?"

There was a moment of silence. "We heard they were searching everywhere, forcing themselves into houses. We waited and prayed. But no one came. It was because of the way we live. They did not think the Cup would be entrusted to such as we."

"Trust in the Lord!" cried Harhas, his voice high and exultant. "He stretched forth His hand and the searchers passed by."

Luke walked to the center of the room. "Joseph of Arimathea left the Cup in my hands and I shall consider myself responsible for it until it has been placed in the frame which we see. It then becomes the property of the church of our Lord Jesus. Every Christian in the world becomes an owner, and it will be for the princes of the church to decide what is to be done with it. Perhaps they will say that it must no longer be laid away in darkness, its whereabouts a secret from those whose eyes long to behold it. Perhaps they will say, 'Send it openly to Jerusalem.' We who will have the privilege today of gazing on the Chalice are not in a position to know what the princes of the church will decide." He turned and pointed to the bundle on the table. "Dorcas," he said, "will you remove the coverings?"

The wife of the vendor stood up. Her husband rose also, placing a hand protectingly on her arm as she walked to the bundle on the table. She stretched out her arms and proceeded to remove the outer wrappings, which consisted of a blanket worn by constant washings as thin as blades of grass. She was still more deliberate in unwinding the lengths of silk, and it was with shaking fingers that she finally reached the end. The Cup looked small when thus revealed to the eyes of the company; very small indeed and plain and, if it might be supposed to have human feelings, very unassuming.

A silence had settled on the room. Every eye was now fixed on the Cup. The wind had died down for the moment, and the candles that had been brought in and placed on the table burned with a clear and steady light.

"Hananiah," said Luke, breaking the silence, "will you now place the Cup in the frame which has been prepared for it?"

The vendor of sweetmeats was taken completely by surprise. "No, no!" he exclaimed. "Not I. I am not worthy to touch it with as much as the tip of a finger."

"I am sure that I speak for the presbyters and all the members of the church," declared Luke, "when I say that no one has done more for the faith than Hananiah and his wife, Dorcas. I can think of no one more worthy of being chosen."

The old man kept his head bent and his eyes fixed on the floor. "You compel me to tell you that I adopted this mode of living in expiation of a great sin I had committed." He stretched out his hands. "These are not clean. They must not touch the Cup. I cannot hope to be declared free of my sin until the time comes for me to die." His manner changed, becoming more calm. He looked down at his wife beside him and smiled. "Dorcas, who shares my punishment without a word of complaint, has no sin on her conscience. Her hands are clean."

"Dorcas shall act in your stead."

The wife of Hananiah hesitated. Then, with fingers that trembled violently, she raised the Cup. Carrying it to the head of the table, she held it suspended for a moment over the silver receptacle. With great care she lowered it into the close embrace of the exquisitely molded frame. The Chalice was complete.

The wind selected this moment to blow against the linen coverings of the windows so violently that they were torn loose. It swept through the room. The candles flickered and went out. As the evening was now well advanced, the company found themselves in darkness.

The boy David, who was standing immediately behind Luke, drew in his breath. "I can see the Cup!" he said in a tense whisper.

Luke turned and laid a cautioning hand on his arm. "Yes, my son," he whispered. "To those who see with the eyes of fullest faith the Cup is never hidden. But say nothing of it here. There are some in the room who are lacking in faith to that degree, and for them the Cup does not shine."

2

For a week after that the house was filled with visitors. The Chalice had been placed openly on view and the Christians of Antioch came in great numbers to see it, quiet men and women who arrived with expectant faces and went away with a satisfied glow in their eyes. Harhas had been overruled by his fellow presbyters and had washed his hands of the proceedings; and so the two guards stood at the head of the stairs and all who entered the room to see the Chalice passed between drawn swords.

It was necessary, because of the menace hanging over them, to observe many precautions. The presbyters took turns at the entrance to scrutinize the visitors and determine when the doors might be swung open. No more than three were allowed in at a time.

It was apparent from the first that the house was being subjected to a hostile surveillance. On one occasion a blind beggar followed a group of visitors up the sloping road, feeling his way cautiously with a long stick and calling out at intervals: "I have no eyes! Pity me and make way!" Basil happened to be at the entrance and he noticed that the feet of the beggar, in an unguarded moment, were careful to avoid a rough spot on the road. He walked out and laid a brusque hand on the man's shoulder.

"You are here for no good purpose, my friend," he said. "I suggest that you do not bother to use that stick in departing, for it is quite certain that you can see. If you wanted to deceive us, you should have learned how the blind use their feet in walking."

"Take your hands off me!" snarled the supposed blind man. His hand went furiously to his belt and produced a dagger. "Yes, my bold one, I have eyes and I came here to use them. If you do not have a care, I shall use them to select a mark for this little toy of mine, perhaps in the small of your back."

He turned and retreated down the road, muttering more threats and stopping at intervals to study the line of the house over his shoulder.

A second attempt to spy out the land was more successful. A supply of fish had been delivered at the back gate in the wall. The cook, carrying the basket in to the kitchens, was conscious that she was being followed, but when she turned her head the vendor had disappeared. He was located on the back stairs, which led up to the part of the house where the Chalice was on display. The cook was a stout woman with muscular arms and it so happened that the intruder was small. She took him by the shoulders and dragged him back to the yard. Here, possessing herself of one of the fish, she gave him a vigorous smack in the face with it.

"Sneak and spy!" she hissed at him. "Do not dare come back or I will turn you over to those who will know what to do with you."

The man laughed at her and said, "I will be back and I will repay you then for filling my eyes with scales."

The wall was six feet high, but he placed a hand on the top and vaulted over with the greatest ease. "I will come back over this wall just as easily, O woman with rough hands," he called from the other side.

Basil saw little of what was going on, being immersed in legal matters. As soon as the Chalice was completed he had sought out a man who had the reputation of being the most learned and versatile of all exponents of the law in Antioch. This was a very shrewd and resourceful Jew named Jehoahaz. To this lawyer he proceeded to tell the story of his experiences at the court of Nero and finished by asking a question, "Would it be safe to apply for another hearing of the case concerning my father's estate when by so doing I might bring myself to the attention of the ministers of the Emperor?"

Jehoahaz gave the matter long and serious thought. "Know this first," he said finally. "We are a long way from Rome. In the imperial city they hear nothing more than the faintest echoes of what goes on here. They regard us as people living on the frontier and take no interest in us. It is almost certain that nothing would be heard in Rome of the case beyond the report that would be forwarded to be filed in a department on the Capitoline Hill.

"There is also this," went on Jehoahaz. "You are a Roman citizen and you broke no law by acknowledging yourself a Christian. Inasmuch as no evidence developed of a conspiracy in the imperial household, there are no possible grounds for disturbing you here. It is my opinion that you may safely apply for another hearing."

If Basil had been in a position to hear Nero say to Petronius, "Sometimes I find myself hoping he will escape," he would have made his decision with fewer qualms. As it was, he said: "It is worth the risk to have it established that Linus had no right to sell me as a slave. Will you, Jehoahaz, take the necessary steps in my behalf?"

A week later Jehoahaz reported to him in a state of self-congratulation. "You are to be allowed another hearing. What is more, it has been set for a week from today. It helped me a great deal that the magistrate who heard it the first time has been recalled to Rome because he had become so barefaced in his dishonesty."

The lawyer began at once to find witnesses who were willing to testify, for the most part merchants who had known Ignatius and had been in his confidence. He paid a visit also to the grimy stone building where the

head of the Roman forces in Antioch made his headquarters, and returned
with more good news.

"The commandant has received the copy of Kester's deposition," he
declared. "He expresses his willingness to turn it over to the magistrate
who will hear the case." The lawyer paused and winked broadly. "The
magistrate is above reproach, a stern custodian of the principles of justice
and honesty who has never accepted a bribe. We can depend on the
utmost impartiality, which will make this hearing far different from
the first."

"How is Linus taking things?"

"With a degree of passivity that rather surprises me," answered
Jehoahaz. "What is the man trying to do? It is certain that he is making
no effort to buy himself a second decision. Why not? I think it is because
he lacks the money for the purpose. The city is full of rumors about him.
He has made some disastrous gambles and he has lost two ships filled
with goods from the South and East." His voice fell to a confident whisper. "A better time could not have been found for the hearing. Linus
is beset with difficulties. He will fight, of course, but he will not carry
matters off again with such a high hand."

On the evening before the hearing Basil paid a visit to the room where
the Chalice was on view. Visitors were still arriving, and Luke, who had
been on duty at the front gate, welcomed him with a tired smile.

"Tomorrow night," he said, "we turn the Chalice over to the presbyters.
It will be a relief in a sense when it is in their hands. I shall be able to
rest again." He added after a moment's pause, "I start for Caesarea in
two days."

Basil felt a sudden sinking of the heart. "So soon?" he asked. "What
are we to do without you?"

"There has been another message from Paul. He is pressing to be sent
to Rome." Luke's eyes, which had been on the Chalice, came to rest with
an unhappy intentness on Basil's face. "None of us will return. We are
old men and the sands are running out fast."

"You are needed here," protested Basil. "More than in Rome. They
depend on you in everything. And you know what the situation is in
Rome. Should you involve yourself unnecessarily in the troubles there?"

"Paul needs me," said Luke simply. "He is a sick and lonely man. He
must not be allowed to make that long sea voyage alone. My place is
at his side."

A woman who had been standing in front of the Chalice burst into loud lamentations at this point. She beat her breast and wept so bitterly that her companions had to lead her away.

"It is hard not to be overcome when standing here," said Luke. "The poor woman is thinking of the shameful death the Saviour died. And yet, my son, it seems to me that tears are a selfish manifestation. Whenever I yield to the impulse, I know it is for myself that I lament. It is true that Jesus wept on many occasions, but it was because of His pity for us. I never see a hint of moisture in the eyes of Paul. That great man of logical mind knows it is weakness to cry out for those who have passed on to a better life.

"We are weak creatures," he continued after a moment, "and we repine for what we have lost. I am telling you this, my son, because I must say farewell to you so soon. I shall miss you; I shall miss you most bitterly. The unhappiness on your face tells me that you will feel unhappy also. Smooth the trouble from your brow, my boy. You have a fine wife and before long you will have a family of fine children. You will enjoy a full and useful life. Always keep me in your memory; the stranger who came to you that night in the Ward of the Trades when your spirits had fallen to such a low ebb. I smile still when I recall that you thought me the angel Mefathiel. It is one of the gems in my crown; if you can call the tiny chaplet I may have earned by such a name." He leaned over and placed an arm on Basil's shoulder. "There must be no tears when we part. Nothing but smiles and heads held high—even though we know it will be a last farewell."

CHAPTER XXXIV

1

Basil was conscious of the scowl of Linus as soon as he entered the courtroom. The usurper sat on the other side, surrounded by a group of witnesses and men of the law. He was sprawled in a low chair with his feet planted wide apart and a belligerent look on his face; an obese figure, a little bent, more coarse of face than ever. He continued to scowl in Basil's direction and to mutter sullenly to those about him.

"He is in an angry mood," commented Jehoahaz. The man of law was confident and cheerful. "It will do him small good. One thing is certain, he has not bribed the dyspeptic Brutus up there on the bench. T. Orestes Flaminius is a young man of extreme rectitude and the custodian of the shortest temper I have ever encountered. We must tread warily and so avoid his wrath. But I suspect that he and Linus will soon be at each other's throats."

Basil looked at the magistrate with mingled feelings. T. Orestes Flaminius was noticeably young for such a post; thin, prematurely bald, and obviously shortsighted, for he was squinting impatiently at the documents in front of him. He would be impartial, that was certain, but also he would be testy and difficult.

On the occasion of the first trial Basil had felt that he stood alone. No one had spoken to him. His father's old friends, knowing him the certain loser, had avoided his eye. The atmosphere of the court was now quite different. Eyes met his with friendliness. People smiled at him and nodded. It had been a dark and threatening day when he tasted the bitterness of defeat; now the sun came triumphantly through the windows of the court and glistened on the polished breastplates of the Roman soldiers standing at each end of the magisterial bench.

Everything was different, but Basil did not find himself reflecting the cheerfulness of Jehoahaz. Deborra had found it impossible to accompany him. That morning she had risen at the same time he did, but she had been slow at her ablutions. "I am finding it hard to be cheerful," she had said. And then, suddenly, she had seated herself and was looking at him with a white face. "Basil, I feel badly," she said. "I—I am very much afraid I am going to be ill. Do not look so disturbed about it, dear heart. I am sure it is just the—the usual symptoms."

As he sat in court now and waited for the hearing to begin, his mind was not on the case. He was thinking of the white face of his bride and fearing that she had held something back from him. She had been so pathetically limp and it had been so hard for her to smile when she said good-by.

Inevitably, however, his mind went on to more cheerful matters and he thought of the son who would arrive after all the customary symptoms had been lived through, the son who would proudly wear the fine clothes the old prince had left for him and frighten other boys by swaggering about in the conjurer's mask.

"It is certain that Linus is in financial difficulties," whispered the man of law. "It is the one thing I am concerned about. Are we fighting over a dead carcass?"

The sharp voice of the young magistrate was raised. "Let us begin," he said.

Jehoahaz pawed through the documents in front of him and found the deposition of Kester of Zanthus. He rose to his feet. "Learned Judge," he said, "I have a paper I desire to lay before you. It is a statement made by one of the five witnesses who was not heard from at the first hearing. His name is Kester of Zanthus and he is a dealer in army contracts, residing in Rome. This statement was given by Kester to the plaintiff when the latter was in Rome."

Linus roused himself from his sprawling position and stared at the lawyer with startled eyes. Clearly he was hearing for the first time of the statement supplied by the missing witness. "Now he will begin to rant and roar," thought Basil. But the man who had won the first legal battle said nothing. There was a flush on his flabby cheeks, and it could be seen that the hirsute hand with which he grasped the arm of his chair was twitching spasmodically.

"I have a copy of the evidence of this man, Christopher of Zanthus," declared the magistrate, lifting a document in front of him. "It has been supplied to me by the commandant of the imperial forces in this district, to whom it had been sent by the witness himself. There is, I understand, an acquaintance of long standing between them."

The legal aides seated about Linus went into action at this point, arguing bitterly about points of law. There was a loud babble of voices for some minutes, and much raising of vehement fists in the air, and then the magistrate cut the discussion off with an impatient thump of his hand on the bench.

"Enough!" he said. "I need no instruction in the meaning of the Twelve Tables. This deposition, copies of which have reached the court now from two sources, is admissible as evidence." He turned in the direction of Jehoahaz. "What witnesses have you?"

The witnesses who went up one by one, to stand briefly in the fierce light of the magisterial eye, were merchants for the most part, men who had known Ignatius well and who testified that they had heard him speak of Basil as his adopted son and his heir. Flaminius allowed no interference with them. He asked the questions himself, sharp, pointed, conclusive. It took no more than a few minutes in each case, and then a wave of the nervous hand of authority would send the witness back to his seat.

While this went on Basil was watching the man he had hated so deeply and for so long and realizing that none of that feeling was left in him. He was conscious, in fact, of a trace of pity for the usurper. Linus was a sick man and a frightened one. Basil no longer felt any desire to tear his opponent down and exult in his fall.

2

It was clear from the beginning of the defense case that it would rest on the evidence of Hiram of Silenus. Basil remembered him as a fat and oily specimen with great yellow freckles on his face. Hiram was both fatter and oilier now and the freckles had multiplied to the density of stars in a constellation. It was quite apparent from the moment he entered the room that he would have preferred not to testify a second time and that he had come under pressure of the law.

The magistrate summoned the witness to a position directly beneath the seat of authority and proceeded to go over his previous evidence step by step. Hiram, perspiring freely and sometimes turning to dart apprehensive glances at Linus and his little circle of advisers, affirmed under this close examination that the evidence he had given at the first hearing had been true. He was still of the belief that the ceremony he had witnessed had not been one of adoption. He did not remember any striking of the gong with the ingot of lead, no affirmation on the part of Ignatius that he was taking the boy as his son.

The magistrate then picked up the statement of Kester of Zanthus and read it aloud. What did Hiram of Silenus have to say about this?

That the memory of Kester of Zanthus was at fault.

Had the father of the boy offered his son for sale three times as prescribed by law?

Yes, but not for adoption.

Had there been a meal afterward of five courses and had five of the finest wines been served as asserted?

He had no recollection of a meal of any kind.

Was it true that Ignatius had given to each of the five witnesses a belt buckle of silver?

He had received no gift of any kind from Ignatius.

Did he have in his possession a silver buckle of the kind described by Christopher of Zanthus?

No, he had no such buckle.

At this point in the examination Basil sat up very straight on the bench he was sharing with his legal adviser, his attention roused to a keener point. There had been something about the appearance of Hiram when he first entered the room that had tantalized him with a hint of familiarity. Could it have been the buckle on his belt?

He got to his feet and made his way through the crowded space in front of the magisterial dais until he stood close to the unwilling and now harried witness. His eyes settled on the buckle of the man's belt. It was of silver and it had five points; it was, in fact, identical in every way with the one Kester of Zanthus had worn.

"This lag-witted ox, this accepter of bribes!" said Basil to himself. "He has been guilty of the stupidity of wearing into court the evidence that will prove him to be lying."

What would be the most effective way of calling the buckle to the attention of the young magistrate with his keen wits and his eyes as sharp as camel-prods? Basil examined the perspiring bulk of the reluctant witness and saw that the leather of his belt was showing the strain of spanning a stomach that had become too wide for it. The belt had worn thin at the back.

Basil carried one of his knives in his own belt and this he now produced, touching a finger lightly to the blade. It was keen and sharp. He edged his way behind Hiram and gave the most frayed part of the leather a quick, deft slash. The leather parted and the belt fell to the floor.

Before the startled Hiram could do anything about retrieving the belt, Basil had it in his hands. He glanced at the inside of the buckle, which was tarnished from long use, and saw that two names and a date had been inscribed upon it. Stepping close to the dais, he held it up in the air.

"Here, Learned Judge, is proof that this witness has not told you the truth," he declared. "This is the buckle which was given him by my father, Ignatius; the same gift which the other four witnesses received."

The magistrate held out a peremptory hand. "Give it to me."

The belt was handed up to him and he examined the inscriptions with an eye that had become cold and accusing. Then he leaned forward and held the article out to the witness.

"Where did you get this?"

"I do not remember. I have had it for many years."

"Do you deny receiving this from Ignatius on the occasion under discussion?"

"I do not recall receiving a present of any kind."

"What explanation do you give of the inscriptions on the back?"

"I was not aware there were any inscriptions."

"And yet you tell me that you have owned this belt for many years? Do you still deny any knowledge of the nature of the inscriptions?"

"Yes."

"I call to your attention that the buckle is inscribed with the name of Ignatius and the name he was giving the boy, together with the date of the ceremony."

The witness had nothing to say. He was now perspiring so profusely that he seemed on the point of melting away like tallow under the rays of the sun.

The magistrate raised a hand for silence. All mutter of conversation in the court ceased. There was no sound even of rustling garments or the scuffing of sandals on the floor.

"It will not be necessary to hear anything further," said the magistrate.

No doubt was left as to what the verdict would be. Basil looked at Linus. The mouth of the usurper had fallen open and his face had become as white as candle wax. Basil said to himself: "Luke was right. There is no satisfaction in revenge. This man deserves no pity and yet I find that I am sorry for him. I have won but I must strive to be generous."

3

Basil noticed differences in the house on the Colonnade as soon as he was admitted. The halls had not been sufficiently aired and his nostrils encountered a thicker mustiness than he had ever detected in the halls of Nero. It surprised him still more, however, that he had been met by Quintus Annius.

The Roman clerk bowed to him solemnly and ceremoniously. "I knew you would come," he said. "As he came the other time."

"Is my haste unseemly?"

Quintus Annius shook his head. "Not at all. The others have been arriving. You are the last."

Basil looked his surprise. "What others?"

The Roman clerk made a gesture with his hands that suggested resignation. "The creditors," he said.

This brought other questions at once to the tongue of the restored owner. "Creditors? What I have heard is true then? Linus has been having losses?"

A morose nod of the head provided the answer. Basil's heart sank very low. Had he won back his inheritance to have it snatched away again in the moment of victory? Did this mean that his hope of security and independence was to be no more than a dream?

He became unpleasantly aware of the silence and emptiness of the halls. Most of the furnishings had been removed, and so far he had seen no trace of servants.

"Where are the slaves?" he asked.

"There was a commotion when word of the decision reached us. I ordered them confined to their quarters."

"What kind of commotion?"

"Linus was a hard master and had made himself hated. When we heard you had been restored to your inheritance there were demonstrations of joy. For a time they got quite out of hand."

Basil smiled without any sense of mirth or pleasure. "I begin to get a sense of welcome after all. But any real satisfaction I might have taken is gone because my mother is not here to share in it."

Quintus Annius nodded gravely. "It is much to be regretted that she could not have lived two months longer. She was very kind, particularly near the end. We had many talks and she was always certain that you would be restored to your rights. The last time I saw her she said it would be soon but that she would not be here to see it. How true that was!" He sighed deeply. "As long as she lived we were able to keep up a semblance of order. It was after her death that the place fell into such shameful neglect. I even found myself wishing at times that Linus had a wife."

"Is he here?"

The clerk raised both hands in the air, the fingers clenched in sudden anger. "He was the first to come. He said he was going into his room and did not want to be disturbed for half an hour. I took this to mean that he would resort to the only honorable way to conclude such—such an inglorious affair as this has been. No sounds came from behind the door and I said to myself, 'He has opened his veins.' I waited the half hour, but when I went in I did not find him on the floor in a pool of his own base blood. The room was empty and it had been ransacked from top to bottom!" The clerk's face, which was usually void of expression, had become red with the intensity of his indignation. "He had seized everything of value he could get his hands on—money, bits of jewelry, documents—and had taken advantage of the absence of the servants to leave by the rear gate. A fitting end after all. He had made himself a common thief!"

"Whatever he managed to steal," declared Basil, "is a small price to pay for the gift of his absence. He will never dare come back. And when we have been robbed of so much, does a little more matter?"

They had reached the door of the circular room. Quintus Annius motioned with his thumb. "They are in there," he said. "Waiting for you. I suggest you come with me first. I have some documents to show you."

In his own small room the clerk seated himself before a neat pile of documents. He looked at them and heaved a bitter sigh.

"Everything is listed here," he said. "Here are the debts, as far as I have been able to compile them. The total will give you an unpleasant surprise. Here is the list of our assets. They have been dwindling fast. What a hopeless mess it has been!"

Basil glanced at the figures, and his heart went down again into the depths. It was worse, much worse, than he had feared. "There will be little left," he said.

"Very little. Those fellows in there have been most demanding. They have been hovering over us like vultures, flapping their wings and screeching." He picked up the documents and frowned over them. "I have done nothing for you. As you do not need to be told, I am a coward. I deserted you the first time——"

"I had refused to take your advice."

"True. But when the second hearing was directed, I did not go into court. I knew the magistrate would look at me and ask, 'Why did you not give this evidence the first time?' The only answer I would be able to make was that I had been afraid. I lacked the courage to face that question, and so I stayed here and skulked in abasement. You will never forgive me. I do not deserve it."

"Put it out of your mind," said Basil. "I assure you that I have no hard feelings."

The young Roman's face flushed with a new resolution. "I shall try to make up for it. I will fight for you against these ravenous dogs. I will fight over every bone that is left. I may even be able to bury a few bones away where they will not find them." He shook his head with a savage resentment. "He was out of his depth from the very first, a midget trying to fill the shoes of a giant. I have been in torment, watching him destroy with his fumbling hands the magnificent prosperity into which he stepped!"

There was a long moment of silence. Basil was realizing how badly shaken he had been. "This is a hollow victory," he thought. "But I have one satisfaction. The stigma of slavery has been lifted from my name. Perhaps I should be content." He asked aloud, "How many slaves are there?"

The clerk consulted a list. "Forty-two."

"Would the balance in my favor allow me to keep ownership of them?"

Quintus Annius shook his head emphatically. "They constitute a very solid share of the estate. The vultures in there are probably figuring now on the prices they will get for them."

Basil thought of the misery that would result if the slaves were sold to help satisfy the claims of the creditors. They would be auctioned off to the highest bidders. That would mean separation of families and the breaking of all ties. Many, without a doubt, would find themselves the property of cruel and demanding owners. He recalled his own sufferings.

"Multiply that by forty-two," he said to himself, "and one realizes what this will mean."

He rose to his feet. "I shall go in now," he said. "I think it will be necessary for me to face them alone."

He realized as soon as he got inside that, if a search had been made for the seven flintiest hearts and the seven coldest faces in Antioch, the result would have been the group that now faced him. He recognized one of them only, a banker who had paid occasional visits to Ignatius. They had taken possession of all the seats the room provided and so he remained standing just inside the door.

"I am told that you all have claims against the estate," he said. "It is proper then for me to join you. I am the biggest creditor."

The banker, who occupied the chair Ignatius had always used, moved uneasily. "I do not understand what you mean by that," he said.

Basil was fully aware of the frigid intentness with which all seven were watching him. He indulged in a silent prayer. "O Lord, look down on me and lend me Thy help," he said. "I am without experience in matters such as this. Enable me, O Lord, to make the things I must say to them sound very convincing."

He addressed himself then to the company. "That good man who adopted me as his son left a great estate when he died. There was this house, which was filled with rare objects of great value; there were the warehouses, the ships, the olive groves, the great reserves of money and supplies. I was to inherit everything. But, as you know, the law permitted a great injustice to be done. Everything was taken away from me. Now that injustice is being righted. The law has said to me, 'You are the rightful heir.' And so I come today to claim that great inheritance which should have been mine at first."

The banker indulged in a sour smile. "How much of it will be left for you after all our claims have been met?" he asked.

"I have a first claim!" cried Basil. "You, my good sirs, have been dealing with a thief. Your claims are based on arrangements you made with an interloper. Do you believe that I am in any sense responsible for the mistakes this man made while in possession of my property, which is now declared to have been illegal and obtained by fraud?"

The banker's smile developed into a laugh, a decidedly unpleasant laugh.

"Fine words," he said. "Would they win you a decision from any judge?"

"I am sure of one thing," declared Basil. "If it comes to a court decision, it will be delivered in Rome. Do you realize what that means, my good sirs and fellow creditors? I have wealth and influence behind me and, if necessary, I shall carry the fight all the way to Caesar."

Six of the seven faces remained fixed and stolid, but that of the banker now showed a deep and resentful flush. "It would be an expensive fight!" he cried.

"Yes," said Basil. "For all of us."

There was a long silence. "I am sure," he resumed, "that you all know how the appeals are mounting up in Rome. It would be at least two years before we could get a hearing in the imperial courts. In the meantime, my good sirs, what will happen to what is left of the magnificent trading concern my father built? If taken vigorously in hand now, it might be saved. It might be brought back to something of its former prosperity. But after two years of litigation and indecision it will not matter much who is given the verdict. There will be nothing left for the victor."

The banker was combing his beard with nervous fingers. "What are you leading up to?" he asked. "What do you propose?"

"A division now," answered Basil. "Give me ownership of the slaves and divide up everything else among you."

The banker searched through some documents on the marble table of Ignatius with hands that trembled furiously. "The slaves!" he cried. "There are forty-two of them. See, here is the list. They are a valuable lot. What absurdity is this?"

"I have stated my terms," said Basil quietly.

Immediately all seven were shouting and waving their arms at him. They got up and surrounded him, gesticulating, threatening, screaming. He made no move except to fold his arms on his chest. He said nothing more and even smiled at the insults they heaped upon him.

When he emerged from the circular room he found Quintus Annius crouched uneasily in his chair. "I thought they were going to tear you to pieces," said the latter.

Basil was carrying a document. He laid it down in front of the young Roman.

"We reached an agreement in spite of the noise," he said. "This contains all their signatures. As you will see, I am to have the slaves. They divide the rest."

Quintus Annius sprang to his feet. "This is a triumph!" he cried. "You have brought them to your terms. I did not think you would have a chance dealing with any one of the seven singly, let alone the lot of them together." He reached for a slip of parchment. "See, I was making an estimate of the value of the slaves on the present market. It is a handsome amount."

Basil did not look at the figures. "I want to visit their quarters now," he said. "Will you come with me and hear what I have to say? I am giving them their freedom."

The Roman looked at him with unbelieving eyes. "By all the laws of the Twelve Tables, you do not mean it!" he cried. "If you did this, you would strip yourself to the skin. There must be reason, even in generosity."

"If you had ever been a slave as I have, you would understand the reason. Will you have the writs of manumission prepared?"

Quintus Annius said to himself: "He is mad! What other explanation can there be of such supreme folly?"

Not knowing the doubts of his sanity that had taken root in his companion's mind, Basil proceeded to give further proof of an unsettled reason. On the way to the slave quarters he stopped suddenly and turned his eyes up to the ceiling. "Father, have you been listening?" he asked. "It is all I can do for you. I hope it will suffice."

CHAPTER XXXV

I

THE DEPRESSION that gained possession of Basil's spirits on his homeward journey was not due entirely to the loss of his inheritance. He had left the house reluctantly in the morning. It was the last day for showing the Chalice and he would have preferred to remain and share the watch with the two guards. He had paid a visit to the vigilant pair before taking his departure and had said to Elidad, who was standing at the door: "Keep your eyes open today. It is their last chance." He was thinking of this as he strode vigorously through the streets of the city, which were emptying fast with the coming of dusk. "I wish," he was thinking, "that some other day had been selected for the hearing." He had spoken to Jehoahaz about the possibility of getting a postponement, but the man of law had been most emphatically against this, saying, "We must not tamper with our good fortune."

The darkness of evening was beginning to settle down over the white houses and the small gardens when he approached his own neighborhood. He had been falling deeper into gloom with each step he took. There seemed to be something sinister about the tints in the sky as they turned from gray to black, in the rustling of the trees in the Grove, in the echo of activity from the city streets below that followed him on his climb. He was certain that something had gone wrong, and this put impatience into his feet. His gait had increased to a jog trot by the time he reached an angle of the road where a space had been provided for the turning of vehicles, but he slowed down when he saw that a number of chariots had turned in here. The drivers, waiting for the return of their passengers, stood in a knot by the side of the road and talked in loud and confident voices. The tenor of their talk was political and they spoke in Hebrew.

"Zealots!" thought Basil. His fears mounted to a sense of certainty. Climbing the hill, he heard a loud shouting from behind the walls of the house. Then he noticed that the front gates were swinging wide open and that no one was standing guard over them. He saw two men climb in great haste over a side wall and vanish into the woods.

"Mijamin has struck!" he cried, racing up the steep road in furious haste. When he arrived, he saw a distracted group of visitors and servants in the outer court. Running through into the inner garden, he found Luke bending over the unconscious figure of Elidad. The young guard, it was apparent, had sustained serious injuries in defending his trust. Fearing the worst now, and filled with a furious and rebellious despair, Basil entered the house and reached the stairway at the head of which the guards were supposed to stand. There was no sign of Irijah. The stair, in fact, was empty, as was the landing above. He took the steps three at a time and came to the small room where the Chalice was kept. It also was empty. It was empty in another sense than in the mere absence of the men assigned to protect the Chalice. The Chalice was gone.

Basil stood for several moments and stared at the space on the table where the sacred Cup had stood. He was too stunned to think, too unhappy to have any coherent reactions to the disaster.

"It will be taken to the High Priest and he will break it with his own hands," he said to himself. "Nothing can be done about it now. All our efforts have gone for naught."

He began then to link what had happened to his personal misfortunes. On the long walk from his old home on the Colonnade, after disposing of it to the creditors, he had become reconciled to the loss of everything he had won in court, but the final victory of the Zealots suggested to him now that there was a pattern in this succession of blows. "Are we being tested?" he asked himself. "As Job was tested in the land of Uz?"

But there was another respect in which the room was empty. From the first he had been conscious of something different about the twelve models on the table, and now he realized that this was due to a gap in the row. He turned quickly and counted them. There were only eleven.

He walked to the table in deep fear of what he would find. The fear became certainty. It was the head of Jesus that was missing.

At first he was conscious only of what seemed a tragic coincidence, that if one had to be destroyed it would prove to be the most sacred of them all. Then he realized that chance had played no part in this. The model had not been broken in the haste with which the invaders had taken possession of the Chalice; it had been carried away. None of the others had been moved. It had been the purpose clearly of Mijamin and his men to steal it as well as the Chalice.

Basil's next reaction was one of resolution. He would make another model of that sad and wonderful face while his memory was still fresh. That much at least must be salvaged from the disaster, for he knew that there was in every Christian heart an unquenchable desire to gaze on the face of the Saviour. He must set to work as soon as the trouble and confusion had died down.

Then a sense of fear and defeat swept over him. His recollection of the sacred face had already become dim! Would he be able to call back the clarity with which he had worked after waking from his dream? Would he be able to replace the lost model with one of equal fidelity? He could not be sure.

He strove to find reassurance by saying to himself that the vagueness of his memory was due to the anxieties that filled him. Later he would be able to put demands on his mind and reclaim the clear recollection of the sacred face. He felt so much urgency about it, however, that he could not wait for this to happen. He must know at once; and he set himself with deliberate effort to re-create in his mind the room in the Wall of David.

It came back slowly. There was no relief for him in the result, for the scene that gradually grew in his mind was clear in every respect save one. As on the first two occasions when it had been shown to him, the space in the center was empty! He waited with the most intense concentration, hoping to see the face of Jesus emerge; but it soon became evident that this was to be denied him.

A sense of irrevocability took possession of him. "Why," he asked himself, "should I have expected that I would be granted a second glimpse of His face? It was given me once, and such a great reward will not be repeated." Then the meaning of this second loss came back to him in full measure. "It is a great misfortune, for I have been the only one in a position to preserve for mankind a vision of how Jesus looked. They will destroy everything, these men from Jerusalem, and the memory of His face will be lost for all time."

He had been a few moments only in the room. In a state of deep despair he descended the stairs and reached the inner court, where Luke was tending the wounds of Elidad. The physician's hands, already stained a deep red with the blood, were working with a sure but at the same time an almost frantic haste. He had cut a soft sponge into pieces and was applying them to the many wounds.

"I must act quickly if his life is to be saved," he said to Basil without allowing himself to pause. "Cataplasms may be necessary, but I am not yet sure. I may be able to check the loss of blood without them. I hope so, for it is a cleaner way and surer to lead to a recovery. The cataplasms sometimes clog the wound and keep it from healing."

An excited voice was heard at this point in the outer court. "It is Irijah," said one of the maids. "I saw him go over the wall after them. Perhaps he has come back with the Cup."

Basil crossed to the outer court and found that Irijah, who was surrounded by what was left of the visitors and by anxious servants, had come off badly in the struggle also. There were wounds on his cheeks and neck from which blood was flowing down over his shoulders. His tunic was so badly torn that he was almost naked to the waist.

"They got away," he said. There were tears of resentment and grief in his eyes. "I followed them over the wall, but they scattered in the woods and I lost track of all of them."

"Did they have the Chalice with them?" asked Basil.

"I did not see it. But one of them must have had it." Irijah's eyes were burning with self-denunciation. "It was given us to guard and we failed. The Lord will punish us."

"Tell me how it happened."

"I did not see the first of it because I was upstairs at my usual post, but this is what they tell me. A woman came to the front and said she wanted to see the Cup. She gave a familiar name. The elder at the door was short-sighted and perhaps too old to be quick of mind. He thought he recognized her and he stepped out to have a closer look. It was not a woman at all. It was Mijamin, who is very short of stature and had made himself up in this disguise. He clamped a hand over the mouth of the elder, and two others came out of the woods and took possession of the gate. Then the rest of the party came in."

Irijah could not face Basil as he went on with the story. "We could have held the stairs, Elidad and I, if Mijamin had not made a noose at the end of a long rope and succeeded in throwing it over my friend's head. He pulled the rope tight and dragged Elidad down the steps, so that he landed on his head and was knocked unconscious by his fall."

"How many were there of them?"

"I think nine or ten. They seemed to be swarming wherever I looked."

Irijah took a quick and shamefaced glance at his questioner and then dropped his eyes. "I did the best I could. I kept on fighting, and some will carry my mark on them as long as they live. But I could not hold the stair alone against so many." He made a despairing gesture. "They got into the room and two of them took the Chalice and jumped out of the window. This again is what I am told. I could not see what was happening behind me. There were two visitors in the room and they have told what happened. All I am sure of, Jehovah forgive me, is that no one will see the Chalice again."

Basil motioned to one of the menservants, who was standing open-mouthed on the edge of the group. "Harness two horses to the chariot," he said. "Have it at the front entrance as quickly as possible."

He returned to the inner garden and spoke to Luke. "I am going to the police. They must be told what has happened. They got their hands on Mijamin once and perhaps they will be able to do it again. The gates of the city must be watched and all ships leaving the port searched."

Luke looked up from his labors. His face was white and drawn, and it was clear that he was badly shaken by what had happened. "If it is the will of the Lord that the Cup be taken from us, we must abide by His decision and not question it," he said. "But we must not sit down and repine. We must make every effort to repair the disaster that has befallen us. Do what you can, my son. I will send word also to Jabez, who may be able to stir the police to greater efforts on our behalf." He straightened his back with a suggestion of physical weariness. "Harhas will say the Lord is punishing us for opposing force with force. He will raise his voice against us in bitterness and triumph."

"I don't think we need to be concerned over his wrongheadedness," said Basil. "Tell Deborra that it will be late when I return. I cannot delay to speak with her."

2

It was several hours later when Basil returned. The horses were weary from the efforts that had been demanded of them, and Basil himself had been finding it hard to maintain his equilibrium as the chariot wove its way through the approaches to the Grove. He threw the reins to the servant who met him at the front entrance and stumped stiffly into the court. Luke came out from the house to meet him.

Basil began at once on a report of what he had done. "It seems that the police ordered Mijamin to leave Antioch when he was given his release. They are angry over his disregard of this and can be depended on to make every effort to track him down. A watch has been set on all the gates. But I am afraid it is too late to accomplish anything." He dropped stiffly into a chair and stretched out his legs. "Mijamin is a careful planner. We have had many proofs of that. He had his escape provided for in advance. I expect they got to the nearest gate and are well away from the city already." He rubbed a hand over his eyes and sighed in sheer weariness. "I drove to the port with the officer who carried the orders. We went to every ship in harbor and gave instructions to the captains to keep an eye out for them. We can be sure of one thing: they will not get away by sea."

"You are very tired, my son," said Luke. He hesitated. "And now I must tell you about Deborra."

Basil sprang up from the chair. "Deborra!" he cried. "What about her? Has she been hurt?"

"She was found after you left. It seems she suspected what the Zealots would do and stationed herself under the window of the room where the Chalice was kept. She attacked them when they jumped from the window. She was using your sword. I have questioned her, but she cannot tell much about what happened. As the point of the sword is reddened with blood, it is apparent that she used it to some purpose. When she was found, she was still unconscious from a blow on the back of the head."

"What will she think of me!" cried Basil. "She knows that I returned and left again without making any effort to see her."

"You have been engaged on a task that had to be done. Deborra knows and understands." Luke gave his head an admiring shake. "She is indeed well named, that brave little Deborra. I had been ill all day and was lying asleep in a back room when the trouble started. I did not see these things with my own eyes, but I have been gathering the story. How splendidly she behaved! While the Zealots were fighting to carry the stairs, she led the servants against them from the rear. It might have succeeded if they had been well enough armed; but shovels and brooms cannot prevail against weapons in the hands of desperate men. They were beaten off roughly and some of the servants were hurt. After that she could not get them to make another effort and she took her place under the window alone."

"And while this happened I was on my way back from a day spent in looking after my own interests!" cried Basil. "I shall never forgive my-self."

"She wants to see you, my son. You had better go up to her now."

Deborra was propped up on pillows, her head swathed in a large bandage. It was clear that she was still suffering from the wound in her head. Her face was a chalky white. She turned her eyes with the greatest difficulty in his direction. "I am glad you are back," she whispered.

Basil took her in his arms and pressed his cheek against hers. "My sweet wife!" he said. "Will you ever forgive me?"

"Forgive!" she protested. "None of this is your fault."

"I left you when you needed me."

"Basil," she said, giving her head a rather feeble shake, "you could not have done anything to prevent this from happening."

"I should have been here. I shall always charge myself with negligence."

"But you had to be in court." He felt her stiffen suddenly in his arms. "Basil, what has happened? What was the verdict?" Before he could an-swer, she went on in a tone of self-accusation. "You have been blaming yourself because you were not here, but I have more reason to do that. I have been so upset that for hours I haven't given a thought to the case. How thoughtless of me when it means so much to you!"

"There are things that mean more. The loss of the Chalice—and you, my dearest one, fighting here alone in my absence."

She began to sob. "You do not tell me and so I know that you—that you lost the case."

He shook his head. "No, I won. I have been declared the legal heir. But also I lost." He went on to tell the story of what had happened when he reached the house on the Colonnade. "So you see," he concluded, "while I am the winner, the victory will not put a single copper coin in my purse."

Deborra had listened with conflicting emotions. "I cannot tell you how happy I am that you have been declared the rightful heir," she said at the finish. After a moment's reflection she gave her head a nod. "You were right in giving the slaves their freedom. No matter at what cost, it had to be done. And I am very proud of you. How well you must have talked to the creditors to make them agree!" Then she had a change of mood and shook her head angrily. "It makes me furious to think that a stupid and dishonest man could take such a flourishing business and ruin it so quickly. Ah, my Basil, what a disappointment this has been for you! What a great misfortune!"

"I confess that I felt very much downcast at first. I had been making such plans in my mind. But"—he tightened his arms about her—"I am more disturbed over this wound in your head than I am over the loss of my estates."

She struggled up to a sitting position. "This makes me so angry," she said, pressing both hands to her temples, "that my head has started to throb worse than ever. Oh, Basil, this is dreadful! Our world is falling in ruins about us and I cannot think! Surely, surely, there must be things we should be doing. We should not be talking about our misfortunes; we should be planning ways of meeting them. But I cannot get anything clear in my mind. Oh, if I could only think!"

Basil seated himself on the side of the bed. "My dearest child," he said, "there is nothing more we can do. Do you remember the story of Job? How the Sabeans came forth and slew all his servants, and then there came the fire of God and the great winds, and his children were killed and all his property destroyed? This may be a test of *our* faith." He shook his head slowly. "The estates are gone. I have signed them away and nothing can be done about it. I believe I am becoming reconciled to that. The Lord giveth and the Lord taketh away. As for the Chalice, do you suppose that the old man, Harhas, was right? That we should have been ready to leave it in God's hands? One thing is certain, there is nothing left for us to do about it now." He took her in his arms again. "My sweet one, do not torture yourself in this way. Things might have been worse. You might have been killed. As it is, you will soon be better, and I ask for nothing more."

Luke entered the room at this point, carrying a cup filled with a medical preparation. He held a hand against a vein in her throat for several moments and then shook his head. "You have been talking too much," he admonished. "Here, drink this. It will ease the pain and allow you to get some sleep." He turned to Basil and nodded. "All she needs now is rest. A long and dreamless sleep. I think you had better go and get some rest yourself."

Deborra reached out an imploring hand. "Not yet," she said. "Stay with me a little longer. Until I get to sleep."

Basil rose and went to the window to allow more air in the room by drawing the curtains. As he looked out into the dark the sky suddenly became so light that the world seemed on fire. He could see each stone in the wall about the house, and beyond that the trees in the Grove of Daphne and somewhere, very far off, the roof of a temple. There had never been such a light before, he was sure, for it lasted no more than a fraction of a second and yet he had felt as though he needed no more than an added iota of time to see far beyond the stars. It left as abruptly as it had come, and the murk and stillness of night closed in again.

The strangest part of it was this, that the coming of this sudden blaze in the sky had brought him a complete sense of peace. The troubles which had filled his mind had taken prompt wings. He could see stretching ahead all the beautiful things he was going to make, chalices and drinking cups and fine platters and imposing lavers, made of gold and silver and rich with precious stones, and back of them figures in bronze and marble, some of them of heroic size; all of this with such extraordinary clearness that he lacked only time to identify each piece and study its artistry of design. Excitement gripped him. He was being allowed, he knew, a glimpse of the future. He knew that in the course of time he would bring all these lovely objects into existence. He raised his hands and stared at them.

"I must set you to work," he said aloud. Then he was ashamed, for the words had sounded plain and bald and, in the exultation of spirit that had gripped him, he wanted to speak in high-sounding voice and flowing phrase.

He realized then that Deborra was sitting up and that her eyes were shining. "Basil, something very strange has happened!" she exclaimed. "The pain has left my head."

"Has it gone completely?" he asked. It was an unnecessary question; he was certain of the answer in advance.

"Completely. And suddenly. I feel happy and content. I know that we must not complain or try to change what is happening. Everything is in the Lord's hands. I feel very humble because of what I said to you, but also I feel very happy." She reached out and put her hands in his. "But there are things we can do, my husband. I can see *that* most clearly. We can, in our own way, make up for the loss of your estates. I know it is our duty to do so. I am able to think again and my mind is filled with plans."

"I am sure," said Basil solemnly, "that we have witnessed a miracle."

"Yes, yes, of course. What else could it be? That strange light was sent to make us see the truth. It was sent to guide our feet."

"I am sure that angels have been flying about the house. We were not allowed to see them or to hear the rustle of their wings. But they were here."

Luke had said nothing. His eyes had turned to the window and he had not moved since the light had come and then so quickly subsided. It was clear that his thoughts had gone with it and were fixed on horizons of which they could not conceive.

He turned now, and they could see that a mood of the greatest exultation possessed him.

"I have said many times, and meant it in all humility, that a prophetic tongue has not been given me; and yet when that light was in the sky I was able to see for a brief moment into the future, so brief a moment that there could not be in any language a word to define it. And what I saw brought great happiness to me. I know that all will be well. The Chalice will not be destroyed. The man who has it is torn already with doubts. He feels the sacredness of it and he does not know what to do. He will find himself so troubled in mind that he will desert the cause for which he has been fighting and bring the Chalice back to us. There will come to him a full resolution of all his doubts."

The voice of the old physician had been kept low, but now it blazed up with passionate conviction.

"Yes, my children, the Chalice will be restored. Tomorrow? In a month? In a year? I do not know. All I could see was that it would be returned to us and that we would be able to keep it in peace. Perhaps, with Jerusalem torn apart and swept with fire, the hands of our enemies will no longer be able to reach us.

"But," he cried, "that is not all! With that one look which was vouchsafed me I saw far on into the future. The Chalice will be taken away a second time. This will not be due to the machinations of evil men. There will be a flood, an earthquake, a convulsion of nature of some kind; and it will be buried deep down and lie in darkness for a very long time, perhaps for centuries. When it is brought out into the light again, it will be into a far different world. The earth will be peopled with new races, tall men, beardless for the most part, with strange talk on their tongues. There will be great cities and mighty bridges and towers higher than the Tower of Babel. But evil will be loosed and they will fight long and bitter wars with frightening new forces of destruction.

"In such a world as this the little Chalice will look strange and lost and very lonely. But it may be that in this age, when man holds lightning in his hand and rides the sky as Simon the Magician strove to do, it will be needed more than it is needed now."